AILEEN ARMITAGE is █
by birth. She began █
obliged her to give up work in the outside world.

Her main hobby is pretending she isn't blind,
which calls for a sense of humour in her friends
when she spills wine all over them and in head
waiters when she stubs her cigarette out in the
sugar bowl.

She is the author of *Hawksmoor*, *A Dark
Moon Raging*, *Hunter's Moon* and *Touchstone*.
She now lives in Huddersfield, West Yorkshire.

20

CHAPTER
OF
INNOCENCE

AILEEN ARMITAGE

Whoever blushes is already guilty;
true innocence is ashamed of nothing.

ROUSSEAU – *Emile*

FONTANA/Collins

First published by William Collins Sons & Co. Ltd 1988
First issued in Fontana Paperbacks 1989

© Aileen Armitage 1988

Printed and bound in Great Britain by
William Collins Sons & Co. Ltd, Glasgow

Life is sweet, brother. There's night and day, brother, both sweet things; sun, moon and stars, brother, all sweet things; there's likewise a wind on the heath . . .

GEORGE BORROW: *Lavengro*

ACKNOWLEDGEMENT

During the course of writing this book I found occasion to ask several people for help, which they gave without stint. I would therefore like to express my deep gratitude to Ruth Kitchen, acknowledged expert on Cleveland Bay horses, to my farmer friend George Statham for his expert help concerning pigs, to Werner Mayer, director of the Jewish Museum in Manchester, and especially to Marjory Chapman for her perceptive editorial advice.

Last but not least, I should like to thank Deric Longden for his constant and untiring help, researching and reading back to me so that I could revise without strain, and for his unfailing reassurance and love. I am blessed among writers.

AILEEN ARMITAGE
September, 1987

PROLOGUE

When Maddie Renshaw was a child the wind whispered to her at the window and called her to the wild places where it was born. Sometimes it moaned and sighed, sometimes it screamed, demanding her to attend, and she knew she was born to hear and to obey.

She had not heard it before Mother died when she was thirteen, not realized it cried out to her. It was only in the loneliness that followed that she understood its meaning, and the terrible ache in her cried out in answer.

Scapegoat Farm, high on the hill overlooking the village, was a lonely place for any child, but it was only then that it came to Maddie just how unwelcoming home could be. She sat on the drystone wall surrounding the farmyard and looked at her home with new eyes. The long, low building surmounted by a lead-grey slate roof held no sign of warmth. Small-paned windows stared at her with the bleared glaze of a blind man. On four-foot-thick stone walls hung rusty iron lamp brackets destined to light the way to the stables and byre, but never in her lifetime had there been light.

It was Mother who once shed light and warmth on all around her, and with her going Scapegoat was thrust into gloom. For seven years Maddie had watched the farm crouch under the onslaught of pitiless grey rain or lie still and silent under its shroud of snow and she had longed for summer to come again. The cold silence of the farm oppressed her, choking her youth. Father had withdrawn into his own world of private grief seven years ago, leaving her to grieve alone. And the worst of it was, she knew he blamed her. There was no one else to listen to her now but the wind.

CHAPTER ONE

It had been a wonderful summer in the Garthdale valley, filled with intoxicating sunshine and sweet-scented with hay and honeysuckle. The sheep clipping and haymaking were finished for the year and only the sheep dipping still lay ahead. And the Fair.

Maddie felt at peace. After the evening milking it was heaven to ride Duster up on the moor, to lie on the coarse moorland grass and listen to the hum of bees as they plundered the heather, to breathe in the pure air and dream of adventures yet to come. And they would come, she was sure of it, even if they were taking their time about it.

Life seemed to teem with activity all year round for the folk down there in Barnbeck and Agley Bridge and Otterley and Thirkett and all the other Garthdale villages but up here on Scapegoat Hill where only Father's farm blotched the otherwise open stretch between Barnbeck village and the moor, nothing ever happened. Not until August, anyway, and the day of the Gooseberry Fair, when every year the villages in Garthdale began to pulsate with excitement and even Father was caught up in the fever.

'I've taken that trophy before and I'll do it again, just you see if I don't.'

The steely tone of James Renshaw's voice was characteristic of the man, thick-set and weathered as the solitary ancient oak on the hillside and dour and enduring as the limestone hills. There was no room for unnecessary frills in his life; even his old sheepdog bore no name other than Dog. Maddie nodded and piled freshly dug potatoes on the stone sink.

'I've no doubt you will, Dad.'

He glanced at her sharply. 'Not been snooping, have you? You haven't been poking at my berries?'

'No, Dad, I've not been near them. I never do.'

He rolled up his shirt sleeves and came alongside her at the sink. Maddie stepped aside.

'Shift them potatoes out of my way, lass. I'll just have a swill before the news comes on.'

She laid aside the paring knife and lifted the enamel bowl out of the sink. Renshaw turned on the brass tap and splashed cold water on his face. She watched the droplets splash off the crazed bottom of the sink and run down his hairy arms to the elbow, splattering the kitchen floor. Renshaw straightened and reached out, eyes closed, for a towel. Maddie handed it to him.

'That's better,' he muttered. 'Now, did you remember to take that accumulator down the village and get it charged like I said?'

He was already tuning in the battered old wireless on the sideboard. Hissing and whining gradually subsided into a recognizable human voice. Renshaw seated himself, open-kneed, beside it and craned an ear to listen. Dog sprawled on the rug before the fire and closed his eyes.

Maddie returned to the task of peeling the potatoes for supper. It was no use trying to talk to him while the six o'clock news was on. For all the years she could remember it had been the same.

Mother used to smile and lay a finger to her lips, and there was a closeness, a conspiratorial intimacy in that smile. A sibilant voice droned on, issuing words like Prime Minister and Chancellor of the Reich, but Maddie paid no attention. What went on on the wireless concerned a world far removed from Barnbeck and the Fair and the need for a new dress.

'And here now to read the postscript is Mr J. B. Priestley,' the voice said. Renshaw groaned and switched off. Maddie saw her opportunity.

'I've been wondering,' she said tentatively.

10

'Wondering what? I ought to have another look at that sick sow before I settle down for the night. How long will supper be?'

'A good half-hour yet. But listen, Dad, I need a new frock. It's three years since I had a new one.'

'Is that all? Your mother could make a frock last ten year if she'd a mind to. Took care of her things, she did.'

Maddie seized the opening. 'Then could I have a look in her wardrobe, Dad? Maybe there's something there that might fit me.'

'That you'll not. You'll make do with your own stuff. Stay out of her room.' There was no mistaking the asperity in his tone. As he turned away Maddie caught the sound of his murmured words. 'You above all people. But for you . . .'

Maddie switched course. 'I've grown, Dad. My best frock's far too small for me now.'

'Then let it down, like she used to do. She was a thrifty woman, was your mother. A woman's best virtue, is thrift.'

The implication was clear, and Maddie rose to it. 'I'm no waster, Dad. I've already let it down, twice. It's not that. It's just not big enough.'

He still didn't catch on. 'I've seen your mother put a bit on the bottom before now, rather than bother me when she knew every penny were spoken for.'

Maddie sighed. 'It's not that. It's that tight on the chest I can hardly breathe in it, and it's faded. How about letting me have a shilling or two to buy a length of stuff – I'll make it up myself.'

From the embarrassed look in her father's eyes Maddie knew that she had won.

'Well in that case happen I'd best find the money from somewhere – but think on to cut it generously this time, lass. Put a good hem on it too lest you should grow more.'

Maddie snorted. 'I'm twenty years old, Dad, nearly twenty-one. I hardly think that's likely.'

'Half a crown, that's all I can manage. That were to have

11

been your Christmas box, so don't go looking for no more when Christmas comes.'

The next evening she told her best friend Ruby about it. It was cosy sitting in the Sykes' little parlour with its gleaming brasses and Royal Doulton proudly displayed on the Welsh dresser, drinking tea from one of Mrs Sykes' Sunday-best cups. Doreen Sykes had never quite got over the disappointment of having to marry beneath her when she settled for a policeman. If it hadn't been for a terrible mistake that summer evening when she'd got carried away she could have done very well for herself. She'd never touched a drop of cider since.

'There's some quite nice stuff in our shop,' Ruby admitted, 'but Mrs Spivey charges over the odds in my opinion. You can do far better if you go down to the market. You'll have to get a move on though.' She sighed. 'I'm really looking forward to the barn dance. All the lads will be there.'

Mrs Sykes gave her daughter a reproving look. 'Now, now, love. Young ladies don't talk like that. Specially in front of our Eunice.' She cast a meaningful glance in the direction of her younger daughter who was leafing through the *Radio Times* quite oblivious to the conversation.

Thursday afternoon found Maddie threading her way through the crowded stalls of the market which straggled up the cobbled streets of Barnbeck towards the squat grey church. It did not take long to come across exactly what she was looking for – a pretty glazed cotton spattered with tiny pink and blue flowers. The stallholder was emphatic in its praise.

'That stuff'll neither run nor shrink,' he promised. 'Some of the best stuff I've ever had.'

'It better hadn't,' Maddie retorted, 'or it'll be back here faster than a ferret down a rabbit hole. I'll take two yards and the thread and those buttons – how much is that?'

'To you, lass, two and six the lot. How's that?'

Maddie widened her eyes in mock disbelief. 'Half a

12

crown? I could buy a frock in a shop for that – and not have all the bother of sewing it neither. Daylight robbery, that is.'

The stallholder chuckled. 'Nay, you'd rob me blind, you would. Tell you what, this is the last of the roll – near enough three yards, there is. How about half a crown for the whole piece, buttons and thread and all?'

For a second he paused, then added, his eyes twinkling amid folds of weather-tanned skin, 'Go on, seeing as it's you, I'll take two bob, only don't tell folks or they'll all want a bargain off me.'

Delighted, Maddie took her bargain and moved on to another stall where she bought a delicate pink hairslide shaped like a butterfly. After supper that evening she spread out the sprigged cotton on the kitchen table and began to cut carefully. Her father sat reading yesterday's copy of *The People* and paid no attention. At ten o'clock he rose stiffly from the rocking chair and made his way outside to the privy, Dog following him. Minutes passed. When he came back he wound the clock and then came to stand behind Maddie's chair.

'Have you done? Time for bed if we're to be up for milking.'

'I've still the sleeves and pocket to set in and the buttonholes to do. I want to finish this tonight.'

He looked down at her. 'Lights go out ten o'clock every night, you know that well, paraffin costing what it does. You'll have to make do with candles.'

'I know.'

His work-roughened hand brushed her shoulder. She saw the look in his eyes and wished with all her heart for some sign of affection from him. But it was no use.

'You'll still have to be up at five, think on. I want me breakfast before milking.'

He blew out the paraffin lamp and clumped away upstairs, leaving Maddie to sew by candlelight. The clock on the mantelshelf struck twelve before she had finished.

Then, holding the frock against her body, she strained on tiptoe to try to see her reflection in the mirror over the sideboard.

The candlelight gleamed on the sheen of the cotton and gave her face an ethereal glow. She held the frock against her cheek, revelling in the feel of its clean crispness. In Maddie's mind's eye the shadowed corners of the farm kitchen were peopled with spectators watching her every move across the slate-flagged floor to the rhythm of fiddle music only she could hear. The day after tomorrow and Gooseberry Fair, with its evening barn dance, could not come fast enough.

James Renshaw lay in bed and wondered why his daughter always made him feel ill at ease. She was an uncomfortable creature to have around, wide-eyed and dreamy half the time as if she were listening to sounds only she could hear, though she did her work about the farm well enough. If only she had been a lad . . .

It was the biggest regret of his life that he had no son to follow him, to take over the farm which Renshaws had worked for centuries. There it was, in the family Bible for all the world to see – he, James, was the eighth Renshaw to run Scapegoat. If only there was a ninth to care as deeply as he did about breeding fine pigs and taking the gooseberry prize. Instead he had only a daughter who was fragile and remote, not the sort of child a hill farmer could boast of when he called in the pub down in Barnbeck.

Not that any of the men spoke of their families these days. They didn't even talk war talk any more, despite the daily rumblings on the wireless. Pacts with Poland or anywhere else were unimportant compared with the contest the day after tomorrow. Down the end of the garden, beyond the privy, hung the fattest gooseberry he had ever nurtured, a good two ounces if it was a gram. Not even Jack Kitchen could ever have grown a beauty like that. Nor that water-bailiff fellow up at Otterley who, so the story went, fed the roots of his gooseberries with dead salmon.

Though the sky was as cloudless tonight as it had been for the past few weeks, Renshaw was taking no chances. On his bedtime trip down to the privy he'd gone to have a look at his precious berries by the light of the harvest moon which hung huge and low in the sky. And he'd taken the precaution of suspending a bucket over the treasured bunch, just in case. Maddie wouldn't miss her mop bucket until she came to swab the kitchen floor.

A two-ounce gooseberry it must be; just think of it. It would break every record in the Fair's book. In his mind's eye he already held the trophy in his hands. There was only one thing missing to complete his happiness. Lily would have been so proud . . .

The following evening James sat in the corner of the Cock and Badger, alone but for his sheepdog at his feet. Conversation around him was desultory but significant. Every man's mind was dominated by one thought. Even the ominous news on the wireless about that upstart Adolf Hitler took second place to the approaching contest.

Eddie Sykes, the village policeman, squinted as he took aim at the dartboard. 'How's gooseberries going up your place then, Jack?'

Jack Kitchen, bent over the domino table, shrugged thick-set shoulders before answering. 'Middling. Just hope there's no rain.'

Heads nodded in understanding. Jack clearly had a plump contender.

'Had a swarm of wasps over at my place,' murmured Eddie. Heads shook in sympathy. 'Did no harm though,' he added as his dart sank satisfyingly into double twenty. 'I've got netting over.'

Every man had netting or some other form of protection such as canvas or discarded curtains over his treasured gooseberries to protect them from predatory birds. Every man in the villages surrounding the river Garth had his own secret weapon for success and his own methods of surveillance. Even closest friends could not be trusted when it came to the Gooseberry Fair.

'What about yours, James?' a squat, balding man at the dominoes table enquired of Renshaw. 'Going to take the prize again this year?'

The darts players paused in their game to look across. Every man burned to know whether Fred Pickering's question would make James Renshaw give anything away.

Renshaw shook his head and tossed off the remainder of his pint. 'I'm saying nowt,' he muttered. 'Tempting Providence, that is.'

'Meant to ask you,' cut in George Bailey. 'Can I borrow one of your horses, James? I need – '

'No,' said Renshaw shortly.

'Whyever not? I've told you oft enough you can borrow my tractor any time you want.'

'Makes no odds. I'm lending nowt.'

'And I've given you two days of my time for harvesting . . .'

'You heard what I said. No.'

'Mean devil, that Scapegoat Jim,' Fred muttered after Renshaw, followed by the dog, had left the Cock and begun the long climb back up to his farm. 'Mean as muck, that fellow. Wouldn't give you the time of day.'

'Miserable sod. Last time I offer him my tractor,' said Bailey.

The landlord smiled as he wiped the mahogany counter. 'Aye, and he'd never let on about his berries any more than you'd tell how much you take in that shop of yours, Fred. You surely didn't expect him to tell us if he had one that looked a winner. Not Scapegoat Jim. Never in all this world.'

'Nay,' agreed Eddie as he threw the final dart, 'No more than he'd buy a man a pint. Beats me how he ever wed and

16

bred a lass like that Maddie of his. Pretty as a picture, she
is. Make some lad a bonny wife some day.'

'That's as may be. Renshaw never hardly lets her out of
the house,' remarked the landlord. 'Reckon maybe a lass is
too much for him to handle on his own. Happen she's a
handful – comes of not having a mother to train her up
proper, I reckon.'

Jack looked up from the row of dominoes stacked in
front of him. 'He's no cause to grumble. She works hard
on the farm, she does, even if she does look as spindle-
legged as a newborn foal. Like Eddie says, she'll make
some young farmer right happy one day. And I'll tell you
summat else, Len Laverack – she's a rare hand with horses.
A natural touch, that's what she's got. Understands them
like she was their mother.'

'Aye,' agreed the landlord. 'For him it's pigs, for her
horses. She'll happen win a rosette at County Fair one day
with yon mare of hers.'

'Wouldn't surprise me at all,' said Fred as he chose a
domino and laid it at the end of the row. 'Give old James a
shock, it would, if she started bringing home prizes in place
of him. Still, his boar's not a bad beast.'

'Wake up, Dad,' muttered Jack Kitchen. 'You've just
played a four to my five.'

The old man crumpled in the corner of the settle
suddenly stirred into life. 'I were thinking about Scapegoat
Jim. It's his gooseberries we need to watch out for right
now,' his reedy voice complained. 'If he's keeping that
quiet, I reckon he's got a corker.' For a moment he ground
toothless gums together in silent contemplation. 'Serve him
right if someone didn't sneak up to Scapegoat one night
and bust it for him.'

Scandalized faces turned to survey the speaker. 'Bust it?
Nay, Seth, that'd be sabotage!' said Eddie.

'Only if it were touched,' the old man said with a
complacent chuckle. 'You couldn't do it, you being a

policeman and all. Nor me neither, only having the one hand left. But someone might . . .'

His pale eyes grew watery as he laid aside his beer glass to pick up his pipe with his one good hand. 'I remember young Thwaite Holroyd back in nineteen-nineteen. He never knew what happened, but he did know he couldn't go on flirting with other fellows' wives after that. Learnt him a lesson, that did.'

Seth leaned back on the settle, puffing contentedly on his clay pipe. Sam Thaw, the present owner of Thwaite Farm, looked across at him with curiosity in his eyes.

'Thwaite Holroyd – up at my place?' he echoed. 'So that's why he sold out, is it? Well, I never did. Odd that, him messing about like that when he had such a pretty wife of his own.'

'Aye, every bit as bonny as Lily Renshaw she were,' agreed old Seth, 'every bit as bonny.'

Fred was rubbing his chin, a thoughtful light in his pale eyes. 'Aye, if someone just overwatered Renshaw's berry a little bit, happen after a very hot day, then nature'd do the rest. Serve him damn well right, that would.'

CHAPTER TWO

'I don't give a damn what that Ruby Sykes is allowed to do
– I want you home by ten, understand?'

'But it doesn't finish till twelve, Dad, and everybody
stays till the end.'

'Eddie Sykes can let his lass get herself into trouble if
he's a mind, but I'm not letting you. I'd have thought he'd
have known better, him being a policeman and all. But
that's his business. You'll be home by ten and there's an
end to it.'

Tears filled Maddie's eyes but she knew better than to
argue further. It was so unreasonable. How could he
humiliate her so, making a girl of twenty be home so early?
How could he deprive her of the only fun she was likely to
get in months? But she was not going to let him spoil her
night. If she had to be home early, then by heaven she'd
make the most of the time she had.

The day of the Gooseberry Fair dawned misty and full of
promise. The milking done and the milk churns standing
ready by the gate for the lorry, Maddie hurried to her room
to get ready while her father prepared his berries. Her
reflection in the bedroom mirror reassured her that she
looked prettier than she had ever done, hair clean and
shining with the pink butterfly nestling amongst the fair
curls, and face scrubbed till it shone and then powdered
with cornflour until it shone less. She pinched her cheeks
and lightly touched the stub of lipstick Ruby had given her
to her lips, so lightly that it barely showed. In the new
frock she felt like a princess.

Her father looked up from packing his precious gooseberries and gave a begrudging nod.

19

'You look nearly as bonny as your mother, Maddie lass. I used to be that proud . . .'

He had never shown it, thought Maddie. Not in words or gestures at any rate. Never once had she heard him tell her mother that she looked pretty, though she could recall the tender way his gaze would sometimes rest on her, especially at the end . . .

'That neckline's a bit low,' her father said sharply.

'It's the fashion nowadays. Ruby's got one just the same.'

'That's as may be. Now mind you behave yourself.' He picked up the cardboard box and carried it carefully to the door. Dog loped out after him.

The earthy smell of the farmyard gave way to the spicy scent of lupins as Maddie and her father made their way out to the farm gate. From the lane she could see the dew beading the new-cut grass in the meadows and she breathed in deeply the heady scent. Dog, relieved of work for the day, scampered up and down the banks of bramble and nettles looking for sport.

Down in Barnbeck the sun filled the cobbled streets with warmth and radiance, and it was joy to Maddie's soul to listen to the excited chatter of the villagers, dressed in their Sunday best and eager to make the most of the holiday. Mrs Spivey was just coming out of her little haberdashery shop, her ruddy face beaming as brightly as her straw hat decked with green ribbons. Old Seth Kitchen was loudly refusing his son's arm and tottering along with the aid of his stout walking stick. Eddie Sykes stood with his hands clasped behind his back outside the Cock and Badger, his uniform buttons and helmet badge gleaming in the morning sunlight, while the landlord crossed the road to greet his old friend Sam Thaw. They were all heading for the field behind the main street, the one relatively flat field the village possessed and which during the winter months doubled as the Barnbeck team's football pitch.

Once in the huge marquee erected for the occasion, Maddie's father became at once preoccupied with the meticulous display of his gooseberries. One by one the other afficionados appeared, all clutching boxes as tenderly as if they contained the Crown Jewels. Each man was preoccupied. It was easy for Maddie to slip away and join the throng in the main street. Ruby was waiting by the market cross, her dark red hair set off by the pale green frock she wore. She swung a pretty bonnet carelessly by its ribbons but eagerness glowed in her eyes.

'Where've you been? The lads have been asking whether you'll be coming,' she giggled. 'They're still hanging about over there. I fancy we're in with a chance today, Maddie Renshaw, and I for one am going to make the most of it. Come on, see if they follow us.'

Conscious of the appreciative stares of the village lads, Maddie turned and walked with Ruby, swinging her hips and with a tilt of the head, proudly aware that her long tawny hair gleamed like silk under the sun. Bob Bailey, the lean-hipped youth who worked on his father's farm next to Scapegoat and who often came to help Dad with the ploughing and the haymaking, left the group and swaggered into step beside the girls.

'You look very bonny today, Maddie lass,' he ventured. Ruby giggled. Maddie tossed her head.

'Don't I always then?'

He grinned. 'Course you do. Only today you look stunning, that's what I meant. Like a film star.'

She looked up at him from under her lashes, the way Bette Davis did. 'Which one?'

He spread calloused hands. 'Any of 'em. They're all pretty.'

'Sabu isn't.'

Ruby dissolved into noisy laughter. Bob threw back his head and chuckled. 'You're too quick by half, Maddie Renshaw, but I like a girl with life in her. Can't stand the dumb ones.'

They had reached the little stone bridge over the river.

Maddie stopped and leaned against the parapet, running a hand through her long hair. Ruby gave her a nudge.

'I've just seen someone I want to talk to. See you later.'

Maddie watched as the girl sauntered across to a tall blond youth. She recognized Norman Pickering, the shop-keeper's son, and smiled at the way Ruby professed surprise at meeting him. She turned to Bob.

'Go on, then. You didn't tell me yet which film star,' she prompted. She didn't care if she was fishing for compliments; she could see the other lads watching Bob's progress from a distance.

He leaned against the parapet beside her, his lean body casually stretched so that she could make out the muscles beneath his shirt.

'Well, when you look at me like that – I'd say happen Pearl White.'

'She's dead,' Maddie objected.

'But when you walk by all hoity-toity like, I'd say Greta Garbo. There isn't a lass more beautiful than that.'

'I like Vivien Leigh – did you see *Gone With the Wind*? She's fantastic.'

He looked down at her with an amused smile. 'Aye, she's got a bit of spirit about her and all, just like you.'

He rolled his length over on the parapet so that his blue eyes gazed closely into hers. 'Are you going to be at the dance tonight, Maddie? Will your dad let you go?'

Maddie shrugged. 'Happen I am. Are you?'

'I am that. If you're there, I'll see you, Maddie Renshaw. Keep a dance for me, will you?'

'Could be.'

And he was gone, sauntering off with easy grace down the lane with his pals, laughing and joking. Maddie looked across the street but Ruby was no longer there. The parish church clock struck two and she turned to walk back to the marquee to see how her father was faring with the contest.

* * *

The air was suffocatingly close and hot in the marquee, but sweet with the scent of summer fruit and trampled grass. James Renshaw stood, stiff and tense, among the group of men clustered about the weighing table. Total silence reigned while all eyes focused on the five men seated there, concentrating on the task in hand. Two judges, spectacles perched on noses, two weighmen in the shape of the chairman and secretary of the Gooseberry Society and the recording clerk all peered intently at the scales. Tiny weights were being placed on the pan to counterbalance the plump berries in the other. Not a muscle moved among the waiting group while the scales quivered and finally fell still. The weighing in of the berries held all the solemnity of a major surgical operation. The tension was unbearable.

A whisper broke the silence. One of the contestants behind James could not bear the agony of suspense any longer. 'Well, has the record been broken or not? Is there one over twenty-five grams?'

A wall of silence met his unwarrantable intrusion into the seemingly interminable deliberation. The recording clerk continued to turn over the yellowing sheets listing the achievements of the last two hundred years, but his inscrutable expression gave nothing away. James held his breath.

The five heads bent close together, nodded, and finally separated. The chairman cleared his throat.

'Gentlemen, we have reached our conclusion. The best berry weighs twenty-seven grams, twenty-two grains. The winner of the heaviest berry trophy this year is Jack Kitchen, of Barnbeck.'

Maddie realized it was all over the moment she ducked her head to enter the green shade of the tent. Jack Kitchen was beaming broadly as he showed off the gooseberry trophy to his admiring friends and her father was nowhere in sight.

'Just goes to show what a bit of good Barnbeck manure can grow – that, and a bit of tender care,' Jack grinned happily.

'Aye, and whatever secret recipe you're not telling,' rejoined Sam Thaw. 'Same as that old lad up Agley Bridge the other year – he fed his berries on dead rats.'

'Dead rats be blowed – that's what he let folks think, but I don't believe it,' growled old Seth peevishly, resentful of the implied slur upon his son's good name. 'Some folks'll say owt – and some folks'll believe owt.'

'Too true,' said Sam. 'As I recall, your Jack said the other night he had nowt but rubbish.'

'He's had better,' retorted Seth. 'You're just jealous, Sam Thaw, because you'll not have that trophy on your sideboard this year.'

The old man took the trophy from his son and cradled it protectively against his chest, his old eyes rheumy with pride.

Maddie's heart sank. Evidently her father had not won the overall prize gooseberry class, but he could still have won a first in one of the other sections. She ventured to ask. Sam Thaw removed his pipe from his mouth and shook his balding head.

'Nay, I don't think so, lass, but have a look at the display for yourself. I'm off to hear the result of the raffle.'

Maddie went round the tables scrutinizing the tickets. It was no use. Individual prizes for red, green, white and yellow berries had gone to villagers from miles around, as well as awards for the best hairy variety and the best smooth one they called slape. Gone to foreigners from miles away were the awards for twin berries on the same stem, the heaviest six and the heaviest twelve. Dad was going to be unbearable during the following weeks. Either he was now in the Cock and Badger knocking back a pint to drown his disappointment, or more likely, unwilling to face the others, he'd gone home to brood in privacy.

But there was still the dance. Ruby appeared from the yard behind the general store when Maddie walked down the main street, starry-eyed as she smoothed down her hair.

'I've got a date with Norman at last!' she confided. 'He

wants to dance every dance with me tonight. Ooh, I do hope he asks me outside with him. I could fancy them big brown arms around me. You'd be all right on your own, wouldn't you, Maddie?'

'Course I would.' Not for the world would she spoil Ruby's fun. Ruby nudged her playfully.

'Got off with Bob, have you?'

'Sort of.'

'Great! All I've got to do now is dump our Eunice. Me mam says I've to mind her, but I reckon I can get out of that if I put me thinking cap on. Let's go and get some lemonade and plan it all out.'

After a sunlit afternoon at last the time for the dance arrived. The moment the two girls reached the marquee Ruby made a bee-line for Norman Pickering and was soon dancing in his arms, her pretty face radiant. Maddie stood, uncertain, by the door. Bob Bailey was standing with a group of friends among a bank of flowers near the band of musicians. He saw her and immediately walked over to her. 'On your own, are you? Where's your mate then?'

Maddie nodded in the direction of the dancers. 'Dancing.'

'You want to dance?'

'I can't do a fox trot.'

'Me neither. We'll make it up as we go.'

He took her in his arms and soon she had found the rhythm. It was blissful to feel the pressure of his firm body against hers. For a time they danced without speaking and she had time to savour the exciting new sensation.

'Been thinking,' Bob said. 'Them bay horses of yours are damn hard work to follow at ploughing. Why don't you get your dad to buy a tractor. My dad's dead pleased with his new Fordson – makes life much easier, come ploughing time.'

Maddie shook her head. 'He won't have anything to do with tractors. New-fangled things, he calls them, can't do the job any better than horses.'

25

'Aye, but tractors is the things of the future. Me dad swears by his – cuts the time by half. Got to move with the times, tell your dad.'

Maddie gazed up at his earnest young face, wishing he would talk of something more romantic. 'Horses were good enough for my grandfather and great-grandfather, and they've done well enough for him, he says. I can plough too, you know.'

He ignored her. 'He won't get nowhere if he don't get mechanized, I'm telling you. Same as motorbikes'll replace the old push bike. I'm saving up for a motorbike.'

'That'll be nice.' She dimpled. 'Will you give me a ride?'

'Aye, happen. If you behave yourself.' He gave her a teasing smile and for a time they danced in silence.

'It's no use, you know, Dad'll never listen. Any road, I wouldn't want to see Robin and Duster put out to pasture.'

He laughed as the music ended and he took her arm to lead her off the floor. 'You and your horses – you're dotty about them, aren't you? The lads were betting about you in the pub the other night.'

'About me? What about me?'

He gave her a look of amusement. 'That you probably take them to bed with you.'

She jerked her arm free of his. 'And what's wrong with that? Yes I have, as it happens – a baby foal once. I wouldn't be without my horses for the world – they're far more reliable than people.'

It wasn't true about the foal, but it was gratifying to see the confident look on his face change suddenly to amazement.

'Horses better than people? Nay, I'll not have that,' he said stolidly. 'They can't be.'

'They are, tons better,' Maddie asserted. 'Give me Duster rather than a lad any day.'

He was good company, Maddie discovered, talking about films, making sure he found a seat for her and fetching her lemonade in the interval. He claimed every dance, and she

26

made no objection. His friends hovered near but did not dare to intrude. It was satisfying to see the gleam of interest evident in their eyes. It must be the new dress. It was a pity that Ruby was so fully occupied with the task of entrancing Norman. Later in the evening Maddie looked for Ruby but there was no sign of her friend. She smiled. They would have a lot of gossip to share when next they met.

During a waltz Maddie caught sight of Joanna Westerley-Kent, the daughter of the local squire, laughing up at her brother. Joanne was wearing a dress of identical sprigged cotton to Maddie's but with a full gathered skirt. She looked radiant and was clearly enjoying herself, and being the focus of many young men's attention. She caught Maddie's eye, nodded and smiled.

Moments later Maddie felt a touch on her elbow. Joanna had her coat over her arm. 'I like your frock,' she said softly. 'I must compliment your good taste.'

Smiling, she moved away. Maddie felt a glow of pride. It was a truly wonderful evening.

Suddenly she heard the church clock striking. She jerked herself free from Bob's arms.

'Dear heavens, I ought to be home by now – I'll have to fly or my life won't be worth living!'

'Come on then,' Bob said good-humouredly. 'I'll walk you back.'

On the way up the lane leading towards Scapegoat Farm she felt Bob's arm slide about her waist.

'How about us going to the flicks together one night, Maddie? Good film on at the fleapit in Agley Bridge next week.'

Maddie bridled. Getting her father to agree to let her go to the pictures now and again with Ruby was one thing . . .

'I haven't been out with any of the village lads. What makes you think I'd go out with you?'

'Only because your dad wouldn't let you, we all know that.'

'Then you know more than I do. I've never asked him.'

'Happen because you daren't. I've seen the way he glowers at anyone who comes near you.'

'Doesn't he frighten you then?'

Bob laughed. 'Not me. Nowt frightens me. I'm a man, not a mouse.'

'Nowt? Not even all this talk of war they keep on about? Dad says the last war was terrible and he should know – he was in it. Millions of men died, he said.'

'War would be the most exciting thing that could happen. Nowt ever happens in Barnbeck. It must be the most boring place in the whole world.'

She looked up and gave him a mischievous smile. 'What, with me in it?'

He smiled. 'Nay, you're the most exciting lass a lad ever clapped eyes on. Merle Oberon, *that's* who you're like – you know, *Wuthering Heights*. She were grand.'

Maddie's eyes grew dreamy. 'She led Laurence Olivier a right dance in that,' she murmured.

'Aye, she did that. Untamed she were, just like a wild creature. That's why she reminds me of you, Maddie. Nobody ever knows just what you'll do next – remember that time at school when Miss Gaunt said – '

Maddie groaned. 'There's Dad out at the gate looking for me.'

She stopped, apprehension filling her at the sight of the stocky figure leaning over the five-barred gate. His anger would know no bounds if he caught sight of her with a young man.

'Then give us a kiss before you go.' Bob pulled her into the shadow of a hawthorn bush. Without resistance she let him kiss her. It was pleasant, but for the thought of her father's brooding presence. She pulled away.

'I must go. Goodnight, Bob.'

'Will you come to the flicks with me then?'

She hesitated. In the gloom she could just discern Bob's expression, pleading and hopeful. 'I'll see,' she promised, then hurried on up the hill alone.

Her father stood back to let her push open the yard gate. 'You're ten minutes late,' he said.

'I'm sorry about the trophy, Dad,' she murmured.

He stood looking down at her thoughtfully in the half-light. 'Aye, well. I'd have won if my best berry hadn't been overwatered. Bloody shame. It must have been well over two ounce, that one. Best berry there's ever been.'

'Oh, Dad! Are you saying – '

'I'm saying nowt, only rain couldn't have touched it under a bucket, could it?'

He followed his daughter as she crossed the yard towards the house, the air heavy with the smell of rotting manure and pig swill, but for Maddie there was only the scent of flowers in the marquee and her inner ear still heard the sound of music. It had been an evening of enchantment.

As she unlatched the door Renshaw said, 'Don't let me see you with that lad again.'

Maddie's mouth gaped. 'You saw me?'

He snorted. 'There's nowt much escapes me. Comes of a lifetime of watching for your own sheep – I can spot one of mine two hills away and know it from anybody else's. That Bailey lad is not for you, and that's final.'

Some days later after supper James Renshaw was ensconced in his armchair, the newspaper over his face. The sound of a Wurlitzer organ and the strains of 'On the Road to Mandalay' filled the room. Maddie was not sure whether or not her father was asleep but she dared not switch off the wireless during one of his favourite evening programmes.

She scraped the remains of the supper off the dinner plates into Dog's bowl, watching the old sheepdog as he nosed into it. As she scoured the plates in the hot, soapy water she glanced over at the old wireless set on the sideboard. Time she tidied away those cardboard boxes alongside it containing those ugly gas masks. They had been delivered during the Munich crisis last summer, like

29

the Anderson air-raid shelters some of the villagers had begun building in their gardens. Ugly things.

She rinsed off the soapsuds under the running tap and stacked the plates on the stone draining board, hoping the clatter might waken her father. She must get away from the farm for an hour or so, see if Bob really had remembered to look for her, or go down and have a gossip with Ruby. But she could not just slip away without letting him know.

The song ended in a series of crashing bass chords and Sandy McPherson began to read a letter from his postbag. When he announced that he was going to play 'Pale Hands I Love' Renshaw suddenly sat upright and snatched the newspaper from his face.

'Turn that thing off,' he ordered. 'If there's one thing I can't stand it's that sloppy, sentimental rubbish.'

Maddie dried her hands and crossed to the sideboard to switch off the offending music. Then she knelt to stroke Dog who was stretching before the fire. It was comforting to feel the pulsating warmth of his body under the fur.

Renshaw leaned forward in his chair and glared. 'Leave that flaming dog alone, Maddie. How many times must I tell you he's a working dog, not a blooming lap dog? You'll make him soft.' He shivered and added, 'We could do with more coal on this fire, lass. It's getting a bit nippy.'

'I'll mend it. There's coal ready in the bucket outside.'

In the farmyard the late sun still glowed on the cobble-stones. It was as Maddie was straightening, bucket in hand, that she caught sight of the dark head beyond the farmyard wall and her heart quickened. Bob was waiting for her. She took the bucket indoors and watched as Dog, his stomach filled and lying content before the fire, moved begrudgingly aside as her father nudged him with his foot. Her father's movements were slow and deliberate as he picked out the coals with the fire tongs.

She had to get out before Dog was aroused. She tried to make her voice sound natural. 'I think I'll just pop down to

Ruby's and see if she got me that material for your new work shirt. I won't be long.'

Her father glanced up. 'Down to Ruby's at this time? Whatever for?'

'You said you wanted another shirt.'

'Aye, but I don't much care for that Ruby Sykes.'

'She can get us stuff cheap, Dad.'

'Happen she can but she's no better than she ought to be, that one, not a good influence on you. Anyhow, it's late.'

'It's not yet eight o'clock, Dad. And I want to make a start on that shirt – you need it.'

He continued placing the coals on the fire. 'Aye, well, in that case . . . Oh, and while I think on – yon Fred Pickering came today – he's to be air-raid warden, seemingly. Says we're to get blackout material up at windows. More blessed expense. You'd best talk to Ruby about getting us some stuff cheap. See you're back before dark.'

She smiled to humour him as she glanced in the mirror to tidy her hair. 'Come on, Dad, this war talk's getting you down.'

'It's not only that,' he muttered. 'There's some funny folk about. I don't want 'em finding you dead in a ditch. So don't you go talking to no strangers.'

She laughed as she put on her coat. 'There's hardly ever anyone up here on Scapegoat. Don't worry so much.'

'You take care, that's all.'

She sped down the lane to where Bob was waiting. He held out his arms eagerly and she let herself be crushed against the rough tweed of his jacket.

Bob buried his nose in her neck. 'I thought you was never coming,' he murmured. 'God, you smell good. What's that scent you're wearing?'

'Californian Poppy.' He too smelt good to her, of male sweat mingled with earth.

He held her at arm's length. 'Where'd you like to go, lass?'

Far away from Scapegoat, where there was air to breathe. 'Up on the moor.'

He frowned. 'Nay, it's too open up there. Let's go where it's private.'

'Like where?'

He glanced up at the clouding sky. 'I can smell rain coming on. There's a cosy barn over at our place. It could rain all it liked then.'

She hesitated. To go all the way to Bailey's farm and back would take too long. 'I've got to be in before dark.'

'Your dad'll not beat you, will he?'

'I wouldn't put it past him if he were vexed enough.'

She heard his impatient sigh, and then he took her arm abruptly. 'There's nowt else for it then. It's got to be your barn.'

The first few drops of rain were falling as they sidled round the back of the house. Maddie was still reluctant. The barn would be dark but at least there was little danger in going there. The milking was done and Dad had fed the pigs so all the chores were finished for the night. By now he'd be listening intently to Robb Wilton and there was little chance he'd venture out of the house again except to go down to the privy at bedtime.

She could hear the chickens clucking as they passed the hen coop. Bob's hand was tight on her arm.

James Renshaw stirred. The newspaper slithered from his lap to the floor. Something had awakened him from his doze, some sound which had alerted him – the chickens, that was what he'd heard, he felt sure. Maybe a stray dog had got into the yard, or a scavenging fox. By rights he ought to go down and check. He lay still for a moment, listening, but all he could hear was the patter of the rain.

Bob kicked open the barn door and sniffed. 'It smells nice, all that new hay. Come on, Maddie.'

He was tugging her arm gently. In the doorway she

paused. It was so dark and close in there. He looked at her curiously.

'What's up?'

'Nothing, it's just – oh, I don't know . . .'

He frowned. 'Come on, it's starting to rain proper hard. We've not got much time, you said.'

Hesitantly she followed him inside and the warm, sweet darkness closed about them. Her heart was lurching in her chest. Bob must have felt it as his arms slid around her and he pulled her down on to the hay.

'Nay, Bob, I shouldn't – '

'Shouldn't what? What the devil's up with you, Maddie Renshaw? I thought you had a bit of life about you. I didn't take you for a yellow-belly, that I didn't.'

She felt stung. 'I'm not.'

He laughed softly and rolled on his back on the hay. 'Oh, I get it now – you haven't been with a lad before, that's it, isn't it? You're not what you make out at all, you with your sexy hips swinging. Well, well . . .'

'I never made out anything – it was you who jumped to conclusions you'd no right to, that's all.' Somehow she felt cornered, as if she was getting out of her depth.

His tone became gentler. 'There, there, there's nowt to make a fuss about, lass. I'll not rush you. I'll do nowt you don't want me to, I promise.'

He was sitting upright again, his arms about her and his weight gently but firmly pressing her down into the rich, warm hay. The atmosphere of the dark barn and the scent of hay and male sweat were strong and intoxicating. She made no move to stop him when his fingers fumbled with the buttons of her blouse. The touch of his hand on her body was stirring wonderful sensations she had never known. 'You got lovely skin,' Bob was murmuring, pulling back the blouse and putting his lips to her breast. The blood sang in Maddie's veins. She closed her eyes and savoured the delicious thrill.

Suddenly the barn door burst open and the doorway was

33

filled with a huge, menacing figure. Maddie leapt to her feet, clutching her blouse. For a moment her father stood motionless as his eyes became accustomed to the gloom.

'Maddie Renshaw!' his voice thundered. 'You little slut! Get back into the house this minute!'

CHAPTER THREE

'I told you to leave the lads alone – you defied me!'

James Renshaw's voice thundered about the farm kitchen; Dog slunk under the table and sank his head between his paws. Maddie hung her head, wishing her father's rage would pass, hoping she could reason with him.

'I meant no harm – we weren't doing anything wrong, Dad. It was only harmless fun, that's all it was. And that's the truth.'

Laying thick fists on the scrubbed deal table her father leaned across towards her. 'Oh aye? And that were the truth when you told me you were off down to Ruby Sykes's? It were that Bailey lad you were off to see. I'd never have known if I hadn't chanced to go down to the barn. Just how often have you lied to me?'

She lifted her chin and said, 'I'm twenty, Dad, not a child. I don't have to be minded all the time like a baby.'

His blue eyes glittered in scorn. 'Grown up, are you? But not grown up enough to know what that sort of bad behaviour can lead to, seemingly.'

She turned away to light the candle for bed, her cheeks burning. As she bent to put the taper to the fire she heard him muttering behind her.

'I can't trust you no further nor I can see you, deceiving me like that! I said that Ruby Sykes were no good for you. Well, you may be too big for me to thrash now, Maddie Renshaw, but I'm master in Scapegoat, and what I say goes. From now on you stay in Scapegoat by nights so I know what you're up to.'

'But Dad –'

He waved his arm. 'Don't you argue with me! I've no

wish to see a daughter of mine branded a trollop, that I haven't.'

She turned from the fire to touch the taper to the candle and caught sight of the vein throbbing in his temple and stayed silent. She could see her freedom slithering out under the door like a boneless barn mouse. The excitement of the evening was gone. Now there was only resentment.

'I'll say goodnight then, Dad.'

He sat by the range and made no answer. It was strange, she thought as she turned back the coverlet to climb into bed, smouldering and resentful still, but she did not feel bitter disappointment at not being able to meet Bob Bailey again. The touch of a man's hand on her body had aroused strange and wonderful feelings such as she had never known before, it was true, but the excitement had come more from the illicit fun of dodging Dad than from Bob's eager embraces. She knew in her heart that Dad was right about one thing – Bob Bailey was not the man for her.

Leaning over to the night table she blew out the candle and closed her eyes against the darkness of the room.

At eleven o'clock on Sunday morning James Renshaw had his head bent close to the crackling wireless set when Maddie came in from the milking shed.

'Foddering's done and the churns are all scrubbed and clean,' she said.

'Quiet, lass, I'm listening.'

She took one glance at his broad figure crouched by the wireless and turned away. Him and his wireless programmes. On such a beautiful morning with the sun flooding the whole of the valley and only the soothing sound of church bells drifting on the air, it seemed such a waste of life to sit pinned indoors. Sunlight and beauty beckoned. After dinner she would ride Duster up on the purple moor and soak herself in light and dreams.

The voice on the wireless was strange, charged with

emotion. James switched off the set and turned to his daughter, his expression stern.

'What is it, Dad?'

'That were Mr Chamberlain. We're at war, lass. Hitler's invaded Poland. England's declared war on Germany.'

Still stunned by the news, Renshaw watched his daughter as she seated herself at the deal table, her eyes clouded. 'What'll we do, Dad? You won't have to go away, will you?'

She looked so vulnerable, so like Lily. He shook his head. 'Nay, I'm too old. It'll be the young fellows as'll have to join up. We'll just go on same as always.'

For a moment she sat there, trying to understand. Then she stood up. 'I'll make us a cup of tea. Then I'll go and see about feeding the chickens.'

He glowered. 'Eleven o'clock and the chickens not fed yet? You're slipping, my girl. We'll have no slipshod ways in Scapegoat. You'll have to make better shift nor that, else how'll you help me run the farm?'

He intended to sound sharp to conceal his anxiety. A man couldn't afford to let tenderness show. He'd made that mistake once before, and just look where it had landed him . . .

'I can't help not being a lad.' Her voice came low but clear from where she stood at the sink.

It was the greatest disappointment of his life not to have a son to follow him, but in that thought lay more pain that he could ever reveal to his daughter. She must never know. It was his cross to bear, not hers.

He muttered, 'We'll get by. We always have. I'm off down to see to the pigs.'

'Anyhow,' her voice pursued him as he went out, 'if I'd had a brother, you'd have to let him go now, wouldn't you? Like you said, all the lads'll have to go.'

* * *

It was fortunate that James arrived at the pigsty when he did. The largest of his sows, all heavily in pig, was just about to give birth to another piglet, the first two already squirming and squealing around her swollen body in search of her paps.

James leaned over the wooden wall of the stall to watch. The sow lay on her side, grunting, and suddenly the newest arrival slithered from the vast rump, all pink and silky and glistening. The moist little parcel dropped into the dung-soaked straw, wriggling and squeaking and struggling to stand up.

Pigging was a remarkably clean process, James reflected, no mess, no blood, no slime. Just a quick, easy procedure as nature intended it to be. Women should be like that.

'Your wife has not had an easy delivery, Mr Renshaw – not as straightforward as one might have expected.'

In the end stall James could hear the old boar snorting and scraping the stall sides with his tusks, scavenging for every last morsel to eat. In front of him the piglet was on its feet now, a good three-pounder, tottering around its mother's huge flank and tugging its cord until it was stretched tight. James never failed to marvel at nature's cleverness, making the newborn piglet deal with its own cord. One final tug, and the cord snapped. At one minute old the piglet had broken the bond and made its bid for independence; James smiled in admiration.

It began to burrow under its mother's body alongside its siblings, its pink rind of a snout searching for milk. The old sow was already giving birth to the next of her litter, and it was then that James caught sight of the little legs protruding from under her belly.

'Hellfire!' he muttered, jerking open the door of the stall and bending to shove the sow's huge body aside. It was as he feared. A tiny piglet lay trapped under her enormous body.

'You daft animal,' he growled as he removed the body and inspected it. It was not breathing; it hadn't had a

38

chance under that massive weight. That was several shillings down the drain, he reflected. 'Stupid bloody sow! Rolling over on him like that you've crushed and smothered the little bugger.'

'*But she and the child are both well, Mr Renshaw. You have a lovely baby daughter.*'

Just as James always turned to his pigs when stressed, so Maddie went down to the stable. The chickens fed, she leaned over the stable door, watching Duster, the mare, as she crunched mouthfuls of hay. In the next stall the gelding munched contentedly.

'Duster, my lovely,' Maddie murmured, 'there's only you I can talk to. There's only you and me who understand each other.'

'*Talking to the horses again?*'

Her mother's voice came soft and low, just as it always had in life. It was so easy to hear her out here, away from the house.

'I can't help being a girl.'

'*I know, sweetheart. It's not your fault. I was the one who failed your father in oh, so many ways.*'

'I feel trapped. It's so unfair, trapped in a girl's body when I want to be free like a man.'

'*Men are not to be envied, darling. They're no more free than we are.*'

'They can do as they like! Look at Bob – if he wants to go somewhere, he just goes. I can't.'

'*Men have it no easier than women, believe me, Maddie.*'

The voice faded away on the breeze and Duster whinnied as Maddie stroked her soft muzzle. The mare looked at her with huge, limpid eyes and Maddie kissed her nose.

The mare nuzzled her under the arm. Maddie ran a hand over her broad shoulder, then added thoughtfully, 'Men should be like you, Duster. Big and strong and kind. You hide such strength under that gentleness of yours. All day long you'll pull that plough without so much as a snort out of you. Yet you could kill a man with a kick if you'd a mind.'

It was Bob Bailey who gave her the idea. She was gathering blackberries in the lanes that afternoon when she came across him, crouched under a drystone wall marking the boundary between Scapegoat and his father's farm. Far across the meadow she could see Dad's broad figure, bending and straightening as he worked on the sheep pens.

Meeting Bob's glance she laid a finger to her lips. He nodded, understanding, and jerked his head in signal. She understood his meaning and moved further downhill, out of her father's sight.

'Crouch down here with me,' Bob urged her. 'I've been trying to pile stones here without him seeing. He'd kill me if he laid eyes on me.'

It was true. Her father had still not forgiven him for the night in the barn. She ducked down in the hollow alongside Bob and placed the bowl of blackberries carefully on the ground beside her.

He hunched his arms round his knees. 'I've summat to tell you. I'm off to join the army next week,' he said proudly. 'I'm going to be a dispatch rider – taking dispatches on a motorbike. Fancy that, Maddie, a bike all of me own.'

His young face glowed with enthusiasm. 'It were Miss Westerley-Kent gave me the idea when I were helping out at Thorpe Gill – she'd been thinking of joining the Wrens, she told me, because she loves boats. So I thought, why wait for me call-up papers? I'm much more likely to get the motorbike job if I volunteer – so I did. I'm off to see the world, Maddie. Wish me luck.'

She touched his hand lightly, a gesture to express how pleased and at the same time how envious she felt. Then she pulled her hand away and picked up a handful of berries. 'I do, Bob, I really do.'

He took her hands roughly in his. 'Don't you wish you could go too – get away from this place? I tell you, I'll be glad to see the back of Barnbeck. For a bit at least.'

She looked down at the crushed berries in her hand and the purple juice trickling between her fingers. To get away, to see the world.

That night she braved her father as he picked up his newspaper.

'You? Go in the Women's Auxiliary? What the devil are you talking about, lass? What could you do, in heaven's name – you're nowt but a lass.'

'Women are going into munition factories, doing a man's job.' After a moment she added tentatively, 'I could go in the Land Army at any rate.'

'Digging potatoes and the like? You'll have to do that here now the lads are off. And where better than on your own place, eh? Scapegoat'll be yours one day. For the Lord's sake stop talking rubbish, Maddie, and get me supper ready. You just get on with what you're born to.'

Maddie turned away, tears scalding her eyelids. It was useless to try to make him understand. So long as nothing disturbed his world he did not care about anyone else.

It was time for the stubble burning. For most of the day James stayed out working in the fields, brooding over the future. Maddie brought sandwiches and beer out to him during the afternoon, and then he carried on, lighting and fanning the flames, guiding their direction and all the time deep in gloomy thought. It was hard work doing all that had to be done on the farm single-handed. He could do with more help, but that was going to be difficult to come by with all the young men of the village going off to war. There was one consolation at least, he thought wryly. He had been spared the pain of watching a son go away to fight.

By nightfall there was only the top meadow to finish. Maddie came slowly across the field to join him, standing

41

alongside him in silence. Together they watched the sparks flying in the wind and the blaze creeping relentlessly across the field.

'I love the light,' Maddie said softly. 'So many colours in it. Isn't it beautiful?'

Not to me, thought James. Somehow the fire seemed symbolic of the death of the old way of life as they had known it all these years. Would to God they knew what lay ahead! For a time father and daughter stood staring at the blaze without speaking.

Maddie broke the silence. 'I've been thinking. What are we fighting a war for anyway?'

James looked down at her. 'War's nowt to do with folk like us, lass. Politicians decide these things. They sign a treaty, we have to honour it. Like it or not, we're stuck with it.'

She continued to stare into the blaze, her chin jutting. 'Why? What's Poland to us? Why can't they fight their own battles?'

He could see the fireblaze reflected in her eyes, and that strange, far-away look that reminded him so forcibly of Lily.

She heaved a deep sigh. 'Well, there's one thing,' she said at length. 'You said things'll go on the same as before but maybe war'll make things change. For the better, I hope. It wouldn't be such a bad thing if it did.'

He watched her slim figure as she walked away and climbed over the drystone wall. Whatever was she on about? Funny creatures, women. He never had been able to understand them.

Winter came and took its time about receding. Snow still lay in scattered mounds on the high ground. James Renshaw trudged wearily down from the moor. There was always one ewe which decided to drop her lamb far too early on a bitter night, and James was more than ready for his bed by the time the little half-formed creature was stillborn.

42

He could not resist a shudder as he limped back from the moor down the hill towards home. This freezing weather was playing up his rheumaticky knee something cruel and Dog had to keep pausing to wait for him. It was high time those agricultural people found him the help he'd applied for, and not just some of them dratted Land Army girls like he'd seen up at Bailey's neither.

It was not only the chill of the night which troubled him but also a memory which haunted him. His gentle Lily would be alive still but for just such a thoughtless ewe, choosing to drop her lamb high on the moor on just such a bitter, rainy night. Tender to the end, Lily had stayed all night up on the open moor to care for the silly creature, soaked to the skin and chilled to the marrow. Pneumonia had made a quick end of her. Lovely, feckless Lily, the light of his life, but he'd never found the words to tell her just what she meant to him. And then it was too late. Loving Lily had brought only pain.

James turned his thoughts to his daughter. He was uneasy about Maddie. She was growing restless, just as Lily had done. He could not let her go away, not when there was no one else, no family in all the world except for Lily's sister Lottie out on that sheep farm in Australia. That lad Ronnie must be all of twenty-two now – he'd be a hell of a help around the place unless the army got him and all . . .

James jerked his mind back to the immediate problem. Maddie was growing rebellious, something Lily had never done, and he did not know how to handle it. How could he let the girl know that his abrupt ways did not mean he did not care? He did care, despite the bitterness that sometimes welled in him.

As he unlatched the farmhouse door and caught sight of the warm fire and the smell of soup on the hob, he felt a moment's gratitude for having a daughter. If only he'd had that son as well . . .

* * *

Maddie leaned her elbows on the windowsill as she watched for her father coming home from the fields. If Scapegoat Farm had been isolated before the war, it seemed ten times worse now with blackout up at the windows and not a glimmer of light being allowed to fall across the cobbled farmyard. Strips of sticky paper criss-crossed each window-pane, barring the wintry daylight, and Maddie felt as if she would choke to death in the suffocating silence of the place.

She pleaded with her father after supper. 'At least let me go down with Ruby to the Church Wives' sewing meetings. I could sew blanket squares for the troops.'

He answered testily. 'For God's sake, give over, will you? It were bad enough before war started, but with the blackout and all now, it's out of the question. Any road, that Ruby Sykes is up to no good, I keep telling you, so you can give over your moithering and do your sewing at home if you must. As if there wasn't more than enough work to do here . . .'

She fretted as she sewed. It was all right for him – he could go down to the Cock and Badger if he wanted to get out nights, but not she. No more chance of an evening spent gossiping with Ruby even – life had come to an abrupt end just as surely as if she were already in her coffin.

But she wasn't dead yet, and she wasn't going to live the rest of her life like a nun because of blackout and those flaming Jerries. Not by a long chalk.

CHAPTER FOUR

Colonel Westerley-Kent, Master of the Foxhounds of the Garthdale Hunt, stood at the dining-room window in Thorpe Gill, hands clasped behind his ample back. Outside a feeble spring sun struggled to penetrate a bank of cloud.

'Looks like rain before long,' the Colonel remarked.

'Still, it's not a bad morning for hunting, Reginald,' his wife replied. 'Good and frosty. I used to enjoy riding out behind the hounds on a crisp morning.'

He glanced quickly across to the wheelchair where she sat, a rug over her knees, and felt a stab of compassion. Autocratic and difficult she might be at times, but Hilary had been an excellent horsewoman once.

'I'm sorry, my love.'

She sighed, 'Ah well, I've learnt to live with it. But it's so frustrating. I could be doing something really useful . . .'

She never accused him directly, never reproached him that it was his fault she had galloped away from him that day six years ago. Hilary was far too shrewd for that. She had learnt how to turn her disability to good use to manipulate her family. Instead she implied reproach in every word she spoke, and he had not the heart to tell a woman with crippled legs that it was her own bad temper which had been her undoing, that but for that she might have seen the barbed wire stretched across the top of the fence.

'Still, I'm not complaining, you understand,' she went on equably. 'I still have my horses. Did you see the lovely foal Mr Thaw's mare produced? I told you Vulcan would sire excellent stock, didn't I?'

Colonel Westerley-Kent nodded. 'You were right, my

dear, as you always are. I trust your judgement implicitly where breeding is concerned.'

It was true. It was her doing entirely that they now owned such fine hunters as Vulcan and Firefly, bred from stock of her choosing. No one had a keener eye for a true thoroughbred and no one had more guts when it came to handling an unruly beast. On a cold day he could still make out the livid scar on her chin where that highly strung horse had back-heeled her, breaking her jaw.

'Pity the children don't take after you,' the Colonel remarked, seating himself opposite his wife and opening his newly arrived copy of *The Times*. 'If only one of them inherited your interest in horses.'

She picked up the embroidery frame lying alongside her chair. 'Their only interest is to ride them into a sweat,' she commented. 'And since Joanna is so set on going away now it hardly seems worth the effort to try and persuade her. And as for Richard . . .'

The Colonel snorted. 'That fellow doesn't seem capable of applying his mind to anything other than enjoying himself. Should have sent him to my old school. He might have learnt a bit of self-discipline then.'

His wife sighed. 'He'll get that in the army soon, I hope.'

'Yes, and high time too. Now what about Joanna – I'm sure you've tried to talk her out of this silly notion of hers?'

Mrs Westerley-Kent selected a strand of crimson silk and squinted as she threaded it into the needle. 'Waste of time, my dear. Her mind's made up, and you know how she is.'

The Colonel sighed and returned to his newspaper. Joanna was indeed her mother's daughter, and if Hilary couldn't talk the girl out of joining one of the Women's Auxiliary Forces, then no one could. Secretly he felt she rather approved of her daughter's wilful manner, as if she were some highly strung filly. Ah well, she'd just have to learn to fend for herself.

Some minutes passed, and then Hilary laid aside her sewing. 'You know, Reginald, the house is going to be awfully quiet when the children have gone. I've been thinking. I want to be up and doing like everybody else. I'm fed up of just sitting here, hardly ever going out.'

He glanced at her surreptitiously over the top of his paper, powerless to help or console, and apprehensive of where her restlessness might lead. Suddenly her frown faded.

'I know! I could sew something useful instead of just more embroidered cushion covers. I'll get in touch with the Church Wives' secretary this morning and tell her I'll organize a sewing group.'

'I thought there was one already,' the Colonel remarked.

'In that case I'll organize that,' his wife said firmly, and the Colonel heaved a sigh of relief. So long as Hilary was organizing something all would be well, for him if not for the Church Wives.

James Renshaw was waiting for his breakfast to be served when the postman delivered the official-looking envelope. Maddie placed the letter before him and Renshaw frowned as he adjusted his spectacles to read it.

'Hey up, they've taken notice of me at last,' he muttered. 'They're sending me some help.'

Maddie scooped eggs out of the frying pan on to two plates and sat down opposite him, elbows on the table and her chin cupped in her hands. 'Are they? Land Army girls? I've seen some of them at Bailey's – they wear green jerseys and trousers like a man – '

'Nay,' her father interrupted. 'I told them I didn't want no lasses – it's a man's muscles I need, what with the shearing and the branding and all. Lasses are no use when it comes to lifting a twenty-stone pig with block and tackle.'

'So who are they sending then?'

'Chap name of Bower.'

Maddie stabbed her fork into the egg, watching the yolk ooze slowly out and spread a vivid stain around the sausages. In her mind's eye she was already trying to visualize the newcomer. Would he be young and bright-eyed like Bob Bailey? she wondered. Or, too old for war service, would he be grizzled and tetchy like her father? No matter. It would be a new face.

Her father was studying the letter as he chewed. 'They don't give us much warning, that's for sure. This Bower's arriving late this aft, seemingly.'

She paused, fork half-way to her mouth. 'Today? Then I'd better get ready for him. Is he to sleep in Mother's room?' she ventured.

The chair scraped noisily on the flagstones as he stood up abruptly. 'The room in the attic'll do him.'

He was still muttering as he put on his old tweed jacket and Dog leapt to his feet. 'Trust them to time it wrong. I could have done with some help this past week. Thank God lambing's nearly done.'

Maddie stacked the dishes. No word of thanks for her part, she noted, though as always she had ridden up the still snow-spattered moor to round up the pregnant ewes and bring them down to the meadows where she had herded them into the pens ready for the lambing. And turn and turn about with her father she had spent nights working in the pens, helping the ewes give birth. Like all other Garthdale men, acknowledged head of the family, Dad expected unquestioning obedience and respect as his due, with no thought of thanks. Those Land Army girls were better off than she was, she thought resentfully. Twelve and six a week they got on top of their keep. Keep. That reminded her – the newcomer would need feeding. At least he'd be bringing another ration book.

The bell on the grocer's shop door clanged as she closed it behind her. She balanced the basket of groceries on the handlebar of Dad's rusty old bicycle propped against the wall and was just tucking away the ration books into her pocket when Ruby's bright young voice wrested her from her thoughts.

'Hi – long time no see! I'm just off to fetch some Woodbines for Mrs Spivey – she's always running out. Beats me how she can sew at all with a fag hanging out the corner of her mouth. Listen, I been thinking about you and that dad of yours.'

'What about him?'

'You got to teach him he can't go on shutting you up in Scapegoat for ever like a blooming nun. Why, it must be weeks since I saw you! All the fun you been missing! Why don't you just tell him what you want to do, then do it? Don't argue with him, that's my advice.'

'Easier said than done. He'd throw me out.'

'No he won't. I trained my folks. Even though my dad's a policeman he soon saw sense. Your dad'll soon catch on that you're a woman, not a child.'

Catching sight of Maddie's basket she broke off suddenly. 'Hey, what's all that lot for? Must be a whole month's rations in there.'

She indicated the bag of flour, the currants and sugar and the tin of treacle in the basket. Maddie smiled. 'We got company coming.'

Ruby licked pin-pricked fingertips. 'Company? At Scapegoat? Never!'

The interest in her young face deepened into excitement as Maddie told the tale. 'So I'm off home to make some dumplings for the stew. See you.' She pulled on darned gloves and swung a leg over the crossbar.

'Hey, I'll be up to see you soon in that case,' Ruby giggled. 'Can't have you getting first crack at a fellow before I've seen him. And mind you don't do yourself a mischief on that bike neither.'

'He'll be old as the hills, I bet you,' Maddie called over her shoulder as she rode away up the cobbled street. 'Bound to be.'

Ruby's vivacity brought a brightness to her day, but by late afternoon, the baking done and filling the farm kitchen with a delicious aroma, the new farmhand had still not arrived and her father was late. Maddie watched from the window as the sky deepened into dusk and a fine drizzle began to fall. She felt the old familiar blanket of darkness closing about her soul, and drew the blackout curtains close and lit the paraffin lamp, then began setting knives and forks for three on the kitchen table.

Dad came in at last, bleary-eyed and bedraggled, and taking off his jacket he shook it vigorously. Dog shook himself and headed for the fire. 'Hasn't he come yet?' her father asked.

Maddie shook her head.

'Good. I want a word with you first.'

'What about?'

'About you – your behaviour.'

He sat down and began pulling off his boots. Maddie stared at him, bewildered.

'Me? What've I done?'

'It's not what you've done – it's what you might do. Just because he's a man there's no call for you to be getting any daft thoughts about him, go leading him on or owt. Understand?'

Maddie continued to stare, and the look seemed to irritate him. 'Don't look at me so stupid, you know what I'm getting at. Just don't you go making sheep's eyes at him, my girl, or you'll have me to answer to.'

Maddie closed her eyes, trying to stem the anger that rose in her. Stay calm, Ruby had advised. She took a deep breath. 'I don't know what you mean, Dad. I'm not like that.' She turned away to ladle out stew from the pan.

Her father put down a mud-caked boot on the freshly scrubbed flags and placed grimy hands on wide-spread knees. 'Aren't you? I don't want no fellows with a hand inside your blouse again, that's what I mean. Just wanted to make it clear before he comes. I don't want no trollops here.'

Maddie's anger boiled over. She turned to face him, the plate of stew in her hand. 'I'm no trollop, and well you

50

know it! I need no lesson in how to behave, but it seems to me that you do, talking to your own daughter like that!'

He rose slowly, uncurling his height from the chair till he towered above her. 'Aye, you're my daughter right enough, so I can talk to you how I like,' he said, his voice full of anger. 'But for me coming in that night, you'd have had a big belly on you by now. I've known it happen before and I'll not see it happen again. And what use would you be to me then, eh, if you got landed with a bastard? Bloody millstone, that's what. Neither use nor ornament.'

Before she could think the plate had left her hand. As if on a film she saw it fly across the room past his head and hit the dresser behind him, sliding down the dark wood and leaving a snail-trail of gravy as it fell. She was aware of her father's face, open-mouthed and purple, and then she was rushing out of the door into the night, tears scalding her eyelids as she ran.

She had no recollection of flying down to the stable and saddling up Duster. She could only feel the black rage that choked her, blinding her to everything but the thought that her father neither loved nor appreciated her. She was of no more value to him than any poor wretch of a farmhand. To him she was only a tool of no greater value than a mattock or a pitchfork, a woman to run his house and work his precious farm, but a failure to him because she was not a son. She could disappear into the night for ever and he would not even care, let alone regret. He had even forgotten that today was her twenty-first birthday . . .

She rode hard, oblivious to the drizzling rain, until at last she became aware of Duster's heavy breathing. She had driven the creature onwards and upwards till now they were on the edge of the moor. Reining in, she turned the horse about and looked down the steep slope to the village far below in the valley. In the rain-dark night it was barely discernible. Not a light glimmered from a window; not a sound pierced the eerie moaning of the wind. From here Barnbeck looked like a village of the dead.

The dead. Oh Mother, how I miss you! How I need you now! Maddie slithered down from the saddle and stood on the scarp edge, tears filling her eyes and hair clinging damply around her face. She could smell the rich sweetness of wet earth as she listened to the wind. It did not fail her.

The voice came low on the gusting sobs of wind, soft and musical. *'Don't fret, my lovely. Close your eyes to the hurt. The world is not all disappointment, I promise you. There is so much else, so much beauty.'*

'And so much pain,' Maddie cried bitterly.

'But don't let it blind you to the beauty. You will find it, sweetheart, alone, and in silence.'

'But I'm tired of being alone, Mother! I need someone – I need you!'

'You need only yourself, Maddie, and what is within you. Alone, darling, and in silence you will find what you seek. Don't expect too much of others.'

The voice faded on the sighing breeze, and Maddie bent her head. The rain swept like a caress across her brow and she sensed peace in its touch. She could take comfort from that and write about it in the little exercise book where she confided all her inmost thoughts, the thoughts she did not dare tell even Ruby for fear of ridicule. Her poems. But for them she would have gone crazy long ago.

James Renshaw was disturbed. As so often happened at times like these, he found himself in the upstairs corridor, outside Lily's bedroom door, reaching up for the key kept on the ledge above the doorframe.

To him it was her room, though once it had been their room, a room filled with love until that final brief illness had snatched her away. The memory of that last day had made the room unbearable except for times like now, when he needed to feel her still close, still loving . . .

He averted his gaze from the bed as he crossed to the

dressing table in the window and looked down on her silver-backed brush and hand mirror. A few strands of dark hair still clung to the bristles and he felt the lump constricting his throat.

'I didn't mean to be so hard on the girl,' he muttered. 'I only wanted to see she was all right.'

Only the silence of the empty room met his words. He traced a stubby finger in the dust of the dressing table. *Lily.* The lump in his throat swelled till it seemed it would choke him. How often he had written her name on the back of his letters to her during the war, before he came home from the army and married her. It was their code. He remembered how she had smiled when he told her.

'The letters LILY spell out a message, love. It means Lily, I love you.'

He fingered the little cut-glass scent spray he had given her, remembering how she always wore the same perfume because he liked it, the one that smelt of violets. She had asked for it that last day, as if conscious that she needed to be at her best for the journey she was about to make. He recalled handing it to her then standing stiffly by the bed, gawky and afraid, ignorant of how to make amends.

'I'm sorry, James. Please forgive me.'

Oh no, Lily! It's me should have asked your forgiveness, but I didn't know how. And you went away from me, the words still unspoken.

'I can tell you, as your physician, that time will heal your grief, Mr Renshaw. In the early stages a bereaved person always feels guilty, but quite unnecessarily. It passes with time, you'll see.'

But the doctor was wrong. He had had no conception of the depth of James Renshaw's remorse. After all these years it still tore the heart out of him.

He stood at the foot of the bed but could not bring himself to look up at the frilled pillows. His voice came hoarsely out of a reluctant throat. 'I'm sorry, Lily love. I am.'

Then he rushed from the room, locking it behind him.

* * *

Maddie remounted the big bay which had been patiently cropping the wiry moorland grass. Steam was still rising from the mare's flanks, but the heat which had blazed in Maddie had finally begun to cool. It must be late, high time she got back to Scapegoat even if she could not find it in her heart yet to think kindly of her father.

Duster was picking her way down the rough pebble-strewn track towards home when Maddie caught sight of the light glimmering in the distance, moving across the fields. It was a lantern, far across the meadow where the sheep pens stood, and it could not have been painted black as regulations demanded. Fred Pickering, in his capacity as air-raid warden, would have a fit.

The light disappeared from sight. Maddie rode across the field towards the pens, dismounting and leaving the horse to graze. Her father was kneeling on a sack inside one of the cubicles alongside a sheep which was lying on its side. Beside him steam rose from a bucket of soapy water.

'She's had it. She can't make it,' Renshaw muttered to his daughter. 'It's stuck.'

Maddie knelt beside him and then she could see clearly what was happening. The lamb's head protruded from the ewe's vulva, distended and swollen to an unbelievable size and its eyes half-closed. A purple tongue lolled from its mouth. Her father sat back on his haunches and breathed a deep sigh.

'It's no use. I've tried – I just can't get my hand in. She's a goner and so is the lamb. It's choked.'

Maddie knew what he was thinking. He could ill afford to lose either lamb or ewe, but to lose both would be a tragedy.

'Let me have a go. My fingers are smaller than yours.'

'Nay, leave it be. She's stretched that tight you'll never make it.'

The swift refusal hurt. She knew what he meant – she was only a girl, useless in a crisis. He would not trust her. Now if she'd been a boy . . .

Suddenly a voice spoke behind her, startling her. 'Its legs are back. It cannot be born like that.'

Renshaw stared up at the face of a man dimly illuminated by the lantern glow. 'I know that. I can't get hold of 'em.'

'Let me try.'

There was curt authority in the voice. Renshaw eased his girth to one side to let the newcomer come closer. Maddie could see him clearly now, a tall, dark-haired man with serious eyes and heavy brows. She watched with curiosity as he knelt, dipped slender hands into the pail of water and then felt around the distended little head for a way to intrude his fingers inside and behind it. The ewe bleated piteously.

'How long has she been like this?'

'Nigh on two hours. She's that swollen now she's choked the little beggar.'

Maddie watched as if mesmerized. How readily her father had recognized the man's quiet, capable manner and given way to him. She felt resentful that Dad should allow a stranger into his confidence where he had rejected her, in a kind of masculine conspiracy. She looked down at her father's thick, stubby fingers. They were red and chapped, while the man's hands were slender and white.

There was a quick intake of breath. 'Have you got it?' asked her father. 'Can you feel owt?'

The man's finger had found an entrance just behind the woolly little neck. Maddie looked at his face. He was shaking his head thoughtfully.

'I find a shoulder,' he said softly. 'I must move carefully.'

'Feel down – find the elbow,' urged her father.

'I have it. I feel for the foot.'

More delicate probing and then, minutes later, he pulled forward gently. A tiny hoof appeared. The stranger nodded. 'And now for the other.'

Minutes passed before he found it, minutes that seemed like hours, and no one spoke. Maddie saw the gleam of hope in her father's eyes as the second hoof appeared. No sooner were the two little legs visible than the ewe seemed to realize that she too could now share the responsibility and took over. A mighty heave and the lamb was born.

Her father exhaled a long, slow breath. The stranger rubbed the lamb gently with a handful of straw and it opened its eyes, then he lifted it gently and put it to the ewe's head. She looked at it blankly for a moment, as if startled by its grotesque appearance, then licked it. The stranger stood up.

'I think all is well,' he said.

The ewe was making low, chuckling noises as she nuzzled her lamb, and it was ducking its swollen little head under her belly in search of the udder. Renshaw nodded in satisfaction and blinked up at the stranger. 'Thanks, lad. I'm grateful to you.' Then, as if conscious of seeming helpless on his own, he added gruffly, 'Lucky you have lady's fingers.'

The stranger bowed his head. 'It was fortunate I came just when I did. I am looking for Mr Renshaw, of Scapegoat Farm.'

'You've found him. That's me.' Realization slowly dawned on Renshaw's weathered face. 'Are you the fellow they're sending me? The new farmhand?'

The man inclined his head. 'Max Bower. I am happy to meet you.'

Resentment fled. Maddie felt a sudden leap of pleasure. He was no aged, crabby creature, nor a lumpish idiot. He was beautiful in the lamplight, his dark hair curling about his head in the rain and those large, black eyes resting on her. She pulled herself together.

'And I'm Maddie Renshaw. We're very grateful to you, Mr Bower. But for you, who knows what might have happened?'

Suddenly she became aware of the biting wind cutting across the top of the hay bales. It was penetrating her wet clothes and the two men must be just as frozen. 'Come on down to the farmhouse and I'll make us all some nice hot soup,' she said. 'I'm sure you could do with something warm inside you, Mr Bower.'

The dark eyes moved from her to Duster. 'I think perhaps you should see to your horse first, Miss Renshaw. I noticed it was steaming when I arrived.'

Maddie felt stung. Who was he to tell her how to care for her horse? As she moved away to take up Duster's reins she saw him bend to pick up a battered suitcase. Her father was following with the lantern, a glow of pleasure on his weather-beaten face.

'Them with their legs back are always the awkward devils,' he remarked. 'Like breech-first ones, they never amount to nowt. Born backwards, always backward. The only thing that's worse is when the sheep's been worried by a dog. It's no joke delivering a dead lamb. Have you ever smelt the stink?'

Her father's conversational tone irritated Maddie. It was so clear that Mr Bower was already accepted in a way she had never been. And all because he was a man and he knew something about sheep.

CHAPTER FIVE

'Look, Joanna, I've told you why I don't think you should go on with this silly idea. I would have thought that you, of all people, were capable of rational thinking.'

Hilary Westerley-Kent sat with her back to the window, her fingers drumming impatiently on the arms of her wheelchair. Her daughter stood moodily by the great marble fireplace, tapping her riding crop against her boot.

'I can't see what's so irrational about wanting to get away from here. After all, Richard's gone. You're always telling me that I'm too inexperienced.'

'Get away from here? You make it sound like a prison. Surely you love Thorpe Gill as we do.'

The girl bridled. 'There you go again, Mother. You always manage to make us feel guilty.'

Mrs Westerley-Kent smoothed down the invisible creases in her worsted lap. 'Well, I shouldn't really think I need to remind you, my dear, of your responsibility. Your father has enough on his hands running the estate and organizing local defence . . .' Her voice tailed away.

Joanna's face reddened. 'Go on, say it! You mean I should stay and look after you because you're a cripple, don't you? Oh, Mother!'

She turned away abruptly. Her mother regarded her averted back and spoke smoothly. 'I didn't say that, Joanna.'

The girl swung round. 'You never say it in so many words – that's the worst part of it. You imply it – all the time, and we all know it. You try to manipulate us.'

Her mother stared. 'You all think that? Oh Joanna, how could you!'

The girl's chin jutted. 'I'm going away, Mother – yes, I am – and someone had to tell you sooner or later.'

For long seconds there was a silence in the room, so tense it was almost tangible. When Mrs Westerley-Kent spoke again there was the faintest hint of a tremor in her voice.

'I didn't know you thought so badly of me, Joanna. It's a dreadful blow to a mother to learn that her child – '

'Stop it, Mother! You're still doing it!'

Joanna was leaning her forehead against the marble mantelpiece and her mother could see the quiver that ran through her slim body.

'To learn that her child resents her, even hates her,' she said in a voice barely more than a whisper. Joanna spun round and ran across to her, kneeling at her feet.

'Oh no, Mother, I don't! We're desperately sorry for you and wish we could do something, but we can't! We don't hate you.'

Her arms were around her mother's waist and her face buried in her lap. Mrs Westerley-Kent stroked the dark head and murmured, 'I'm so glad, darling. It would break my heart.'

The girl looked up at her with tear-filled eyes. 'No it wouldn't, Mother. You're stronger than all of us, you know you are, and we've always admired it.'

Her mother smiled and patted her head. 'We do what we have to do, my dear.'

The girl sat back on her haunches, letting her hand linger in her mother's. 'But I'm still going away next week. Don't send me away feeling guilty. Wish me luck.'

Hilary turned the wheelchair around to look out over the grounds. 'See what they're doing to our lovely lawns?' she murmured. 'Dig for Victory, they told us, so the lawns have to be dug up for vegetable beds. Imagine it, carrots and turnips and things! Such a shame, after all the trouble Vernon has taken.'

Joanna rose slowly to her feet, disappointed. Her mother was clearly not going to give her blessing. Instead she was ignoring completely something she did not wish to recognize.

'I'm going upstairs to pack, Mother.'

'So smooth they were this summer, something to be proud of when your Aunt Rebecca came to stay. Ah well, we have to make sacrifices, I suppose.'

James Renshaw pulled on his old tweed jacket. 'I'm off down to the Cock and Badger for a bit. Where's Bower?'

Maddie glanced in the direction of the staircase. 'Upstairs. He'll be down to hear the nine o'clock news most likely.'

'Aye well, just remind him we've to get the lambs marked and the branding done tomorrow afore we send the sheep back up on the moor. I did tell him.'

'I'll tell him,' she sighed. 'Not that I'll get an answer. Can't get a word out of him. Never met a man so quiet.'

'He's got more sense than to waste time nattering. That's a woman's game.'

'More's the pity 'cos he talks so nicely, have you noticed? Like the BBC fellows on the wireless. Not like folks round here.'

It was true, thought James as he picked his way down the pitch-dark lane with the help of his torch. The new farmhand had a very precise way of talking and was certainly a cut above anyone he'd ever employed before. He worked well too and ate the food Maddie set before him without comment and then took himself off to his attic room without bothering anyone. The fellow must come from a pretty decent family. As Lily used to say, breeding always shows.

In the warmth of the Cock and Badger he forgot about the newcomer to Scapegoat as he sat in his usual corner sipping his pint. As always, no one bothered him and he sat listening to the conversation.

'The bugger's invaded Denmark and Norway now,' Fred was saying to the landlord. 'He must think he owns the bloody world.'

Old Seth took his clay pipe out of his mouth. 'Aye, I heard Al Barley Dell telling us that on the news. Well, Hitler's not going to get me eating a measly one-and-tenpenny-worth of meat a week, I can tell you, war or no war. I've been used to a good bellyful of food all me life – how else would I have got to ninety?'

'You're nearing eighty, Seth,' said the landlord. 'Don't go trying to have us on.'

'How do you know, Len Laverack? Seen my birth certificate, have you?'

'I've seen your identity card.'

'Well any road, I'm going to get my share of good beef same as always,' muttered the old man, 'Hitler or no bloody Hitler. I'd teach that bugger a lesson if I still had me left hand.'

Fred chuckled. 'What'd you do to him, Seth?'

The old man chewed toothless gums for a moment. 'I'd string him up into sausages, and any other ruddy Germans, I would. Pity of it is I were too old last time and all.'

Fred glanced across at James before he spoke again. 'Well now's your chance, Seth. There's one of 'em walking around free right here in Barnbeck.'

Seth stared, mouth agape. 'A Jerry, do you mean? Here, in Barnbeck?'

Fred nodded. 'That's right – isn't it, James?'

James put down his glass and surveyed the shopkeeper for a moment before answering. 'What's right? What are you on about?'

'That fellow up at your place – he's a Jerry prisoner they've released, isn't he? What's he like to live with, James? Aren't you afeared he might rape your lass or stick a knife in your back? I wouldn't sleep sound in my bed of a night if I were stuck with one of them.'

James felt the blood chill in his veins. He was conscious that every eye in the pub was turned on him, watching for his reaction. He tried to gather his wits.

'What makes you think he's a German?' he asked cautiously.

'Nay, I don't think, I know. Eddie Sykes were notified by Otterley police station that an alien were coming, and Donald Fearnley said the fellow asked the way to your place the other night when he got off the train. He knew straight away, did Donald, said the chap talked funny, not like us. Didn't think you could keep it quiet, did you, James?'

There was challenge in Fred's tongue. James felt dizzy – why hadn't he tumbled to it before? Why hadn't the War Ag told him? Maddie had spoken of Bower's accent only tonight – but his name was a good English one. He rose and drained off his glass.

'Seems to me you get to know more than is good for you, Fred Pickering. Happen it's time you minded your own business for a bit.'

'Nay, it is our business when one of our own is sheltering an enemy,' countered Fred, and there was a murmur of assent. 'What does that make you?'

James felt the anger rising in his throat. 'Hey,' said Seth as a thought struck him, 'happen you'd best put a stop to him before he invades Whitby.'

Gales of laughter were ringing in James's ears and he could feel the eyes on his back as he followed Dog out into the night again and began the climb back uphill. Whatever his feelings about what he'd just discovered, he wasn't going to let those gossips see how he felt.

Not them. But he'd certainly let that devious bastard have a piece of his mind. A Jerry, was he, and he taking advantage of James's hospitality under false pretences? Those bloody Jerries had wrecked his life twenty years ago, and he was damned if he was going to give shelter to one of them now . . .

Maddie sat alone at the kitchen table, chewing the tip of her pencil. Before her lay the exercise book and the few

62

lines she had written in the private time while her father was out.

> *Whisper to me, wind, of happier times,*
> *When I was young and knew no care.*
> *Whisper to me of times to come*
> *And happiness to share.*

She cocked her head to one side and looked at the lines again, but they looked no better from that angle. It wasn't what she wanted to say; it sounded more like a message in a birthday card than her vague but certain belief that some day something would happen to make life incredibly beautiful. Real poets seemed to find the way to say it, but if you couldn't understand the words, you could feel the sadness and hope in them.

A heavy footstep on the stairs behind her made her start and out of habit she closed the book and pushed it under the newspaper. Mr Bower came across the room and looked at the clock on the mantelshelf.

'Is it past nine o'clock already?'

She turned to look at him. If he had a little more flesh on him he would look better, she thought. His cheeks were hollow and those dark, piercing eyes and long nose gave him a hungry look.

'Twenty-five past. You've missed the news.'

'What did they say?' His tone was curt, demanding.

'Hitler's invaded Norway and Denmark.'

The black eyes swung round to stare at the ceiling, ominously thunderous. 'First Czechoslovakia, then Poland, now this! There is no end to his evil.'

His voice was low, as if speaking only to himself. Maddie felt uncomfortable. It was as if she were not there and the strange light in his eyes troubled her.

'That's what Dad says – he's downright evil,' she agreed. Bower turned his glittering, black gaze at her.

'He's a fiend, an emissary of Satan! No torture is too great for such a swine!'

Maddie recoiled before the savagery of his words and the terrible light in those eyes. But suddenly it was gone. He seated himself opposite her at the table and sank his head in his hands. Maddie sat immobile, unwilling to disturb him. At length she remembered what she had to tell him.

'Dad says to remind you about the branding,' she ventured.

Mr Bower made a murmur, and then sat upright. His hand reached out to the newspaper and she caught sight of the scratches and the ingrained dirt. In only a few days those slender hands were losing the appearance of a gentleman's hands.

'What is this?' he asked, in that deep, sombre tone that sent shivers down her spine. He was holding her exercise book, flicking over the pages. She snatched it from him.

'It's mine. It's private.'

'A diary?'

'No.'

For a moment he surveyed her curiously. Maddie felt as she used to in the old days at school, when Miss Gaunt called her to make account for some misdeed, and felt the flush spread on her cheeks.

'Do not worry,' he said quietly. 'I will not intrude upon your privacy.'

At once she repented of her sharpness. He was a strange man, this Mr Bower, but somehow she sensed an undercurrent of sincerity. She hesitated. He was clearly an educated man, and perhaps she ought to take advantage of it, but maybe he would laugh at her. No, she did not know him. She could not confide in him, not in a man who could change mood so suddenly and unpredictably.

They were sitting in silence when the door burst open and her father's bulky frame filled the doorway. He leaned against the doorjamb as if his leg were troubling him again, but his face wore an expression of fury. Dog sidled in round him and made for the fire. Her father raised an arm and pointed at Mr Bower.

'You! Out!' he roared. Maddie caught her breath. Mr Bower did not move. 'You heard me – get out of my house this minute!'

Maddie sprang to her feet. 'It's all right, Dad. He wasn't doing anything – we were just talking.'

Her father ignored her and came forward a step, his arm still upraised. 'Did you hear me, Bower? Get your things packed and get out of here! I never want to see you again, deceiving me like you did!'

She caught hold of his arm, fearful lest he might strike out. 'What's up, Dad? What's he done?'

He shook her off and turned ferocious eyes on her. 'Talking, were you? And did he tell you he was a Jerry, 'cos he never told me?'

Maddie turned incredulous eyes on Mr Bower. 'Is that right? Are you a German?'

Mr Bower shook his head. 'I am no German, Mr Renshaw. I am an Austrian.'

'Same difference,' snorted Renshaw. 'Hitler's lot. And you never let on owt about it.'

Bower rose to his feet, and Maddie noticed for the first time that tall as her father was, Mr Bower was an inch or so taller. 'No, Mr Renshaw,' he said fiercely, 'I am not Hitler's lot. I am a Jew.'

'A Jew? A German Jew in my house?' Renshaw's eyes glittered. 'Get your bags packed this minute and get out like I said.'

Bower regarded him coldly. 'I cannot leave here without government permission.'

Maddie saw her father's look of amazement. He was not accustomed to such cool defiance. 'You'll at least get out of my house,' he ordered. 'No government on earth can make me give shelter to a man who cheated me.'

'I did not cheat. You did not ask.'

The purple in her father's face turned to white. 'Don't give me your insolence, man – get out!'

Without a word Mr Bower turned and went up the stairs.

65

Maddie stared at her father. 'Where's he to go at this time of night, Dad?'

He shrugged. 'That's his business.'

Moments later Mr Bower reappeared carrying his battered suitcase. Dog lifted his head as he opened the door and a flurry of rain spattered the flagstones, then Mr Bower went out into the night. Renshaw, his face impassive but still pale, pulled a letter out of the drawer then bent to the oil lamp to peer closely at it.

Maddie searched for a way to ease the tension. 'I'd never have believed it if he hadn't said so himself. How did you find out?'

'The fellows in the pub. How was I to know? It says here his name is Bower. I knew some folks called Bower once, good, honest Yorkshire folk, they were.'

'Was he right – he said you can't sack him?'

Renshaw shoved the letter back in the drawer. 'It says he can't go away for more than forty-eight hours without permission on account of the restrictions. But he'll not set foot in here again. He can sleep in the barn or where he will, but I'll not have a Jerry in my house . . .'

She realized what was worrying him. After his years in the army fighting the Huns he would hate anyone to believe he was willingly harbouring one in his home. But was Mr Bower really a German? He said not.

'The War Ag people should have told you,' she muttered. 'Fancy not mentioning it.'

'Any road,' said her father, 'he's a Jew. Never had no time for them neither. Never knew one as didn't do well for himself by charging other folks high.'

'But he's a human being, Dad. It's cold out there.'

Renshaw made no answer, but sat down by the fire. She knew he would not climb down.

'Well, I'll take him a blanket then,' said Maddie.

'That's if he's still here and hasn't buggered off,' her father muttered.

Mr Bower was still in the yard, sitting on an upturned box, the suitcase beside him and his jacket collar turned up against the rain. She could barely make out his features in the darkness as she handed him the blanket.

'Come on, I'll help you get settled in the barn,' she offered. He stood up abruptly.

'No need. I can look after myself.' He picked up the suitcase and strode away towards the barn.

'Shall I bring you a lantern?' she called after him. She was anxious to help, to prove that everyone was not against him. In the darkness she heard the barn door slam. Startled chickens in the hen coop uttered a few protesting squawks and then silence returned.

With a sigh she turned back to the house. Her father was sitting slumped before the fire.

'Well?'

'He's in the midden.'

He grunted. 'And there he'll stay so far as I'm concerned. Middens is the place for pigs.'

Max Bower lay in the straw with the blanket pulled over him and hated the bitterness that welled in him. From a young man whose life had once seemed so full of prospect, a young man full of hope and dreams, he had somehow turned into a creature of despair and self-pity, robbed of self-respect.

It was the Nazis' doing. When they came to power he, like thousands more Jews, had applied for a visa to America, but as the danger grew and no word came, flight had become the only solution. England was the refuge of the persecuted, they had told him, but how wrong they had been! Ever since he had come to this country more than a year ago he had met nothing but rejection. Even changing his name by deed poll from Bauer to Bower had had no effect. No work, they had said, for aliens, and for Jewish aliens in particular.

And when the war came at last the British government

had made no apparent distinction between refugee and enemy aliens. Interned under Section 18b on the very eve of war, he had found himself housed in a horse box on a peacetime racecourse. And not only that, but housed with rabid Nazi prisoners of war, to whom the very name of Jew was anathema.

Hatred, ridicule, torment. This had become the pattern of his days in the camp. The English guards either did not know or did not care about the suffering of the Jewish internees, the daily terror that they might be victimized yet again by those sadistic Nazi prisoners. His best friend Leo, chained and castrated by Nazis on an English racecourse – it was unbelievable.

And then suddenly came blessed relief for Max at least.

'*I am informed that your visa for America is granted,*' the commanding officer had told him. '*You may go to Epsom at once to collect it from the American Embassy. You are freed from internment.*'

But the sudden hope that leapt in him had been quickly stilled. '*You are free to go, but to get a berth on a ship to the States will take time – thousands are waiting and it could take years, the way things are.*'

'But I may leave the camp?'

'*Yes, today. Subject to certain limitations you can go where you please.*'

As far from Lingfield as he could get, he was determined, and he had snatched at the offer of voluntary work on a farm in the north of England.

Only a week ago he had been so full of hope that country life would help to restore his faith in humanity. He recalled how he had seen Scapegoat Farm for the first time, neglect obvious in its bleared windowpanes and shabby, peeling paint, but the occupants had seemed reasonable people despite the heavy oppressiveness of the place.

The farmer looked like any peasant the world over, his bloated, porcine face disappearing, almost neckless, into a blue-checked shirt. A face of peasant anonymity, Max remembered thinking, and as it turned out, of peasant obstinacy too. No, that was harsh. There had been others who should have known better who had laboured under the same misapprehensions as Renshaw.

Max shivered. It was damn cold out here in the barn. He thought with envy of the warm farm kitchen with the rusty bicycle leaning against the dresser, cycle clips swinging from the handlebars. A bicycle – he doubted whether the farmer knew that vehicles of any kind, even a bicycle, were forbidden to aliens. Even the rough stone sink, the rickety chairs around the table and slate-flagged floor with its worn and frayed rug seemed attractive compared to this. Still, the outside privy was convenient.

If it wasn't for that girl the place would be unbearable. Pleasant little thing, even if she did lack education and sophistication. There was a glow in her eyes and an other-worldly quality about her that rendered her somehow different from anyone else he had ever met. He would never be able to eradicate from his memory the sight of her riding that huge horse along the moor's edge the night he arrived. Wild, she had looked on horseback in the rain, a totally different creature from the rather subdued and faded mouse she was when she was with her father. A veritable Valkyrie she had been up there on the moor, wild and free and beautiful, just like sister Heidi used to be, before they took her away to concentration camp . . .

But Maddie was still a child, an unformed creature whom that stupid if well-meaning Renshaw would finally mould to his liking. She had no chance, locked up with him alone in this bleak and cheerless place.

Poor child. She would have to suffer the gloom and oppression of Scapegoat Farm until it finally drained her of life. It was inevitable.

As for himself, Max no longer cared. The wretched place suited his mental and spiritual desolation. He was already doomed, for the face of God was turned away from him.

CHAPTER SIX

'This is the BBC Home and Forces Programme. Here is the six o'clock news.'

Hilary Westerley-Kent moved with amazing speed in her wheelchair, crossing the expanse of Persian carpet to the sideboard. With one swift movement she snapped off the switch. 'Don't want to hear any more of that depressing stuff, do we, dear?'

Reginald knew better than to protest too forcibly. 'I know there's very little happening, but there could be more rationing changes or something.'

His wife spread her hands expressively. 'Whatever the changes, they won't do us any good. Just look what Lord Woolton did as soon as he became Minister of Food. Nothing but shortages ever since.'

'We don't do so badly – we can always top up the rations with a duck or rabbit, or even the odd trout or pheasant in the season.'

She gave him a withering look. 'If you had to do the cooking, you'd know. I mean, twelve ounces of sugar a week! You take that in your tea alone – and you always expect home-made lardy cake or scones with it. Whose sugar ration goes to make them, do you think?'

Reginald did not answer. Secretly he thought it was more likely to be Mrs Barraclough who made the sacrifice rather than Hilary. The cook was a good soul, so he could tolerate her pursed lips when she found the undissolved sugar left in his teacup if only she could go on producing her mouth-watering lardy cake . . .

'Are you listening to me, Reginald?' he heard Hilary's

voice demand. 'What do you think? Should I send for the girl and put the idea to her?'

Reginald's army training had not been in vain. He thought swiftly. 'Whatever idea you propose, my dear, is always worth listening to. By all means put it to her.'

Hilary nodded. 'I doubt very much that she'll refuse a chance like that. After all, it isn't every day a person of her standing gets the opportunity to have her mare covered by a stallion like Firefly. I'm dying to know what kind of foal he'll sire.'

Reginald's eyebrows arched in surprise but he was saved from having to comment by the sudden arrival of his son. Richard swept into the room full of enthusiasm and good humour, bringing a draught of fresh air with him. Hilary held out her arms to him, her face irradiated by a warm smile.

'Darling, you look so handsome in your uniform – come and give your mother a kiss.'

Reginald watched as his son dropped a swift kiss on her forehead, deftly avoiding her embrace. 'I think I'll go out for a ride, Mother – which horse would you suggest?'

Her face fell. Richard had only three days' leave and so far he had spent it all out of Thorpe Gill. 'Firefly,' she pronounced firmly. 'He's in need of exercise and I still can't get Archie to ride him enough.'

'Still the same old Archie,' Richard laughed. 'Can't think why you've employed him all these years when he hates horses so.'

'Not horses, only the Cleveland Bays. He's never been able to understand my enthusiasm for the breed. Which reminds me, Richard – would you send Archie to me – I've got an errand for him.'

'Can I do it for you, Mother?'

She considered for a moment. 'I want that girl at Scapegoat Farm to come and see me – you know the one, the little fair-haired creature?'

71

'The Renshaw girl? Yes, yes of course I'll go. Shall I tell her why?'

'No need. I'll explain when she comes.'

Richard was in high good humour as he left the drawing room to go down to the stables, his father noted. The boy had not changed during his short time in the regiment – he still had an eye for a pretty girl.

The coals in the brazier were glowing fiercely red. The two men stood facing each other across it, each man's image shimmering in the heat rising on a cold morning. Renshaw straightened his back and spoke gruffly.

'I reckon it's ready. Done any branding before?'

Bower shook his head.

'You know summat about animals, though.'

'A little.'

Renshaw grunted. A rotten Jew he might be, but at least the man didn't boast; that was to his credit. 'I'll hold 'em then, and you brand 'em. Good and hard on the horn, remember. And take care how you handle that branding iron.'

The sheep stood ready in the pens, sniffing the strange scent of hot iron. Renshaw took hold of one by the horns and dragged it, struggling, towards the brazier. Then he forced the creature down between his knees and gripped it tightly.

'Now. On the horn, till I tell you to stop.'

Bower stood for a moment, branding iron upraised, until the animal seemed to sense a superior will and lay still between Renshaw's knees. Bower came close, and bent so that his face was within inches of Renshaw's, and the older man could see a strange look in the fellow's eyes. It had a haunted, desperate quality and Renshaw could feel on his face the heat of the iron in Bower's hand.

Bower drove the iron firmly home as the sheep squealed and the smell of burning horn filled the morning air. Bower stood back. The letters of J. C. R. Stood out clearly.

A shadow detached itself from the shadows. The blond young Nazi officer billeted in Max's hut stood there, feet astride, barring Max's path, and he was not alone.

'Stop, you Jewish bastard, we want you!'

A companion in the shadows chuckled. 'We have a Christmas gift for you, Jew boy.'

'Specially made for you – and your circumcised brothers,' drawled the blond youth. 'Your own Star of David. We took a lot of trouble over it.'

'Come on, Heinrich, let's stoke up the bonfire and let the lads have their fun,' a third voice complained. 'There isn't much else in this damned camp to amuse us.'

Heinrich smiled. 'Go ahead. It is the winter solstice and we must celebrate our pagan rites. Teach these greasy money-grubbing Jews a lesson. Mark them out for all to see.'

Max made to dart, but strong arms seized him, then a sickening blow to the pit of his stomach drove all the air out of his lungs. He fell, gasping. Boots began kicking his head and excruciating pain seared his body. He was aware that his stomach heaved, spilling its contents on the muddy grass. It began to seem as if pain could do no more to hurt him and blackness began to seep through his brain, blocking out the crimson glow of fire.

'Leave off, don't kill him,' a voice protested. 'He'll be no fun dead.'

Muscular arms lifted him to his feet. Max hung limply between two tall figures, helpless and unable to breathe. His lungs felt as if they would burst within him.

'It's ready, Heinrich. Now?'

Max was dimly aware of the vivid orange glow of the branding iron, of someone baring his forearm, and then the smell of his own burning flesh and savage pain ripping through his arm before blackness enclosed his brain . . .

'Right,' said Renshaw. 'That'll do.' His muscles relaxed as he let the ram go free. It stood staring for a moment, then shook its head and ambled away. One after another the sheep were brought out, branded, and released. After a time Renshaw was beginning to sweat profusely.

'Let me,' said Bower. He dropped the iron back into the fire and crossed to the pen to drag out the next sheep. Renshaw watched. The man was no expert but his lean frame concealed powerful muscles. And he must have been watching closely, for he held the beast correctly between his knees. Renshaw took up the iron. Bower wasn't shaping too badly at all – he'd let him carry on.

For a time both men worked in silence. Renshaw was so preoccupied with the task in hand that he did not notice Maddie until she set down the large jug covered with a saucer and a plate draped with a cloth.

'Some hot tea and some sad cake with dripping on,' she said.

He grunted. 'We can't have done more than fifty. A long way to go yet.'

He watched her pour tea into tin mugs as he squatted on the grass. It would be quicker if he let Bower try to handle a sheep alone, as he himself could. He took the mug from her and tossed off the tea in a gulp, blinking as it scalded his throat.

'Come on, let's get on with it.'

Bower put down his mug, the tea only half-drunk. Maddie cut in. 'Oh, have a proper break, Dad! There's that lovely dripping I brought – '

'Later,' he said testily. 'Come on, Bower. We'll take one apiece now.'

Jerry or not, all credit to the fellow for showing no surprise or dismay. He dragged out the next sheep to the fire and took up an iron. Renshaw could see the fellow's muscles ripple beneath his shirt as he strained to control the struggling animal and the muscle tense in his forearm as he pressed the iron firmly into place.

'What's that?' said Renshaw, indicating the farmhand's arm. 'Tattoo?'

'No,' said Bower quietly. 'A brand.'

Renshaw stared at the mark, an irregular shape like a star. 'A brand, eh?' he echoed. 'Whatever for?'

'It is the Star of David, the mark of my race.'

The heat of the iron pierced the horn and the familiar bitter smell filled the air. Suddenly a flame leapt; the horn had caught fire and begun to blaze. Bower stared at it, then took the iron away.

'Douse it,' commanded Renshaw. Bower looked about him.

'*Gib' mir!*'

Renshaw saw the startled look that sprang into Maddie's eyes as Bower snatched the jug from her and poured tea over the animal's head. The flame died and Bower let the sheep go free.

'Nowt to fret over,' said Renshaw. 'Often happens.'

Bower gave him a long, slow look then turned away to fetch another sheep from the pen. Renshaw saw Maddie's gaze resting on the fellow, and felt a stab of irritation.

'It'll not be long before we need this lot taken back up on the moor. You might as well get saddled up.'

She turned away without a word. As she walked down the meadow with easy grace, he saw Bower pause to watch, his dark eyes glinting under the bushy brows.

'No time to waste,' Renshaw muttered savagely. 'We've the lambs to mark and the cows to turn out again. For the Lord's sake get a move on.'

Maddie was deep in thought as she climbed the stile into the lane, thinking about the strange foreigner and the unexpected touches about him which intrigued and somehow disturbed her. She was not aware of the rider until he was close, a tall, rangy figure in the saddle, sunlight glinting on the brass buttons of his uniform. He was watching her intently as he approached.

She recognized him, the son of the Westerley-Kent family down at Thorpe Gill. He must be home on leave for the whole village knew he had gone away to be an officer.

Ruby had recounted in rapturous detail how magnificent he looked in uniform, and Maddie could see she had not exaggerated.

He rode up beside her and dismounted. 'Aren't you Miss Renshaw?' he asked, and there was a smile in his eyes.

She saw his appraising look, and blushed. 'Maddie Renshaw, that's me.'

'I'm Richard Westerley-Kent. My mother sent me to invite you to come up and see her – at your convenience, of course.'

Maddie's eyes widened. 'She wants to see me? What on earth for?'

He spread his hands, and she noted their slender whiteness. 'She didn't say. A cagey lady, my mother.'

He had a wonderful smile, she thought, one that lit up his whole face. He fell into step alongside her, leading the horse by the rein. It was a very fine Cleveland stallion, beautifully groomed till it gleamed in the sunlight.

As the farmyard came in sight he slowed his step. 'Well, what answer shall I give her? Will you come?'

Maddie hesitated, but then curiosity won. 'Yes, I will. Tell her I'll call this afternoon, after I've got my jobs done – that's if it's all right with her.'

'I'm sure it is.' For a second he paused, looking down at her and tapping the rein lightly on his palm. She sensed he was searching for something to say, something which could delay his leaving, and the thought pleased her.

'I say, I'm told you have a Jerry prisoner working for you,' he said suddenly. 'Is that right?'

Instantly the pleasure fled, giving way to a defensive feeling. 'No, it's not. We have an Austrian, though – and he's a refugee, not a prisoner.'

'A refugee? What's he running from?'

His eyes were wide now. Maddie grew impatient. 'Who said he's running? He's a Jew, that's all, and you know what they're doing to Jews over there.'

His expression changed from surprise to repugnance.

'Ugh! You mean you have to have a Jew living with you? How dreadful! It must be very distasteful for you.'

Maddie glared up at him. 'No it's not. Mr Bower's a very good worker – and what's more, he's a gentleman.'

She walked on purposefully towards the gate. He was not to be dismissed so easily.

'I'm sorry. I didn't intend to be rude. Do you really mean you can find something in common with a – well, a foreigner?'

Maddie turned to face him squarely, her hand on the gate latch. 'Yes, I do, as a matter of fact.'

'Like what?' He was peering at her closely.

She shrugged. 'In our different ways, we're both outcasts, I suppose.'

He threw back his head and laughed. Maddie was both incensed and confused that he should laugh at her. 'What a dramatic little soul you are, Maddie Renshaw! That line was worthy of any of our finest actresses. Oh Maddie, we must meet again, you and I. Will you come out with me tonight?'

She was flustered but even so he intrigued her. 'I don't know – my father doesn't let me go out with boys.'

He clearly read her words to mean she would like his company if only she were permitted. He smiled and touched her hand, ever so briefly, but it sent shivers of excitement through her body.

'Leave it to me, Maddie. Was that your father up in the meadow branding the sheep? The old, grey-haired man?'

'He's not that old,' she countered, and again she saw the smile irradiate his handsome face.

'I only have two more days. Don't worry, I'll charm your old man and we'll go to the pictures together tonight. Would you like that?'

'Oh yes! There's a film in Agley Bridge I've been dying to see!'

'Then that's settled. I'll pick you up at seven – I'm certain I can get Father to let me have the car.'

Maddie watched him ride away, a fine-looking man on a superb beast, and wondered whether she could believe what had just passed. If he could achieve the miracle of persuading her father, there was the prospect of a handsome gentleman escort, a ride in a car for the first time in her life, and Errol Flynn in the darkness of the Roxy as well. Ruby would never believe it.

Hilary Westerley-Kent eyed the girl speculatively as Maddie stood beside the wheelchair in the stable yard. A pretty little thing she was, slight and vulnerable-looking, but she clearly knew a good Cleveland Bay. Hilary looked appreciatively again at the girl's mare tethered in the corner of the yard.

'Hold him steady, Archie.' Archie Bottom was growing restless as he held Firefly's head, his whiskered lips set in a tight line of thinly veiled impatience. 'Well, what do you think of him then?' she asked.

Maddie nodded. 'He's a very fine horse, Mrs Westerley-Kent. I thought so this morning when I saw your son riding him.'

'Ah yes, you've met Richard. He goes back to Catterick the day after tomorrow. Well, what do you think of my idea about your mare and Firefly? We'd have to try and establish your mare's claim to a pedigree, of course, otherwise I'd have the Society on my back.'

'Duster's not in the stud book,' Maddie said.

'But you know her dam, don't you, and it's the mare's line that counts in Clevelands.'

'Well, yes. We got both her and Robin from Thwaite Farm, from Sam Thaw.'

'Then we go back to Mr Thaw and establish the line. I think we'll have little difficulty because I know local farmers are as keen on pure Cleveland blood as the Society.'

Maddie nodded. 'Clevelands are far better than Shire horses for hill work. No hair on the legs, so they don't get clogged up with mud. But I don't understand why you're interested in breeding with Duster, Mrs Westerley-Kent.'

'Because like you I can recognize a good horse when I see one. She'll breed a fine hunter.'

'Hunter?'

'Oh yes. Clevelands are superb hunters, you know, the very best.'

'I'd never thought . . .'

'Then think about it. There's money to be made from breeding good hunters, Miss Renshaw. I don't want a stud fee. My interest is purely in seeing what your mare and Firefly will produce. The foal will be yours, of course, but if you decide to sell it, I'll have first choice.'

The young face still looked concerned. 'But I'll need two horses for the ploughing –'

'Tractors, my dear. You could borrow one. They're taking over from the Cleveland. The idea does appeal to you, doesn't it?'

'Oh yes! But I still don't see why you're doing it.'

'Because, like you, I love the Cleveland and don't want to see the breed die out. What with wartime rationing and the tractor, they will die out soon if we don't protect them.'

'Oh no!' Maddie protested.

'And I have not much time. Oh, the Cleveland Bay Society will go on, of course, but I'd dearly love to see someone carry on doing the work I've loved. I fancy you would be perfect.'

Hilary reached out a hand and touched the girl's lightly. 'Don't pass over this opportunity, my dear. You'd be doing an old lady a great favour.'

The girl looked down at her and smiled shyly. 'I'll have to talk to Dad about the tractor. He's not keen on them at all.'

Hilary patted the slim hand. 'I'm sure if anyone can coax him, you can. And we'd better not waste too much time. We'll need to get her covered soon, during June I suggest, and then the foal will arrive with the new grass next spring.

Now wheel me back into the house, my dear, and we'll have Mrs Barraclough bring us some tea and scones.'

'Nice girl,' Hilary told her husband later. 'Bright. Not like some of your village clots. Knows horses, too.' She sighed before adding wistfully, 'Would have been gratifying to have had a daughter like her.'

Maddie's feeling of excitement was soon dispelled. Her father was in the farmyard when she rode home again and dismounted.

'Bloody nerve!' he rasped. 'Fancy that fellow thinking he could talk me into letting him get his hands on you! Was it you put him up to it?'

Maddie's heart sank. Richard's faith in the power of his charm was obviously misplaced. There would be no car, no Errol Flynn and no blood-tingling embrace in the arms of a handsome young man tonight.

'No, I did not.'

He grunted. 'You must have led him on. Haven't I told you, Maddie Renshaw, there'll be no messing with lads for you, not now nor ever. Any road, I sent him off with a flea in his ear. He'll not be back.'

She led Duster towards the stable without answering. This was not the moment to tell him about her visit to Thorpe Gill. As she entered the stable she caught sight of Mr Bower just inside the gloom of the barn. He was watching her with dark, thoughtful eyes. For a second their gaze met and held, and then he moved away out of sight.

When supper was ready Mr Bower sat and ate in silence. As he lifted the fork to his mouth Maddie caught sight of the red weal on the back of his hand where the branding iron must have caught him. For a moment she wondered about that star-shaped brand on his arm and then, taking a deep breath, she told her father about Mrs Westerley-

Kent's proposition. He continued to eat in silence as he listened.

'I'll never get a better chance, Dad,' she urged. 'Much better than using the stud stallion that comes to Barnbeck every summer and everybody uses.'

'And what about ploughing time?' His sober eyes probed hers.

'I've thought about that. We could borrow Mr Bailey's tractor. He'll not mind.'

'You know what I think about tractors.'

'Or I could borrow another horse.'

Renshaw pushed back his chair and stood up. 'Well, I've to get on with the books. Never a moment's peace.'

'What do you say, Dad? Can I do it?'

'I can't think about that when I've the books to do. Bloody headache, is that.'

He took his books from the drawer in the dresser and Maddie knew it was a signal to leave. Renshaw never disclosed his figures to anyone. She took the dishes from the table and left them in the sink, then put on her jacket to go down to the stables. As she opened the door she heard Mr Bower speak.

'Can I perhaps be of assistance, Mr Renshaw?'

She paused and looked back, certain that the offer would produce an outburst. Instead her father licked the stub of his pencil and looked at Mr Bower over the top of his spectacles.

'Know summat about keeping ledgers, do you?'

'I used to run my own business.'

'Did you now?' The light in his eyes could have been either of disbelief or new-found respect, Maddie could not tell, but since she was obliged to close the door behind her she could witness no more.

'Well, well,' she murmured to Duster as she piled oats into the mare's manger, 'there's maybe more to Mr Bower than we thought. If he can get Dad to let him see his books, he's done more than I could. And more than Richard Westerley-blooming-Kent could do either.'

She fetched water in a pail to refill the iron horse trough and watched the mare's soft muzzle dipping into it. 'Just think, Duster, if I get my way you could have a foal by next spring. Firefly's foal.'

The mare paused and raised limpid, enquiring eyes. Maddie laughed softly and rubbed the soft nose. 'Nothing but the best for you, Duster. You shall have a pedigree mate or nothing. And come to that, so will I.'

She left the mare's stall and went to feed and water Robin. Half an hour later she returned to the farmhouse. As she neared the door she heard the sound of low voices in the kitchen and paused outside to listen.

'Your daughter has a natural feel for horses,' Mr Bower was saying. 'It might be a good idea to consider the tractor and let her – '

'You can mind your own business,' her father cut in. 'You don't know the trouble young girls can be, you not having none of your own.' There was a moment's pause, and then he mumbled, 'I know what's in her blood. There's a wild streak as needs taming.'

'I was only trying to say – '

'Nay,' cut in Renshaw, and Maddie could hear the impatience in his tone, 'funny how folks fancy they can tame a kicking donkey except them that has 'em. I'll take your advice on figures but nowt else, do you hear?'

Maddie opened the door. Catching sight of her, her father started drawing his papers together and she could see again the angry purple flush on his weathered face.

Mr Bower rose to his feet. 'I think it is time I went to the barn,' he said, and there was a stiffness in his voice. Her father was looking down at his papers and did not look up.

'Aye. Goodnight to you.'

Maddie stood aside to let him pass. As he did so their bodies almost touched, and she did not move away. The

Jew's eyes were on her, and she was fascinated by their mesmeric darkness and intensity.

'Goodnight, Maddie.' The voice was husky.

'Close that dratted door,' snapped her father. 'The draught's blowing my papers about.'

CHAPTER SEVEN

It was a warm spring day and the kitchen door stood open. Renshaw lifted his nose as he entered and sniffed. 'Summat smells good. What is it, Maddie?'

'Rabbit stew with dumplings and then apple pie for afters.'

He nodded appreciatively. 'Not had a bit of boiled bacon lately, have we? Nothing like a bit of bacon with cabbage.'

'We've run out. None of the last lot left.'

'Kitchen doesn't smell the same without a flitch or two hanging up. Time I killed another pig, I reckon. I could do with Bob Bailey's muscles for that.'

'Not the right time, Dad – there's no "r" in the month,' Maddie pointed out. 'Anyway, you'll have to get a permit from the Food Office.'

He snorted. 'Be damned to regulations! Do they seriously think we'd manage on only two pigs a year, after what we been used to? They must be off their chump if they do.'

'You'll get found out sooner or later. The food inspectors can turn up any time.'

'We'll just have to keep us eyes and ears open.'

'And folks talk.'

Renshaw growled. 'Aye, busybodies. But it's surprising how they keep their mouths shut when all them sheep keep breaking a leg and have to be put down.'

'Food Office is bound to cotton on sooner or later. We can't expect things to be the same as they were, now there's a war on. Any rate, we're lucky, we still have our own bread and butter and eggs.'

'Happen so, but even the bread's not what it was. That

National Flour's a damn funny colour. I don't like grey bread.'

'A tasty bit of pork dripping'd help.'

'I'll kill that old sow – she's good and heavy again now after farrowing – and I'll only let on about the ones I kill at Christmas. I'll need help though – where's his nibs.'

'Gone down to load the milk.'

'Did you get five gallon this morning?'

'Yes. It's all gone down.'

Renshaw grunted. 'That's one good thing, any road. Before they started this Milk Marketing Board we were never sure of nowt. Makes a difference having that cheque come in every month.'

'My geese and ducks help out,' Maddie pointed out.

He ignored her. 'Aye, things have changed. Not so long back I were lucky to get three bob for a pig. Remember·the times I've been stuck at Otterley market last thing at night and had to let ten of my piglets go for a quid? Aye, war's not done us so bad, lass.'

'It's not done Mr Bower a lot of good.'

'Rubbish. He's well off compared to some.'

'Being separated from his family,' Maddie murmured. 'I suppose he has a family. He never tells us anything. He seems such a lonely man.'

Renshaw gave her a shrewd glance. 'He's nowt to us, lass, and just you remember it. He's a Jew boy, that's all he is.'

A shadow filled the doorway and Maddie looked up. Mr Bower stood silhouetted against the bright sunlight behind him.

Renshaw pushed past him and went out without a word. Maddie came forward. 'Take no notice, Mr Bower. He really does think well of you, you know, despite his ways.'

He looked down at her thoughtfully. 'You think that? You, of all people?'

'How do you mean?'

He shrugged and sighed, a deep, weary sigh. 'No matter. I'd better get back to work.'

Maddie intervened. 'No you don't. You just sit a while and I'll make a cup of tea.'

He did not argue, but seated himself and watched as she pulled the kettle off the range, poured hot water into the teapot, swirled it round and emptied it into the sink. As she spooned tea into the pot he spoke. 'I saw that young man in the lane – the one from the big house – I think he's waiting for you.'

Maddie looked up in surprise. 'Richard, you mean?'

'I think he is trying to avoid your father.'

Maddie poured boiling water into the teapot. The last thing she wanted now was to face Richard Westerley-Kent after the way her father had treated him. But on the other hand, he had stirred excitement in her in a way Bob Bailey had never done . . .

'I'd better go and feed the chickens now,' she said as she drained her cup. Mr Bower stood up.

'And I to work. Thank you for the tea, Miss Renshaw.'

'Oh, please call me Maddie – everyone does.'

He gave a thin smile, and it seemed at odds with the gaunt, hollow look in his eyes. 'Very well, if you will call me Max.'

'Ah, well, my father might not like it – '

The smile faded. 'As you wish.' He turned to go out. Maddie felt ashamed, for he was clearly hurt.

She sighed and took up the bowl of meal for the chickens. As she crossed the yard towards the hen coop she saw her father disappear into the pigsty, a large knife in his hand.

'Psst!'

Beyond the farmyard wall Richard was waving to her, keeping a wary eye on the pigsty. She had to pass him to reach the chicken coop.

'Had to see you, Maddie,' he whispered urgently. 'Can you get away?'

She glanced back nervously over her shoulder. 'Go away, for heaven's sake – my dad'll see you.'

She pushed open the door of the coop. Instantly he threw one leg over the wall and clambered over. Maddie entered the darkness of the hen coop and he followed.

'You're asking for trouble,' she scolded. 'If my father catches you he'll kill you.'

He ducked his head under the sloping roof and seemed unaware of the eager chickens clucking round their feet. 'Oh, Maddie, I couldn't go back without seeing you again,' he whispered, and the urgency in his tone gave her pleasure. 'I haven't been able to get you out of my mind since I saw you. I've got to go back to camp tomorrow.'

The pleading in his eyes was accompanied by an equally persuasive touch. She did not stop him, encumbered as she was by the bowl in her hands. His arm slid about her waist and he drew her close. She held the bowl out behind him. It was exhilarating to feel the warmth of his body in the dark secrecy of the hut.

The sound of voices in the yard made her start.

'Mr Renshaw – please come here.' It was Max.

Maddie clasped Richard's arm. 'Dad's out there – I warned you, Richard – '

He let go of her and bent to peer through a crack in the wooden wall. Then he straightened. 'It's all right – he's gone into the barn.'

He turned and took her in his arms again. 'Oh, Maddie, you feel so good,' he murmured into her hair. 'Anything's worth daring to hold you like this.'

'Even my father?'

'Even him.' His voice was barely audible with his face buried in her neck. And his hands were moving gently up from her waist to her breast. Maddie took a deep breath. This was too wonderful to make him stop. For long moments they stood entwined, their bodies melting against one another, and Maddie felt dizzy with rapture.

There was a sudden piercing squeal and the chickens

squawked and fluttered around them. The squealing continued, hideous terror in the sound, and then suddenly it
stopped. Richard started. 'My God! What the hell was
that?'

He let go of her, his eyes wide. Disappointment filled
Maddie. 'Dad's killing a pig.'

Richard bent to look through the crack again. 'I'd best
get out of here,' he muttered. 'If he's got a knife – '

'He won't be coming out yet if he's just killed the old
sow. It takes a long time – '

'There goes that farmhand of yours, off over to the byre.
Now's my chance.'

Richard opened the door and slithered out like a grass
snake. Maddie watched him go, mesmerized. It was all so
unsatisfactory, not like Errol Flynn would have behaved at
all. And Richard hadn't even said he'd see her again.

Ah well, she thought ruefully as she scattered the last of
the corn, if real-life heroes could be so disappointing, there
was always the new copy of the *Picturegoer* to look forward
to reading. There was a lovely photograph of Mae West and
Cary Grant on the front page.

She emerged into the sunlight and recrossed the yard
towards the house. Her father's voice called out from the
pigsty.

'That you, Maddie? Come here and catch the blood for
us.'

Max Bower stood beside him at the bench where the
great sow lay motionless on her side, the hole in her neck
spurting a crimson fountain on to the salt in the bucket on
the floor. Over her father's bent back Maddie could see
Max's expressionless face. She knelt, taking up a stick to
stir the blood while her other hand pressed on the sow's
shoulder blades.

Renshaw straightened. 'I'll fetch hot water and we'll take
turns at scraping off the bristles, Bower. Maddie's got to
keep stirring while the blood cools else it'll be no good for
black pudding if it clots.'

Maddie concentrated on pumping out all the blood while he was gone, stirring the creamy red liquid in the bucket with the other hand until she heard the sound of her father's heavy boots clumping back.

'Can't think what got into you, Bower, calling me to look at that calf,' he muttered. 'Sack's tied tight enough. There were nowt wrong with the way I wrapped it at all.'

He set the pail of hot water down on the stone floor and reached for the scraping knife. Maddie sat back on her haunches. The hole in the pig's neck no longer oozed blood. The look Max directed at her behind her father's back was strange. She lowered her eyes and carried on stirring.

Renshaw was applying the water to the pig's skin with care, bending close to see in the half-light.

'Aye, I reckon that's hot enough to do the trick. Don't want it too hot neither, making black marks on the skin.'

He was sweeping the knife across the skin in deft, easy strokes when a thought occurred to him. He turned to his daughter.

'Tell you what, you can drive down to the station this aft, lass, and get them calves on the afternoon train. Bower'll give you a hand while I get on with cutting up the pork. We can have a bit for us supper tonight then.'

He handed the knife to Max and nodded. The younger man hesitated, then moved forward and began the same rhythmic movement over the pig's body and for a few minutes Renshaw watched.

'Funny thing, that,' he said quietly, as if talking to himself. 'The old sow wouldn't die as fast as they normally do. Tough old beggar she were. Just stared at me, she did. You could swear she knew what I were doing. Them eyes . . .'

He jerked himself out of his reverie and went outside. By the time he returned the blood was cooled in the pail and the pig's body stripped of bristles. Maddie watched as her father made ready with the block and tackle.

'This is where your young muscles'll come in handy,'

Renshaw remarked to Max. 'Hoisting twenty stone up on the cambril is no joke.'

It was a pleasure to watch the men's muscles strain beneath their shirts as they heaved, making the task of hoisting the massive carcass up to the beam look easy. Maddie noted the droplets of blood on Max's shirt front and the glaring splashes of crimson on her father's trousers. She left them to it and went back to the house. It would be a pleasure to go down into Barnbeck on such a sunny day.

By the time she came out of the farmhouse that afternoon her father had already loaded the calves on to the cart where they lay, their soft brown eyes wide in bewilderment. Inside the sacks they could not move, but she knew they were not uncomfortable. Renshaw watched as she led Duster out from the stable and backed her between the shafts of the cart.

'Sam Thaw told me he lost a pound on the Derby last year,' he remarked. 'I told him he were daft. There's only one way to back a horse, and that's between the shafts.'

Maddie climbed up on the cart. Renshaw looked about him. 'Where the devil is that fellow?' he said irritably. 'I told him he were to go with you.'

Maddie shaded her eyes against the sunlight. 'There he is – down the lane. I'll pick him up,' she replied, and cracked the reins. Her father turned back to the pigsty.

Max Bower was leaning against the drystone wall. He straightened as she approached and climbed up to join her on the driving seat. He made no move to speak as she drove downhill, the cart bumping over the rutted wheeltracks. Maddie felt compelled to thank him.

'You saw me with Richard,' she ventured.

'Yes.'

'And you distracted Dad so he wouldn't know. I'm grateful.'

'No need. It is I who should be grateful to you.'

'What for?'

'Caring for me. You are very thoughtful.'

90

She felt suffused with pleasure. It was a new experience to be thanked for doing only natural, everyday tasks. Suddenly the sun seemed to shine a little more brightly.

'You do not appear to share your father's distaste for Jews,' she heard him say, and she frowned.

'I never thought about it. Or that you were a German either. Funny, that.'

'An Austrian, Maddie. It's another country – or at least, it was, until Hitler took it prisoner.'

A prisoner. Maddie felt her heart lunge in pity for the man. 'I heard what you said to Dad last night – that was nice of you.'

She half-turned to him, smiling. The sombre eyes looked away, and she saw how pale he looked. 'Are you all right, Max? You look funny.'

'Thank you, yes. I needed air, that is all.'

'Is that why you didn't come in for lunch? Why you were down the lane?'

'Yes.'

'It was the pig, wasn't it? Oh Max, I am sorry! Slaughtering's not very nice if you're not used to it.'

He shook his head. 'Don't worry, I am well now.'

The station master nodded to Maddie as they arrived at the station and watched in silence as she and Bower carried the calves on to the one little platform. When Max was out of hearing he pushed back his cap and scratched his head.

'You got that Jerry with you?' he said to Maddie, jerking his head in Bower's direction.

'He's an Austrian, Mr Fearnley, not a German.'

The station master replaced his cap. 'Oh aye? But he's a Jew, isn't he? Never seen one of them before.'

Bower appeared not to hear. When the calves were safely stowed away in the guards' van on the afternoon train Maddie had a sudden desire to lengthen the brief spell alone with the enigmatic farmhand, away from the claustrophobic atmosphere of Scapegoat.

'We don't have to hurry back,' she said impulsively. 'Let's leave the cart here and go for a walk.'

He looked uncertain. 'Won't your father need us?'

'Not yet. He'll want me to soak the joints in brine when he's done, but that won't be for a bit yet. Let's go along the riverbank. You haven't seen the river, have you?'

Max shook his head. 'Not from down here, only from the top of the moor.'

'Come on then.'

There was no one about as they sauntered along the hot, dusty main street. A few sheep ambled about the pavement and into the front gardens of the little cottages, intent on munching grass and flowers, and they showed little interest in the passers-by. The sheep might be uninterested, thought Maddie, but the villagers would be sure to be curious about the stranger. No doubt at this very moment curtains were twitching as they passed.

At the end of the street Maddie pointed to the low grey building next to the church. 'See that school house? That's where I went to school,' she told Max.

He looked across at the building. 'Did you enjoy your schooldays, Maddie?'

She shrugged but made no answer. How could she tell a stranger that the world had seemed a sunny place then, full of fun and giggling confidences with her best friend Ruby in the next desk, plotting how they would creep under the hedge on one side of the schoolyard and escape into the fields during the dinner break? How Ruby had always copied Maddie's exercises into her book and never learnt that Miss Gaunt was far too shrewd to be taken in? How Maddie's only concern in those days had been envy that Ruby had a lace-edged hanky tucked up her knicker leg while Maddie had only a piece of clean rag in hers? And how that light of carefree youth had vanished that bitter-cold day they told her her mother was dead? She held her tongue as she and Max cut off across the meadow down to the riverbank.

The river was no wider than a stream at this point, meandering like a lazy snake between the trees bordering its banks. At the edge of the wood Maddie caught sight of rabbits leaping and frolicking, unaware of their approach.

'Oh look!' she cried. 'That one's drumming his hind legs! And there's a black one! That's good luck, I always say.'

'I thought it was a black cat which was supposed to be lucky,' Max replied.

'You can make whatever you want be lucky for you,' Maddie rejoined firmly. 'Black pigs if you like.'

She saw the wry smile that came to his lips. 'I hardly think so. Jews are not supposed to eat pig. It is regarded as unclean. The pig to us is a symbol of gluttony.'

She stared at him, wide-eyed. 'But that's silly – hang on, is that why you never have the pork sausages at breakfast? And helping Dad handle the pig – is that why you were feeling sick just before? Oh, Max!'

He gave a weary smile. 'There could be no greater penance for a Jew than to have to assist in the killing of a creature he is forbidden to touch.'

'And you never let on.' Maddie plucked a blade of grass, turning over the thought in her mind. Then she ventured another question. 'Do you eat rabbit, Max?'

He threw back his head and laughed, and Maddie took pleasure in the sight. 'Strictly speaking, no. We should not eat any creature which swarms, crawls or uses its front feet as hands. But I have eaten and enjoyed your excellent rabbit stew, Maddie. And what of you? Can you bear to eat rabbits, admiring them as you do?'

She nodded. 'Oh yes, but I hate to think of the way they're caught. I hate suffering.'

'Traps, you mean?'

'It's no better when the men send muzzled ferrets down the burrows after them. They catch the rabbits running out with nets, poor, terrified little things. Cheating, I call it. But at least it's not as cruel as hare coursing. I won't watch when they set the lurchers on chasing hares.'

'They could become pests if man didn't hunt them, Maddie. A she-rabbit can have as many as seven litters a year – did you know that? And that she can conceive again before she even gives birth to the litter she's carrying?'

Maddie hunched her arms round her knees and frowned. 'I know Dad hates them because of eating the corn – eating his profit, he says – and he enjoys shooting them up at Bailey's when they run out of the way of the tractor. But I think it's terrible that people have to be so cruel.'

She was staring into the middle distance, unaware of his scrutiny. 'Do you love all animals so much, Maddie?'

She shrugged. 'What else is there to love?'

'People. Don't you have any other family besides your father?'

'No. My mother died years ago. Well, there is Aunt Lottie and my cousin Ronnie, but they're in Australia. There was Uncle Arthur too, but he's dead. I've never even seen them. Anyway, people aren't the same as animals.'

'People fail you, is that it?'

'Animals are more reliable. You can get to understand them. Like my horses, for instance. I understand every mood they're in, and they understand me.'

He reached out a finger and touched her lightly on the arm. 'Poor Maddie, poor child,' he murmured.

She snatched her arm away angrily. 'I'm not a child!' she protested. 'I'm over twenty-one. And I'm sick of being treated like a child. Maybe it's time we went home.'

Suddenly the beauty of the riverbank glowed less invitingly, and she resolved she would not tell him about Duster after all. As they neared the railway station Ruby was just coming out of Mrs Spivey's haberdashery and tailoring shop where she worked. Her lively eyes darted straight to the man at Maddie's side. Maddie felt in no mood to introduce them.

'Hey, Maddie! Where've you been? Oh, I say! I can see why you've been hiding yourself away. Right little dark horse you are.'

'We've been busy,' said Maddie. 'Got to get back and get supper ready now – it's got to be on the table for half-six.'

'Hold on a minute.' Ruby tossed back her hair and rolled her eyes. It was all for Max's benefit, Maddie knew. 'Did you know Richard Westerley-Kent was home on leave? He looks absolutely gorgeous in his officer's uniform. You can keep Clark Gable!'

'Yes, I know. As a matter of fact, he asked me out.' Maddie could not resist saying the words with pride.

Ruby's eyes widened even further. 'He did? And what did you say?'

Maddie glanced at Max but his face was averted. 'I said no.'

'More fool you,' laughed Ruby. 'See you.'

Renshaw was in a taciturn mood over supper, and afterwards he announced that he was going down into the village. 'They're setting up some sort of army unit – Local Defence Volunteers – and I said I'd think about joining.'

'Why, Dad? You fought in the last war.'

He glanced at Max, but the farmhand's pale face was expressionless. 'We all have to do us bit,' he muttered. 'I'll not be late.'

Max rose. 'I shall return to the barn then,' he said.

'Aye,' said Renshaw, 'it'll not do you any harm to have an early night.'

Max was still standing in the yard after Renshaw had gone. Maddie approached him and looked up at him shyly.

'I didn't mean to snap at you this afternoon,' she said softly. 'It's just that I get annoyed being called a child all the time.'

He turned and looked down at her. 'You are a child in the ways of the world, Maddie.'

'Stop mocking me!'

'I'm not, I assure you. I envy you. You should enjoy your youth while you can, Maddie. A time of innocence

95

and charm. Age and experience bring sadness, and we long to recapture what you still have. We envy you your youth.'

She frowned. 'But you're not that much older than me, you can't be.'

She heard the deep, long-drawn sigh before he answered. 'In years, perhaps. But I would give anything to live again that chapter of my life when I had your enthusiasm for life, your innocence, your hope.'

'You must be daft, wanting to be like me! Can't you see how I'm trapped in this place? But I'm not going to let it go on for ever. I'm going to do what I want for a change, just you see if I don't.'

His eyes searched hers for a moment before he answered. 'You will, I know you will. I only hope that your impetuous nature does not make you act in a way you may regret.'

She turned away, puzzled, and looked up to the high open moor where the sun was setting in a deep, crimson glow along the ridge. 'You said you'd seen the moor,' she remarked. 'When?'

'At night. I often walk there when everyone is sleeping.'

She turned back to him, filled with pleasure. 'Do you? Do you like the moors?'

He nodded, and his dark eyes held again that deep unfathomable air that intrigued her. 'It is only when I am alone up there that I can feel at peace.'

She was savouring the thought that someone else should share her feeling, when he said abruptly, 'Goodnight, Maddie.'

She was alone again, and the sun had set. More than anything she would have liked to pursue this puzzling but fascinating man and question his meaning, but at the same time she felt irritated. Who was he to patronize her, to talk as if he were as wise as Solomon and she only a stupid donkey?

The farm lay still under the moonlight. Maddie was about to light the candle to go to bed when she heard the farmyard gate creak and knew her father was home.

'Who the devil did that?' she heard him roar. 'Bower! Come out here!'

Dropping the box of matches she ran out into the yard. Bower was emerging from the barn, barefoot and his shirt open to the waist. She could see the dark hairs on his chest as he stared, blinking, at her father.

'See that?' her father demanded, pointing towards the gate. In the moonlight his face looked drained of blood. 'Did you do that? And if you did, in God's name, why?'

She followed the direction of his finger. Just beside the gate stood a wooden stake driven into the earth. On the top of it grinned a pig's head. Bower approached it slowly.

'It's off that sow I killed today, isn't it?' Renshaw said savagely. 'What did you want to go and do a thing like that for, eh? Some kind of stupid gesture, is it? After all we've done for you?'

Maddie saw Max straighten slowly and shake his head. 'This is not my doing, Mr Renshaw. I rather think the gesture was meant for me.'

He turned away from the ghastly grinning head with a look of distaste, brushing past Maddie and back into the barn. Maddie approached the head, filled with a sense of unease. A piece of paper was nailed to the stake, and she pulled it off. She peered closely. There were words on it but they were hard to decipher by the light of the moon.

'What's it say?' her father rasped.

She frowned. 'It says *Dirty Yid*. What does Yid mean, Dad?'

Behind her she heard him give a deep sigh. 'Nowt. Let's get back into the house.'

CHAPTER EIGHT

Time was slipping by and Renshaw remained in an intractable mood, refusing to discuss with Maddie what should be done about Duster.

'I'm fed up of hearing about that mare. I've other fish to fry.'

'But if ever I'm to breed off her, I'll never get a better chance, Dad. We've only got a gelding, not an entire, and Firefly is the finest Cleveland stallion you could find. And after all, Duster is mine.'

'She belongs to Scapegoat, like everything else here. Nowt's yours till I'm dead and gone, so you'll just have to bide your time.'

'Are you saying I can't mate her then?'

'How can she when she's needed for ploughing? And I don't want to hear no more about Bailey's bloody Fordson tractor neither.'

'Am I to tell Mrs Westerley-Kent I can't then?'

'For God's sake shut up. I won't discuss it any more.'

Maddie pounded the clothes in the zinc washtub, watching the water gradually turn to grey as the posser eased out the dirt. Fury and frustration boiled in her. Why wouldn't he listen? Was her life going to be for ever like this, growing greyer by the minute like the sudsy water?

The washing finally done and hung out in the yard to blow in the breeze, she stamped away down to the stables. The warmth of the spring day hung under the low rafters, enhancing the sweet smell of the hay. Tears brimmed under Maddie's eyelids as she buried her face in Duster's wiry mane.

'I'm not going to let him spoil your life, Duster, or mine either. He's a selfish brute!'

A quiet footstep behind her made her start guiltily. Max stood in the doorway, dark fronds of hair clinging damply to his forehead. He was carrying a bucket of whitewash. Duster threw back her head, showing the whites of her eyes, and whinnied.

Maddie brushed a hand quickly across her eyes. 'Don't worry, Max. She doesn't recognize you, that's all.'

He put down the pail and regarded her thoughtfully. The mare was still wide-eyed in distrust. Maddie rubbed her nose.

'There, there, it's all right, Duster.'

'She does not trust me,' Max said.

'You don't need to be afraid of her, you know. She'll get to know you.'

'Dumb animals understand a great deal.'

'More than people give them credit for. Still, once you've won her trust, she'll do anything for you. She'll carry a sheep on her back for me, and that takes years of training as a rule.'

She hesitated, wondering whether she should reveal her thoughts. On an impulse she decided. 'Listen, Max,' she said urgently, 'have you ever handled horses? Not just ridden them, I mean.'

He smiled, a thin, weary smile. 'Yes. I used to work with the Lipizzan horses in Vienna.'

'Lipizzan?' She frowned. 'I haven't heard of them. Would I know them by another name, like some folk call the Cleveland Bay a Chapman?'

He gave a dry laugh. 'No, Maddie.'

'What then? Is it a plough horse too?'

He turned away, and she could swear she heard a chuckle. 'Not a plough horse, no. It's a dancing horse.'

For a moment she stared, and then grew suspicious. 'You're teasing me, aren't you? Who ever heard of a dancing horse except in a circus? You're mocking me again, Max. You're treating me like a child again.'

'And so you are.' He was smiling broadly now, and she still could not be sure whether he was teasing her. 'I came in here to whitewash the walls as your father told me. Is it inconvenient? I can do it later . . .'

'No, wait.' She took a step towards him, then scowled and turned away. 'Oh, what's the use? There's no one I can rely on – except my horses. The world is a rotten place.'

She saw him frown. 'How do you think the people in Holland and Belgium are feeling now they've surrendered to Hitler? And now it is the turn of the French. You are lucky compared to many.'

She heard the infinite sadness in his tone and felt guilty. 'You've never talked about yourself and your family, Max. Are they still in Germany – Austria, I mean?'

'Who knows? May I begin the painting now?' His tone was clipped to the point of rudeness, but Maddie was not to be deterred.

'You don't want to talk about them. I can understand that, Max, really I can. I don't like to talk about my mother.'

'Why not?'

She shrugged. 'Because I loved her so much – because no one else knew her like I did.'

'Not even your father?'

'Him least of all! I hate to hear him talk of her, making her out to be silly and useless. I try to close my ears to him. I don't want him – well – reshaping my memory of her. She was wonderful.'

'Now you know why I too do not wish to speak of those I love.'

He turned away from her and she felt a sudden surge of compassion. He too had suffered.

'Damned Nazis!' he muttered. 'Twenty years ago your people defeated those devils, yet you did not hang on to

100

your victory. Now look what is happening – we must suffer them all over again.'

He swung back his foot and kicked the door of the stall so violently that it banged against the frame. Duster laid back her ears and whinnied.

'Easy now, Duster,' Maddie said soothingly. 'You should take care, Max, or you'll frighten her.'

His dark eyes clouded. 'Forgive me. I should not have let my feelings take control.'

'Duster might have kicked out at you,' she murmured. 'Look, Max, I want to get Duster down to the stallion at Thorpe Gill – today, while Dad's gone down to buy the seed corn. I'd take her myself, but I might have to go with Dad. Will you take her for me?'

Max hesitated. 'Your father has told me I must white-wash the barn.'

'Then after that – you'll have finished before we get back?'

'I should ask your father whether there is any other work I should do first.'

'No!' Maddie swallowed hard. 'No, really, I don't think you need talk to him. In fact, I'd rather you didn't mention this to him at all.'

Dark eyebrows rose in silent query and she hastened to reassure him. 'Just take her for me, Max, that's all, and get her back here this evening. Archie Botton, the stableman, will see to the rest. Will you do that for me?'

There was the briefest of pauses before he answered. 'Very well. Now if you will take the horses out I'd better get on with the whitewashing.'

'Tell me all about it, Joanna,' Mrs Westerley-Kent was saying to her uniformed daughter. 'I really thought you would have been given a position in clerical work with all your education.'

'They graded us and I was one of the few who could drive a car,' Joanna explained cheerily, 'and I can't say I'm sorry. Driving officers has its perks, you know – lots of parties and dining in smart hotels. It's almost like civvy life in a way.'

Her mother regarded her thoughtfully. 'I see. Well, I hope you're not getting into bad habits, that's all. I know your penchant for fun and games.'

'Now, now,' said Joanna. 'You forget, I am a responsible member of His Majesty's armed services. I say, who is that gorgeous man coming up to the house?'

Hilary spun her wheelchair around and moved across to join her daughter at the window. She frowned. 'I don't know him. ARP, perhaps, or one of those officious Food Office inspectors again. Go down and see what he wants, there's a dear.'

Joanna still hung around the drawing room when the handsome young man entered and handed over an envelope. She did not take her eyes off him as her mother read the letter. He was tall, muscular and held himself well, his manner just the right combination of earnestness and insouciance. As Hilary finished reading she refolded the sheet of paper.

'I understand the mare is in season. You have brought her with you?'

'Yes.' His voice was deep and resonant, but his manner was not as deferential as one might expect from a farmhand. 'Miss Renshaw was not able to come herself.'

'Pity. I see she says here that she must have the horse back again by evening. You do realize that the stallion may or may not have covered her by then, don't you?'

'Yes, madam.'

Hilary sighed. 'Most unsatisfactory. I'd much prefer the mare to stay longer so that we could be certain. Still, I'll send for Archie and see what can be done.'

'There is no need, madam. I can handle the servicing if you will permit.'

Hilary's eyebrows rose. 'Are you accustomed to horses?

Can you supervise if my stallion were to be run with the mare now?'

'I can.'

She eyed him appreciatively. With his air of authority and confidence he was clearly no common villager. He was very good-looking too, in a dark, saturnine way. Knowing most of the people in Barnbeck as she did, it was strange she had not come across him before.

'Do I know you, Mr – ?'

'Bower. No, madam.'

Hilary then became aware of Joanna's speculative gaze. 'Joanna, I would like to take Mr Bower down and show him Firefly. I wonder if you could get Archie – '

'Don't trouble yourself, Mother, I'll see to it. It will be a pleasure,' said Joanna. 'Come this way, Mr Bower.'

Renshaw had just unloaded the seed corn from the cart and settled down at the table to eat his supper when Ruby arrived. Her lively eyes flicked around the kitchen as she took off her jacket and flung it over the back of a chair.

'Just popped up to see how you was going on, Maddie,' she remarked. 'Haven't seen sight nor sound of you in ages, only in passing the other day. Well, I see nowt much has changed here.'

Maddie gave her a cup of tea and watched the door for Max. She knew full well why Ruby had come, but she was far more concerned to know how Max had got on with Duster down at Thorpe Gill.

As soon as he came in Ruby swivelled round on her chair, green eyes appraising. 'My, my, you look all hot and bothered,' she said with a dimpling smile. 'I know we've met but I didn't catch your name.'

'Max Bower,' he told her tersely, and turned away to the sink to wash his face and hands.

'And I'm Ruby – Maddie forgot to introduce us the other day, but I reckon she's not as daft as she looks. Why haven't we seen you down in the village, Max? Don't you never get time off?'

Max was splashing water over his head and did not appear to hear. Maddie could see the droplets clinging to the black of his hair as he rubbed his face with the towel.

Renshaw pushed away his plate and crossed to the sideboard. As he turned on the wireless and seated himself next to it, his frown of irritation was clearly visible.

Ruby turned her attention to Maddie. 'Hey, I say, we've had some new dress patterns come in at the shop. You ought to come in and have a look, Maddie. Happen there's summat you'd like to have made up – after all, it must be a year since you made that one.'

'Hush,' said Renshaw. 'I'm listening.'

'A girl needs a decent frock or two,' Ruby went on. 'Did you know there's a Saturday night hop at that army camp up at Otterley? I've been asked to go.'

Maddie laid a finger to her lips, but either Ruby did not notice or she was deliberately ignoring it. 'Come to that, I've been asked by somebody else to go to the flicks on Saturday too. Might as well, seeing as Norman's off in the air force shortly. Oh, that reminds me – have you got last week's *Picturegoer*? One of them rotten cows at work must have pinched mine. There's a photo of Greta Garbo in it, you know, *I vont to be alone* – I don't think!'

All the time she was speaking she kept her eyes on Max who sat eating in silence. Maddie sat toying with a cup of tea, longing to ask him about Duster. Renshaw curled his hand round his ear and leaned closer to the wireless.

Ruby leaned her elbows on the table and bent forward confidentially. 'This chap, this soldier who's asked me to the dance, Maddie – you should see him. Shoulders big as an ox. He's the spitting image of that chap in the pirate film – you know, what's his name?'

'For Christ's sake, shut up, girl!' Renshaw bellowed. 'Haven't you got a home of your own to go to? France has fallen to the Jerries, our lads have had to be pulled out of Dunkirk and any minute now we could be invaded by them bloody Germans, and all you can do is rattle on about frocks and lads!'

Ruby sat open-mouthed with shock. Renshaw, muttering, turned the volume up. 'Now bugger off home if you've nowt better to do,' he growled. Maddie pushed back her chair.

Ruby got up abruptly, her pert little nose in the air. 'Well, really, Mr Renshaw! There was no call for that.' She turned to Maddie. 'I was thinking of asking you if happen you'd like to come with me to the hop next Saturday – '

'No,' snapped Renshaw. 'Now bugger off like I said.'

Maddie was no longer listening to the interchange. Behind Ruby's back Max had caught her eye. He gave a slow, deliberate nod.

Her heart leapt. She understood his meaning – Duster had been successfully covered by Firefly, and with luck she had now conceived her foal. Ruby's chatter outside as she left made little impact on her.

'I reckon my mam was right after all,' Ruby sighed, 'much as I hate to admit it. You know how she goes on about being ladylike and self-confident and all that. Difficult parents make for withdrawn children, she says. No wonder you're like you are with a dad like that.'

Joanna Westerley-Kent felt irritable. She lay wide awake in the sticky heat of her large canopied bed and found no way to make herself comfortable. She had already thrown off the counterpane and blanket, but still the sheet clung annoyingly to her naked body.

Still, it was more comfortable than her barracks bunk would be on a summer night like this. She wondered what the others would be doing tonight – punting on the river, perhaps, mooring up on a beautiful Thames-side bank overhung with willows and indulging in a midnight picnic of champagne and canapés. Life in the ATS was fun with

105

companions like Mabel and Jessica, and young officers like Vivian and Roger and Nigel to escort them and dream up wonderful pranks.

By now they would probably be dizzy with champers and amphetamines, sidling away two by two to the privacy of a secluded copse. Thank God for Volpar – girls could have so much fun these days, released from parental surveillance and the dread of pregnancy. She could never have known such freedom if it hadn't been for the war.

Mabel would be making a bee-line for Nigel now that Joanna was out of the way. She tossed the sheet aside and turned over to peer at the bedside clock. Nearly two, and she still felt wide awake. Damn Mabel. It would be a hollow victory for her, however, if Joanna could appear indifferent, casually dropping the information that Nigel was no longer of interest because she had found someone far more interesting. Positively exciting, in fact – that would be one up for her.

'I came across this absolutely fabulous farmhand, darling – and he's a foreigner. Jewish, I believe.'

Joanna allowed her imagination to run riot with the scene of Mabel's amazement and ill-concealed envy when Joanna went on to recount the farmhand's imaginary mastery of the arts of love.

'And such stamina, my dear! I was exhausted! You simply wouldn't believe how indefatigable these Jews can be!'

She rolled over on her back and stared up into the darkness. That Mr Bower had certainly excited something more than her imagination this afternoon down in the heat of the meadow, but he had been so engrossed in handling the stallion that he had remained blind to her interest in him.

It wasn't only the inscrutable expression on his handsome face which gave him such an exciting air of mystery, but the way he had managed Firefly with all the dexterity of a trained handler, quiet but powerful in his control of the

106

excitable beast. From the moment he led Duster to the field where Firefly grazed and introduced the two horses over the gate, it had been clear he knew what he was about. The mare had caught Firefly's scent and begun to gallop and rear, filling the air with those piercing cries that betray a mare's eagerness. When the stallion had responded to the mare's welcome, her hind legs spread and tail upraised, the laconic Jew struggling to control him, Joanna had felt herself infected with that eagerness too. She had watched the man as if mesmerized, the muscles straining under the thin shirt and the dark eyes afire. He was a beautiful animal himself, this Jew, a stallion any thoroughbred filly would be proud to welcome.

'I'd have you to cover me any day, you gorgeous creature,' she murmured in the darkness of her room. 'Come to me now, straight from the stables and smelling of hay and good, honest sweat. Take me in your arms . . .'

Closing her eyes she slid her hand slowly down over her naked body and made soft moans of pleasure. Once again in memory the sun beat its relentless heat on a glossy stallion's back as it mounted a quivering bay mare.

At length Joanna fell asleep, her longings assuaged by fantasy.

CHAPTER NINE

Renshaw was shepherding the newly arrived calves along the lane to the meadow when the postman came panting up the hill on his rusty old bicycle.

'By heck, but it's a long climb up here,' he gasped, pulling off his peaked cap to rub the sweat from his forehead with his sleeve. 'Don't half make a man thirsty.'

Renshaw ignored the hint. 'Just look at these calves,' he grumbled. 'Just look at the colour of them.'

The postman stared. 'Why, what's up with 'em?'

'They're filthy, that's what. Did you ever see any of mine that colour?'

'Grey, you mean?'

'It's smoke, is that. Comes of buying from a mucky place like Halifax. I might have known. Well, what have you got for me?'

'Just one today, official.'

The postman pulled out a buff envelope with OHMS printed on the corner. Renshaw groaned.

'Nowt but bad news comes in that. Give it us.'

He took the letter and turned away, shoving it in his pocket and leaving the postman to climb back on his bike and freewheel downhill.

The calves safely in the pasture Renshaw went back to the farmhouse. The tantalizing scent of frying bacon and eggs filled the air and Maddie was just cutting another strip of bacon off the joint hanging from the beam.

'Fat's a bit on the yellow side, Dad,' she commented. 'Are you sure you mixed some of that corn in with the swill – you didn't feed it all to the cows?'

'Course I did. No one knows better nor me how to feed

pigs right. More likely it were you as forgot to use rock salt in the curing. T'other sort's got iodine in.'

He was already tearing at the envelope as Max came in, ducking his head under the lintel as he entered. Renshaw laid the sheet of paper to one side of his plate and tore a chunk of bread to dip into the egg yolk, scanning the contents of the letter as he chewed.

'Bloody hell!' he muttered. Maddie looked up from the frying pan.

'What's up?'

'The War Ag – they only want me to plough up some of the wild land for arable, that's all. Want me to grow wheat or oats. Well they know what they can blooming well do with their oats.'

Max pulled out the chair opposite and sat down. 'Is that such a bad thing?' he enquired quietly.

'Bloody district committee,' grumbled Renshaw. 'Think they know everything, they do. Never been near a farm in their lives some of them, yet they have the nerve to tell us how it's done. Just listen to this – we should get a ton of wheat or oats to the acre – on this soil? They must be crazy!'

Maddie brought a plate of eggs and fried bread and placed it before Max. 'They keep saying on the wireless we need all the food we can grow now the ships can't get through.'

'Plough up with tractors and then put in potash or phosphates,' sneered her father, reading aloud from the letter. 'Subsidies available and free use of their tractors – that'll mean yet more ruddy forms to fill in, more time wasted. What do they think we are, farmers or blooming clerks?'

'It could mean an opportunity to develop the farm at the government's expense,' Max pointed out. Renshaw glared at him.

'Oh aye? And what do you know about farming, eh?

109

They offer two pounds for every acre of grassland turned over to arable – how rich do you think we'll get on that?'

Max shrugged. 'You say farming has been in the doldrums for years. New methods and the use of mechanical aids could change all that.'

Renshaw was studying the letter again. He scowled. 'Bloody cheek of it! They say I could face penalties if I don't comply, even face eviction.'

Maddie poured fresh tea into his pint pot. 'Could be a good thing, Dad, like Mr Bower says. The start of a whole new way of life.'

He snorted. 'A fat lot he knows! Evict me, from a place my family's owned since God knows when, will they? A land fit for heroes they promised us back in 1918 – some joke! Churchill wasn't joking though when he promised us blood, sweat and tears. Seems a man can't call nowt his own these days.'

Over his head Maddie could see the look in Max's dark eyes, and knew he too was powerless to alleviate her father's resentment. She hastened to change the subject.

'How's your berries coming along, Dad? It'll be time for the Gooseberry Fair again before long.'

He grunted, rose stiffly and limped outside. It was curious, she thought, how his leg always seemed to trouble him more when he was disturbed. She followed him out into the sun-drenched yard.

He was standing by the drystone wall, looking down on the village. She came up close beside him, longing to reach out and touch his arm by way of reassurance, a sign that whatever their differences, she understood and sympathized. He glanced at her from under bushy brows and cleared his throat.

'It's pigs I were born to, and pigs is what I know best,' he muttered, 'but we'll have to do as we're told, I reckon, for the time being at any rate. When it comes to it we're not so important as we like to think we are. Like my old dad used to say, we've only been put on this earth to make

110

the numbers up. But when this bloody lot's over we'll show 'em who's master at Scapegoat.'

He turned and limped away towards the gate, his shoulders bowed. Dog loped after him, his shuffling movements seeming to reflect his master's dejection. Maddie felt sorry for her father. It was not easy for a man as proud as he to concede to officialdom.

'Dear me,' said Colonel Westerley-Kent, 'what will they ask of us next?'

He laid aside the morning post and reached for his pipe. Hilary looked up from her newspaper. 'Why, dear, what is it?'

'Not content with making us keep separate dustbins for our bones, pigswill and paper, they now want us to give up our metal. They've commandeered our railings. It really is too bad.'

'What, all of them? All round the grounds?'

The Colonel struck a match and lit his pipe. 'Afraid so. They're needed for aeroplanes. What sacrifices we are obliged to make! Did I tell you that the Oval cricket ground has been dug up? Sacrilege!'

'Still,' said his wife reflectively, 'we're not being bombed like those poor people in London. I used to think all those precautions we were obliged to take against air raids were all a waste of time. We really can't object to our railings being made into bombers to stop all that, can we?'

'I suppose not.' Reginald puffed on his pipe and did not voice the apprehension he felt. Hilary was far too intelligent to be diverted by idle talk; she was just as aware as he of how critical the situation had become. France and Holland now fallen to the enemy, British troops rescued from Dunkirk in a crushing retreat thinly disguised as a victorious manoeuvre, there was now no defence left to protect England against invasion from Europe. This nightmare bombing of London was clearly a calculated move to destroy morale, a prelude to yet more bitter attack.

And where were Richard and Joanna at this critical time? Joanna was certainly in the London area. Neither he nor Hilary voiced their fears. Bless her, Hilary was a true British lady, stiff upper lip and all that. A woman to be proud of. He regarded her profile with pleasure. An arresting, impressive if not handsome woman – he had been wise in his choice of wife.

She laid aside the newspaper. 'Dreadful pictures of people bombed out of their homes,' she remarked. 'Poor children. They really can't understand why all this is happening to them. I feel so sorry for them.'

She picked up a bundle of papers. 'These Food Facts leaflets really are surprisingly useful,' she remarked. 'I must make sure the ladies at the sewing circle learn about the tips they suggest. Carrots to make a cake – who'd have thought it? Woolton Pie, made only from vegetables and Marmite – very tasty and nourishing, they say. And I must suggest to Mrs Barraclough that she tries out this substitute for spinach.'

'Spinach substitute?' echoed Reginald. 'What's that?'

'Nettles. We've got acres of them since the under-gardener left to join the Fire Service.'

Reginald swallowed hard. This war was going to be greatly unpalatable if Hilary carried her patriotism to extremes. He was rather glad the Ministry of War had suggested he might be useful in London, in some area other than the organization of the Local Defence Volunteers . . .

Maddie walked alone through the leafy evening shadows of Folly Wood. She was thinking about her father's taciturn but intriguing farmhand when she suddenly caught sight of him.

He was sitting on an upturned tree trunk, his legs spread wide and his elbows on his knees, deep in thought. For a moment she hesitated, wondering whether to take the opportunity to speak or to slip away and leave him undisturbed. After all, his day's work was done and he might resent the intrusion into his privacy.

'Max?'

He looked up and caught sight of her. At that moment there was a sudden piercing shriek close at hand and Maddie stiffened. She recognized the sound.

Max started to his feet. '*Mein Gott*! What is that?'

'A rabbit in a trap! Here, this way!'

She plunged into the undergrowth in the direction of the sound and Max followed. In a hollow under a tangle of brambles they saw it, a small, furry body struggling to free itself from glistening steel jaws. Max bent over it.

'For God's sake, make it stop! Get it out,' Maddie pleaded. She could not bear the piteous sound of the rabbit's agony. She watched Max's hands, those slender fingers like a woman's, as he strained to prise the trap open. At length it began to yield.

'Here, you pull the rabbit out while I hold the teeth apart,' he muttered.

She took the furry little creature in her hands, feeling its body quiver in terror as she lifted it. 'Poor thing,' she murmured. 'Its legs are broken.'

Max straightened and stood looking down at her. The rabbit's eyes stared wide, its ears laid back and its hind legs dangling uselessly. It was no longer screaming, but uttered faint squeaks now and again. A tiny rivulet of blood from its hindquarters trickled down Maddie's hand.

'Poor little thing,' she whispered, feeling tears begin to prick her eyelids, 'What's it done to suffer like this?'

Max squared broad shoulders. 'Don't cry. Give it to me.'

She stroked the little body and pressed it against her cheek. 'I can't help it. It hurts me to see pain.' She felt the tears beginning to trickle down her nose.

Max took the rabbit in his hands and squatted in the hollow, cradling it in his lap. Maddie watched as he stroked gentle fingers down the length of the quivering body, murmuring words in German until the little thing at last lay still. Then, with the utmost tenderness, he lifted its ears with one hand, laying bare the neck.

She caught her breath. In one swift movement he raised the other hand and brought the edge of his palm down sharply, and she heard the crack as the spine severed. For a moment he remained crouching still, and then he looked up at her.

'There, it is at peace,' he murmured.

Maddie nodded dumbly and flicked away a tear. 'Thank you, Max.'

He gave a thin smile, and all the weariness of the world seemed to be in his smile. Maddie longed to reach out to touch his hand, to feel his warmth and let him know that though words failed, they were for once in total harmony. For a fleeting second she believed she saw in his eyes a sentiment which answered her own.

He stood up and held out the body, towering above her like some dark demon of the woods, his lips set in a hard line. 'If only all suffering could be resolved so easily,' he murmured. 'My people have had to suffer pain such as you have never known.'

'I have! Memories bring me a lot of pain.'

'Memories?' he echoed, and his tone was harsh. 'I have seen the Nazis break the legs of old men. I have seen them tear a woman's body because she was beautiful, and Jewish . . .'

He turned away suddenly and strode up the brambled bank out of the hollow, oblivious to the thorns tearing at his trousers. Maddie stood staring after him, the corpse of the rabbit still in her hands. *I have seen the Nazis break the legs of old men . . . tear a woman's body*.

She laid the rabbit aside on a grassy knoll and climbed the bank. Max was already out of sight.

Misery lay heavy on her heart as she made her way home. For a moment she had savoured a magical closeness to another human being . . . It was only as Scapegoat came in

114

sight again that she became aware of the blood still staining her hands. She hurried indoors to wash it off.

Some time later her father limped indoors from the pigsty. He seated himself with difficulty and stretched out a leg towards her.

'Pull me boot off for me, lass, and give me leg a rub, will you? I've got cramp, I think.'

Maddie knelt before him and did as she was asked. He lay back in the chair and gave a deep sigh. She could see the pallor of his cheeks behind the weather tan.

'Does it hurt bad?' she asked.

'Now and again, but I'll live.'

'Maybe we should get the doctor,' she suggested. 'That leg seems to cause you a lot of bother these days.'

'Nay. Doctors cost too much. It's nowt but a bit of rheumatism.'

'In this weather? It's been hot for weeks.'

'Then it's about to change, mark my words. When my gammy knee plays up like this, we're in for rain.'

The colour was coming back to his cheeks. Maddie stood up. 'The weather forecast's good. According to the wireless it'll stay fine till long after harvest's done.'

Renshaw sat upright and wagged a stubby finger. 'You never heed what the wireless says. You just listen to my knee. Now, is my supper ready?'

Max did not come in for supper. Maddie kept it hot in the range oven till dusk fell, then went to look for him. He was nowhere to be found. Dad seemed unconcerned when he came back from the privy at bedtime.

'Don't bother waiting up for him,' he muttered. 'He's a law unto himself is that one. Get off to bed, lass – he knows we've to be up before five.'

Maddie had barely closed her eyes when the unfamiliar wailing sound began. She sat up in bed, puzzled for a moment, before she recognized it. She heard her father's hurried steps as he came to her door and threw it open.

'Sirens,' he muttered excitedly, 'them's air-raid sirens! And I heard aeroplanes too.'

He crossed to the window and pulled back the blackout curtains. At the same time Maddie heard the distant sound of a dull thud. And then another.

'Them's bombs,' her father exclaimed. 'God, I can see 'em!'

Maddie jumped out of bed and came to stand by him at the window, clutching her nightdress round her in alarm. Far away in the distance she could see a dull red glow in the sky.

'North of here,' Renshaw muttered. 'Looks like they're having a go at Middlesbrough. God help 'em.'

Maddie sank back on her bed, stunned. War had come at last to Scapegoat.

A week or two later war brought its victims to Barnbeck in the shape of a bunch of bedraggled evacuee children. Snatched from the nightly bombing of their town, they were decanted from the train at the village railway station and shepherded into the church hall. There they stood, some still red-eyed from weeping at being parted from their mothers, others curious about this strange new world so different from their back-street tenement homes in the town.

Mrs Chilcott, the vicar's wife, stood surveying the straggling line of children. Alongside her stood Mrs Pickering who was wearing her Sunday-best hat although it was only Friday.

'So I've been appointed billeting officer,' Mrs Pickering was saying, hugging her ample bosom higher with pride, 'probably because I'm the air-raid warden's wife. It's up to me to find homes for all of them. Now, I'm sure you have room for a couple at the vicarage, Mrs Chilcott?'

Mrs Chilcott's wide green eyes inspected the children. They looked a very unhappy lot, luggage labels attached to their coat buttons and an assortment of luggage in their grubby little hands. They looked bewildered, mouths agape, and one little boy at the end of the row had green running down from his nose which he kept trying to lick away.

'Very well,' said Mrs Chilcott, conscious of the eyes of the other women in the hall, 'I'll take that little girl over there.'

She had to set an example, so she took care to choose the cleanest-looking child. Mrs Pickering looked pleased.

'Right. Now, you're Hilda, aren't you?' she said to the child. 'You're lucky, Hilda. You're to stay at the vicarage with this lady. Take your things and go with her.'

The girl pouted. 'Only if my sister can come with me,' she said fiercely. 'My mam said we wasn't to be parted.'

Mrs Chilcott sighed. 'Very well. Come along.'

She left the hall, followed by Hilda and her smaller, cross-eyed sister. One by one the other women walked along the row of children, inspecting each little face closely and choosing until at last only three children remained.

Doreen Sykes sniffed as she lifted a tray of half-eaten buns to carry out to the kitchen. Not for all the tea in China would she allow one of these slum children to contaminate her new loose covers.

'What about you, Mrs Sykes?' Mrs Pickering called. 'You've got room for one, surely?'

'I'm sorry. Our Eunice is just coming down with something – I think it's chicken pox. Wouldn't be safe. Oh, Ruby – I'm glad you've come.'

Mrs Pickering sighed and addressed the girl who had just come in.

'Give me a hand, will you, Ruby? I've still got to find homes for these three before teatime.'

'Leave it to me,' said Ruby. 'I've got the afternoon off – I'll get them settled. Come on, kids, follow me.'

Maddie was never quite certain that she actually agreed to Ruby's proposal, only that somehow Ruby had gone and a surly little girl now sat in her father's chair with a ticket attached to her coat buttonhole which read *Eva Jarrett, age nine*.

She was a pretty little thing, if a trifle on the skinny side, but the smell from her small body threatened to overpower even the scent of the hams hanging from the rafters of the kitchen. Her pointed little face was grubby from the constant attention of grimy fingers and her coppery hair hung lank and unwashed. A frayed cotton skirt dipped unevenly with its unstitched hem above dirty knees, and torn socks disappeared into split sandals.

'That's why she wasn't picked by any of the other women,' Ruby had confided in a whisper. 'Still, she won't look so bad after a good scrub.'

But Ruby could not have noticed the way the girl scratched. She must be riddled with lice. Thank heaven the range boiler was full of hot water and there was a new bar of Sunlight soap in the cupboard ready for bath night.

An hour later, despite the child's squeals of protest, the transformation was remarkable. Eva looked positively angelic with a scrubbed and rosy face and her hair shining. Maddie could see the child herself was amazed at her reflection in the mirror, for she kept fingering her hair in disbelief.

'I rinsed it in rainwater,' Maddie told her. 'That's how I keep mine all soft and shiny.'

She was still scratching her head, however, and Maddie knew she was going to have to get to grips with the lice. But the immediate problem was going to be persuading her father to let the child stay. Poor little thing, torn from her mother and father; she must be terrified.

Maddie smiled encouragingly. 'Well, what do you think of Barnbeck, Eva? Pretty village, isn't it?'

The girl gave her a surly look. 'I don't like it. It's daft.'

Maddie's eyebrows rose. 'Daft? How do you mean?'

Eva shrugged. 'It's like we're still nowhere. There's no streets and trams and lamp posts and that. It's the middle of nowhere here. I don't really have to stay here, do I?'

'We don't have bombs here, Eva. It's safe.'

'I want me mam.' The voice grew plaintive and Maddie spoke gently.

'You can write and tell her about us and the farm. She'll be glad to hear from you. And it'll be nice for you, won't it, having letters from her?'

'I'm not very good at writing. Me teacher said I were messy.'

'You'll be going to school here soon, I reckon, after the holidays. You'll soon be able to write beautifully, I'm sure.'

It seemed pointless reassuring the child when her father might well rage and insist on her leaving, but Maddie felt certain the child's surliness was born more out of anxiety than hostility.

Renshaw and Max came back at supper time from the fields where they had been dipping sheep all day. Renshaw came in from the yard first, filling the kitchen with the pungent smell of disinfectant still clinging to his clothes.

'Hey up, what's this?' he demanded, seeing the small figure already seated at table, knife and fork gripped tightly in her fists. Dog moved forward to sniff curiously at the stranger's legs, then moved away to inspect his bowl.

'This is Eva, Dad. She's one of the kids who've been evacuated from Middlesbrough because of the bombing. A lot of the village folk have taken some of them in.'

'Oh aye? Well, we've no room.'

He took off his jacket and hung it on the peg behind the door. Maddie knew he considered the subject closed.

'We've got one room empty, Dad,' she said quietly.

He turned and stared. 'If it's your mother's room you're talking of, lass, then you know what I feel about that. It'll stay empty. No one goes in there but me. In God's name, they can't make me give that up too!'

'There's the attic room,' Maddie persisted, and at that moment Max entered. Realizing that he was interrupting a conversation he stood silent.

Renshaw snarled. 'There's three folk living here already and three rooms. There's no more space.'

'Are you saying the attic room is Mr Bower's, Dad?'

He gave the farmhand the briefest of glances. 'Course it is.'

As he moved to pull out a chair at the table Max came forward. 'Thank you, but I do not want your room,' he said coolly. 'I am quite content as I am.'

Sensing the tension, Maddie began serving the meal and both men ate in silence. Only Eva could be heard, squelching and guzzling as she devoured the stew. When she had finished she put down her knife and fork and began scratching herself fiercely.

'That child's got lice,' said Renshaw. 'And look at the state of her – she's through to the blacking on her shoes. She'll not stay here.'

'She will. She'll sleep with me.'

Maddie rose from the table and cleared the dishes away with deliberate movements. Renshaw glared.

'Are you defying me, lass?'

Maddie shrugged. 'It's only common decency, Dad. She stays here.'

'You could at least give her a dousing in the sheep dip first. Wouldn't do her no harm,' muttered Renshaw.

Max got up from the table abruptly and left. Maddie turned to the child. 'Come on, Eva. Time for bed. We get up very early on the farm – very early indeed.'

In the bedroom Maddie helped the child to unpack. There was very little clothing in the pathetic little bundle of belongings.

'Nightie?' said Eva. 'Nay, I sleep in me vest and drawers. I always do.'

Bombs fell again that night to the far north. Maddie lay awake beside the sleeping child, listening and wondering. Eva moved only once, murmuring in her sleep.

'Mam – cuddle me.'

Compassion flooded Maddie. Lice or no, she put her arms around the little body and cradled her close.

CHAPTER TEN

The long hot days of summer continued until after the corn had been reaped. Now it stood in neat stooks dotted over the meadows, and village children and evacuees alike were revelling in the newly provided playground.

'I've told you, Eva,' Renshaw said severely, wagging an admonishing finger, 'leave them stooks alone. You city kids are all the same. Daft as they come.'

The evacuees, at first a source of curiosity to the villagers of Barnbeck, soon became a nuisance. Freed from the surveillance of parents and teachers, they ran wild in the fields, chasing butterflies and building nests in the bracken on the hillsides, then scrumping unripe apples and chasing chickens.

'Would you believe it,' a scandalized Joan Spivey remarked to her neighbour, 'Mrs Chilcott told me she even came across that little cross-eyed vaccy going through her handbag! No money were gone, however – she just pinched a box of matches and all but started a grassfire up the hill.'

'Bet it was that young urchin Stanley who put her up to it,' replied Mrs Woodley. 'Caught him smoking one of our Bert's Woodbines down the lavvy the other night.'

'Did you tell him off?'

'What? Told me he was allowed to smoke at home, bold as brass he were. Said if the gang leader didn't smoke, the other lads would think him a cissy.'

'I hope you put him right,' said Mrs Pickering.

'Our Bert did. He's only to start unbuckling his belt now and young Stanley thinks twice about answering back.'

Eva seemed to have settled down at last. Apprehensive as she had seemed when she first arrived, she quickly overcame the humiliation of having her copper-red hair daily fine-tooth combed until the last of the head lice had been eradicated and she had not taken long to surrender, grumbling, to wearing a cut-down nightdress in bed. She seemed at last to welcome Maddie's help, allowing her to plait her hair into stubby pigtails of which she was immensely proud.

'Just like you do Duster's mane,' she commented, and the comparison seemed to please her. She seemed to have become self-appointed leader of the evacuees, and it was not long before she took over possession of Scapegoat Farm.

'You get your foot off our gate,' Maddie heard her say fiercely to a small boy who dared to swing on the five-barred gate. 'It's our farm, not yours.'

One day Renshaw jerked open the back door. The yard was full of children laughing and scampering around. One of the evacuee children held a mongrel dog which was straining on a lead, and the chickens were shrieking and fluttering wildly.

'What the devil's going on out here?' he demanded. Eva stopped running and turned.

'What's up, Mr Renshaw? We're only playing.'

'Not here, you don't! Get out, the lot of you!'

He chivvied the rest of the gang out of the gate, then turned to Eva, his face purple. 'Where's Maddie? Why didn't she stop you? Do you know what you could have done, frightening the chickens like that?'

Eva gave him a mischievous smile. 'We meant no harm, Mr Renshaw. Like I said, we was only playing.'

He grunted. 'Playing, is it? Chickens think a dog is a fox, don't you know that? Fright'll make 'em stop laying.'

'I'm sorry, Mr Renshaw.'

But then other complaints began reaching Maddie about the child's behaviour.

'I wouldn't care, only them apples were nowhere near ripe,' complained George Bailey. 'And they damaged my fence climbing over too.'

'Are you sure it was Eva though?' Maddie asked.

122

'Know it for a fact – first one over, my missus said, and the rest of the pack followed her. Not one little apple left when them little hooligans had done. Bloody locusts, they were. There'll be no apple jam for us this year.'

Eva just hung her head when Maddie questioned her about it. But a few days later it was Mrs Pickering who waylaid Maddie outside her husband's shop.

'How about paying for them oranges your Eva pinched off the front yesterday?' she demanded. 'I don't reckon as she'll have told you she never paid.'

It was no use arguing with Edna Pickering. 'She's a thorough bad lot, is that one. Bet she wets the bed and all, like that little cross-eyed Betty up at the vicarage.' Maddie paid up and went home, full of determination to deal firmly with the child. Motherless or not, she couldn't be allowed to go on like this.

'I never,' Eva protested shrilly when Maddie confronted her with the story. 'I wouldn't dream of doing a thing like that – honest!'

The child stared with such open, horrified eyes that Maddie found it impossible to punish her. But it must be true, she thought; so many complaints could not all be unfounded. The suspicion began to dawn that Eva was not as angelic and honest as she would like people to believe. Maddie was chewing over the problem as she plaited Duster's mane.

'What should I do, Duster? I know she misses her mum so I can't be too hard on her.'

The mare looked at her with a soft, trusting expression. At that moment Max entered the stable.

'Talking to your horse again, Maddie?'

Maddie shrugged. 'I'm worried about Eva. I was just talking it out.'

'About Eva? Why?'

She told him. He listened with dark, attentive gaze. Then he sighed.

'I think you are right, and she misses her family. But

she'll be starting at the village school soon, will she not? Once the new term starts?'

'True,' Maddie agreed.

'Then she will be fully occupied. You know,' he added thoughtfully, 'we have something in common, the child and I. We have both been dispossessed by the Nazis, both strangers in a foreign place and therefore distrusted. Don't be too severe with her, Maddie.'

Strange, thought Maddie that night in bed, but she had felt an unreasonable surge of jealousy at his words. But why should she feel envious that he should feel close to Eva? It was only his natural sense of compassion, the same as when he showed concern for the rabbit in pain.

Distant bombs fell again during the night, a long, persistent bombardment which could only mean that Middlesbrough was taking yet another hammering. Eva slept on, undisturbed, but as Maddie stood at the window and lifted the blackout to watch the far-off flashes of light, she felt guilty. The child's family were in mortal danger; she had no right to feel envy of Eva.

On Thursday morning Renshaw called Max early from the barn to eat breakfast.

'We've to be up early at Bailey's to start the threshing. Every man in the village will be there, do the whole lot at once. Just hope the rain keeps off.'

Dark clouds were gathering on the horizon as the two men trudged over the hill to George Bailey's farm. Bailey, cloth-capped and pipe in hand, stood watching as horses and carts trundled in with sheaves of corn from the fields and men stoked the Fowler Tiger traction engine with large lumps of coal.

Bailey gave Max only a passing glance before turning to Renshaw. 'Steam's got up ready now,' he said. 'This double summer time's a blessing. Gives us an early start.'

Alongside the traction engine stood the great threshing machine. A raw-boned Land Army girl was dragging a pile of hessian railway sacks alongside to be hooked on. Max stared at the wire balers and the big flat belt which turned the engine. Men moved around him, but no one spoke.

'Come on,' said Renshaw, tugging his cap down more firmly over his eyes. 'Now you'll find out what hard work is. But there'll be good grub at the farmhouse after.'

Max looked surprised. 'Maddie has packed bread and cheese and onion for us.'

'Aye, but farmer's wife gets extra allowances for workers. We'll do all right today.'

Renshaw had not exaggerated, Max discovered, for it was a gruelling and dirty job. Before long every man was covered in dust as the machine flailed and the husks flew. His skin was itching, especially at the back of his neck where the dust found its way beneath his collar. And the itching was made worse the more he sweated. Renshaw was sneezing incessantly and wiping his nose on his sleeve as he worked. The other men too were scratching and sneezing, but none of them spoke to Max.

During the brief dinner break the Land Army girl helped Bailey's wife to serve up food in the farmhouse kitchen. Max was aware that the men around the table spoke to each other in monosyllabic bursts, but they were deliberately avoiding speaking to him.

By mid-afternoon the rain came on. At first it seemed like relief, cooling the sweat on his head, but it made no difference to the discomfort. Renshaw paused and looked up. 'Still itchy?'

Max nodded.

'It'll get no better, you'll see. Rain just makes the dust stick even more. Mucky devils, these machines.'

The rain began to come down hard. Renshaw paused again to look up at the sky. 'Raining stair rods now,' he remarked to Bailey. 'It's not going to ease up.'

'Nay, happen you're right, but we'd best keep on while she's going,' the farmer replied, casting a wary glance at the traction engine. 'She could start slipping any time.' No sooner had he spoken than the belt began to slip. Again and again.

'It's no use,' said Bailey. 'Any road, corn's getting wet. Best leave it now while morning and hope to blazes the sun'll dry it out.'

Maddie had made certain there was plenty of water ready in the range for the men to bathe after they had eaten. Eva giggled when she saw Renshaw scratching his shoulder blade during supper.

'Hey up, it's you that's got the itch now,' she said impishly. 'How about the sheep dip, then?'

'Enough of your lip,' said Renshaw, but Maddie thought he spoke with less severity than he might have once. When the meal was cleared away she took Eva upstairs, leaving the men to take turns in the zinc bathtub in the kitchen.

'Get Dog out of the way too,' her father said as she was ushering Eva up the stairs. 'Daft devil keeps dipping his nose in the bathwater.'

'I'll take him,' said Eva.

She led Dog upstairs and he sprawled on the cool linoleum of the bedroom floor. Maddie crossed to the window and gazed out over the fields. Eva climbed on a chair next to her.

'Which way is home?' she asked.

Maddie pointed north. 'That way.'

'Oh. What's that stuff on the fence?'

'Where?'

The girl pointed. 'Down there, on the fence.'

'That's sheep's wool, stuck on the barbed wire down at Rowan Tree farm.' Maddie's eyes grew dreamy, recalling how she had asked her mother the same question, many years ago. 'Did you know that rowan trees are magic, Eva? They protect you against witches.'

Witches, spells, enchantment – mother's stories had had a magic all their own, keeping her spellbound by the hour in those far-off, happy days. Childhood was a magic time – and

Eva was being robbed of hers by war. Now if only Maddie could remember some of those wonderful stories . . .

'I can hear doves,' Eva pronounced. Maddie listened and then laughed.

'Not doves, Eva. That's wood pigeons.'

Eva scowled. 'I want them to be doves. My mam said doves mean peace.'

Maddie turned quickly to the child. 'Don't worry, Eva. She'll be all right.'

'She won't. You haven't read her letter.' The girl took an envelope from the drawer. 'Here, you read it to me.'

Maddie read it aloud, slowly. It was written in an untidy scrawl on a torn sheet of exercise paper but the mother's love was clear.

'We've had a terrible lot of bombing in Middlesbrough but so far we been lucky. Mrs Plunkett down the road got hurt last week and is in hospital but only broken legs. The street is a heap of rubble and we had a lot of flames. Your in the best possible place, Evie love, so be a good girl for your mam.'

Maddie folded the letter. 'You see, she's all right. Shall I help you write back to her?'

'I can do it myself,' the girl said defensively. 'I'll tell her we'll be all right – we got a round tree to protect us.'

'A rowan tree. Yes, you do that. She'll be glad. And tell her she can come and visit any time.'

At that moment she heard knocking at the door of the farmhouse and jumped up. 'I'd best go down. You write your letter, Eva, and then I'll make you a cup of Namco before you go to bed.'

The child was rooting in the drawer. Maddie left her to put the letter away and went downstairs. At the bend in the stairs she could see down into the kitchen, the zinc tub before the fire, the pools of water glistening around it on the flagstones and the gleaming wet body of the man just standing up in the bath. It was Max, and he had his back towards her. She stood, fascinated. He clearly had not heard her coming.

'Oh, it's you, Eddie Sykes,' she heard her father say. 'Come in.' Then she heard the sound of the door closing.

Max stepped out of the bath and bent to reach for a towel. She stood mesmerized by the sight of him. In the glow of the firelight he looked like some beautiful animal, lean, well-muscled and lithe. He had filled out since he had first come to Scapegoat, she noted, and wondered at the pleasure the sight evoked in her.

With a start she realized that at any moment he could turn and see her. She was heading back up the stairs when her father spoke.

'It's not often you come paying a visit, Eddie Sykes,' he was saying. 'There must be a reason.'

'Aye, there is,' Eddie replied. 'I had word from the Food Office. I want to have a word with you in private about some hams.'

Maddie's heart sank. It would be a crying shame now if Ruby's father were to get her father into trouble.

'Word gets about fast,' said Renshaw. 'You'd best sit down.'

Renshaw then waited until Max had towelled himself down, put on his trousers and left.

'Now tell us what you've come about,' he said to Eddie. 'I'll not offer you a drink if you're here on business.'

Eddie took off his helmet and placed it on the kitchen table. 'Nay, I'm not. I can see there's hams up there but that's not why I've come.'

'You didn't get word from the Food Office then? You're not here to snoop?'

Eddie smiled. 'Nay. I knew about that pig, of course. Walls have ears, as they keep telling us. And the squeals of a stuck pig carries miles.'

'Well then?'

Eddie leaned forward, hands on knees. 'It's about this farmhand of yours.'

'Bower? What about him? Hey, it wasn't you as stuck that pig's head at the gate, was it? Fair upset us, that did.'

'Nay, James, I know nowt about that, but just hear me out, will you? Some folks think he could be a spy. What do you reckon?'

Renshaw snorted. 'Rubbish, that's what I think.'

Eddie nodded. 'Aye, so do I. He seems right enough to me, but he's been seen up on the moor by night. Late at night, by himself.'

'So what? His time's his own once his work's done.'

'He's not using your bike, is he? Cos it's not allowed, you know.'

'Is he heckas like! He must walk up there.'

'It's just that there's been all this bombing of late.'

'Nowt to do with him. How could it be?'

'You're certain he can't have a radio or owt? Any way of contacting his own folk?'

'I'm certain. Any road, he's no German. He hates Nazis like we do.'

Eddie gave a sigh. 'Good. If you're satisfied, then I am. It'd take a canny devil to pull the wool over your eyes, I reckon.'

Renshaw made to stand up. 'If that's all you came about –'

'No, hang on. I wanted to tell you summat, but you're to keep it to yourself, mind. You're in the auxiliary fire service now, I'm told?'

Renshaw stiffened. 'Aye. Colonel wouldn't have me in the LDV.'

Eddie spread his hands. 'Does it matter how we help so long as we all do our bit? Now listen. There's an idea going about as we could happen cheat them Jerry bombers that come over here most nights.'

'Cheat 'em? How?'

Eddie leaned further forward, glanced over his shoulder and then spoke in a whisper. 'They got bombs to get at our shipyards and munitions factories. If we could make 'em drop 'em up on our moors . . .'

Renshaw was staring at him. 'On the moors? Make 'em think the moors was a shipyard or summat, you mean?'

'If there was a fire blazing up there they could think it was a city on fire, Middlesbrough or Hull or summat, and they'd keep hammering at it. Waste their bombs on nowt more than a sheep or two. We'd make sure it was far enough away to do no real harm.'

Renshaw was rubbing the stubble on his chin. 'Aye, I see what you're getting at,' he murmured.

'But we couldn't have the Fire Service rushing in and putting our fires out, do you see?' Eddie said.

'Nay, of course not. Oh, I see – yes, I could see to that,' Renshaw muttered. 'No problem at all. But it's Dai Thomas's hearse we're to use – '

'Dai knows of the plan – he's OK.'

There was the sound of a door opening upstairs. Renshaw sat upright and put a finger to his lips. Eddie nodded and rose, taking up his helmet from the table. 'Just think on,' he whispered, 'not a word to a soul.'

Maddie came down the stairs humming a song. 'Oh, hello, Mr Sykes. How's Ruby?' she asked.

Eddie scowled. 'Don't talk to me about that lass,' he said severely, but there was pride in his voice. 'She's just told us she's planning to go off to work in the city. Going to be a munitions worker, she is.'

Maddie felt a stab of disappointment. It was not only Ruby's freedom she envied. Life would be dismal without her exciting presence.

'Eva, what've I told you about that dog?' Renshaw demanded. Maddie turned. Eva was standing on the bottom step of the stairs and beside her stood a rather bewildered-looking dog, his long ears looped up over his head and tied together with a large pink bow.

Eddie's mouth twitched at the corners. 'Well, I'd best be off. Like I said, James, there's fellows in the Pig Club like me as'd be glad of a bit of advice from an old hand like you when you've a minute.'

'What? Oh, aye,' said Renshaw.

'How to choose a good weaner, how to feed it up right

and all that. Meetings on Tuesday nights at the Cock and Badger. Goodnight to you.'

Maddie watched him go, then turned to her father. 'What's this Pig Club then, Dad?'

Her father stared past her. 'Did you hear me, Eva? Get that thing off Dog this minute.'

Eva, bending over Dog as she tried to fasten another ribbon to his tail, pouted. 'He's pretty now with my Sunday-best ribbon on. You never do nowt to make him pretty.'

'Get it off, you hear? He looks daft.'

'And he needs a name too. I've decided to call him Lassie, like him on the picture.'

Renshaw sighed. 'You can't call him that. He's a lad. Come here, Dog.'

'Come here, Lassie,' said Eva, seating herself by the fire. Dog looked uncertainly from master to child, then crouched on the hearth, torn between the desire to put his muzzle in the bathwater or scratch the offending constriction away from his ears. Finally he lay with his head between his paws and worried at the ribbon until it came loose. By that time the bath had been cleared away.

In the Cock and Badger the men had abandoned their games of darts and dominoes to sit hunched around the table and discuss more earnest business.

'So it's OK, then, is it?' said Fred. 'You told Scapegoat Jim he'd either have to shit or get off the lavvy?'

'Aye,' said Eddie. 'He's with us. And he vouches for the Jerry. We can make a start whenever we like.'

'The sooner the better,' said Jack. 'No time like the present. Ought we to let the Colonel know?'

Fingers rubbed chins thoughtfully and faces turned towards the policeman for a lead. 'Happen it'd be best,' said Eddie. 'After all, he's in charge of the LDV.'

'Aye,' cut in old Seth, 'but how can we be sure that Jerry fellow won't cotton on and sabotage our plans, eh? He might let his mates know as they're dropping their insanitary bombs on nowt but sheep.'

'Incendiary bombs, Dad,' said Jack, 'and didn't you hear Eddie? Scapegoat Jim'll tell no one, and any road the fellow isn't a Jerry.'

'Jerry or not, he walks up the moors by night,' muttered Fred. 'We must make shift to keep him away.'

Dai Thomas joined in, his deep Welsh baritone voice drowning the old man's treble protests. 'Renshaw won't interfere, that's for sure, since he'll need my hearse and I'll make certain he doesn't take it. And he'll make certain the foreign fellow doesn't butt in. All we need is the makings of a good bonfire.'

'We've got that all right,' said Jack. 'We've plenty of wood and we can all chip in with a drop of paraffin.'

Len stopped polishing glasses to look at the barometer on the wall behind the bar. 'I'd leave it while tomorrow if I were you, lads. It's still teeming with rain. Just time for another half before I close up.'

'Right, first things first,' said Seth, banging his one good fist on the table. 'Whose turn is it?'

Faces turned expectantly towards the undertaker. 'It's you, isn't it, Dai the Death?' said the landlord.

The Welshman turned pale. Old Seth chuckled.

'He looks as if he will and all. Come on then – mine's a pint.'

CHAPTER ELEVEN

'I didn't sleep a wink last night,' Hilary Westerley-Kent told her husband over breakfast. 'Not only the heat and the noise of the bombing but there was the most tremendous fire blazing up on the moors. Did you see it?'

'Jerries offloading incendiaries on their way home, probably,' the Colonel said briefly over his newspaper. 'Better there than on Middlesbrough again.'

'I don't think so, dear.' He looked up and watched her expression as she buttered toast. 'I heard the aeroplane engines, but there was no sound of bombs falling – not close at hand, anyway.'

She was too shrewd by half. Hilary was not a woman one could delude easily; he resolved to explain.

'I see,' she said as he finished, 'a very commendable plan. One tends to underestimate these people, Reginald. They're very tough and determined, and their altruism is remarkable.'

'Indeed.' He hoped that her praise would atone for the fact that he had betrayed the locals' confidence in him, and decided to avoid any further questioning by telling her about Renshaw.

'Had to turn the fellow down for the Local Defence Volunteers,' he said tersely. 'Poor devil. Think he thought it insulting after he'd campaigned in the First War. Still, I'll be out of all that once I join Intelligence down at Latchmere House.'

'Why did you turn him down?'

'Because he's such an awkward devil, that's why. Questions everything I say. Couldn't have a Bolshie undermining my influence like that.'

'Poor man. I hope you let him down gently.'

'Oh yes, I think so. Put him in charge of local fire-watching and fighting. Arranged for that Thomas undertaker chappie to have a hearse fitted out with hosepipes and all that to tackle any blaze until the proper Fire Service can get here. Two-man team to man it, Renshaw and Thomas. Renshaw can boss away for all he likes now.'

'Good idea,' said Hilary. 'And Archie Botton tells me the villagers have set up a Pig Club too – another good idea. We must tell them how to mix their pigswill – no, it's pigwash they call it, isn't it? Mix it with boiled turnips and swedes, and then mix the balancer meal into that. Makes the meal go much further.'

The Colonel stared at his wife in amazement. How on earth did she come by all these amazing snippets of information?

'And by the way,' said Hilary, 'you'd have been wasting your time if you thought you could have kept the business of the fires on the moors from me. I'd have got it out of Archie sooner or later.'

Maddie stared at the letter in her hand. *'I really miss you, Maddie,'* Richard Westerley-Kent wrote. *'I haven't met a girl on this camp or anywhere else who can match up to you. All the chaps here have got a pin-up on their locker doors, and I'd like to have a picture of you on mine. The other chaps' eyes would pop out if they saw you. Be my girl, Maddie, write to me. I shall look forward so much to having letters from you, and to holding you in my arms again . . .'*

Renshaw put his head round the kitchen door. 'I'm off up to see to my berries. Have you fed the chickens?'

'Yes, Dad. I'm just off to feed and water the horses now.'

She pushed the letter into her pocket as she made her way to the stables. Across the fields she could see Eva scampering around Max who was busy with the sheep. Dog crouched in the long grass watching her.

Richard wanted her to be his girl. She mulled the thought

over in her mind as she filled the iron trough with fresh water and watched the mare's nose dip into it. She could not help wondering how her father would react if he knew. He'd be outraged perhaps, or proud that the only son of the Westerley-Kent family should choose her. Strange. Only months ago the invitation would have filled her with excitement. How could it be that now the letter left her completely unmoved?

Maddie fetched a bucket of wheat to mix with the mare's meal and set it down to take the letter from her pocket again. She stood leaning against the doorway in the sunlight to re-read it.

'*It would be nice to know I had my own girl waiting for me at home,*' Richard wrote. '*Someone who'd write me letters I could treasure. I think you're fantastic, Maddie, the most beautiful thing I've ever seen, and I want to know for certain that you are mine and no one will ever take you from me.*'

Maddie felt resentful. Why should he want to tie her down? She wasn't his girl, never had been, never even hinted she wanted to be . . .

'*Just remember that while I may be only in Catterick now,*' Richard went on, '*I could be sent abroad on active service any time now basic training's over. Just think if I never came back, Maddie, how would you feel then?*'

She frowned, feeling anger rising in her that he should try to make her feel sorry for him. A voice at her elbow startled her.

'Is something wrong, Maddie?'

It was Max, his dark eyes searching hers. She thrust the letter away in her pocket.

'No, no, it's all right.'

'Is your father about?'

'He's gone up to see to his gooseberries. Why, what's up?'

Max gave a deep sigh. 'It's the lambs. Some of them have got the maggot. Do you have disinfectant?'

135

'Jeyes fluid, in the kitchen. That's what Dad uses. Shall I give you a hand?'

He gave her a quick glance. 'You have done this? It is not a pleasant task.'

She laughed shortly. 'I've grown up on the farm, Max. Lots of jobs aren't very pleasant, but they have to be done.'

Together they rounded up some of the affected lambs in one of the pens. It was clear Max was right for the creatures were growing irritable with the itch. Maddie could see where bluebottles had laid their eggs in the crust of excreta on their backsides.

'Have to get that crust scraped off, then cut the wool before we can bathe them,' said Max. As he had said, it was a smelly and offensive task, scraping away wriggling maggots before they could cut away the soiled wool and apply the disinfectant, but at last the job was done.

Maddie was carrying the bucket back across the yard when she suddenly remembered Duster and the feed. Max heard her quick gasp.

'I left the corn in the bucket in Duster's stable – I meant to mix some of it in the horses' feed – she may have eaten it.'

Max was behind her as she rushed into the stable. As Maddie looked over the door of Duster's stall her heart sank. The bucket was empty; the mare lay on her side on the straw and she was groaning.

Max was beside her as she bent over the mare. 'She has colic,' said Max. 'We must make her get up and move around or it could be too late.'

Maddie tugged and coaxed, but Duster refused to move. Max stepped forward and gripped the nose rein firmly. 'Get up, you brute, you hear me?'

The mare lifted her head and stared at him for a moment with dull eyes, then staggered slowly to her feet.

'Come on, outside!'

He led her out into the sunlight and dragged her around

the yard. Her feet stumbled and slithered but she struggled to keep moving.

'Take her,' Max said to Maddie, 'and whatever you do don't let her lie down.'

Maddie took the reins. 'She's in pain, Max. Awful pain.'

'I know. But keep her moving. That's the one thing which will relieve it. And her life depends on it.'

Maddie knew he was not exaggerating. Colic in a horse could lead to a twisted gut which could be fatal, and if Duster had been precious before, she was doubly so now she might be in foal.

By turns they walked the mare around the farmyard until the attack began to subside. As Maddie's anxiety eased, she realized how indebted she was to Max.

'Thanks, Max,' she murmured.

'No need to thank me.'

'You were firm with her. I couldn't have got her up on her feet on my own. I once said you didn't understand horses. When it came to it, you were more help to her than I was.'

It was a humiliating admission to make: that she, Maddie Renshaw, who loved her horses more than anything else in the world, had failed them in a crisis. Max seemed to understand as he nodded in acknowledgement.

'I know how you feel about them. You will learn that caring can sometimes mean firmness.'

She felt stung by his words, the implied reproach that she was too soft. As she turned to answer the challenge she saw Eva's small figure climbing on the gate.

'I work them hard, Max, ploughing in all weathers, pulling the cart to market when it's heavy laden – they know what hard work is, Duster and Robin. And they never refuse.'

Max stared at her for a moment and then slapped the reins in her hand. 'Then you should take better care of them and not let distractions make you endanger their lives. I think she is all right now. You can stable her again.'

He turned away abruptly towards the gate. Maddie stood bereft of speech then, as she led the mare into the stable, she heard Eva's voice.

'You two been quarrelling?' she demanded of Max. 'Me and that rotten Eunice Sykes have been having a row too. She says she's not going to be in my gang any more. She called me a daft name and thought she were a right clever devil.'

'Take no notice,' Maddie could hear Max reply. 'You have to get used to people calling you names. They only do it because they don't understand you.'

'Know what Eunice said?' went on Eva. 'She said my name was Eva Kewey. Get it? Eva Kewey – evacuee. Dead clever she thought she was. Kept saying it, till I bashed her on the nose. She didn't say it again.'

Maddie could swear she could see the corners of Max's lips curve into a smile as she came out of the stable. Then she caught sight of her father standing at the gate watching.

'Had any bother?' he asked. Max looked away.

'Only a bit,' said Maddie. 'We found some of the lambs had maggot.'

'Aye, I thought as much when I saw they'd been shaved. Well, now that's done happen we can have us dinner.'

'Can I go down the shop and get me toffee ration?' said Eva.

'You had your toffee ration this morning,' Maddie pointed out.

'Well I could have Mr Renshaw's then, couldn't I, 'cos he never eats his.'

'You can't have eaten all yours already,' said Renshaw. 'You've never gobbled the lot.'

'I had chewing gum,' said Eva. 'And when I was walloping Eunice Sykes I swallowed it. You can't really say I had my fair share. So can I have yours, Mr Renshaw?'

Renshaw chewed his food without replying. Maddie changed the subject.

138

'Dad, do you think you could take your cap off in the house? It's not right, you know.'

He looked up in amazement. 'Take me cap off? Whatever for?'

'Well, we've got company.'

For a moment he continued to stare. 'For all the years I've run Scapegoat I've worn me cap. I'm master here, think on.'

Long seconds passed while the four ate in silence. Maddie rose to fetch milk from the dresser and as she resumed her seat she saw that her father had laid his cap aside.

'Saw that Westerley-Kent woman out in her motor car this morning,' he remarked as he poured the creamy liquid into his mug. 'Says she's been looking out for you since yesterday dinner. Wants a word with you, lass.'

Maddie put down her fork and faced him. 'That'll be about Duster, I reckon.'

Her father eyed her from under his brows. 'Oh aye? She wants to know if she's in foal, do you mean?'

Maddie glanced quietly at Max and back to her father. 'You knew?'

He stabbed a piece of meat. 'Of course I knew. I've not been a farmer all me life for nowt. There's not much escapes me, lass.'

'I made a decision on my own,' said Maddie defensively. 'You always said I'm airy-fairy about things. I decided it was time she foaled.'

Renshaw continued to eat. 'Right then. But if she is in foal she'll still get the ploughing done, whether or not. I'm not having that tractor and that's a fact. If you want a job doing right, do it for yourself, I've always said, and there's not a man on earth who'll shift me on that.'

He picked up his cap and put it on. Maddie caught Max's eye and smiled. 'That's right, Dad. You stick to what you believe in.'

'I will,' he growled, 'make no mistake. But next time just think to ask me before you decide owt.'

Eva seemed to sense concession in the air. 'Now can I have your toffee ration, Mr Renshaw?'

He surveyed the child for a moment, rubbing his knee thoughtfully. At last he swallowed the mouthful. 'Aye, go on then.'

'Oh great! And I promise I'll keep the kids away from the yard – specially that daft cow Eunice Sykes.'

Seth straightened up from filling the jerry cans with the offerings of paraffin the lads had brought round for tonight's blaze. It had not been an easy task to do one-handed, but he'd promised Jack. His back was aching and he rubbed it gingerly. As he did so he caught sight of a copper-headed child with her hair in plaits who was walking jauntily down the village street. Seth recognized the dog bounding alongside her.

'Hello,' he said, straightening slowly and putting himself between her and the jerry cans. 'You must be the little evacuee lass from up Scapegoat Jim's – that's his dog, isn't it?'

She tossed back the plaits. 'His name's Lassie and I haven't to talk to strangers.'

'Oh aye? Well, you got a strange fellow up your place, haven't you? That queer Jerry fellow?'

'Mr Bower's not queer. He's all right,' the girl countered defensively.

'Mr Bower, is it? And what do they call you?' Seth enquired.

'What they call me is nowt to do with you. Me name's Eva.'

Seth chuckled. 'And where are you off to, Eva?' He took hold of a swinging plait and tugged it playfully, but the child wrenched her head away.

'Don't do that!' she yelped, 'or I'll kick you!' There was a low growling sound. The dog had laid back its ears and Seth saw, to his alarm, that its lips were pulled back, laying bare gleaming teeth. He let go of the plait.

'Nay, there's no need to take on,' he muttered. 'I were only playing.'

'Come on, Lassie,' said the girl. 'Let's go and get us toffees.'

She marched off down the street, her head held high. The dog gave one last menacing growl and loped off after her.

'Strikes me they're all a queer lot up at Scapegoat,' Seth muttered to himself. 'Funny buggers the lot of 'em.'

Later that night Maddie, having spent half the evening cutting up newspapers into squares and threading them on to a piece of string, made her way down to the privy before bedtime. It was then that she caught sight of the dull red glow over the ridge. As she paused to look, she saw Max standing by the yard wall and the probing arcs of searchlights behind him.

'What is it?' she murmured, coming up close to him. 'It can't be Middlesbrough they're bombing – I can't hear any bombs.'

'The moor's on fire,' he replied. 'The heather must be as dry as tinder after all the hot weather. Someone probably dropped a match.'

'Then I'd best tell Dad.'

But her father expressed no surprise when she came indoors to tell him. 'I know,' was his laconic reply.

'Then oughtn't you to get the fire-fighting stuff up there?' Maddie asked. 'I thought you had to cycle down to get Dai Thomas and the hearse?'

'Not this time. I know what I'm doing.'

From her bedroom Maddie could see the extent of the blaze – a long swathe of fire curving across the very topmost reaches of the moor, dimming the distant searchlights with its brilliance. It was still burning when the wail of the air-raid siren disturbed the still of the summer night, and when the dull, distant roar of aeroplane engines heralded the coming of the German bombers.

Then came the first strange sound – a whine which grew in volume and ended in a terrific crash. Eva awoke with a start.

'What's that, Maddie?' she said fearfully, her eyes wide.

Maddie pulled back the blackout curtain. High on the moor she could see a great dancing sheet of flames. Again came the whining sound and Maddie's fingers flew to her ears as another resounding crash told her that a bomb had fallen.

'They're bombing the moor,' she whispered. 'They think it's a city. Come on, down to the cellar, quick!'

Of course, she realized as she pulled on dressing gown and slippers, her father had known. Instead of getting out of bed Eva had disappeared under the bedclothes and was whimpering. At that moment Maddie, her eyes growing accustomed to the darkness outside, made out the figure of a man high on the moor road, and he was running. It was Max, she was sure of it, for the figure held arms upraised, shaking his fists at the night sky. She knew, as surely as if she could hear him, that he was shouting oaths and imprecations upon the enemy above him.

The bombing stopped, but then another unfamiliar sound came to her ears. It was the drone of an aeroplane engine but the droning was erratic, as though an engine were faulty. She strained her eyes to see into the blackness of the sky. When she looked down again the figure of the man had gone.

Eva lay quiet again. The sound of the engine came closer, stuttering and pausing for whole seconds together. Maddie hurried downstairs.

Renshaw was standing by the window, the curtains pulled back. Dog lay before the embers of the fire, his head between his paws, eyes wide and his ears laid back.

'There's a plane in trouble,' her father muttered without turning. Even as he spoke the sound of the engine died. Maddie held her breath and neither of them moved. Only Dog lifted his head, his ears pricked.

Renshaw caught his breath. 'I can see it! It's a plane on fire! Oh God! It's coming this way – it could hit the village!'

Maddie stood rooted to the spot. Then she heard it, a long-drawn-out sound like the hissing of a high wind increasing to a gale, and then a deafening crash and the sound of splintering.

'It's hit the hillside – quick, they'll need help, if it's not too late!'

Renshaw moved like a young man to grab his tin helmet from the sideboard and wheel his bicycle out into the yard. Maddie raced out after him, tying the cord of her dressing gown tightly as she ran.

'My God, just look at the blaze!' gasped Renshaw. 'I'll go for the fire-engine – you get Bower and see if there's owt can be done for the poor buggers.'

Renshaw sped off down the lane towards the undertaker's. Thank God the ride was downhill for his gammy leg could never have stood the strain of cycling uphill.

Dai already had the trailer pump hitched to the hearse and the engine running. He was standing beside it, staring uphill at the hideous glare that filled the horizon. 'Bloody awful crash. Knew you wouldn't be long.'

Renshaw clanged the bell which had been mounted outboard while Dai drove at speed up the lane towards the moor. The forty-foot extension ladder fitted to a rack inside the hearse rattled precariously. Dai's face was white.

'Thought that thing was going to hit the village,' he muttered. 'It skimmed the rooftops, took Mrs Spivey's chimney off. Lucky it went on past the vicarage and up on the moor.'

Not far above Scapegoat Farm they found it, scattered wreckage glowing in the fierce light of the fire. The scene was as brilliantly lit as if it were a midsummer day. Men were moving like ants around the blaze, and Renshaw could see Bower. He plunged into the burning wreck and

143

moments later dragged out a body which he laid by a blackthorn hedge before darting back into the blaze.

'Thank God there's the pond,' said Dai. 'You get the suction-pump pipes down to it and I'll connect up the hose.'

He drove the hearse off the road and Renshaw could feel the trailer behind leap and wobble over the rutted field. Drawing the hearse to a halt Dai leapt down and began unravelling the hose. Renshaw grabbed the suction pipe and dragged it towards the pond. As he slithered down the bank he could hear Dai shouting for one of the men to give him a hand.

It was no easy task to lower into the water the heavy basket which served as a makeshift strainer to prevent leaves and debris from being sucked into the pump. When it was done Renshaw scrambled back up the bank, conscious now of the pain in his knee. He limped hastily back to the hearse, pushing his way through a gap in the blackthorn hedge.

In the shadow of the hedge his foot caught on something and he looked down. At first the body lying there seemed to be that of a negro, and then Renshaw realized with a leap of alarm that the fellow was so badly burnt that hardly any skin was left intact. He was undoubtedly dead. Nausea filled Renshaw as he went back to help Dai thrust the coupling home on the delivery outlet of the pump.

Fred Pickering, in his ARP uniform, was running out the first section of the hose. Renshaw took command.

'I'll do that,' he said shortly. 'Dai, you take the second and branch pipes. Pickering, you start up the engine.'

Pickering swung the starting handle and the pump's engine roared into life. Renshaw picked up the first section of hose and ran towards the fire, unravelling the hose.

As he neared the wreck the heat of the fire scorched his face. He turned and waved a signal to Pickering to turn on the water, and at once a powerful jet emerged from the pipe. As he directed it into the heart of the blaze he knew it was going to be useless. He became aware of Bower at his side.

'I can't reach the others,' Bower said.

'No one on earth could reach them now,' shouted Renshaw. At that moment there was a sudden explosion, and Bower grabbed his arm.

'Ammunition – it's exploding. Quick! Take cover!'

The men who had been milling around the wreck fled, disappearing into the darkness. Renshaw kept on playing the jet into the fire, feeling more and more helpless that it was having no effect. Dai came up to him, coughing and beads of perspiration gleaming on his ruddy face.

'Leave it, Renshaw. The AFS should be here any time now – they're better equipped to deal with it. Come on, we've done our best.'

Renshaw waved a weary arm to signal Pickering to turn off the water. As he trudged back across the churned-up heather he could see Dai's face, illuminated by the light of the blaze. He was standing by the hedge, looking down.

'My God, just look at that!' said Dai. Renshaw looked down. The body of the dead airman had been rolled over, its arms outflung and the face unrecognizable. Then he saw what was holding Dai's attention. Around the blackened wrist was a circle of white flesh.

'Would you credit it?' muttered Dai. 'While we was busy with that fire some rotten bugger pinched his wristwatch.'

CHAPTER TWELVE

The full horror of war had come to Barnbeck and for days the villagers spoke with hushed voices of what had taken place.

'I think we ought to have got a medal for bringing that Jerry plane down,' grumbled old Seth. 'Can't be many civilians who's done that. Exciting, that were.'

'Nay, it's not that exciting when you see all them charred bodies,' murmured Eddie.

'What happened to them dead Jerries?' asked Seth. 'Never saw 'em meself – Colonel Westerley-Kent wouldn't let us near.'

'The military took 'em away,' said Fred. 'Same as they requisitioned the wreckage and mounted a guard over it. Can't see what was so secret like, seeing as we'd all seen it.'

Dai sipped his beer mournfully. 'They could at least have let me bury them,' he muttered. 'Haven't done a decent burial for best part of a year now.'

'There were one of 'em not dead though, weren't there?' enquired Sam. 'Parachuted out, got caught in a tree near the vicarage, I heard.'

'They took him and all. Reckon he didn't last long though,' replied Fred, but he no longer spoke with relish of his superior information.

'Funny about that wristwatch that wcre pinched,' murmured Eddie. 'Don't know whether I ought to have reported it or not. Rum do, that. Who'd ever think of stealing off a dead man?'

'Nay, we don't know that owt were pinched,' cut in Fred. 'Can't tell, with a body as burnt as he were.'

'It wouldn't be one of us at any rate,' said Sam. 'Not an Englishman's way, isn't that. Not cricket.'

There were murmurs and heads shook in disgusted disbelief.

'True,' agreed Fred. 'A Nazi might do summat like that, but not one of us.'

Old Seth nodded. 'Aye, well, we all know who that'd be then, don't we?'

He leered knowingly at his son. Jack drained off his pint. 'We don't know as he had owt to do with it. He went in and pulled that airman out of the wreck, think on.'

'One of his own folk,' murmured Fred. 'One of his own.'

Sam pulled his pipe from his mouth. 'Nay, Eddie told us that Scapegoat Jim vouched for him – he's no spy.'

Fred looked at him meaningfully over his glass. 'He's a Jerry, isn't he? A leopard don't change its spots.'

'That's a fact,' agreed Seth. 'Funny-looking chap he is and all – right gloomy-looking. Wouldn't look me in the eyes. Don't trust fellows that won't look at you straight. Can't abide 'em.'

He gave a mock shudder and drank deeply from his glass. Fred gave a slow nod.

'Aye, it's fellows like him we could well do without. No joke having the enemy in your midst. A man never knows what'll happen next. Thieving off a dead man, I ask you! Evil bugger.'

'Aye,' agreed old Seth. 'Downright wicked, is that.'

'Needs teaching a lesson,' averred Fred. 'One he won't forget in a hurry.'

George nodded. 'Aye, he does that.'

Fred nodded. 'Right. We'll lie in wait for him coming down off the moor.' He picked up his glass of beer. 'We'll make the bugger wish he'd never come to Barnbeck.'

Eva squatted alongside Dog, watching Renshaw as he bent over his most prized gooseberry bush.

'Me and Lassie's hungry,' she said, twirling one of the dog's ears. 'When's dinner?'

'Thought I told you to keep away from these bushes,' Renshaw growled. 'What you doing here?'

'I were just coming back from Eunice's and I saw you here,' the child replied.

'Thought you and her didn't speak.'

Eva shrugged. 'That were ages ago. She's my best friend now. She's got a real posh house, she has, all lace covers on the chairbacks and potted plants. And a big doll's house.'

Renshaw grunted. It was a well-known fact in Barnbeck that Doreen Sykes kept a tidy house, smarter by far than anyone else's, and that it was more than Eddie Sykes's life was worth to set foot in his own parlour until he had divested himself of uniform and boots and had a good wash in the scullery. And it was said she even washed the bar of soap after he'd finished.

'So she's not calling you names any more,' he remarked.

'Nay. It's that cross-eyed Betty up at the vicarage who's getting it now,' Eva said complacently. 'We all call her Specky Four-eyes.'

Renshaw squinted against the sunlight to glance at the child's expression. 'That's not very kind,' he remarked.

'Nowt to it. There was a whole gang of the village kids chasing your Mr Bower up the hill the other day, calling him names. He said nowt.'

'Oh aye? What were they saying?'

'*Yid, Yid, dirty Yid.* He were mucky and all, 'cos he'd been digging that manure stuff. He didn't mind 'em.'

She rolled Dog over on to his back and began tickling his stomach. 'Know what? Eunice says they took one of the Jerries to her house the other night. The one with the parachute. Mrs Sykes wouldn't have him in, Eunice says, 'cos he was all burnt and it would have messed up the cushions. Any road, the soldiers took him.'

She reached out to tweak a plump gooseberry. Renshaw spotted her and slapped her wrist.

148

'What've I told you? Get off down the lanes and pick blackberries if you must, but leave my berries alone or I'll have the hide off your backside, young lady.'

Eva nursed her wrist against her thin chest and glowered at him. 'I'll set Lassie on you,' she threatened. 'Any road, blackberries aren't ripe. I got bellyache from 'em last week.'

'Serves you right. Teach you to leave stuff alone. I've told you, these berries are for the contest and I'll not have no one touching 'em.'

She stared, wide-eyed. 'You can't want 'em all – there's millions of 'em! Go on, let me have some.'

He straightened and looked down into the earnest little face. 'Tell you what,' he said at last, 'not now but after your dinner, you can have some off that bush there – but only off that one, mind. If you touch any others – '

She stood up, grinning happily. 'I won't, I promise. I knew you'd let me have some in the end – you're a nice man really, whatever they say. Come on, Lassie.'

Before he could speak she was dancing away towards the farmyard, Dog trotting after her.

Maddie listened patiently to the child's chatter as she ate her bread and soup at dinner time. It made her angry to hear about the children taunting Max, but with difficulty she managed to control her tongue.

'I'm off now,' said Eva, climbing down off her chair. 'Eunice and me's going to look for asks, she says. What's asks?'

'Wriggly things in ponds. Some folk call them newts.'

'Oh – them.' Eva rushed off out to meet Eunice.

Shortly after Renshaw came in and slumped on a chair. He stretched out his legs and gave a deep sigh. 'Could do with a mug of tea.'

'Kettle's boiling. I'll brew up.'

She was just drawing the kettle from the hob when she heard her father's quick intake of breath.

'What the devil – !'

Maddie looked up. A dark shadow leaned against the doorframe, silhouetted against the bright sunlight.

'Max? What's up?'

It was then that she saw the blood. It was gushing from Bower's face and running down on to his shirt. Her breath caught in her throat as she saw how pale he looked.

'Max! What on earth has happened?'

Renshaw clicked his tongue. 'Don't plague him with daft questions, lass. Come here, Bower.'

Max stumbled into the room and sank on to a chair. As he closed his eyes she could see the deep, jagged cut that ran across his cheek. She was barely aware of the shrunken figure of a man by the door as she took a clean rag and soaked it under the tap.

'Who are you?' rasped Renshaw.

'Lorry driver – taking coal over to Thwaite. Thought I'd best bring him in.'

'Oh aye, I've seen you about. What've you done to him?'

'Me? Nowt. I just found him in the lane.'

Maddie touched the rag to the cut, wincing as she saw how deep it was. Max moaned as she cleaned it with the utmost care and gentleness.

Renshaw leaned over her shoulder. 'It's bad, is that. Needs a doctor.'

'No,' Max said quietly. 'It's only a cut. No bones broken.'

'Ought to be stitched,' said Renshaw, and turned to the lorry driver. 'Can you take him over to the doctor's in Otterley?'

The man shrugged wiry shoulders. 'Lorry's stuck. Any road, he's a Jerry, isn't he? Why fret over him?'

Maddie was taking iodine from the cupboard as Renshaw turned on the man. 'German he may be, but he's my hand and I'll take care of him. He needs a doctor.'

The man made for the door. 'Then you see to it if you're

so fond of Jerries. I've to see to the lorry or the boss'll have my guts for garters.'

And he was gone. Max still lay back in the chair, eyes closed. He made no sound as the iodine bit into the wound, but Maddie saw his eyelids tighten.

Renshaw tossed off the mug of tea. 'You all right, Bower?'

'Yes.'

'No,' said Maddie. 'If he doesn't have stitches he's not to move or he'll start the bleeding off again. It's nearly stopping.'

Renshaw eyed the farmhand with curiosity. 'Villagers, were it?'

Max made no answer. Renshaw got up from his chair. 'Aye, well, I've work to do. Come back out when you're ready.'

He made for the door. Without opening his eyes Max spoke. 'No need to worry, Mr Renshaw. We heal fast, we Jew boys.'

Renshaw made no answer as he strode out. Maddie turned to lift the teapot.

'There's fresh tea here – I'll pour you some. Tell me, Max, what happened?'

For a moment the dark eyes stared hard at her, then his gaze slid away. He picked up the mug without answering. Maddie persisted.

'Were you attacked? I've heard how the village kids tease you – they'll have picked that up from their folks.'

'I do not question you. Friends do not question.' He gulped back the tea and rose, his head a clear foot above her own. Maddie looked up at him.

'Are we friends, Max? I'd like to think so.'

Without warning his right hand seized her arm, the fingers digging into the bare flesh until she winced. Black eyes bored into hers as if probing into her very soul, and she felt a strange and heady sensation, mesmerized by the power of that fierce look.

'Would you call a thief a friend?' he muttered, the vice-like hand shaking her arm.

'How do you mean? You're not a thief.' She was bewildered by his words, his terrifying look, but at the same time she felt a surging excitement. Suddenly he flung her arm away.

His voice came softly from his throat, filled with infinite bitterness. 'My people should be accustomed to branding after all these years,' he muttered.

'Branding?' Maddie echoed.

'They're saying I stole a dead man's watch. I am branded a thief, a spy, a Jerry – and a Jew.'

His lips were compressed into a tight line below the still-seeping wound as he swung around to leave. Maddie snatched hold of his sleeve.

'You're a good man, I know!'

For a second he let her hold on to his sleeve, looking down into her flushed, impassioned face. Slowly he raised a hand and let his fingers move lightly down her cheek to rest, for the briefest of moments, on her chin. Then without a word he pulled his hand away and stumbled out of the kitchen.

That night heavy rain put an end to the weeks of incessant heat, but Max was too troubled in spirit to remain in the shelter of the barn. Midnight found him walking alone along the high ridge of the hill.

In the dark and the rain the moors seemed vast and endless, a sweeping expanse where nothing moved nor lived. In this land of strangers he felt even more estranged and reviled than ever before. The rage inside him began to curdle into despair.

God had truly forsaken him, he was convinced of it. But for Eva's childish chatter he might not have learnt what the villagers were saying, not realized the reason for that stone which had been hurled at him from behind a bush by a faceless figure. Alienation from these people had been bad enough, but to be unjustly accused of such a despicable theft!

The mind hummed with memory, a confusion of tangled glimpses of the past mingled with imagination's horrifying scenes. Max stood looking down at the moonlit surface of the river below, watching its gentle curve down through this quiet land on its steady journey towards the sea, and then he turned to retrace his steps along the ridge. As he caught sight of the patch of earth, churned and blackened, where splinters of wreckage still showed, a shudder of apprehension ran through him. There had to be something eternal and imperishable in this hideous world, something of true beauty . . .

'You're a good man, I know!'

He heard again Maddie's voice fiercely protesting his innocence, and he smiled. How young and innocent she was, how filled with that youthful wild rapture which reminded him so much of his sister Heidi. So earnest, her soul laid open to view with all the delicate transparency of a butterfly's wing. She was a thing of beauty, in all truth – but would she too, despite all her defiance, be crushed and broken in the end? Oh no, Lord; let her at least remain whole and perfect in her innocence.

He walked on through the rain without raising his head, yielding to the depths of weariness within him. At last, shivering and realizing that he was soaked he turned, bracing his shoulders, and headed downhill again in the darkness towards Scapegoat Farm.

A candle was burning in an upstairs window and for a fleeting second he caught sight of Maddie's face before he went into the barn. She must have forgotten to draw the blackout curtains.

Maddie was still awake and dressed and listening for Max to come home. She heard his footsteps stumbling across the yard and could hear the hopelessness in his dragging feet. Her heart ached with pity and as she heard him fumble with the latch of the barn door she made up her mind. Late though it was, she must talk to him. Making certain that Eva was asleep she crept downstairs and out into the rain-soaked yard.

The barn door opened and she went in slowly, uncertain of her welcome. She stood bewildered in the light of the stable candle, her eyes searching him out in the gloom. He was standing, jacket in hand, by the bales of hay and he watched in silence as she walked across and seated herself on one of the bales.

Finding no words, she held out her arms to him. He let the jacket fall and sank to his knees at her feet, burying his head in her lap, and she felt his whole body begin to shake with silent sobs. She bent her head and held him close, and her heart ached for his suffering.

At last he lay still, his head still pressed into her lap, his hands clutching about her waist. He gave one deep, convulsive shudder and she drew his head gently against her breast.

'I know, I know,' she murmured.

His voice was indistinct as he replied. 'I'm sorry, Maddie.'

She leaned back, lifting his face to smile gently at him. Her hands were cupping his face, one finger gently tracing the wound.

'Take no notice what those stupid folk are saying – they just don't know any better. They don't mean to be so cruel.'

He gave a dry, humourless laugh.

'I mean it, Max – you must believe that things will work out right in the end.'

He gave a weary smile. 'Forgive me, Maddie. I think the old me died with the war.'

Maddie let her hands fall from his face, conscious now that they were too close, too intimate for comfort. Max stayed kneeling for a few moments, his hands in her lap, as if reluctant to lose contact. Then he sighed deeply and sank back on his heels.

'I should not stay here, Maddie. I should move on.'

Maddie gasped. 'Go away, you mean? Where could you go?'

He rose to his feet and turned away. 'America, perhaps. I have a visa – I was one of the lucky ones.'

Maddie's hands flew to her lips. 'America? Oh no!'

He was speaking into the shadows of the barn, his voice weary and far-away. 'Maybe there I can start again, where no one knows me.'

Maddie leapt to her feet. 'Then take me with you, Max!'

He turned, black eyes wide. 'Take you with me?'

Excitement blazed in her eyes. 'Why not? We could make a new start. We could both be free.'

She saw the light dawn slowly in his eyes, and then he took a step towards her. 'You would do that, Maddie? Leave your father and Scapegoat Farm?'

She stood, feet apart and a defiant recklessness in her eyes. 'Why not? There is no one in the world I would trust sooner than you.'

The amazement in his eyes softened into a smile, and he came close. 'Maddie, oh, Maddie!'

Somehow she was in his arms, her face pressed against his shirt. For long moments they clung together in silence, and she found his strength gave new resolution. At last he let her go. She looked up at him earnestly.

'You do mean it, Max? You would take me?'

He turned away with a deep sigh. 'It's a big step, Maddie. It means more than you realize.'

'I don't care – I want to go with you.'

'Let me think about it for a while. Go back to bed now.'

Max lay in the straw after she had gone and marvelled at her innocent trust in him. It was far too big a responsibility to take on without consideration, but his heart was warmed by her loving, childlike faith in him.

There were many reasons why he should not take her away from this place, but on the other hand Maddie's eager, questing spirit cried out for freedom, and there was nothing he would like more dearly than to give it to her. Away from this village and its restrictive, narrow-minded influence she would grow and blossom into the beautiful, fulfilled woman she had every right to be.

It was a vexing problem, one best to sleep on for a while. Max drifted off into uneasy dreams.

Dawn was spreading a faint, rosy glow when he awoke suddenly, disturbed by a sound. It was not the usual crowing of the old rooster but a quieter, more insidious sound. He rolled over to face the door and saw, framed in the doorway, the figure of a girl.

He struggled to sit upright and throw the blanket aside to rise. The girl closed the door and came towards him and he saw it was not Maddie. It was the girl from the big house down in the village, the Westerley-Kent daughter who had watched as the horses mated, and she was smiling.

'I've been out riding,' she said in a casual tone. 'I heard you slept in the barn, so I thought I'd pay a social call. I'm supposed to give you a message that Mother wants to see the Renshaw girl anyway.'

Max felt bemused. He stood, rubbing his eyes and trying to think of what to say. He heard her chuckle.

'Not accustomed to lady visitors in your boudoir?' she teased. 'I felt sure you'd be awake by now. Shall I go out and come in again? Speak to you in your own tongue if you're still only half-awake – *Guten Morgen, Herr Bower. Hier kommt eine niedliche Dame mit Ihnin zu sprachen.*'

He looked up at the high small window where dawn was still streaking the eastern sky. 'What time is it? Am I late?'

'It's not yet five. Relax, Mr Bower.'

He seated himself again on the hay and she sank down gracefully beside him. 'Caught you napping, haven't I?

Still, they say that's the best way for a woman to catch a man. At least you're decent – got your trousers on, I mean.'

He could hear the amusement in her tone as she twirled a blade of straw between her fingers. Then suddenly she tossed it aside and leaned forward to lay a hand on his trousered shin. Looking up into his eyes she slid her fingers gently up to his knee, murmuring softly.

'*Ich denke oft an dir, Herr Bower.* I've thought a great deal about you ever since that day you brought the mare to the stallion. Oh indeed I have! I've dreamt a lot about mares and stallions since that day – in fact, I did again last night. That's why I'm here, Mr Bower. You intrigue me more than any other man I've ever met.'

He looked down at her blankly, trying to ignore the fingers slowly rising above his knee. 'Me? That's nonsense,' he muttered.

'You intrigue me. What is that mark on your face? A duelling scar?'

Her hand left his thigh to touch his cheek. He laid a hand over hers to remove it. 'Nothing so dramatic, I'm afraid. Now if you would excuse me – Mr Renshaw will be calling me . . .'

'Not just yet, I think. There is still time for us to get to know one another better. Come, lie back and relax. I shall show you what none of the village or Land Army girls could teach you. You will not forget Joanna in a hurry . . .'

She was reclining full-length in the hay now, giving him a lazy smile as she began slowly to unfasten her blouse, one button at a time. He could see her pale flesh; she wore nothing underneath. She was incredibly beautiful, he realized, with her dark hair falling loose on her shoulders, not rolled up as he had seen her before, and the white skin of her shoulders glowing luminous in the half-light. Beautiful, yes, and very desirable. To a man so long deprived of a woman's body she was irresistible.

Her breasts lay bared to his view, full and rounded and the nipples erect. She pulled her skirt high around her knees, then stretched her arms above her head with all the luxurious elegance of a cat.

'Come, my stallion,' she murmured in a husky tone. '*Komm, mein stolzes Tier*. You will find me a receptive mare.'

Max felt the blood rise, inflaming him and driving reason from his brain. He knelt beside her and reached out his hand. Her breast was warm and responsive as he stroked it gently for a moment. 'It's been a long time,' he muttered.

She smiled. 'Don't tell me you haven't had that little girl of Renshaw's – Maddie, or whatever her name is.'

Instantly his hand stiffened and then he drew it away, sitting back on his haunches. Joanna raised her head.

'What's wrong? Go on, I like it.'

Max rose to his feet and turned to look for his shirt. 'I think you came to the wrong place, Miss Westerley-Kent. Perhaps you should look in the stables.'

His shirt over his arm, he strode out of the barn, leaving Joanna to stare after his retreating back in fury. The last she saw of him as she went to remount Firefly was a weather-tanned figure, naked to the waist, dousing his head under the yard pump.

CHAPTER THIRTEEN

Hilary Westerley-Kent was pouring the breakfast tea into her best china cups and surreptitiously surveying her daughter's face at the same time. The girl looked decidedly pale. Forces life was evidently rather draining for the child – still, she wouldn't be told.

'Did you deliver the message to Miss Renshaw?' she enquired. Joanna nodded. 'Is she coming down today?'

'I don't know. I left the message with the farmhand.'

Joanna was clearly moody today. Hilary resolved to find out the reason.

'You rode out early, I believe. I imagine it was very pleasant on such a fine morning, though perhaps a trifle wet underfoot after the rain?'

Joanna shrugged.

'Was Archie annoyed about having to saddle up so early?'

'I did it myself. No need to wake him.'

So it wasn't Archie's taciturn manner which had irritated the girl. It must be something that happened up at Scapegoat. 'Was there anyone else about at the farm when you called? Apart from the farmhand, that is?'

Joanna snorted. 'He was enough. Never met such an uncouth creature. Changed my mind about him – he's not so attractive after all.'

So that was it, thought Hilary with satisfaction. The fellow had evidently crossed Joanna somehow. It wouldn't do the girl any harm to realize she couldn't push everyone around. Hilary's estimation of the farmhand rose. He was evidently a man with strength of mind; the kind of help Hilary would give her eye teeth for – how on earth Renshaw had managed to come by him was a mystery.

'The Renshaw girl is pleasant though, didn't you think? Obviously knows a thing or two about Clevelands. I do so hope that mare is in foal. Such a nice girl.'

Joanna flung down the half-nibbled piece of toast and rose from the table. 'You're not the only who thinks so, Mother. Richard apparently thinks she's a cracker too.'

'Richard? I didn't know he knew her that well. Still, it shows he can recognize a nice girl when he sees one after all. I was beginning to wonder; all those rather weird ones he's picked up in the past.'

'Those were passing things, for entertainment only. This time it's different.'

Joanna's tone sounded casual but Hilary was not deceived. Pouring herself another cup of tea she spoke diffidently.

'I see. And how do you know?'

Joanna turned to face her. 'Because Richard told me himself. He's writing to her, asking her to go steady with him. Next thing you know they'll be engaged. He's in deadly earnest about this one, Mother, says he's madly in love with her.'

'Is he now?' Hilary's tone was still mild for she was too well disciplined to betray her alarm. For Mrs Westerley-Kent, the wife of Colonel Westerley-Kent of Thorpe Gill, to befriend and patronize the daughter of a local hill farmer was one thing, but for that girl to get ideas of trapping her son into marriage was quite another. Something would have to be done – and quickly too, before matters got too far out of hand.

'I should go and change if I were you, darling,' she remarked. 'There's a smear of mud on the back of your skirt.'

That afternoon Joanna could not resist hanging about in the drawing room for a few moments longer when Miss Renshaw was announced. Her mother wheeled her chair behind the side table and put her spectacles on her nose, a sure sign that she meant to talk business.

The Renshaw girl came in, looking about the room, and gave a hesitant smile. She was wearing a cotton frock of the same material as that one Joanna had had made last year, and was dutifully carrying the regulation gas mask slung over her shoulder in a cardboard box. Joanna could not help envying her slim legs, bronzed by the sun and not, like her own, with the aid of gravy-browning mixed with face cream. She was attractive, in a plebeian sort of way, with her long fair hair and pretty snub-nosed face, but even so, she couldn't possibly be the reason why the Bower fellow had been so unresponsive this morning. Not a little faded thing like her.

'Good afternoon, Miss Renshaw,' said her mother. She did not, as was her custom, invite the visitor to sit. 'Would you be so kind as to leave us, Joanna?'

'Of course. But I'd like to ask Maddie Renshaw to pass on a message for me before I go.'

'What is that, dear?'

'Tell your Mr Bower this, Miss Renshaw. *Hoffentlich wird' ich ihn niemals wiedersehen.* Just tell him that from me, will you?'

Joanna gave the girl a thin smile as she passed her. 'You know, I used to have a frock of that stuff once. Whatever happened to it, I wonder? Mrs Barraclough probably tore it up for dusters ages ago.'

The girl's lips parted, but she said nothing. Once outside the door Joanna could not resist the temptation to listen. It was a pity Thorpe Gill's doors were so solid.

At first the voices murmured unresolvable words, and then her mother's voice came loud and clear. 'Let me make myself clear, Miss Renshaw. I will not have it, do you understand? My son is far too young . . .'

The girl did not seem to argue very much. No spirit, thought Joanna with contempt. But just as she was turning to leave, the Renshaw girl's voice rang out.

161

'You've got it all wrong, Mrs Westerley-Kent. I don't want your son. There's someone else I care for. It's Richard you should be telling off, not me. I don't even like him.'

Her mother's answer, though low, was equally clear. 'To be truthful, Miss Renshaw, sometimes I do not like him very much myself. But I must protect him. The matter is at an end.'

Joanna sped away down the corridor. The Renshaw girl had some spirit after all.

Later Hilary appeared in her wheelchair in the conservatory where Joanna sat, and Joanna could detect the determined gleam in her eyes. She made no mention of the Renshaw girl's visit.

'The village police constable brought up some trout for us this morning,' she said conversationally. 'Chap called Sykes. That awful brown trout – totally inedible, I'm afraid. When will they realize there's far too much alum in the river? Pity we haven't had a flood for so long – that's the only time we get salmon up this stretch of the river.'

Joanna made no response. Hilary sighed and began plucking withered leaves off the azaleas. 'Reverend Chilcott telephoned this afternoon. He says the church needs a new window and asked my help to raise funds. I thought a bridge drive, perhaps. The only trouble is, I couldn't let Ernest Chilcott take part in it. He cheats like mad. But I'll think of something – when I want something I usually get it.'

'What happened with the Renshaw girl?'

Hilary rolled the handful of withered leaves into a ball and crushed them firmly in her fist. 'Oh, there was no real problem there after all. She's completely taken up by that German fellow. Now all that remains is to talk sense into Richard.'

Old Seth tottered along behind his son towards the beehives at the bottom of the herb garden.

'One hand or no, I've helped take the bees afore and I can do it now,' he was saying stubbornly. 'Any road, you've no veil – you lent it to that fellow up Otterley and he never brought it back.'

'Don't need it,' muttered Jack, trying to ignite the rolled-up newspaper he was carrying stuck in the end of a metal spout.

'And it ought to be done when it's hot,' persisted Seth. 'Rained last night.'

'I know. That's why Ivy's nagging me.'

Old Seth lingered by the rhubarb patch. 'Been missing me bit of heather honey lately,' he complained. 'Nowt better for me cough.'

'Then push off out of my way and let me get on.' Jack was trying vainly to set the newspaper alight to give off a fume of white smoke. The match-end burnt his finger and he swore. Seth leaned on his stick, grinning a toothless smile as Jack removed the lid of the first hive.

'I told you it were a two-handed job,' the old man said with satisfaction. 'Let me hold the puffer for you while you take the panels out.'

Jack growled. 'How the devil can you puff the bellows, Dad? Just clear off, will you?'

He was struggling to pull out a sticking panel from the hive and at the same time to puff the bellows. Seth made no move to leave.

'What were the lads on about in the pub this dinner?' Seth enquired mildly. 'I couldn't catch it all. Summat to do with that Jerry up at Scapegoat, weren't it? What do they want with him this time?'

'Less you know, the better,' muttered Jack. 'Bloody hell!'

'What's up? Got stung? I told you, didn't I? Nay, you'll never listen. Too clever by half, you.'

'Shut up, Dad. Pass us that bucket.'

★ ★ ★

163

The honeycombs at last safely retrieved, the two men returned to the upper garden. Seth lowered himself, breathing heavily, on to the bench next to the big drum with the revolving blades and watched while his son placed the honeycombs inside. Seth took hold of the handle and began turning it, chewing his gums as he watched the drum spinning and the honey spattering on the drum sides. He was frowning as he thought deeply.

'What about that Jerry, Jack? Throwing stones is kid's stuff. Now me, I'd have taken him on man to man,' said Seth, aiming an uppercut at the drum with his stump.

Jack smiled. 'Spin away, Dad, and I'll go tell Ivy she's got honey for us tea.'

Maddie clenched her lips tightly together as she served supper to Eva and the men and then sat in silence, trying to force the food down her throat but it seemed strangely unwilling to swallow.

Eva was filling the air with chatter. 'Mrs Sykes told me off for not having me gas mask,' she was saying brightly. 'Daft, is that. She said the teacher, Miss Gaunt, always has hers, but she doesn't go running in the woods like us.'

'You're supposed to carry it at all times,' said Renshaw. 'Don't you read the leaflets? Suppose there was an air raid.'

'Jerry planes haven't been over for ages now,' said Eva complacently. 'Anyhow, why should they bomb us? We're nowt. Here you are, Lassie.'

'I've told you to stop feeding that dog at the table, haven't I?' said Renshaw. 'What's for afters, Maddie?'

Maddie watched them as they ate the steamed pudding. Eva put down her spoon and smacked her lips. 'That's nice. I think I could eat some more – I think.'

'No you don't – you'll only leave it,' said Maddie.

'Aye,' said her father. 'Think on what they tell us – Waste means Want. When in doubt, do without.'

Maddie was watching Max covertly, wondering why the sight of his handsome, scarred face filled her with anger and resentment. It was that Joanna Westerley-Kent girl who had done it, sending him messages no one else could understand.

'I'm off out then,' said Eva, jumping down off the chair.

'And just you keep clear of the pond this time,' warned Renshaw. 'Don't want you coming home with your sandals all soaked again.'

'I'll be all right. They only got wet 'cos Eunice and me used 'em as boats to have a race. Come on, Lassie.'

Maddie poured tea for the men and then curled herself up in the easy chair by the fire, exercise book and pencil in hand. Renshaw glanced across at her.

'You've always got your nose in a flaming book,' he grumbled. 'What is it this time?'

'It's not a book, Dad,' she answered quietly. 'I've had a letter from Richard Westerley-Kent. I'm going to answer it.'

Renshaw's craggy eyebrows rose. 'A what? What've I told you – ?'

'Don't fret yourself, Dad. I'm telling him not to write again.'

'Oh.' Renshaw's brow furrowed in thought. 'What did he want to write for in the first place?'

Maddie took a deep breath. 'He wanted us to go steady. I don't want to.'

For a few moments there was silence in the kitchen, a silence so tense Maddie dared not lift her head to see Max's face. She waited, half-expecting her father to burst out with angry words, but when at last he spoke it was in a far-away, considering tone.

'Go steady, eh? Fancy that – you mistress at Thorpe Gill one day.'

Maddie leapt up from the chair and stuffed the exercise book back in the drawer. 'You didn't hear me right, Dad. I said I don't want anything to do with him.'

She went out into the yard, slamming the door behind her, leaving the two men staring.

* * *

'What do you make of that then?' murmured Renshaw.

'I don't think I understand women,' Max ventured.

'Nor me neither,' said Renshaw. 'Never have.'

'Perhaps you would have liked to see her as mistress of a big house.' There was silence for a moment. 'Is this Richard a good man?' Max asked.

Renshaw shrugged. 'Hardly know him, him being one of the nobs like. Not like you, he isn't. He couldn't do a day's work. Still, he could make life easy for her. Better not having to slave to make this place pay when I'm gone – too much for a woman is that. She doesn't appreciate that. Stubborn as they come, is Maddie. Take a whip to her, that's what she needs.'

'Did you ever beat her?'

Renshaw looked away. 'Happen I should have done, but it's no use crying over spilt milk. Too late now by many a long year. Always was a wild thing, and always will be, I reckon. Take a tough fellow to tame her, by God it will.'

Maddie sat, arms hunched round knees, on the heather and stared moodily at the vast, expressionless surface of the reservoir. Beyond it rose the hills, their purple heather deepening to black in the evening light and the sinking sun spreading a crimson glow along the ridge. Nearby Duster, reins trailing, stood cropping the wiry grass.

It was not easy to try to sort out her tangled emotions. She was growing dependent upon Max for her happiness and that was not good for her. She must stop watching for him, hanging on his every word and action.

But Max Bower had come to mean so much – he was the man who could re-create her entire world if he agreed to take her away from Scapegoat before it choked her to death . . .

Duster whinnied and she started, aware that someone was standing close behind her. Turning, she saw Max, his tall figure silhouetted against the evening sky.

'You startled me,' she said accusingly. 'I didn't hear you coming. Did you follow me?'

He swung himself down beside her. 'I was concerned. Why did you leave so suddenly?'

Maddie plucked a blade of grass and chewed it in silence for a few moments. He continued to watch her face closely. Suddenly the vexation rose up and spilled over.

'I hate rich people, Max. I feel uncomfortable with them. We've got nothing in common.'

'What makes you say that?'

'Mrs Westerley-Kent is a pompous prig. I saw grouse and sherry up there and all the things they could want – they're not stuck to rations like us. And they think they can give other people orders. Rich people can have all they want, seemingly.'

'But they aren't always happy, Maddie.'

Maddie flung the blade of grass aside. 'Well they're not telling me what to do, Cleveland foal or no. I'll have nothing to do with Richard. I hate the snobbery in that family. And that Joanna is a cat.'

'Thorpe Gill is cultured, class-ridden, and just as suffocating as Scapegoat, Maddie. You are right. It's not the place for a spirit such as yours.'

'At least there's no snobbishness at our place,' said Maddie defensively. 'I bet Mrs Westerley-Kent wouldn't have a foreigner living there. Oh, I'm sorry – I didn't mean –'

He smiled gently. 'Don't worry. I would not wish to live in Thorpe Gill with all its luxuries. I would hate the restrictions. I much prefer the wild moors and open spaces.'

Maddie stole a sidelong glance. 'You mean you wouldn't want anything to do with them either? What about Joanna – she's very pretty.'

Dark eyes probed hers. 'Yes, she is, but why do you ask?'

'I'm not jealous, you know.'

He was still regarding her closely. 'What is there to be jealous about?'

'I'm not just trying to get my own back, not telling you she sent you a message. It's just that I couldn't understand it.'

He looked bewildered. 'Message? What message?'

'I told you – I couldn't understand it. She just said something in a foreign tongue.'

'I see.'

'What are you thinking, Max? You never say what you're thinking.'

He came close to her, so close she could feel his breath on the back of her neck. His hand touched her arm. Maddie moved away out of his reach. When she turned she saw that he was smiling. 'The message is not important, Maddie. Don't let it trouble you. Forget it.'

'I can't help it.' She was conscious that she sounded like Eva, like a sullen child who could not get her way.

He came close and touched her shoulder lightly. 'Would you like to leave here – go away and start a new life?'

Maddie spun round to face him, her face radiant. 'Oh yes! You do mean it, don't you, Max? You're not just teasing me?'

His expression was sober as he drew her close. 'I mean it, Maddie. But it will take a little time.'

She thought swiftly. 'Next week it's the Gooseberry Fair. Dad's got a real chance of winning this time – let's go away as soon as that's over.'

'To go to America will take longer than that, Maddie. I have to wait for a ship, and that could take a year or more.'

Her face fell. 'Oh no! I can't wait that long.'

He placed a finger under her chin. 'We shall hope, Maddie, and plan. But it is getting dark now and we should go back.'

Her face was upturned to his, all the fire and eagerness of youth radiant in her expression. Without a word he bent and kissed her gently on the forehead. Maddie pressed close against him.

'Oh, Max! I do so love you!'

He looked down at her thoughtfully. 'Don't confuse love with gratitude, Maddie. And do not be too hasty. Making a new life may not be easy.'

'With you I can't go wrong,' she replied trustfully. 'I want to be with you always.'

Suddenly he was kissing her again, but on the mouth this time, and there was no gentleness. He strained close to her, pressing his mouth hard against hers and startling her with his fierceness. But then, slowly at first and then erupting into flame, a fiery, irrepressible sensation came over her, a feeling more powerful than any she had ever known. It was savage, but it was wonderful . . .

A shrill sound cut through the still evening air, sweeping over the surface of the reservoir. Max broke away. 'Oh, my God! The air-raid siren!'

'Come on,' said Maddie. 'We'd better get back home – Eva will be worried.'

CHAPTER FOURTEEN

No German aeroplanes came over Barnbeck that night, although searchlights and the sound of distant ack-ack guns to the north indicated that they aimed for Middlesbrough yet again.

Over the course of the next week the wireless announced the devastating news. The Germans had begun a heavy and systematic blitz on London and the south-east, a fierce bombardment which was to be kept up for weeks. Renshaw was glued to the wireless daily, scolding Eva if she dared even to breathe while the news was on.

Seven of our aircraft are missing. Renshaw groaned. 'Looks bad,' he muttered. 'There's always more of ours missing than Jerry planes. How long can we keep this up?'

Two of our merchant ships were sunk. Eva looked up. 'My dad's in the merchant navy,' she commented.

'I've told you to keep quiet,' snapped Renshaw then, seeing Maddie's look, he added, 'It'll not be your dad's ship any road. He'll be all right.'

'Me mam'll be listening and I bet she's wondering,' said Eva. 'Poor mam, all on her own.'

Poor woman, thought Maddie. Somehow she'd never really conjured up a picture of Eva's mother. Despite invitation Mrs Jarrett had not yet come to visit the child, writing instead that her job in the aircraft component factory demanded all kinds of shift-hours. Maddie had a hazy vision of a harassed-looking woman with her hair covered by a headscarf tied turban-fashion and with a couple of metal curlers peeping out at the front. She must feel desperately anxious every time a merchant ship went down, eager and yet fearful to learn its name.

The news ended and Renshaw took out his papers from the drawer, setting them out in piles on the table. The music of Harry Roy's band filled the kitchen, and Maddie turned the volume down so as not to disturb him.

'*If you go down to the woods today, you'd better go in disguise,*' sang Eva. 'Can I go down to the woods, Maddie, me and Lassie? We'll be back for us tea.'

'No,' murmured Renshaw. 'You can go down to the shop with Maddie and fetch the rations.'

'Oh, do I have to?' moaned Eva. The song ended and another began.

> *Can I forget you, when every song reminds me*
> *How once we walked in a moonlit dream? . . .*

'Shut that bloody thing off!' roared Renshaw, jumping up from the table and crossing to the window to look out. Maddie hastened to do as he asked. She knew what had troubled him, but nothing in the world would make him say it. The memory still hurt too deeply.

'Come on, Eva. Fetch the basket and we'll get off.'

It was as they were coming out of Pickering's shop that Maddie caught sight of Ruby. She was wearing a new tweed jacket over a cotton frock and high heels and a heavy layer of make-up. Scarlet lipstick glowed on her lips and her lustrous hair was coiled neatly into a long, continuous fat curl all round her head like a halo. Her arm was hooked through that of a good-looking young soldier.

Ruby withdrew her gaze from his face and spotted Maddie. 'Hi, there! Maddie! I was thinking of calling up to see you if we had time – I'm only home for the weekend. Meet Gordon Ormerod – he's my steady.'

Eva's mouth gaped. 'Lovely to see you again, Ruby,' said Maddie.

'You know, you really ought to have come with me to work in the munitions factory, Maddie,' Ruby enthused, hugging the young man's arm. 'I've never had so much money in me life – and so much fun! You'd love the girls I work with – they're a great bunch, wouldn't she, Gordie?'

'I'm sure I would,' said Maddie.

'Can't think how you can stand this place any longer,' Ruby went on, glancing around and giving a mock shudder. 'I wouldn't come back here to live if you paid me. You know, I thought once as you might make shift to leave, but now it's too late, I reckon.'

'Oh, I wouldn't say that,' said Maddie, then hesitated. It would not be wise to say too much in front of the child. 'You never know.'

Eva was eyeing Ruby over with evident appreciation. 'How do you keep your hair like that?' she asked, cocking her head to one side.

Ruby laughed. 'It's easy. Top off an old stocking, put it round me head, tuck me hair in. I'll show you if you've got an old stocking. Seriously though, Maddie, you ought to come to work in the city. Big army camp there – so much fun going on – this place is dead compared to what we get up to. Gordie could tell you, couldn't you, love?'

The young man smiled down at her good-humouredly. 'I could that, if you didn't mind me splitting on you,' he chuckled. Ruby gave him a teasing nudge.

'Go on with you – you've got a one-track mind, you have,' she dimpled. 'Still, we'd best be getting on. We're off to Agley Bridge tonight to the pictures to see Bing Crosby. Oh, by the way, don't tell nobody about Gordie and me, will you? It's not official-like as yet, and you know how folks talk.'

'She's pretty,' remarked Eva when Ruby had sauntered away arm in arm with Gordon. 'Why don't you dress up all smart like that, Maddie? You know, you're pretty too only you don't really notice it.'

Maddie felt the blush that crept over her cheeks. 'Farm's no place for fancy clothes, Eva – you know how mucky it is.'

'You must have some Sunday-best clothes, haven't you?'

172

'What for? We never go anywhere.'

'You could go to church all dressed up like other folks do. I'd like to do that and all.'

Maddie smiled. 'I'll make you a Sunday frock then, only you won't have to wear it other times and mucky it up – all right?'

'And make one for you too,' said Eva. 'Then we'll both go out and show off on Sunday.'

That evening Maddie took stock of herself in the mirror. The child was right. She did look decidedly dowdy. Something would have to be done before taking off into the great world outside – she wouldn't like Max to be ashamed of her. She had enough money to buy a bit of stuff to make a frock, but a jacket like Ruby's and high-heeled shoes . . .

And then it came to her. All those things were to be found here, in this very house. Upstairs in Mother's room the wardrobe still harboured a collection of pretty dresses, scarves and shoes. And in the dressing-table drawer lay all Mother's jewellery – not precious stuff, just cheap Woolworth's jewellery, but pretty enough to brighten up a plain dress. It was stupid just to leave it all lying there, unused. It was hardly likely her father would recognize them after so long.

It was no use asking his permission for his reply was predictable. All she had to do was to get into Mother's room when he was out. She knew where he kept the key, above the door . . .

Her chance came next day. Eva went down into Barnbeck to play with Eunice and the men were both busy working in the fields. Maddie glanced out of the kitchen window to make certain she would not be disturbed.

As she opened the door of Mother's room she held her breath. Somehow going in there still had the feel of entering a church, the same slightly damp and chill atmosphere, though in Mother's room there still lingered just the faintest trace of that familiar perfume of hers. Maddie moved slowly towards the bed, hesitated, then turned back the covers and knelt to bury her face in the pillows.

Oh Mother, I can still remember when I used to creep into your bed. Only a child knows the comfort of the warm smell of a parent's body.

'Easy now, Maddie, darling. There is nothing to fear. I am proud of my little Maddie.'

There was so much I wanted to tell you, how you brought joy to my life, but I had no words to tell you. Now you'll never know . . .

A tear escaped Maddie's eye and ran down her cheek. It was cruel that Mother had gone so suddenly that there had been no time for farewell, no chance of a last word.

'I have not gone away, sweetheart, not really.'

It's hard to believe I'll never see your dear, kind face again, Mother. I want so much to talk to you – about life, about Max, about why I have to go away with him – things that only you could understand.

'I am still with you, Maddie. I am thinking of you always. I failed your father, but I shall never fail you . . .'

Oh, Mother! Always so loving and eager to help – I am beginning to understand the words you spoke to me as a child. I could not understand them then.

'It is love that gives the wind under my wings.'

Excitement burns in me like a fever. Wish me luck, Mother, for that wind will soon bear me away from here, away to a life of freedom and hope.

On the day of the Gooseberry Fair no one could speak to Renshaw. He seemed totally oblivious of the sweet scent of the blackberry and apple jam Maddie was stirring in the big copper pan over the fire, and when the milking and all the chores were finished he had eyes only for his precious gooseberries as he laid them carefully amid piles of tissue paper in the box. It was only when he was at last ready to leave that he caught sight of his daughter and raised bushy eyebrows.

'Where are you off to then, all done up like a dog's dinner? Haven't seen that frock afore, have I?'

Maddie avoided his gaze. 'Been busy sewing, haven't I? Seen Eva's new frock too?'

Eva pirouetted around the floor to show off the pretty pink cotton and the matching ribbons in her plaits. Renshaw nodded.

'Aye, you're a right bobby-dazzler and no mistake,' he commented then, lifting his nose, he added, 'What's that I can smell?'

Maddie caught it too, the faintest whiff of violets. 'It's the jam – I've left it to cool on the slab.'

She moved further from him, towards the open door. He hadn't recognized the frock she wore, but the lingering perfume could give the game away. Renshaw pulled on his cloth cap then picked up the box of gooseberries with infinite care.

'Will you be in the weighing tent today?' he asked. She understood. No power on earth would induce him to ask her to be there, to give moral support, no more than he would welcome good luck wishes.

'Course I will. See you there, Dad.'

Doreen Sykes was plaiting Eunice's straggly brown hair, jerking her head back whenever the child winced and tried to pull away. When she had done she scrutinized the girl's neck critically.

'You haven't washed behind your ears,' she scolded. 'And what've I told you about your eyebrows? A young lady always smooths them down when she dries her face, else they stand up all spiky-like, just like your dad's. Go on, I've finished.'

Eddie appeared not to notice the implied suggestion of his peasant origins, a fact which clearly irritated his wife.

As she turned to the mirror to fasten a triple string of imitation pearls around her thick throat, he heard her sigh.

'I do wish this jumper was a cashmere one like Mrs Westerley-Kent wears. Still, beggars can't be choosers.'

He wasn't going to point out, yet again for the thousandth time, that a police constable's income did not stretch to cashmere and cultured pearls. He had learnt by now that it was a useless exercise for she had always had an answer and a regretful sigh at the ready. It was always wiser simply to change the subject.

'Didn't you say young Eva was coming down, Eunice?' he enquired. 'It's twelve o'clock – she should be here now if she's coming with us.'

'Punctuality is a sign of breeding,' said his wife as she picked up the new feathered hat from the sideboard and placed it carefully on her head. 'You really can't expect the likes of – '

'She's here now!' shouted Eunice who was kneeling on the settee looking out of the window. 'And Maddie Renshaw's with her. Ooh, she does look nice!'

Mrs Sykes came to stand behind her at the window. 'My, my,' she commented. 'The Renshaw girl's smartened herself up a bit – and not before time, if you ask me. Who's that young fellow with her?'

Eddie took a quick glance out of the window and then let the lace curtain fall. 'That's the Jerry – the chap who works with Renshaw. We don't have to go out and join them, do we?'

His wife gave him a look of shocked pain. 'Good heavens, no! Eunice, don't you dare go out!'

'It's all right,' said Eunice who was peeking under the curtain again. 'Eva's coming to the door – the others have gone on.'

Mrs Sykes gave a deep sigh of relief. 'Thank heaven for that! It would be asking too much, even of a lady, to be polite to an enemy. What on earth can the Renshaw girl be thinking of, bringing him down here, on Fair day of all days too?'

'Aye,' agreed Eddie. 'Bit tactless, that. Go and answer the door, Eunice.'

'We shan't acknowledge them if we chance to meet them,' Mrs Sykes warned her husband in a loud whisper. 'If she wants to be seen with him, that's her business but she'll not involve us. Oh, hello, Eva dear. What a pretty frock. Pity you haven't got some nice new white socks to go with it. Right then, let's be off or we'll miss the Punch and Judy.'

Taking one last glance in the mirror over the sideboard to assure herself that the new hat was perched at exactly the right angle, Mrs Sykes ushered her little troupe out into the sunshine.

The mingled scent of trodden grass and ripe fruit pervaded the green shade of the marquee. Renshaw could see where Maddie and Eva stood on tiptoe on the far side of the crowd of spectators around the weighing table. His heart was pounding.

The chairman rose to his feet and adjusted his spectacles as he held out a slip of paper to bring it into focus. No one moved; no sound broke the silence but happy laughter and the tinkle of a bell from somewhere outside in the field.

'The heaviest berry, and therefore the overall prize for this year,' intoned the chairman with all the solemnity due to such an auspicious occasion, 'weighs twenty-eight grams exactly.'

James held his breath, feeling his heart lurching so violently against his ribs that it seemed it would burst from his chest. Was it his berry? For God's sake, man, speak up!

'And the owner of the berry is Mr James Renshaw, of Barnbeck. Come forward, Mr Renshaw, to receive the trophy.'

A polite spatter of handclaps rippled around the tent as James took the cup in hands which felt numb. His heart was so filled with pride and joy that he felt his lips twitching into a smile. He turned away from the table and Maddie appeared before him, a wide smile irradiating her pretty face.

'Well done, Dad.' She gave him a quick hug, but he could only stand, stiff and unresponsive, still not yet fully believing it.

'I knew you'd win,' said Eva, tugging at his hand. 'You were bound to, 'cos I never touched your big berries. Can I go and have another go at the hoop-la stall now, Maddie? I want to win a goldfish.'

Faces around them were melting away, murmuring and avoiding his gaze. James felt a sudden stab of disappointment and shook his hand free of Eva's. It was clear that his was not a popular victory. Recalling the scene last year, when Jack Kitchen held the trophy aloft to the accompaniment of teasing and laughter and genuine pleasure, James suddenly felt that the glow had gone out of his day. He nudged Dog out of his way sharply with his foot as he turned to go.

'Going for a drink to celebrate?' asked Maddie. He brushed past her.

'Happen I will later. Don't keep that kid out late.'

Maddie watched her father's broad figure disappear, closely followed by Eva who was anxious to rejoin her friend and get on with the fun of the Fair. Maddie strolled out into the sunlight. Now, perhaps, he would be less edgy and irritable for a time. She was pleased with herself; the mirror had told her that the soft blue frock of Mother's suited her well, matching the colour of her eyes exactly. Even Max had noticed.

'Blue becomes you, Maddie. You should wear it more often,' he had remarked. Where was he now? He had declined to accompany her and Eva to the marquee for the contest, and he had not said where he would be.

For a time Maddie sauntered among the stalls, watching animals in pens being inspected by solemn-faced judges and enjoying the sight of excited children trying their hand at the coconut shy or sinking happy faces into a cloud of pink candy floss. Somewhere Eva, an extra Saturday sixpence in her pocket, would be revelling in the fun too, all fears for parents and bombs forgotten for the moment.

Throughout the rest of the afternoon Maddie saw no sign of Max, and felt a sense of disappointment. It would have been a perfect opportunity to talk to him at length, undisturbed, but he seemed to have melted out of sight in the crowds. Evening approached, and farmers loaded up animals and drove them away up the lanes and stallholders began to dismantle their stalls. Mothers tugged reluctant, tired children away home for supper, and all the day's activity in the field behind the church came to an end and it began to take on the forgotten quiet of a graveyard.

Maddie lay down by the hedge in the long grass still saturated with the heat of the day and watched the swallows arrowing across the sky. Her eyes grew heavy. After a time she started upright, conscious that she must have dozed.

'There's no barn dance this year,' she heard a voice behind her say. Turning, she saw the squat figure of Mr Pickering in his ARP uniform, wearing a tin helmet and with his gas mask slung over his shoulder. He was standing, hands on hips, addressing old Seth Kitchen whose bleary eyes shifted quickly away as he caught sight of Maddie.

'Blackout regulations, you see,' said Mr Pickering. 'Can't have the marquee all lit up after dark.'

'No, course not,' muttered Seth. 'Are you off down to join the others at the Cock?'

'Happen I will, after I've done me rounds and checked all's well.'

'Don't forget you owe me a pint,' said Seth, wagging a finger. 'Jack's berry were bigger than yours, like I said it would be. I've won me pint.'

'A half,' said Mr Pickering. 'I'll be down later.'

The two men moved away without acknowledging her, but Maddie shrugged it off. It was probably because she

179

was Renshaw's daughter, and he had hurt their pride by taking the trophy.

It was a pity about the dance, in a way. But the idea of dancing no longer held the magical appeal of a year ago, as if somehow the eager enthusiasm of youth had slipped away during the last twelve months. Perhaps it was because Ruby was no longer here to stir excitement, giggling as the village lads eyed them across the street. But nearly all the village lads had gone away to war now. Or maybe it was just that last year, the last long hot summer of peacetime, seemed so far removed from all the dreariness of rationing and blackout.

Or perhaps it was because she was going away. Maybe she had outgrown Barnbeck and everything it stood for. A new life was beckoning.

Maddie stood up and brushed the grass from her skirt then walked across to the far edge of the meadow, watching dusk spreading grey over the fields. It was then that she spotted the figure squatting on the grass under one of the guy ropes of the marquee. It was Eva.

'Where's Eunice?'

Eva pulled a face. 'Her mam made her go home to bed, rotten cow.'

Maddie tried not to smile. 'You shouldn't talk about Mrs Sykes like that. It's rude.'

'You should hear what she says – she hasn't a good word to say about nobody – you included.'

'Me? What've I done then?'

Eva shrugged. 'Oh, dolling yourself up like a tart, going out with a Jerry – you're no better than you ought to be – all that sort of stuff.'

'Did she say that?'

'I told her off. Told her I wouldn't let her say nowt about you.'

Maddie smiled. 'What did she say?'

'Nowt. Told you, she took Eunice home. I'm fed up,' the child complained. 'And I'm cold.'

Poor Eva – she had to suffer for Maddie's crimes. Maddie pulled the child to her feet. 'Come on, love. I'll take you home.'

Eva stumbled along wearily beside her. 'And I didn't win no goldfish neither. And – ' She stopped suddenly as the worst insult of all came back to her. 'And Eunice's mam said I had old socks on and dirt under me fingernails. She said I weren't half as smart as her Eunice.'

'Rotten cow,' said Maddie, putting her arm about the child's thin shoulders. 'Come on – we'll have a nice hot drink by the fire.'

Eva was struggling up the lane behind Maddie, half-heartedly pulling leaves from the hawthorn hedge, when Max's tall figure came striding down towards them, his chest bared in an open-necked shirt. Maddie's heart leapt at the sight of him.

'Where've you been all day? I've been wondering. Oh, poor Eva's so tired . . .'

His gaze flitted from her face to Eva's, then without a word he swung the child up in his arms. Eva sighed and settled against his chest, a smile curving her lips.

Maddie smiled. 'It's been a good day, Max. Dad won the trophy.'

He gave her a sidelong glance. 'And you? You have had a good day too?'

Maddie sighed. 'Yes. And you? Where were you?'

He nodded uphill. 'Up on the moor. I could see you coming from there.'

It pleased her to know he had been watching for them, like a protective guardian angel. 'Why didn't you stay at the Fair, Max?'

He shrugged. 'It would be embarrassing.'

It was on the tip of her tongue to question further, but then the thought came to her that perhaps it was not his feelings he had wanted to spare, but hers. He knew his company brought the villagers' contempt upon her, that was it. Max Bower was a gentleman.

They reached the farmyard gate. 'Eva's fast asleep,' Maddie whispered. 'Perhaps you could carry her upstairs for me.'

She unlatched the door and watched him cross carefully to the foot of the stairs, then turn and look at her questioningly. 'The first door on the right,' she whispered.

At the top of the stairs he nudged the door open gently with his shoulder and carried the sleeping child to the bed. He laid her gently on the coverlet and began unlacing her shoes. Maddie stood in the doorway, feeling a surge of tenderness for the solicitous way he cared for the child. She stood savouring the moment, enraptured by his tender concern and the close, warm feeling of being part of an intimate scene, almost as if they were a family, she, Max and Eva. She stepped forward.

'Thank you, Max. I'll undress her now and get her into bed.'

It took only moments to unbutton the little pink frock and slip it off. Then she pulled the sheets carefully over Eva's vest-and-drawers-clad figure and tiptoed from the room.

Max was waiting in the corridor. He nodded towards the door next to Maddie's room. 'What is this room?'

Maddie hesitated for only a moment. 'Let me show you.' Reaching up, she took the key from its hiding place over the doorframe, then unlocked the door. Flinging the door wide open, she stood back to let Max enter.

He took one step inside, then lifted his nose and sniffed. 'Violets?' he murmured. 'This must be your mother's room.'

CHAPTER FIFTEEN

Inside the door Max stood looking down at the girl's pretty face, eager and alive as only the young and innocent can look.

'Yes, it is Mother's room. Dad doesn't like me to come in here but I feel she's still near to me in here. You know, she died so suddenly.' The eager look gave way to a wistful sadness. 'I never had a chance to tell her how much I loved her. It still hurts.'

'I am sure she knew just the same.'

'Not one loving word . . .'

He understood now. The poor child had had no word of love spoken to her since her mother's death – that was what she yearned for. Old Renshaw was incapable of filling that need, even if he was capable of recognizing it.

'She had a sad life really,' the girl whispered, fingering the lace edge of the pillow. 'I think she was lonely too.'

She looked so fragile, so vulnerable. Max ached to touch her, to soothe her like the rabbit in the woods that day. He took a hesitant step towards her, searching for words.

'It was all a long time ago now, Maddie.'

Max leaned forward to touch her hand. It was as cold as a dead woman's. She uttered a sigh so deep and long-drawn that he felt his heart lunge in pity. Her voice was barely audible.

'Trouble is, I've got nobody now.'

He pulled her arm, turning her to face him. 'Don't feel so sorry for yourself, Maddie. People do care, you know – I care.'

She turned her face up to his. 'Do you? Do you really?'

Suddenly the tears erupted and she clung to him. 'Hold me, Max, please hold me!'

Max heard in her voice the loneliness and rejection he knew all too well. He cradled her close, stroking her trembling back and crooning words of comfort. She put her arms about his neck.

'Love me, Max, for God's sake, love me!'

He looked down at the tear-stained face and felt a surge of emotion. She was no child but a woman, and a woman who needed his love. Wisdom fled. His lips came down on hers, tender at first, and meeting the eagerness in her mouth, he felt the old familiar fire within him kindle and then burst into flame.

'Maddie, my lovely Maddie!'

With a deep sigh she pulled his face to hers, covering it with kisses. For the first time he could remember in years he felt the glowing fire of life, the eagerness of youth, stirring in his body and marvelled that she could reawaken in him sensations he had believed dead and gone for ever. He murmured into her ear.

'*Magda, ich hab' dich lieb.*'

Suddenly there was the sound of footsteps approaching and Renshaw's burly figure filled the doorway. His mouth gaped as he took in the scene and understanding and fury dawned in his eyes. Maddie broke away from Max's arms.

'My God! What in heaven's name . . . ?'

The words rasped from Renshaw's throat, his eyes glittering hatred and contempt. He took a step towards Max, his great fist upraised. Max could see the whites of his eyes glowing in the gloom and as his fist swung Max ducked, intercepting the blow with his forearm and then pinning Renshaw's big body back against the door.

Renshaw's look of rage changed to bewildered surprise as he struggled to break free. He glared at Max with venom.

'You – you evil bastard,' he hissed. 'I'll never forgive you – taking my hospitality and then seducing my daughter – here – in this room! I'll kill you, I swear I will!'

'No, Dad, no!' Maddie cried. Renshaw managed to pull one arm free and was writhing like a snake, his eyes wild and a thin gleam of saliva dribbling from the corner of his lip. Max held him tight, and the older man's struggles became feebler.

'Here – in her room, you little bitch!' he panted. 'My beautiful Lily's room! But for you she'd be alive still – you killed her!'

Maddie stared at his contorted face in horror. 'Killed her? No, Dad – I didn't . . .'

'You killed her! If only you'd come and told me she were up on the moor that night . . . And not content with killing her, you have to commit this – this sacrilege!'

'She made me promise not to tell! Oh, Dad, you can't blame me!'

There was agony in her eyes, and at the same moment words seemed to choke in Renshaw's throat and his clenched fist suddenly uncurled to clutch at the air. His legs staggered under him, his eyes glazed over. Startled, Max released him and stood back. Renshaw's eyes closed and he fell heavily to the floor.

Seconds passed and he did not move. Maddie stared down at his inert figure and then looked helplessly at Max.

'Oh my God! Max, what have we done?'

Max bent over the prostrate figure. Maddie watched in horror. 'He's dead, Max! We've killed him!'

Max slid a hand under the shirt front, felt for a heartbeat, then squatted back on his haunches and shook his head. 'No. His heart beats. Let us put him on to the bed.'

It was no easy task. Not once did Renshaw open his eyes while Max lifted him on to the bed. Maddie looked down at his unconscious face in desolation.

'Are you sure he's all right, Max?' she asked anxiously. 'Shouldn't we fetch the doctor?'

'It is probably only an excess of emotion which has caused him to pass out,' said Max quietly. 'There is a doctor in Barnbeck?'

'No – in Otterley. I'll go and get him.'

She was heading for the door when Max intervened. 'No. I shall fetch him. Saddle up a horse for me.'

He came out into the yard as Maddie was leading Robin out from the stable. She handed over the reins to him and spoke in a fearful whisper. 'What's the worst that could happen to him, Max? Tell me, please.'

He put a foot in the stirrup and swung his leg over the horse's back. 'Apoplexy, or a seizure. Too early to be sure. Watch over him. Keep him quiet if he wakes.'

Out in the lane Maddie watched him urge the horse into a canter, then she turned to go back into the house. Max's manner showed that the situation was serious, and it was she who had brought it upon her father. Anxiety mingled with guilt as she sat by the bedside, watching his sleeping face and listening for the sound of returning hoofbeats. If her father were to die now . . . Here in Mother's bed . . .

Max came back at last, and Doctor Ramsay arrived close behind in his mud-stained car. Max was still stabling Robin while Maddie watched the doctor examine her father. He looked so old, his lined face yellow against the white sheets.

The doctor's expression betrayed nothing as they came downstairs from the bedroom. Max was standing by the kitchen table, his eyes wide in silent question.

'It is too early to tell yet whether any lasting damage has been done,' Doctor Ramsey said in a matter-of-fact tone. Maddie felt he was so accustomed to life and death that he had forgotten how nerve-racking it was for those waiting to hear his verdict.

'Just let him sleep, and if he wakens in the morning and behaves normally, then there is nothing to fear. Let me know if it turns out otherwise.'

At the doorway Doctor Ramsay paused as he pulled on his hat. 'I understand Mr Renshaw was in a heated state of mind when this happened. Make certain nothing disturbs him again which could cause another attack. It could be far more serious next time.'

Maddie drew in a deep breath. 'How bad, Doctor?'

'Stroke, seizure – a man of his weight and choleric disposition – it would be wise not to upset him again. The consequences could be very serious, even fatal.'

To Maddie's immense relief her father wakened in the morning. His eyes were wide open as she carried in his morning cup of tea, and he looked for all the world as if he had just awakened from a good night's sleep. Any moment now he would speak; if he did not rage about last night he would be sure to protest about being in Mother's bed.

He lay watching her with expressionless eyes as she bent to place the cup on the bedside table.

'Now you've not to try and get up, Dad,' she murmured in the soothing tone of a mother to her child. 'The doctor says you've to rest.'

He made no attempt to argue as she had expected. Looking at him closely she saw there was no expression on his weather-beaten face, no anger, no resentment, almost as if he had forgotten last night. It was only as he was sipping tea from the cup that she noticed the dribble down his chin, and saw that one corner of his mouth appeared slightly twisted.

'How are you feeling, Dad?'

He grunted but made no answer. He had never been one to complain, for it there was anything he despised it was hypochondriacs like Joan Spivey, forever complaining of her rheumatics and her bad bronicals, as she called her wheezy chest. Maddie remembered how he had asked her to massage that troublesome leg of his, but only because the soaking rain had caused it to play up badly.

She went downstairs and out into the farmyard. Max, shirtless, was mucking out the stable. In the hot August sunshine the fetid smell of soiled straw filled the air as she told him about her father's condition.

'I can't make it out. You go up and have a word with him, Max,' she urged. 'Perhaps you can tell how he really is.'

Max looked down at her soberly. 'After last night I'm the last man he'll want to see.'

She gave him a pleading look. 'Please, Max. You know about these things.'

With a sigh he propped the pitchfork against the stable wall and went indoors. When he emerged, some minutes later, Maddie saw his face was flushed and her anxiety deepened.

'What is it, Max? Is he all right?'

Max nodded. 'Your father appears to be much better.'

Maddie gave a deep sigh. 'Oh, I'm so glad. A day or two's rest should put him right then. We can manage to run the farm till then, can't we?'

Max turned away. 'I think you will find he is already up and on his way downstairs. You do not need me.'

Suddenly she became aware of the strange tension in him, the way the scar on his cheek stood out white against the surrounding flush.

'What are you saying? We do need you – Max, what is it?'

He turned towards her, but his gaze avoided hers. 'I am leaving. I go now to pack my belongings.'

He moved away towards the barn. Maddie scurried after him. 'We can't leave now, Max – I must see he is all right. Give me time – a day or two.'

'I must leave now. Your father has commanded it.'

She stared, bewildered, as he began thrusting shirts and socks into the battered old suitcase. 'He told you to go?' she said faintly. 'Why didn't you stand up to him, for heaven's sake? He needs help now, of all times.'

Max straightened and faced her. 'He told me to piss off, to use his own words.'

'Take no notice, Max – he's upset. He's always been too stubborn for his own good. I'll go and talk to him.'

She was turning to go when Max stopped her. 'No, Maddie. Your father has made it very clear he does not wish me under his roof, and I can't blame him.'

She spread her hands helplessly. 'But what about me, Max? I was going to go with you.'

Turning, he gave her a long, slow look and she could see the strained patience in his black eyes. 'You must choose for yourself when you are ready to leave here.'

'I can't just walk out now – I can't leave Dad and Eva – and there's the sheep still to be rounded up for dipping.'

He turned back to the suitcase. 'I know. I will help you round up the sheep before I leave.'

'Where will you go?'

He shook his head and made no answer.

'I said, where will you be, Max? I want to know.'

'I cannot tell you. I do not know myself.'

'Will you be coming back for me?' Her voice was small, contrite, like a schoolchild who has failed its teacher.

He looked down at her thoughtfully before answering. 'I don't know, Maddie. I cannot promise anything when I don't know what I'm going to do yet.'

Turning away from him, she stood leaning against the barn doorway, biting her lip.

Max paused in his packing. 'I am sorry. I know you feel let down, but you must see I can't promise anything yet.'

Maddie kicked the doorframe, muttering to herself. 'Go away then, Max. I'm getting used to seeing people go away.'

She rushed away across the yard towards the house. Eva stood in the doorway.

'I was wondering where you was. I'm hungry.'

'Come on then. I'll get your breakfast.'

'I been thinking. I ought to have a pet of my own, oughtn't I? Eunice has got a cat, and some of the other vaccies have got rabbits and things.'

Maddie was in no mood to listen, aware of the dark brooding proximity of the man who was going to walk out

189

of her life today, robbing it of the only enlivening excitement she had known.

'You've got Dog,' she pointed out. 'Be satisfied.'

'Oh, Lassie really belongs to Mr Renshaw. I want something that belongs to me. I want me own goldfish.'

Seeing Maddie's total lack of interest the child added in a surly tone, 'And I'll get it, somehow, just you see if I don't.'

Darkness was falling over the valley when Max left Scapegoat Farm that night. No one had seen him go; no one had wished him farewell. Eva had been missing since supper time, no doubt down in the woods with her gang of evacuee friends, searching the pond for newts or cooking up new forms of mischief, and James Renshaw had taken good care to stay out of his way. And Max had no desire to stir more pain for Maddie by making an emotional leavetaking from her, though he would have been glad to have a last glimpse of her before setting out, a last opportunity to reassure her.

He closed the farm gate quietly so as not to disturb the chickens in the coop, and set off down the lane. The handle of the battered suitcase had given out at last and he was obliged to carry it under his arm. Below him stretched the village, enveloped in blackout gloom, and he reflected how appropriate it was for this part of the world, for Scapegoat especially, the shabbiest, bleakest home he had ever come across. Poor Maddie.

There was a sudden slithering sound behind him and Max stiffened. It was no rabbit scurrying up the brambled verge or a fox scavenging for food, but a heavier step and the snap of a twig breaking. He had an uneasy feeling that all was not well, and put down the broken suitcase. There it was again. The furtive sound was reawakening memories. A year ago . . . the internment camp on the racecourse at Lingfield . . . the arrival of the first prisoners of war, Nazi sailors captured from a torpedoed ship . . . the night of the winter solstice. He felt the hairs on the nape of his neck begin to prickle.

'Get him, lads!'

Suddenly there was a stampede of running feet, voices shouting and a flashlight pointed at his face, dazzling him so that he could not see. Bodies surrounded him, several of them, and he felt his arms being caught and pinioned to his sides, and then a crashing blow to his stomach drove all the air out of his lungs.

'*A Jew, Franz, a Jew! We can celebrate the solstice with a bit of fun with him. Ritual sacrifice.*'

'*Get his trousers off, Heinrich, and we shall see whether he is a Jew.*'

Max struggled to free himself, but in vain. There were too many of them.

'*He is! He's had the snip, Franz! See for yourself.*'

'*But not enough, mein Freund. We shall do it better and so ensure that he will beget no Jewish bastards to defile our blood.*'

Punches were raining on Max's face and chest, and reason deserted him. He saw no Englishmen in the lane, only the hate-filled faces of Nazi Junker officers and a gleaming knife, and a scarlet mist engulfed him. He gave a great cry of fury and, gathering his strength, flung his attackers off so that they fell away like flies from a horse's mane. Only one man, his face indistinguishable in the darkness, hurled himself again at Max's chest.

There was no premeditation. Max raised a clenched fist high in the air, then brought it crashing down on the bridge of the attacker's nose. The flashlight swung away from Max to focus on the man, and Max could see clearly then the disbelieving look as the man touched a hand to his face. His nose was split from bridge to tip and splayed out across his cheeks. Something leapt on him, and again Max raised his fist.

The flashlight swung towards them. By its light Max saw that the wizened creature hanging on his arm was an old

191

man, and he was already lowering his fist when he caught sight of the empty sleeve.

'Leave off, Seth, or he'll do for you and all,' a voice cried. The old man stared for a moment, and then let go.

'Mr Bower? What you doing?'

Eva's voice penetrated the gloom. For a second no one moved, frozen in a darkened tableau, and then voices muttered.

'Away, lads! Let's be off!'

Feet began to scurry away downhill towards the village, fading fast into the distance until silence returned. Eva approached Max as he bent to find his suitcase.

'Was you fighting just then? Did them lot ambush you like the cowboys on the pictures?'

Max straightened. 'Go home, Eva. Maddie's looking for you.'

The girl looked puzzled, and then nodded. 'Aye, I expect I'll get a rollicking for being out in the dark. Never heed. She'll not wallop me.'

He strode away down the hill, anger satiated. A single blow, that was all, and he was master of the situation. Just as he had been in Lingfield camp that night of the winter solstice.

For the first time in months Max took a deep breath of satisfaction and made purposefully downhill towards the railway station.

Len Laverack shook his head mournfully as he brought out a bowl of water and a cloth to the counter. 'I told you it were daft, Fred Pickering. You wouldn't be told. You came off worse than him, seemingly.'

'Nay, I wouldn't say that,' growled Fred. 'You haven't seen him, have you?'

'Aye,' agreed Jack. 'It must have hurt him real bad when your nose hit his fist. You'd best clean the worst off before your Edna sees you.'

The landlord dabbed carefully. Old Seth peered over his

shoulder with a frown. 'It's bad is that, Fred. You won't be able to hide it, you know.'

Jack stood impatiently by the door. 'Come on, Dad, it's time we were home else we'll be in Ivy's bad books and that wouldn't do at all. Come on.'

Dai stood up. 'Aye, I'm away home to my bed too.'

'Where's Donald?' asked Fred.

'Had to go and see the last train off. Anyway, it's near enough closing time.'

Seth was edging towards the door, reluctant to leave. 'You should put him some iodine on that, Len – there'll be no hiding it from his Edna then. By heck, Fred, I'm glad I'm not in your shoes.'

'Bugger off,' growled the shopkeeper.

'Nay, that's no way to thank us,' said Seth. 'We did a good job tonight, we did, teaching that Jerry a lesson. We stood up for old Scapegoat Jim – he couldn't have tackled the fellow, though I'll wager he'd have liked to. After all, we had to go to the help of a fellow countryman.'

'Aye, he's a good enough chap, and his family's lived here for centuries,' agreed the landlord.

'S'right,' muttered Fred. 'Renshaw's one of us, even if he is a funny bugger. Pity he wasn't there to give us a hand.'

'Happen he'd have got worse than a bloody nose, him being an old fellow,' said Jack.

'Nay,' protested his father. 'I'm older than him, and I were all right. Mind you, I had me wickenwood.'

'Your what?' said Dai. 'What the hell's that?'

'Me wickenwood. Old name for a bit of rowan. Magic, that is, protects against harm. I've carried this bit in me pocket since I were a lad.'

Seth was pulling a desiccated stick from his pocket when his son stopped him. 'Come on, Dad. Fat lot of good it were in the sawmill when you got your arm chopped off. Now come on or our Ivy'll kill us.'

He was holding the door of the pub open for his father.

Without warning a slight figure suddenly burst in, fair hair flying and eyes blazing. The men stood, transfixed, as Maddie, her face scarlet, glared at them.

'Just what the devil's been going on?' she demanded. 'Our Eva tells me you set upon Mr Bower in the lane.'

She looked a diminutive figure of fury, her feet astride and hands on slender hips. Fred brushed aside the iodine Laverack was holding and stood up unsteadily.

'Nay, now look here, Maddie Renshaw – '

'I won't look here! I'm ashamed of you, a gang of you setting upon a man in the dark like that! Cowards, that's what you are, all of you! You hate him because he's a foreigner and that frightens you – you're jealous of him and want to destroy him. Well, let me tell you, he's a better man than all of you put together, and if he's hurt I'll report you to the police, that I will!'

Donald Fearnley, the station master, was standing listening in the doorway. He pulled off his peaked cap and spoke nervously. 'He's gone, Miss Maddie. He went off on the last train. He can't be hurt that bad.'

Maddie spun round, her cheeks suddenly turning pale. 'He's what?'

'Gone – I know for certain, I sold him his ticket. And he booked a single too, not a return.'

CHAPTER SIXTEEN

Renshaw never mentioned Max's name. In fact, he had spoken little since the night of the attack. It was almost as though he had put the farmhand out of his mind, as if Max had never existed, and it angered Maddie. It seemed that as far as her father was concerned Max, like Mother, would be obliterated from memory, forgotten and unmourned. Too late now she realized how deeply she had come to care for Max – and he would never know it.

For her the world held an air of unreality, sombre and bleak despite the sunshine. Max was gone – that was the reality. And he had gone without a word of farewell, just as Mother had done. The old familiar feelings of chagrin, of bitter disappointment and a sense of loss, filled Maddie's heart. She needed Max, she longed for him, and he had turned his back on her. Life was bitterly cruel, robbing her of those she loved and needed.

September swept over the Garthdale valley in alternating bouts of showers and sunlight. One misty Tuesday morning a whole new world began for Eva with the reopening of the village school.

Maddie watched Eva's excited little face as she hung her jacket on the iron peg in the school cloakroom and sniffed the dusty air smelling of Jeyes disinfectant mingled with chalk dust. She watched as Miss Gaunt, whose plump, haughty face belied her name and did not seem to change with the years, blew the whistle and marshalled her charges into lines in the schoolyard.

'First line, forward,' she commanded and Maddie watched as the children trooped into the school doorway.

Miss Gaunt nodded as she caught sight of Maddie standing by the gate.

'Madeleine Renshaw, is it not? I never forget a face. Let's see, four or five years ago?'

'Six,' said Maddie. 'I've brought our evacuee down to start today. Eva Jarrett.'

The teacher's lips curved into a hint of a smile. 'I'll watch out for her. I'll need to if she's anything like the daydreamer you used to be.'

She ushered the last of the children indoors and followed them. Maddie turned away to walk on down the road.

As she pushed open the door of the little village shop with its pungent smells of acid drops and cheese she saw Doreen Sykes, propping her ample bosom on the counter and leaning across it to talk confidentially to an overalled Edna Pickering.

'Well, of course, far be it for me to judge others,' she was saying, 'but if they can live in the same house and neither of 'em speak for seventeen years, then they've no right to call themselves sisters if you ask me.'

'Well, like you said, it's not for us to say,' said Edna, catching sight of Maddie. 'Us not being the sort to gossip.'

Doreen glanced over her shoulder, then straightened. 'No, not us. It wouldn't be Christian. I've no time for uncharitable folk, specially when there's all this blitzing going on in London. Give us a tin of mustard, Edna, and I think that'll be all.'

Edna lifted down the tin off the shelf. 'That'll be eight and fourpence altogether, Mrs Sykes.'

As Doreen delved into her purse to find the coins she could not resist a final comment. 'Course, if I had to live with a woman who always smelt of chips, I probably wouldn't want to talk to her for seventeen years neither. Still, it takes all sorts, and there's worse creatures about than Dulcie Parfitt.'

She gave Maddie a tight-lipped look as she picked up her

basket to leave. Maddie had a sudden recollection of Fred Pickering's bloodied nose in the Cock and Badger.

'Were you by any chance referring to me, Mrs Sykes?' she challenged. 'Or our farmhand?'

The older woman gave her a fierce glare. 'If the cap fits,' she snapped.

'I did nothing except speak my mind, Mrs Sykes, tell the men what I thought. And Mr Bower did nothing except defend himself against a gang of bullies.'

'Defending a spy, you were, and going into a pub all brazen-like on your own. Not ladylike, isn't that. Nor is shouting the odds in public – I know, I heard about it.'

'No worse than shouting the odds about a poor old lady behind her back,' murmured Maddie.

Doreen gave her a furious glare, sniffed loudly, and went out into the street. As the door clanged shut behind her Edna gave an embarrased little laugh.

'Take no notice, love. Now, what can I do for you?'

'Just the sugar and tea ration, please.'

Edna eyed her covertly as she weighed out the sugar. 'Your farmhand's done a bunk, I hear? Happen it's as well, in the circumstances.'

Maddie kept a tight rein on her tongue. 'He's gone, yes.'

'Aye well, good riddance, as they say. It'll be a lot quieter up at Scapegoat now, I reckon. Just you and your dad and the vaccy girl. We've had it a lot quieter since our Norman went off.'

She was pouring the tea from the scales into a curled cone of paper when she spoke again. 'Take no heed of Doreen Sykes, Maddie. She weren't gossiping about you, you know. She'd just had a bit of a run-in with one of the Miss Parfitts and you know how she is.'

'Yes,' said Maddie. 'A busybody. Minds everybody's business but her own.'

'Nay, now, she's never said a word against you, not to my knowledge, any road,' said Edna reprovingly. 'There's no call – '

'Only picks on old ladies and little girls who can't hold their own,' pronounced Maddie. 'Like somebody said the other day, she's a rotten cow.'

Edna gasped. 'That'll be three and six, please. And here's your ration books back.'

James Renshaw came out of the pigsty into the sunlight to draw a deep breath of air into his lungs. He still felt far from well though he would be hard put to it to describe exactly how he felt.

It was a strange, uneasy feeling that all was not well, a light-headed sensation and a strange reluctance in his lungs to work unless he concentrated on the habit of breathing. In fact, it was as though his whole body might at any minute refuse to function, and the sensation gave rise to a deep feeling of dread. And the dread seemed to permeate his day, making fearful happenings out of what had been everyday things.

Like the pigs, for instance. The big old boar had always been an evil beast, ravenous and untrustworthy, but today those piggy little eyes set deep in the ugly, snouty face had seemed to be watching and waiting, as if at any moment the creature might catch his master off-guard. Renshaw could visualize the ugly brute's gusto if it should find a human leg added to its supper, and he was glad to escape the noise and stench of the pigsty. He leaned against the doorframe, welcoming the cool breeze on his brow.

Eva came whistling through the yard gate, carrying a bundle of comics and a jam jar.

'Look what Stanley gave me,' she said, holding out the bundle. 'All these *Dandys* and *Beanos* for a measly five marbles. Now I can find out what Desperate Dan's been up to. Think Maddie'll make us a cow pie for supper?'

Maddie was watching from the kitchen doorway. 'What's that you've got there?' she asked.

'What? Where?'

198

'In that jam jar. It's a goldfish, isn't it? Where'd you get that?'

'Off the rag and bone man. He were outside school.'

Maddie surveyed her with suspicion. 'He only gives balloons as a rule. What did you give him to get that?'

Eva was peering into the barn. 'Hey, look!' she said excitedly. 'That stray cat's in the box I made her – is she going to have them kittens now?'

'Eva,' said Maddie sternly. 'What did you give him?'

'Only me cardy – I didn't need it. It's too hot.'

Before Maddie could say more she had disappeared into the barn, goldfish and comics with her. Renshaw took a deep breath and levered his weight off the doorjamb.

Maddie caught sight of her father's face.

'Come on in, Dad. I'm just brewing up a nice pot of tea. You look like you could do with a cup.'

Renshaw heaved a deep sigh. 'Not for me, lass. I think I'll go have a lie down for a bit.'

She watched him cross the kitchen towards the stairs, conscious of his boot-marks on the clean floor, but she had not the heart to scold him. He looked so weary, so old . . .

Eva came in and flopped down on a chair at the table. 'I just gave Duster a handful of hay,' she told Maddie. 'She's never let me near her before.'

'Nonsense. She likes girls, not men though.'

'She frightened me, she's that big.'

'You've no need. She's gentle as a lamb.'

Eva squinted up at her. 'Think she'd let me ride her? Would you teach me?'

Maddie nodded. 'Perhaps I will, but not today. She's cast a shoe so I'll have to take her down to the blacksmith's in the morning.'

'Mr Bower always took her down there before.'

Maddie's heart lunged. 'Anyway, Dad's not well so it might be just you and me to do the milking tonight, Eva. Time you learnt how to make yourself useful.'

* * *

Renshaw had not reappeared by milking time. Eva grumbled but to Maddie's surprise she soon picked up the knack of milking, her touch as gentle and at the same time as firm as any woman's. By supper time Maddie was growing anxious and went up to her father's room with a mug of tea.

He lay half-propped up on the pillow, his eyes open, but he made no sign of recognition as she came close and put the mug into his hand.

'How do you feel now, Dad?'

He made no answer and as she moved around to the far side of the bed the mug slithered from his fingers, tilting over and spreading a large yellow stain on the flowered counterpane.

'Never mind,' she said reassuringly. 'I'll fetch a towel.'

She was turning to go when she heard the sound. It was no more than a gurgle, but alarm leapt in her. She turned back anxiously. Wide eyes stared back at her, and he seemed to be straining to speak, but only the strangled, gurgling sound would come. Then she saw that one side of his mouth hung lop-sidedly and a thin trickle of saliva was running down his chin.

'Dad – Dad! What is it? Tell me.'

Only the choking rattle in his throat answered, and Maddie's heart filled with fear. She seized his hand, but there was no answering pressure in the limp, cold fingers. Then the terrifying truth hit her – her father could neither speak nor move, and the look in his eyes was one of sheer terror.

Maddie stood leaning against the doorway of the smithy watching Dick Farrow, the huge-shouldered blacksmith, as he stood with his back towards her, Duster's hoof between his knees, pulling out the iron nails. She could feel the heat of the fire on her face even at this distance, but her mind was filled with the latest disaster to strike her life.

Farrow was lifting the new shoe, glowing red from the

fire, and placing it on the anvil. She heard the sound of his hammer ringing around the rafters, shaping and turning the shoe. Blow after heavy blow, and with each she heard the fateful words.

'Stroke! Stroke!' Doctor Ramsay had said. 'Bed! Bed!'

Each blow of the hammer emphasized the finality of his words. Her father was paralysed, he had said. Maybe some use might return to his arm and leg one day, maybe he might be able to speak again, but it was foolish to hope . . .

She saw the horseshoe being lowered into the pail of water and heard the hiss as it cooled. Then Farrow applied it to Duster's hoof and a curl of smoke rose, filling the air with the sharp smell of burning. Sheep and branding, a horn alight, Max snatching tea from her hand; memory returned unbidden and brought with it a twist of pain.

The blacksmith drove home the nails and filed down the edges of the hoof, inspected it critically then stood back, rubbing his nose with a stubby forefinger. 'There, Miss Maddie, reckon that'll do to be going on with.'

Maddie straightened up and came forward to take the reins. She rubbed the mare's nose gently. 'Aye, we'll do to be going on with, won't we, lass? We'll have to do, God help us.'

James Renshaw lay helpless in bed and railed inwardly, but his anger could not match his fear. For a man built like a bull, broad-shouldered and strong, suddenly to find that not only could his legs no longer bear the weight of his body, but even his fingers could not hold a cup nor his tongue find words was terrifying beyond belief.

The words came clear in his head all right, but during the journey from brain to tongue they seemed to become tangled and lose direction, and the effort to spill them out was almost too much. He watched his daughter move about the bedroom and longed to shout out to her, to tell her how frustrated and helpless he felt, but only incoherent sounds

201

and the occasional word tumbled out, and the fury and frustration grew.

Powerless, that's what he was, powerless either to give orders or explain his helplessness. Treated like a child he was, fed and watered, washed and changed as if he were a baby. For days black rage festered inside him, and then at last it began to recede, giving way to desolation and retreating inside himself.

The most frightening thing of all was losing his memory, Renshaw concluded. Some days, watching Maddie's figure silhouetted against the window, he could remember everything clearly, from her babyhood up to the events just before his illness. But other days he had only fleeting memories, Maddie seeming to become inextricably confused with the lovely girl he had courted down the meadows, the girl he wrote to with painstaking effort, always remembering to inscribe the message LILY once the envelope was sealed.

Perhaps losing his memory was no great loss after all, he tried to console himself; it was no longer a prop because it hurt too much, bringing bitterness in its train. It was terrifying to realize his mortality however; there was nothing left now of his youth, only regret, and even that too was fading.

What was the point of fighting any more? He felt so unutterably weak. He was doomed to a vegetable existence, dependent upon Maddie both physically and emotionally. She would care for him, be a dutiful child now that disturbing Bower was gone. He might as well sink into oblivion for a time and let others do the worrying . . .

He opened his eyes. Eva was sitting beside the bed, sucking her thumb as she concentrated on reading the comic in her hand.

'Oh, you're awake,' she said, laying the comic aside. 'I'll tell Maddie and she'll fetch your supper.'

He made an effort to speak. Eva frowned as she listened.

'You what? Towel, did you say? What towel?'

He glared. He'd asked for the chamber pot, he knew he had. What was wrong with the girl? Suddenly Eva's frown vanished.

'The po, that's what you want, isn't it?'

It had taken her long enough. He managed a nod and Eva brightened.

'Right, I'll tell Maddie, don't you fret.'

She was gone, and within minutes Maddie reappeared with the chamber pot. She looked at him curiously as she helped him lever his weight over it.

'How did Eva know what you wanted, Dad? She said you told her.'

Renshaw concentrated on the task in hand, then lay back. A tumble of words came from his mouth, explaining that it wasn't his fault if the child was slow. Maddie's frown deepened as she drew the blackout curtains.

'I'm sorry, Dad, but I can't make out a word. If Eva could, then that's good. No, don't worry, it doesn't matter. Just you lie easy now and I'll fetch your supper.'

He lay in the half-light, waiting for her to reappear with the oil lamp and his supper tray. What on earth was up with them all? Still, what did it matter? Nothing was important any more.

Maddie felt in no mood to scrub out the milk churns. Up at half-past four to do the milking at five with Eva's grudging help, carting the milk down to the gate ready for collection by the lorry at seven, then Eva to feed and get dressed ready for school was only the start of a long, tiring day. Horses, pigs, chickens to feed, her father to see to – and then the rest of the normal everyday tasks could be started. Today she must ride up to see how the sheep on the high ground were faring, so the milk churns could wait.

A grey drizzle hung over the moor, low, dark clouds which threatened heavier rain to come. Maddie swung herself down out of the saddle and left Duster to nibble among the purple heather. Turning her back on Scapegoat she determined to try to swallow the hatred she was beginning to feel for the place.

It wasn't her father's fault this time, she had to admit. He hadn't planned illness to keep her here, but she felt more trapped now than she had ever done. Once there had been the possibility of escape, but now . . .

A lifetime of bleak loneliness spread ahead of her, and it hurt the more because she had come to know Max, come to love him as she never would love any man again. She would always love him as powerfully as she did right now. 'I told you I knew no peace when you were near,' she murmured into the wind, 'and I shall know none now you are gone.'

Life was darkness without him and she could not find her way. But for her father she could have gone with him. Anger bubbled inside her, anger at being trapped for ever in this desolate place. But how could she rail against her father, once so strong, bullying and implacable, but now like a helpless child whose total disinterest in life frightened her. The desire for revenge was gone.

Routine was the only antidote to her misery, she concluded, the unthinking round of daily tasks which would leave no room for hurtful memory. Somehow she had to banish from her mind the joy of Max's presence, the fire he had stirred in her when he held her in his arms, a surge of joy and tenderness which no other man had ever roused in her.

But the strange state of unreality seemed to stay with her, a curious sensation of heightened awareness of everything around her. Leaves on the trees, wisps of wool clinging to the hedgerows, droplets of rain sparkling on the leaves of young cabbages like fairy teardrops – everything throbbed with a clarity so beautiful and significant, magnified by a heart rendered more sensitive than ever before.

An ant crawled upon her bare shin. Maddie stared, mesmerized. It was as though the creature lay exposed to her gaze under a powerful microscope, and the intricacy of its construction made her heart constrict with pain. It was so exquisitely beautiful and precious, and the joy of it was unbearable. Maddie began to feel light-headed; she thought no one could ever have experienced such heightened perceptions before, except perhaps saints in ecstasy. Oh, Max! My beloved Max – where are you? I need to share it all with you! It's too much for anyone to experience alone.

She started up suddenly, scooped up armfuls of heather and called to Duster, then rode at a canter down towards the track and home.

Maddie had just persuaded Eva to have a wash before putting on her nightdress for bed when a knock came at the door.

'Whoever can that be?' said Eva in a whisper. 'No one ever comes here.'

'Off to bed with you, young lady. I'll see to it.'

Eva lingered on the stairs long enough to see that the visitor was Ruby, and she leapt down again in delight.

'Ooh, you look lovely!' she enthused. 'Hey, Maddie, look at her fingernails!'

Maddie glanced at the scarlet nails and then shooed a reluctant Eva off upstairs. Ruby watched.

'You look proper done in,' she remarked as Maddie came back. 'I heard as how your dad were ill – that farmhand made him have a stroke, they tell me.'

'He did nothing of the sort,' snapped Maddie, 'and if you've only come to spread gossip – '

'Hey, hang on,' protested Ruby, 'I'm your friend, remember? I came 'cos I wanted to tell you how great it is living up in the city, how easy it is to make money.'

'You told me,' said Maddie flatly. 'It's no use, Ruby, I can't leave here.'

'No, not now, I suppose.' There was no disguising the disappointment in Ruby's tone. 'Pity. You've no idea what you're missing. My friend Geoffrey – '

'I thought he was called Gordon.'

Ruby laughed. 'That were ages ago, before I found out

it's better to stay free. There's a lot more to be had that way.'

'How do you mean?' Maddie could not help the lack of interest in her voice; she felt so tired she could fall asleep by the fire right this moment. Ruby was not to be deterred.

'I've got me own place in town, lovely little bedsit, and I can have visitors there whenever I want,' she said proudly.

'Very nice,' said Maddie.

Ruby's eyes twinkled as she gave her friend a nudge. 'You don't get me, do you? Friends in whenever I want, Maddie, day or night – women or men either. Get it?'

Maddie stared for a moment, bemused, then understanding began to dawn. 'You mean – ?'

Ruby chuckled. 'Slow, but you get there in the end, don't you? Yes, of course I mean – nowt to it, really – easy as pie once you get used to it. And the money – Maddie, do you know what this costume cost me?'

She stood up and pirouetted around to show off the flared skirt of the well-cut blue suit. 'I'd never have got this in a million years if I'd stayed here, lass, nor me perm neither.'

The sparkle in her eyes faded as she caught sight of Maddie's expression. 'Oh, I'm sorry – it's not fair, is it, seeing as you're stuck here now. But remember, love, if ever you do get a chance to come, I can put you on to all the tricks – like I said, there's nowt to it once you get going. Some lovely fellows I've met, and lots of 'em come back regular-like. You can't blame a girl for looking after herself best way she can these days. I mean, when you think of all them getting killed in London. Live for today, as they say, for tomorrow we could all be dead.'

After she had gone Maddie dragged herself across to the dresser and took out the old exercise book and a pencil. By rights she ought to go to bed now, having to be up again at the crack of dawn and to save the precious paraffin too. After a moment's hesitation she blew out the lamp and lit a candle, and by its guttering light she scratched laborious words in the book. It was no use. She could not find the words to capture the feelings she wanted so much to convey.

Maddie laid down the pencil and stared into the dying embers of the fire. In her mind's eye she saw again the star-shaped brand on Max's arm, and she brushed away the tear that trembled on her eyelid. She rose from the chair and put the exercise book back in the drawer, then picked up the candle. Time for bed. Life must go on; there must be no space in it for bitterness or regret, only for the determination to survive.

CHAPTER SEVENTEEN

Autumn gave way at last to the first frosts of winter, and for Maddie work on the farm seemed never-ending. Even when the chores of the day were finally completed and she sank, exhausted, into her father's chair by the fire, there was still the paperwork to be done. Leaflets arrived in profusion from the War Ag, Growmore pamphlets about soil nutrients and urging higher production, pamphlets advising on ploughing and drainage. After absorbing these there were still the milk and egg yields to be filled in on the official forms if ever-diminishing feed supplies were to continue – a tedious chore but it had to be done. Maddie struggled to stay awake long enough to finish.

Eva appeared, sleepy-eyed, on the stairs.

'When you coming up, Maddie? It's awful late.'

'I know, love. I'll soon be done.'

'You got to get up at four, you said. I wanted a story tonight. Can't somebody else do that?'

'No, love, there's no one but me.'

'Haven't you got no brothers or nowt then?'

'Only a cousin far away in Australia. He's no use.'

It might make sense to seek help, Maddie reflected, either to ask George Bailey to let her borrow one of his Land Girls or apply to the War Ag committee for help. She could manage the sheep dipping alone, but the winter ploughing would be no easy task single-handed.

No, best leave the War Ag out of it, she decided. To approach them might mean stirring up questions about Max and so far no one had come seeking him. It was best to leave well alone.

* * *

Maddie was herding sheep into the pens in the lower meadow one frosty morning when a car passed in the lane and she heard its engine slow. A voice hailed her. 'Miss Renshaw!'

It was Mrs Westerley-Kent, peering out of the half-lowered window. Maddie paused, then walked across to the drystone wall, conscious of the disreputable figure she must cut in the shabby mackintosh and her father's mud-caked gumboots with three pairs of socks inside.

'Good morning, Mrs Westerley-Kent.'

She saw the older woman's eyelids flutter under the veiling on the blue hat. No doubt she was thinking of how she had put a stop to her son's liaison with her, thought Maddie. It all seemed such a long time ago . . .

'I expect you're finding things rather heavy going these days,' said Mrs Westerley-Kent. 'I mean, with your father incapacitated as he is. I was wondering whether we could help in some way? Lend you one of our men, perhaps – just for a day or two, you understand?'

It was on the tip of Maddie's tongue to refuse, but then she hesitated. It would be foolish to let pride get in the way of help, and God knew, she needed it.

'Very good of you,' she said abruptly. 'Come ploughing time I'd be glad. I can manage till then.'

'Very well,' said the other woman. 'Let me know when, and I'll send him down. Perhaps at Christmas then you'll be able to relax for a day or two. You look as if you could do with it.'

'No such thing as days off on a farm,' Maddie retorted. 'Christmas Day's the same as any other.'

Mrs Westerley-Kent appeared not to notice the rebuke and went on smoothly. 'I don't suppose there was any good news about your mare, otherwise I'm sure you'd have let me know?'

Maddie looked down uncertainly at her mud-caked feet. In the tumult of recent events she had almost forgotten her hopes for Duster. 'No,' she muttered. 'Nothing seems to have come of it.'

'Never mind. There's always another time,' the liquid voice soothed. 'In the spring perhaps you'd like to try again. Think about it, Maddie.'

She was about to wind the window up again when a thought occurred to her. 'Oh, by the way,' she said casually, 'Richard's just gone back to camp – did you see him?'

'No,' said Maddie.

'I just wondered. He was out late the last night he was home – said he'd been to the cinema with one of the village girls. I just wondered whether it was you.'

'No, it was not,' said Maddie emphatically.

'Ah well, never mind.'

Was it imagination, or did Maddie detect a note of disappointment in the older woman's voice? Disappointed because she was being kept in the dark about her son's activities, Maddie concluded, and it damn well served her right.

Eva was not going to be put off from her ambition to ride. Day after day she pestered Maddie.

'You promised!' she wailed one night as Maddie tried to coax her into the bathwater. 'You promised, and I'm not going to have a wash again until you teach me!'

Maddie, exhausted though she was, relented at last. 'All right then. Tomorrow – it's Saturday, no school, and when you've helped me get the cheese done, then we'll start. All right?'

Eva had somehow gone missing when Maddie set about the churning in the dairy next day, and when the job was done she found Eva in the stable, cradling in her arms one of the week-old kittens belonging to the stray who had taken up residence with the horses.

'He's my special kitten,' Eva confided, ''cos I saw him being born. He was the last one, and he's the littlest. The others keep pushing him out of the way, so I tell them not to bully him – it's not fair.'

Maddie smiled, touched by her fiercely protective love for the little creature. Duster gave the little family in the box an incurious stare as Maddie saddled her up.

Once she had overcome the strange sensation of sitting up so high above the ground Eva proved as adept in the saddle as she had done with the milking. Duster's gentle expression seemed to show she realized her responsibility and she behaved beautifully. Several times Maddie paraded her around the stable yard before leading the mare up to the field.

'Sit up straight now, Eva, not like a sack of potatoes. Grip with your knees and sit down hard in the saddle. That's it – now hold the reins tight – just tight enough to feel Duster's mouth, that's all, no more. Good.'

Eva was exhilarated by her progress, and after the lesson was over she asked if she could fodder and water the horses tonight. And even though by bedtime she was complaining loudly, her enthusiasm remained undimmed.

'My bum's that sore I'll never be able to sit down at school on Monday,' she told Maddie. 'Happen I'll have to stay at home?'

'No you won't. And you'll have a sore backside again if you ride again.'

'I don't care. I like it, and so does Duster. I'm going again tomorrow. Hey, when I can ride properly on me own, without you holding the reins, we can ride up the moor together, can't we, you on Robin and me on Duster? Hey, that'll be great!'

It afforded Maddie pleasure, despite her weariness, to see the child's ecstatic delight. Few letters came from Middlesbrough these days bringing news of her mother and Eva deserved some happiness to lift that troubled look from her young face. Somehow, she determined, in spite of the volume of work to be done she would find the time to continue the riding lessons.

Her father seemed to make little progress as the days passed, limp and uninterested in everything about him still. At least his face seemed to have lost its lop-sided look but his speech, though often in recognizable words, made no sense in their tangled arrangement. Maddie found it painful as well as embarrassing to listen to him as if she understood. Eva seemed to find it far less difficult and would spend hours at his bedside, listening to the flow of words.

'They're right in wild barracks and went in albert so realize a nisty to batter,' he would say, with a confidence which indicated that he believed he was making sense. Eva would nod in apparent understanding.

'The boil whiling get a shottering two or three among I cooky,' he would continue to explain. Maddie looked helplessly at Eva. The girl frowned, her head bent in attentive silence.

'Every leafy a tyke is it. They cleat and chope a dunnery box day.'

The girl looked up. 'I think it's his pigs that are bothering him, Maddie. The big one especially. I think he wants it dead.'

Maddie was about to protest, to point out that he'd never spoken a single word that could possibly be construed as pig, when she caught sight of her father's face. A light had sprung into his eyes and he reached for Eva's hand, nodding repeatedly. Maddie watched the way his fingers gripped on to the child's, as though desperate to hang on to a lifeline. She bent to him.

'Is that right, Dad? You want the old boar killed?'

There was a rattle in his throat and a nod of the head before the answer came. 'Nisty. Bugger.'

Later she tackled Eva. 'How did you know, Eva?'

The girl shrugged. 'You don't have to listen to the words really. It's how he says it, somehow.'

And that was the nearest she came to explaining it. But

as the days passed, Maddie found that though her father remained totally incomprehensible to her, Eva seemed to understand most of the time. Sometimes she slipped up, taking him tea when he'd evidently asked for bacon, but his face lit up whenever she came to his side, and Eva seemed to find it no imposition to see to his wants. It was clear to Maddie that the old man was coming to rely heavily upon the child.

'You don't have to spend so much time with Dad,' she told Eva one day. 'Don't stay with him if you'd rather be out playing. Won't be long before the bad weather sets in.'

'Nay, I don't mind. It's a bit like having a dad of me own to see to.'

Maddie's heart contracted. 'I'm sorry, love,' she murmured. 'You must miss your own dad a lot.'

The girl stiffened. 'I don't. He were no good, him.'

'But he's your father, Eva!'

Eva sniffed. 'You wouldn't know it. Always drunk, he were. Always giving me a clout when he come home.'

'But didn't your mother stop him? She cares about you, I know she does.'

'He belted her and all. She didn't like folks seeing her with a black eye, but he didn't care. Rotten devil. Me mam's far better off without him. Your dad doesn't knock folk about.'

Maddie felt chastened. Wrapped up in her own problems, she had never taken the time to delve into Eva's. Poor child. No wonder she and her father had somehow drawn closer to each other over the past few weeks . . .

When Eva was asleep Maddie sat by her father's bed. He seemed to be either sleeping or unaware of her presence. She pulled out the latest War Ag leaflet from her pocket and began reading, and then became aware that her father was watching.

'Huh?' he said. She glanced across at him. He seemed to be asking what she was doing.

'Just reading this leaflet, Dad.'

213

'Huh?'

'They're suggesting we could get more ploughing done by working nights as well as daytime. Use dimmed lanterns, they say, and carry on all night if need be. That's all very well . . .'

She pushed the pamphlet back in her pocket and sank back into the chair. Renshaw turned over with slow, cumbersome effort to face the wall.

'Rubbish,' he said. Dog edged his way in around the bedroom door and came to sprawl full-length alongside the bed.

Hilary Westerley-Kent moved speedily in her wheelchair to intercept her husband in the hallway of Thorpe Gill. He was just putting on his overcoat and gloves.

'Reginald! I want a word with you!'

'What is it, my dear?' he enquired patiently. 'I've a meeting at ten and the car's waiting.'

'I need your advice. About the Renshaw girl. I promised her weeks ago that we'd give her some help if she got stuck, and she's just sent word.'

'Seems only charitable, in the circumstances,' the Colonel agreed. 'Poor old Renshaw won't be much use to her now, I hear. Always thought that choleric temper of his would get him in the end.'

'You don't see the problem, Reginald. We haven't got anyone to spare now, with Barraclough leaving us in the lurch like that. What can I do?'

Colonel Westerley-Kent shrugged. 'There must be someone – haven't we got anyone left, or are they all too old?'

'Well, there's Vernon, but he's only a gardener. I suppose he would do,' Hilary said carefully. 'He's only tenpence to the shilling, but he can follow instructions if they're spelt out to him . . .'

'Then that's settled,' said Reginald with relief. 'Now I must be off.'

'No letter from Joanna today? Or Richard?' his wife enquired as he made for the door.

'No – were you expecting to hear?'

'I thought from Richard, perhaps. After what I wrote to him.'

Affecting ignorance would be the best policy, the Colonel decided. 'You're bound to feel anxious about him, my dear, in the midst of all that dreadful bombing, but he'll be all right. Bad pennies and all that.'

That was the wrong thing to say; he realized it as soon as he said it, but too late. 'Exactly,' said Hilary. 'He's a fool unto himself, that boy. Picking up with all the wrong kinds of girls, getting himself entangled . . .'

'It's only to be expected if he has a bit of fun, my love, with all that danger around him. We'd probably do the same in his circumstances. Live for today, and all that.'

His wife ignored him. 'He usually makes some kind of protest when I put a stop to his *affaires*. I felt sure there'd be a letter today.'

'But you won't stop this one apparently, my dear. He's made it quite plain that he's going to marry the girl. Says he's going to speak to her parents when he's home on leave again. It seems pretty final to me.'

'Hmm. We'll see about that,' murmured Hilary. 'The daughter of a policeman, indeed! Whatever can he be thinking of?'

'Goodbye then, dear,' said her husband from the doorway. 'I won't be late home tonight.'

'Put your scarf on, Reginald. It's bitterly cold out and teeming with rain. You know how easily you catch cold.'

But the Colonel was already out of sight.

Day after day the rain came down, turning the fields into a bog. Maddie grew impatient. At this rate the ploughing would never get done. At the best of times this clay soil was heavy going, but now the horses would have to paddle in mud.

At last the rain eased off and, true to her word, Mrs Westerley-Kent sent up a man from Thorpe Gill. Maddie eyed him over. He was comparatively young, late thirties possibly, with stained breeches and a cloth cap pulled down over his face, pudgy and pink as a baby's bottom.

'What's your name?' she asked as they led the horses out from the stable.

'Vernon.'

He wasn't very communicative and his mouth did tend to hang open as Maddie explained what she wanted, but he seemed willing enough.

'Done any ploughing before, Vernon?'

He shook his head. 'I'm gardener at Thorpe Gill. Have been, man and boy this twenty year.'

She sighed. Still, his help was better than nothing. 'We'll take a two-horse hitch and plough the lower field to a depth of ten inches. Then at the upper end we plough to no more than an inch and a half where the sheep graze, OK?'

'A two-horse hitch?'

'Two horses in the yoke. Now there's a fair slope on that field, and the clay's thicker at the bottom than at the top, so you'll have to set the rig properly. Have you handled horses before?'

'Oh aye. Archie Botton's had me helping him out in the stable from time to time.'

'Good.'

A bitter easterly wind was blowing as they began. Maddie took the handle of the plough, instructing Vernon as they walked behind the horses.

'Straight furrows, mind, every inch turned and there should be no muck left on the blades. Make sure it's cutting, not ripping and tearing the ground and making a mess.'

They reached the end of a row. Maddie turned the horses about.

'Bring her round gently – and come back, always keeping

in line. The furrows have to be a penny's width apart, and they should be that neat they look like they've been drawn with a ruler. Gee up there, Duster, pull away, Robin.'

The two horses were pulling hard, so hard it felt as though they would nearly pull Maddie's arms from their sockets. 'Good boy, Robin. Lovely girl, Duster. You have to praise them, Vernon, give them credit.'

'I've never seen horses walk that fast,' he muttered, 'and in the mud too.'

'Bays are like that. Some farmers can't keep up with them. Keep them in rein, though, else you'll make a mess of the field.'

For a time they plodded along behind the horses and there was silence except for the squelch of the mud and an occasional snort from the horses. This was a time Maddie enjoyed on a sunny day, a feeling of companionable closeness with her horses, but it was no pleasure on a bitter winter morning with the mud sucking at her boots.

The green of the grass was disappearing as the furrows turned. Vernon seemed to be watching closely and as they reached the end of the furrow Maddie handed over the reins.

'Right, now you have a go. Bring her round. Everything firm, remember, no slack in the reins. We're well set in, turn – easy now – close the rig. Keep in line, always in line. Lovely.'

For a time Vernon plodded on, growing pinker in the face. Maddie smiled. 'You need strong wrists in this game, Vernon. Steady now, keep to the pattern. All the green has to go, right up to the hedge.'

'Not as easy as it looks,' he muttered, chewing his bottom lip.

'You're doing all right. You see, cut neatly like that it turns over like roast beef off a sharp knife.'

'Aye, I see.' His face glowed with pleasure. Maddie let him carry on. It soon became clear that, although he would never make a draughtsman, Vernon's strength would make up for it and she left him to it.

By midday the lower field was done and they trudged back down to the farm for a bite to eat. Eva was afire with news.

'I've had a letter from me mam!' she cried excitedly, hurling herself on Maddie. 'She's coming to see us on Saturday!'

Maddie smiled, pleased by the child's delight. 'That's great, love. We'll bake a cake specially.'

Hot soup and bread and cheese soon restored Vernon's flagging energy. He chafed his arms as they made their way to the upper field.

'It's hard going with them big devils tugging me arms out of me sockets,' he confided, 'but I'm getting the hang of it.'

'This'll be easier,' Maddie promised. 'Only an inch and a half deep.'

By mid-afternoon the skies lowered menacingly, and it was clear rain, sleet or snow was on the way. Maddie left the pigs and went back to see how Vernon was faring. He cocked his head to survey the furrows.

'How'm I doing?'

Maddie nodded. The lines were far from straight but certainly not the wavering mess she could have expected from a beginner. Vernon had a feel for ploughing all right.

'Not bad at all.'

He grunted with satisfaction and pulled down the cloth cap further over his eyes as he carried on. The horses were growing restive, and Robin banged Duster with his shoulder.

'Easy now, quieten down,' Maddie murmured, but she could sense their unease. Vernon, lolloping from side to side with one foot in the furrow, glanced at her.

'What's up? Are we to pack it in?'

'I think maybe we should.'

At that moment there was a quick flash in the darkened

sky, followed almost at once by a deafening clap of thunder. Duster whinnied and made as if to rear.

'Easy now!' Maddie commanded. 'Hold her head, Vernon!' Both horses were showing the whites of their eyes. Maddie took the reins and rubbed Duster's muzzle, murmuring words of comfort.

'Gently now, love. It's all right.'

But both Robin and Duster were trembling. Maddie knew that if another thunderclap came, either of them could start and rear, even make a bolt for it.

'Come on, we'll get them back to the stables,' she told Vernon. 'A good rub down and they'll be right as rain.'

It was on the way back to the farm that she saw the fox. Vernon saw it too.

'By heck, look at that! First time I ever saw a black one,' he gasped.

It was a vixen, and its blackness was no trick of the light. She was snuffling in the ground, no doubt looking for earthworms in the freshly turned soil. For a second Maddie stared, memory rekindled.

'*A black rabbit, Max – that's lucky.*'

'*I thought it was black cats that were supposed to be lucky.*'

'*Anything black's lucky if you want it to be – a black pig, even.*'

How little she had known about him then. With effort she put him from her mind and concentrated on the task in hand. Once the horses were rubbed down and fed and Vernon gone on his way back to Thorpe Gill, there was still a meal to be prepared before the evening milking.

Milking. She looked down dispiritedly at her blistered hands and felt the ache burning between her shoulder blades. God alone knew when she would find the time and energy to mend the roof of the chicken coop loosened by the high winds and rebuild the drystone wall near the farm gate where the lorry had backed into it.

* * *

It was the next day she saw Dai Thomas's hearse climbing the rutted lane beyond the farm gate as she came out of the chicken shed, pail in hand. He waved to her through the window and drew the hearse to a halt, engine running. Maddie went to the gate.

'Not a fire, is there?' she asked as he wound down the window and leaned one pudgy elbow on it.

'No, more's the pity. I could do something about a fire, but not a death,' he replied mournfully. 'So young too. I don't like burying 'em young. Anyway, I'm not burying this one. She's to go back to her own folk.'

Maddie felt a sinking feeling in the pit of her stomach. 'A death?' she repeated. 'Who's died?'

'Oh, haven't you heard? Land Army girl up at George Bailey's place. Tragic, it was, and her only nineteen and all. Break her mammy's heart, it will.'

Maddie swallowed hard. It was difficult to think of it, a girl near her own age. 'What happened, Dai? Was she ill?'

'Accident, it was. Driving George's big Fordson tractor last night. No one knows just how it happened, only that she was found under it, crushed she was, but still conscious.'

'Oh, poor thing!' cried Maddie. 'God, how terrible!'

'She'd driven the thing before, George says, and no problem. Doing the ploughing by night, she was, tractor and a five-furrow plough behind. She must have got down, left the engine running or something and it moved.'

Maddie could see it. A bright-eyed girl, full of life and cheerfulness, leaping down, lantern in hand, to bend and swear at a wayward mechanical piece, looking up in horror at the gleaming steel monster as it advanced upon her . . .

'Such a sight, she was,' Dai went on. 'Leila Bailey told me they found her with the wheels on her chest and blood spurting out of her eyes.'

Dai's voice was funereally resonant and he seemed to speak the words with relish. Maddie could visualize the scene, the crimson blood spattering the dark green jersey,

220

and felt her stomach turn queasy. Life on the land was always raw, brutal even, but to rob a girl so young of the life she could have expected, far from her own home – it was so cruelly unfair.

'Anyhow, she didn't last long,' concluded Dai. 'Just as well, maybe. Poor soul – I remember when those girls first came – George said they were green, but green sticks bend easy, he said. Well, this one's snapped altogether now. Makes you think, doesn't it? You don't have to be in the firing line to snuff it these days. We never know when our number's up.'

Revving up the engine, he put the hearse into gear and continued to climb the hill. In chastened mood Maddie went indoors. And then another thought struck her. If her father had been able to understand he would have wagged a righteous finger at her.

'Always told you them machines were no good to man nor beast,' he would have said. 'Now will you believe me?'

CHAPTER EIGHTEEN

Eva could hardly wait for Saturday. All dressed up in her Sunday-best frock she hovered at the window all morning. Mrs Jarrett turned out to be not the plain, angular, headscarfed woman Maddie had visualized at all, but a shapely young woman with dark, naturally curly hair and a shy smile. Her clothes, though clearly cheap, were bright and brought a welcome touch of colour to Scapegoat. When she managed to abstract herself from Eva's effusive hugs she smiled shyly at Maddie.

'I hope as how our Eva hasn't been too much bother only I know what a pest she can be. She means no harm, though. She's a willing enough lass.'

'No bother at all,' Maddie assured her. 'Sit down and we'll have a cup of tea.'

She sat down at the table and ate jam sandwiches and sponge cake with evident appreciation. 'I don't get no time for home-baking these days,' she said apologetically. 'What with shift work and all.'

Maddie gave a weary smile and watched how Mrs Jarrett held the cup of tea with her little finger outstretched, the way Mrs Sykes did. When at last the time came for her to leave, Eva began to sob noisily.

'Don't go, Mam! You've only just come!'

Mrs Jarrett looked flustered. 'I've got to, love – the train goes in twenty minutes.'

'Then I want to come home with you.'

'Don't be daft, Eva. These folks have been so kind to you – and any road, it's that much safer here. Can't be doing with worrying about you in the bombing. You've got

222

that rowan tree you wrote me about, remember? That'll keep you safe, you said so yourself.'

'Wickenwood they call it round here, Mam,' Eva corrected her, proudly showing off her local knowledge. 'But I've not seen you for so long – '

'Would you like to stay until tomorrow, Mrs Jarrett?' Maddie cut in. 'If you're not working, that is. You could have a little more time with each other then.'

'Well, no, I can't as it happens,' the other woman said nervously. 'You see – I'm being met off the train in Middlesbrough.'

Eva stiffened. 'Me dad's not home, is he?'

Mrs Jarrett gave an embarrassed little laugh. 'No, love. It's Mr Bakewell – he's factory foreman at our place – he said he'd meet me and see me safe home.'

'Oh,' said Eva, clearly relieved. 'And will you come and see me again soon – at Christmas, happen?'

Her mother looked questioningly at Maddie. 'Of course you must come, whenever you can,' said Maddie, 'and Mr Bakewell too, if you like.'

'Oh thanks,' said Mrs Jarrett. 'In the New Year then. That'd be very nice. I'll tell him.'

That night when Maddie pulled off her gumboots she discovered the chilblains on her legs. No wonder it had hurt when the boots rubbed against her calves. She sat dejectedly by the dying fire, elbows on knees, visualizing the days of winter still ahead, the chapped hands and aching limbs, the digging and lambing and all the interminable daily work of chickens and pigs and horses yet to be done before the wintry weather finally gave way to spring . . .

And her father. It seemed unfair that she should feel guilty but there was just no time to sit with him, talk to him and try to understand him. He probably wondered at her apparent lack of interest, and the pity of it was that she could not explain to him, incapable as he was of understanding anything but his own needs.

Her feet were beginning to grow numb. Maddie went upstairs and undressed, then wriggled under the bedclothes next to Eva's warm little body. Thank God for Eva. But for her her father would have no pleasure at all.

Winter came on with sudden swiftness, bringing icy winds which found their way in through the gaps in the window-frames of Scapegoat Farm. However high Maddie stoked up the fire in the range, the bedrooms of the old farmhouse still remained freezing, and though she and Eva cuddled close under the thin, threadbare blankets long overdue for renewal, her father could not be kept warm. With Eva's help, Maddie made up a bed in the corner of the kitchen and with difficulty they managed to bring him downstairs.

Meanwhile the myriad tasks about the farm continued to occupy her from dawn until long after dark, and she was often so exhausted that, taking one last glimpse at her sleeping father to ensure all was well, she would stumble upstairs, supperless, to crawl into bed alongside Eva. Her body ached with fatigue, her fingers throbbed with pain, chapped and bleeding from washing the milk churns under the yard tap in icy water. Sleep was not easy, but inevitably exhaustion overcame her.

Christmas was approaching. Maddie determined that, what-ever the difficulties and the shortages, an effort must be made to provide some kind of festivity, for Eva's sake at least. The child's face had been full of eager anticipation when she brought home the hand-made Christmas card from school, painstakingly made out of an old cardboard carton and with the words *Merry Xmas* untidily written in coloured crayons.

'I wish I'd had a chance to sew her a new frock,' Maddie said to her father on Christmas Eve after Eva had gone to bed, 'but there just hasn't been time.'

Renshaw stared from his bed in the corner at his daughter slumped in the armchair, but there was no light of understanding in his eyes. Dog was nuzzling the hand that hung from the bed but there was no answering pat on the head, and Dog gave up.

'Maybe I'll make her a cake anyway,' said Maddie, talking more to herself than to her father. 'And I've some new ribbons in my sewing basket she can have – that'll be a start.'

His eyes were upon her as she gathered together the flour and sugar and began the mixing, but by the time she lifted the cake from the oven he was deeply asleep. Maddie fetched the ribbons from her box, a rosy apple from the loft and took out a sixpence from her purse, then crept upstairs. In a drawer she found the pink butterfly hairslide, and smiled as she remembered the barn dance, so long ago, then placed ribbons and hairslide and the other meagre offerings in Eva's waiting sock hanging on the bedpost.

'Church,' said Eva emphatically on Christmas morning. 'Everybody goes to church on Christmas Day, no matter what. Me mam always used to take me, and we're going. Pity you can't come with us, Mr Renshaw, but Lassie'll take care of you till we get back. Sit there, Lassie, and don't move.'

The dog followed her pointing finger and sat obediently alongside the bed. Maddie smiled as she saw the pink butterfly attached to the fur at the back of his left ear.

Maddie sat in one of the back pews of the village church next to Eva, and let her senses find comfort in the peaceful atmosphere. Carols drifted across the chilly air:

> *While shepherds watched their flocks by night . . .*
> *Once in Royal David's city . . .*

There was great solace in the sound of so many voices raised in divine praise, in watching the pools of coloured light cast by the sun filtering through the high stained-glass windows on to the grey flagstoned floor. Maddie almost forgot the cares of the farm, of her father's illness, but not Max. Never in her life would she forget Max.

They had left the church before the other villagers emerged. Eva bounced along happily, dreaming up new means to celebrate.

'We could have music,' she suggested. 'Haven't you got a gramophone?'

'Well, yes, up in the attic. And some records. But we mustn't disturb Dad.'

'He likes music, and he hasn't had the wireless on for ages,' Eva pointed out. 'He'd like it.'

Maddie was still thinking about Max and what he had told her of Jewish celebrations at Christmas time. She told Eva about it.

'The Festival of Light, Mr Bower called it.'

'What's that?' asked Eva.

'Jewish children light a candle every day for the week before Christmas.'

She could still recall the far-away look in his eyes as he had recounted the story of the Maccabees and the miracle of the lamp, telling her how he loved to see the glow of anticipation in his nephew's eyes. The Festival of Light. Oh Max, how I need your light!

Eva considered for a moment. 'Pity you didn't tell me before,' she remarked. 'We could have lit a candle every day too. Never mind. We'll dance instead when we find them gramophone records.'

After the dinner was cleared away Maddie brought down the old gramophone. When the accumulation of dust and cobwebs was cleaned away it worked quite well, although the few remaining needles had long since lost their point and the music filled the air with a scratchy sound. Eva didn't care.

'*I wonder why you keep me waiting, Charmaine, my Charmaine,*' she sang rapturously while she swept around the

226

kitchen in her version of a waltz. 'Come on, Lassie – you dance too.'

The dog looked on, bewildered, while Eva tugged Maddie up from her chair.

'*Is it true what they say about Dixie?*' was her next choice, followed by '*Smoke gets in your eyes*'. When she picked up '*Have you ever been lonely?*' Maddie protested.

'Enough, Eva, enough! I'm fagged out! Let's have a cup of tea now – I'm sure Dad's ready for one. And I've a bottle of Tizer for you tucked away where you couldn't find it.'

When at last the child lay asleep in her bed, Maddie looked down at her innocent face by candlelight and gave thanks. If Eva had not been with them this would have been a very dreary Christmas indeed. Carefully she put away in the drawer the little package Eva had given her this morning, the Carters Little Liver Pill box containing five sticky toffees. She touched a finger to her cheek where she fancied she could still feel Eva's enthusiastic wet kiss.

With a sigh she left the room to go down to the stables to fodder the horses and Dog padded silently alongside her. As she leaned over the door of the stalls to watch the horses eat, she could not help feeling saddened to see how thin both Duster and Robin were becoming. Working horses should not be allowed to get fat, she knew, and in any event they always grew thinner in the winter time, but these wartime rations were inadequate for creatures their size, taking into account the amount of hard work they did. It was only as she turned to leave, lantern in hand, that she caught sight of the pink butterfly bow still nestling in the fur behind Dog's ear . . .

January's icy weather turned to February snow, the moors shrouded under an ethereal veil of white as Maddie trudged homewards, her cheeks tingling and her earlobes throbbing with pain. There seemed little time these days to admire the beauty of winter, the virgin snow delicately patterned by the wind, whipped into waves and settling into deep drifts by the drystone wall. From under a hedge a single set of tracks led across the home field, the neat footprints of a fox, and Maddie wondered whether it was the black vixen, searching desperately for food.

The shadows of the farmhouse stretched blue across the snow-covered yard and it was good to reach the warmth of the kitchen at nights. Her father was always dozing in his bed and Eva's bright chatter filled the air. She at least was enjoying the winter.

'We had a snowball fight after school, me and Stanley against Eunice and Hilda. I didn't half land one in Eunice's face – she were boiling mad – she chased me into the woods, she did, but I got away from her. Got a hell of a stitch though, I did. That were this dinner.'

'Bet she was waiting for you this afternoon at school then,' said Maddie. Doreen Sykes's daughter was not likely to let her off easily.

'Aye, she were. Her and Hilda got me down in the playground. Gave me a Chinese burn, she did. Just look at that!'

Eva rolled up her sleeve to display the red mark still visible on her forearm. 'Rotten cow. Cheated, she did, two of 'em on to one. But I'll get even with her.'

'What'll you do?'

'Don't know yet,' muttered Eva darkly, 'but I'll come up with summat. Happen I'll belt her hard with the rope next time it's my turn to twist at skipping.'

The snows melted at last into February slush and sleet. Eva bounded in from school one day, flung her gas mask on the sideboard and drew herself up to her full height, bursting with important news.

'Guess what?' she challenged Maddie. 'Guess what I've been told.'

'Take your muddy shoes off in the house,' said Maddie sternly.

'No, listen,' said Eva impatiently, 'Eunice told us her Ruby's home, and she's got engaged.'

'Shoes,' said Maddie, pointing at the offending feet. Inwardly she felt disappointed that Ruby had not come to tell her news in person.

Eva perched on the stool, pulling off her shoes. 'Don't you want to know who to?' she said with an impish smile. 'You'll never guess.'

'Then you'd better tell me, hadn't you?'

'Only Richard Westerley-Kent, that's who,' said Eva. 'Eunice says she's got a big diamond ring, and Reverend Chilcott is calling the banns on Sunday, whatever that means. They'll be getting married real soon, and Eunice is going to be bridesmaid. Can I be bridesmaid when you get married, Maddie?'

'Time enough for that,' said Maddie shortly. 'Peel some potatoes for me while I get the pigs fed.'

Eva pulled a face. 'Do I have to?'

'Would you rather feed the pigs?'

'Ugh, no. I hate them pigs. Ugly buggers, they are. Little piggy eyes and all pink – like Eunice looks when I make her cry.'

'Did you make her cry today?'

'Aye, I did. Dropped the desk lid on her fingers. Serves her right for bragging.'

Maddie sighed and rose wearily. Eva followed her to the door. 'Know what she were bragging about, Maddie? She said her mam were dead proud 'cos their Ruby were marrying a real gentleman and she were going to be a lady. Now she's looking for somebody with a title or summat for Eunice.'

'Snob,' said Maddie.

'I told her they were just jealous 'cos they couldn't find anybody really handsome, like a film star. Eunice said she could – she'd find somebody just as gorgeous as our Mr Bower.'

Maddie stopped in the doorway, startled. 'Max? Whatever made you think of him?'

'Because he is gorgeous, and Eunice always used to say as their Ruby fancied him rotten. I told her she never stood a chance. He'd want somebody much nicer than her. She'll have to make do with a Valentine from her Richard, won't she?'

Wilf Darley stood drumming his fingertips impatiently on the counter of the taproom at the Cock and Badger.

'Come on, Seth, it's up to you to buy this round. There's no pockets in shrouds.'

Jack Kitchen chuckled. 'Nay, if me dad can't take it with him, he's not going.'

Dai glanced up. 'No. He's too mean to put money in my pocket.'

The old man frowned. 'It's not easy reaching into me pocket with only the one hand.'

'Nay, specially when you keep your change in the pocket over the other side,' remarked Sam.

'I'm not as daft as the rest of you,' muttered Seth. 'It were me as found the way to get you sorted out, Sam Thaw, when yon bull were too small to serve your cow, remember. It were me suggested standing him on a mound and backing the cow up to him. Credit where credit's due.'

The landlord smiled. 'Aye, I know your credit well enough, Seth, by heck I do.'

'Are we having another half then or not?' demanded Wilf.

'Aye, go on then.' Seth reached, growling, into the pocket of his stained corduroy breeches. 'Hey, you've not told us who sent any Valentines this year, Wilf.'

'How should I know? His Majesty's mail is strictly private,' protested the postman. 'I know who got summat like cards but not who sent 'em. There were one for Ruby Sykes, one for Mrs Sykes . . .'

230

'It'd be more than Eddie's life were worth not to send her one.'

'Nowt for the Renshaw lass then?' asked Sam. The postman shook his head. 'Beats me,' said Sam, 'how the prettiest lass by far in the whole Garthdale valley doesn't seem to have a lad.'

'Can't be Scapegoat Jim who keeps 'em away now, any road,' said Seth.

'Must be of her own choosing,' said Jack. 'Too much on her hands if you ask me. I heard as she even had to borrow that gardener fellow off Thorpe Gill to help with the ploughing – you know, that fellow who's lost his marbles. She could do with a chap who's all there.'

'Aye, well, running that place on her own don't leave much time for courting.'

'All the more reason to find herself a man then,' said Seth. 'Wouldn't even have to pay him then if she got wed.'

Maddie was stumbling through sheer fatigue as she unlatched the farmyard gate that night. Every muscle in her body seemed to be crying out with pain, and she longed for the comfort of a hot drink and the warmth of her bed. Exhausted as she was, she was still acutely aware of everything about her, the sweet, strange smell of night and the aching loneliness within her.

Suddenly she stiffened. There was a sound, so faint it was almost indiscernible but somehow alien to the usual night sounds of the farmyard. Reaching into her pocket she pulled out the flashlight and as she did so, a footstep sounded so near to her that she gasped. Then sudden hope leapt.

'Max? Is that you?'

She flicked the torch on. In the circle of light she saw the face of a young man, tall and broad-shouldered and dressed in some kind of uniform.

'Who are you? What do you want?' The words issued from her throat in a whisper. His reaction was startling, for

231

he seemed to leap forward and then she felt her arm seized in a tight grip.

'Open the door, for Christ's sake, and let's get inside.' His voice was low but the urgency in his tone was clear and his fingers were digging deep into her arm.

'Why? Who are you?' she asked again. 'Why are you up here at this time of night?'

'You Maddie Renshaw?'

'Yes.'

'Well I'm your cousin – Ronnie. You've heard of me haven't you? Come all the way from Australia. Now for Pete's sake open that bloody door.'

CHAPTER NINETEEN

In the lamplight of the kitchen Maddie could see him clearly, his khaki greatcoat spattered with melting snow-flakes, the blond hair that leapt into view as he took off his cap and shook it, and the deep green eyes watching her intently. She stared in bewilderment from his tall figure to that of her father lying in the bed. Dog looked up and, seeing a stranger, leapt up, a growl rumbling in his throat.

'It's all right, Dog. Be quiet,' Maddie commanded. The sheepdog came forward, nose to the ground, sniffed the newcomer's leg, then backed off and lay on the mat, head between paws but eyes alert and watching.

'Well now,' said the newcomer with a slow smile and an equally lazy drawl as he dropped his knapsack to the floor, 'Aren't you going to give your cousin a welcome then?'

Instinctively Maddie turned away and out of lifelong habit she drew the kettle over the range. 'Of course we're glad to see you,' she said. 'It's just that I'm – well – taken by surprise, that's all. I mean, I knew I had a cousin in Australia, but I never thought – '

'Never thought to see me in the flesh, eh? Well, here I am, Cousin Ronnie, large as life and twice as ugly. That your old dad? Uncle James?'

He nodded in the direction of the bed where Renshaw lay, his eyes open but giving no sign of life or recognition. Ronnie gave him only a fleeting glance then peeled off his greatcoat, tossed it over the back of a chair and sank down into the armchair, heaving a sigh. Maddie noted how completely at ease he was, like man coming home to his own fireside after a day's work in the fields. She took off her coat and hung it on the peg behind the door.

233

'My father's ill, I'm afraid,' she explained. 'A stroke last summer – he can't walk or talk properly now, otherwise I'm sure he'd tell you how delighted he is.'

'Yeah, I reckon he would. Reckon you could do with a man around this place now Uncle James is sick. Kind of a spooky place for a girl on her own.'

'No it isn't. I've never been afraid in Scapegoat.' Strange, she thought, how quickly she leapt to defend the prison she'd hated for so long. It was just something about Cousin Ronnie which annoyed her and made her react defensively.

'Are you here on your own then?' he enquired, watching as she moved to and from the fire with the kettle.

'No. There's Eva.'

'Who's Eva?'

'Evacuee from Middlesbrough. How is Aunt Lottie?'

He raised his arms above his head and stretched. 'Fine, last letter I had from her. She said to send her love if I got around to seeing you and Uncle. Been meaning to call for months. Tell me about yourself, little cousin. Not married yet, I see? No ring on your finger?'

'No,' said Maddie shortly. 'You've got leave, I take it – how long for? Oh, I mean you're welcome to stay for as long as you like, but I know leave is usually only short . . .'

He leaned forward on the chair and gazed into her eyes. Maddie could see the deep green intensity in that stare. 'As long as I like, Maddie? You mean it?'

She felt flustered by his searching stare and looked away. 'Of course.' Even if his leave was for several days, she could put up with him since he was kith and kin, son of Mother's only sister . . .

She poured out a cup of tea and turned to hand it to him. That green stare still rested on her as he took it. Then his mouth curved up at the corners into a smile and he opened his lips to speak. 'In that case – ' he began.

At that moment a gurgling sound came from the bed. Maddie set down her cup with a rattle and went to bend over her father. 'What is it, Dad? Look, your nephew Ronnie has come to visit us.'

The old man turned blinking eyes on the soldier, then took Maddie's hand in his.

'Me spittens nursen big clernag,' he gasped. 'Bloody wanag boiler larty.'

Maddie listened, then shook her head helplessly.

'I'm sorry, Dad, I don't know what it is you want. Tea, is it? I'll pour you some.'

He still clung to her hand and mumbled, staring wide-eyed at Ronnie as he did so. Maddie patted the hand reassuringly.

'It's Cousin Ronnie, Dad, all the way from Australia. He's in the army now, and he's come to see us.'

She half-turned to explain to Ronnie over her shoulder. 'He's worried about having a strange man in the house. Never liked young men anywhere near me. I'll have to set his mind at ease.'

Turning back to her father she went on in a soothing tone. 'Ronnie's staying with us for a day or two, Dad, so he can tell you all about Aunt Lottie, can't he?'

'Longer than that,' she heard the quiet voice behind her. 'Quite a lot longer, I should think.'

Letting go of her father's hand she turned back to the visitor. He was lying sprawled in the armchair, his legs stretched towards the fire, a smile of amusement on his lips. His boots, she noticed, lay on the floor alongside his chair, melting snow shaping into a puddle around them.

'Pardon?' she said. 'What did you say?'

The lazy smile continued to play on his handsome face as he half-closed his eyes. 'I said longer than a few days, Maddie my love. I'll be staying here for quite some time, I reckon. Not that you need worry 'cause anyone with half an eye can see you need a man's help around this dump. Falling apart, it is. Wouldn't see a farm as shabby as this back home.'

'I'm doing the best I can,' Maddie countered, angered by

235

his insulting attitude, 'but what do you mean, stay for some time? When have you got to get back to camp?'

'That's what I'm trying to tell you, little cousin, I haven't got to get back. I've left. I'm never going back. This war game's not for me.'

Maddie's mouth gaped. 'Are you saying – are you telling me you've deserted?'

He shrugged. 'If you like. They should never have made me join up. Don't believe in war, I don't. Killing's wicked.'

'Ah, I see. You're a conscientious objector, is that it?'

'Reckon that's what I am. Anyway, I'm not going to let myself get sent into battle with the rest, and that's a fact. So are you going to accept my help to get this old place on its feet again, cousin? Best offer you'll ever get.'

'You know about hill farming?'

He smiled. 'I've run our sheep farm back home ever since me dad died. Yours is mainly sheep, isn't it?'

Maddie hesitated, but only for a second. She glanced back over towards the bed. Her father had already lost interest in the newcomer and was chewing idly on a cracked fingernail. There was no one with whom to discuss the offer, no reason to refuse. Scapegoat was in desperate need of help and Cousin Ronnie could turn out to be worth his weight in gold, even if he were a deserter. First impressions could be misleading.

'All right, then.'

He sat up slowly and held out a hand. 'Good. Then let's shake on it.'

His grip was firm and the green eyes steady as they met hers. Weariness flowed throughout her body, but a slow feeling of optimism was beginning to thread her veins. Suddenly a thought struck her, and she sat upright.

'The police – if you've deserted, they'll come looking – '

'The army knows nothing about me having relatives in this country. Nobody knows I'm here.'

'But Fearnley, the station master – '

'I got off the train in Otterley and walked across the moor. Like I said, nobody knows I'm here.'

'I see.' He'd evidently thought it all out well in advance. 'Well, I suppose I can think up some excuse to explain how I came by a new farmhand,' she ventured.

'Farmhand?' he echoed in surprise. 'Oh well, fair enough, for the time being. Now for Pete's sake, Maddie, show me to a bed, will you, girl? I'm bushed.'

Next morning over breakfast Eva eyed the newcomer with evident distrust. When he was out of earshot she stood in the open doorway, hands on hips.

'You didn't tell me we had a new farmhand coming,' she said truculently. 'You should have said.'

'I didn't know either,' Maddie answered truthfully. 'Now for heaven's sake close that door, will you? It's freezing.'

'I don't like him,' said Eva flatly.

'Now really, Eva, don't be so silly. And don't forget your gas mask or Miss Gaunt will be after you.'

'And Lassie doesn't like him either,' Eva retorted with an air of finality. 'We're not going to bother with him, Lassie and me.'

'I'm sure that'll bother him,' said Maddie. 'Ronnie's got far too much to do to fret over you and a dog. Now be off with you or you'll be late for school.'

Leaving the dishes in the sink Maddie went upstairs to make the beds. Her own room tidied, she went into her father's room, and felt a curious sensation of being an intruder. Ronnie's belongings lay scattered around the floor, his wallet and some papers on the dressing chest. As she opened the wardrobe to put his clothes away she saw the greatcoat already hanging there, and felt a stab of apprehension. His army uniform was a forcible reminder that she was sheltering a deserter, committing a criminal act.

Then she saw that some of her father's clothes were missing. Of course, that blue shirt and the corduroys –

Ronnie was wearing them at breakfast. Irritation rippled through her. He could at least have asked . . .

But of course it made sense. He could not be seen out in the field wearing army khaki. She would have offered some of her father's things if she'd had her wits about her. Ronnie had just anticipated her.

During the succeeding days it gave Maddie pleasure to find that Ronnie, being a sheep man, discovered for himself the tasks around the farm which needed attention. He worked with good humour, never needing to be told what to do, and even found time during the day to mend the roof of the chicken coop. Over supper Eva glowered at him without speaking, but he seemed not to notice. It was curious though, Maddie noted, that Dog seemed to take his lead from Eva and always avoided Ronnie, even when her cousin tried to stroke him or feed him a titbit.

'He's not used to being fed from the table,' Maddie explained, attempting to cover the embarrassing lack of response from child or dog. 'He only eats from his bowl.'

'More fool him,' said Ronnie. 'He should grab where he can.'

Whether feeding Dog was Ronnie's way of trying to win over Eva, Maddie could not tell, but his next attempt met with no greater success.

'Here, I've made a little dolly for you,' he told Eva one evening over supper. Maddie saw him hand over a peg doll, carefully whittled from wood.

Eva took it, glanced at it with total lack of interest, and put it down on the table. 'I've got me own piece of wickenwood,' she said coolly. 'It protects me against evil things, and people.'

'Suit yourself,' said Ronnie with a shrug.

One morning on her way to the stables Maddie met Ronnie emerging from the pigsty.

'Bloody pigs,' he muttered. 'That big porker's an evil

beast. Can't trust pigs an inch. I wouldn't have 'em if it was my farm.'

'Nor I,' she agreed. 'I'd get rid of them, produce more milk to make money, and buy more horses.'

'Make more sense to breed your own,' he remarked.

'Oh yes, I'd do that once I could afford a good stallion. Ah well, some day, maybe.'

'Never mind the maybe. Do it. I know I would – that and the sheep, of course.'

'It's not my farm. One day it will be.'

'It's as good as, your dad ill as he is.'

'I can't just take decisions like that, without him agreeing,' Maddie protested.

'Why not? He bloody well can't. He's only a drag on you now.'

'He's not! What if he was your father?'

'I wouldn't give a shit. I'd make the farm pay.'

'Ronnie!'

He smiled and shrugged, as if he found her shocked expression amusing. 'Isn't it time the ewes came down to the pens ready for lambing? Some of 'em look big enough to drop 'em any minute.'

What a strange man he was, Maddie thought later as she went over the incident in her mind. He seemed almost cherubic with his blond good looks and easy good humour, yet he said such vile things at times. A complete contrast to Max with his black-eyed, wary look and disinclination to speak at all unless drawn, yet under it all simmered that sudden, explosive heat . . .

There, she was doing it again, allowing herself to wallow in the memory of him, steep herself in the luxury of recalling his arms about her and the passion born in her at that moment. Oh God, Max, now I've lost you I must learn somehow to forget you.

When lambing started there was little time left for yearning. Maddie found herself once again crouching over bleating ewes by day and by night, helping to guide infant lambs into the world. Ronnie proved himself an adept midwife.

'This one's stuck,' he muttered as Maddie, shielding her lantern against the wind, came to the pen where he squatted. 'Tried every-which-way I have, but she can't get it out. Come on, you silly bitch, push!'

In her mind's eye Maddie could see again Max's gentle manner with the labouring ewe that other night, coaxing words but firm, persuasive fingers. Ronnie's hands knew their work, but his language was far from coaxing.

'Can I help?' said Maddie.

'Nope. I'll get it, with or without her help. You go back and get me some supper ready, for Christ's sake. I'm starving and me balls are dropping off with cold.'

The stew was ready and Eva just pulling up her chair to the table when Ronnie stumbled in. Maddie heard Eva's cry of delight.

'Oh, let me have him!'

Turning, Maddie saw the infant lamb in his arms and Eva holding out her hands to take it. She looked at him questioningly.

'Ewe's done for,' he said shortly.

'Oh – is there another who's lost her lamb?'

'No. But I know what I can do. Let me have some supper first.'

'Hasn't it got a mam?' asked Eva. 'Or a dad? Is it an orphan? Poor little thing.'

Throughout the meal she sat on the hearth, cradling the lamb in her arms and allowing only Dog to come near it. She refused to touch her supper until Ronnie, satisfied, rose from the table and took the lamb from her. He disappeared out into the night and reappeared some time later.

'Goat's suckling it,' he said briefly. 'Thought she would.'

'Good,' said Eva. 'Now he's got a stepmother, hasn't he?'

Her manner towards Ronnie was visibly warmer, Maddie noticed. And she had to confess that she too had a higher opinion of her cousin than when he first arrived. He was a good and knowledgeable worker, and his help was invaluable. His manner might leave something to be desired, but he was fast becoming indispensable.

Colonel Westerley-Kent was more than ready for bed. It had been a gruelling journey back from London in an unheated train and the big bed, heated by hot water bottles, was heaven for his aching limbs. But Hilary, sitting up in bed smoothing Pond's cream into her face, was eager to hear his news.

'In the morning, please, my love,' he mumbled into the pillow. 'I really must sleep.'

'But you haven't told me a thing about London yet,' his wife remonstrated. 'Did you get to see Joanna or Richard?'

'No.'

'What? Not in five days there?'

'I told you. My time was wholly taken up with work.'

'Interrogations again? Who this time? Prisoners of war?'

'Hush, Hilary. Walls have ears, you know. Top secret work.'

'Don't be silly. This is Thorpe Gill, Reginald, not some sleazy café. It's pillow talk, really – confidences between husband and wife. It will go no further, you know that. Tell me just something that happened. You know I can't get out.'

That touched the right chord. Reginald rolled over towards her with a sigh and watched as her fingers stroked her neck. 'Well, yes, interrogations. There was one fellow I had to deal with who might have interested you. Refugee, he was, Austrian Jew who fled here before the war. Police had picked him up for not notifying his change of address. A bit suspicious about him, they were – thought he could be a spy. Turned him over to us for examination.'

'And was he a spy then?'

'No evidence in his background to think so. Seemed OK

to me. Intelligent chap, but very reticent. Took me ages to get him to talk.'

'But you did in the end, I know.'

'Oh yes. Gained his confidence, I think. Seemed very bitter about what the Nazis had done to his family. He escaped at the time Hitler annexed Austria but his mother and sister were sent to a concentration camp before he could get them out. He knows they're probably dead by now.'

'Poor man. What was he like?'

'Like I said, very intelligent. Had a degree in veterinary science and practised as a vet in Vienna before the *Anschluss*.'

'What was he doing over here?'

'Seems he'd worked on a farm before he ran off.'

'Did he say why he ran away?'

'Has a visa to go to America. I didn't see why we shouldn't make use of his skills while he waited for a berth on a ship. Horses, that's his speciality.'

'Horses?' Hilary pricked up her ears. Screwing the top back on the face-cream jar she laid it aside on the night table and snuggled down beside him.

'Yes – remember that time we went on holiday to Vienna long before the war?'

'Of course, it was our honeymoon.'

'Remember that equestrian school we visited?'

'The Spanish Riding School – the Lipizzan horses?'

'That's right. Well, he worked with them.'

'Really?' Hilary was clearly impressed. Only a top-class vet would be allowed near the famous Lipizzan horses.

'Anyway, I've suggested we might make use of him in the meantime with military horses. He seemed pleased, as far as I could tell. A very impassive kind of man – hard to know what he was really thinking.'

'The strong, silent type,' murmured Hilary. 'Wasn't going to tell why he really ran away. I'll bet he was being harassed, being Jewish as well as a foreigner.'

'Very likely. He didn't say.'

Hilary sighed. 'You need some women in the Corps, someone like Joanna who speaks fluent German. She'd have got through to him. Yes, I bet he was being harried. Somewhere down south, probably, on one of those pretty picturesque farms in Somerset or Worcester. Pity he wasn't sent up here – our north-country people aren't a bit silly like that, far too bluff and honest.'

Her voice sounded sleepy and satisfied. Reginald breathed a deep sigh and settled himself down to the sleep of a man content that he has done his day's duty well. There had been no need to tell her that the fellow had once worked at Scapegoat.

Hilary reached out and snapped off the light.

'Reginald?'

'Mmm?' came the sleepy reply.

'Five days is a long time. I missed you.'

'*I miss you so much, Max. My heart aches for you.*'

Maddie closed the notebook, put it away in the drawer and went upstairs. Taking the key of the door from above the doorframe, she unlocked her mother's bedroom and went in.

Strange, but it was still difficult to realize that nowadays she was free to do as she pleased without asking the withered old man in the corner downstairs. No one would scold and rage if she opened up Mother's room. It would afford her great pleasure to move her things in here and leave Eva to enjoy her room alone.

With an effort she wrenched her mind away from the memory of Max in this room. Words of love had been spoken here, and it hurt beyond bearing to recall them now. Instead, she took her time to open and explore the drawers of the dressing table, secure in the knowledge that no one would accuse her of sacrilege, clamp an angry hand on her shoulder and order her to leave. Poor Dad. Never again would he raise his voice in protest, for all memory of the past seemed to have deserted him. Even the present was too much for him to cope with.

Faded photographs lay under the neatly pressed chemises and petticoats. Maddie lifted them out, bending to the light of the window to see better the sepia figures posing against a sepia vista of hills. Two girls, arms about each other's waists, smiled back at her, and she recognized Mother in her youth. In another snap the same two girls sat side by side on a horsehair sofa, a baby in the arms of the other girl. It must be Aunt Lottie.

Maddie shuffled the photographs together and took them downstairs. She would show Ronnie the snap which could be of himself, and who knew? Perhaps they would help to prompt her father's memory.

The old man lay propped up in bed, his hand resting on Dog's head. Dog lay with his chin on the edge of the bed, wide eyes watching his master. Maddie patted him as she sat down.

'Look at these photos, Dad. That's Mother, remember?'

He took the snap and tried to focus his eyes upon it. Maddie pointed to the other woman. 'And that's Aunt Lottie, isn't it? Before she went to Australia with Uncle Arthur.'

Noises rumbled in the old man's throat. Maddie nodded. 'Arthur Whittaker, you remember? He's dead now, of course, but it's his son and Lottie's who staying with us – Cousin Ronnie. You know Ronnie?'

He looked up at her for a moment. 'Lottie,' he said, and Maddie laughed.

'That's right! Good!'

He stared down again at the photograph. Maddie pointed at the baby. 'That's Ronnie, before they went away, when he was just a little baby. Do you remember?'

'Lottie nardle pram.' It was a struggle, but the words emerged. Maddie seized his hand.

'Yes!'

244

The door opened suddenly and Ronnie strode in, his handsome face clouded in anger. Maddie leapt up.

'Ronnie, he recognized your mother in the photo! Could he be getting better, do you think?'

Ronnie ignored her. He pushed past and grabbed hold of Dog's collar. 'What the hell do you think you're doing, beast?' he demanded. 'You buggered off just when I needed you with them sodding sheep. I'll take my belt off to you if you do that again.'

Maddie stared. 'Did you hear me, Ronnie? Dad – '

'I don't give a shit if he gets better or not,' he growled.

Noises gurgled in the old man's throat again. Maddie looked down and saw he was staring, wild-eyed, at Ronnie. His hand rose slowly in the air, curled itself into a fist, and he shook it feebly while the noises gurgled. Even if there was no recognizable word in his speech, the hatred in his eyes was unmistakable.

Maddie knelt to take the shaking fist in hers. 'It's all right, Dad – it's only Ronnie, your nephew. Nothing to worry about.'

But the malevolent look did not shift away from Ronnie's face. The younger man turned for the door. 'Stupid old bugger, he's off his chump,' he muttered as he went. 'One foot in the grave already – don't know why the hell he doesn't get it over with.'

Maddie rushed out after him, eyes blazing and totally oblivious to the icy air. Seizing hold of Ronnie's arm she pulled him to a halt. 'You've got no right to talk about my father like that! You're sheltering under his roof, remember. Don't you ever talk like that about him again.'

He looked down at her, a sneering lip curled. 'Oh yeah? Or else?'

'Just don't you dare – and don't dare lift a finger against my dog either.'

Turning away, she rushed back into the farmhouse, anger scalding her throat. Her father lay back on the pillow, a fearful look in his watery blue eyes.

'Don't you fret, Dad. He'll not get the better of us,' she muttered savagely. 'Only trouble is, he's put me in a hell of a hole now. I can't very well tell him to leave.'

Nor would she want to try to manage without his help, she had to confess to herself. Funny, Eva had been right about him from the start. Strange how perceptive children could be. Cousin Ronnie was showing himself in his true colours now, and he was not half the man she had taken him to be. Not like Max. Now there was a man . . .

The air was tense over supper that night. Eva was quick to sense it.

'You been quarrelling?' she demanded, looking from Ronnie to Maddie.

'Hell, no,' said Ronnie. 'We're dead beat, that's all. Dying for a bit of shut-eye.'

Maddie took her father soup and a spoon. He waved the spoon in the air. 'Nisty a bugger,' he croaked. Eva looked up from her plate.

'Who is, Mr Renshaw? Who's been annoying you then?'

Renshaw waved the spoon again. 'Larty wanag nor many a school. Nisty a bugger.'

Eva's gaze turned to Ronnie. 'What you been doing to him then? You leave Mr Renshaw alone. He can't hurt you. Only bullies pick on littler people.'

Ronnie stared. 'You understand what the old fool says?'

'More or less. He doesn't like you, seemingly. Can't say as I blame him.'

Maddie pushed back her chair. 'What are you going to do about your stuff upstairs, Ronnie? Wouldn't it be best to get rid of it?'

'Me uniform? Maybe I should, but that coat's too good to chuck away. It'll come in useful one day.'

'I was thinking – if you're staying long, people will ask your name.'

'So? Oh, I see. Whittaker, and Dad coming from Otterley, you mean. OK then, choose me a new name.'

'I could think of a good name for you,' said Eva. Ronnie ignored her.

'Not many folk come by here, and those who've seen me in the fields don't ask much. There was a fellow asked if I was sent by the War Ag, whatever that might be. I said I was, and that seemed to satisfy him.'

When Eva had gone to bed Maddie took the farm ledger out of the drawer and, pulling out the envelope of papers for the month, drew a deep sigh.

'Those the farm accounts?' asked Ronnie from the depths of the armchair.

'Yes, and returns to be done.'

'Give 'em here.' The outstretched hand waved peremptorily.

Maddie hesitated. 'I can't do that. It's private. There's Dad's income figures over the last year.'

'You said there was returns to be done.'

'That's right, for the milk yield, so we get the feed allocation as well as the payment.'

'So all right, I'm doing you a favour. I'm good at figures – comes natural. Give it here and stop making a fuss, woman.'

He took them from her and glanced through the pages. 'Nothing to it. From now on you can leave all this to me,' he said quietly. 'Business is a man's job anyway.'

Maddie felt uneasy. Cousin he might be, but he was being far too familiar for comfort. 'Any idea how long you might be staying?' she asked.

He shrugged. 'As long as it takes for things to quiet down. After that . . .'

So he was only making use of them till there was no more need to hide, Maddie realized. She would miss his help around the place, but somehow her heart felt lighter at the prospect of his going.

'People come, people go,' she murmured to Duster that night as she saw to the horses. 'Nothing's fixed in the world, is it? Nothing you can really rely on.'

She sighed, burying her face deep in the mare's mane, savouring the smell of horseflesh and recalling how Max stood over there by the door, watching her with that dark, inscrutable gaze of his, and as she did so she felt the love swelling inside her again and the terrible, aching sense of loss.

'Never mind, Duster,' she muttered through threatening tears as she stroked the strong, smooth neck, 'We'll always stay together, won't we? Who cares about men anyway? The sooner Cousin Ronnie clears off, the better.'

CHAPTER TWENTY

The lambing was coming to an end, and Ronnie said he was quite capable of doing the branding and marking on his own.

'Done millions of 'em in me time – no problem doing this little lot,' he said cheerfully. 'Same goes for shearing – I'll be able to strip these in a day or two.'

So he was still planning to be in Scapegoat in three months' time, Maddie thought. By then, at the rate he was going, he'd have got the place ship-shape again; already the fences were repaired, the chicken coop roof fixed and most of the drystone walls rebuilt.

One morning the postman knocked at the door.

'Not often I call here, not with personal letters, it isn't,' he remarked as he handed over the letter. 'This one's postmarked Middlesbrough. From young Ruby Sykes, I'll be bound.'

'Most likely. Thanks, Mr Darley.'

It was from Ruby, a letter glowing with excitement and happiness. *'The wedding date is fixed and I'm to be a June bride. You must come to the church, even if me mam won't let me have you as bridesmaid. Oh, Dick is so gorgeous. I'm going to adore being his wife.'*

Maddie smiled to herself. Of course I'll be at the church to see you marry the man you love, Ruby, no matter what your snobby mother thinks.

Daily the wireless gave news of the war, of horrific attacks on British merchant ships and the thousands of tons of shipping being sunk by German submarines. In Barnbeck and Otterley and all the other villages in the Garthdale valley people watched anxiously for the telegraph boy, fearing the dreaded buff envelope.

'*We regret to inform you . . .*'

Maddie watched closely Eva's reaction as the sonorous voice on the wireless droned on, telling of the Battle of the Atlantic. The child's face remained impassive.

'Are you worrying, Eva?' Maddie asked.

'Only 'cos you say that's why treacle's rationed now. I like my treacle pudding. That Ronnie always gets most of it.'

Spring was filling the valley with fresh green grass and pale-budded trees. Funny, thought Maddie, how yellow flowers always seem to be the first to greet the spring – crocuses, primroses, and then the stately golden daffodils, Mother's favourite. She took a bunch down to the graveyard.

Sunlight trickled through the trees overhead, casting dappled shadows on the ancient grey tombstones. There was a tranquil air in the deserted graveyard, only the birds singing and the distant sound of men working their horses in the fields. Maddie felt a sense of calm, of closeness to those she loved. As she pulled away the weeds and placed the flowers on the neglected grave she thought of Mother for a moment, and then the image was quickly replaced by Max. Words began to shape in her mind, words she must remember so that she could write them down in the little exercise book when Ronnie was out of the way.

Ronnie was chopping logs in the yard when she arrived home. He looked up momentarily, and then continued swinging the axe, his blond head and the fair hairs on his forearm gleaming in the sunlight.

'Where you been?'

'Just down to Mother's grave with some flowers.' She

sighed. It was just like the old days, having to account for her movements.

'I'm going to have a look through them accounts tonight,' Ronnie muttered between blows. 'I'm not satisfied.' —

'Satisfied with what? I've kept them regular as clockwork,' Maddie protested.

'Not that.' He gave a final blow, severing the last of the beech logs, and flung down the axe. Then he turned to Maddie and eyed her with all seriousness. 'The farm's just not making what it should. It needs rethinking. I could make it show a profit.'

'Rethinking?' Vaguely she was registering that he had said that he, not they, could make a profit.

'You been wasting your time with pigs. Money comes from selling milk and lambs. We should concentrate on cows, sheep and horses.'

'The pigs are Dad's – he's an expert.'

'Maybe he was, but not any more. Cost of feeding is higher than what sales of piglets brings in, according to the books, so they can go for a start.'

He wiped the sweat from his forehead with the back of his arm. He had not asked her opinion, Maddie noted. The decision was made as far as he was concerned. The old, familiar streak of rebellion flared.

'You're forgetting something,' she said firmly. 'We've got government regulations. War Ag committee tells us what we can and can't do. You need to read all the leaflets as well as the accounts.'

'Bloody governments,' he muttered. 'Just look where they've got us.' He stamped off into the house.

Maddie, reluctant to follow him, lingered in the sunlit yard. After a time she heard the creak of the farmyard gate. Eva was coming in, one pigtail unplaited and flying about her face.

'Hi,' she said breezily. 'Where is he?'

'If you mean Ronnie, he's indoors.'

251

Eva looked towards the house, 'Go and get Lassie for me, will you, Maddie?'

'Fetch him yourself, lazy.'

'Not if he's in there.'

'Why not? He won't eat you, you know.'

'I just don't like him. I wish he was dead.'

'Eva!'

The child pulled a sullen face. 'Well, I wish he'd go away anyway. I wish Mr Bower would come back. I liked him.'

Maddie put a hand on the child's shoulder, feeling a leap of warmth. 'Yes. But we can't always have what we want. Not straightaway, at any rate.'

Eva nudged one of the logs with her foot. 'You know, Maddie, I wished my cousin was dead once. He was a lot older than me. He kept teasing me something rotten.'

Maddie curled her arm around the girl's shoulders. 'We all feel like that at times. I know I do.'

'My cousin did die – in an accident down the pit. Pitfall, me mam said it were. They brought his body to our house. He were lying on our kitchen table – I can remember it, although I were only little.'

Maddie finger's tightened on the girl's shoulder. 'Oh, love! It wasn't because of you, you can't believe that!'

Eva's face was still clouded as she reached back into memory. 'His fingernails were all black and broken. Me mam said he must have been struggling to get out. I watched while me mam and me auntie washed him and put a white sheet on him. Combed his hair, they did, just like he weren't dead at all.'

Compassion flooded Maddie. 'Oh love, and you felt you were responsible. That's nonsense. It was an accident, Eva, a pure accident.'

The child sighed. 'Aye, that's what me mam said but I know different. God heard me when I wished him dead. God'll catch up with me one day.'

Then, just as suddenly as the melancholy had come upon her, a burst of sunshine irradiated the child's face. 'I got to find Lassie – he'll have been waiting for me for ages. I promised him I'd take him down the woods today to look for rabbits.'

The sound of Renshaw's voice whined from the kitchen, querulous and demanding. When Maddie entered, Ronnie was sitting at the table leafing through the accounts, a hand cupped over the ear nearest the bed. Her father's stricken face showed he needed the chamber pot.

'For Christ's sake, see to the old bastard,' Ronnie muttered. 'He's a bloody pain in the arse.'

'He's not, he's sick,' Maddie said sharply. 'How would you feel if it was you?'

'I'd shoot myself rather than let that happen to me.' He frowned down at the papers, the old man clearly already forgotten. After a time he pushed the papers aside, stretched his arms above his head and yawned. 'What is there to do in this rotten place? By way of a change, I mean? Got a gun? I could do a bit of shooting.'

She was loth to tell him about her father's gun under the stairs. 'You'd only draw attention to yourself,' she pointed out. 'That's the last thing you want.'

'Where's the kid?'

'Taken Dog down to the woods.'

He threw back his head and laughed. Somehow, thought Maddie, his laugh never rang with pleasure like other people's did, only with a harsh and jeering sound. 'What a bloody stupid name for a dog. Why couldn't you have called him Gyp or Rover or some doggy name like everybody else?'

Ignoring him, Maddie turned away, irritated but unwilling to argue with him. Carping, criticizing all the time – Cousin Ronnie's company was beginning to become unbearable.

She was leaning over the sink, running the tap to rinse the mud off the potatoes for supper, when she became aware of Ronnie behind her, his body so close to hers she could smell the rank smell of sweat from his armpits.

'This place gets bloody boring,' he muttered.

'I know.' She busied herself wielding the paring knife.

'It stands to reason farmers have a lot of kids when there's little else to entertain them,' he went on.

'Oh, they go ratting or ferreting or play quoits in the summer – and there's always the pictures in Agley Bridge.' She looked past him at the clock. 'Nearly six, Ronnie. The news'll be on in a minute. Shall I switch on?'

He stood square, blocking her way. 'No need. I'll do it when I'm ready.'

He stood looking down at her, a hint of a smile quirking his lips. Maddie stiffened. She was trapped between him and the sink, and fiercely aware of his physical closeness. Her irritation and unease began to give way to apprehension. Proximity with Bob and Richard had caused fluttering excitement, with Max a deep and passionate stirring such as she had never known, but with Ronnie there was only dread.

She took a deep breath, the paring knife still in her hand. 'Excuse me, I want to pass,' she said quietly.

He smiled. 'And what if I don't want you to?'

'You'll get no supper. Now stop annoying me – can't you smell the meat is catching?'

Angrily he flung himself down at the table and hunched over the papers again. Maddie stirred the contents of the pan over the fire, relieved that he had not realized the meat wasn't really burning.

He examined the papers without speaking for a time. Maddie chewed her lips as she cooked, wondering what he might have done. Would he have made a pass at her? The idea was unthinkable.

Eva burst in, Dog trotting happily in alongside her.

'I saw Stanley down in the woods. He lives next to Mr Pickering's sweet shop and he told me Mr Pickering got a telegram today. He said Mrs Pickering had to have the doctor 'cos they couldn't stop her screaming.'

Maddie looked up sharply, apprehension stabbing her. 'Telegram? Not Norman?'

'That's his name,' said Eva. 'Norman Pickering got killed. His ship got sunk.'

'Oh no,' said Maddie. 'He's their only child. It's not that long ago they were celebrating his twenty-first.'

It was unbelievable. She could see him still, the cheeky blond lad in her class who was the bane of Miss Gaunt's life, the bright-eyed and proud youth walking with Ruby on his arm at the Gooseberry Fair barn dance . . .

Ronnie pushed aside his plate. 'So what?' he muttered. 'You've not had any war casualties in the village up to now. You couldn't expect to escape. Now you see why I wanted out.'

'He's not the first,' Eva said coldly. 'There were that Land Army girl up at Bailey's who got squashed.'

'I said war casualties,' growled Ronnie. 'That were an accident.'

'It's still a casualty,' argued Eva. 'So there.'

'You mind your lip, girl.'

Eva stamped out of the house. 'Where you going?' called Maddie.

'Down the lavvy,' came the sullen reply.

Maddie was not looking forward to fetching the week's rations from the village shop. She could not bear the thought of seeing the harrowing look in Edna Pickering's eyes. What could she possibly say to alleviate the woman's suffering?

As luck would have it Doreen Sykes was sitting on the stool on the customer's side of the counter, shopping bag at her feet and one plump arm resting on the deal counter. Mr Pickering was not at his usual station behind the grille of the post-office section of the shop.

'I don't know, Edna,' Doreen was declaring loudly, 'you must be a woman with a brain and a half if you can fathom out all this points nonsense they've started. What with all the rationing we've already got, and now clothes to be rationed too – if this keeps on we'll be going about our business stark naked before this lot's over.'

Maddie recognized her strategy at once. It was better by far to talk as though life went on. Edna, red-eyed and blotchy-faced, served Maddie's needs and only nodded without speaking when Maddie offered a few words of regret. Doreen listened without acknowledging her until Maddie's purchases were made.

'Now, like I was saying, Edna,' she went on as Maddie turned to go, 'it might be a good idea to organize some sort of exchange system, specially for kiddies' clothes. Good second-hand stuff won't go amiss with all these vaccies to be seen to. I've some nice things our Eunice has grown out of . . .'

The moment Maddie had left the shop Doreen leaned across the counter. 'Now there's a quiet lass if ever there was one. Wouldn't have known she'd got herself a new farmhand but for Eva. She does chatter, that child.'

Edna nodded. 'I heard tell there was a fellow up there – big, blond-haired lad, they say. Wonder why he's not gone off in the forces?'

Doreen laid a finger to her nose. 'Ah well, according to Eva he's not quite all there, if you know what I mean. She told me herself, no prompting. She doesn't get on with him at all. Right funny devil, she says. Reckon he must have been turned down for the army – it's only the best who get in, you know.'

Edna gave a thin smile and wrapped up the bacon. 'Aye, reckon you're right.'

Maddie went on her way. As she was making her way along the main street a well-built figure in a tweed suit was coming towards her. It was Miss Gaunt, the schoolmistress, who peered over the top of her spectacles.

'Ah, Madeleine – I was planning to have a word with you – about little Eva.'

'Oh – she's not been causing trouble, has she?'

'No, no. Not that she can't be a little mischief at times, but I've noticed over the years that all the bright ones are. That's what I wanted to talk to you about. The scholarship exam. She'll be old enough to sit for it soon. Is there any chance you could send her to the grammar school if I put her in for it?'

'Well, I don't know – I hadn't thought about it – '

'Only I remember your father wouldn't send you, so I wondered . . .'

'Well, it's for her mother to decide really, I suppose,' said Maddie. 'I'll have to write to her about it. I'll let you know.'

Ronnie was busy preparing for the lambs to go to market. He gave the shopping basket a scathing glance. 'Enough food for one there,' he remarked drily. 'What are the rest of you going to eat?'

'I haven't a ration book for you,' Maddie pointed out. 'Good job Dad doesn't eat much, and we got our own bacon and eggs and milk, or else we'd be in queer street.'

The hens were laying well when the government announced strict control over egg distribution. Maddie wasted no time. She mixed bucketfuls of waterglass and requisitioned Eva's help to pickle eggs for the winter.

'I don't like pickled eggs,' Eva protested. 'They taste funny and the yolks are always broken.'

'Better than no eggs at all,' said Maddie. 'I can't make cakes without 'em.'

'We got loads of hens, millions of eggs.'

'But hens don't lay in the winter. Now put those eggs in the bucket carefully else you'll crack them and they'll be no use at all.'

All the time she was speaking Maddie was aware of Ronnie's tall figure, leaning against the doorway watching and listening. If Eva noticed, she did not deign to acknowledge him. From the corner of her eye Maddie could see the sunlight on his fair head, the negligent way he lolled, arms folded, and knew his eyes were following her every movement. He made her uneasy, and she wished he would go away.

'Did you want something, Ronnie?' she asked at last.

'Nothing you'll give me – yet,' he replied lazily, and she saw the teasing light in his eye as he turned to go.

The following day after the milking was done Maddie took the cows from the byre out into the meadow. On a fine June morning it was pleasurable to feel the warmth of the sun on her bare arms, and she wondered idly what Ronnie was doing now the lambs had been safely dispatched to market. She was nearing the top end of the meadow before she caught sight of him.

Ronnie was lying on the grass, his head propped on one hand, watching her as she herded the cows upfield. When she came back down towards him, she could see that the expression in his green eyes was no longer teasing nor jovial. There was no kindness, no gentleness in that stare, only a deep, searching, grasping expression as though he was soaking up the image of her, trying to absorb her whole, to take over her being and possess her outright, and the thought filled her with revulsion.

'What do you want?' she demanded. 'Haven't you got work to do?'

He plucked a blade of grass and put it between his teeth, then leaned back on one elbow. 'Wanted to talk to you.'

'What about?'

'Horses. We said we'd talk about breeding.'

She could see the way his gaze was travelling over her, from her face down her body and up again. 'Yes – we said we'd think about it some time, when the farm was paying better.'

'No time like the present. Get rid of the pigs, like we said, get the mare covered. This is the time of year for mating, isn't it? She's in season.'

'Yes.' This time a year ago, hopes had been so high for

Duster. Max taking her down to Thorpe Gill, Mrs Westerley-Kent's enthusiasm . . . 'But it's a question of getting the right stallion anyway,' she said lamely. 'Just any stud won't do.'

'I'd like to watch a really virile stallion covering your mare,' Ronnie said, and there was a quiet emphasis in the way he spoke the words which sounded obscene to Maddie's ears. 'If I go and find a really good thoroughbred . . .'

'No!' cried Maddie. 'You don't know about horses – Duster needs another Cleveland Bay; you can't taint the blood with thoroughbred!'

He was eyeing her with narrowed eyes. 'That makes the foal more valuable?'

'No – well yes, because it's pure, it has a pedigree. But this isn't the right time. Next year, perhaps.'

'I don't understand you. Not long ago you were crazy to get her mated.'

'That was then. Now things are different. Oh, I don't want to talk about it.'

'Maddie,' he said, tossing the blade of grass aside and getting to his feet, 'this farm has got to be made to pay. Women are no use when it comes to business, coming over all hysterical.'

'I'm not. And I've got work to do.'

She turned hastily and made back for the farmhouse. She was aware that Ronnie was close behind her and, as she entered the kitchen, she began talking brightly to her father.

'Would you like the wireless on, Dad? It's time for the news.'

Tuning in the wireless she saw Ronnie loitering by the door and knew he was anxious to pursue the conversation. Ignoring him, she busied herself tidying her father's sheets as the music came to an end and six pips sounded.

'*Here is the ten o'clock news. Today the Cabinet has announced that the German Army has invaded Russia . . .*'

Maddie caught her breath and swung around to face

259

Ronnie. 'Russia,' she breathed. 'Is there no stopping Hitler? Is he going to take over the world?'

Ronnie was chewing his lip thoughtfully. 'Maybe the old bastard's bitten off more than he can chew this time,' he murmured. 'But he won't get here.'

'Please God he doesn't,' said Maddie fervently.

Ronnie straightened and opened the door. 'Nope, he won't. I won't let him take over this place, that's for sure.'

Maddie could not help the smile. 'Very noble of you, cousin, but I hardly think you could stop the whole German army on your own.'

He looked down at her, a frown rutting his forehead. 'I mean it, Maddie. Nobody's going to take the farm off us. It's ours, and it'll stay that way.'

The old, familiar feeling boiled up inside her. 'Ours? Dad's, you mean, and one day it'll be mine, but you've got nothing to do with it.'

A slow smile spread across his face. He jerked his head in the direction of the shrunken figure in the bed. 'He's not long for this world, and you know it. Soon Scapegoat will be yours and you can't run it without me. You need me. Together we can make a real good go of it. On your own, you're useless.'

Maddie stood by the bed, open-mouthed, then drew herself upright to flare back at him. But before she could speak he had taken two steps across the room, seized her roughly and was pressing his mouth down on hers. Maddie fought to free herself, but his grip was too strong for her, bruising her arms and her lips. Somehow she felt remote from what was going on, disembodied and looking down on the scene from somewhere overhead. She could see the man, forcing his attentions on a girl, and nearby an old man in bed watching, puzzled and helpless. At last Ronnie stood back, a hint of a smile on his lips.

Maddie wiped the back of her hand across her mouth and glared at him, filled with hatred and revulsion. He perched on the edge of the table.

260

'Why don't we get together, Maddie? I fancy you'd make me a good brood mare.'

Before she could think her arm had swung up in the air and come down across his face. She heard the crack, then watched, mesmerized, as red fingermarks bloomed on his cheek. To her surprise he simply smiled.

'I like a woman with spirit,' he said drily. 'It isn't true what they told me about tame English girls. I think I'm going to enjoy schooling you.'

'Is that supposed to be a proposal?' Maddie demanded. 'Because if so, let me tell you I wouldn't marry you if you were the last man on earth!'

'Hell, no, little cousin, I'm not proposing marriage at all,' he drawled. 'No need for that. In the outback we don't bother with formalities like that.'

For a moment Maddie stared, then at last she found her voice. 'Get out,' she said in a low voice. 'Get out and don't come back. I never want to see you again.'

'And have me run in by the police?' he said in a voice which was clearly relishing taunting her. 'And not only me – but you too, for harbouring a deserter. Can't have that, Maddie. Whatever would happen to Uncle James then, eh? And to Scapegoat? Oh no, little cousin, I'm afraid you're stuck with me for the duration – and then some.'

CHAPTER TWENTY-ONE

Maddie sat trembling on the edge of Mother's bed, filled with mingled hate, fear and fury. At length she heard Ronnie's footsteps on the stairs, and held her breath until she heard him go into his room and shut the door.

She dared not undress for fear he should come in. For half the night she lay on the bed, still fully dressed and listening for any sound from him, but only the usual night noises of creaking beams and settling furniture came to her ears and at last she drifted into a fitful sleep.

She awoke to the sound of the old rooster crowing and the lowing of the cows rising to shrill insistence, showing their impatience to be milked. Maddie crept downstairs and looked at her father's sleeping face. Gone now was the man of strength, the man ready to meet all crises. In his place lay a yellow-faced old creature who understood little and was powerless to help himself or her.

The fire was low. She filled the kettle with water and then raked out the ashes, built up the fire with coal, then held a sheet of newspaper before it to draw it up. A step on the stair behind her made her stiffen, but she could not turn to face him.

The newspaper burst into flame. She watched it, mesmerized, for a second before thrusting it into the fireplace and watching it blacken and disintegrate. The footsteps came closer.

'You told me not to do that.' It was Eva's accusing voice, and relief flooded Maddie.

'I know. I had to. Have you seen Ronnie?'

'Oh – him. No, and I don't want to neither. How are you today, Mr Renshaw?'

She crossed to the bed, and Maddie could see that her father was awake and watching. He muttered sounds and Eva bent close.

'What's that, Mr Renshaw?'

Maddie heard him mutter.

'Who?' said Eva. 'You mean Ronnie?'

'Arg.'

'Is he now? Well, never mind. You'll have your breakfast in a minute.'

She came back to the table. 'Mr Renshaw don't like that Ronnie neither, seemingly. What's he done to him?'

'Nothing that I know of. Now, will you have porridge today?'

'He's done summat. He's a bugger, is Ronnie.'

'What've I told you? Porridge?'

'I'd rather have a lump of parkin.'

'None left, and there's no more treacle to make any more.'

'Porridge then. Oh, here he comes.' She rolled her eyes ceilingwards as Ronnie clumped down the stairs. 'Where's my pocketknife?' he said abruptly.

'I know nothing about it,' said Maddie with studied indifference, stirring oatmeal into the pan of water. 'It's probably where you left it.'

'No it isn't. I left it on the dressing table.'

Eva looked up at him with a mocking glance. 'Oh aye, it's just walked then, has it?'

He scowled at her. 'None of your lip, girl. You know where it is, do you? Come on, have you nabbed it?'

'No I haven't, so there!' Eva's voice was full of offended innocence.

'Well somebody did,' he growled.

'Well it wasn't me. You're daft, you are, losing something and then saying I pinched it.'

'I've told you, brat . . .'

Maddie heard a resounding crack and spun round to see the child's face crumple as she reeled from her chair, and then a howl filled the air. Eva clapped her hands to her head and jumped up, her little body shaking as she shrieked at him in fury.

'You're rotten, you are, as well as soft in the head if you think anybody here'd pinch owt from you! You've got nowt we want, any road! I wish Mr Bower was here – he'd thump you, you big bully!'

As the child ran crying out into the yard Maddie saw her father sitting up in bed, his mouth agape and his whole body trembling. She ran out after Eva.

'I'm not coming back!' Eva howled. 'Not while he's there! I'm off to school, and I'll tell 'em all what a rotten bugger he is!'

'No, Eva, you mustn't – you'll get us all into trouble if you do!'

'Well he's not going to belt me like me dad did – he's nowt to me, isn't Mr Clever Dick! I wish somebody'd give him a right good hiding!'

'I couldn't agree with you more,' said Maddie with heartfelt sympathy. 'Still, let's keep private things to ourselves, and we'll sort him out somehow or other.'

Eva rubbed a fist across her eyes. 'Promise?'

Maddie sighed. 'Yes, love. I don't yet know how, or when, but we will.'

'OK then, I'll be off now. See you this aft. Hey – go in and get me gas mask for me, will you?'

Maddie could not help admiring the child's resilience as she walked off jauntily down the lane. The girl had probably grown up accustomed to blows and raised voices, but it was unfair that she should have to meet violence again here, in Scapegoat, where she had come for shelter. It was a kind of betrayal of the child's trust, and Maddie felt personally responsible. Affairs could not be allowed to continue like this, for her sake.

* * *

That afternoon Maddie sat down and wrote to Mrs Jarrett. The letter finished and sealed, she decided to go down to the village to post it.

The children were playing in the schoolyard as she passed. Eva's diminutive figure was leaping in deep concentration from one chalked square in the playground to another in an earnest game of hopscotch, and she did not see Maddie.

The letter posted, Maddie walked along the street under the trees edging the churchyard, deep in thought. Again the image of Max leapt unbidden into her mind. Oh Max, what shall I do? What would you do if you were here with me now? Oh God, if only I could wipe Ronnie out of our lives and bring you back into it, Max!

Maddie was wrenched from her reverie by the sight of a figure crouching on the wooden seat in the shadow under the lych gate. As she approached she could see a floral print overall and wrinkled stockings and as the woman raised her head she recognized the tear-stained face of Edna Pickering. Hastily the woman wiped her eyes with a crumpled handkerchief.

'Oh, I'm sorry – I didn't expect to see anybody here,' she mumbled. 'Only, I've got to weep me tears somewhere, and I can't do it at home and upset our Fred. I'm that sorry.'

'No,' said Maddie gently. 'Don't apologize. Can I help or would you rather be alone?'

The pudgy face crumpled again. 'I can't bear to think of him drowning like that. Our Norman hated being shut in anywhere – he loved open places like the moors, he did, and he always said he got claustro-thingummy if he hadn't space to breathe. I were that glad when he got sent on a ship and not in a submarine – he'd have hated that – but what good did it do him?'

The shoulders hunched again and shook. Maddie sat down beside her and put an arm about Edna's shoulders, saying nothing but hoping the woman would take comfort from the warmth of human closeness. For a time she felt Edna's shuddering sobs, and then the woman straightened.

'I could bear it,' she managed between sniffs, 'if only I'd have said a proper goodbye to him. I'll never rest, knowing I didn't.'

Maddie squeezed the shoulders. 'I know just what you mean, Mrs Pickering. I never had the chance to say goodbye to my mother.'

It was curious, she realized, but she had managed to say it without it hurting. Maybe Max had been right about time healing all . . .

Edna raised enquiring eyes, and Maddie could see the new light in them. 'Didn't you? And did it bother you too?'

'For a time, but not any more.'

'I wanted to find a way to get in touch with him – you know, Spiritualists or summat, but Doreen said that were wicked, meddling with the devil and it might stir up evil. But I still wish I could.'

Maddie felt the old irritation rising. 'Doreen Sykes has too much to say for herself sometimes. What does she know about it?'

'Aye, that's what I thought.' Edna dabbed her eyes again and put the handkerchief away. 'There, I feel a lot better now. Thanks, Maddie lass.'

She stood up, straightening her cardigan and smoothing down her overall. Maddie stood too. 'I'd best be off home now,' she said, giving the woman's arm one last squeeze. Edna stared into the distance.

'You know summat else Doreen said?' she murmured in a far-away tone. 'She said it wasn't over yet, 'cos these things always come in threes.'

'What do?'

'Deaths. First that Land Army girl, then our Norman. There'll be another death before long, she said, somebody from our village.'

* * *

Some days later Ronnie was sitting in the farmyard on an upturned box in the heat of the summer afternoon, his discarded shirt lying over the wall where he had tossed it. Maddie could see him from the kitchen window, his muscular back lightly bronzed and his blond head bent over some object in his hand. Once another man had sat on that same box, a man with an air of mystery and infinite sadness in eyes as black as night.

She shook off the thought. Max was never coming back, he had said so clearly, and it was foolish to keep on dreaming of him.

'Maddie!'

Ronnie was looking back over his shoulder, an impatient frown on his face. Sunlight glinted on the metal in his hand, and she saw that it was her father's gun. Irritation pricked her again. Ronnie had been rooting in the cupboard under the stairs.

'What is it?' she called.

'Where's the ammo for this gun?'

'Same place as the gun was. Why?'

She wiped her hands on the towel and went to stand in the doorway. He looked up and grinned. He was remarkably good-looking, she thought, and he knew it, but his good looks could never make him attractive. There was no warmth in his face or in his soul. He was far too self-centred to be truly attractive.

'You'll only draw attention to yourself if you use it,' she remarked. 'We already talked about that.'

'They know I'm here. Plenty of people have seen me.'

'They'll be wondering . . .'

He shrugged. 'I told you, I've spoken to some of 'em. I let 'em think I've come to replace Eva's precious Mr Bower.'

'Hardly,' said Maddie. 'He was an Austrian.'

'You had a prisoner of war here? I wonder you didn't keep this gun cleaned and primed in that case.'

'He was a refugee. Has Eva come home yet?'

He made no answer, busying himself instead by spitting on a piece of rag and polishing vigorously. Maddie went to the gate and looked down the lane. Eva was struggling slowly uphill, her face flushed.

'Whew!' she said as she neared the gate. 'We ought to have holidays on days like this. There ought only be school on wet days.'

'It's nearly the summer holidays now,' said Maddie. 'Only another week.'

'Aye, and then he'll have me working.' She scowled at the seated figure in the yard. 'Have you heard from me mam yet?'

'Give her a chance, love. She hasn't had my letter long. She'll be writing soon.'

It was another week before the letter came. Mrs Jarret made rather tortuous explanations for not having had time to visit Barnbeck again, then went on to tell of the new home she had moved into.

'*I know our Eva will like it, up in the posh part of town. Mr Bakewell helped me find it. Our old house got a bit knocked about what with the windows broken and the slates all dropped off but there's not much bombing going on now so maybe I'll be able to have her back here soon. As for the scholarship Mr Bakewell says we have a very good grammar school near here that would suit Eva.*'

Maddie fully expected Eva's face to break into smiles of delight when she read the letter aloud to the child that evening after supper, but Eva only stared gloomily at her feet.

'Aren't you pleased? You might be going home soon,' Maddie prompted.

'She's full of that Mr Bakewell,' said Eva. 'What's he got to do with me and school?'

'Well, she probably feels she needs a man's advice, what with your dad being away.'

Maddie glanced across to where Ronnie sat, but he made no sign of having heard. Eva snorted.

'She never listened to him! And I bet she's not told him her new address neither. She wants shot of him, and I don't blame her, but I don't want no Mr Bakewell telling her what to do about me neither. I don't know him. Why can't she ask Mr Bower? He knows me.'

Ronnie looked up. 'I keep hearing about this fellow,' he remarked. 'He must be quite something. Tell me about this Bower, Eva.'

The child shrugged. 'He was my friend. He was nice and kind. He wouldn't like you. I wish he'd come back, and he will one day, I know he will.'

'Oh, Miss Hoity-Toity,' laughed Ronnie. 'He won't if he has any sense. He's well off out of this dump.'

'Sticks and stone may break my bones but names'll never hurt me,' chanted Eva.

'That kid needs a thrashing,' said Ronnie to Maddie. 'Too cheeky by half. Now if she were a kid back home on Merlin's Crossing she'd get the buckle end of the belt. That'd whack the cheek out of her.'

Suddenly a distant sound cut through the still evening air, a high-pitched, plaintive sound. Eva sat upright. 'What was that?'

'A fox,' said Ronnie.

'It sounds terrible,' said Eva. 'Is it crying?'

'Hungry, probably. Hope the chickens are well locked up.'

'It's a vixen,' said Maddie suddenly. 'A black vixen.'

'It's an awful noise,' said Eva. 'I don't like it.'

And well you might not, thought Maddie as she prepared Eva for bed. In country folklore the cry of a fox foretells evil. Maddie was uneasy as she undressed for bed, filled with a strange sense of foreboding.

Three days later came the letter from Ruby. *'I shall be home almost as soon as this letter, Maddie, so expect me by Saturday.*

*Such a lot we got to talk about – my lovely wedding dress and
the ring Richard's going to give me of his grandma's. He was
here yesterday and we sneaked off together to the woods on our
own. It was lovely.'*

Maddie went out into the sunlit garden, puzzled that the
letter had caused such a feeling of loneliness. She bent to
inspect the ripening berries on her father's favourite gooseberry bush, the one handed down to him by his father, and
felt a deep sense of regret that never again would he be able
to compete for the coveted Gooseberry Trophy. He would
be saddened if he could see the condition of the bush now,
forgotten and neglected during the recent heat with the
result that the berries, burgeoning without sufficient water,
were already beginning to shrivel and fall. Maddie was so
preoccupied that she did not notice the portly figure
dismount from a bicycle on the far side of the wall.

'Ah, good afternoon, Madeleine.'

She looked up to see the brightly flushed face of Reverend
Chilcott as he leaned his bicycle against the wall. Maddie's
eyebrows rose. Visitors to Scapegoat were rare, and
especially the vicar.

'Oh, hello, Mr Chilcott. Have you come to see Dad?'

Blue eyes flickered away from hers. 'Ah, no, actually, I
came to see you. A sad errand, I fear. Most dreadful news
to report.'

A sinking feeling clutched at Maddie's stomach. 'Bad
news? What is it?' Eva's father? Or her mother?

'Mrs Sykes sent me to break the news to you. She did
not feel up to coming to see you herself, but she felt you
ought to know, being her best friend all those years.'

'Oh God! Nothing's happened to Ruby, has it? Oh,
please no, not Ruby!'

'I fear so, my dear. A dreadful accident. She was killed
in a motor-car mishap in the blackout. Her body is being
sent home for burial and Mr and Mrs Sykes both felt that
you would probably wish to attend the funeral on Friday.
So very sad. So young and full of spirit, but there we are.'

Tragedy strikes even the innocent in these terrible times. God moves in mysterious ways.'

'I can't believe it,' Maddie whispered. The vicar cleared his throat and flung a leg over the crossbar.

'I must be off to inform other friends now. I'll tell them you'll be there on Friday then, shall I?'

As Maddie turned, stupefied, to go back into the house she heard a sudden echo of a woman's voice.

These things always come in threes.

On Thursday afternoon Eddie Sykes stood in the centre of the living room while his wife inspected the black serge suit he was wearing. Rain was hurling itself against the window like dirty grey handfuls of gravel.

He could smell the pungent odour of moth balls emanating from the suit, and tried to recall the last time he had worn it, but his heart was too heavy with the knowledge of Ruby's death. Bright-eyed, bubbling Ruby, the joy of his life, snuffed out and gone . . . Doreen seemed to have taken the news with remarkable self-control, and he was proud of her.

'Your trousers seat is all shiny,' she said, but her tone was far more restrained than usual. 'You'd better let me have a go at it. Can't have you looking scruffy.'

'I could wear me uniform,' he offered. She shook her head.

'Nay, you wear that every day. And somehow a helmet's out of place at a funeral. Got to show some respect, we have, specially when your Alice and Bill will be all done up like a dog's dinner.'

'Nay, they'll not be worrying about things like that on a day like tomorrow,' he muttered.

'I don't know so much. She's all for show, is your Alice. Likes folk to think she's posh, she does, even if all else she's got is shabby. All lace curtains and no knickers, is your Alice.'

She drew her mouth into a tight line of obstinacy and

slow sympathy welled in him. He understood. It was Doreen's defence against breaking down, to talk as if life was as normal as it ought to be. He decided to fall in with her.

'Nay, don't be sarky, love,' he murmured.

'I'm not. Did you see that coat she wore at Easter? Must have cost her a fortune, but she gave us tea in them cracked old cups she's had this twenty years to my knowledge. No pride, she hasn't.'

She stood close to him, brushing specks of imagined dust off his shoulders, and he could see the reddened rim of her eyes. She sniffed.

'Take your suit off and give it me,' she said tersely. 'Try that black tie on with your shirt. And you'd best try them shoes while you're at it – you've not had 'em on your feet since last Gooseberry Fair.'

She sat on the settee, clothes brush in hand, and attacked the suit while he struggled to fasten a brass collar stud in the neck of his shirt. It was no use.

'This collar's far too tight, love. It must have shrunk in the wash.'

'You criticizing my washing? Try the shoes then.'

They were tight too. He stood uncomfortably on one foot, feeling the corn on his big toe starting to stab. Doreen sighed.

'I'll rub castor oil in – that'll soften 'em.'

She prodded a plump finger into the pocket of the suit. 'What've I told you about not bulging your pockets out with stuff? What's this?'

She withdrew a dog-eared photograph, and bent to peer at it in the fading light. 'Oh, Eddie, look – it's a snap you took that time we went on a charabanc trip to Whitby,' she murmured, then thrust it hastily back into the pocket. 'Can't think why you had it in there.'

He knew why she did not show it. He could remember clearly that hot August afternoon, the picture of Doreen,

272

slimmer and prettier then, with her two little girls on the jetty. He had been so proud of his little family . . .

A watery sun poked warm fingers round the edge of the curtains. Eddie could not bring himself to speak for the lump in his throat, and after a time his silence seemed to anger her. He could see the way her body stiffened as she rose from the settee and laid the suit aside.

His voice came gruffly. 'Shall I make us a cup of tea, love?' he offered. She shrugged thick shoulders, her back towards him. He went round in front of her and offered stiff arms, but she stood rigid.

'What are you doing?'

Without answering he put his arms about her, something he had not done in the daylight for years. She stood, still stiff and unyielding like a pit prop in his arms, and he heard the slow tick of the clock on the sideboard. At length he felt her body relax against him. Then she lifted her face and gave him a peck on the cheek, quickly and shyly, before she pulled away.

'We'll get through it, love,' she murmured. 'It'll not be easy, but we'll show them Westerley-Kents we're every bit as proud as they are. They'll not get another wife for their lad as good as our Ruby'd have been, God rest her. She was a lady.'

CHAPTER TWENTY-TWO

Ruby's Aunt Alice was plump and well scrubbed and in the softness of her yielding body lay all the warmth and beneficence of an earth mother. As she enveloped Maddie in an effusive embrace, all flesh and sharp-edged jet beads, Maddie could see the moustache on her upper lip and marvelled how she could register such a stupid detail when Ruby's body lay out there, in Dai Thomas's hearse, waiting to be buried in the black earth.

It was barely believable that Ruby, always so eager and pulsating with life, only a week ago lying in Richard's arms in the woods, now lay white and lifeless wearing a shroud in place of her wedding dress. It was ironically cruel, just as she was on the brink of a whole new life with Richard. Maddie caught sight of him in uniform waiting, cap in hand, by the church door for his bride . . .

Maddie sat near the back of the church, watching as garlands of flowers, the country folk's symbols of virginity, were carried before the coffin up the length of the aisle. Mrs Westerley-Kent sat in a wheelchair alongside her son in the front pew, a black fur stole about her neck despite the heat of the day, and to Maddie it looked like a dead cat. Or a fox. Once again she could visualize the foraging black vixen in the snow.

Eddie Sykes stood stiff and expressionless alongside his wife who wore a black-veiled hat and clung tightly to the hand of a white-faced Eunice. The Reverend Chilcott spoke gently and briefly about the untimely fading of a country rose, then led the singing of a hymn.

> 'Oh for a heart to praise my God,
> A heart from sin set free.'

Doreen Sykes's shoulders heaved, and Maddie could guess at her thoughts. What sin had Ruby known in her brief time on earth? Only the impatience and eagerness of youth had ruffled the surface of her life. Ruby had never known the walking emptiness that was Maddie, giving rise to hatred and bitterness and envy.

At the graveside Maddie hung back on the fringe of the mourners, full of pity for the sorrowful, bewildered look in Richard Westerley-Kent's eyes. His mother sat stiff and erect in her wheelchair, her gloved hands folded in her lap and her face composed. Eddie and Doreen Sykes leaned towards each other, not touching, and only an occasional sniff could be heard from under Doreen's veil. Eunice was sobbing quietly into Aunt Alice's ample bosom. Distant figures stood watching by the lych gate, caps in hand.

Maddie stood, hands clasped and head bent, recalling the day of Mother's funeral and feeling again the terrible sense of loneliness and desolation. Mother gone, then Max, and now Ruby. She felt cheated, and at the same time felt a curious twinge of guilt for being still alive, as though some day she might be punished for it. She marvelled at the sober air of resignation in the little churchyard, the feeling of stolid, proud endurance, and could not help feeling pride in her people. There was no drama of public tears, no one spoke or fidgeted. Tragic though Ruby's death had been, there was in these people acceptance born of centuries of familiarity with hardship.

'*Ashes to ashes, dust to dust.*'

As earth clattered on the coffin lid she could not help reflecting how significant the phrase was for country folk, people close to the earth they nurtured and which gave them their livelihood, and never closer to it than in death. The earth was claiming back its own.

'When the day of resurrection comes,' intoned Reverend Chilcott, 'may I be acceptable in Thy sight.'

Acceptable? Ruby was beautiful, thought Maddie

angrily. She envied her, young and beautiful and dead, the object of pity. If Maddie had died, maybe her father would have repented of his harshness in the past.

She began to speculate how she might die, dramatically like Ruby in an accident perhaps, or heroically saving a life, of maybe lingeringly in a hospital bed of some dreadful, incurable disease. Not among strangers but here, where she was known and word might eventually reach Max. He at least would care.

The service was ending. Maddie thrust aside the self-pitying thoughts as she watched Eddie Sykes helping his wife to stumble away from the open grave. Having no wish to linger and be obliged to speak to Richard, Maddie followed. Mrs Sykes stood by the lych gate. She spoke to Maddie in a jerky, strained voice.

'I told Edna it were a daft idea to try and get in touch with her Norman, but now I know what she meant. I'd give owt to be able to talk to our Ruby now.'

'I'm sure she understands,' said Maddie.

'And if ever I find a way, I will,' said Mrs Sykes. Her husband took her elbow.

'Come on, love. What we need now is a nice cup of tea.'

'Aye, well,' she said with a sigh, 'your Alice left the ham sandwiches and everything ready. Where's she got to now?'

There was no invitation to Maddie to come and eat the funeral tea, and she was relieved. As she reached the foot of the lane leading up to Scapegoat she could not help noticing the rowan tree. Someone had been lopping it, and Maddie stared at the resinous sap oozing from the cut branch. It seemed for all the world like blood seeping from a wound.

Outside the lych gate, Hilary Westerley-Kent sat waiting for the chauffeur to open the car door. She looked at her son's pale face in concern.

'You bore up well, Richard,' she said approvingly, 'but I

think you need some diversion while you're home on leave. Doesn't do to brood.'

Richard shrugged but made no answer. His mother continued relentlessly. 'You found that Renshaw girl quite sympathetic, I remember, so why not call on her, just for a chat and a cup of tea? She must be very tied to that place with her father so ill – I'm sure she'd be glad of a visitor.'

He mumbled something as he pulled on his peaked cap, then held out his arms to her. 'Here, let me support you while the wheelchair's put in.'

She ignored the waiting chauffeur. 'Listen to me, Richard. You need diversion. You weren't well even before this dreadful thing happened. I don't want you ill on my hands. I've got enough on my mind worrying about your sister.'

She stood swaying in his arms, looking up at him anxiously. Richard clicked his tongue.

'Oh, for pity's sake, Mother, I'll be all right.'

'But you will go and see her? She's a very sensible, down-to-earth girl, and I know she'll help.'

'All right then. Now let's get you into the car.'

Back at Thorpe Gill Hilary found her husband in the drawing room. He lowered his newspaper to smile at her.

'Hello, love. Just got back from London half an hour ago. How did Richard take it?'

'Very well, in the circumstances. But I'm worried about him, Reginald. And I'm concerned about Joanna too. I haven't heard from her for weeks.'

'You'll never stop being the anxious mother, will you? You fret too much, my love. No news is good news. Now let's have a nice pot of tea and you can tell me what's been happening while I've been away.'

'I'm serious, Reginald. There's something wrong with Joanna, I'm sure of it, and I wish I knew what it was.'

In a little teashop in Marlow Joanna gazed out of the window gloomily at the willow trees overhanging the sun-dappled river, but she was unaware of the beauty of the day. Two flies were crawling lazily around the dusty pane.

'Oh, come on, Joanna,' said her friend Mabel. 'It probably isn't what you think. I know, I've been late so often it doesn't bother me any more.'

Joanna prodded the cream cake around the plate with her fork and grunted. 'Not as late as I am. Nigel won't want to know anything about it – he's told me often enough, and God knows how my parents will react if I tell them. Pack me off to my Aunt Rebecca's or something so as not to bring disgrace.'

Mabel eyed her curiously. 'You don't know for certain yet, do you? Or have you been holding out on me?'

'Certain as I can be, short of seeing the M.O. Oh God, what a mess I've got myself into!'

Mabel sighed. 'In that case you've only got two choices. Get Nigel to marry you, or tell your parents. You can't cope with a baby on your own, that's for sure.'

Joanna stared at the café window, watching the two flies. Both of Mabel's solutions were unpalatable, but something had to be done. The flies began a slow descent towards the windowsill. For some reason the larger one, the bluebottle, made her think of Nigel, big, dominating and overbearingly selfish. She made a sudden decision. If the bluebottle reached the bottom of the pane first, she would speak to Nigel, coax and plead with him. If the smaller fly won, it would be Mother she had to tackle . . .

Mabel sighed. 'We'll have to be setting off soon if we're going to get a share in that bottle of wine Jessica brought back off leave. I think I'll just have another slice of gateau or something while we're here. Let's see.' She flicked the menu out of the holder on the table and Joanna held her breath. The flies continued their tortuous, downward trek.

'What are you staring at?' asked Mabel, turning to look out of the window. 'I can't see anything.'

The bluebottle changed its mind and flew up to the top

278

of the window. The smaller fly reached the bottom and began investigating the windowsill. The die was cast.

'Nothing,' said Joanna. 'I've decided I'm going to write home tonight. Come on, let's pay the bill and go.'

Maddie stood against the drystone wall edging the upper meadow, looking down on the valley below and savouring the warmth of the sun on her bare, freckled arms. Then she became aware that Ronnie had paused in rounding up the sheep to stand and stare at her, and she felt embarrassed. His green eyes rested on the curve of her breast where the breeze pressed the thin shirt taut against her body.

His lips curved into a smile. 'As my old dad used to say, and he was a wise old bird, small-breasted women are the most passionate. Did you know that, little cousin?'

Maddie turned away, whistling to Dog. Ronnie, undeterred, went on. 'And passionate women's the only kind I'm interested in. My mother was flat-chested, and yours too.'

Irritation flooded her. 'Don't talk about my mother. You didn't know her.'

He shrugged. 'I seen pictures of her. I guess the old saying was true in her case.'

'Shut up,' snapped Maddie. 'You don't know what you're talking about! She wasn't like that.'

He laughed, a deep, mocking laugh. 'How little you know, Cousin Maddie. She was wild and wilful, not like my mother – she was dull and conventional and boring. Lily was a scatterbrain, she used to say, a feckless woman who'd drive a man nuts.'

Maddie turned and flared at him. 'No, she wasn't! She was capable and determined. She never gave way to despair, an optimist, she was, and she'd be appalled to see you. She was a real lady.'

He was shaking with silent laughter. 'You little fool – you've no idea, have you? All these years you've been idealizing the memory of a woman who isn't worth it.'

'Shut up! Don't you dare try and spoil my memories! I'm off back down to the farm.'

Seething with rage, Maddie turned and ran down the meadow, Dog racing after her.

Hilary laid the letter aside with a deep sigh. Her husband reached across the table and put a hand over hers.

'I know. It's a terrible blow, my love, but it isn't the end of the world. We'll sort something out.'

She pulled her hand away. 'You mean I will. You have your mind filled with London and Latchmere House. It's up to me, as always.'

He gave a rueful smile. 'You have a knack, that's why. The children know, as I do, that you're the strongest of us all, wheelchair or no wheelchair. We all lean heavily on you.'

Hilary refolded the letter and replaced it in the envelope. 'He must be a spineless creature, this Nigel, not shouldering his responsibilities like a man. I suppose I could tackle his father, but there seems little point in forcing the boy to marry her if he's so weak.'

She clicked her tongue in annoyance. 'As if I didn't have enough on my hands now that Archie Botton insists on retiring. Now I've got to find someone to replace him, take over the horses and relieve me.'

'What about that gardener fellow – what's his name?'

'Vernon? He's useless with horses, and anyway, he smokes too much. He'd probably set fire to the barn and endanger their lives as well as his own. No, it's got to be somebody younger, someone who knows and loves horses as I do and who'll take over the business.'

'Ah, well, maybe I can help there,' said Reginald.

'I should hope so. You've got more contacts than I have. You can't leave everything to me.'

Reginald ran a finger down his nose, a far-away look in his eyes. 'Someone connected with horses – there was somebody recently, I feel sure . . .'

'My first priority is to make enquiries to get Joanna into a private nursing home and arrange for an abortion. I'll leave the rest to you. You think you might be able to come up with somebody then?'

'There was someone – I can't just remember. Let me check my records when I get back to Latchmere House next week.'

'And maybe you could find time to go down and see Joanna – she's not far from you, is she?'

'Thirty or forty miles, I'd say.'

'Reassure her we'll see to things. Oh Reginald, I feel so tired.'

He looked at her drawn face with concern. For the first time he could see the lines of care and age beginning to etch her handsome features, and the complacency bred in him over the years began to slip a little. Joanna's careless mistake and Richard's strangely distant behaviour were both understandable and transient, it was to be hoped, but for Hilary to let the reins of government slip from her hands and to admit to weariness . . . An uneasy feeling began to flicker in his veins.

Ronnie, having ridden Robin out on the moor to round up the sheep, was making an excellent job of clipping them. As Maddie passed by the meadows, trying not to catch his eye, she could not help noticing the deft expertise of his calloused hands which spoke of years of practice. Now had he been her father or Max she would have been close by, folding and rolling the fleeces and stacking them neatly into a pile . . .

It was during the evenings, however, that she found it impossible to avoid Ronnie's company, and it was a relief as well as a complete surprise when Richard Westerley-Kent came to call.

'I don't want to talk about what's happened, Maddie,' he said shortly as he stood, cap in hand, by the kitchen table,

281

unaware of Ronnie's scrutiny, 'only to have your company for a while.'

'Of course. Sit down, Richard.'

There was an embarrassed silence for a moment. She was unwilling to introduce Ronnie, much less to admit he was her cousin. Fortunately Ronnie, having eyed over the newcomer with ill-concealed contempt, finally rose and trudged outside. Eva looked Richard over curiously.

'You from Thorpe Gill?' she asked.

'Yes.'

'Thought so. Officer's uniform. Eunice told me about you.'

Maddie intervened. 'Eva, Mr Westerley-Kent doesn't want to chat – he wants a rest. Go out and play for a while, there's a good girl.'

Eva pouted. 'Don't want to. He's out there. Can I put some records on instead – I promise I won't make a noise?'

Maddie looked across at Richard's vacant expression. He suddenly started.

'Music? Yes, I'd like that,' he murmured. 'Music.'

Poor Richard, thought Maddie as she pored over the gramophone records for something restful. He was taking Ruby's death very badly.

Beethoven. That had been one of Mother's favourites. Maddie wiped the surface of the record clean of grease and placed it carefully on the turntable. Scratchy music filled the air. Eva listened for a moment, pulled a face, and went upstairs. Dog trotted after her.

Richard, seated in the armchair, leaned his head against the chairback and closed his eyes. Not once had he seemed to notice the old man in the bed. As the music gathered speed Maddie saw his fingertips beating time on the arm of the chair, then he opened his eyes and stared at the ceiling, a strange, desperate expression almost amounting to ecstasy in his blue eyes. Poor Richard. He had a face as innocent as a flower's and transparent as Eva's.

As the sonata ended he rose abruptly to his feet. 'Thank you. I'm going home now,' he said.

'So soon? You've only just come?'

'I must go. I'm grateful to you, Maddie. Goodnight.'

And he was gone. Maddie picked up Eva's cardigan and started to sew on a button. When Ronnie came back into the kitchen there was a wry smile on his lips. 'Your friend didn't stay long,' he remarked drily.

'I don't think he's well,' said Maddie.

'Well? He's crazy as a dingbat, he is! Best not have him here again, little cousin – I'd say he'd got shellshock only I know he's never been into battle.'

'He's had a rough time,' Maddie argued. 'He's just lost his fiancée.'

'I tell you he's a nutcase. Let his own people have the worry of him, not us.'

'He's a friend,' said Maddie. 'People ought to help their friends.'

'People ought to help themselves first. I don't want to see him here again. You got that?'

Maddie stabbed the needle forcibly into the cardigan and felt it sink into her finger. She let the sewing fall on her lap. 'Hold on a minute – I think you're forgetting something, Ronnie. This is my home. I say who I want here, not you. If Richard wants to come and visit, then he can, whether you like it or not.'

Ronnie's eyes glinted as he leaned forward, his face thrust into hers. 'Oh no, he can't. I'm the man of the house and what I say goes. Neither him nor any other fellow comes here. Have I made myself clear?'

Anger burned like fire in Maddie's throat. 'Now just you look here,' she said with quiet emphasis. 'Ever since you came here you've been trying to take over this place. Well, I won't have it. You're not master here, and never will be. You've got your own farm to go back to once the war's over.'

'It isn't mine.'

'It will be one day, when your father dies.'

'He's dead. Died a year last Christmas.'

Maddie stared, mystified. 'Well then –'

'He didn't leave it to me.'

'Didn't he leave you anything?'

Ronnie's face registered a strange expression. 'Oh yes, he left me something all right. A letter.'

'A letter? What letter?'

'One I'd sent him years before. One where I told him what I thought about him, what a mean old skinflint he was, and how nobody would give a shit when he died. The cunning old bastard. He gave it to his solicitor with instructions that it was to be given back to me when he died. And that's all he left me, the vicious old bugger.'

'I'm sorry,' said Maddie. 'But you can't have Scapegoat. It's ours.'

'For the time being, maybe.'

'What do you mean by that?'

He took a deep breath. 'I mean one way or another it will be mine, see? So you might as well get used to the idea.'

Maddie sprang to her feet, the cardigan slithering to the floor. 'I think you'd best get out of here – now,' she raged. 'Get out before I fetch the police to you!'

'You wouldn't do that, little cousin.' There was a curl of amusement on his lips which infuriated her.

'Oh yes I would! Then we'd be free of you!'

The smile slid away. He turned and walked over to the cupboard under the stairs and took out the gun, then turned back to face her. 'If you do that, little cousin, then I tell you this. There'll be a bloodbath. I wouldn't give in easy, I promise you. They'd have to shoot me – but not before I got you and the kid and your old man first.'

The cold, malevolent look in Ronnie's green eyes showed only too clearly that he was in deadly earnest. For the first time in her life Maddie knew real fear. She looked helplessly down at her hands and saw the smear of blood on her fingertip.

There was a small body curled up in Maddie's bed when she went upstairs. By the light of the candle she could see large eyes surveying her over the top of the sheet.

'I heard him shouting,' Eva whispered. 'What's he mad about? Is it me?'

'No, love. It's nothing. His bark's worse than his bite.'

She saw the little body shiver. 'I don't like him. Can I stay here with you?'

'Yes, if you like, just for tonight. But there's nothing to worry about, really there isn't.' Maddie wished she could feel the conviction she mouthed.

She nipped out the candle and slipped into bed. Warm arms encircled her neck. 'I wish he was dead,' murmured a sleepy voice. 'Please God, make him be dead soon.'

CHAPTER TWENTY-THREE

Hilary clapped her hands together in surprise as the new-comer entered the drawing room.

'So you are the Mr Bower my husband told me about! I should have recognized the name. You used to work at the Renshaw place – you came here once with the mare!'

Max inclined his head. 'It is good to see you again, madam.'

She surveyed him up and down with appreciation. 'You have put on some weight, I see, and that's no bad thing. Quite undernourished, you were, when you came here that time. I remember you well, Mr Bower, and the fact that you knew how to handle my stallion.'

'I am honoured,' he replied. 'And also that you wish me to work with your horses. I know how deeply you care about them.'

She nodded. 'My stable has had to be cut down to four horses since the war started, but I am anxious to breed more again. I was dubious about handing them over to a stranger, but my husband told me the new man used to work with the world-famous Lipizzan horses, and now I see who it is, I am confident that I have made the right decision.'

'I shall endeavour to honour your trust.'

Hilary sighed. 'There are so many other matters on my mind that I am glad to be able to hand over my horses to someone I can trust, and I do trust you, Mr Bower, though I know little about you beyond the fact that you are an Austrian refugee. Bower is not an Austrian name though.'

'It was spelt Bauer before I changed it by deed poll.'

'And where did you live?'

'My home was in Vienna – '

'Ah, Vienna! A beautiful city! I visited it once, on my honeymoon. Such elegant buildings and beautiful fountains – *Kaiserlich, koniglich* they called it. I remember walking down those lovely tree-lined streets and in the Prater Park, wasn't it? And there was music and laughter everywhere, I remember.'

'That was in the old days, madam, in the time of the old empire, before the Nazis came. Vienna was no longer a city of laughter afterwards.'

She searched his thin, handsome face. 'Of course, you are Jewish. That is why you had to flee. And your family – you have a family?'

The penetrating black eyes lowered. 'My father died when the Nazis burned down his bookshop.'

'He died in the fire?'

'No. He was found dead outside in the street. It could have been a heart attack when he saw what they had done to his precious books.'

'And your mother?'

'My mother and sister were taken away to a concentration camp. I never heard from them again.'

'But you were not taken.'

'I was away from home, at the equestrian school. I escaped over the border to safety.'

For a moment she regarded him thoughtfully, then cleared her throat.

'I don't know whether my husband told you, Mr Bower, but there is a small cottage available. My former stableman, Archie, retired and went to live with his sister in Guisborough. You may have the use of it if you so require, rent-free of course.'

There was a hint of a smile as he bowed his head. 'You are most kind. I am grateful.'

'You'll find it beyond the stables – go and settle yourself in now, and we'll talk again in the morning. I am beginning to feel fatigued, and so must you after your journey. Goodnight, Mr Bower.'

She watched him turn to go and felt a deep and indescribable sadness. Here was a man she could admire and respect, without truly understanding why or questioning it. Somewhere, from the back of her mind, came words she must have read or heard somewhere long ago.

If I ever forget thee, my Jerusalem, may my hand lose its cunning and my tongue cleave to the roof of my mouth.

Max placed his battered suitcase down on the little sofa and went to look out of the window at the sun dipping over the ridge. He had not planned to return to Barnbeck, not without a berth and a clear-cut plan for the future, but life had a strange way of making decisions one had not contemplated. It was almost too overwhelming a dream to allow oneself to dally with – horses, security, and the proximity of the one person he had come across in this alien land who gave succour to his soul . . .

Even on the train journey here he had felt the first flickerings of hope as the fertile femininity of the southern countryside swathed in the lush green heat of an English summer receded behind him. Mile after mile spun past the soot-grained window, until the view began to give way to greyer, harsher vistas where men had to struggle to wrest a living, and he almost felt that he was coming home.

The little cottage looked cosy enough, and Max was eager to breathe clean, fresh air and rid his lungs of London smoke. The prospect of earning a living from exercising horses on those high, wild moors filled him with pleasure. He opened the cottage door and walked out into the warmth of the sunset.

Now, at last, life was holding out hope again. With the thought an image flitted into his mind, a vision of a tawny-haired girl seated alone in a twilit room, and the image heightened the flicker of hope. He clung fiercely to the image, rejecting the hateful thoughts. It was as though his mind had been lying in wait for this memory . . . But would she welcome him back now, after a year had gone by and after the way he had left her? Would her father even let him come near Scapegoat Farm?

He should not have gone away go abruptly, not taking the time to try to explain his hurt to her. Even if the villagers would never accept him, maybe she, in the wisdom of her innocence, would find it in her heart to forgive him. It was not going to be easy, trying to make amends now, but more than anything in the world he wanted to soothe away the pain he must have caused her, to bring her close again, a loved and trusted friend.

The last crimson rays of the setting sun spread out along the ridge like some great, glorious sunburst. Max paused, leaning against a drystone wall to watch. Suddenly a figure cut into the sunburst, and his heart leapt. It was the figure of a girl on horseback, riding fast so that her hair streamed loose behind her. Within seconds she had vanished from sight, over the crest of the hill in the direction of the moors. It was the Valkyrie, the figure which had welcomed him on his first arrival in Barnbeck more than a year and a half ago, and his heart thudded. It was an omen. Perhaps, with luck, she would welcome his return after all . . .

Maddie rode wildly, urging Duster on and far away from Scapegoat. Her mind was humming like a hive of swarming bees, tangles, inexplicable thoughts. All she was aware of was that they had delved into regions they should never have ventured to explore, and the consequences had left her stunned and fearful.

It was all Doreen Sykes's doing, she and poor Edna Pickering. The two women had trudged up the hill to Scapegoat after tea, carrying a brown paper parcel and begging Maddie's help. It was impossible to refuse two such sad-eyed bereaved mothers. Eva had regarded the parcel with evident interest until Doreen jerked her head in the child's direction and spoke across her in a loud whisper.

'Best if we didn't have someone's company,' she hissed. 'This business is only for adults.'

'I don't care,' said Eva, tossing her plaits. 'I'll go down the stables and talk to Duster.'

When the child had gone out, Doreen set about unpacking the parcel and bringing out a three-cornered board with a hole in each corner. Edna, twitching nervously, went to have a look at the old man in the bed and then returned to the table.

'Shame about your dad, Maddie,' she murmured.

'Our Alice brought this round,' said Doreen, laying the board down reverently. 'She reckons we can get in touch with our loved ones like she did.'

'What is it?' Maddie was intrigued, watching as Doreen wedged a pencil into one of the holes, then spread a sheet of white paper on the table and placed the board over it.

'She called it a planchette. Now, all we have to do is sit round the table, one hand on the planchette, and all of us think of the dead person we want to contact. Then we can ask the planchette a question.'

'And the pencil will write a message,' added Edna. 'Isn't that what she said? Oh Doreen, do you think we should? I'm starting to come over all creepy.'

'Don't be soft,' said Doreen. 'You want to get in touch with your Norman, don't you? So sit down – and you too, Maddie. I thought of you 'cos you have a dead relative, though it's a fair while since your mam died, I know. Never mind, the more the better, our Alice says. Put your finger on like us.'

Maddie hesitated. Ronnie was down in the barn feeding the pigs and it could not be long before he returned. Still, he could hardly complain about two middle-aged ladies coming to call. She looked at Edna's face, white and eager, then took her place at the table.

The late sun was casting low beams aslant the flagstoned floor and the three heads bent over the board. Doreen spoke in a hushed, reverential tone.

'Is anybody there? Do you want to tell us anything? If you're there, spell out your name.'

Nothing moved, not the board nor the pencil nor the women. In the distance a dog barked. Maddie found it hard to concentrate on anything, especially Mother; somehow a dark-skinned face with sombre, brooding black eyes kept intervening in her mind.

Edna was fidgeting. 'Nothing's happening, Doreen,' she whispered.

'Probably 'cos you're not concentrating. Think hard about your Norman.'

For several minutes only the ticking of the clock on the sideboard broke the silence in the kitchen. Then Edna's lips parted.

'I can feel Norman's near. He is, he's near.'

Doreen frowned. 'Speak to me, love,' she murmured in a voice charged with urgency. 'Speak to me, Ruby! Tell me all's well with you and you've no more pain.'

Maddie felt her finger, pressed hard on the board, beginning to grow numb. Edna, her eyes tightly closed, muttered under her breath.

'Oh Norman, love! I want to know you don't feel terrible, shut in down there in the dark – are you all right, love?'

Suddenly Maddie stiffened. The board was beginning to lift under her hand, to jerk and sway as if it had a life of its own. At the same moment she heard the hiss of indrawn breath as the others gasped.

'It's moving!'

'Hush!'

The board sprang and writhed in a staccato, clumsy dance, then shuddered and lay still. The women stared at the sheet of paper and the scrawl left by the pencil. Suddenly the door opened and Ronnie stood there. His mouth set in a tight line when he caught sight of the strangers.

'What the devil's going on here?' he demanded.

No one answered. Maddie twisted her head round to try

to decipher the scrawl. Her heart leapt in her throat as she read the words.

For God's sake let me rest!

Doreen blanched and Edna began to sob. 'Whatever does it mean?' Doreen whispered.

'It's evil – I told you we shouldn't!' Edna's voice was no more than a whimper.

Maddie heard the crash of her own chair as she leapt to her feet and then she was aware of nothing more till she found herself high on the moor, riding hard through the night to escape the terrible unknown shadow that overhung Scapegoat.

Memory stabbed like a wound. Mother's voice came softly on the wind, crystal-clear and urgent.

'*We must find the answer from within ourselves.*'

Next morning Eva was helping in the cowshed, deft fingers milking the udders while she grumbled to Maddie.

'Whatever got into you last night, rushing off out like that? There I were, talking to Duster, and you came rushing in and took her off without a blooming word.'

'I'm sorry, love,' said Maddie quietly. 'I was a bit upset.'

'You might well be. That Mrs Sykes . . . Still, it were me was copped it after you'd gone,' Eva muttered. 'Right miserable bugger he were.'

'Ronnie, you mean?'

'Aye, grousing about you having strangers in and telling him nowt about it. Who does he think he is, miserable sod? I tell you this, if he don't clear off soon, then I will.'

'Don't be silly, love. Come on, help me fill up the churns and then we'd best get started on the chickens.'

'I wish I were back at school, then I wouldn't have to put up with him. Mr Bower never clipped me round the ear like what he does.'

A handsome face with sloe-black eyes and high cheek-bones leapt into Maddie's mind, and the liquid, mellow sound of his voice. She pushed the memory aside and sent Eva back indoors to fetch chicken feed.

The chickens fed and milk churns stacked ready by the gate at last, she went back into the house. Eva was standing staring miserably out of the window. Her nose trailed, snail-like, across the pane, leaving a smear of wet.

'It's Gooseberry Fair today. Are you going down?'

'I don't think so, love. I've the washing to do.'

Eva turned away from the window and sighed. 'It must be rotten being old like you. Nothing exciting to do. Must be even worse if you're really ancient like Mr Renshaw, all falling to bits.'

She walked across to the bed in the corner. The old man's face twitched as if attempting to smile. Eva patted his hand. 'You haven't got Lassie to keep you company, have you, since he come here? He's no business to take our Lassie away all the time.' She turned to Maddie. 'Well I'm going out before he comes back.' There was a defiant tone in the girl's voice.

'It's coming on to rain. Where are you going?'

'Just out. It's too wet to go to my little house.'

'Little house? Where's that?'

'It's a secret. Nobody knows, not even Eunice.'

'You going to meet Eunice?'

'She's busy.'

Maddie watched the small, dejected figure as she picked her way through the muddy farmyard towards the gate. Poor Eva. There was little joy in the child's life since Cousin Ronnie had come to Scapegoat. She could understand Eva's need for a private place, a tree-house or tunnel in the undergrowth where she could feel safe.

Maddie sighed and put a saucepan of milk on the fire to boil for the bread sops Dad seemed to favour for breakfast these days. Soon it would be time to ladle the steaming water out of the range boiler into the washtub to start on the week's washing. She sighed again. If the rain came down in earnest then Ronnie was going to grumble loudly

293

yet again about wet washing hung up on the creel to dry. Already she could visualize the handsome face stiffening as he entered and the harsh light leaping into those sharp green eyes . . .

But it was Eva who came home first that afternoon, bursting into the kitchen with a wild whoop and flinging herself on Maddie in a fierce hug. 'I seen him!' she cried ecstatically. 'He's back home again! I seen him outside the blacksmith's!'

Maddie disengaged herself and the armful of wet vests from Eva's clutching arms. 'Seen who, love? Mind out, or you'll trip over the washboard. I should have put it away.'

'Mr Bower – I seen him taking a horse to get new shoes! Oh, Maddie! He's back – he'll not let that bugger belt me any more, I know he won't! Will he be coming back to our barn, do you think?'

Maddie let the pile of washing fall on the table and sat down abruptly. 'Mr Bower? Oh no, you can't have – it must have been somebody else, love. Mr Bower's a long way away.'

'No he's not – he's here! You ask Betty!'

'Who's she?'

'You know – kid from the vicarage. Mind you, you can't trust owt she sees – she's as cross-eyed as me Auntie Molly were, and she were blind as a bat. But I did see him, and I know Mr Bower better nor anybody. It were him, Maddie, honest it were.'

Maddie chewed her lip, unwilling to believe too readily what might turn out to be only the child's wishful thinking, but hope leapt unbidden. 'Are you sure, though – did you speak to him?'

The child's face fell. 'No, I couldn't – Mrs Spivey came out and grabbed me. She made me pick up all the toffee papers on her front door step, and it weren't all me. Betty bought the toffees and she only give me one. It weren't fair, but Mrs Spivey wouldn't listen. By the time she let me go he were gone.'

Eva's excited chatter only dried up when Ronnie came in and sat down at the table to be served with his evening meal, heedless of the trail of mud left by his boots.

'Raining cats and dogs out there,' he grunted. 'I could see tents down in the village – some sort of jamboree going on, I reckon, but they must have got rained off, whatever it was.'

No one answered. Maddie served up the food and he ate without attempting to speak again. Eva kept her attention firmly fixed on her plate until the meal was ended.

After Eva was safely tucked up in bed that night the picture she had drawn still glowed vividly in Maddie's mind. She could see him, tall and darkly mysterious, his black eyes serious as he handed over a horse to be shod.

But how could he be here in Barnbeck? Whose horse was it? And if he were, why had he not tried to contact her? The whole idea was preposterous. It was much more likely that Eva, in her desperate need to be rescued from the tyranny of Ronnie, had conjured up the vision of her hero. Maddie smiled to herself. It was just like those far-off days when, as a child, she too had called on her friend, the imaginary Jamie who had no substance except that born of her need, to whom she could pour out the secret hopes and fears of her heart. Jamie had always had a ready ear to listen.

Ronnie put down the paper he was reading and stretched his arms above his head. 'Rain seems to have eased off at last,' he remarked. 'I'm off for some shut-eye. Want to be up early to make a start on reshaping this place.'

Maddie looked up sharply. 'Reshape what?'

He gave a short laugh and got up from his chair, coming over to stand by her. 'There you go again, coming over all bossy. Look here, Maddie, I know how to make this place pay. Why don't you just let me get on with it – tell you what, let's get married then we'll both be the boss here.'

'I'm in charge here – I've told you,' she replied quietly. 'That way there'll be no argument.'

'I'm not arguing. I'm telling you.'

'But you didn't say no. Think about it, Maddie. As Mrs Ronnie Whittaker you'll have a protector and a free farm worker. Can't be bad.'

'I'm going out.' She stood up and walked with slow deliberation to the door and took her jacket from the peg.

'That's right, girl, take a walk and think of the advantages. Then in the morning we'll fix the date.'

He pulled off his boots and made for the stairs. Slamming the door behind her Maddie went out into the night.

Max had taken much pleasure in the day despite the rain. It would take time to win the trust of Firefly and Vulcan and the two mares, but it had been a good opportunity to begin the acquaintanceship with Firefly, taking him to be shod. And considering how forcefully the villagers had bidden him farewell a year ago, waylaying him on the dark lane the night he left, he had been pleasantly surprised by their lack of animosity today.

True, they had been rather preoccupied with their festival in the sodden marquee, but none had glared at him and one or two had even granted him a curt nod. The big and powerful blacksmith, laconic at the start, had become gruffly affable by the time Firefly's shoeing was complete.

Mrs Westerley-Kent had sent word she wanted to see him before she went to bed. Max left the cottage to cross the stable yard towards the house. Muffled in blackout with sandbags piled high outside the main door and no sound issuing from within, it seemed like a house of the dead. Strange how this wartime blackout could affect the brain, he reflected, making even one's thoughts seem as if wrapped up in straw.

Mrs Westerley-Kent sat alone in the drawing room already wearing a dressing gown and sipping a cup of Horlicks. Beside her a standard lamp cast a soft light on her face, and he could see the lines of fatigue.

'Ah, Mr Bower,' she murmured, laying the cup aside

'Have you found the cottage to your liking? Is it comfortable enough? I know Archie was very spartan in his ways – you know what crusty old bachelors can be like.'

'It is very comfortable indeed.'

'We could do something about brightening it up, I suppose. New curtains for a start, only in these days of coupons – '

'There is no need, but I appreciate your thoughtfulness.'

'Make do and mend, they tell us. That's an idea – we have spare curtains here in Thorpe Gill which we don't need. Cut down, they would suit the cottage perfectly. Joanna could do that, and add a few other feminine touches to the place for you.'

'Joanna?' He was startled. He had believed her away at some army camp.

'Yes, she came home today. I'm planning a little holiday for her and myself shortly – at my sister-in-law's in Harrogate – but that won't be for a week or so. She can make herself useful in the meantime.'

'A holiday will be of great benefit to you, madam.'

She sighed. 'Yes, I think I am in need of a rest. Children are always a source of worry to a mother, however old they may be.'

'I'm sorry to hear that.'

She leaned back in her chair and regarded him thoughtfully for a moment. 'It's funny how I feel I can talk to you, a stranger. You ask no questions, you simply accept.'

He bowed his head in acknowledgement of the compliment but remained standing stiffly before her. She closed her eyes. 'There is no one else I'd tell that my son is sick, and I fear for him. And Joanna is the cause of much concern to me. She is like a wild filly, Mr Bower, a filly as yet unbroken. Somehow I failed her. She needs a man well versed in managing untamed fillies, to break and school her and keep her on a long rein.'

He was still standing, silent and eyes downcast, when the door opened and Joanna entered. For a second her eyes

297

gleamed and her mouth opened when she caught sight of him, and then she turned her back on him.

Hilary smiled at her daughter. 'I was just telling Mr Bower, our new stableman, that you would probably enjoy riding while you're at home, dear. Help him exercise the horses.'

Joanna turned slowly and surveyed him, her eyes travelling up and down again. 'Indeed,' she said in a slow, affected drawl, 'life is pretty tedious in this dull place and I must confess I do become rather bored. It might be quite fun for us to ride together.'

She was staring straight into his eyes, challenging and mocking. Max's gaze slid away, but he was sure that her mother's sharp eyes were missing nothing of the interchange between them.

'If you will excuse me now,' he said stiffly. He could feel the two women's eyes still on his back as he left the room. It was a relief to escape the claustrophobia of the place and get back out into the damp summer night. He decided to take a walk around the grounds before going back to the cottage and bed.

The grass was wet underfoot and although the rain had stopped droplets still fell from the branches overhead on his face as he walked. He turned a corner and crossed the lawn to the gravel path, then suddenly he felt the hairs rise on the back of his neck and had a strange sensation that he was not alone. He stood stock-still, straining his eyes in the gloom, and then he saw it. A shadowy figure detached itself from the yew hedge and moved silently across the lawn towards the boundary wall.

His heart leapt. The figure was familiar, he was sure of it, a girl's slight figure. He hurried towards it, arms outstretched. 'Maddie?'

The shadow stopped and turned. A voice came softly in the darkness.

'Yes.'

CHAPTER TWENTY-FOUR

The moon emerged from behind a high bank of cloud and he could see her face, small and pearly-pale. She looked up with a shy half-smile.

'I didn't mean you to catch me, snooping around in the grounds here like a burglar. I'm sorry. I didn't mean to pry, but I had to know . . .'

Without thinking he took hold of her hands, conscious of the odd excitement within him, like a tingling under the skin.

'Maddie – how are you? Are you well?'

He searched her face, looking for a sign of pleasure, the innocent betrayal that she had missed him. She shifted awkwardly from one foot to the other.

'Whatever must you be thinking of me?' she murmured. 'I meant to go down to the marquee, but I had to find out whether Eva was right. She said she saw you at the smithy today.'

'Eva? Is she well too?' It wasn't what he wanted to say, but somehow her sudden appearance had thrown him into a spin.

Maddie shrugged. 'She's fine. She was thrilled to bits about you. I didn't know whether to believe her.'

'So you came to see for yourself,' he said, and he felt touched by her caring. 'Does that mean you forgive me?'

'What for?' She sounded awkward and ill at ease.

'You know full well – the way I left here, no explanations, and I owed you that at least.'

'You didn't owe me anything.' There was a stiffness in her tone, a defiance he had not expected. 'If you thought you did, why didn't you visit me?'

299

Her eyes were not meeting his. He cleared his throat. 'In time I intended to, but after what your father said to me –'

She broke free from his hands. 'Oh, that was all a long time ago. A lot of water has gone under the bridge since then, Max. Things change.'

'I was forbidden his house,' he reminded her. 'I couldn't push in again uninvited.'

'Not even when you knew I wanted to see you?' Her blue eyes challenged his now. He smiled gently.

'Now that I know that, I will come, Maddie.'

She gave a shy half-smile. 'I must go home. It's late.'

She turned and he walked alongside her. At the gate she stopped and faced him. 'Don't come any further, Max. I'll go back alone.'

He took her hands in his again. She looked so small and vulnerable in the moonlight, but there was a wariness about her now that he did not remember. The child was growing up. For long seconds they stood without speaking and the silence flowed between them like waves lapping on the shore, giving a sense of peace. Then she withdrew her hands.

'Goodnight, Max. I'm glad you're back.'

And she fled up the lane, fading quickly from his sight like some fragile wraith dissolving back into the miasma which gave it birth.

Over the course of the next few days Max found that although he was fully occupied with the horses, his mind could not shake off the image of Maddie. He must see her again soon.

Vulcan seemed to be having trouble with a hind leg as he rode down from the moor. Max dismounted to have a look. He had just removed the cause of the trouble, a small pebble lodged in Vulcan's hind hoof, when a stocky man with a stubble of beard came striding across the heather.

'You the stableman from Thorpe Gill?' he demanded.

300

'My name's Bailey – my farm's over there. Know owt about calves?'

'A little,' Max admitted.

'Only our vet's away. Come and have a look at my poorly calf.'

Max followed him, leading Vulcan by the rein. Stooping to enter the ramshackle shed he saw the calf lying on its side in the straw. 'It's not really my job,' he murmured. 'Still, let's have a look.'

He bent over the animal, running his fingers over its belly and noting its dull eyes. 'Has he been eating as he usually does?' he enquired. The farmer shrugged.

'He were off his grub a day or two back, but he's keeping it down again now.'

'I see. You know if a calf is prone to colic it's best to get rid of it early on. Still, there doesn't seem to be much wrong with him now.'

'Reckon I need to send for the vet from Otterley then or not?' asked Bailey.

'I don't think so. He's over the worst, from what you tell me.'

'Nowt special I should do, then? Could have saved meself the trouble of running after you, couldn't I? Still, I'm grateful to you. There won't be no fee then, seeing as you've prescribed nowt.'

'No,' said Max. 'No fee.'

'Didn't you used to work at the Renshaw place? I seem to recall your face.'

'A year ago, yes. Now I work at Thorpe Gill.'

'Mrs Westerley-Kent must think well of you to let you handle them Clevelands of hers. Expect you worked with them at Scapegoat. Nowadays it'll be that new farmhand, the fellow none of us can get a word out of, old Renshaw being laid up as he is.'

Max frowned. 'Laid up? What is this expression?'

'Laid up – you know, bedfast. Never been the same, hasn't Scapegoat Jim, since that stroke. It's young Maddie and the new fellow does all the work now, and he's only tenpence to the shilling, they tell me. Still, she's a sturdy little lass for all she looks so scrawny. Pretty lass and all, that Maddie Renshaw. Aye, he's never walked again, hasn't Renshaw, and they tell me he never will.'

Max emerged from the shed into the sunlight. Bailey followed him. 'Aye, well, I'd best be getting back down to the meadow – harvesting, we are, and them silly devils are sure to bugger up my tractor if I don't keep an eye on 'em. Much obliged to you. Good day.'

Max took up Vulcan's reins. The horse walked easily beside him to the gate, no trace now of a limp. If only all problems could be cured so easily . . .

His ears would have burned if he could have overheard the conversation down in the lower meadow.

'That Jerry's back,' said Bailey. 'You know, that one that used to be at Scapegoat. Working at Thorpe Gill now. Just seen him.'

'Oh, him. Fellow that pinched that watch,' grunted old Seth.

'We don't know as he did. It's Fred who says that. Any road, he can't be such a bad bloke – he knows about calves. Just told me what were wrong with mine.'

'What made you ask him?'

Bailey bridled defensively. 'Vernon told me he were a vet. Anyway, Colonel's missus wouldn't let just anyone near her precious Clevelands.'

'True enough,' said the blacksmith. 'I like the look of the fellow, foreigner or not. Can't say the same about that funny bugger who's working at Renshaw's now – daft or not, he looks shifty to me.'

There was no comment from the other men as they stacked the cornsheaves. If the big blacksmith, rarely known to comment at all, liked the look of the Jerry then, as Bailey said, he couldn't be all bad.

* * *

Hilary watched as her daughter fastened the buttons on her blouse and then put on the neat navy skirt. Four months now. It wouldn't be long before she'd be unable to pull up that zip.

'Have you seriously thought, Joanna, about keeping the baby?'

Joanna glanced at her mother. 'That's a turn-up for the book. I thought you wanted the whole thing hushed up.'

'A natural first reaction, my dear, the shock and all that. But I've been thinking. It's what you want that really counts.'

'But I don't want to marry Nigel.'

'All right then, don't. But you could still have the baby and foster it out. Then when you do marry – '

Joanna swung round. 'Mother, really! Who do you think is going to take on another man's brat? No, I've got to get rid of it. Kids are a load of trouble anyway.'

'Don't I know it?' murmured her mother.

Seating herself at the dressing table Joanna began brushing out her hair with long, smooth strokes. After a moment she paused, looking at her mother's reflection in the mirror. 'Tell me, why the change of heart, Mother?'

'There must be lots of women who'd be glad to earn an extra few shillings a week fostering a child,' murmured Hilary. 'Not too far away, but far enough not to cause any embarrassment.'

Joanna laid down the brush and swung around. 'Out with it, Mother. I know you and your ways too well. Just what is going on in that scheming head of yours?'

'A grandchild, that's what. I want a grandchild to inherit what we've built up.'

Joanna stared. 'Can't it wait till I'm married – or Richard is? Why now?'

'Because I believe that the way Richard is, he'll never marry. No one wants a man with a psychiatric problem.'

'Then wait till I have a baby in wedlock.'

Hilary sighed and began wheeling her chair towards the

bedroom door. 'I'd like to, my dear, but I honestly don't think I have the time.'

Joanna sat staring, bereft of words, as the wheelchair glided away down the corridor. Mother, ill? Is that what she was saying, so ill that there was very little time left?

Or was she simply up to her old tricks again? Joanna sat toying with the hairbrush, tracing the leaf design etched in the silver-gilt back until the dinner gong sounded.

The stables mucked out and the horses fed and watered, Max was at last free of work for the day. Mrs Westerley-Kent had said he could go to the kitchens for his meals, but this evening he was in no mood to eat. A much greater hunger burned in him – the desire to see Maddie again.

She was in the little garden plot when he reached the top of the lane, kneeling in the evening sun to tend the plants. He stood by the chicken coop, just out of her sight but close enough to watch for a moment, unobserved, and take pleasure in the sight of her.

The scent of herbs filled the air, mint, sage, parsley and thyme. He watched small slim hands firming round young plantlings as she separated and transplanted them, and somehow there was infinite beauty in those earth-grained hands. He wanted to touch them, to lift them to his lips . . .

He took a step forward. 'Hello, Maddie,' he said gently, trying not to alarm her. He was so close now he could smell the sun on her warm flesh and see her skin browned with freckles. She turned her head, and he saw the light of pleasure that leapt into her eyes.

'Hello, Max. I hoped we'd meet again soon,' she said, rising and coming over towards him. She seated herself on the drystone wall, swinging her legs and never taking her eyes from his face. He leaned against the wall beside her, feeling the sun's warmth soaked into the old stone.

'I came outside. It was too hot in the kitchen. I've been baking,' she said. He could smell now the aroma of fresh-

304

aked bread drifting from the direction of the open doorway. She looked up at him shyly. 'I hoped this last year
you'd been all right. I thought about you often.'

She looked down again, letting her fair hair fall so that it
screened her face.

'Did you, Maddie?' said Max quietly.

'You didn't get a ship yet then?'

'No, not yet.'

'What are you doing at Thorpe Gill?'

'It's a long story. When they picked me up I was kept for
a long time in a house in London where they interrogate
aliens. The Colonel offered me a job working with his
horses.'

'With the Clevelands? Oh, how wonderful!'

The leg began to swing again, and the slim ankle
mesmerized him. She tossed back the curtain of hair. 'I was
afraid you might still be unhappy,' she murmured. 'I didn't
like to think that.'

He gave a short laugh. 'I was a fool, Maddie. I was like
the Flying Dutchman, sailing to the edge of doom and
believing I should never find peace.'

'And have you found it now?'

He shrugged. 'I think so. At least I no longer feel full of
hatred. The Buddhists say that he who feels hatred in his
heart has already murdered his brother – they call it murder
of the heart.'

'Funny, Eva said something like that once. She hated her
cousin, and he died,' said Maddie thoughtfully. 'She's a
strange child.'

'And a wise one,' rejoined Max.

'Yes. She's a smashing kid. I do hope she'll be happy.'

There was a wistful tone in her voice, a distant sound
which concerned him. He touched her hand lightly, and
she did not move it away.

'She will, I know. She's found someone to love and that
brings happiness.'

For a few moments she stared down at her swinging feet.

'Max, tell me something.' Her voice was small, tentative just as it had been when he came across her in Thorpe Gill's gardens. 'Have you found it – love, I mean?'

'I think so, Maddie. I have found her.'

He was reaching for her hand, already anticipating the feel of the grit on her fingertips, when a sudden voice cut through the still air.

'Maddie, what the devil you doing out here? I hope my flaming dinner's ready on the table.'

A tall, broad-shouldered young man with a tangled mass of blond curls came striding in at the gate. Max saw his green eyes scrutinizing him as he spoke to Maddie.

'Thank Christ the bloody harvest's nearly done. Takes twice as long without a tractor. We'll have to get one, girl.'

He strode on into the farmhouse. Maddie jumped down off the wall. 'I'll have to go, Max. He doesn't like being kept waiting.'

'Who is he?' asked Max. 'The new farmhand?'

Her eyes slid away from his. 'Yes – Ronnie – he's called. And he's good, especially with the sheep. I must go now, Max.'

'But we shall meet again, won't we?'

'Yes. Riding on the moors.'

She was hurrying away, across the yard. 'Tomorrow afternoon, two o'clock,' he called after her.

'Yes, yes, all right. On the ridge.'

In the kitchen Ronnie was poking a grubby finger into one of the loaves cooling on the wire tray. 'Who's he?' he asked, tearing a chunk off the end of the loaf as Maddie entered.

'The man I was talking to?'

'Who else? Who is he, and what's he doing here?'

'He's the stableman from Thorpe Gill. An old friend of mine.'

'We don't want no snoopers here, friends or not. Just keep him away from this place, do you hear?'

* * *

Eva was radiantly happy when she came home. 'I been with him, Maddie. I took Mr Bower to see my den.'

'Mr Bower, eh?' said Ronnie. 'I don't notice as you call me Mr Whittaker.'

'I don't call you nothing,' said Eva, and Maddie could not help smiling. The child's haughty look clearly showed that she did not consider him worthy of any name at all – none she could repeat in his hearing, at any rate.

Ronnie tried to change the subject. 'I reckon the old boar's got something wrong with him. He's off his grub.'

Eva was not to be deterred. 'I'm glad Mr Bower's back, Maddie. He's terrific – he's going to show me how to tie proper knots so my rope ladder will stay up.'

'What rope ladder, love?'

'In my den. He's a real gentleman, is Mr Bower.' Eva gave Ronnie the briefest of glances. 'He's going to meet me tomorrow.'

Maddie was no longer listening. Her heart was leaping in tremulous hope. Max had come looking for her, and wanted to see her again. The only cloud was his strange talk of love – he had found it, he said, but he had spoken no name. Could it be what she hoped to hear, or had he found someone on his travels during this last year?

The cloud did not dim her sunny horizon – after all, Max had come looking for her . . .

Joanna slithered down off the mare's back and handed the reins to Max. 'I enjoyed the ride, Mr Bower. We'll do it again early tomorrow. Make sure you give Ladybird a good rub down.'

Max watched her slim figure receding across the stable yard. She had spoken little during the ride in the mist-laden morning, in fact only once had she made a remark, turning in the saddle to look at him.

'Beautiful countryside hereabouts,' she said drily. 'How would you like to be master of a place like this?'

He had made no answer, and she seemed to expect none.

In fact her manner indicated that she considered him a servant rather than an acquaintance. He could not help remembering the day she had come to the barn where he slept, and the feel of her body. Perhaps she was paying him out now for his lack of response. She knew she was desirable, but a truly beautiful woman did not taunt and tease with her sexuality the way Joanna did. Mrs Westerley Kent was right; the girl needed schooling.

A woman's beauty lay in her soul as well as her body, thought Max, his mind flitting, for the thousandth time since breakfast, to a slender-waisted creature with trusting blue eyes and wild, tawny hair that blew about her face in the breeze. Now if he lay close to *her* . . .

CHAPTER TWENTY-FIVE

Maddie rode alongside Max on the highest part of the moor, glancing sideways under her lashes at intervals to make certain she was not dreaming.

He was really here at last, black hair gleaming in the afternoon sunlight, glossier than she remembered it in the old days, shirt sleeves rolled up and his head held high and the reins lying easily in his slender hands. He seemed to have lost that wary air of a forest creature alert for danger which always used to surround him.

Neither of them spoke for some time. The dale spread away below them and through the shimmering heat haze she could just make out the glint of water where the reservoir lay. From under the horses' hooves rose the familiar smell of heather in bloom, filling the air with its heady scent. Far away from Barnbeck and the farm, they might have been the only two people in the world.

An outcrop of tall rocks came in sight. As they neared them Max slithered down out of the saddle. Maddie followed suit.

'Let's sit,' said Max. He flung himself down in the shade of the tallest rock, gazing out over the dale. Maddie sat too, revelling in the feel of the sun's warmth on her back through the thin cotton of her frock.

'They call this place Thunder Crags,' she said softly. 'I've come here a lot, ever since my mother died. Somehow I feel close to her here. I used to come when you were away. I always thought of you then, but somehow it was spoiled without you.'

She saw the corners of his lips lift in a slow smile. 'It's strange,' he said, 'I used to come here too. Somehow I

always felt at home here on the moors. I felt lost for s‹
long, until I came to Barnbeck.'

'Then you should make it your home.' She could sens‹
the loneliness in him beginning to ebb, and felt grateful
She lay back on the grass, her arms behind her head.

'Tell me about Vienna, Max, about those dancing horse‹
– what were they called?'

Maddie closed her eyes, anticipating the mellow, liqui‹
voice. Deep and sonorous, only the slightest trace of
foreign sound differentiated it from Richard's culture‹
tones.

'They are called Lipizzan horses, and they're trained i‹
dressage at the Spanish Riding School in Wels. They ar‹
very beautiful, Maddie, all pure white stallions with broa‹
shoulders, sturdy legs, powerful haunches with a narrov
head and big dark eyes.'

'They sound beautiful,' she murmured, letting the word
fall like feathers. 'Are they big?'

'They are big and gentle like your Cleveland Bays, an‹
quick to learn. Most of them are carefully bred for th‹
purpose at the National Stud.'

'In Vienna?'

'A place called Piber. Only the best are chosen, and thos‹
selected are branded then in three places, with an L on th‹
cheek meaning Lipizzan, and with a P and a crown on it
flank if it's been bred at Piber – not all of them come fron
the National Stud.'

'And the third brand?'

'That's burnt in his side, over his ribs, to indicate hi‹
breeding.'

Maddie opened her eyes. He was staring down thought
fully at the star-shaped mark on his arm.

'His sire and his dam?'

'That's right. Once he's trained, a Lipizzan is a ver‹
valuable animal.'

'And did you ride them?'

'For exercise only, not on display. Their riders, th‹

Bereiter, train for years. No, my job was at the Stud, breeding and caring for the Lipizzans.'

Max rolled over on the grass to face her. 'Now tell me about you, Maddie. What have you been doing while I've been away? Does your friend Richard still come to call?'

Maddie shook her head. 'He's ill, you know. He was engaged to marry Ruby and she died.'

'Ruby? Oh, no, that is very sad.'

'A car accident. In Middlesbrough. I miss Ruby.' Maddie half-sat up, leaning on one elbow. 'It's odd how much has happened since you left, Max. And yet nothing has really changed.'

He plucked a blade of grass and put it in his mouth. She watched his lips close around it, and somehow it put her in mind of Rosie Bailey's baby and his tiny mouth sucking at his mother's nipple.

They talked in desultory snatches, letting the heat and peace of the day soak into them. It was a day of sunlit pleasure, words flowing gently between them. She felt bathed in contentment.

'I hear your father can no longer walk,' said Max. 'Was it a result of that stroke he had?'

'No – he had another, after you'd gone.'

He fell silent, and she was glad he did not ask more. It would only bring him pain to know the second stroke had happened directly after his quarrel with her father.

'So you have this farmhand – what is his name?'

'Ronnie. I don't know how I would have got through all the work without him. He's good – especially with the sheep. Had years of practice.'

'And the horses?'

'He doesn't handle them, except when we're rounding up the sheep. He rides well, but I prefer to see to them myself.'

'I'm glad. It takes a special kind of temperament to manage horses, and from what I saw of your man, he doesn't have it.'

311

'No.'

Max cocked his head to one side. 'You don't like him, d[o] you? Why do you keep him?'

She could not bring herself to meet that searching gaze 'Eva doesn't – she can't stand him. But then,' she adde[d] with a laugh, 'no man will ever match up to you in her eye[s] – you're her hero.'

He smiled that languorous smile again. 'Then I hav[e] much to live up to. Come, let's walk along the ridge.'

Leading the horses, they walked together, the heathe[r] springing under their feet. After a time Max turned sud denly to her.

'Maddie – remember when you wanted Duster to foal[?] Why not now? I'm sure Mrs Westerley-Kent would agre[e] to let us try again. And your father can't stop you now.'

Maddie hesitated. 'Well, I don't know – it's not the righ[t] time – '

'Not now, but perhaps in the spring. We could wor[k] together. I know of no one else who knows and loves horse[s] as well as you do. I don't know of anyone else with whom I'd rather work.'

Her heart leapt in pleasure. He reached for her hand an[d] for a time they walked in silence. She was recalling the las[t] time she had felt so close with him, the night they embrace[d] in her mother's room.

'You know, Magda,' he said dreamily, and somehow th[e] name gave her pleasure, 'some ancient Greek philosophe[r] once said that God created the horse from wind, just as h[e] created Adam from clay.'

'Oh yes,' she breathed. 'Have you listened to the wind Max? It's magic, it's mysterious, and oh, so powerful!'

From far below in the valley came the sound of a bell Maddie started. 'Heavens, it's six o'clock! Oh Max, I mus[t] be getting back.'

She turned, meaning to remount. Max caught hold of he[r] by the shoulders and she looked up into his dark eyes. '

meant what I said, Magda. Since I came back here the world has grown beautiful again.'

She lowered her gaze, fearing that he might feel her heart bumping in her chest. 'I'm glad, Max. It has for me too.'

'When shall we meet again?'

'Soon.'

'I'll call to see you.'

'No, no – you mustn't come to Scapegoat – I'll meet you here.' She turned away, taking hold of Duster's rein.

'Magda! Look at me.' She turned back slowly, unwilling to meet that searching gaze. 'What is wrong? Are you afraid your father and I may quarrel again?'

'No. It's not that.'

'What then? I know there's something – what is it?'

She climbed up into the saddle, then sighed. 'Leave it alone, Max. I can't tell you.'

'It's that farmhand, isn't it? He spoke to you rudely, I remember. Why do you let him talk to you like that? Are you afraid of him? Because if you are, I'll – '

'No, Max, you mustn't do anything! Promise me you won't come, Max! I've got to sort things out for myself.'

He came close to Duster's head, looking up at her. She could see the earnest fire in his eyes. 'Are you sure? Whatever problems you have are mine too. Can't I handle it for you?'

'No, Max, please. Trust me.'

For a moment he regarded her thoughtfully and then he nodded. 'Very well, if that is what you wish.'

He turned away to gather up Firefly's reins and climb into the saddle. Maddie followed until she was riding alongside him again.

'You are right, Max, it is Ronnie who is the problem. But I must sort this thing out alone and I want to do it my way. You do understand, don't you?'

He sighed. 'I can't claim to understand since you have told me nothing. But I do trust you. You will tell me when you are ready.'

'I will, I promise.'

They had reached the cart track now. Ahead of them a diminutive figure sat on the low drystone wall, a dog sprawled at her feet. It was Eva.

'What's up, love?' said Maddie. 'Why are you up here?'

A little tear-stained face looked up at her. 'It's that rotten bugger. He did it.'

Maddie felt a stab of apprehension. 'Did what?'

Eva's voice was choked with tears. 'Lassie – just look what he done to our Lassie.'

Maddie saw it then, the red streak on the dog's coat where he licked and then laid his head down again. Max swore in German and swung down out of the saddle to bend over the dog. Then he looked up at Maddie.

'Laceration,' he said briefly. 'There could be internal damage.'

'The swine! Give him to me.'

'No. I'll carry him for you. You take Eva.'

Eva's little body pressed warm against Maddie's. She was still sobbing gently. 'He kicked Lassie, hard, with his great working boots on. I bit him.'

'You bit Ronnie?'

'Well, he were asking for it, big bully, picking on Lassie.'

'But Eva, he could have hurt you – did he hit you?'

'Did he heck – I were too quick for him. But I daren't go home till you come.'

Max was riding in silence, the sheepdog cradled in his lap, and Maddie could see his lips set in a tight line. When they reached the gates of the farm Max dismounted and carried the dog straight across the yard towards the kitchen. Maddie lifted Eva down and hurried after him.

He stood in the centre of the kitchen, looking about him. Renshaw lay wide-eyed in the bed in the corner, but there was no sign of Ronnie.

Her father half-rose on his elbow and made a wincing sound. Max went towards him, holding out the dog's body. The old man's hand rose, then fell gently on the dog's

314

shaggy head in a gesture of affection. Maddie watched as her father's pale blue eyes rose to look at Max, stared for a moment, and then his hand moved slowly from the dog's head to rest on Max's arm. Muttered words escaped his lips, and Eva came to listen.

'He can't talk any more, Max,' said Maddie.

Eva bent forward. 'You what, Mr Renshaw? Say it again.'

Garbled words, pauses, then more strange phrases; Eva nodded. 'You thought he were no good – you mean Mr Bower? Oh, till Ronnie came – yes, I see. You're sorry – is that it? Am I to tell him?'

She turned to look up at Max. 'Well, you're in his good books any road, which is more than that other bugger is. Seems Mr Renshaw's bothered about summat that went wrong between you and him – '

'It's all in the past,' said Max. 'Forgotten.'

'Put Dog down here,' said Maddie, 'and then go, please. I'll wash the cut and see to him.'

Max laid the dog down gently, then knelt and probed over its body with gentle fingers. Then he sat back on his haunches.

'No bones seem to be broken, but watch to see if he can eat. Let me know if not.'

He rose and crossed to the bed. Renshaw, who had been watching, lay back on his pillow and his face twitched into a smile. Max's hand rested lightly on the old man's shoulder for a moment, dark eyes meeting her father's blue ones. For long seconds no one spoke, but Maddie could sense the tentative attempts both men were making in silence to bridge the void. Then Max turned away.

'Are you sure you still want me to leave? A man who can behave like that – '

He touched her cheek gently. Maddie smiled.

'Yes, please go. He won't hurt me. I'll let you know if I need help, I promise.'

He strode away across the yard. Eva watched him from

the window and then went back to sit on the edge of Renshaw's bed. 'I'm glad you like our Mr Bower, Mr Renshaw. Pity that bugger wasn't here,' she added wistfully. 'Mr Bower'd knock the living daylights out of him. Still, I made his hand bleed, and that's summat.'

Maddie was laying the table for supper when Ronnie came in. His face was contorted with anger. 'That bloody mare of yours!' he exploded. 'She just tried to kick me!'

Eva shrank back into the corner. Maddie looked up at him sharply. 'Why? What did you do to her? If you've taken a whip to her – '

'No I didn't, but if you ask me that's what she needs. Stupid creature! I was only forking hay and she damn well lashed out at me.'

He sat down to pull off his boots. Maddie caught a whiff of an earthy smell. 'Did you go straight from the pigsty to the stables?'

'And what if I did?'

'Don't you know horses can't stand the smell of pigs? Anyway, I've told you often enough to leave the horses to me. You just don't understand them.'

'Not like Mr Bower,' said Eva from the corner.

'And you can hold your tongue too, brat.' Ronnie swung round to face Maddie. 'Do you know what that little bitch did to me today? Did she tell you she bloody well bit me? That's kid's going to get herself a damn good hiding and locked up in her room, she is.'

'No she isn't,' said Maddie quietly, continuing to lay knives and forks on the table. 'From what I hear, you asked for it. No thanks to you, the dog is all right. We need him, and just you remember it.'

'Now look here,' shouted Ronnie, 'there's no call for you to come over all hoity-toity with me. The kid's a handful, and if you can't tame her, then I will. God, what a bloody household! A useless old man, a spoiled brat, damn stupid animals, and you!'

316

'I do my share of the work and I give you shelter. What more do you want?'

'You could be a damn sight more biddable. Get out in the fields and pull up the grass roots for a start.'

'I'm not wasting my time picking out wittens. I've work enough to do. And I'm going to be going out as well.'

'Out? Where?'

'Down to Thorpe Gill, with Max Bower.'

'Oh no, you're not. You've work enough to do here and I need you to do the pigs. I've had a bellyful of that old boar. The old bastard keeps trying to bite me.'

Maddie heard Eva's snigger. 'I'm going to spend time with Max, Ronnie. I've told him I will.'

'Are you now?' He walked around the table, his green eyes never leaving her face, and sat down on the armchair, draping his long legs lazily over the arm. 'And what if I say you're not?'

'Ronnie – please!'

He glanced at the child. 'Eva – outside. We got private things we want to talk about, so clear off.'

Eva's face crumpled. 'I haven't had my supper yet!'

Ronnie started up from the chair. 'You heard me, kid – bugger off!'

The child darted for the door, keeping well clear of his reach. Ronnie waited until he heard the door click behind her, then rose easily in one smooth movement and came to stand behind Maddie. The smell of pig manure was overpowering.

'We'll get along real well, sweetheart,' he said in a husky tone. 'I'll make you a good husband and father some fine kids for you.'

'Marriage is not the answer,' Maddie murmured.

'Oh no. And why not?'

'I don't love you.'

'That doesn't matter. Like I said, we'll get along real fine.'

Maddie felt his hand reach round to cup her breast and

317

looking down, she could see calloused, dirt-grimed fingertips and small, red teethmarks on the back of his hand. 'I'll
show you just how well,' the voice rasped as his fingers
tightened.

Maddie picked up the carving knife from the table and
half-turning, held the point directly to his throat. 'Take
your hands off me,' she whispered. 'I'll never marry you –
I loathe you, and I'll never give up Scapegoat to you. It's
mine – and his!'

The hand fell away from her breast. Renshaw was staring
from the bed, his blue eyes glittering hatred and contempt.
Ronnie stood open-mouthed for a second, then grinned and
moved back.

'Aw, come on now, honey – no need to get all hysterical
about nothing. Put the knife down, there's a good girl, and
we'll talk.'

Ronnie sat down and watched her for a moment, then
said easily, 'Tell you what, I won't rush you, eh? Now you
must see the sense in marrying your cousin – you don't get
chances like that every day out here in the outback. You
could get stuck with some hick like that stablehand at the
big house, and what's he got to offer you, eh, tell me that?'

'A damn sight more than you'll ever know,' snapped
Maddie. Ronnie threw back his head and laughed.

'So that's it! You're on heat for the horse-man! Well,
well, you needn't fret, little cousin. Marrying me needn't
stop your fun. I won't mind him having a poke at you now
and again – after I've had my fill.'

'You beast! You disgust me! The best thing you could do
is pack your bags and get out of here!'

Flinging the knife down on the table, Maddie rushed out
into the yard.

She'd reached the end of the garden before she heard the
drone of aeroplanes overhead. It was at the same moment
that she caught sight of something moving on the moorland
road, lorries painted in green and khaki, pulling trailers
behind them on which were mounted large guns. It must

318

be soldiers from the army camp at Otterley on manoeuvres, she reflected, but she had an odd feeling of resentment that they were moving across her moors like trespassers. They and the planes brought the reality of war too close.

Overheard gulls were wheeling and dipping, shrieking coarsely as they scavenged for food. The day had somehow taken on the quality of a dream, she thought, a dream where she was a player and yet somehow outside of it all. Dreams were strange things, where matters had an odd way of taking unpredictable turns. She could not suppress the uneasy, almost superstitious, feeling that at any moment her new-found happiness with Max could be snatched away . . .

Joanna opened the front door of Thorpe Gill, puzzled by the scratching sounds. A small girl in a grubby cotton frock was pushing a large stone on the doorstep and was just about to climb on it.

'What are you doing?' Joanna asked.

'I been knocking – nobody heard me. I were trying to reach the bell.'

Joanna eyed her curiously. 'Are you one of the evacuee children? What do you want?'

'I want to see Mr Bower. Is he in?'

'No, he doesn't live here.'

'He does. He said he were here. I want to see him.'

The child's confident manner amused Joanna. 'But does he want to see you, I wonder? He's finished work for the day – he's probably resting.'

'He'll want to see me. I'm his friend. Where is he?'

'Down at the cottage. Come, I'll show you.'

The little figure trotted along at her side until they reached the stable yard. 'That's his house, there,' said Joanna. 'I'll tell him you're here.'

'You needn't bother. I want to see him in private.'

The child ran ahead and knocked at the door. Joanna saw him answer, his expression of surprise and the questioning look directed at her over the child's head. Then, before she could speak, he had ushered the little girl indoors.

Joanna turned back up the path towards the house. That intriguing fellow evidently attracted children as well as adults; that was no bad quality for a man who might one day be the father of a family.

Eva flung herself on Max. 'Oh, Mr Bower! I can't stay there with him no longer!'

Max stared, bewildered, at the tear-stained little face. 'Come, sit on the sofa and let me dry your eyes.' Eva took the handkerchief from him and began rubbing her eyes with it. 'He's a right bugger, Mr Bower,' she muttered between sobs. 'He don't like me at all. He said he'll give me a walloping and lock me up in me bedroom. I don't like him, Mr Bower. He wants Maddie all to hisself. Can I stay here with you?'

Max stood, bewildered. 'What about Maddie, Eva? Surely she knows – she'll stop him bullying you.'

'I reckon she's scared of him too.'

'Then she can send him away.'

Eva shook her head firmly. 'No. He's going to stay for good. He said so.'

'No, Eva. He's only there because Maddie needs him to help run the farm. She'll send him away in time.'

'She can't. He's her cousin.'

'Her cousin? I didn't know that.'

'From Australia,' Maddie said. 'I wish he'd go back there.'

'I don't think you need to worry, even so, Eva. Maddie will sort things out.'

'I know she needs him for the work,' Eva said miserably, 'but I don't see why it can't be you.'

Eva sniffed and drew a deep sigh. 'If you don't let me stay here with you I reckon I'll have no choice, Mr Bower. I'll have to go home to me mam.'

Max made no answer. Eva was whimpering quietly again. 'I had a letter from her today. She said happen I can go back home soon but I don't really want to, not if she's with Mr Bakewell. I don't know him. I'd much rather stay here with you and Maddie. Mr Bower – are you listening to me?'

Max knelt and took hold of the child by the shoulders. 'Eva, listen to me. I love you, but you have to go back to Scapegoat. It's getting dark and Maddie will be worrying about you.'

'Oh, Mr Bower! How can I stay there with a rotten bugger like him, and after he kicked our Lassie and all? Can I stop here with you, Mr Bower, can I?'

He rose slowly to his feet. 'I'm afraid not, Eva. Come, I'll walk back up the lane with you.'

Eva was still muttering when they reached the gate of the farm. 'If he hits me when I get in, then it's your fault, not letting me stay with you.'

'He won't. I'll wait out here till I know you're all right.'

'And if he does you'll come in and beat hell out of him, won't you, Mr Bower? You'll have to, 'cos Maddie can't. He might hit her.'

'He hasn't touched her, has he?'

Eva shook her head. 'No, but there's never no telling with a bugger like him. He got mad with her just for talking about you.'

She unlatched the farm gate. 'Come in with me, Mr Bower, and tell him off. Tell him he's not to hit me.'

Max looked down at her pleading face. 'I can't do that, Eva. Go in now, and I'll see you're all right, I promise.'

He gave her a quick kiss on the cheek and pushed her inside the gate. At the doorway she paused and looked back, waving and smiling bravely.

'I love you too,' she whispered, and then she disappeared inside.

CHAPTER TWENTY-SIX

On the way back down the muddy lane to the cottage, his hair clinging about his face, Max tried to stem the tumult in his head.

Confused thoughts were running through his mind. Eva's revelation had taken him by storm, but why on earth had Maddie not told him? Why hadn't she said the fellow was her cousin? And why was he in England while the war was on? Maddie had been evasive about him, but there must be a reason. She knew what she was doing.

'*Trust me, Max.*'

But was she in need of help? Should he have gone into Scapegoat to find out? He was in no position to claim any rights over her but he'd spelt out his feelings as clearly as he could. Though words of love had not been spoken, he'd thought she understood. If she had felt anything in return, why hadn't she told him then that she was having trouble?

Because she was proud, perhaps. Maddie Renshaw was not the woman to be pushed into anything she did not want. She had far too much spirit to be forced into anything against her will.

There could be another reason. Perhaps Maddie and that fellow were closer than Eva knew. Maddie and Ronnie had been close to each other in that gloomy farmhouse while he had been away – how close? Anguish filled him to remember how he had yearned for her while he lived up there in Scapegoat, and that Ronnie might not have been as reticent as he had been. And to a girl who needed love as much as Maddie did, the proximity of a handsome, active young man could have led to intimacy, and possibly even more.

Max had a vision of a slender girl in the arms of the muscular blond farmhand, and nausea overwhelmed him.

If she and the fellow were already close his visit would only be a source of embarrassment to her, and could even bring her harm. No, he could not risk that.

The kindest thing he could do for both of them was to leave her alone. But he could not do it. The thought of life without her was unbearable.

Deep pain tore in him like an open wound. He was scarcely aware of walking, not up the gravel drive to Thorpe Gill, but along the river towards the woods. Jealousy was tearing him apart.

The next thing he was aware of was hearing a cry like that of a wild animal in pain, of flinging stones against the tree trunks, hurling them with all his might, again and again, until exhaustion overtook him. He flung himself down heavily on a fallen elm in the clearing and he found his forehead bleeding, blood trickling down his nose and shreds of bark under his fingertips.

He knelt, shivering and hunched like a child fearful of the dark. Lord God, do not forsake me! Having shown me the light, do not cast me back into the darkness of despair!

By the time he retraced his steps to the cottage he was in chastened mood, ashamed now of the passion he had allowed to overcome him. But as he took out his key to unlock the door the image leapt again into his mind of Maddie in the arms of that brutish lout.

Before his mind could reason, his fist rose and lashed out, smashing through the pane of glass in the little door and sending a myriad fragments flying. He gazed down at his hand, bemused by the blood trickling from his palm.

The men gathered around the bar in the Cock and Badger were for once more intent on slaking their thirst after a day's threshing than on the darts board. Jack raised his pint.

'Here's to us, lads, all on us, me and all.'

Seth put down his clay pipe to raise his half-pint. 'May we never want nowt, none of us, nor me neither.'

The door opened to admit another figure and heads turned. Wilf Darley came in followed by Edna, who stood just inside the door, smiling shyly. 'I just popped in to see if Eddie Sykes were here – oh there you are. Eddie – I wanted a word with you, about this watch.'

She came forward, taking a wristwatch from her pocket. Eddie put his ale glass down, conscious of the other men's eyes on him.

'What's up with it then? I'm no master clockmaster, you know, Edna.'

'Aye, but everybody knows you're a wizard with clocks that won't go. I'd be obliged if you could do owt with this – it were our Norman's, you see.'

'Give us it here.'

The others looked on over his shoulder as he turned it over. 'It's a gold watch, is that,' said Seth reverently. 'Must have cost a bob or two.'

'Aye, I reckon it did,' said Edna. 'Our Fred got it for Norman's twenty-first. He wouldn't take it with him when he went off, it being gold and all.'

The men fell quiet. Eddie was inspecting the back of the watch. 'There's summat written on it,' he remarked. 'I can't quite make it out.'

'I reckon it's the name of the maker,' said Edna.

'Let's have a see,' said Seth.

'You haven't got your specs,' said his son. 'Let me have a look.'

Jack peered closely. 'It says summat like for Hans zum Gluck. That's a queer name.'

'Oh, I don't know,' said Dai. 'Gluck – that's a good name in watches if I remember rightly. A real quality name.'

Edna gave him a shy smile. 'Well, our Fred thought the world of our Norman. He's not a man to do things by halves, isn't Fred. But can you do owt with it, Eddie?'

324

The policeman prised off the back and looked at the works. 'Seems little enough wrong with it,' he murmured. 'Mainspring's OK – it probably only needs a good clean. Leave it with me for a day or two, Edna. I'll take good care of it for you.'

Edna beamed. 'I knew you'd be able to help. Well, I'd best get back to me pot roast before it spoils. Goodnight to you.'

When the door closed behind her Len leaned forward over the counter. 'Gold, eh?' he murmured. 'Fred must be making more out of that shop than he lets on. But I'd never have thought he'd spend that much, twenty-first or no twenty-first.'

'It means a lot to Edna, whether or not,' said Eddie. 'I shall do my best for her.'

'I know a bit of German,' said Dai. 'I were in the first lot.'

'What's that got to do with owt?' asked Jack. 'You Welshmen are all the same – showing off for no good reason.'

'I had a postcard from a Jerry once,' Dai went on unperturbed. 'After the war, of course. It said zum Gluck.'

'The watchmaker?' said Len. 'Whatever for?'

'I had it translated. It means for luck. And it says Hans on the back of that watch too, doesn't it?'

Eddie looked down at the watch in his hands . . . 'Aye, that's right.'

'For Hans, wishing him good luck. I reckon I know where that gold watch come from, and it weren't from Fred dipping into his till, neither.'

Realization dawned slowly. At length Eddie cleared his throat and gave the others a significant look.

'I think, in the circumstances, although it's up to me to report anything suspicious, it'd be best if we all forgot about it,' he said with deliberation. The others nodded and murmured agreement.

325

'You were only kidding about the quality name, then,' said Jack thoughtfully.

'I thought it best,' admitted Dai.

'Well, at least it's a mystery solved,' muttered Len.

'Indeed,' agreed Dai. 'I always thought that Jerry fellow wasn't such a bad sort. If ever he comes down from Thorpe Gill and pops in here for a drink, I reckon I'll stand him a pint.'

'Nay, no point in going over the top,' growled Jack. 'Make it a half.'

It was growing dark and there was still no sign of Eva. Maddie went down to search in the privy, then went to the stable. Beyond Robin's glossy rump, protruding from his stall, she could see Eva's rag doll lying crumpled on the ground.

Duster lay in her stall. Maddie spoke gently as she approached. 'It's only me, beauty, don't fret.'

The mare rose to her feet, small ears pricked and liquid eyes questioning. Maddie held out a carrot and the mare snickered in pleasure as she bent her head to receive it. She looked unhappy, Maddie thought, her mane and tail hanging limply, her eyes dull and her coat rougher than usual. Maddie ran a hand down over her withers and on down her neck, but there was no sign of sweating.

'Come on, girl, we'd best go look for Eva,' she murmured gently. The mare seemed to understand. As Maddie backed her out of the stall she could see the feed uneaten in the trough, the drinking bucket empty. The mare was clearly unhappy. Just like the rest of us, thought Maddie. Odd how unhappiness could be so infectious. And Ronnie was the root cause of it all; like a cancer, eating away the living flesh . . .

Maddie rode uphill to the open country. Eva banished was more likely to seek solitude than the company of others in the village. But although she rode as far as the reservoir, its

326

brooding surface steely in the half-light of dusk, there was no sign of the child, only the gleam of headlamps as a convoy of army lorries snaked along the moor road towards Otterley.

Maddie turned the horse about to head for home. As she rode downhill again night tumbled like a dark blanket over the valley, a clouded, moonless night where only the stars glittered. Far below Barnbeck lay shrouded in regulation blackout and Maddie grew uneasy. No one would be out on the streets now but Mr Pickering, the air-raid warden, and the men still drinking at the Cock and Badger.

Droplets of rain began to fall, spattering her bare arms, and she shivered, urging the mare on. She must find Eva soon. The poor little thing must be cold and hungry by now.

A hazy shape materialized in front of her in the narrow lane just above the lane. Maddie stood up in the stirrups. 'Eva – is that you?'

The shape did not answer, but continued stumbling on down the lane. Maddie urged Duster on until she overtook it. It was a stray sheep; evidently it had found its way out through a gap in the drystone wall. She slithered down out of the saddle and turned back.

The sheep sensed her presence, stopped and bleated. Maddie came closer. The creature backed away, stumbling and crying out.

'Come on, you daft thing,' said Maddie impatiently. The rain was falling faster now, her cotton skirt clinging damply to her thighs. The moon suddenly came out from behind a bank of raincloud and she caught sight of the ewe's face as it twisted its head this way and that. There were curiously dark patches around its eyes.

'Whatever's up with you?' said Maddie, advancing cautiously on the animal. 'It's only me.'

The ewe, its back against the wall, stood still. Maddie put a hand to its head and felt a strangely sticky sensation. She moved her fingertips slowly about the face and the ewe made no attempt to escape. Maddie stiffened. Above the creature's nose warm liquid met her touch.

'Oh, my God!' Maddie drew back in horror. Where its eyes should have been were only gaping, oozing hollows. 'Oh my God! The gulls!'

'Eva, love! I've been worried out of my mind!'

Maddie knelt alongside the child, her knees hunched against her little chest in the gloom of the stable. Her face was a picture of misery.

'I got bellyache,' the child moaned. 'Terrible bellyache. When you wasn't in I waited out here.'

'What have you been eating?' Maddie drew her to her feet. 'Or is it hunger pains? Maybe you just need some nice hot soup.'

Eva shook her head. 'I couldn't eat it. I ate too many goosegogs already.'

'Gooseberries?'

'Mr Renshaw didn't want 'em for the Fair this year, and there were millions of 'em all going rotten on the bushes. Oh Maddie, I feel sick!'

The rain was drumming on the corrugated-iron roof. Maddie put her arm around the girl. 'Come on, indoors. I'll give you some Syrup of Figs.'

'Not if he's in there. I don't want to.'

'It's all right. Come on.'

They stood in the stable doorway, watching the rain bouncing on the cobblestones. Maddie cuddled Eva close.

'Where were you all that time, love? You weren't in the stable when I came out looking for you.'

'I were at Mr Bower's.'

'Down at Thorpe Gill? No wonder I couldn't find you. Come on, let's make a dash for it.'

Bending their heads against the rain they ran through the puddles in the yard to the house. As she lifted the latch Maddie spoke again.

'Did you tell Max about the gooseberries?'

Eva shook her head. 'I had them after. I were that hungry, waiting out there. I didn't go to the lavvy in case he came down.'

They stood in the kitchen. Only the firelight glowed, showing the old man asleep in the corner.

'It's all right – he's not here. What did you and Max talk about then?'

Eva shrugged. 'We talked about you.'

Maddie felt a shiver of apprehension. 'About me? What did he say?'

'He didn't say nowt. I told him about Ronnie being your cousin.'

Maddie swallowed hard. 'Look, love, let's get those wet things off and we'll get you into bed before Ronnie comes back. Do you know where he is?'

'He must have gone out while I were in the stable.'

Maddie got Eva into a clean nightdress and settled in bed with hot soup. 'Now tell me again just what you told Max, Eva.'

'Only about Ronnie being your cousin from Australia and him saying he's staying here for good. You wouldn't really let him stay here for always like him and you was married, would you, Maddie?'

The child's eyes were huge and eloquent in the lamplight. Maddie patted her arm.

'I'd kill myself first,' she muttered.

The rain had eased off by the time Maddie made her way up the drive of Thorpe Gill, stepping carefully on the gravel so that crunching footsteps did not disturb anyone in the big house. She moved quietly round the back to the stable yard and the cottage Eva had described.

The cottage was silent and in darkness. Perhaps Max was not at home. As she raised a hand to tap at the door she saw the shattered pane of glass.

'Max,' she called out softly. 'Max, are you in?'

Hearing no answer she tried the handle. The door opened

and she went in. By the firelight she could see him, crouching on the hearth.

'Max?'

He looked up, a bewildered look in his eyes, then rose to his feet. 'Maddie – I didn't hear you – come in. I'll light the lamp.'

'No, don't. The curtains aren't drawn.'

She came to stand by him, looking up into his face and wondering how to tell him.

'Max – Eva told you about Ronnie. I want to explain.'

'You don't have to.' His voice came dark and sombre, full of pain. She ached to take hold of him but he kept his face averted.

'I had a duty to him, seeing he's my cousin.'

The words, meant to soothe and explain, seemed to have no effect on him except to harden the lines of his body. 'I know,' he murmured, still looking at the floor.

'Please, look at me. I've got to tell you – '

Her words seemed like offerings, attempts to bridge the gulf, but he was not making it easy for her. He remained immobile, and she felt threatened by his silence.

'Look at me, Max, please.'

Slowly he looked up, his eyes strangely old and his face drained of colour, and she saw a dark mark on his forehead, a bruise or a scratch . . .

'I know it's none of my business and I have no right to pry, Magda, but I have been worrying about you. I can't help it – the two of you so close – wondering whether there was anything between you and him. It seemed there were things you didn't want to tell me . . .'

The sombre resonance of his voice made her shiver. Maddie took a step closer to him. 'There's nothing between us, Max, I promise you. I can't stand him. The sooner we see the back of him, the better.'

A light began to creep back into Max's black eyes. 'I can't tell you how relieved I am. I've been mad with jealousy, Magda. I fancied I could see you in his arms. You

330

would be ashamed of me if you knew how I have behaved tonight,' he murmured.

She smiled. 'I asked you to trust me, remember?'

'I'm sorry.'

She traced the outline of the star-shaped scar on his arm with gentle fingertips, and felt him quiver.

'If I lost you,' he murmured, 'I could not live without you. Say you forgive me.'

Penitence glowed in his eyes. If only, if only he would say the words . . .

'I forgive you, if you promise never to do it again.'

'I swear it.'

'Now tell me how to get rid of Ronnie. He's a deserter from the Anzacs and he's been hiding out at our place. Eva didn't tell you that.'

'No,' said Max thoughtfully, still standing close. 'But in that case there's no problem – inform the police.'

'He's got Dad's gun – and he's sworn to use it on us if anyone comes for him. Some bastard he is, threatening to kill a child and a paralysed old man, but now you see why I had to keep quiet. But I've got to find a way to get rid of him, Max. Eva's so terrified of him she wet the bed again last night.'

'I'll come back with you to the farm now,' said Max, breaking away to reach for his jacket. Maddie stopped him, taking hold of his sleeve.

'No, Max, not tonight. Let me give him a warning first. He is my cousin after all, and I know my mother loved Aunt Lottie dearly. I'll tell him if he's not gone by midday tomorrow, we'll tell the military – they're up on the moor on manoeuvres.'

Max hesitated, frowning. 'He has threatened you with a gun. I can't let you go back there alone.'

'I have to, Max. Eva is there. And if you come he will go for the gun. Let me go, please.'

Max laid his hand over hers. 'If he is your cousin . . .'

'I'll be all right, don't worry.'

'I still can't let you go alone.'

He was standing so close now she could feel the warmth of his body. No sound broke the silence of the little room but the slow ticking of the clock on the mantelpiece, and suddenly the intimacy of the room and the proximity of Max brought a memory flooding back . . . lace-edged pillows, crisp, clean sheets and the pervasive scent of violets . . .

Max inclined his face till his mouth was close to her ear. 'Once before we came close, Magda, as close as we are tonight.'

'I remember,' she whispered.

'Let's continue where we left off, the night I left Barnbeck.' The murmuring voice rippled softly through her hair, and the wild, surging sensation she had known once before rose in her like black smoke.

By the flickering embers of the fire she could see him peeling off his shirt as she unbuttoned her frock and let it fall. Max's skin glowed pearly-translucent as he knelt before her, and she revelled in the touch of his dark hair against her body as his mouth sought her breast. Then he looked up at her, black eyes intense.

'I watched you once, and you did not know it. I watched as you bathed before the fire.'

She remembered how she too had watched him, excited by the gleam of his wet body in the firelight, and the thrill of spying unobserved. Max touched her shoulder.

'Oh Magda,' he murmured. 'I've never seen a vision so beautiful. You stood that night with the sponge by your face and squeezed it, and the water trickled down your body, here' – he kissed the hollow at the base of her throat, 'and here' – his mouth moved down to the hollow between her breasts, 'and dripped from here' – his lips touched her nipples and she shivered, 'and flowed down here' – he buried his face in the hollow between her thighs. Maddie stretched her throat and gave a soft moan of pleasure.

'I love you, Magda. I love you more than life itself.'

He had spoken the words at last! The words, hoarse but

tender in the darkness, made Maddie's heart soar. Max lifted her and carried her to the rug before the fire, smiling tenderly and murmuring words of love.

'*Magda, Ich hab' dich lieb!*'

Gentle hands moved over her skin, caressing her into infinite rapture, and she moved in answer until at last minds and bodies fused in a communion of ecstasy. The world outside was forgotten. All time and space were shrunk to this little dusty room.

They were still lying, naked and intertwined, when there was a sound, faint but unmistakably obtrusive. Maddie sat up.

'What was that?'

He ran a finger over her breast. 'Nothing to concern us, *mein Liebling*. You are beautiful, Magda, the most beautiful woman I've ever known. We were meant for one another, you and I.'

She sighed, a deep, long sigh of contentment. 'I know. Once Ronnie is gone . . .'

He sighed and sat upright. 'Ah yes, we must come back to reality, I suppose, for the moment.'

Maddie was pulling her frock over her head when she remembered the sheep in the lane. 'You know, Max,' she said quietly, 'I've got this funny feeling that something's going to happen. Ever since I found a sheep with its eyes pecked out by the gulls.'

Max looked up from fastening his shoelace, a frown cutting his forehead. 'Superstition, my lovely Magda. There's nothing to fear when I am with you.'

Maddie stood up. 'No, when I am with you I am afraid of nothing. Ronnie was out when I left but he should be back now. Take me as far as the gate, Max. What's that behind the door?'

She bent to look at the square of white and picked it up. It was a folded sheet of paper. Max took it from her, then poked up the fire into a blaze and peered closely at the paper.

'It's a message, from Eva.'

'From Eva? Let me see.'

Maddie's fingers trembled as she took the crumpled paper and bent to read it by the light of the flame.

Mr Bower, i can't stay here no longer. i only wanted a drink of water and he hit me. Sorry if you mind me going, but i can. put up with him no more. i threw his bullets away in the pig sty but even my bit of wickenwood cant save us from him. Eva.

'Oh my God!' moaned Maddie. 'I must get home! With luck I can catch her!'

'No,' said Max firmly. 'I am going to take over now.'

'But Max –'

'You cannot go back there alone. First the dog, then Eva – he has done enough. It's time Ronnie was taught a lesson. Come.'

Maddie found it hard to keep up with him as they hurried back up the lane towards Scapegoat. Max strode into the yard ahead of her, flinging wide the kitchen door and stepping inside. Maddie followed him in, breathless. The only occupant was her father, sleeping deeply in the corner.

'There's no one here, Max.'

Max crossed to the staircase and ran upstairs. Moments later he reappeared. 'No sign of either of them,' he said tersely. 'I'll search the outbuildings.'

Maddie followed him out into the yard and saw him disappear into the pigsty. She headed for the stables. Duster's stall was empty.

'Max! Duster's gone!' she called. Max came running. 'It must be Eva who took her, Max – Ronnie always rides Robin.'

'Does she ride?'

Maddie nodded. 'She learnt while you were away. Oh Max! Where can she be?'

Max seized her by the shoulders. 'I think I know where she may be. Saddle up Robin for me.'

Turning to do as he said, Maddie murmured, 'Wha

334

about Ronnie, Max? You don't think he's taken her, do you?'

'No. The letter said she was running away.'

'I could go and look for her.'

'It is better that you remain here in case she returns.'

'You're right. If Ronnie comes back everything will seem normal then.'

Max took the reins from her and laid a hand on her shoulder. 'Make sure he suspects nothing unitl I come back. Say nothing, remember? The first priority is to find Eva. After that, I shall deal with your cousin.'

She watched him canter away up the lane towards the moor. Please Max, find Eva and bring her back safe soon!

CHAPTER TWENTY-SEVEN

It was closing time at the Cock and Badger and Len Laverack was just draping a towel over the beer pump when Fred hurried in.

'Draw us a half before you shut up shop, Len,' he said, taking off his tin helmet and laying it on the counter. 'Hot things, them hats. Fair makes you sweat.'

In the far corner the dominoes players looked at each other. Dai's lips twitched. 'And that's not all that makes him sweat,' he murmured. 'I'll bet Joan Spivey's in a bit of a lather too.'

'Hush, Dai,' said Jack. 'He'll hear you.'

Eddie, having thrown his last dart, turned away from the dartboard and caught sight of the air-raid warden. 'Ah, Fred – I've got summat for you.'

He drew a gold watch from his pocket and handed it to Fred, who thrust it quickly away in his pocket.

'Good watches, them German ones,' remarked Eddie. 'Tell Edna it works a treat now. You'll have no more trouble with it.'

Fred glanced about the room nervously. 'Aye, thanks. What do we owe you, Eddie?'

Eddie picked his words with care. 'You don't owe *me* nowt,' he said deliberately, his voice lingering significantly on one word. 'But I wouldn't wear that watch too much around the village if I were you.'

Around the bar not a man moved or spoke. Fred cleared his throat.

'Aye, well, I'll see you right one of these days.'

Without waiting to finish his glass of ale Fred picked up his tin helmet and went out.

* * *

It took some time before Joanna felt able to return to the house. The image of what she had witnessed through the window of the stable cottage would not leave her mind.

She could see it still, Max's body gleaming in the firelight as he knelt before a woman standing in the centre of the room. God, but he was a magnificent creature, black-maned and endowed like no other stallion she had known – and Nigel thought he was fortunate . . .

But admiration quickly gave way to envy. It was some other woman who stood there ready to receive his embrace. Her back was towards the fire, her slender body silhouetted against the glow and her face in darkness. Joanna stood, scarcely breathing, close to the windowpane and watched in fascination as Max caressed her.

She watched his lips move, travelling that body, and saw the woman respond, arching her back so that the long hair almost reached her waist. Joanna grew hot and felt her heart thudding, her own body growing moist with desire for him.

And when he lifted the woman, carried her to the hearth and laid her gently on the rug, a soft moan escaped Joanna's lips. Mesmerized, she could not tear herself away. He was taking his time; he was clearly a man well skilled in the arts of love. Whoever the little whore was, she was getting a good run for her money. Joanna's breathing quickened.

Rise and fall, rise and fall, slowly at first, then gathering momentum . . . Joanna could hear herself panting softly. At the end, she almost cried out herself in unison.

The woman sat up, and Joanna backed away, but not before she had caught sight of the pale face in the firelight. It was the Renshaw girl from Scapegoat Farm.

That was half an hour ago. Only now did Joanna feel sufficiently calm again to go indoors. Mother was sitting by the fire with a mug of Horlicks between her hands.

'Ah, there you are, my dear. I was wondering where you'd got to.'

'I took a walk in the grounds. Down by the stable cottage.'

Her mother looked askance over the rim of the mug. 'I see. And did you see him? After the telegram from Nigel too? I thought you were considering it.'

'I am. I promised I'd think about it, but a proposal of marriage takes time to consider.'

'Not when you're four months pregnant and the alternative is abortion, Joanna. It's now or never.'

'I saw him all right – the stableman, I mean. He was screwing one of the girls from the village.'

'Joanna – really!' Hilary's tone was only mildly reproving. 'You didn't happen to notice who she was, I suppose?'

'That girl from Scapegoat Farm. Disgraceful, I call it. I wonder you keep such a randy creature, Mother, I really do.'

'*Judge not, lest ye be judged,*' observed her mother. 'You're hardly in a position to criticize. I keep him because he's good – very good. And I've got a lot of respect for the Renshaw girl too – she knows about Cleveland Bays. No, if it was her, then that's all right.'

'All right? You never said it was all right for me! Honestly, Mother, you are a hypocrite! There he was, stark naked, screwing away like mad, and her like a bitch on heat –'

'Joanna, darling, if you must describe the picture in such graphic detail, I wish you would use more delicate terminology. You know, I wouldn't have thought it was quite you, Joanna, to be a voyeur – or should it be voyeuse?'

Joanna slumped moodily in a chair. 'Oh, what's the use? What's sauce for the goose, and all that – and it was saucy, I can assure you.'

'Jealous, darling? Well, you have the remedy in your own hands.'

'I suppose so.'

Hilary's voice grew dreamy. 'It could be such a lovely wedding, darling. I can just see it – marquee on the lawn with the smell of grass and banked roses, the sound of music drifting over the lake – it would be so romantic.'

'Yes, maybe you're right. Nigel isn't such a bad sort. Forty-eight hours' pass did he say?'

Joanna fell silent. Forty-eight hours wasn't long, but one could cram a lot of passion into that time if one set one's mind to it.

Maddie was distracted by the time Ronnie showed up. She had searched the house, the barn and stables again, even the chicken coop and pigsty just in case Eva was hiding, but all she could find was the little piece of rowan twig, Eva's wickenwood, lying on the bed.

Ronnie was swearing under his breath as he came in, the necktie knotted about his throat all awry. 'I'll kill that bloody pig yet,' he muttered, and took off his waistcoat and flung it on the chair.

'Where's Eva?' Maddie demanded. 'I can't find her anywhere – do you know where she is?'

'How the hell should I know?' he rasped in irritable tones. 'I got more to worry about than kids. Sodding boar's in a foul mood 'cos he can't get at the sow, and the bloody gulls have pecked the eyes out of three of my sheep, did you know that? I'll take the gun to them tomorrow.'

He rooted around in the cupboard and took out the shotgun, then leaned it in the corner near the door. 'Got anything to drink in this damn place apart from that god-awful wombat-piss you call home-brew? I've got a thirst on me like a flaming desert.'

'Ronnie – for God's sake, listen! Eva's missing – where on earth can she have got to?'

'Search me. So the brat's done a bunk, has she? Well, not before time, if you ask me. Good riddance.'

Maddie faced him squarely. 'You made her do this – you hit her.'

Ronnie shrugged. 'I gave the kid a clip round the earhole

339

for giving me lip. She ran off bawling – I haven't seen her since. I went out.'

Fury boiled in her. Ignoring Max's advice Maddie took a deep breath and glared at her cousin. 'Now look here, Ronnie, I've had about enough of you. It's time you left here and moved on. Cousin or not, I want you out of this house, do you hear me? I won't have you here a day longer. If you haven't left by midday tomorrow, I shall send for the military. Do you understand?'

As her words soaked in, a slow grin spread across his face. 'You're talking out of the back of your neck, girlie. Nothing's going to shift me – I know when I'm on to a good thing. So you can shut your trap.'

'You heard what I said – I'll turn you in.'

'Only if you want to see your old man shot.' He jerked his head in the direction of the bed in the corner, then let a calloused hand fall on the gun's barrel in a brief caress. Maddie glanced across at the bed. Her father was looking on with vacant eyes.

'I'm not the only person in Barnbeck who knows you're a deserter,' she flared defiantly. 'You'll be caught.'

He chuckled. 'You don't give up easy, I'll give you that, little cousin, but bluffing won't work. I'm staying put, you stupid galah, and you better believe it.'

He began prowling round the room, jerking open cupboard doors. 'Now where the devil do you keep the liquor in this dump, eh? There must be some booze somewhere?'

Maddie was standing by the window, peering out under the blackout. Eva was out there somewhere, and Max too, looking for her. Please God he would find her soon.

'You hear me, woman? Where's the liquor?'

'There isn't any.'

For a moment he stood staring at her, then slumped on to a chair. 'Come to think of it,' he said, fixing his gaze on the pegged rug, 'I couldn't find you tonight. Where in hell were you?'

'Out.'

He clicked his tongue in irritation. 'I know that, stupid. Hey, wait a minute – you been to see that Pommie bastard, that great Pommie ape working up the big house, haven't you? You still got the hots for him.'

'You're wrong, he's not a Pommie,' replied Maddie quietly. 'He's Austrian.'

Ronnie glared at her. 'You're asking for a smack in the mouth, my girl.' He rubbed his bristly chin for a moment. 'Austrian, is he? That's the same as a Jerry. We had Jerries back on the sheep farm in Merlin's Crossing. On Saturday nights, them and the Italians, they used to go into town on the truck, get drunk and poke a sheila or two. The Italians got interned when the war started.'

He was talking more to himself than to her now. Maddie continued to look out of the window. Come on, Max, find Eva and bring her back, please!

Ronnie sprawled back in the chair. 'Yeah, just like anyone else, them Jerries. Like that stupid galah up at the big house – I seen him, "Thumb in bum and mind in neutral", as a mate of mine used to say.'

'Don't talk about him like that!' Maddie could not help the sharpness in her tone. Ronnie eased himself up and turned to look at her.

'I talk about him how I like,' he said mockingly, but his voice was charged with menace. 'And you too, little cousin. I'm boss around here, and don't you forget it. I won't forget you threatening me like you did, and I'll make you pay for it.'

'You're a bully! You've made Eva's life a misery, but I won't let you do it to us any longer!' Maddie came across the room to him, standing before him and hurling the words defiantly. Ronnie rose unsteadily to his feet.

'And what will you do to stop me? I bloody own you, Maddie Renshaw, you and the farm – yes I do – I bloody own you!'

There was a strangled sound from the direction of the bed. Renshaw was sitting upright, his hand to his mouth and his eyes wide with fear. Ronnie was chuckling to himself and moving round the table towards her. Maddie backed away.

'You don't own me! Get away from me!'

'And I can prove it,' Ronnie muttered. 'I don't reckon the old man told you, did he? He wouldn't want the world to know, but I found out in the end.'

'Found out? What?' Maddie held her breath.

'I'm your brother, girl, not your cousin. Well, half-brother, to be precise. We had the same mother, Maddie, if not the same father. So you see – '

'No! No! I don't believe it!' Maddie's fingers flew to her lips. It was too horrible – not Mother.

Ronnie was laughing. 'Lily wasn't the angel she was cracked up to be, whatever the old man led you to think. He wouldn't want to tell the world his girl was busy screwing another fellow while he was away fighting for King and country.'

'No,' breathed Maddie. 'It's not true . . .'

'It's true all right. Some farmer called Holroyd. She had this bastard no one wanted, so she gave me to her sister. My folks were just setting off for Australia, so no one was any the wiser.'

Maddie looked to her father. He was sitting, shoulders hunched, and his face buried in his hands. Maddie's brain raced, trying to find some way to refute this hideous accusation.

'You're making all this up, I know you are, but it won't work!'

'Nope. My old mum told me last year – least, I thought she was my mum till then. You ask your old man.'

Renshaw's shoulders were heaving silently. Maddie grew desperate. 'You can't be my half-brother – you wanted me to marry you. Now who in his right mind would propose to his sister?'

'So what's wrong with a fellow screwing his sister? It happens all the time, specially in farming country, and

342

hould know. Brothers and sisters, fathers and daughters –
on't tell me the old man there never tried to poke you?'

'You evil bastard! What a foul, disgusting creature you
re!'

'Well,' said Ronnie, spreading his grimy hands, 'a fellow
a the prime of life don't want to miss out – he needs a bit
f pokey when his old woman's dead. Keep it in the family,
o to speak.'

Maddie was not conscious of thinking or of moving; the
ext thing she knew she had hurled herself on him and was
lawing at his face. Ronnie began to laugh, throwing up his
rms to fend off her hands, but after a moment his grin
anished. Maddie lashed out again, and this time saw where
er nails had scored his face, raking long red lines in the
esh.

Ronnie put a disbelieving hand to his cheek. 'You bitch!'
e snarled and, leaping on her, he pinioned her arms and
ushed her back against the table. Her mind registered the
our smell of sweat choking her nostrils. 'I'll teach you a
esson, my girl,' he hissed, 'one you won't forget in a
urry.'

His right arm rose in the air and came swinging down,
racking her hard across the face. Maddie felt the breath
riven out of her by the shock and violence of the blow.
he struggled to free herself, writhing and twisting, kicking
ut at his shins, but Ronnie was too strong for her. She was
eld in a grip so tight that every bit of air was squeezed
om her lungs. Over his shoulder she was aware of her
ither's agonized face.

Again she saw Ronnie's right hand rise and come swing-
ig down and tried to twist her face away. The first blow
aught her and she felt the quick warm burst of blood spurt
om her nose. The hand came smashing down again and
ie heard a sudden, high-pitched squealing sound, and
ealized the sound came from within her head and was
ccompanied by a piercing pain in her ear. Dizziness welled

over her, and in the haze she saw her father struggling to
lever his legs out of the bed.

'I'll teach you, you little bitch!' she heard Ronnie spit,
and felt a hand release her. She opened her eyes. Ronnie
was still holding her with one hand and unbuckling his belt
with the other.

Not a beating too! As she struggled still, Ronnie let the
belt fall to the floor and began unfastening his trousers.
Maddie felt nausea and rage well up inside her and, making
a desperate effort to find strength, she seized her chance.
Wrenching from his grasp she tore at his face, and felt the
flesh give under her nails.

She heard Ronnie bellow like an enraged bull and tried
in vain to dodge the welter of blows to her face. She was
dimly aware of the ferocious violence of the blows, with the
fist now and not the flat of his hand, and the searing pain in
her head until it began to seem if all life had been pain.
Then the pain began to fade and no longer seemed to
matter. Her knees were buckling under her and the room
swirling into darkness.

'You won't forget who's master now!'

There was a sensation of being swung around and thrown
down face first on a hard surface, then of her clothes being
torn and cool air against her skin. But nothing mattered
any more, only darkness and oblivion . . .

Edna lay in the darkness of the bedroom waiting for her
husband to get into bed.

'I'm that glad Eddie were able to fix that watch all right,
Fred,' she murmured sleepily. 'Now you'll be able to wear
it – on Sundays, happen, when you wear your best suit for
church.'

'Nay, I don't think so, love,' she heard him reply. 'I'll
not risk owt going wrong with it again. I'll put it by, for
Norman's sake.'

Edna's face grew soft with memory as she remembered
her son's birthday. He had been so proud of the watch, so

ateful. It was thoughtful of Fred to decide to put it by
d treasure it, for his sake.

'You're a good man, Fred,' she murmured, throwing
ck the covers to let him into bed. 'I'm that glad I were
cky enough to get a husband like you.'

ight and sound began to permeate Maddie's consciousness
last. There was a high-pitched squeal in her head and a
avy, aching dizziness as she struggled to open her eyes
d she found herself slumped on the floor of the kitchen,
ousered legs in front of her and Ronnie's white face
nding over her.

'Get up, you silly bitch,' he was muttering. 'There's
thing wrong with you – get up!'

She shook her head slowly, trying to clear the fog from
r brain. Her face and her body ached. There had been
ows – anger – Ronnie – . He was staring at her, and she
w him touch gingerly his torn cheek.

'Get up – your dad needs help. He fell out of bed. Did
u hear me? Get up, you stupid whore.'

Maddie levered herself up on her elbow, her head
vimming, and attempted to rise. It was no use – her legs
ere weak and every inch of her body seemed racked with
in and useless. Memory flooded back, and with it came
rror and a sickening sense of revulsion.

'You – you raped me!'

She could hear her own voice, no more than a whisper
agged out of a hoarse throat. Ronnie swung away and
ced around the far side of the table.

'Bollocks. Get up like I told you and see to the old man.'

She could see her father lying on the floor near the bed.
is eyes were closed and his body sprawled in an untidy,
ngled heap. 'You bastard,' she croaked. 'What have you
ne?'

'Didn't touch the silly old coot. Told you, he fell out of
d.'

Trying to come to my help, thought Maddie bitterly, and

tears welled in her eyes. It was ironic; all those years yo
tried to protect me from men . . .

With an effort she managed to pull herself into a ha
sitting position, trying to rearrange her clothes, but h
head swam and she leaned back against the rough sto
wall and closed her eyes. She must pull herself together a
go to her father – he might be hurt.

The singing in her ear was easing a little now but t
pain remained. Something hard in her pocket was diggi
into her thigh. Her fingers closed on a piece of wood
Eva's twig. Then, through the humming in her ear, s
heard a sound outside.

Maddie lifted her head, holding her breath and listenin
Yes, it was the sound of footsteps on the cobbles outside
the yard – and they were coming closer . . .

CHAPTER TWENTY-EIGHT

onnie heard the sound and turned just as the door was
rust open and two figures stood there.

'Maddie – I found her!' Max's voice was triumphant.

'He found me and Duster hiding in the – ' Eva's shrill
y died away. Maddie could see Max's eyes darken as he
ok in the scene, herself half-lying by the table, her father
rawled by the bed, and Ronnie standing in the centre of
e room, his face bleeding. The two men held each other's
ze, the one tall and slimly built, the other shorter but fit
d powerful. For seconds no one moved. It seemed like a
isly caricature of one of those Christmas tableaux Miss
aunt worked so painstakingly to produce for the parents
ery year . . .

Then Max hurled himself across the room to kneel by
addie, reaching out a finger to touch her swollen, bruised
ce. She hung her head, conscious that she must look a
rrible sight, her face streaked with tears and blood and
er hair tangled in wild disorder.

'He raped me, Max,' she whispered. 'He raped me.' She
lt her stomach retching as she said the words.

Max lifted her gently and carried her to the armchair,
en knelt and cradled her head in his arms, black eyes full
concern. Then their expression began to change. He
rned his head to look at Ronnie, and Maddie could see
e cold, steely fire that dawned in his eyes.

'Take no notice of her – she's a whore,' said Ronnie.
Anyway, this is none of your business. You just sling your
ok and leave us be.'

'That's just where you're wrong,' said Max, rising to his

feet, and there was icy determination in his tone. 'It is n
business.'

Ronnie suddenly came to life, racing across to t
shotgun propped by the door. He snatched it up ar
pointed it at Max.

'You heard me – bugger off now or I'll blow your brai
out.'

From behind him Eva's voice piped up. 'He won't, M
Bower – I threw his bullets in the pigsty.'

Max hesitated, looking from Eva to the gun, then took
step forward. Ronnie took aim. 'Don't come any closer –
got both barrels loaded, so you and her'll get it,' he snarle
moving the barrel fractionally in Maddie's direction.

'No you haven't then – there's no bullets in, I know 'c
I looked, so there!' There was no disguising the triumpha
tone of Eva's voice.

Max did not hesitate any longer. As he moved in, Ronn
pulled the trigger. Maddie gasped as the gun clicked, a
then clicked again.

'See!' cried Eva.

Ronnie grabbed the barrel end of the shotgun and swu
it. It caught Max a fierce crack across the shoulder, and f
a moment he stumbled. As Ronnie swung the gun agai
Max ducked and closed, seizing him around the waist a
struggling to pull him down. The two men whirled in
crazy dance around the kitchen.

'Mind Mr Renshaw!' Eva cried out then, eager to hel
she snatched up the cast-iron frying pan from the hear
and clouted Ronnie with an almighty whack at the back
his knees. With a yelp he stumbled backwards, knocki
Eva off-balance. Max brought the edge of his hand sharp
across Ronnie's throat. Ronnie's eyes bulged and he f
backwards, trapping Eva under his weight, Max goi
down with him.

Maddie could hear Eva's squeal from somewhere und
the heap, and there was the clanging sound of the fryi

an meeting bone, then to Maddie's relief Eva's little figure rawled out to squat by Renshaw's motionless body.

The two men rolled over and over, Ronnie's bleeding ace appearing briefly only to disappear again. Then it was Max sitting astride him, bunching his hand into a fist and unching.

'Give him one for me, Mr Bower!' cried Eva, and clapped er hands as Max fetched him a great, open-handed blow. Beat him to a pulp – he's asked for it!'

Max's eyes dilated as he took hold of Ronnie's ears and mashed his skull down, again and again, on the flagstoned oor, but Ronnie's fingers had found Max's throat and ocked deeply into the flesh. Maddie tried to stagger to her eet, but dizziness made her lurch against the table. She aw Max raise both hands above his head, lock them ogether and bring them crashing down on Ronnie's nose. Ronnie's eyes seemed to swivel in their sockets. From ridge to tip his nose was split wide open, splayed out in a et, pulpy mess with blood spurting down his face.

'I think he's had enough, Mr Bower!' cried Eva. 'Don't ill him!'

Ronnie lay motionless, eyes closed. Eva came close and ooked down at him. 'He's a right mess, isn't he?' she said onderingly. 'We gave him what for, didn't we?'

Maddie sank back into the chair. Max got slowly to his eet and came to squat by her. 'Are you all right, Maddie? od, what a fool I was to leave you alone with him! It's all y fault!'

She shook her head. 'It was my own fault, Max. You arned me.'

For a moment he laid his head in her lap, then straight-ned and stood up.

'I must lock him up until the military comes. Somewhere afe – no windows. I know – the pigsty, then I shall fetch e doctor.'

'There's no need, really, I'm all right, Max.'

He raised a hand to touch her cheek, and she caught

sight of his bleeding knuckles. 'I'll ride for the doctor,' he repeated. 'Your father needs help too.'

While he was dragging Ronnie's inert figure out of the doorway and across the yard Maddie made her way stiffly to where her father lay. Eva was bending over him in concern, patting his cheek.

'He won't open his eyes, Maddie. I think he's bad.'

She was right, Maddie could see. His skin had a ghastly pallor about it and his breathing was shallow. Max came back and lifted the old man into bed.

'I'll go now. Lock the door and rest till the doctor comes.'

At the door he glanced back at her over his shoulder and she could see the black fire still smouldering in his eyes. 'Evil bastard,' he muttered hoarsely. 'Prison is too good for a swine like that. He shall be punished according to his deeds one day.'

As in a dream Maddie set about cutting bread and cheese for Eva.

'We showed him, didn't we, Maddie, Mr Bower and me? That bugger won't come back here no more.'

'Where were you, Eva, when Max found you?'

'In my secret house, up in the cave, of course. Nobody ever goes there. I don't know how he found me, 'cos I wasn't never coming back.'

'Up in Thunder Crags?'

'That's right. I must have told Mr Bower about it once, him being my best friend and all – next to you, I mean. I wonder what I did with my wickenwood – I can't find it nowhere.'

'Here.' Maddie produced it from her pocket. Eva pounced on it with delight. 'Oh, it did save us after all! And there was me thinking it were useless . . .' She stowed it away in her cardigan pocket.

'Time for bed,' said Maddie, and hugged the child close for a moment. Somehow it was reassuring to watch Eva climb the stairs smiling, content that, as in all good fairy stories, the good had been vindicated and the villain punished.

The night was close and the smell of blood lingered on the air. Maddie mopped the flagstoned floor clean of stains, trying to banish from her mind the evil thing that had happened. Then she filled the bowl with hot water, stripped off her clothes and with a scalding sponge washed away all trace of the attack. She scoured every inch of her body vigorously, ridding herself of the stench of Ronnie.

'You bastard!' she muttered under her breath. 'You filthy, filthy bastard! I wish you were dead!'

Ronnie struggled slowly back to consciousness. The first thing he was aware of was a snuffling sound and the foul stench of manure, then as his eyes began to focus he recognized where he was.

'Shit! – the bloody pigsty!'

He sat up slowly, putting a hand to his aching head and trying to recall what had happened. Then it came back – the need for Maddie, then that bloody Jerry – the fight . . .

His nose! Christ, it hurt! He put a hand gingerly to it and was horrified to feel its hideous shape, splaying out across his cheeks like a Bantu and soggy as a squashed melon. Fury boiled in him. None of the boys back at Merlin's Crossing had ever got the better of him, and yet that blasted Jerry – and in front of Maddie too . . . By God, but he'd pay that bastard back one of these days, and with good interest too!

He attempted to stagger to his feet, but his head was pounding like an anti-aircraft gun and blood spurting down his shirt front. The pain in his nose was excruciating. Christ, if only he had the shotgun he'd go back in there and put an end to the lot of them, that god-awful brat as well!

The gun – it was still in the house, but the cartridges – hadn't the kid said she'd put them in the pigsty? Or did she say pigswill? He looked across at the boiler where the scraps were thrown in ready for boiling.

Under the lid a mass of foul-smelling cabbage leaves, left-over dinner, breadcrusts and turnip tops swirled in a watery mess. Ronnie plunged his hand in deep and groped around. Blood dripped from his nose into the boiler. If the kid had left the cartridges in their box there was just a chance one or two might not have got soaked.

After a moment he gave up, wiping his arm on his shirt and peering around the gloomy shed. Where the hell had the kid put the cartridges, blast her? Light, that's what he needed. Alongside the boiler his fingers found the niche in the stonework where the candle-end was kept. No bloody matches – he'd taken them indoors after feeding the pigs. But there was a box in the niche – the cartridges! Now all he needed was the shotgun.

He made for the door, still staggering slightly, and swore aloud when he found it locked.

'Fucking Jerry!'

The bastard knew what he was doing – no windows in this place and the door a huge, solid thing it would take five men to batter down. Ronnie could hear the old boar grunting and banging against the side of his stall and the sound of his tusk grating against the timber. The beast was still restless with the old sow out of reach in the next stall.

But then he saw it, the only ventilation in the sty, a small opening in the stonework high above the boar's stall. Perhaps, with luck, a man could just squeeze through. Wiping away the stream of blood still running down his face, Ronnie picked up a spade.

'Shift, you stupid beast,' he said. The boar looked back at him with small malevolent eyes. These middle whites were no creatures to be trifled with, powerfully built, short-nosed and with tusks like a rhinoceros. And this one was in a foul temper already. Ronnie opened the door of the stall and the boar watched him suspiciously.

'Back off, you silly bugger.' He swung the spade and caught the animal a crack across the shoulder. The boar roared and lowered its head. Ronnie moved forward.

'That's better.' He dropped the spade and felt for a fingerhold in the stone wall. There was a rush of movement behind him and he felt a hideous pain in his leg as it gave way and he slumped. Venomous eyes glared at him as he sank, and he saw blood on the boar's tusk.

His leg was ripped from the ankle up to the knee, a deep, hideous wound, and there was a fire in the pig's eyes. It lifted its nose and sniffed, and Ronnie felt fear rising in his guts. If a boar smelt blood . . .

It was lowering its head again. Ignoring the pain, Ronnie leapt up and threw himself at the wall, scrambling to get free. But the creature's blood was up. With a roar it lowered its head and thrust forward again, and this time the tusk tore into Ronnie's thigh, blood spurting over the animal's face, and Ronnie screamed.

He was down now, on the rotten, stinking straw of the stall, and the boar coming at him again. Ronnie felt the point of the tusk drive deep into his chest, and then the filthy yellow teeth closed in on his face. He could smell its fetid breath, feel his eyes bulging and heard the crunch as his jaw snapped . . .

Agony was ripping through his whole body, and then blackness came . . .

Maddie was dozing in the kitchen when Doctor Ramsay at last knocked at the door. The first light of dawn was streaking the eastern ridge as she let him in. Relief flooded her to see Max's tall figure across the yard going into the stable with Robin.

The doctor gave her a quick glance, assessing the bruising on her face. 'You were attacked, I gather. Any bones broken?'

'No – I'm all right. It's my father.' She indicated the bed in the corner. Dog lay alongside, his head between his paws. Doctor Ramsay set down his bag on the table and took out a stethoscope.

'He fell, I believe. Has he woken up?'

'Not since the fall.'

The door opened and Max came in. The doctor moved the dog aside with his foot and drew back the sheets, unbuttoning the old man's shirt. Then he sat on the edge of the bed and frowned as he applied the stethoscope to his chest and listened. Max moved forward to stand behind Maddie, sliding one arm about her waist.

At last the doctor laid aside the instrument and for several seconds sat silent. Maddie grew alarmed.

'He'll be all right, won't he? He's slept ever since – '

'I'm sorry, my dear.' The doctor rose and pulled the sheet up over her father's face. 'The shock – it must have been too much for him.'

She felt Max's hand tighten on her waist. 'He's not – oh no, he can't be!'

'Another stroke, I fear. He wasn't strong enough to survive another. I'm sorry. If it's any consolation to you, at least he didn't suffer.'

Words choked in Maddie's throat. She turned to Max and felt his arms enfold her, his hand caress her back in silent sympathy. She laid her head on his shoulder, her mind still struggling to register the fact that her father was dead. He must have died while she was sleeping. It was too cruel, so stupid and unnecessary! Not suffered? It must have been agony for him to want so much to come to her help and not to be able to do anything to stop –

'Now you'd better let me have a look at you,' Doctor Ramsay murmured. 'If you would please unbutton your frock . . .'

Max released her and moved away. Maddie let herself be examined, but her mind still recoiled from remembering just what her father had been trying to prevent. The thought of that evil creature penetrating her body. She could not bear to think of it. And Max – what of Max?

'No bones broken, no real damage apart from bruising and minor lacerations,' Doctor Ramsay pronounced at length. 'You won't care much for looking in the mirror for the next day or two, but the discoloration will soon fade. Is there anything else?'

His shrewd eyes were searching hers. Behind him Maddie caught sight of Max's dark expression. No, I can't tell him about the rape, thought Maddie. Never, never would she speak of it again. Only Max knew . . .

'A sedative, perhaps?' Doctor Ramsay said in a kindly tone. 'You've had a double shock tonight, what with the attack and your father. A sleeping pill – '

'No,' said Maddie quickly. 'No thanks.'

He was closing his bag now and reaching for his hat. 'I'll see to the death certificate and have a word with Dai Thomas for you, if you like. He'll arrange to take your father's body and do all that is necessary.' He glanced at Max. 'See to it that she gets some rest now.'

'Thank you, Doctor.' Her mind was still numb. Doctor Ramsay was making for the door.

'Have you spoken to the police, my dear? They'll need a statement.'

'No, not yet. I – I don't feel – '

'I will see to it, Doctor,' said Max quietly.

The doctor nodded. 'I'll say goodnight then. Or good morning, rather. I've got to get back to Otterley now to deliver a baby which is on the way – curious how a birth and a death often go together in my line of business . . .'

After the doctor had gone, Maddie turned to Max. 'Is Ronnie still out there in the pigsty?' She could not help shivering as she spoke.

'Never mind about him. What about you, Magda? Why didn't you tell the doctor?'

She shrugged. 'There's nothing he could do. I'd rather not talk about it.'

She looked across to where her father's body lay in the bed, silent and unmoving, the way he had lain for months. 'Oh Max! I can't believe he's gone. He was trying to help me, you know.'

She stood beside the bed and drew back the sheet,

conscious of Max's hand on her shoulder. Her father's lined face looked peaceful in death, almost as though he was happy to be freed from care and reunited with his Lily. Dog had resumed his position, head between paws, beside the bed. Suddenly outside she could hear heavy footsteps on the cobblestones, and looked enquiringly at Max. He let go of her abruptly.

'It's the military,' he said, making for the door. 'They've come for Ronnie.'

He went out, leaving her alone in the kitchen. The early morning sun was poking fingers of light around the blackout but Maddie could not bring herself to draw back the curtains and let the radiance into the room. To look out would mean to see the pigsty.

Eva was moving about upstairs. Maddie tried to compose herself, unwilling to let the child see her turmoil. The door opened and Max came in, and behind him came Dai Thomas, his normally cherubic face composed into the sober lines of his professional manner.

'Go upstairs, Magda, and see to Eva,' said Max, and she recognized his meaning. To watch her father being carried away from Scapegoat would be too much to bear . . .

She stayed in the bedroom with Eva until Dai was safely away from the farm and her father's body with him. From the window she watched Dai's hearse disappear round the bend in the lane. Eva was heartbroken.

'I thought he was only sleeping, Maddie! How was we to know he were dead? It were that bugger Ronnie – he killed him!'

'Hush now, love. Wash your face and then come down and have your breakfast.'

As they came down the stairs there was a knock at the door. 'I'll go,' said Max. It was the postman, a letter in his hand and his eyes wide with curiosity.

'I heard the news,' Wilf said in a loud whisper. 'Very sudden, wasn't it?'

'Yes,' said Max. 'Mr Renshaw had another stroke.'

'Eh, I'm that sorry. Tell Maddie, if there's owt we can do . . .'

Eva wept uncontrollably for half an hour, burying her face in Dog's shaggy neck and murmuring words of comfort to the animal.

'Don't cry, Lassie, you've still got Maddie and me to look after you,' she wailed. 'We love you, Lassie, so don't cry.'

Maddie was moving about mechanically, making up the fire and putting the kettle on to boil. There would be the cows to milk soon. Max sat watching her.

'The letter, Magda. Will you leave it until later?'

'I'd forgotten.' She took it from him and tore it open and stared at the words, unable to take them in. Then she handed it back to Max. 'You read it.'

He did so, then put it aside and rose, coming to stand before her and take her gently by the shoulders. 'Magda, there's something I must tell you. It is not pleasant, I'm afraid, but you must know.'

She looked down at the sheet of paper on the table. 'Not bad news? Oh no, not more trouble!'

'Not the letter – that can wait. Magda, I'm sorry – you've taken enough already, but you have to know. It's your cousin.'

She gave a quick glance towards the door. 'Is he still out there? Oh Max – '

'No, Magda – he's gone.'

Relief flooded her. 'Thank God. What is it then?'

'The boar got him.'

Maddie's breath caught in her throat. She had seen what pigs could do; once they had bitten another's tail the scent of blood drove them crazy. 'It gored him?' she whispered.

'Worse than that. It ate his face. Nearly killed him. The military have taken him away to hospital and they think it's unlikely he'll survive, but if he does he'll never look normal again. He'll be badly disfigured for life.'

Maddie sank down on a chair, burying her face in her

hands. The hideous picture Max had painted somehow made it harder to hate a man who had suffered such a punishment, whatever he might have done . . .

'God, how awful,' she murmured.

'It serves him right,' said Max quietly.

Eva looked up. 'That's right, Mr Bower, it does, after what he done. We won't cry over him, will we, Lassie? Come on, Maddie, we better milk the cows before the milk van comes.'

Eva picked up the sheet of paper from the table. 'Hey!' she cried in delight. 'This letter's me mam's writing! Come and read it to me!'

The letter was brief but to the point. '*So taking all in all, Mr Bakewell and me has decided it might be best to leave things as they are for the time being. Eva loves that school and her Miss Gaunt, so if it's all right with you we'll leave Eva with you for the duration.*'

Eva whooped with delight and, milking forgotten, ran out to the gate. 'I got to go and tell Eunice,' she shouted back. 'I got to tell her I can be her best friend for years and years now. Come on, Lassie!'

Dog rose and then hesitated, looking back at the empty bed. Maddie bent to pat his head. 'It's all right, Dog – Lassie. You go and look after Eva.'

The dog loped out. Maddie smiled. All was not darkness when a child's face could bring her such happiness. Max came to her. 'I'd better be getting back to see to the horses,' he said quietly. 'Are you sure you'll be all right?'

Maddie nodded. 'I'll be all right. Will you come back soon?'

He held her close for a second. 'I'll be back soon and often. Nothing on earth will keep me away from you.'

She reached out a hand and he took it eagerly. 'Thank you, Max. It means a lot to me, especially after – after – '

He squeezed her hand, pulling her close. She tried to pull her hand away and turn from him, but he held it tight. 'Oh Max! I feel so dirty, so degraded.'

'No,' he said firmly. 'You are what you have always been – innocence itself. It was your innocence which brought me back to life, Magda, and you will have it till the day you die, whatever happens.' He kissed her gently, murmuring, 'You are beautiful, Magda. I will be back soon.'

Maddie watched him go out of the gate and turn to wave. As long as Max was coming back she could cope . . .

September was dying away into October, drenching the Garthdale valley with beauty, gilding the trees down in Barnbeck and bronzing the heather on the moor. The first crisp air of autumn tinged the morning as the valley began to move imperceptibly into winter. But all was warmth and peace in Scapegoat Farm.

James Renshaw was laid to rest one windy afternoon in the little graveyard alongside his Lily and as Maddie's tears dried she began to emerge from a twilight state and memories of that hideous night began to fade. Max never spoke of it, as though he understood her need to forget. Eva was happy now the new school term had begun and there were stimulating diversions for her active young mind. Even Duster was holding her head high again, her ears pricked and alert and her coat glossy. Maddie rode on the moor, revelling in the wild wind that tossed her hair and savouring the peace that had come back into her life.

At Thunder Crags she reined in and turned to face the wind, hearing in its howl the sound of weeping.

'There will be no more weeping, Mother,' she whispered into the bluster. The wind snatched at her words, carrying them away over the moor. 'No more weeping, for the world has grown beautiful again.'

She listened for a moment, but knew no answering words would come. Then, turning Duster about, she rode back down to Scapegoat.

Max was late today. Every day at noon he had come since her father died, giving a hand with the heavier jobs, helping with the books and forms. Yet the day must come when he would hear that there was a ship to America . . . Alone in the kitchen with only the dog to hear, she hugged a cushion to her chest and poured it out.

'I love you, Max, with all the passion of my soul. You make life so beautiful. Never leave me, Max, never go away again because you are all that makes life worth living. I'd go to the ends of the earth with you, I'd give up everything for you, my darling. I'd die for you.'

There was a sound outside, footsteps, and then silence. Maddie flung aside the cushion and opened the door. He was sitting, as he had done once before, on the upturned box by the pump.

'Max?'

He turned his head, those magnificent black eyes taking her in, and then he smiled.

'I was remembering,' he said, and the vibrancy of his tone made her shiver.

'Come indoors. Eva's not back from school yet.'

He stood up slowly, uncurling his length in graceful, catlike fashion, and his gaze still rested on her face. Despite the chill in the air his shirt sleeves were rolled up and she could see the rough star branded on his forearm, and somehow the sight moved her.

'What were you remembering, Max?'

He gave a rueful smile. 'Oh, how full of self-pity I was when I first came here, how meeting you brought hope and light back into my life. You didn't know what a miracle you wrought.'

'I was a child. I knew nothing then.'

'It was your innocence I needed, Magda. I need it still. You're different from any other woman I've known. You're my light in this wilderness of a world.'

She did not interrupt. She wanted to hear more. He stepped closer to her. 'I love you, Magda, more than anything in the world. I want to be with you always.'

She looked up at him. 'Are you sure? Ronnie – '

He put an arm about her waist and drew her indoors. Do you know the Song of Solomon?'

'No.'

'There's a line in it. *You are wholly beautiful, my love, and without blemish.*'

As he kissed her Maddie clung to him, feeling she could almost choke with love. Suddenly a voice cut in.

'Mr Bower, Eunice don't believe me about you and them dancing horses.'

Eva was standing in the open doorway, the shy face of Eunice behind her. 'Tell her it's right, Mr Bower – I haven't made it up, have I? You really did have horses what danced in Venice?'

'Vienna, Eva.' Maddie could hear the gentle amusement in his tone.

'Summat like that. Well any road, come out to the stable with us.' She pulled him by the sleeve, tugging him away from Maddie's arms. Maddie could see the smile on his lips as he allowed himself to be dragged through the open doorway into the farmyard.

'Why? What is it you want, Eva?'

'I told Eunice you could do it – you can do owt, you can – so come down to the stable with us and show Duster how to dance.'

Maddie smiled, standing in the open doorway and watching them cross the dusty cobbled yard together. The diminutive figure of Eva was gazing up at Max with adoration in her eyes. Oh yes, thought Maddie contentedly, it's all right with me, Mrs Jarrett, if you leave Eva with us for the duration, or even for always . . .

Contemporary Women

Powerful, compelling novels about today's women . . .

Decisions
Freda Brigh

The moment every working woman longs for . . . and ever married woman dreads.

When Dasha returned to law school, her husband Jorda backed her all the way. And when she got a job with a to law firm, no one could have been more proud – unt Dasha's career began outstripping his own. Now Dash must make the most important decision of her life . . .

Friends of the Opposite Sex
Sara Davidso

'A lively, intelligent novel remarkable for its thoughtf honesty' EVENING STANDARD

Lucy is an independent woman with a flourishing caree and plenty of love affairs. But she is thirty, and marriag and motherhood are suddenly appealing. Then she meet Joe, who wants both more and less than love – a workin partnership – and Lucy must decide if they can ever be 'ju good friends'.

The Rich and the Mighty
Vera Cowi

The news of billionaire Richard Tempest's death shake the world's financial markets – and sends a tremor c anticipation through his rapacious stepchildren. Bu control of the Tempest fortune passes to a stranger Elizabeth Sheridan, already a top model, has a cool hea and a streak of ruthlessness. But are they enough to ensur her survival in the dangerous, decadent world of wealth t which she is suddenly heiress?

FONTANA PAPERBACKS

Fontana's Family Sagas

Molly   Teresa Crane

Molly is a spirited young woman who escapes poverty in
Ireland for a new life in Victorian London. Courageous
and passionate, she fights the prejudice against her sex
and her class — and wins.   A compelling story.

The Cavendish Face   Jane Barry

A love story to sweep you off your feet. Set in London of
the 1920s and '30s, it tells of a young woman's struggle
against the stifling conventions and corrupt morals around
her and how she seeks a way to love freely the only man
who has ever had a place in her life.   A captivating novel.

Futures   Freda Bright

Caro Harmsworth is the perfect twentieth-century woman
— young, liberated, independent, and determined to be a
success in the high financial world of Wall Street. A strong
contemporary story of love and success — and of the
woman who has to chose between the two. . .

FONTANA PAPERBACKS

Distant Choices
Brenda Jagger

In a world of mill barons and railway kings, two sister
Oriel and Kate share the same uncaring father. Bu
whereas Kate is legitimate, Oriel is not.

Oriel learns from an ambitions mother to be cool, t
calm the fire in her heart. Kate, with emotions untame
and no mother at all, yearns to break free from he
loveless life.

Drawn together by fate as well as by birth, th
two sisters are friends. And then Squire Franci
Ashington, poet and explorer, comes back to live i
Gore Valley . . .

Also available
A Song Twice Over
A Winter's Child
Days of Grace

FONTANA PAPERBACKS

New British Writers

Three rich, wonderful novels
by outstanding young British authors

A Splendid Defiance   Stella Riley

Justin Ambrose, a dashing and cynical Cavalier, was bored
with garrison life – until he fell in love with Abby, the sister
of a fanatic Roundhead rebel. With their hearts and
loyalties divided, and caught up in a passionate, forbidden
love affair, Abby and Justin watched the rival armies
prepare for a bloody confrontation.

The Skylark's Song   Audrey Howard

Zoe was born in the poorest street in Liverpool. As the
youngest of five children her life in the Merseyside slum
meant brutality, degradation and appalling poverty. But
Zoe was bright, sensitive and determined to escape.
Freedom would bring her wealth, luxury and love – and
heartache she could never have imagined . . .

A Season of Mists   Sarah Woodhouse

Ann Mathick had a dream. She wanted to make the run-
down Norfolk farm, which she had inherited from a
disreputable uncle, prosperous again. None of the county
believed she could do it. But the only man who could stop
Ann was Sir Harry Gerard, her dashing, reckless
neighbour – a very dangerous man to fall in love
with . . .

FONTANA PAPERBACKS

Fontana Paperbacks: Fiction

Fontana is a leading paperback publisher of fiction
Below are some recent titles.

- ☐ CABAL Clive Barker £2.95
- ☐ DALLAS DOWN Richard Moran £2.95
- ☐ SHARPE'S RIFLES Bernard Cornwell £3.50
- ☐ A MAN RIDES THROUGH Stephen Donaldson £4.95
- ☐ HOLD MY HAND I'M DYING John Gordon Davis £3.95
- ☐ ROYAL FLASH George MacDonald Fraser £3.50
- ☐ FLASH FOR FREEDOM! George MacDonald Fraser £3.50
- ☐ THE HONEY ANT Duncan Kyle £2.95
- ☐ FAREWELL TO THE KING Pierre Schoendoerffer £2.95
- ☐ MONKEY SHINES Michael Stewart £2.95

You can buy Fontana paperbacks at your local bookshop
newsagent. Or you can order them from Fontana Paperback
Cash Sales Department, Box 29, Douglas, Isle of Man. Pleas
send a cheque, postal or money order (not currency) worth th
purchase price plus 22p per book for postage (maximum postag
required is £3.00 for orders within the UK).

NAME (Block letters) _____

ADDRESS _____

_____

FLAME OF DESIRE

"Little one, ah little one . . ." His warm breath caressed her face. Slowly, like the figure in her dreams, he bent his head. His lips touched hers, closed over her mouth.

She was lost in his deep probing kiss and felt the impact of the intimacy all the way down to her chilled toes. A warmth spread through her. Her limbs began to shake.

His voice rumbled huskily. "You are cold?"

Unable to speak, she shook her head no. Cold was the furthest thing from her mind—her body aflame with desire. . . .

MORE TEMPESTUOUS ROMANCES!

GOLDEN TORMENT (1323, $3.75)
by Janelle Taylor
Kathryn had travelled the Alaskan wilderness in search of her father. But after one night of sensual pleasure with the fierce, aggressive lumberjack, Landis Jurrell—she knew she'd never again travel alone!

LOVE ME WITH FURY (1248, $3.75)
by Janelle Taylor
When Alexandria discovered the dark-haired stranger who watched her swim, she was outraged by his intrusion. But when she felt his tingling caresses and tasted his intoxicating kisses, she could no longer resist drowning in the waves of sweet sensuality.

BELOVED SCOUNDREL (1259, $3.75)
by Penelope Neri
Denying what her body admitted, Christianne vowed to take revenge against the arrogant seaman who'd tormented her with his passionate caresses. Even if it meant never again savoring his exquisite kisses, she vowed to get even with her one and only BELOVED SCOUNDREL!

PASSION'S GLORY (1227, $3.50)
by Anne Moore
Each time Nicole looked into Kane's piercing dark eyes, she remembered his cold-hearted reputation and prayed that he wouldn't betray her love. She wanted faithfulness, love and forever—but all he could give her was a moment of PASSION'S GLORY.

Available wherever paperbacks are sold, or order direct from the Publisher. Send cover price plus 50¢ per copy for mailing and handling to Zebra Books, 475 Park Avenue South, New York, N.Y. 10016. DO NOT SEND CASH.

KATHARINE KINCAID

ZEBRA BOOKS
KENSINGTON PUBLISHING CORP.

ZEBRA BOOKS

are published by

KENSINGTON PUBLISHING CORP.
475 Park Avenue South
New York, N.Y. 10016

First printing: February, 1984

Printed in the United States of America

For my parents,
who have always believed in me

When the sun sets
In crimson splendor
Followed by darkest night,
Fear not, oh my beloved,
You will not be alone
In the fiery dawn.

Prologue

November, 1794

Dear Aunt Margaret,

So much has happened since last I wrote to you, I scarcely know where to begin. Indeed, since it will be months before you receive this letter, it seems foolish to begin at all. But I must. You are my only kin and I think of you so often, wishing we could visit and I could share these thoughts in person. You must often wonder how Papa and I have fared since we arrived in the Ohio Country one year ago last month.

The good news first: I am now married to a man I love with all my heart. His name is Kin-di-wa, which means Golden Eagle in the Miami language, and in many ways he is exactly like that wild free bird. He is also tall and handsome, with straight black hair and eyes the color of a blue winter sky. (In case you wonder, his eyes are his only legacy from a white father who abandoned him before he was born.)

Please do not be shocked that I have chosen to marry a "savage," but I am no longer the foolish flighty girl who longed to come to Philadelphia and be courted by fine gentlemen. I am a woman of eighteen who has learned much in the wilderness, and my husband is not only a fierce Miami warrior but a man of great courage, honor, and gentleness. I am proud to be his wife. Among the Miamis, he is exceeded in esteem only by their great war chief, Little Turtle.

Now for the bad news: Papa is dead. He was killed by a war party of Shawnee last spring. I would be dead too had I not been rescued by Kindi-wa. I confess that at the time I didn't know I was being saved from the Shawnee. I thought I was being assaulted and kidnapped. (Indeed, believing myself alone, I was taking a bath inside in an old rain barrel.) But that is the way life is here in the Ohio Country: things are not always as they seem.

Poor Papa. Perhaps it is just as well he didn't live to see his greatest hero dishonored. I am speaking, of course, of General Anthony Wayne. No doubt you have heard by now how Mad Anthony defeated the Miami Confederation at Fallen Timbers this past August—the Moon of the New Corn. No doubt all Philadelphia celebrated the victory. But I must tell you, Aunt Margaret, there was nothing honorable about that battle. The Indians were misled by British promises of arms and support and then betrayed at the last moment.

It was wrong for the United States Army to engage in such a battle. The Northwest Territory belongs to the Indians. They have fought these many years only for what they own, and I hope and pray that President Washington will instruct General Wayne to deal with them fairly at the Treaty Council next summer.

Oh, Aunt Margaret! If you could know the Miamis and live among them, as I am doing, you too would weep to see them defeated. Their villages and crops have been destroyed. They have lost their finest young men and several great leaders. A bitter cold winter lies ahead, but they will never ask for mercy. They are a proud unbending people—yet peace between our peoples is all most of them have ever wanted. Peace and protection from land-hungry whites.

Well, enough of history. What is done is done. When we journey to the Treaty Council, I will try to post this letter. I shall never get to Philadelphia now as Mama dreamed—God rest her and Papa's soul!—so it eases my mind to have written to you. Life this winter will be harsh, but please know I would rather be here than anywhere. The destiny of my husband and his people is my destiny now; Kin-di-wa is my reason for living.

9

May the Great Spirit who holds us all in the palm of his hand keep you safe from harm. Affectionate regards.

Your niece,

Rebecca McDuggan

Part One

One

January, 1795

The mist in the Shawnee graveyard was thicker than Rebecca remembered. It snaked between the mounded graves like a living breathing thing and coiled itself around her naked body as though she were its prey.

Wake up, Rebecca, wake up, her inner voice warned. *You've got to get away from here.*

Shivers rippled up and down her spine. She tried to run but her feet were mired in the undulating mist. Sinuous white chains held her fast and forced her to look back—back into a past she'd thought she'd long since buried.

She pulled her flaming red hair around herself like a veil and crossed her arms over her breasts in an anxious protective gesture. "Kin-di-wa!" she called. "Where are you?"

13

The only sound was the hiss of steam from a small sulfurous pool nearby. She drew a deep shaky breath, the stench of sulfur and death making her feel nauseous. This place was evil—evil. Why had she returned here? She was safely married to Kin-di-wa now, and all the ugly hurtful things that had happened—even those that had happened here—could never hurt her again.

But now the past came rushing back to her: Papa's death in the swamp. The pain and degradation she had suffered at the hands of a man named Will Simpkin. The Battle of Fallen Timbers. Her frantic search for Kin-di-wa among the dead and wounded.

But it is all over now! she insisted. Kin-di-wa's wounds are healing well, and I have even made peace with Two Fires—Kin-di-wa's other wife.

Then she remembered how Kin-di-wa had tried to send her away to her own people after the battle, and her heart gave a sickening lurch. Yes, he had sent her away, tried to spare her the suffering of his defeated tribesmen—but then he had come after her and brought her home again. Home. Home was where Kin-di-wa was, and no matter what they'd been forced to endure—or what remained to be endured—they would never part again. He had promised her this. "Without you, there is no reason to live," he had said. "No reason to go on."

She twisted and turned in the mist, looking first one way then the other. Where was Kin-di-wa now? Why was she here? Why didn't he come and

14

take her away from this awful place?

"Kin-di-wa?"

Her voice echoed faintly, bouncing off a ledge of rock in the very center of the mounded graves. A tinkling sound came to her ears—shells brushing together. Shells and gourds and feathered amulets decorated the stakes marking each grave. She turned toward the sound, calling softly, "Kin-di-wa, is that you? Have you come for me at last?"

But the man coming toward her through the mist was not Kin-di-wa. Kin-di-wa was tall and regal, with the bearing of a chieftain. His body was perfectly proportioned, broad of chest, narrow of hip, and rippling with smooth muscles. Her husband's face knew no beard, nor did it know fear, greed, lust, cunning or any other base emotion.

Not so with this man. He lumbered toward her with a heavy tread, his huge body calling to mind the dimensions of a grizzly bear. And he was covered from head to foot with crinkly curling black hair. The only ornament on his otherwise naked body was a necklace of shriveled and dried human fingers that she knew had been taken from the neck of a dead Shawnee warrior.

"Will. Will Simpkin." She spoke his name calmly as if to do so might dispel the dread he aroused within her, but waves of nausea and fear washed over her. He had no right to invade her dreams, no right whatsoever. "What are you doing here, Will Simpkin?"

"I come fur ya, Becky," the man growled. "I come t' take ya home ag'in."

15

"My home is with Kin-di-wa," she answered coldly. "I am his woman—his wife."

The man called Will Simpkin came closer. His rank body odor assaulted her, and his tiny pig-like eyes glittered dangerously above the bristling growth of black hair on his face. "I done tol' ya once, Becky. Y' b'long t' me—only me. An' I'll kill any man whut says ya don't."

Too upset to reply, she couldn't stop herself from rediscovering every detail of his repulsive hairy body. Once, he had forced himself upon her—here, in this very place—after leaving her father to die of his wounds in the swamp. If only the Shawnee had shot him too! If only Will had died instead of Papa!

Her gaze came to rest on his extended manhood, springing straight out from a tangled nest of hair. A flush spread hotly across her shoulders and up her neck to her cheeks. His swollen organ seemed to grow larger, shocking her, as he chuckled throatily. "Like whut ya see, little red-haired spit-fire? Ya want ole Will t' make ya feel like a woman ag'in?"

"You never made me feel like a woman. You forced yourself on me and made me feel like an animal. That's all you know how to do—force yourself on a woman. Why don't you go off in the forest and rut with the bears? I'm sure a female black bear would enjoy your love-making far more than I did."

Now, he reared up over her, and his hands became two enormous curving-clawed paws. His nose lengthened to a snout, and his body hair thickened into a shaggy coat of fur. He snorted and growled, causing fear to pump through her veins like snow water. His breath smelled of rotted fish, but she refused to step back from him—to show any sign of her mounting terror. Kin-di-wa had taught her never to run from a menacing bear. Stand still, he'd told her once. Stare him down, and the bear will retreat.

"You don't frighten me, Will. I know you for what you are—a coward. You're afraid of your own shadow. Yes, a coward, a skulking whining dog—that's all you are, Will."

In the face of her taunts, the bear image faded. The man became pitifully human again as his self-confidence oozed out of him like blood from a suppurating wound. "Who're you callin' coward?" he whined. "I ain't no coward!"

"No? Then why do you shoot Indians in the back, Will? Why don't you face them and fight?"

"How do you know about that?" he cried. "You wuzn't there! You didn't see it!"

"Did you think no one would ever find out? Did you think you killed both Indians?"

"They wuz savages! Worthless savages! I done my country a favor by killin' off them stinkin' animals!"

"One of them did not die, Will. One of them lived to tell the story: how you tricked and betrayed them. How you offered your hand in friendship, then shot them when they turned their backs. How you stole their furs, then left their bodies to rot . . . and it wasn't the first time, was it, Will?" She looked pointedly at his necklace.

17

One of his huge furry hands groped upwards to the dangling human fingers. His pig-eyes narrowed defensively, and she was conscious of his rising anger. "No, it wuzn't the first time, Becky—and by God, it won't be the last! I'll kill every one o' them slimy bastards! An' you—a white woman—oughta thank me fur it!"

He took another step toward her, and her courage fled. The instinct to flee was overwhelming, but before she could turn and run, his hand shot out and grabbed her about the neck. "Let go of me, Will. I warn you!"

Her voice quavered, and she was disgusted and ashamed that he should know of her fear. "You won't degrade me again! Kin-di-wa will kill you if you touch me!"

He threw back his head and laughed—a thundering mocking laugh that rolled out over the graves and rattled the bones in the treetops. "Ain't nobody gonna keep ya from me, sweet Becky! Not yur Papa an' not that stinkin' half-breed ya call yur husband—ya hear me?" He began to shake her by the neck. "He ain't yur husband—I am! An' I'm takin' back whut's mine!"

"No!" she screamed. Her teeth rattled as he shook her. "Kin-di-wa! Kin-di-wa, help me!"

"I'll make ya furget that half-breed," Will snarled. Fingers locked in her long flowing hair, he dragged her naked body to him and enfolded her in his crushing grip. "I'll make ya beg fur me, little spit-fire. I wuz the one yur papa meant fur ya—he promised ya t' me!"

18

She twisted and fought him, but it was futile. He was too strong for her. "Before Papa died, he cursed you, Will! He cursed you with his dying breath. I found him after you ran off and left him—I found him and heard him curse you!"

Will's hands dug into her buttocks, forcing her body to rub against his swollen organ. "Whut do I care fur a dead man's curses? This time I'll teach ya, little spit-fire. I'll teach ya t' run away from me inta the arms of a stinkin' half-breed!"

He bent her backwards, heedless of the blows she rained down upon his neck and shoulders. His body odor was thick in her nostrils, sickening her, making her gag. How she hated him—despised him! "No—I won't let you do this to me again!"

But he was doing it, almost breaking her in half as he bent her backwards, forcing her to the mist shrouded ground. His teeth moved down her neck—not kissing, not nibbling—but seeking to inflict pain. Pain was the only thing he knew, the only way to possess a woman, to break her spirit.

The mist reached up with clawing fingers to draw her down, down, and further down. Will's teeth found her breasts, and his rough hands dug into her woman-place. She writhed against him, writhed against the pain and terror which swirled around and through her—snaked over her like the mist. "No-no-no-no-no . . . animal! Animal!"

Then he was shaking her, shaking her. And suddenly, she heard Kin-di-wa calling her from some far distant place. "Cat-Eyes! Cat-Eyes!"

Kin-di-wa's voice came closer, more insistent. "Cat-Eyes, wake up!"

19

Two strong hands held her shoulders, shaking her gently. "Wake up, little Cat-Eyes, it is only a dream."

"A dream! But—but . . ." She opened her eyes to see Kin-di-wa's face—his beloved handsome face with its granite jaw and chin, its dazzling blue eyes, and its finely-chiseled nose. He was bending over her, eyes alight with concern and dismay.

Unable to believe for a moment that he was truly there, she ran her fingers along his jawline, then up to his forehead where the tender pink of a new scar stood out sharply against his bronze skin. Her husband's eyes darkened. "What is it that makes you cry out in the night? You woke us all with your screams and insults."

She glanced toward the three recumbent forms on the other side of the lodge. They were unmoving. A log fell heavily in the stone-ringed fire, sending up a tiny shower of sparks, and she turned her gaze back to him, soothed by his nearness and relieved that she had only been dreaming.

"I see no one else awake," she whispered. "Or if they did wake, they went quickly back to sleep again."

"They knew I would soothe your troubled mind—and find out the reason for it." The shadows shifted like thunderclouds in his startlingly blue eyes, and she twined her fingers in his straight, black, shoulder-length hair.

"Kiss me, my husband," she begged. "I need to know I am safe here in your arms."

Stiffly, he bent down and brushed her lips with

his, and the stiffness, she knew, was from his still mending rib. The rib had been shattered by a near death blow from a Long Knife at the battle of Fallen Timbers.

"Now, tell me what you dreamed," he commanded. "For you know a dream can foretell the future, and if our future is again threatened, I would know now so I can prepare for it."

"It was not the future of which I dreamed—it was the past. A past that is best forgotten." She sought to divert his attention from the dream by drawing him down again and offering her lips. The sweetness of his gentle kiss had already made the dream fade into the dark shadows rimming the lodge fire.

But persistently, he held her away from him. "Was it my brother's murderer of whom you dreamed?"

She couldn't meet his eyes. Instead, she looked again toward the sleeping forms, one of which was Two Fires, the widow of his dead brother. "Yes, I dreamed of Will Simpkin, the man who shot *Kat-a-mon-gli*. But it was only a dream, Kin-di-wa, a dream of no importance."

Kin-di-wa sat up and turned his back to her. He stared moodily into the fire. "All dreams are important. And I too have dreamed of him. I have dreamed of his necklace of fingers. You know as well as I do, Cat-Eyes, what the dreams mean."

She scrambled to her knees beside him. "No, Kin-di-wa! There has been enough killing— enough death." She gestured to the sleeping forms. "Would you leave us all to starve while you again took up the trail of vengeance? Two Fires has lost one husband—must she lose another? There are no more brothers to take her as wife if you should be lost!"

Sudden amusement tugged at his lips. "So it is Two Fires for whom you worry, is it? I had hoped you might have some fear for your own possible widowhood."

She was not in the least amused. "I do have a fear for it—but if you will not forsake vengeance for me, perhaps you will do so for them: Two Fires and her son—your son, now. Must little Walks-Tall grow up fatherless? Will there be no one to show him how to track and how to hunt? Must he . . . ?"

Kin-di-wa turned to her, grinning, and placed a finger across her lips. "Hush . . . you will wake them yet. And what about Crow Woman?" He nodded to a cocoon of skins from which protruded a grizzled white head. "Have you no word for her, about how I will be neglecting my duty to an elder—one to whom I owe my life?"

"You will be neglecting your duty to her if you go off and get yourself killed! If it weren't for her wisdom with herbs, you'd already be dead! Please, Kin-di-wa . . ." she grasped his hand. "We almost lost you at Fallen Timbers. Please don't go on any missions of vengeance now—when you are almost well again."

The amusement faded from his eyes. "I will not go now, little one. Winter is not the time. But in the spring, when the winds blow warm again, my brother's murder must be avenged."

22

"Kin-di-wa . . ." She would beg if necessary. "Can't we put vengeance and bloodshed behind us? Soon, there will be a treaty council, an opportunity for new beginnings. So many on both sides have been killed—maybe even Will Simpkin. Couldn't we just forget past wounds and grievances? Start out fresh and new?"

His hand came up to caress her cheek. "My beautiful green-eyed woman, wife of my heart . . . do you not know how much I wish for that to happen? A new beginning—where the drums of war will never again be heard." His eyes blazed with some deep emotion—was it hope?—then became shadowed and guarded once more. "But you must not expect too much, Cat-Eyes. We have been at war so long, I do not know if we can remember how to live in peace—even when we are starving."

"Oh, Kin-di-wa!" She pressed his hand to her lips, then gently took it away. "Come now . . . you must sleep if you would go hunting again tomorrow."

The thought of him roving through the cold bleak forest made her shiver. He ought not even to be out in such bitter cold weather. His wounds had healed well, but the injured muscles of one shoulder and the area around his broken rib still gave him trouble. Moreover, the game in the area had been over-hunted and driven off by the armies of red men and white, so he usually came back with nothing more than stiffened joints and near frozen extremities.

"Cat-Eyes . . ." He held onto her hand, and a

husky note came into his voice. "Must you always pull away whenever I come too close?"

"Kin-di-wa, you—you must save your strength for hunting." Or else we all shall soon die, she added silently.

"I would seek my strength from you, Cat-Eyes . . . not from sleep. You are all the strength I need."

"But you are still so weak," she protested. "And Crow Woman says you must abstain from that which men and women do together—if you are ever to recover fully."

"Crow Woman—pah! I doubt not her wisdom with herbs, but when it comes to mating, she has long forgotten all she ever knew."

Surprisingly, there was no weakness in the hand that drew her closer, and Rebecca found herself trembling. It had been so long—so terribly long. She could hardly remember the last time their bodies had joined and their spirits soared. Only that it had been before the battle, before Kin-di-wa had been so badly wounded . . . before the heartbreak of the Miamis' defeat and the onslaught of the bitter cold winter.

She stole a glance at the sleeping figures and was embarrassed by the lack of privacy—and by the presence of Two Fires to whom Kin-di-wa also belonged.

Kin-di-wa brought her chin around to face him. "Do you still find my people's ways so strange, little one? Does it still bother you that a man may have more than one wife?"

She couldn't lie to him. It did still bother her to

24

think of sharing him—even though she knew he'd taken Two Fires to wife only because it was his duty. He couldn't shame his brother's name nor abandon those who needed him. "Yes," she whispered. "But I am trying, Kin-di-wa. Two Fires and I—we have made our peace. Only I— I—what if one of them awakens?"

"They will pretend to see nothing and will go back to sleep. Come, little Cat-Eyes . . . I have waited a long time to take you to my buffalo robe. Longer than necessary, for I assure you, my manhood suffered no injury from musket or long knife."

She stifled an impulse to laugh. "I'm sorry to hear that. I had been planning to massage your— manhood—the way I massage your shoulder. I had thought it might need soothing after having been so long neglected."

Suddenly light-hearted and reckless after so many weeks of gloom and sorrow, she allowed him to lead her to his fur-heaped pallet. It lay on the other side of the fire from the two sleeping women and the sleeping child, Walks-Tall, who was laced snugly into his cradleboard. Kin-di-wa turned back his buffalo robe, smoothed down some skins for her to lie on, then turned to her with sparkling eyes.

Feeling as timid and shy as a new bride, she knelt down on the skins and began to undo the laces at the neckline of her beaded doeskin smock.

"Let me do it," he whispered, kneeling down in front of her. "If I have not forgotten how."

"You would never forget so important a thing,"

25

she whispered back, smiling to cover her nervousness. She would have undone her hair from its long braids, but he pulled her hands away.

"I would do that too," he commanded. And his fingers moved nimbly to untie the rawhide thongs that tamed the heavy masses of her bright red hair. He took the braided hair and lifted it in his hands, pulling his fingers through it and shaking it out until it fell across her shoulders like a flaming red curtain.

"Mayhap, I should have called you Sun Woman." His voice was a soft throaty growl. "For your hair is like the sun in the long hours of the evening. It is the color of fire, and I would warm myself in its glow."

Using her hair like a tether to draw her to him, he sought her lips, and it did seem that a flicker of fire raced between their mouths. He drew her hair about his neck and shoulders as though he would bind her to him. She looked deeply into his blue eyes, finding her own green ones mirrored there. Licking flames were leaping in the depths of both blue eyes and green.

"Do you not know how lovely you are, Cat-Eyes? Do you not know you are the wife of my heart—as no one else could ever be?"

"If I am as you say—the wife of your heart—then prove it to me, Kin-di-wa. This night, I have great need to know I am your woman." The dark wings of her nightmare beat at her briefly, then the terror was forgotten as he pressed his lips to hers, claiming her mouth in a long searing kiss.

Breathless, she put her hands on his chest. He

was half naked, as he always was, even in the dead of winter, and his muscles beneath her fingertips rippled fluidly—except for his one shoulder where Crow Woman had dug out a musketball. Lightly, she traced the scar where she herself had placed the white-hot blade to cleanse and close the wound.

His hands moved along her back, then tugged at the fringed edge of her doeskin. Obediently, she raised her arms and allowed him to pull it over her head. "Let me look at you," he whispered. "I want to be certain I am not dreaming—for even when I lay ill with fever, I could not help dreaming of the perfection of your body."

Gently, he eased her back onto the skins, his eyes devouring every inch of her as she lay open and waiting before him. His hunger filled her with delight—made her feel young and free and happy again. She felt as if she had entered a new world, their own private place, where grief and sorrow could never find them. For this had she been born—to love and be loved by this man who was her husband.

"When you lay ill with fever, it was not of my body you dreamed," she teased. "You had nightmares too—worse ones than mine."

"True," he grinned. "But in between my nightmares, I dreamed of you like this—waiting for my kisses to make your body sing with life."

"Sing with life! I am no dead woman," she laughed softly, "nor am I an empty gourd such as you once accused me of being."

"An empty gourd? Did I call you such? Ah, but

that was before I knew you." He stretched out beside her and lazily brushed back the mantle of hair from her breasts. "I did not know, when I stole you screaming out of that rain barrel, that what I saw as a spitting wild cat, was only a purring kitten—one who could be tamed with gentleness."

"I was taking a bath," she reminded him. "I thought myself completely alone. How was I to know you were only saving me from the bloodthirsty Shawnee?"

"Even had there been no Shawnee that day, I would have stolen you, Cat-Eyes. What man could resist flame-colored hair and leaf-green eyes—and skin that begs to be touched?" His hand strayed to the creamy white mounds whose rosy tips were already hardening in anticipation of his caress.

"When I touch you here," he whispered, "I feel as though I am the first man on earth—the one the missionaries taught me about in my boyhood. I am Adam, and the land I journey through is filled with every good thing—all manner of ripe and delicious fruits. All manner of good things to pleasure me."

His caresses made her forget that there was anyone else in the lodge—indeed, in the whole universe—except the two of them. "And will you taste the fruit I bring you?" she sighed. "It is the best kind—that which is offered with love."

"Yes, my ripe sweet Cat-Eyes, I will not only taste, I will consume you . . ." He bent his head and kissed the valley between her breasts, then his lips rolled over the tender sensitive flesh of each curving hillock. He licked her nipples, took one into his mouth and suckled gently.

Desire flooded through her like golden sunlight —liquified into wild sweet honey. She entwined her fingers in his hair and urged him onward, afraid for him to go on, afraid for him to stop. Did the miracle still exist? Could he still move her to a depth of passion and forgetfulness that was like nothing she had ever known? Nothing she could describe with mere words?

"I have missed you so, Kin-di-wa," she moaned. "I have missed being loved by you."

"Then let us make up for the time we have lost, little one.".

His hands, his mouth, his lips moved across her willing flesh like the hot breath of wind that precedes a forest fire or a summer storm. She was caught up in the rushing excitement, the sense of things whirling, whirling, beyond her control. She surrendered joyously. Her entire world narrowed to the exquisite sensation of his seeking lips, his questing fingers.

She began her own exquisite explorations. His hair was straight and fine—not silky like a woman's—but possessed of masculine vibrancy, some inner source of strength. The skin of his back and shoulders was warm and smooth, the muscles firm and fluid, inviting her fingertips to make small circular motions that set the muscles trembling.

Down his back and lower, she went exploring —until her fingers came to the knotted rawhide that held his breechclout in place. Swiftly, she undid the thong and removed the last barrier to the full enjoyment of their bodies. Then, she pressed herself against him, glorying in his hard contours. He was ready for her, his breath coming in ragged gasps as he sought to hold himself in check.

"Not yet," she begged. "I don't want it to end so soon." But even as she spoke, the tide was sweeping her along. The hot wind became a flaming bonfire as he moved over her, then bent down and parted her lips with his tongue. She moaned and clasped him to her. Her hand found his manhood and stroked and fondled. Shivering with excitement and passion, she guided him into the very core of her—the center of her being.

His tongue and his manhood did a probing dance, then he was thrusting, thrusting deep within her, and she could hold back no longer. The world exploded in brilliant shards of light and flame.

She was consumed, lifted out of herself, turned inside out. The miracle was repeated. She and Kin-di-wa were one—man and woman merged and joined in the most ancient mystery of all creation.

They clung to one another, immersed in wonder, and when at last, they disengaged, a tear slid down her cheek. She was startled, but no less than he was.

"Tears?" he questioned. "Was my loving so distasteful to you?"

"Of course not! I—I always weep when I'm happy."

He nibbled on her ear. "Then I shall make your tears fall like summer rain—until the whole world is flooded, and we must make our home in a canoe instead of a lodge."

"Oh, you! You find humor in everything!" Once, she had thought him impossibly stern, even grim—but then he'd had so little joy in his life until she came along. She would die before she destroyed his trust or brought him any more injury or sorrow. She hugged him happily— pleased that he could be so playful.

"Ouch! You're hurting my rib," he complained.

"You didn't seem to mind the pain a few minutes ago," she teased.

He sat up and reached for his breechclout. "The pleasure then was worth a little pain—but now, I am reminded of how stiff and sore my body still is."

"My poor Kin-di-wa . . ." she mocked, then she too sat upright. Kin-di-wa never voiced his discomfort. Now, his face wore a small grimace, and he was even rubbing his side. Had she managed to hurt him? "Here . . . let me see. I knew it was too soon! We should never have . . ."

"Enough!" he laughed. "I only wanted to see if you would continue to treat me like a papoose now that you know I am a man again."

"Oh, I know you are a man—a man who sometimes acts like a papoose." She reached for her doeskin, watching him covertly. He was moving stiffly as he fastened his breechclout back in place. She wished he needn't venture out in the morning—but if he did not, none of them would eat. A low rumble in her stomach reminded her that they had been boiling the same bones for three days now, and their supply of nuts and roots was almost exhausted.

A small sound from the opposite side of the lodge made her start and pull on her doeskin in one single hasty movement. The sound came again—a dry hacking cough, and she realized who had awakened: little Walks-Tall. Despite Crow Woman's chants and chest poultices, and Two Fires's herbal teas, his cough seemed to be growing worse day by day.

Quickly re-lacing her neckline, she got up from Kin-di-wa's pallet and crossed the lodge to the baby's cradleboard. It was propped up against a roll of skins and partially covered with a soft warm blanket made entirely of rabbit furs. Walks-Tall whimpered when he saw her, then coughed again and tossed his head restlessly.

Concern lanced through her. The baby's round black eyes were enormous and accusing, as if he couldn't understand why he should feel so miserable. Only last summer, when she had first come to live among the Miamis, he had exuded health and happiness. His mother's milk had been bountiful, and someone was always stuffing him with tender tidbits of meat, mashed roots, or berries.

But now, the long weeks of the Snow Moon,

the month of January, were taking their toll. At the tender age of sixteen months, his body was no longer plump and dimpled. His unruly thatch of straight black hair had ceased to shine, and his eyes had lost their sparkle. He whined often, suffered from a chronic dry cough, and seemed listless and dull-witted.

These changes astounded Rebecca and frightened her. She had never before realized how slim was the margin between life and death—especially for the very young and the very old. Of the four of them in the lodge, Crow Woman and Walks-Tall seemed to suffer most from the short rations and howling cold winds.

I must make do with less myself, she resolved silently, so that the two who need it most might have more.

Walks-Tall lay quietly while she exchanged the soiled moss in his cradleboard for a handful of clean. She washed and greased his skin, noticing that it too seemed to have lost its glow and vitality. The bones of his rib cage stood out sharply above his oddly round belly, and she noticed that though his face was still rounded, his cheeks were no longer like apples begging to be plucked.

"Would you like some broth, little brother?" she whispered. "There must be something left in the pot." She wrapped his clean naked body in the rabbit fur blanket and carried him over to the lodge fire.

Kin-di-wa was stretched out on his pallet

watching her. "Is Walks-Tall hungry? Mayhap you should awaken Two Fires."

Rebecca shook her head. "Why should she get up when I am awake? I will feed him some broth and rock him back to sleep."

"Pah—he is a man-child. He does not need rocking." Kin-di-wa's blue eyes narrowed. "You must not pamper or spoil him, Cat-Eyes. His mother's breast should be enough to soothe him."

Rebecca didn't want to tell him that only that afternoon Walks-Tall had cried with frustration when he sought to nurse and got so little. Two Fires had hastily given him a boiled bone with a few scraps of meat still clinging to it, but even then the baby had continued to whimper. He was hungry and not used to going without.

She dipped a gourd in the small caldron nestled in the ashes near the fire's edge. A portion of broth remained from their evening meal, and Walks-Tall drank it greedily, slopping some on the rabbit fur. Then he hiccuped and looked around for more. Rebecca wished she could open her bodice and give him what he really wanted and needed.

Sadly, she replaced the gourd in the pot and went to her pallet, intending to sit and rock the baby there, but Kin-di-wa motioned her to his.

"Stay near me, little mother. It pleases me to watch you care for my adopted son. And it shall please me even more one day to watch you care for our son."

Rebecca sat down cross-legged, forcing herself

34

to smile. She wished for nothing more than to one day bear his son—or daughter. Only she hoped, when that day came, it would be during a time of plenty, not of want.

Kin-di-wa voiced her unspoken concern. "Do not be afraid, Cat-Eyes. Tomorrow, I shall find meat. I feel it in my heart. Tonight was a good omen. You have made me strong again, as I knew you would. And now, my skill in the hunt will be great enough to keep my family from starving."

Rebecca cradled the baby in her arms and rocked her body back and forth in a slow easy motion. Her stomach growled loudly in protest—both of its emptiness and of the exercise. "No one in this lodge has ever doubted your skill as a hunter . . . And if we do starve, it won't be because of you."

"We will not starve," Kin-di-wa insisted. "I shall see to it—one way or another."

Now, what does he mean by that? Rebecca wondered. She glanced at him over the baby's nodding head, but Kin-di-wa pulled the buffalo robe across himself and offered no explanation. He lay on his stomach, chin resting on his folded arms, and stared into the embers of the lodge fire.

She knew from the set of his jaw that even if she asked, he wouldn't tell her. When he wanted her to know something he would speak—and not before. It was his way, and no amount of pleading, cajoling, or complaining would change him.

When at last the baby slept, Rebecca gently

laced him back into his cradleboard and re-covered him with the rabbit fur. She put another log on the fire and returned to Kin-di-wa's pallet, only to find that he too had fallen asleep. She was glad. The etched lines of worry on his mouth and forehead—lines that were usually concealed behind a stern mask of discipline—stood out sharply, but he was still the most handsome man she had ever seen.

She tucked the buffalo robe more closely around him. "Sleep now, my husband, my hunter-warrior, my bronzed Greek god."

Another voice from the past popped into her head: Papa arguing with Mama in his lilting Scottish brogue. "'Ee be fillin' the lass's 'ead with all kinds o' foolishness, techin' 'er t' read an' write an' cipher . . . an' study hist'ry of all things! Now, she declares she won't marry unless the man has the looks an' th' virtues of some statuary over in Greece!"

Rebecca lay down on her own pallet and drew the skins up around her. The memory of her father was so strong, so warm and familiar, she could almost feel his presence. Dear Papa, she told him softly, I have found my Greek god—my husband, my lover, and my closest friend. And I pray God I have a chance to enjoy him!

A cold breath of wind stirred the mat that screened the smoke hole, keeping out snow and wetness. Rebecca shivered—more from dread of the uncertain future than from cold, for the lodge was snug and warm. She burrowed further beneath the skins and made herself a promise: I will enjoy Kin-di-wa. I'll seize life with both hands and refuse to let go. Nothing will defeat us—not winter, not hunger, not the greed of my own people. And not my jealousy over Two Fires!

Tomorrow, she resolved, the first thing she'd do would be to hang a blanket from the ceiling so she and Kin-di-wa could have privacy.

No matter what Crow Woman thought, it was time.

Two

Rebecca awoke to the sound of coughing, and a band of fear closed around her heart. She leaned on one elbow and saw Crow Woman stirring a pot over the fire while Two Fires bent over little Walks-Tall. Kin-di-wa was nowhere to be seen. His bow and quiver were gone from the spot where they always hung from the side of the lodge.

"Crow Woman? Is Walks-Tall getting worse?"

The old woman nodded, but her wrinkled face, nutlike in color and appearance, broke into a toothless grin. "I make tea for him from dried leaves of chestnut tree. Soon, cough go away. He feel better."

An astringent odor rose from the caldron, and Rebecca wrinkled her nose. She had come to have great faith in Crow Woman's noxious remedies, but she wondered how effective they could be if

Walks-Tall did not soon have more food in his stomach. It was food the baby needed, not tea or poultices.

Two Fires turned just then with Walks-Tall in her arms, and Rebecca was struck anew by the girl's dark beauty: large black eyes that fairly shimmered in the pale perfection of her face and long, shining, black hair, parted in the middle and braided. Her hair hung down across her shoulders and immediately drew one's attention to the full curve of her voluptuous breasts—breasts that little Walks-Tall was now grabbing at insistently.

"When he awoke last night, I gave him what was left of the broth," Rebecca said.

"That good." Two Fires knelt down close to the fire and undid the thongs at her bodice with one hand. Immediately, Walks-Tall helped himself, but he suckled only a moment then pulled away and began to whimper.

"Milk all gone . . ." Two Fires's voice held a note of panic. Her lovely face betrayed no emotion, but she set Walks-Tall down with an angry gesture that made the baby stare up at her with a surprised look before he began to howl in earnest.

Rebecca herself was shocked, especially when Two Fires got up then, snatched a large skin from her pallet, and stalked out of the lodge—leaving her wailing son behind.

"Two Fires!" Rebecca hurried to the lodge entrance and drew back the flap, but Two Fires was striding quickly away, her moccasin-shod feet making small crunching sounds in the thin gray layer of snow. A draft of cold blustery air whistled through the lodge, and Rebecca drew back from the doorway and re-secured the heavy flap. It was another dark frosty morning, and the feeling inside her chest was also dark and frosty.

"Here, now, little warrior . . ." Crow Woman crooned as if nothing had happened. She held out a string of white *wampum*—beads and shells strung on a thong. "Tea be ready soon."

The baby took the beads to his mouth. "Won't he cut his mouth on the shells?" Rebecca asked.

"Eh?" Crow Woman tilted her grizzled white head.

Rebecca repeated the question, being more careful to enunciate the difficult guttural syllables of the Miami language.

"Shells all rounded," Crow Woman pointed out. "I string them on myself. They never come off . . . Besides, is good Walks-Tall cut teeth on peace belt. Peace belt give off good medicine."

Rebecca resolved to keep an eye on the baby and began to straighten up the lodge. Two Fires's behavior filled her with worry. The girl was upset—and as usual, determined to hide her feelings. This too was the Miami way, but Two Fires took it to the extreme.

Rebecca recalled how it had taken Kin-di-wa's brush with death—the night he'd almost died of fever brought on by his wounds—to open the wound of Two Fires's loss and let the infection come pouring out. It had probably been the first time the girl had allowed herself to grieve normally for her dead husband, to weep herself

41

into a stupor. Over and over, she had called his name: "Kat-a-mon-gli! Kat-a-mon-gli!" But all the while it had been Kin-di-wa who lay dying.

If only Two Fires would speak up and admit what she's feeling! Rebecca thought. She shook out and folded Kin-di-wa's buffalo robe, and the memory of the previous night jostled out other memories. The shaggy heavy skin still bore the faint odor of Kin-di-wa's body: a pleasant masculine scent that was as much a part of him as his frequent baths in icy rivers.

She smoothed down the robe and lovingly placed it on his pallet. Should she really put up a blanket to divide the lodge and make it more private? The lodge did belong to Two Fires as the senior wife; it might upset her even more if Rebecca took to making changes. And wouldn't she too expect to be taken behind the blanket?

While Rebecca was pondering this question, Walks-Tall began to cough—a raspy, ragged cough that shook his whole body. Rebecca swept him into her arms and snatched away the beads, and the baby began to cry as well as cough. "Isn't the tea ready yet, Crow Woman? This child needs something in his stomach!"

"Patience—you must learn patience." The old woman dipped out a gourdful of steaming liquid, blew into it, and handed it to Rebecca. "Give him this. I make poultice now."

The tea was too hot to give the baby, and Rebecca sighed with frustration. She jiggled him in one arm and held away the dipper with the other as Walks-Tall reached for it. At least, his eagerness was a good sign. As long as he still showed an inclination to fight, she could keep her fear for his welfare in abeyance.

When the tea had cooled enough, she sat down on the mats and allowed Walks-Tall to drink. He took one sip, stopped, and nearly upset the gourd with his flailing hands. For a moment, Rebecca thought he was refusing the sharp smelling brew, but then in his desperation, he pulled the gourd back to his mouth.

"There, there . . ." she crooned softly. "Maybe tonight you will have rabbit or venison stew—and your mother's milk will come back again."

The baby looked at her with wide trusting eyes. A lump rose in her throat. What could be more bitter than to watch a child go hungry? She would take the last handful of nuts and roots and pound them into a mash soft enough for him to eat. And she would whisper a silent prayer that today Kindi-wa would find game.

Walks-Tall grew sleepy after the tea, and Rebecca laid him down and covered him. As Crow Woman had promised, his cough had stilled, but the lodge seemed unnaturally quiet. Even before he was a year old, Walks-Tall had learned to turn order into chaos. Toddling from one basket to another, he would quickly overturn them to see what was inside each, then he'd sit laughing and cooing as Two Fires stoically cleaned up the mess.

"See?" Crow Woman grunted in Rebecca's ear. "Did I not tell you tea would soothe him?"

"Will he sleep long, do you think?"

43

"Long time," the old woman assured her. "No need to stand and watch. You not go outside—go now, if you wish. I stay here."

Crow Woman has a habit of guessing what others need, Rebecca thought. She smiled at the old woman, who looked like a sack of bones thrown carelessly together. Who would ever guess that the old crone's heart was as big as the open sky?

"I want to go down to the river—and then to visit Sweet Breeze. But I will not be gone long. Perhaps, if I see Two Fires, I can send her back before Walks-Tall awakens."

Crow Woman shook her head. "Two Fires strange squaw. She feel things too deeply. Is better you leave her alone, and she come back only when ready."

Ready for what? Rebecca wondered. If Walks-Tall were her child, she would never leave him when he was sick and hungry.

Quickly, she went to her place in the lodge and tugged on sleeves and leggings of soft fringed doeskin, securing them into place with rawhide thongs. She threw a small cape made of thick otter skins over her shoulders, stuffed dried moss into her beaded moccasins to deter cold and dampness, then completed her outfit by pulling a worn blanket over her head.

As a child she'd always dreamed of wearing silk and lace, but now, she'd come to appreciate the advantages of simple doeskin. Warm in winter and cool in summer, it resisted dirt, and could easily be cleaned by brushing or rubbing with crushed herbs. Compared to rough and scratchy homespun, a comparison she always made when dressing, doeskin felt wonderful.

She stepped out of the lodge and stood still a moment to adjust to the shocking change in temperature. Her breath came out in a frosty white plume as she glanced about, shivering. The large clearing held fifty or sixty other lodges, and the rounded, mat-covered structures looked like cowering beehives huddled down against the biting cold. Each one emitted a thin spiral of smoke and was entirely surrounded by a grayish layer of snow that hadn't melted once since late October, the leaf-falling moon.

East, west, north, and south of her, the clearing was hemmed in by naked woods. The south side was bordered by a frozen river—the Miami of the Lake. A stream called Swan Creek, running almost parallel to the river and sheeted now with ice, meandered nearby. It led back into the marshland from which the waterfowl had all departed.

Rebecca pulled the blanket more closely about herself, thinking how bleak and barren the scene appeared. Tracks led around and between the lodges but few figures ventured out. Normally, no matter what the weather, a Miami campsite was a cheerful busy place, but this year, the usual winter activities of feasting, visiting, story-telling, and snow games had been replaced by an eerie silence.

Shaking off regret and sadness, Rebecca hurried down to the river, picking her way with confidence through the crunchy snow. There she found her favorite spot, a tree-secluded indentation in the bank where she could perform her daily ablutions. These frosty mornings, the ice had to be re-broken each day with a stone, but a few scoops of river water rubbed across her body under her doeskin did wonders—both for the maintenance of her self-esteem and for good grooming. She'd become accustomed to the Indian habit of cleanliness and, as she splashed, ignoring her chattering teeth, she thought how pampered and unhealthy had been her earlier life on Papa's farm in Pennsylvania.

When she completed her morning ritual, she rewrapped herself in cape and blanket and headed for the lodge shared by her best friend, Sweet Breeze, and her father, Little Turtle. Their hut was set apart from the rest and identified by a decorated lance standing upright in the ground before it. Feathers and amulets, indicating his status as war chief, rattled forlornly in the wind as Rebecca approached. An arrangement of sticks in the snow further indicated their willingness to accept visitors, but Rebecca nonetheless clapped her hands loudly to give warning of her approach.

The lodge flap was pushed back almost immediately, and a small slender girl peeked out. Looking more like a child than a married woman or the daughter of an aging war chief, the girl drew back the flap with a delighted squeal and a spontaneous gesture of pleasure.

"Cat-Eyes!" she exclaimed in English. "Come in. I no see you in plenty long time!"

Rebecca reveled in the warmth of the reception.

46

The lodge fire beckoned, and she hurried inside. "Sweet Breeze, dear friend. I hope I'm not interrupting."

A long recumbent form stirred beside the fire. She was interrupting. Little Turtle had obviously been resting, but he now struggled to his feet and stood swaying before her like a tall noble oak tree—one that had recently been battered by windstorms. Rebecca could barely conceal her alarm. Could this gaunt, hollow-eyed old man really be Little Turtle?

It had been several weeks since she'd last seen him, and now, she understood why. There was an odor of sickness in the lodge, and even as she watched, Little Turtle's chest heaved in a dry paroxysm of coughing that sounded distressingly familiar.

Sweet Breeze took her father's arm. "Lie down, my father. Cat-Eyes come to visit me—not you. She not mind if you sleep instead of talk. We make squaw-talk anyway—not talk-talk of her people."

"Yes, please . . ." Rebecca insisted. The habits and customs of the Long Knives was one of Little Turtle's favorite subjects, but right now Rebecca would have cursed had she spoken of her people. They had done this to the Miami war chief. They had broken this strong proud man.

"Forgive me, little white woman . . ." The old chieftain's magnificent voice—which could ring with the authority of thunder—was little more than a whisper.

Little Turtle lay back on his buffalo robe, and

Rebecca wanted to weep. She remembered how she had first seen him: tall and strong and regal, his long hair still black and shiny, and his eyes so knowing and kind. Even an outsider like herself had felt welcomed—had known instinctively that this man possessed rare wisdom and compassion.

Now his eyes were haunted and filled with pain, and his hair had turned completely white—almost, it seemed, overnight. Anger coursed hotly through her. Fallen Timbers had made Little Turtle an old man—grieving for the young warriors who would never see old age.

Sweet Breeze drew Rebecca to the other side of the lodge fire. "Sit, Cat-Eyes. I make tea. Until good friend, Peshewa, returns from hunting, I no have more to offer you."

Rebecca sat. She had been planning to tell Sweet Breeze of Walks-Tall's hunger, which would have been the same as asking for food, but now the words stuck in her throat. How could she ask for help when Sweet Breeze herself was destitute? "Kin-di-wa is hunting too. I pray Manitou they both find game."

Sweet Breeze frowned, as she maneuvered a caldron over the fire. "Kin-di-wa hunting? His wounds be healed already?"

Rebecca shrugged to hide her own concern. "He seems to think so. He goes hunting every-day."

"Why he not ask Peshewa to keep you in meat?" Sweet Breeze crumbled some dried leaves into the caldron. "Peshewa bring meat for us, for his mother, and for one or two other lodges.

Peshewa no have wife or papoose to hunt for—he glad to help those who need it."

"Kin-di-wa would be ashamed to accept any more help from his friend," Rebecca explained. "It was Peshewa who kept us alive during those awful weeks after the battle—when we didn't know if Kin-di-wa would live or die. But as soon as Kin-di-wa got better, even before the snows came, he began to refuse the gifts of meat."

Sweet Breeze sighed and glanced toward her father whose eyes were closed exhaustedly. "Pride," she whispered. "My father, too, refuse to eat when Peshewa first bring food. He say if he not fit to hunt for us, better we die of hunger . . . and maybe we die of hunger yet."

"Oh, Sweet Breeze . . ." Rebecca studied her friend's drawn face, thinking once again of how much Fallen Timbers had devastated their lives. Sweet Breeze's enormous black eyes—normally dancing with mischief and endless optimism—were now shadowed with sorrow, and the small smile that had always played about her delicate mouth was more often turned upside down than right side up.

Rebecca knew that her friend, like everyone else, mourned the battle, the defeat, and the loss of so many lives. But most of all, Sweet Breeze mourned her lost love, Apekonit, or Captain William Wells as he was known among Anthony Wayne's Long Knives. Rebecca toyed with the fringe on her doeskin, wondering if she dared broach so sensitive a subject. "What do you hear of—your husband?"

49

Sweet Breeze nearly dropped the ladle with which she was stirring the tea. "Apekonit?" she asked in a whisper.

The girl's eyes went to her sleeping father, and Rebecca bit her lip, ashamed at her own stupidity. If she were going to mention Apekonit, the least she could have done was not to mention him in front of Little Turtle. Sweet Breeze's husband was also the adopted son of the great war chief—a son who had fought at his foster father's side through two bitter battles against the Long Knives, and then had broken that same father's heart by returning to his own people and becoming the chief Indian scout for Anthony Wayne.

But Apekonit had been part of a final peace effort before the battle—one that had also involved Kin-di-wa, to the great risk of both men. Was it too much to assume that the breach between father and son might have been mended?

"Forgive me, Sweet Breeze. I had thought your husband's efforts to help obtain peace had smoothed out the difficulties between him and your father—even though the efforts failed. I—I had no right to pry into your affairs."

Sweet Breeze smiled, a shy sad smile that nearly broke Rebecca's heart. "You no pry . . . you friend. I tell you everything. As for difficulties between Apekonit and my father, there never be any. My father and Apekonit always understand that no man can escape his destiny—even if he wants to . . . Only reason my father and I be very sad now is because Apekonit no come home to us. No send message. This we do find difficult to understand. Now that battle over, son should come home to father. Come home to wife who wait for him and love him so many moons."

"Perhaps . . . something happened to him during the battle," Rebecca ventured. She couldn't bring herself to mention the possibility she was actually thinking—that he was dead.

Sweet Breeze shook her head. "No . . . if he killed at Fallen Timbers, I know it here." She tapped her heart. "Apekonit no could die and I not know it."

Rebecca understood her friend's certainty. She too believed she would know instantly if anything ever happened to Kin-di-wa. Sighing inwardly, she sought to turn the conversation to more pleasant matters, such as the possibility that spring might come early or that the pending Treaty Council might result in a better relationship between red man and white in the Northwest Territory.

But conversation soon dwindled, for neither Rebecca nor Sweet Breeze really felt too hopeful at the moment. Sweet Breeze stirred the bubbling tea which both of them had forgotten. "I wish I know why Apekonit not come, Cat-Eyes." She looked up from the pot, tears sparkling in her eyes. "We wait for him—my father and I. We wait, but mayhap he has forgot us."

Rebecca didn't know what to say. There seemed to be no reasonable explanation. If Apekonit came back to the Miamis now, he'd be returning as a respected warrior and victor—especially if he made an effort to help the starving tribe. He could at least bring food to get Sweet Breeze and Little Turtle through the winter, Rebecca thought. Or didn't he realize that his wife and his foster father were suffering?

In silence, she drank the tea her friend ladled out for her. Someday, she wanted to meet this Apekonit, this Captain William Wells. Whoever or whatever he was, white or Indian, he had no right to make her friend so miserably unhappy. Her thoughts turned to her own husband: Would Kin-di-wa find meat today? And if he didn't, what would they do tomorrow?

It was quite late when Kin-di-wa returned that night. Two Fires and Walks-Tall were sleeping after a pitifully small meal of mashed roots and nuts, and Crow Woman was sitting in the corner of the lodge, crooning to herself, as she laced quills through a decorative piece of rawhide.

The snow crunched warningly outside, and Rebecca leapt up from her own quillwork as the lodge flap was pulled aside. Kin-di-wa and another brave entered. The other brave was Peshewa, and Rebecca felt a thrill of hope. She would not have worried so much about Kin-di-wa if she'd known Peshewa was with him. Were not two men together a safeguard for one another— and could they not out-think any wily moose or deer?

But neither man exuded anything but cold and exhaustion as they went directly to the fire, threw off their furs, and held out their hands to its flickering warmth. Then Kin-di-wa's blue eyes found hers: "Put on the caldron, Cat-Eyes. I am hungry."

Happiness leapt in her breast. "You found meat!"

"Hush . . ." Kin-di-wa cautioned. He looked toward Two Fires who had not yet awakened and saw Crow Woman regarding him questioningly with her beady bright black eyes. "Yes, we found meat—but I had rather it go into the pot without anyone studying it too closely."

"But . . ." Rebecca looked from one man to the other. Kin-di-wa stared back defiantly, and Peshewa kept his head bowed, the bright red quills of his scalp lock quivering as if in shame. "Why? Whose meat is it?" she demanded. "Where did you find it?"

"We found it where we have always found meat," Kin-di-wa snapped irritably. "At the end of a long hard trail." He jerked his head at Peshewa who left the lodge as if on signal, and came back a moment later with a large chunk of bloody meat.

Rebecca took it from him and dropped it into the biggest of their iron caldrons. The meat looked fine to her, and she was overjoyed that she and Two Fires had been spared the work of butchering the kill. Then she thought of the skin—surely they hadn't left something so valuable out in the woods! "Where—is the skin?" she asked timidly.

"No skin . . ." Kin-di-wa grunted as he sat down on the mats near the fire to await his hard-won dinner.

Rebecca was amazed and apprehensive. Since Kin-di-wa offered no further explanations, she fastened her glance on Peshewa. What she saw did not please her. The short, powerfully built brave, whose homely, bashed-in face gave him a ferocious look that was often at odds with the gentler aspects of his character, seemed afraid to look into her eyes—or anyone's.

He shuffled his feet, fingered the rawhide thongs holding up his buckskin leggings, then cleared his throat. "I go take meat to Little Turtle—and others who need it."

Kin-di-wa nodded. "I thank you for your help, my brother. We hunted as we did when we were boys—as you and I and Apekonit hunted. It was a good kill. Do not worry. Manitou cannot be angry with us."

But Peshewa did look worried and seemed only too happy to leave the lodge. Rebecca was embarrassed for him. Fear and sheepishness did not sit well on a man who plucked his entire head free of hair, leaving only a quill-bedecked scalp-lock to taunt his enemies into trying to take his scalp as a trophy. The very name, Peshewa, meant Wild-Cat.

When Peshewa was gone, she blurted, "Kin-di-wa, what happened? What sort of meat is this?"

"Cook it," he growled. "And be glad of it. One meat is the same as another." He removed his buckskin shirt, his only concession to being out all day in below freezing temperatures, and flung himself across his pallet.

Two Fires stirred and woke, and Crow Woman tottered over to help Rebecca build up the fire and cook the meat. "Good red meat . . ." she grinned. "We cook it long and make plenty broth so Walks-Tall can eat." Then she laughed and pointed to her toothless gums. "Me too."

The mysterious meat, when boiled for as long as anyone in the lodge could stand to smell and not eat, tasted better than anything Rebecca could remember. She reflected that it was probably just her own hunger that made the meat taste so succulent, but she could not recall ever having eaten meat of this particular flavor. It reminded her a little of everything—and of nothing in particular. What was it—venison, bear, buffalo, wild-cat, moose, elk . . . horse? Maybe, it was dog.

So large a chunk of meat had to have been taken from a fairly large animal. Had Kin-di-wa and Peshewa stolen a horse or oxen? She combed through her knowledge of the nearest human habitations the men could have reached in a single day. The British Fort Miamis lay a short distance upriver, but the traitorous Saginwash, as the Indians called the British, had been so decimated by fever, they'd departed downriver to Lake Erie and gone to Fort Detroit for the winter.

Still further upriver were two new forts that belonged to the Long Knives. One was Fort Deposit at *Roche de Boeuf,* a small fort where Anthony Wayne had stored his supplies and ammunitions. It too was now deserted. But what about Fort Defiance? she wondered. Could the men have traveled more than fifty miles in a day through the cold and snow? And had Anthony Wayne left anyone there over the winter? He might have, she decided.

Wayne had built the fort and named it Fort Defiance, as a gesture of defiance to the Indians. She had heard that he'd shaken his fist and "defied all the devils in hell to take it!" So perhaps he wouldn't go off and abandon it so easily.

The thought that she might be eating meat stolen from her own people almost made Rebecca smile, then she thought of the dangers involved and could hardly swallow her last bite. If the remaining tribesmen took to stealing from their conquerors, it might go quite hard on them at the Treaty Council in the spring.

She and Two Fires cleaned up the dinner mess without speaking. Two Fires was anxious to try nursing Walks-Tall, but the baby was so sated with meat and broth, he went to sleep before she could get to him—and he slept without coughing. Rebecca herself felt warm, relaxed, and sleepy. But she was not too sleepy to wait until everyone was quietly settled down for the night, and then to move her sleeping pallet closer to Kin-di-wa's.

Kin-di-wa had gone to sleep immediately after eating, but as she lay down next to him, he awoke and put his arm around her, drawing her close and pulling his buffalo robe over both of them. "A full stomach is a fine thing, is it not?" he murmured in her ear.

"Wonderful," she sighed. "Even when that which fills it is stolen."

"Stolen? No, little Cat-Eyes, we did not steal the meat."

She turned over to face him. "Then where did it come from? As sparse as game is, I'm amazed you found some. Do you think you'll be able to find more?"

He began to undo her braids in a slow lazy manner. "Wolf. It was wolf you ate tonight, and only Manitou knows whether we shall ever find another. We found no pack—only one single wolf."

"Wolf!" She jerked away in surprise. "But I thought . . ."

"You thought right. My people never kill wolf. The animal is considered sacred."

"Then—won't everyone be angry?"

Kin-di-wa leaned forward and nibbled her ear. "Not if they don't know. And I doubt that starving people will ask if the information is not freely given . . . We buried its skin far away from here and brought back only the meat—stripped off the bones and cut into chunks that no one will recognize."

Kin-di-wa's nibbling felt good, but Rebecca suddenly remembered the shamed look on Peshewa's face. "What would happen if someone did find out?"

"Do not worry, little Cat-Eyes. Peshewa would die before he betrayed me. It was I who put the arrow through the animal's heart, and once it was dead, not even Peshewa could see the sense in wasting its flesh."

Rebecca wound her arms around her husband's

neck. "Do you believe a wolf is sacred? Never to be killed?"

Kin-di-wa pressed his hands against her back so that she could feel his body firm against hers. "I believe all animals are sacred. Manitou gave life to each one—and why it is permissible to kill one and not another, I have never fully understood. I kill only to feed my family, and I never waste the meat. Besides, I pray both to Gitchi-Manitou and to the manitou of my prey." He leaned back and looked into her eyes. "Should I pray to your God too—since you eat the meat and use the hide?"

"No . . . my people never ask God's permission to kill his animals—or to cut down his trees or change the course of his streams and rivers," she added thoughtfully.

"Hmmmmm . . ." Kin-di-wa began nibbling on her ear again. "Mayhap that is why your people are considered savages by more enlightened peoples—such as my people."

She began to giggle then. A full stomach was wonderful. Disease and starvation now seemed like something that could happen only to others, never to her or to those she loved. She allowed her fingertips to rove playfully over his chest muscles. "How is your rib tonight?"

"Sore—very sore," he murmured. "The cold ate into my bones today, and they are waiting for you to warm them."

"And so I shall," she promised.

Pushing back the buffalo robe, she knelt and gently began to knead the muscles of his chest and side. With a sigh, he closed his eyes, and in every stroke, she told him of her love. Soon, the stiff muscles relaxed, became more pliant to her touch, and his entire body lay loose and open, inviting her to continue. "Turn over now," she ordered. "And I will rub your back."

Eyes still closed, he grinned. "It is not my back that needs attention but the lower half of my body."

Pretending to mistake his meaning, she moved quickly down to his feet. "Here, let me take off your moccasins." And when she had done that, she bent and kissed the big toe of his left foot. It was cold as ice to her lips.

"I don't need your kisses down there," he grunted.

"Ah, but your feet are cold—so cold." She warmed them between her hands, then undid the bindings of his buckskin leggings and removed them. His legs were straight and muscular, like strong young saplings. These she kneaded with slow deliberation, from foot to knee, and from knee to thigh. While she was working over his right thigh, he suddenly reached up and grabbed hold of her hair.

"Enough, you little she-cat. Am I never to sleep this night? You tease too much. Off with your doeskin now, and I will warm your bones." His eyes looking up into hers glowed a brilliant blue fire, and she drew off her doeskin gladly. This was the way she loved him most—reaching for her with love and desire.

"Oh, Kin-di-wa . . ." she murmured as he took her into his arms. "I wish it could always be like this. If only we could be safe and warm forever and have nothing to think of but our loving."

"You dream of the impossible, little one. Not all our days can be perfect. We must live each day as it comes." His lips closed over hers, and the sudden wave of passion that engulfed her obliterated everything else.

There was only his mouth, his hands, his thudding heart, pulsing beneath her fingertips. She gave and took with a greedy hunger that might have embarrassed her, had she thought about it. And she did think about it, finally. Later, much later, she remembered the blanket she hadn't put up.

Tomorrow, she thought sleepily, tomorrow—first thing—I will put up the blanket.

But in the morning, there was no time to think of blankets. Someone shook her roughly, and her eyes flew open to find Kin-di-wa standing over her, eyes blazing with anger and worry. "Why didn't you tell me Little Turtle was sick?"

"Wh—what?" she stammered. "I—I thought perhaps you knew, or else . . ."

Hands planted on hips, feet rooted to the floor, he glowered at her—all trace of the gentle lover gone as he faced the challenges of this new day. "Or else what?" he demanded.

"Or else it wouldn't matter if you did know. There's nothing you could do about it that Sweet Breeze isn't already doing." And Peshewa too, she added silently.

"Am I not a man?" he thundered. "My chief and my son lie dying—and yet you tell me nothing!"

"Your son!" She bolted upright and looked frantically around for Walks-Tall. Then she spied him, wrapped up in his rabbit fur blanket and nestled against his mother's shoulder. "Why—he looks all right to me." Indeed, she thought, it's Two Fires who looks ill.

Two Fires's face was pale and drawn, her eyes accusing, and Rebecca wondered if the girl might not have awakened during the night and witnessed some intimate moments she wasn't meant to see. Had she exaggerated Walks-Tall's condition out of envy?

"The blanket . . ." Rebecca muttered. "I should have put up the blanket yesterday."

"What did you say?" Kin-di-wa barked. He seemed to be waiting for her to do something.

"I said—let me look at Walks-Tall. What's wrong with him this morning?"

But she hadn't taken two steps in his direction before a strange sound, something between a cough and a whoop, issued from the rabbit fur. The awful sound came again and again. Then Walks-Tall began to cry, and Rebecca rushed over to Two Fires and pulled aside the blanket to see him better.

The baby's face had turned bright red, and his breath was wheezing. Rebecca put her hand on his naked chest and fancied she could feel something moving insidiously inside him to shut off his air altogether.

"Where's Crow Woman?" she asked. For the first time she noticed that the old woman wasn't in the lodge.

"She's going from lodge to lodge looking for some kind of herb," Kin-di-wa snapped.

"Then why didn't you wake me?" Rebecca moved away from the baby and began heaping more wood on the fire. "How could you let me sleep when all of this was happening?"

"I wasn't here." Kin-di-wa waved his hand in a helpless gesture. "I went out early to see Little Turtle—that was when I discovered how close he is to journeying into the spirit world. Then I came back here and found my son wheezing exactly like him. Two Fires told me where Crow Woman had gone, and after that, I woke you."

Rebecca could only concentrate on one thing at a time. "Little Turtle—journeying into the spirit world? He can't be that bad!" She paused in the act of dipping water from an earthenware jug. "I saw him only yesterday, and he was ill—but not close to death!"

She put the water on to boil, noticing that Two Fires had taken the whimpering baby over to her mat, where she was now rocking him and chanting as if no one else were in the lodge. Rebecca glanced back and forth between Walks-Tall and Kin-di-wa. Was this really happening? Could Walks-Tall and Little Turtle both be dying?

Kin-di-wa peered into the caldron. "What good is plain water? Crow Woman said she needs Itch Weed to stop the cough."

"If she doesn't find it, at least Walks-Tall can inhale the steam to loosen up his chest. That's an old remedy of my mother's."

Kin-di-wa looked doubtful. "What would you have me to do help? Tell me and I will do it."

The near panic in his voice made Rebecca's heart go out to him. Even when he was lying ill of wounds and fever himself, he had never looked or sounded so vulnerable as he did now: if anything happened to Little Turtle or Walks-Tall, Kin-di-wa would be devastated. "There is only a small portion of meat and broth left over from last night. Why don't you go and find Peshewa and bring back another portion? Take some to Sweet Breeze too—if there's any left in this hungry camp."

Kin-di-wa bolted toward the lodge entrance. "If there isn't any left, we mustn't waste a moment in going out to hunt for more."

But as the flap opened and shut behind him, a swirl of fresh snow blew inside, and Rebecca became aware of the whining sound of the wind. It was clawing with more than its usual fury at the mats and skins covering the lodge. She stopped feeding small twigs to the fire and listened. A storm was heading in from the worst direction, the northeast—off the big lake of the Eries. This small corner of the earth, the northwest section of the Ohio Country, was being pounced upon by a blizzard.

"No, Kin-di-wa," she whispered. "You cannot hunt again today, or you would be the prey."

Three

The blizzard predicted by Rebecca raged for a full day and night, trapping everyone inside the lodges. High winds and deep snows buffeted the little camp near the river. The storm itself would not have been so bad, but Crow Woman had come back from her search for the proper herb for curing Walks-Tall with discouraging news: many other children and grown-ups had been struck down with the same mysterious malady—debilitating spells of coughing that were usually followed by distinctive-sounding whoops as the victims gasped for air.

The remnants of Kin-di-wa's wolf kept the inhabitants of several lodges from going hungry for the duration of the storm, but both Peshewa and Kin-di-wa became increasingly agitated: because of the battle which had taken place in late August, the Moon of the New Corn, and now because of the coughing sickness, the number of able-bodied men in camp stood at no more than twenty or thirty.

"Weak though we are, we must do something—and soon," Kin-di-wa snapped, as he paced up and down the lodge.

Rebecca could hardly hear him over Crow Woman's chanting and Walks-Tall's coughing—so anguished and so persistent that he could hardly draw breath except in a frightening whoop. "Keep his head inside the blanket," she instructed Two Fires. "So he gets the benefit of the steam."

Two Fires nodded. Circles ringed her large black eyes, and she was trembling from a combination of too much heat and near-exhaustion. But she dutifully held the baby—with a blanket tented over his head—over the steaming caldron.

"Here, Crow Woman, help her a moment, will you?" Rebecca asked.

Unable to find the herb she needed, Crow Woman had resorted to ancient prayers and the shaking of gourds to ward off evil spirits. The noise got on Rebecca's nerves, but now, the old woman put down her gourds and came over. "Pah! This steam not hot enough! We need sweat lodge to break up cough."

"No! Not for a baby!" Rebecca cried. She had observed the sweat lodge ritual as it was performed by grown men; after hours of sweating in an enclosed place where heated rocks were repeatedly sprinkled with water, the men would then immerse themselves in the icy cold river.

From the corner of her eye, she saw Kin-di-wa pull on his buckskin leggings and shirt. "Where are you going?"

"To find Peshewa. We must make plans. None of us will survive the winter if we do not take our destinies into our own hands." Kin-di-wa's eyes were a cold hard blue.

"What kind of plans?" Rebecca got up from beside the fire and crossed the lodge to him. When her husband's face took on such an expression, she could never be sure of what he would do— only that nothing in the world would stop him from doing it.

"If I must go begging to save my family, then I will do so." Kin-di-wa's lip curled downward with distaste. "And perhaps, there are others in the camp who have come to feel the same. Pride is a small price to pay for the lives of those you love."

Rebecca was relieved he hadn't suggested something worse. "But—to whom would you go? Even the tribes whose villages and crops were not destroyed would have little to share with us. No one had time to hunt, and by the time they returned home after the battle, their crops must have been ruined by the birds and squirrels."

"I was not thinking of the Shawnee, the Ottawa, or the Delaware. I was thinking of the Saginwash."

"The Saginwash!" Rebecca could hardly believe her ears. A scene flashed in her mind: scores of dead and dying Indians heaped around the closed walls of Fort Miamis. The English had refused to open fire on the Long Knives even when the Indians had pounded on the walls for entrance, begging and pleading for the help they had been promised. "Must you go to the Saginwash?" she whispered.

Kin-di-wa's mouth set into a firm grim line. "I would go to the Evil One himself—the one the missionaries speak of—if it would save my people."

He threw a blanket around his shoulders and started toward the lodge entrance. Then Rebecca thought of something. "Kin-di-wa—wait! Why not go to Sweet Breeze's husband? Why not go to Apekonit?"

Kin-di-wa's eyes widened, and Rebecca knew she had made a good suggestion. Anthony Wayne himself might refuse to help, but surely Apekonit, once he knew that his own wife and adoptive father were suffering, could find some way to persuade the hard-nosed general. And it would be easier for the Miamis to humble themselves before a man they knew and trusted, than before those who had betrayed them.

"I will go to each brave and suggest this, little Cat-Eyes. It is a good idea, and the tribe will be pleased to hear it. Indeed, it is so good I don't know why I didn't think of it myself." Kin-di-wa smiled. He suddenly bent forward and brushed her lips with a gentle kiss. "Of course, I will not tell them it was thought of by a mere squaw."

"It wasn't thought of by a mere squaw," Rebecca retorted. "It was thought of by Kin-di-wa's woman—the wife of his heart. And everyone knows that so wise a brave as Kin-di-wa would never choose a stupid woman for his mate."

She unfastened the lodge flap to let Kin-di-wa go out, and snow fell into the lodge. The drifts around the lodge were thigh-high in places, the snow sparkling like heaped jewels. False jewels, Rebecca thought gloomily, as she began to worry about the journey.

"I will prepare a pack for traveling," she called after her husband. "Though I don't know what you can take for food."

"Just prepare it," Kin-di-wa called back. "Today, I will also find out how much food is left in the camp."

Rebecca put together a pack with everything she thought Kin-di-wa might need: buffalo robe, weapons, a small clay pot of glowing embers from the fire, and an extra pair of moccasins. Now, if she only had food to put in, the pack would be complete. She sighed and went through the items again. If everyone else in the village were as destitute as they were, Kin-di-wa might have to embark on his journey with an empty stomach.

She wondered who would accompany him. Peshewa? But then someone would have to take care of all those who had been under Peshewa's care. And someone would have to take care of her, Crow Woman, Two Fires, and Walks-Tall. Then she began to wonder how long the journey might take. Anthony Wayne, or Chenoten, the whirlwind as the Indians called him, had gone back to Fort Greenville for the winter. Fort Greenville was somewhere near the forks of the Great Miami River, but she had no idea how long it would take to get there, especially in winter.

The day passed slowly, measured by the frequency of Walks-Tall's fits of coughing. When at last Kin-di-wa came back through the lodge entrance, it was already growing dark and increasingly colder. Glancing anxiously toward the sleeping Walks-Tall, Kin-di-wa handed her a deerskin pouch. "Corn seed. It was being saved for planting in the spring, but we have gathered together all we have and will now share it among those in need."

With a sinking heart, Rebecca took the pouch. Someone had gone to great trouble to save and protect the precious seed, and now, it would have to be eaten instead of planted. "When do you leave for Fort Greenville? Is Peshewa going with you?"

Kin-di-wa shook his head. "I go alone in the morning. Peshewa will stay here and try to keep you in meat until I return."

"Not alone!" Waves of alarm surged through her. "No, Kin-di-wa—you mustn't go alone! Fort Greenville must be more than a hundred miles away!"

His hands gripped her forearms. He looked down into her eyes with a suppressed anger she hadn't noticed until just this moment. "No one else will accompany me. I asked each man who could possibly go."

"But why? Surely they don't intend to stand

70

around and watch their families die of disease and starvation!"

"That is exactly what they intend." Kin-di-wa made a despairing gesture. "Most of them say it is Manitou's will whether we live or die. If He wants us to live, He will put game into the forest again. He will crack the ice on the river and begin the fish run early. He will bring back the waterfowl and make the sap run in the trees."

"That's foolishness! Superstitious clap-trap!" Rebecca raged.

"It is what they say," Kin-di-wa repeated. "Even Peshewa. Manitou has turned his back on his red children. If he wishes us to die, we shall die."

"Manitou is not responsible for what has happened to the Miamis! What did Little Turtle say? Did you speak to him?"

Kin-di-wa walked past Crow Woman and Two Fires, who were watching from the shadows, and squatted down before the fire. "Little Turtle is suffering, and I did not wish to add to his burden. Besides, he can do nothing. Our future is out of his hands now."

Rebecca wanted to throw something. She paced up and down the lodge, inwardly cursing the stoicism and superstitious attitudes of the Indian. A child, a man, or a whole tribe could sicken and die, and once convinced it was Manitou's will, not a single person would ever complain or try to fight it. Was it Kin-di-wa's early contact with Moravian Missionaries or his own half-white heritage that gave him the ability to think for himself?

She whirled on her heel. "Then I will go with you to Fort Greenville. Two of us have a better chance of getting through the snow and ice than one alone—especially when that one is just getting over severe wounds."

Kin-di-wa glanced up at her. "No, Cat-Eyes. It is not the place of a squaw to set out on a dangerous journey. Your place is here—keeping the lodge fire."

Rebecca bristled. There were two other women in the lodge who could keep the fire as well as she could. And she did wish Kin-di-wa would stop referring to her as a squaw. She was an educated white woman—here of her own choice. And if she chose not to be here, no one could make her stay. Not even Kin-di-wa.

"I will go," she repeated stubbornly.

Kin-di-wa's eyes locked with hers. "You will not."

"You cannot stop me."

"We shall see." Kin-di-wa glowered.

The night seemed exceptionally long and cold. Fearing that Kin-di-wa would steal away without her, Rebecca hardly dared sleep. Twice, she arose and put more wood on the fire, but no matter how high the flames leapt, her insides shook with cold.

Quarreling with Kin-di-wa was something she never did—at least not since she'd found him half-dead on the battlefield. Up to that moment, she had always fought him, pitted her will against his, but now, she surrendered to him in most things.

She and Kin-di-wa were meant to be together—for always and ever, two in one flesh. She was not going to risk losing him again! He was very good at pretending that his wounds gave him no more trouble and that his old strength had returned. But she knew better. Two nights of lovemaking didn't mean that a man was ready to face several weeks of bitter cold without decent shelter. Why couldn't he be sensible? She was strong and healthy; she would be a help to him. Besides, it would be a chance for them to be alone together, and suddenly, desperately, she wanted him to herself. Alone. With no one to awaken in the night and to spy on them.

And then a sense of guilt stole over her. Would she ever stop resenting the fact that Two Fires was also his wife? And what about Walks-Tall? How could she go off and leave him?

Walks-Tall has his mother and Crow Woman to look after him, she scolded herself firmly, but who will look after Kin-di-wa if I don't go along on this journey?

Long before dawn, she heard Kin-di-wa arise from his pallet. Swiftly and silently, he donned his warmest clothing and took up his pack. Through slitted eyes, half-closed in feigned sleep, she watched him unfasten the lodge flap. Then he turned, and in the flickering firelight, she saw him smile. He thought he had gotten away with it—stolen away without awakening her. Well, she would show him!

She forced herself to lie still and breathe

73

normally, as if asleep, but as soon as Kin-di-wa exited the lodge, she threw off her own skins which concealed the pack she had made for herself. It took only seconds to dress in her warmest clothes, wrapping up in an extra blanket for good measure. Then she too stole out of the lodge.

The air outside was breathlessly cold, and a tiny sliver of new moon made the silvered landscape seem even colder. She couldn't see Kin-di-wa, but it was easy to follow his trail through the deep snow. It led straight to the frozen river and from there headed west. A short distance upriver, his footsteps disappeared, but she saw him ahead of her—a tall black figure striding easily across the ice which had been swept clean of snow by a sharp biting wind.

With her heavy pack clutched awkwardly in her arms, she broke into a run to keep the distance between them from growing any larger. She'd brought a headband so she could balance the load on her back with the strap going around her forehead, leaving her hands free, but it was inside the pack. And there was no time now to stop and get it out. Nor were they far enough away from camp that she could risk calling out to Kin-di-wa and urging him to wait for her.

Over the windswept ice she ran, forgetting the cold, forgetting the weight of the pack, forgetting everything except keeping Kin-di-wa in sight.

The frozen river twisted and turned, growing wide in some places, more narrow in others. Islands dotted its center. These broke the wind somewhat, allowing the snow to drift in spots so that Kin-di-wa's footprints seemed to begin and end mysteriously—as if a ghost were making his way upriver.

An hour or more later, the snow-lined river-banks began to lighten, to stand out more whitely, and the sky behind Rebecca became a pure crystalline blue along the horizon. She would have liked to turn and watch the sunrise but she was too far behind Kin-di-wa to risk stopping. She settled down to a brisk walk, lugging her pack on one hip and ignoring the dull pain in her chest. It felt good to gulp down the cold air, and she knew if she could just keep going, Kin-di-wa would not send her back alone when he discovered she was following him.

The sun rose in dazzling splendor behind her, causing icicles along the riverbank to sparkle like shards of glass. Streaks of soft pink and dark rose criss-crossed the blue dome overhead. The day would be bright and sunny, she guessed, too cold for any more snow.

As she strode along, she imagined the river was a road—leading to untold riches, and when the walls of Fort Miamis loomed out of the snow on her right, she was startled at how far she had come—eight miles? Nine?

Abandoned now, the fort and the cleared area around it was a welcome change from the frost-limbed trees crowding the riverbank. Seeing such a broad expanse of unsullied whiteness, broken only by neat squares and rectangles, she felt glad and hopeful: how could Anthony Wayne refuse to help them?

She herself would tell him about the suffering of the defeated Miamis. She'd tell him about Walks-Tall, and perhaps he would send back medicine along with the food they needed. And blankets too. Not all of the Miamis were as comfortable in their lodges as she and Kin-di-wa. Two Fires had managed to save most of their belongings when Wayne burned down the camp, but others hadn't been so fortunate. Blankets, robes, and sturdy mats had all been lost.

Before departing Fort Miamis, the British had given blankets and foodstuffs to the Indians, but not enough to get them through the winter. Indeed, now that she thought about it, she recalled one particular blanket: Two Fires had traded some skins and mats for a fine heavy rug she sometimes threw over Walks-Tall.

That blanket is probably what made Walks-Tall sick, Rebecca thought darkly. Anything the Saginwash have touched or used must surely be tainted.

The river curved slightly, and a high bluff now rose on her right. She was approaching Fallen Timbers, the site of the battle with Anthony Wayne. Scanning the white-blanketed bluff, she saw only the naked trees, their upraised arms weighted down with snow as if they'd been frozen in attitudes of supplication. The devastation of an ancient windstorm during which the trees had been toppled like twigs was partially hidden now by younger competing growth.

But she knew what was up there on the hill

overlooking the river: an impenetrable mass of brush and fallen timbers which gave the place its name, a name that would be remembered because so many had fought and died there. She hurried by with a feeling of dread, picking her way through frozen rapids where rocks jutted up from the ice—as if to purposely trip her.

The sun had arched well up into the sky as she came to the next landmark in the river, Roche de Boeuf. Named by early French traders, Roche de Boeuf was a large limestone outcropping in the middle of the river. Carved by wind and water, the rock resembled a man's face—or so the Indians said, but Rebecca saw only a towering white object rising straight up in front of her. She glanced toward the bank, looking for the Council Elm, and soon saw it: an ancient gnarled tree which had witnessed scores of tribal meetings.

And she saw something else beyond it: Fort Deposit, the small, hastily thrown-up fort Anthony Wayne had built to store his ammunition and supplies.

It too was abandoned now—given over to drifting snow, and she wondered if anyone had thought to search it. In the spring, the soldiers would surely return, so perhaps they'd left some supplies there. Then she remembered the harsh vengeance of Anthony Wayne. No, it was unlikely he'd leave behind anything that the Indians might find useful.

Slipping and sliding, she hurried through the next set of frozen rapids. Kin-di-wa was so far ahead now she couldn't see him. The river undulated west like a snake: what would she do if she couldn't catch up with him? The camp had been left far behind—too far to make it back before nightfall in her present state of near exhaustion. Soon, she would have to stop and rest. Her heart fluttered, half with anticipation, half with fear. Would he be terribly angry when he saw her? What would he say?

A long thin island now lay on her left, and just past it were two smaller islands. She wondered if the view upriver would be clear when she passed the islands. It was hard to remember. The last time she'd seen this section of the river, she'd been in a canoe going in the opposite direction.

Between the last island and the riverbank, the river passage became quite narrow and was heaped with snow. Head down, she followed Kin-di-wa's footsteps and looked up only when she heard something zing past her ear. Kin-di-wa suddenly stepped out from behind the western-most tip of the tiny island, bow in hand and eyes flashing with surprise and anger.

"Cat-Eyes! You little fool, I almost killed you!"

Having assumed that he was far ahead of her, Rebecca was no less shocked than he was. "Kin-di-wa! What . . . ?"

She turned and eyed the path of the arrow she had heard. A splash of red and gray in the snowy underbrush told her the arrow had flown true to its mark. "You've made a kill! What is it?"

Dropping her bundle on the ice, she sprinted toward the fallen animal.

"Stay back!" Kin-di-wa warned, coming up

behind her. "It was a badger I shot, and if my arrow did not kill him, he can be very dangerous."

Rebecca slowed down and approached more cautiously. The first thing she saw was the badger's long curving front claws, and the second thing was the small white animal in its mouth. "Kin-di-wa!" she breathed. "It's got a rabbit!"

Kin-di-wa prodded the dead badger with the tip of his bow. The large, silver-gray, flat-headed mammal did not move. The arrow was buried deep in its furry fat side. "The old fellow was a better hunter than I am," he grunted. He got down on one knee and touched the white-furred rabbit. "Still warm. I knew if I waited long enough Brother Badger would soon come hurrying back to his burrow with his dinner."

"But how did you know he was here? Don't badgers sleep through the winter?" Rebecca almost felt sorry for the fallen creature whose blood was staining the snow a bright steamy red.

"I saw his tracks on the riverbank and followed them back to his burrow. Badgers do not sleep the winter through. They often come out and go searching for food. The rabbit was unlucky. Either it too had ventured out or it was dug out of its own burrow by the badger's sharp claws."

Rebecca, always fascinated by the extent of Kin-di-wa's wood lore, examined the badger's tracks. The front paws toed in and clearly showed the long lethal claws. They were also slightly larger than the hind paws. "They look somewhat like skunk or weasel tracks," she noticed.

Kin-di-wa shot her an amused glance. "You are

learning . . . And I only hope you know enough by now to find your own way back to camp." He unsheathed his knife and removed it from his waist thong, took the rabbit from the badger's mouth, and slit open its belly.

Rebecca looked away, not wanting to watch the cleaning and gutting of the animals. No matter how often she did it herself, she still found it unpleasant, as unpleasant as the subject Kin-di-wa had just reopened. "I'm not going back, Kin-di-wa. I've come this far, and I'm going on to Fort Greenville with you."

"Oh?" Kin-di-wa never even looked up. "And how did you propose to keep from starving on this journey?"

"I thought I'd eat whatever you eat." Rebecca brushed the snow from a nearby fallen log and sat down on it. "This badger could make do for us a good long time."

"It could serve one all the way to Fort Greenville," Kin-di-wa responded. "If he took care to eat it slowly."

"Then we shall have to find another badger. I am coming with you, Kin-di-wa. I'll follow your tracks the entire way if necessary."

Kin-di-wa finished working on the rabbit and turned his attention to the badger. "I have good reason for not wanting you to come with me to Fort Greenville. But even if I did not, a good squaw obeys her husband. Must I beat you to make you mind me?"

Rebecca bristled at the threatening tone of his voice. "It would make no difference if you did.

My decision is made."

The odor of fresh blood and innards was strong in the crisp air. "Stubborn," Kin-di-wa snorted. "You are the most stubborn woman I have ever met. There . . ." he gestured to a clump of twisted intestines. "Dispose of these. At least, you could help instead of watching as I do the work a man's wife usually does."

"That's why I came—to help you." Rebecca left the log and made an indentation in the snow. With her bare hands, she scooped the intestines into it. She was determined to show him just how sweet and submissive she intended to be—as long as he allowed her to accompany him. "Is that good enough?" She patted fresh snow over the buried innards. "Where did you leave your pack? Shall I go and get it for you?"

Kin-di-wa was tying the gutted animals together with a length of thong. "Do not bother. I am ready." He fastened the animals to his waist thong, and his eyes sparked a cold blue warning. "Do not expect me to wait for you if you cannot keep up. We have no time to lose. Would you have my people starve to death because of your foolishness?"

"They are my people too," Rebecca reminded him stiffly. "And you needn't worry: I won't hold you back." She swallowed several nasty comments that sprang instantly to mind. She must remember that it was Kin-di-wa's nature— indeed, the nature of all Miami braves—to expect total obedience from their women.

Kin-di-wa led the way back to the river, and

soon they were on their way again. Rebecca had to struggle to match Kin-di-wa's long strides, but she dared not complain. When she could no longer continue at so brisk a pace, she slowed down, only to find that Kin-di-wa simply continued onward as though he were walking alone.

"Oh, all right then . . . don't wait for me!" She hollered after him. "I'll catch up to you tonight."

His straight arrogant back proceeded silently upriver, as if he were saying, "You see, I told you so. You should have stayed at camp."

It was a long tiring afternoon. The bright sunshine and the exertion of walking kept Rebecca warm enough, but by late afternoon, her energy was spent. She began to feel shaky from cold and hunger, and her feet lost all sensation. Kin-di-wa was out of sight again, and she wondered how long he'd go on without stopping to make camp. She might have to keep walking until long after dark.

Well, you asked for this, she reminded herself. And if you don't keep going, he probably will leave you to freeze to death.

The sun moved down the western sky in lonely, crimson-gold beauty, and even before it sank behind the horizon, Rebecca's teeth were chattering. A single star hung like a precious jewel just above the rim of the earth, and Rebecca thought she had never seen anything so cold and lovely. The sky darkened to a purple-blue, and more stars began winking.

Then, far ahead on the riverbank, she spotted a tiny orange glow. The glow grew brighter as the night grew darker, and she plodded toward it in a daze. If the fire was not Kin-di-wa's, it would make no difference. She could go no further.

"I was about to come after you," Kin-di-wa growled, as she staggered up the riverbank. But his careful camp preparations belied his harsh tone.

The snow had been banked in a semi-circle around the fire to make a shelter from the wind. A stack of kindling and several large broken pieces of log lay near at hand, and Kin-di-wa's buffalo robe had been spread on the ground only inches from the flames. Best of all, several big chunks of meat were turning on a spit, and as the fat dripped into the flames, loud crackling noises could be heard.

Rebecca sniffed appreciatively, wanting nothing more than to join Kin-di-wa on his outflung buffalo robe. But she was still uncertain of his mood. Did he intend to be gruff and snappish all night? She plunked down her pack and began to untie it.

"Sit here by me." Kin-di-wa pointed to a spot close beside him. "We will use your robe as a covering."

"Thank you." Rebecca did as he suggested, then removed her moccasins and began to rub her numbed feet.

Kin-di-wa's free hand—the one that wasn't turning the spit—reached over and began to massage her toes. She was touched by the gesture but said nothing as prickly sensations began to flow upwards from her extremities.

"You will be warmer after you eat," he said. Kin-di-wa removed a chunk of meat from the spit and handed it to her. It burned her fingers, but she blew on it and took a bite. The outside was crusty black but the inside was pinkish red and tender. Juices ran down her fingers as she ate slowly, savoring each strong-flavored morsel, and wondering what Crow Woman, Two Fires, and Walks-Tall were eating this night. She hoped that somehow, against all probability, it was something equally delicious.

When the cooked meat was gone, Kin-di-wa placed one of the large logs on the fire, while Rebecca scooped up a handful of snow and ate it to quench her thirst. She felt warm and good and sleepy, and would have curled up then and there had Kin-di-wa not turned to her suddenly, his eyes glinting in the firelight and revealing his consternation. "I did not want you to come, Cat-Eyes, because Fort Greenville is no place for a woman—especially a white woman."

"But I can be of help to you!" she argued. "Who else but a white woman could persuade Chenoten to come to our aid if Apekonit's plea should fail?"

"And who else but a white woman could turn an entire garrison of women-hungry men into a bunch of savages?" The grooves around Kin-di-wa's mouth grew deeper.

"I hadn't thought of that," Rebecca conceded. "But why does the entire garrison have to know that I'm a white woman? I'll keep my blanket pulled up over my head so you can hardly see my face, let alone my hair."

Kin-di-wa gave a short sharp laugh. "And will you also keep your eyes closed—those big green cat-eyes that can set a man's heart to racing with a single glance?"

"Of course not! But who will bother about the color of a squaw woman's eyes? Your eyes are blue! Does that make you any less a Miami?"

"Among some, it might . . . but we are not talking about me. There may be many soldiers who might favor a taste of conquered female flesh, squaw-woman or no. Even your blankets and skins cannot hide those curves I love to touch."

The conversation was taking a decidedly personal turn, Rebecca thought, but it was a turn toward the familiar. She'd much rather talk about what Kin-di-wa might like to do to her than what the soldiers might like to do. "My curves are somewhat cold at the moment, my husband. Would you mind putting your arms around me, please?"

Kin-di-wa obliged her. With her robe on top of them and his on the bottom, and the fire crackling in front, they were now quite snug. The press of her husband's arms helped more than anything else to make Rebecca feel cozy, and she moved her body slightly so one of his arms passed over her breast. "Are you comfortable?" she asked.

He nuzzled the top of her head. "You know me too well, little Cat-Eyes. You have only to sit close to me, and I cannot even remember why I am angry with you."

"So much the better," she purred. "Would you

rather sleep out here in the cold alone?"

"You know I would not." Kin-di-wa's hands began to explore beneath the buffalo robe, seeking out her breasts. "Promise me you will do what I say when we reach Fort Greenville. And promise me you will do it without an argument."

"Mmmmm . . . that feels good," Rebecca murmured. Her breasts became warm and tingly under his knowing touch. Then she jumped as he pinched her nipples.

"Promise me," he insisted.

"All right, I promise . . . but I think you worry too much."

"And I think you worry too little."

She tilted her head back to look up at him, and he took advantage of the movement to press his lips to hers in a searching kiss. When he drew back, his eyes were smoldering. "I could not bear for any man to taste your sweetness, little one. You belong to me—only to me."

Rebecca was struck by a fleeting thought: I wish I could say the same thing about you, Kin-di-wa, but you do not belong only to me.

Then the thought was driven out of her mind, as he began kissing her with more insistence. They began the slow spiraling ascent of desire and passion, made sweeter than the sweetest honey by the knowledge of their mutual love and longing. In all the cold dark snowy world, there was only the two of them, warmed both by their inner fires and by the small hot fire that burned without.

"Love me, Kin-di-wa," she begged. "Love me, love me, love me . . ."

His kisses made her feel weak and dizzy, as if he were drinking every drop of her strength and resistance, as if he were swallowing her into himself. He undressed her with eager hands, keeping the buffalo robe between them and the sharp night air.

Then she undressed him, discovering anew the planes and curves of his long hard body. She would know his body by touch no matter how black the night or how long the days or hours between one moment of lovemaking and the next. She knew the ripple of every muscle, the texture of every hollow.

He rolled her over on her back and began mouthing her breasts, then his mouth strayed lower—kissing, licking, giving. His lips found the core of her womanhood, and desire radiated upwards through her body so that she had to push him away and breathe deeply. Her body was no longer her own. He possessed and controlled every inch of it.

A soft low protest escaped her. She hadn't yet had enough of him for it to end so soon, and if he kept on, she'd be finished before he even entered her. She rolled over on top of him, and now, having the controlling position, began to consume his flesh with her own mouth, her own lips, until he lay writhing beneath her—a willing prisoner of the web of exquisite anticipation she was skillfully weaving about him.

Down his lean hard belly, she trailed her kisses, but when she came to the root of his manhood, his fingers entwined themselves in her hair. He seemed to be urging her on and begging her to stop with one and the same quick motion. Then suddenly he groaned and cried out, dragging her up, twisting and turning her, until she was pinned beneath him. "Little she-cat, little demon . . . if you play with fire, you will only get burned."

"Then burn me," she whispered in a voice she hardly recognized as her own. "I am yours, Kin-di-wa. You are the only man I shall ever desire."

He thrust into her with the force of a wild free creature who knew no restraint, no hesitation, and she exalted in it. She could never tame him, never make him conform to any notion of civilization, but in their lovemaking she could possess him. She could know him. And the wildness she found in him called forth an answering wildness in her.

She met his thrusts with abandoned thrusts of her own, and received his manseed with a shuddering force that engulfed her in wave after wave of ecstasy. She called out his name in sweet release, then lay back panting in wonderment.

Here, beside the frozen river and under a cold sickle moon, she had been able to respond to him in a way she never had before—a way she could understand was different only by comparison to what had gone before. This time, she had experienced no timidity, no fear of being watched or of awakening someone else. This time, there had been no barriers to be overcome, no silence to be maintained—and her pleasure had been far greater than she had ever dreamed possible.

Kin-di-wa chuckled against her ear. "Had I

known what joys awaited me beneath a winter sky, I would have carried you out of a warm lodge and camped outside with you long before this."

She made as if to push him away, to disengage her body from his, but he held her tightly in his arms.

"No, my little she-cat. Let me remain inside you. Your body is my lodge, and only when I am warming myself at your inner fire am I truly happy and at peace with myself."

She stroked his long black hair, her fingers finding the two white feathers he always wore tucked into the back and pointing downward toward the ground. "Then stay where you are, my Golden Eagle, my Kin-di-wa. My lodge is ever welcoming."

Kin-di-wa fell asleep in her arms, but she lay awake watching the stars overhead. Thousands of them twinkled with cold brilliance in the vast black heavens. From somewhere far distant across the river came the lonely haunting call of a hungry wolf. Rebecca shivered. Perhaps it was wrong for her to be so happy and content, so filled with love and joy. What right had she and Kin-di-wa to know such bliss when others were suffering?

It was the darkest coldest time of year and the darkest moment in the entire history of the Miamis. Yet for her, it was the happiest time she had ever known. Would she have to pay for such selfishness? And if so—how?

The wolf howled again, and a single large black cloud moved slowly out of the east to obscure the sickle moon. Rebecca hugged Kin-di-wa closer, determined to resist the sense of foreboding that prickled her naked flesh. No matter what unknown sorrow lay ahead, she would have this time alone with Kin-di-wa. She would have it.

It is only when life itself is threatened that you learn the importance of storing good memories, she reflected. Kin-di-wa is right. We must snatch happiness while we can.

But the distant howling of the wolf awoke her several times that night, and each time she glanced up at the sky, more stars had disappeared behind persistent wisps of cloud.

Four

Rebecca and Kin-di-wa took more than a week to arrive within a morning's walking distance of Fort Greenville, but that week was everything Rebecca had hoped for: a quiet passionate time alone together such as they had never before experienced in their married life.

Even Kin-di-wa seemed almost reluctant to reach their destination, though he had maintained a fast pace the entire way. "Do you know where we now are, Cat-Eyes?" he asked when they arose on a particularly cloudy cold gray morning.

"Near Fort Greenville, I think," she responded. "You said we had to come up the Miami of the Lake to Fort Defiance, where the Auglaize and the Miami of the Lake come together, and then go up the Auglaize, cross over the portage to the end of the St. Mary's, and continue on overland until we reach Fort Greenville. We've done everything but reach the fort, haven't we?"

Kin-di-wa grinned. "I didn't think you were listening when I explained the trail we were taking."

"I always listen," Rebecca huffed with mock severity. "Especially when you say something that's important."

"Everything I say is important." Kin-di-wa slipped his arm around her. "And what I have to say now is most important."

Rebecca had been putting their things together, but now she paused and eyed him warily. Gone was the teasing playful lover and companion. The "head of the lodge" had returned and was about to issue orders. "I am listening."

Kin-di-wa tilted her chin, his eyes a smoky blue-gray. "I want you to stay here, Cat-Eyes, and wait until I return. It should not take long. I will go to the fort and ask for Apekonit, then he and I together can explain our situation to Chenoten."

"Oh, Kin-di-wa . . . are you sure you don't want me to come with you? These are my people—my first people," she amended, "and I know I could do a better job than either you or Apekonit of persuading Anthony Wayne to help us! After all, I'm a woman!"

Kin-di-wa's eyes darkened. "That is exactly my concern . . . and remember, you promised you would not argue."

"I—I'm not arguing. Just asking."

"Then I am answering: you must stay here. Besides, it looks like it might snow. You can keep busy building a lean-to—unless you wish to

92

awaken tomorrow morning in a snow drift."

He handed her his war club, a small sharp-edged axe decorated with eagle feathers. "Last evening before we arrived here, we passed through a grove of pines. Pine branches will make a good roof for a lean-to. Do you think you can find the grove again?"

"Of course, I can find it. I noted the pines myself." Rebecca took the axe grudgingly. "Will you be back before dark?"

"I will try. I do not like to think of you spending the night alone. Finish the rabbit I snared yesterday. I will take my chances that food will be offered at the fort."

Already clothed and ready for the last leg of the journey, Kin-di-wa turned to leave, but Rebecca quickly threw her arms around his neck. "Go with Manitou, my husband. And may you have good fortune."

Kin-di-wa bent his head and kissed her long and deeply. "You are my good fortune, little one. And I am pleased you came along on this journey."

A lump rose in Rebecca's throat. She hated to see him go striding off through the tall trees without her. If he did not return by dark, it would be a long lonely night.

She spent the rest of the day building a sturdy lean-to and collecting firewood. The pine grove provided for both needs, and sheltered her from the wind which was rising out of the north. By late afternoon, a heavy wet snow was falling, but the lean-to was reasonably warm, dry, and comfortable. Rebecca made a steaming broth from the bones and remaining meat of the rabbit, pleased that she'd thought to bring along a small caldron. Kin-di-wa knew how to fashion a cooking pouch from animal skins, but she was not about to give up all the white man's comforts if she didn't have to.

She ate her evening meal in silence, a silence made even deeper by the hush of falling snow. Outside the lean-to, she could see nothing but a solid wall of white, and as darkness swallowed even that, she knew that Kin-di-wa wasn't coming. She curled up in the buffalo robes, determined to maintain her good spirits. Everything she needed was close at hand, except the one thing she wanted most—Kin-di-wa's arms around her.

Sleep came in snatches throughout the night. The fire had to be kept going, regardless of the snow. At one time, Rebecca awoke and thought she saw a pair of eyes gleaming on the other side of the fire. She threw a piece of wood and shouted, and the creature slunk away—leaving her shivering with unease and frustration. Had Kin-di-wa been there, he might have put an arrow through the intruder's heart, and they could have had meat for breakfast.

Morning revealed a silent, beautiful, white world. The sky was still overcast, but the snow had stopped. Rebecca busied herself with brushing snow off the firewood and shaking it from the pine branches covering the lean-to. She finished the broth from the night before and wondered what she would eat for dinner. It was unlikely that the woods would contain anything edible this time of year, but she would soon grow stiff and cold from inactivity if she huddled much longer in the lean-to.

She banked the fire carefully to keep it burning slowly while she was gone, then tucked her skinning knife and Kin-di-wa's war club in her waist thong. The first rule of the deep forest was to keep a weapon handy at all times, and she thought longingly of Kin-di-wa's musket—left at home for lack of powder and balls.

Indentations in the snow revealed that some animal had visited her fire during the night, but the tracks were now blurred and indistinct. She headed for the pine grove, and her thorough search for more animal signs was rewarded when she found several trees with "brouse lines," where the lower branches and bark had been stripped away by hungry deer. If deer droppings were nearby, a deer or two might be in the vicinity, making it worthwhile for Kin-di-wa to hunt before they left on the journey homeward.

All around the trees, Rebecca searched and searched. But she found nothing and wearily turned back to the lean-to with another armload of firewood.

A second night passed, and still, Kin-di-wa did not return. Rebecca was becoming truly worried now. Knowing she had no food, Kin-di-wa would never willingly leave her alone for so long. Could he still be at the fort, or had something happened to him along the way? If he didn't come today, she'd have no choice but to go to the fort and look for him. Again, she banked the fire and went searching for more wood and animal signs, her stomach growling in hungry protest.

Coming back from these futile ramblings, she came across a furrow made recently under the snow. The trough resembled a white snake slithering across the ground. The little animal, mink or otter most likely, had forged its own tunnel, and at the end of the tunnel were tracks—about three or four inches wide and perhaps half as deep.

It wasn't much, but it was something. When Kin-di-wa returned, he could go after the creature. She hoped it was mink; the meat was barely edible, but mink fur was soft and beautiful, and she could add it to some other furs she'd been saving to make a robe for Walks-Tall.

She trudged back within sight of the lean-to and saw smoke curling up from the fire. It had obviously been stirred and new wood laid on top. Happiness bubbled in her. "Kin-di-wa!" she cried, and dropping her firewood, ran toward the lean-to. Then she stopped in surprise. The man leaning over the fire was not Kin-di-wa.

Hurriedly, she tugged her blanket over her hair and around her face, as the man looked up with a sly crooked grin, then spoke to her in English. "Well, now . . . this fire must be yourn, ain't it?"

Rebecca went closer, gesturing with her hands in the universal sign language she knew most trappers could understand. My fire, she said with her hands, but you are welcome to warm yourself.

"Why, that's right nice o' ya, little squaw-woman." The man, dressed in typical trapper dress of heavy fringed buckskin and coonskin cap, made the sign for thank you, then craned his neck to see past her. "Y'all alone out here, are ya'?"

Rebecca pretended not to understand. She gestured again: you are welcome at my fire. My husband will be along shortly. Then, to emphasize the point, she glanced back the way she had come. If only Kin-di-wa would come now. It was growing late in the day and had begun to snow again, a fine light snow that reminded her of powder.

"Looks t' me like you is half froze," the man grunted. "Best come over and git warmed up." He motioned for her to sit beside him—on the buffalo robe belonging to Kin-di-wa. Rebecca's insides began to flutter. What if Kin-di-wa didn't make it back this afternoon? This fellow was already acting as though he owned the lean-to, and it wouldn't take long for him to realize that she was alone and at his mercy—though surely he must wonder what she was doing here by herself.

She approached the fire slowly, keeping her blanket wound around her face and hair. Her feet and hands were numb with cold, but she dared not go into the shelter. Instead, she knelt down in the snow on the opposite side of the fire and held out her hands to the crackling flames. The man had added some pine branches, and the resinous wood burned bright and hot, emitting a pungent, piney odor.

"I'm on m' way to th' fort," the man said. "Fort." He pointed in the direction of Fort Greenville. "Got bizness there. But my belly's rumblin' an' when I saw yur shelter, I thought I'd quit fur th' day. Been on th' trail since sun-up."

Rebecca kept her head down, giving no indication she had understood. If she looked straight at him, he couldn't fail to notice her green eyes.

"Ya' got any grub t' cook up?" the man asked. "Grub. Eat." He made eating motions with his hands.

Rebecca shook her head no, then on impulse, tried to tell him with gestures that she expected her husband to return soon with fresh meat. Her blanket slipped back a bit from her face, and his eye caught hers, an expression of recognition dawning on his weather-beaten face. Hastily, she pulled the blanket back into place.

"Hey, little squaw-woman. What you tryin' t' hide?" One hand snaked around the fire and yanked at Rebecca's blanket. Her numbed fingers could not move fast enough to hang onto it, and the blanket was jerked aside.

"Well, I'll be a stinkin' polecat! You ain't no squaw-woman—yur a white gal!" The man's mouth curled up, revealing rotted yellow teeth beneath the reddish-colored hair on his upper lip. Slowly and insolently, he looked her up and down. "My oh my, this must be a lucky day fur ol' Jake Potts."

Rebecca snatched the blanket out of his hand and held onto it tightly, glaring at him across the fire. "It will not be so lucky for you if my husband comes back and finds you sitting on his buffalo robe."

"Yur husband? Ya' mean t' say yur married to some thievin' no-good red-skin?"

"My husband's name is Kin-di-wa, and he's not a thief. He's a Miami warrior and a trusted friend of Little Turtle."

"A white woman—married to a Injun." Jake Potts shook his head. His eyes—watery, bloodshot, and of a color somewhere between gray and brown—narrowed in scorn and disbelief. "Why would a pretty red-haired gal like yurself wanta marry up with a no-good Injun?"

"I don't believe that's any of your business, Mr. Potts." Rebecca kept her voice as crisp and cold as possible. "Perhaps you might want to ask my husband when he returns in a moment or so."

Potts looked around. It was snowing harder now, and the afternoon light was failing. "An' jus' what're ya gonna do if'n yur husband don't make it back b'fore dark? Even a Injun ain't gonna chance gittin' lost in the woods at night."

"He'll make it back," Rebecca insisted with more confidence than she felt. She inched closer to the fire, aware of the man's eyes following her every move. If Kin-di-wa didn't come in the next hour or so, he wouldn't be coming tonight—and Jake Potts knew it. They would be alone together in the lean-to throughout the lonely dark night.

It was a cold uncomfortable hour. The trapper rummaged through his pack and produced several strips of dried beef. He gnawed at one and laid the other two on the buffalo robe beside him. Then he grinned at Rebecca. "If'n ya come inside th' lean-to, ya kin have some jerky—but I don't share my grub with folks who is so unfriendly."

"I'm not hungry," Rebecca lied, but she was becoming stiff with cold. Outside the shelter of the lean-to, whirling snowflakes and biting wind were finding their way through her layers of blankets and skins.

It grew darker. The world narrowed to a single patch of golden light cast by the campfire, and Jake Potts became more jovial. He withdrew a corked jug from his pack, uncorked it, and took a swig. "Gittin' cold, little squaw-woman? This 'ere kin warm ya up in a hurry. Why not come inside an' relax? It don't look like yur Injun is gonna make it back t'night."

"My name is not sq-squaw-woman." Rebecca's teeth were chattering. Maybe, if he heard her real name, he would realize that she was a white woman—and worthy of more respect than he obviously had for Indians. "M—my name is R— Rebecca McDuggan, or rather it was, before I married. M—my Aunt M—Margaret and my Uncle H—Hardin in Philadelphia are quite a p— prominent family."

"Oh?" Jake Potts sneered. "Prominent, huh? Well, Philadelphia is a long way away little squaw-woman, an' out here in th' wilderness, we don't stand on no ceremonies. B'sides, I reckon yur kin ain't heard nothin' of ya' in a mighty long time."

Rebecca shivered, remembering the letter she

had written to Aunt Margaret in November. Why hadn't she thought to bring it along and let Kin-di-wa post it from the fort?

Jake Potts took another long swallow from his jug and watched her with slanting eyes and smirking mouth. His nose had a peculiar hook to it, as if it might have been broken once and had healed without being properly set—and the very tip of his hooked nose was getting redder with each successive sip from the jug.

Finally, Potts put the jug aside and moved his musket from his lap to the edge of the buffalo robe. Had he been keeping it handy in anticipation of Kin-di-wa's arrival? A spasm of fear made Rebecca shiver even harder.

"Well, Miz Rebecca McDuggan . . . yur Injun ain't a-comin'. Ya might as well git in here outa th' cold, less'n ya got a mind t' freeze t' death t'night."

Sighing inwardly with defeat, Rebecca groped her way into the lean-to and knelt down. Jake Potts was right. She couldn't spend the whole night outside the shelter, but neither did she intend to permit this stranger to become too familiar with her. Her frozen fingers worked at her waist thong to release her skinning knife. If Potts didn't keep his hands to himself, she would use it.

But suddenly, Potts reached up beneath her blankets and effortlessly snatched the knife away. "Hah! Jus' like I thought! Y'ain't learned t' keep yur thoughts hid like a Injun, 'ave ya, little squaw-woman? I knew soon as ya reached up t' yur belt what ya had in mind."

Rebecca's spirits sank. Why hadn't she waited until her hands were warmer? Her thoughts turned to the war club, still dangling against one hip.

"Take off yur belt," Jake Potts growled. "Let's see whut else ya got fastened to it."

With shaking hands, Rebecca undid her waist thong, and Potts quickly grabbed the feathered tomahawk. His face split into a nasty grin. "Pull up yur dress now an' let's see yur legs. Injun squaws sometimes wear sharp little daggers stropped onto their thighs."

"I don't," Rebecca protested. "And you'll have to take my word for it."

In a single split second, before she could stop him, Jake Potts knelt behind her, threw one arm around her neck, and pressed the cold blade of her own skinning knife to her throat. She struggled against him, but his wiry strength surprised her: she could no more get away from him than free herself from a bear hug.

"Pull up your dress!" Potts snarled. "An' let's get a look-see at them legs o' yourn."

Gingerly, Rebecca raised the fringed hem of her doeskin. One of Jake's hands felt around the bindings of her leggings, while the other kept the knife at her throat. When he was satisfied that she spoke the truth—no knife was lashed to her thigh—his hand went exploring higher. She gasped as he clasped her intimately, pressing her against him so she could feel his maleness hardening against her buttocks.

"D—don't think you can use me and get away

102

with it!" she warned in a trembling voice. "My husband will track you to the ends of the earth and see that you die a slow and painful death."

"I'll be gone b'fore sun-up," Potts chuckled into her ear. "An' I know these woods like th' back o' my hand. Maybe it'll even keep snowin' an' wipe out m' tracks . . . Now, let's ease off that dress, so I kin see if m' luck has held out. A gal with green eyes an' red hair has just gotta 'ave somethin' real purty underneath all them blankets an' skins."

Rebecca could hardly believe that he meant for her to undress—without even a blanket or robe to protect her from the wind. The wind had shifted to a new direction and was now gusting icily into the lean-to. But Potts laid the gleaming cold blade to her throat and snarled, "Go on, git a move on. I wanta see ya stripped down naked as the day you was borned."

While she tugged at knots and binding with fingers that had lost all feeling and control, her attacker kept up a stream of half-drunken prattle. "Ain't had me a piece o' white meat in a good long time . . . an ain't never had me a piece whut looked like you. Ya puts me in mind o' sweet juicy peaches an' thick curdled cream—like ya kin git down south o' here in th' summer. Ya' ever et peaches an' cream?"

When she didn't answer, he reached down and prodded her leg with the tip of his knife, leaving a bright red pin-point in the flesh of her thigh, from which she was struggling to remove a legging.

"Y—yes. B—back home on my P—Papa's farm."

"Had ya a farm, did ya? I did too once . . . til the land give out on me. Never did have no luck with farmin'. Never did have no luck with nothin'—leastways, not til t'night. Hurry up now, an' let me see yur tits . . . a woman ain't nothin' without big tits."

Maybe he won't think I'm big enough, Rebecca thought half-hysterically. She was shivering so hard she could hardly remove her otter-skin cape. But her hope that he might be too disappointed with the swell of her embroidered doeskin bodice, was dashed when he reached out and fondled one of her breasts. "Oh, them promises t' be real purty . . . Does yur Injun know whut t' do with purty tits? Does he touch 'em and squeeze 'em like this?"

She tried in vain to remove his exploring hand, but Potts squeezed so hard that tears leapt into her eyes. "P—please don't hurt me," she whimpered. She was chillingly reminded of that other time, when Will Simpkin had hurt her—just like this Jake Potts was now hurting her—inside and out. Indeed, Will had left deep unerasable scars, but only she, and perhaps, Kin-di-wa, knew they still existed.

Jake Potts now seized and bent her backwards, staring down at her with hungry, greedy, cruel eyes. "Now, you do jus' whut I tell ya, little squaw woman, an' I promise not t' hurt ya . . . but ya gotta do whutever I ask. Ya' hear?" He gave her breasts another sharp twist, then shoved her upright. "Now, undo yur hair . . ."

Rebecca pulled her braids across her breasts as

though to do so would protect her—both from the cold biting wind and any further cruelties. She fumbled with the thongs binding the tips of her braids.

"Hurry up!" Potts snarled. "I'm gittin' cold jus' watchin' ya!"

When her hair was undone, the wind blew it back across her shoulders, and the campfire leapt and crackled, so buffeted by snow and wind that it hardly cast any warmth. I could die out here tonight, Rebecca thought. The lean-to should be turned around to stop the wind. Why doesn't he think of it?

Then she realized that she didn't care if she did die. After this, how could she ever face Kin-di-wa? How could she bear to have her husband touch her—after she'd once again been defiled by a man more animal than human? She had vowed the last time, when Will degraded her, that it would never happen again.

"Here . . ." Potts handed her his jug. "Have a swig o' this. It'll make ya warmer."

Rebecca took the jug and nearly dropped it, lifting it shakily to her lips. Did it matter anymore if she ate and drank what was offered? Her pride was already broken. She couldn't fight a man with a knife—or could she?

The liquid in the jug burned her throat and made her gasp. Her eyes began to water, and for a moment, she could hardly breathe. Jake Potts gave a throaty laugh. "I like my women willin', an' there's nothin' like a snort o' firewater to loosen 'em up a bit."

And to give them courage, Rebecca thought. She managed to take another long swallow before Potts snatched the jug away. "That's enough now, damn ya! Save some fur me!" He took another drink himself, then leaned back on the buffalo robe, toying with the knife. "How many ways you done it, little squaw-woman?"

"Wh—what do you m—mean?" Rebecca quavered. A flush of false warmth from the whiskey enabled her to get her voice under control again. "I don't know what you mean."

Potts's eyes, fastened to the curves of her body which was shaking beneath the doeskin, glittered dangerously. In the uncertain light from the fire, his face looked evil and brooding. "You know whut I mean. Tell me about all th' ways you ever done it with a man . . . go on, tell me!"

Rebecca's insides squirmed. Was the man crazy? She glanced toward the war club lying near him on the buffalo robe. Perhaps, she could distract him long enough to get to it. "Well . . . I . . . I guess the first time was just normal."

"Normal how?" Potts reached over and took a strand of her hair. He curled it around one finger, never taking his eyes from her. "Whadda ya mean—normal? Did he git on top o' ya? Is that what ya mean?"

"Why—yes. Yes, he did," Rebecca stammered. It galled her to speak to this loathsome man of that beautiful thing she and Kin-di-wa had done together. More determined now, she inched her way nearer to the war club, as if in response to the tug on her hair.

Then Potts reached out and grabbed her, pulling her over on top of him. "You ever do it on top?" He clasped her to him in a powerful bear hug, leering into her face. "How does yur Injun like it? Or does he like best stickin' his long red pole down yur throat?"

Rebecca was unable to answer; her breath was squeezed from her lungs. But she saw that the war club was now within reaching distance, and her fingers closed stealthily over it. Slowly, she drew it nearer, but before she could swing it up and then down again, she felt the prick of the knife in her back.

"Throw the tomahawk away, little squaw-woman, or I'll carve my mark on yur purty little white behind b'fore I'm through with ya' t'night."

Bitter determination replaced Rebecca's fear. "Go ahead!" she hissed. "I'd rather die than be raped by the likes of you!"

"Ya' sure about that, little squaw-woman?"

The knife pressed deeper into Rebecca's lower back, imparting a swift hot pain as the blade penetrated her doeskin and edged into her flesh. She tried to swing the tomahawk. The trapper made a sudden shifting movement, and without realizing quite how it happened, she found herself lying pinned beneath him.

Potts's face bulged with fury. The tip of his misshapen nose gleamed crimson. "Now, yur gonna do ever'thin' I tell you, little squaw-woman, an' yur gonna do it with no tricks. Ya' hear? I ain't foolin'; I'll carve ya' up like a side o' venison . . ." He licked his lips, his eyes gleaming with lust. "I once had me a red-haired whore like you, an' she wasn't half as purty—but she kept my pole jumpin' up an' down til I couldn't hardly stand it."

"I'll do nothing. Nothing! If you're going to kill me, do it now. I don't care what happens—I won't play your filthy games!"

Potts drew back and waved the knife under her nose. "Oh, you'll play all right!" He grabbed hold of the fringe at the top of her bodice and hooked through the doeskin with the tip of his knife, as if he meant to slash open her dress from breast to thigh. "Now, I want ya' t' smile real purty an' say, 'yes sir, Mister Potts. I'll do anythin' ya' say—startin' with takin' off my clothes.'"

Rebecca stiffened and said nothing. She remembered how the dying Indians at Fallen Timbers had refused to make a sound. Some of them had suffered terribly, but the bitterness of their defeat had somehow turned into proud triumph when they died without complaint. So too would she die—finding victory in defiance.

"All right, if that's th' way ya' want it . . ." Potts snarled.

Rebecca closed her eyes and held her breath against the expected assault, but a stealthy noise outside the lean-to suddenly drew her attention. Potts also became aware of it and whirled around—too late. Something large and heavy crashed down through the pine branches and struck him across the head. Snow, pine branches, and Potts's heavy body collapsed on top of Rebecca with a thud. She had no doubt as to the identity of her rescuer.

"Kin-di-wa! Kin-di-wa!" she cried, and a moment later, Kin-di-wa hauled the trapper off her and threw him into the snow. Then he was kneeling beside her, brushing away the debris and gathering her into his arms. "Cat-Eyes! Are you hurt?"

Crushed against his broad chest, she could barely answer. "N—no. Only a little cold and scared."

Kin-di-wa wrapped her in a snowy blanket, his eyes blazing with a dangerous blue light. "We will find your cape and leggings as soon as I rid us of this vermin. Watch carefully, little Cat-Eyes, as I show you what a Miami warrior does to his enemies." His hand reached for the knife.

"No, Kin-di-wa!" Rebecca held onto his arm, shocked to the soul by Kin-di-wa's suggestion. She had never seen her husband so savage. "You mustn't—do that! You mustn't kill him!" She searched for the arguments that would bring Kin-di-wa to his senses. "We're too close to the fort! He said he was going there—that he had business! Maybe they'll send someone to look for him. You know who they'll blame for his death . . . if not you, then some other Indian!"

But Kin-di-wa's face seemed carved of stone. "No man may threaten my woman and escape with his life and his scalp."

"Please, Kin-di-wa . . ." she begged, holding tightly to his arm. "For my sake! Don't kill him. He never touched me."

"He would have killed you after he took his

pleasure. Do you think he would have allowed you to live to spread the tale of his wrong-doing?"

Rebecca shuddered, remembering Potts's threats. She would have killed him herself if she could have, but she didn't want Kin-di-wa to kill him—or to torture him in the process. "Chenoten will kill us all to revenge a white man," she argued. "Besides, are we no better than he is—allowing our hatred to turn us into animals?"

"What would you have me do?" There was deep frustration in Kin-di-wa's voice. "A man must protect his own!"

"You have no need to prove you are a man . . . Why not just tie him up? When we're ready to leave, we can loosen his bonds and leave him here. In time, he will work himself loose. But by then, we will be gone—gone without anyone getting hurt."

"Tie him up—pah!" A muscle worked in Kin-di-wa's jaw.

Knowing that her husband was still fighting an urge to seek revenge in the ancient Miami way, with knives and fire, Rebecca laid a restraining hand on his arm. "Please, Kin-di-wa . . . we must think of what might happen to others if we react too hastily. The danger he brought is now past; let's not create new dangers."

Her pleas finally convinced him. With a long drawn sigh, as if something were being torn out of his heart, Kin-di-wa gave the knife back to her. Wordlessly, she took it and hid it while Kin-di-wa found several lengths of rawhide among their belongings. Then he tied Potts's hands and feet with angry grudging gestures. The trapper lay sprawled in the snow, feeling nothing, and Rebecca was glad. If he had awakened and complained of his treatment, Kin-di-wa would have found it excuse enough to kill him after all.

Hurriedly, she dressed, then helped Kin-di-wa put up the lean-to, facing away from the wind. When at last the shelter was snug and warm, and the still unconscious Potts had been allotted a single blanket and a spot half-inside the lean-to, Rebecca curled up in Kin-di-wa's arms, anxious to question him about his success at Fort Greenville.

But Kin-di-wa hugged her to him, his body still shaking with raw emotion. "If he had succeeded in what he set out to do, little Cat-Eyes, nothing on earth could have prevented me from killing him."

"I know," Rebecca whispered. "But he did not succeed. Thank God, you came when you did."

"If anything should ever happen to you, wife of my heart . . ." Kin-di-wa's voice broke, and having no words to comfort him, Rebecca took her husband's face in her hands and kissed him gently on the lips. His agony was the same as she had known when it was his life that was threatened.

Oh, dear God, she thought, are we never to know the blissful joy of ordinary everyday living?

When she and Kin-di-wa were in control of their feelings, Rebecca began pawing through Potts's pack until she found his cache of dried food. At least, the ugly incident had yielded one good thing: there was enough jerky to give them a good start on their homeward journey. Kin-di-wa accepted the proffered meal with a hungry grunt that told her she had succeeded in distracting him.

"Is General Wayne going to help us?" She took a bite of the leathery meat, suddenly reminded of how hungry she was.

Kin-di-wa chewed a mouthful slowly, then swallowed and shook his head. "The mighty Chenoten graciously granted me the opportunity to enjoy the comforts of his guardhouse while he thought on the matter, and then he told me no—defeated Indians are much more likely to agree to peace terms if they dread another winter next year such as they have experienced this year."

Rebecca practically choked. "You mean he wants us to starve?"

"He wants us to suffer. He does not think we are starving. Word reached him sometime ago that the Saginwash were still helping us."

"The Saginwash!" At this mention of the British, Rebecca lost her appetite. "What they gave us in the autumn was not sufficient—and I think their blankets and foodstuffs were probably also tainted!"

Kin-di-wa lowered the jerky from his mouth, one eyebrow raised in doubt. "Tainted? I cannot understand your hatred for the Saginwash, Cat-Eyes. Nor Chenoten's either. Your War of Independence was fought many years ago, yet the name of the Saginwash need only be mentioned, and both you and Chenoten grow angry. The Saginwash did not even help us when we most

112

needed it—so why should they be considered so threatening?"

Rebecca sighed. She never had been able to make him understand how close Fallen Timbers had come to being the opening battle of another war with Great Britain. But Anthony Wayne had understood. If British soldiers had fired on American soldiers, there would have been a cry of outrage from every man, woman, and child in the United States. Memories of the previous year were still too raw and bitter for such effrontery to go unavenged.

Perhaps, she thought, I too ought to be glad instead of angry that the British betrayed the Indians at the crucial moment.

She tried once again to explain the situation to Kin-di-wa. "As long as the Saginwash maintain any presence on American soil, the whites will continue to feel threatened."

"On *American* soil?" Kin-di-wa's eyes flashed an angry blue, and Rebecca hurried to amend her statement.

"Of course, it's not American soil, it's Miami soil. But that's the problem: the Americans think it does belong to them because they defeated the British . . . Oh, what difference does any of it make now? What I don't understand is how Chenoten can allow innocent women and children to suffer—no matter what the reason! Did Sweet Breeze's husband speak to him?"

Kin-di-wa shook his head. "Apekonit was not there. He had been sent to Fort Recovery, only a short journey from here, but when I suggested he

113

be asked to return, Chenoten refused. He said he already knew what his Chief Indian Scout would say: Apekonit has been urging fairness—or leniency, as Chenoten himself would call it—for the Miamis ever since their defeat."

"At least, Sweet Breeze will be glad to hear that," Rebecca murmured. "She doesn't understand why Apekonit hasn't come home to her and Little Turtle."

"I doubt he is able to," Kin-di-wa said darkly. "It is part of Chenoten's plan to keep us all unhappy—so unhappy that we will be glad of the chance to make a strong peace next summer. And many land concessions too."

"Oh, Kin-di-wa!" Rebecca drew up her knees and laid her head on them to hide the rush of tears to her eyes. "What shall we do now? If we go back empty-handed, how will we make it through the rest of the winter?"

Kin-di-wa drew her close as if to shut out the black night, the snow, the wind—and the bleak future. "Winter will not last forever, little one. Only the Hunger Moon lies ahead, and then the sap will run in the trees again and the birds will begin to return. We are a strong people. Somehow, we shall survive."

But Rebecca wondered. February was not called the Hunger Moon for nothing. Even in time of plenty, food was scarce during February.

Rebecca awoke quite early—to the sound of Jake Potts alternately cursing and moaning. Kin-di-wa was not in the lean-to, but the direction of his footprints in the fresh snow told her that he'd probably gone hunting. She wished she had remembered to tell him about the mink tunnel.

After stretching her stiff muscles, she went off by herself behind the trees, and by the time she returned, Jake Potts was sitting up and trying to wriggle closer to the fire. "Y' tryin' t' make it look like I somehow froze t' death?" he complained.

"It would only be what you deserve." Rebecca began to gather up their things, knowing that as soon as Kin-di-wa returned, he would want to start for home.

"Ya' can't jus' leave me here tied up like this," the trapper whined.

"Oh, I'm sure you'll find some way to get loose." She tugged Kin-di-wa's buffalo robe out from under him and rolled it up tightly.

"You stealin' m' food an' whiskey too?"

"We have more need of it than you do." Rebecca removed both jug and jerky from Potts's pack. "When you get to Fort Greenville, they will likely give you more."

Looking a sorry sight, Jake Potts sat and glared at her. His reddish-colored hair—matted with dried blood—stuck straight up. His moustache and short growth of beard were likewise matted and frost-whitened. A slender thread of clear liquid trailed from his beaked red nose, and his bloodshot watery eyes glittered with a feverish hatred. "Yur gonna be sorry, little squaw-woman. Noboby messes with old Jake Potts an' gits away with it."

"Nobody messes with Kin-di-wa's woman and gets away with it either," Rebecca retorted.

"Kin-di-wa, eh? An' whut did ya' say yur name was, yesterday—Rebecca McDuggan?"

Rebecca had a moment's remorse, wishing she'd never mentioned her name or Kin-di-wa's. "It makes no difference. You will never see either of us again."

Jake Potts hawked and spat. "Oh, I wouldn't count on that, little squaw-woman. You an' me's got unfinished bizness. Personal bizness, iffn' ya' know whut I mean."

Rebecca paused in the act of refastening her skinning knife to her waist thong. "The only unfinished business we have, Mr. Potts, can be finished quite nicely with one slash of my knife. The next time, should we both be so unfortunate as to meet again, I won't be so careless: I'll go for your throat—or whatever's handy—first thing."

Potts's response, if he had one, died on his tongue as Kin-di-wa strode toward them.

"If you wish to speak to my woman, white eyes, you had better ask my permission."

Potts squirmed still closer to the dying fire. "I only wanted t' know if yur gonna go off an' leave me like this."

"Better we leave you like that than to leave you naked and scalpless, slashed into a hundred pieces," Kin-di-wa growled.

Potts had no more to say after that. He merely sat and scowled as Kin-di-wa showed Rebecca the beautiful fur and butchered meat of two fat minks he had snared that morning.

She stroked the rich brown fur with trembling fingers. "I am so happy you found them. Now, I do not feel as though we are returning home with nothing."

They broke camp hurriedly then, leaving Jake Potts tied up with rawhide thongs that had been secured into a series of knots. Kin-di-wa assured Rebecca the knots could be undone in the space of a few hours, but as they departed the area, Potts began to shout defiantly.

"Half-breed bastard! Whore! Th' devil take ya both!"

Kin-di-wa would have gone back to silence him but Rebecca took her husband's arm and hurried onward. "Home! Let's go home! I warn you, Kin-di-wa, if you cannot keep up with me, I shall be forced to leave you behind."

Her jest was enough to soften the anger glinting in Kin-di-wa's eyes. He took her hand, and they started the long journey homeward, concealing their disappointment as best they could that the trip hadn't been more successful.

Five

Two days later, as Rebecca and Kin-di-wa made their way along the frozen Auglaize River, they discovered they were being followed. Rebecca saw the single lone figure coming after them on the ice when she sat down to rest her ankle. It had been twisted the day before and was now aching intolerably.

"Kin-di-wa! Look behind us!" she cried. "Who could that be?"

The figure was still far distant and didn't appear to have noticed them. It was a tall man, walking with head down and shoulders hunched, as he pulled some sort of conveyance, heaped high with bundles, behind him.

Ever alert to the possibility of danger, Kin-di-wa took her arm and dragged her to her feet. "Quick—get out of sight on the bank," he snapped. His other hand was already going for his weapons, both bow and war club.

"But—won't he think it odd if he looks up and finds us gone? I mean, if indeed, he has been following us."

Kin-di-wa shot her a warning glance to remind her it was his job to see to their safety, not hers. Then a light came into his eyes. "You are right. You keep walking, and I shall wait here. I had rather you be far ahead anyway when I take away those bundles and see what is in them."

"You—you're going to steal his things?"

Kin-di-wa's glance was cold and level. "If he has any food, I will take it. The rest I do not care about."

Rebecca glanced back at the advancing figure, but the man had momentarily disappeared behind a bend in the river. She thought of Walks-Tall whimpering with hunger. "All right—but don't kill him, Kin-di-wa."

"Start walking," Kin-di-wa said. "You needn't tell me yet again how you feel about killing."

Rebecca set out limping, the pain in her ankle all but forgotten. A little discomfort was nothing compared to the possibility of getting food. She fought her twinges of conscience. Could it be considered stealing to take food to help those who were starving? Then a shocking thought occurred to her: what if the man was already taking food to hungry people?

The temptation to look back was overwhelming, but Rebecca dared not stop or appear to notice anything going on behind her. The river had gently curved again, and she knew she wouldn't be able to see much anyway—but she could listen, and this she did with great attention.

She heard the soft shush, shush of her padded moccasins on the snow-filmed ice, the creak of the pack on her back, and the constant distant rattle of tree limbs stirred by the wind. But there was no sound behind her—not a single cry or shout. She glanced up at the pale gray sky, trying to judge the passage of time. It was early afternoon or thereabouts. How far should she go before stopping to wait for Kin-di-wa?

Her ankle began to throb painfully, reminding her of yesterday's spill on a wind-swept patch of ice. Having forgotten how uncertain the footing was on the river, she had been walking freely and carelessly. Then suddenly, she hadn't been walking anymore but was lying sprawled out awkwardly, her arms and legs going in every direction. Kin-di-wa had burst out laughing—until he saw she was hurt.

They had bound the ankle tightly, relieving the pain, but the remainder of the day had been slow going, and this morning had been little better. If it hadn't been for my ankle, Rebecca thought ruefully, the man behind us would never have caught up so easily.

On upriver she limped, hoping with each painful step that she would soon hear Kin-di-wa's call. When she finally did hear it, she was taken by surprise. He sounded so joyful and excited; what had happened back there on the ice?

She turned and waited. Kin-di-wa came trotting around the last bend in the river, dragging the stranger's crude sled behind him. His face shone with triumph and delight. Rebecca looked past him, and her stomach did a flip-flop. The bundles of the sled appeared not to have been touched, and the stranger was nowhere in sight.

"You killed him!" she accused, as Kin-di-wa loped breathlessly to her side.

The sled jumped and bumped on the ice, and the radiance faded from her husband's face, to be replaced with puzzlement. "Killed him! Who? Do you mean Apekonit?"

"Apekonit!" Rebecca craned her neck to see around the obstruction of the bend. The same tall figure reappeared, only this time, he was striding rapidly back in the direction from which he had come.

"That was Apekonit?" She could not believe it.

Kin-di-wa nodded, his good mood returning. "That was my blood brother and Little Turtle's adopted son. Bringing food, medicine, and blankets. I knew he could persuade Chenoten to help us, once he knew of our need."

"You knew!" Rebecca sputtered. "It was my idea to come! But how did he succeed in changing Anthony Wayne's mind?"

Kin-di-wa adjusted the sled rope on his shoulder. "He did not exactly persuade him. But he did collect some money he was owed—'back pay' he called it. Then he made a few purchases from the Army storehouse. Chenoten allowed him to do so, but only on condition that he take no more than a day or two to find us and get back again to the Fort."

"Oh, Kin-di-wa!" Rebecca threw her arms around her husband's neck, practically dancing for joy in her happiness. "It must have been Manitou's will that I hurt my ankle—or Apekonit would not have found us in time!"

Kin-di-wa swept her off her feet. "If you are not more careful, my little she-cat, you will break your ankle. Will that be Manitou's will?"

She hugged and kissed him. "I can't believe it! Food, medicine, blankets!"

Kin-di-wa set her down again and eyed the carefully packed bundles. "But it is not so much as Apekonit would have liked to send, nor nearly so much as we need. We shall have to be careful; only those who need these supplies the most will receive them. Those who are strong and can still hunt must do without."

"Walks-Tall will not do without." Rebecca set her jaw stubbornly. "Nor will Two Fires. Walks-Tall needs her milk."

Kin-di-wa's eyes twinkled. "Is this my jealous wife who is speaking—the one who finds it so hard to share my affections with another?"

In spite of herself, Rebecca had to smile. Perhaps she was adjusting more rapidly than she realized. But then it was easy to be gracious to the lovely Two Fires, when the girl was so far away. Rebecca limped over to the make-shift sled and climbed on top of the blanket-wrapped bundles. "Well, my husband, are we going home now? Please pull as fast as you can."

Kin-di-wa took up the long tumpline attached to the sled. "Not even a canoe could skim the water any faster than we shall skim the ice. Hold tight, little one."

But as the sled lurched forward up the river, Rebecca wished they could have delayed their leave-taking a few moments longer. She wanted to meet their benefactor: Captain William Wells. But no doubt he had been as anxious to return to the Fort and keep his commander happy, as they had been to continue onward. She would have to wait until another day to meet Sweet Breeze's husband.

It was bitter cold and snowing again by the time they passed the familiar landmarks on the Miami of the Lake—Roche de Boeuf, Fallen Timbers, and Fort Miamis. The Snow Moon had given way to the Hunger Moon, and both Rebecca and Kin-di-wa were in a fever to get to the camp. Once she'd had a chance to stay off it for several days, Rebecca's ankle had healed without any difficulty, and now, she helped Kin-di-wa pull the unwieldy sled across the ice.

They plodded head-down into the wind, and neither felt like talking. Making the effort to speak would only deplete their strength and lessen the likelihood they would make it home before nightfall.

Rebecca peered through the curtain of whirling snow. Her face felt raw, and her lips were cracked. This last leg of the journey seemed to go on forever. But it's been worth it, she thought. She could hardly wait to see Walks-Tall again—and to try out the medicines in the bundle. If the baby was still suffering from his awful cough, she felt certain that she could now cure him.

She reflected that she would even be glad to see Crow Woman and Two Fires. The old woman had long ago won her affection, and this time alone with Kin-di-wa had deepened her sympathy for Two Fires. Two Fires had never been first in Kin-di-wa's heart; she would always be the woman he had taken as wife only to fulfill an obligation. And to Rebecca, the mere idea of marrying for convenience sake was abhorrent. She would rather die than live with someone she didn't love.

As they came within sight of the lodges, Rebecca tugged at Kin-di-wa's sleeve. "Let me go ahead," she begged. "I can't wait to see their faces when I tell them we have food and medicine. Maybe—we could have a feast tonight!"

"No feast . . ." Kin-di-wa grunted. "These supplies have to be distributed with great care, remember? As soon as the camp finds out we've returned with food, everyone will feel like feasting, and by tomorrow, it will all be gone."

Rebecca knew he was right, but she couldn't resist some small celebration. "Couldn't we at least invite Little Turtle and Sweet Breeze to come for a meal? There's ground corn in the packs, and we could make sagamity." She wrinkled her nose, "I don't much care for corn meal mixed with fat, dried vegetables, and whatever else is handy, but you know how much Little Turtle likes it."

Kin-di-wa frowned. "I only hope Little Turtle is

better now than when I saw him last. I hope he is able to join us for sagamity."

Taking his comment as assent, Rebecca ignored her sudden feeling of worry and handed Kin-di-wa her end of the tumpline. Then she scampered across the ice to let Crow Woman, Two Fires, and everyone else know of their return.

Their lodge stood at the near end of the clearing, and Rebecca was so excited to see it that she didn't at first realize how strange and alien it looked. But as she drew closer to the domed shelter, which was almost totally buried in snow drifts, she noticed that no footprints led to and away from the lodge and no smoke was coming out of the smoke-hole.

"Crow Woman? Two Fires?" Rebecca swept aside the skin hanging across the entrance.

No one answered. The lodge was cold and dark, as if no one had lived there for some time. Heart thudding wildly now, Rebecca waved and called to Kin-di-wa: "They're not here! I'm going to Sweet Breeze's lodge to find out where they've gone!"

"Wait!" Kin-di-wa called back. "I'll go with you . . ." Leaving the sled near the river bank, he came quickly.

A dozen questions leapt to Rebecca's tongue, but the worried set of her husband's jaw discouraged her from speaking—he too must be thinking the worst. Wordlessly, they set out through the heavy snow which was much deeper here in the clearing than on the river. All of the lodges were rimmed with snowdrifts, but at least, trails led back and forth between them. Theirs was the only one that seemed abandoned.

They passed several lodges where they might have stopped to demand explanations, but Kin-di-wa steered Rebecca past them. "Let us go to Peshewa's first—not Little Turtle's. It was Peshewa who said he would care for my family in my absence."

"Our family," Rebecca corrected. Her stomach was in a turmoil. They had come so far, endured so much: what could have gone wrong now?

They arrived at the lodge belonging to Peshewa and his mother, and Rebecca was relieved to see that smoke was spiraling out of the smoke-hole. As Kin-di-wa clapped his hands at the entrance, hope fluttered anew in her breast. Maybe Peshewa had taken Crow Woman, Two Fires, and Walks-Tall into his own lodge for protection. Maybe they were all seated inside, at this very moment, awaiting a glorious reunion. She held her breath as the flap was unfastened, and the face she saw peering out was that of her old friend, Crow Woman.

"Crow Woman! Oh, I knew it! I knew you were safe!" Rebecca jostled past her into the lodge. "Where's Walks-Tall—where is he? I have been so worried about him!"

Eagerly, she looked around the dimly lit lodge, but there was only one other person in it: Peshewa's stocky, heavy-boned mother who sat unmoving by the fire. Rebecca whirled around. "Where's Walks-Tall? Where's Two Fires and Peshewa?"

Kin-di-wa came into the lodge behind her, and Crow Woman tried to explain. Her hands moved. Her mouth opened. But no sound came out. Her grizzled white hair stuck straight out from her head, and in her unsuccessful attempt to speak, she looked like a dead woman trying to commune from beyond the grave.

"Answer me!" Rebecca shouted.

But the old woman began to cry soundlessly, tears running down her withered cheeks. Her hands made jerky uncoordinated gestures as, with sign language, she tried to tell what had happened. Rebecca could make neither head nor tail of it.

"Tecumwah," Kin-di-wa finally said, and the woman at the fire lifted her head and stared at them.

Rebecca gasped. Tecumwah, Peshewa's mother, had always been a squat, well-padded woman whose love of food showed in her plump cheeks and pendulous breasts. But now, the plumpness was gone, and the folds of skin that remained made her face look sunken and cadaverous.

"Tecumwah . . ." Kin-di-wa repeated. "Tell us what happened. Where is Walks-Tall and his mother? Where is Peshewa?"

"Peshewa hunt," the woman grunted. "Hunt all the time, but find little. One rabbit, two weasels, one day a fox . . . Peshewa good son. Try hard. Is not his fault he no find more."

"Tecumwah, where is my son—the child of my slain brother?"

Tecumwah's shoulders slumped. "He dead.

128

Walks-Tall dead. No more hungry. No more hurt. No more cough-cough until he choke. He gone now, Golden Eagle, gone to join his father in land where winter never comes."

"No!" Rebecca refused to believe it. She grabbed Crow Woman's thin bony shoulders. "Crow Woman! Where is Walks-Tall? You must tell us! We brought medicine, food, blankets to make him well again. Where is he, Crow Woman?"

"Cat-Eyes . . ." Kin-di-wa's tone was thick with defeat. "Crow Woman can tell you nothing different than what Tecumwah has already told us."

"Crow Woman?" Rebecca felt as if a skinning knife was being twisted in her heart.

Crow Woman choked and sputtered, then finally found her voice. "It true. Walks-Tall die of coughing sickness, and Two Fires . . . she . . . she . . ."

"She what?" Kin-di-wa rasped.

"She take and put Walks-Tall in his cradle-board. She put him on her back. She say she go out in marsh and bury him in secret place. She . . . she go out and never come back."

"What do you mean—she never came back?" Kin-di-wa's voice echoed with such harshness that Crow Woman put up her birdlike hand to ward off a possible blow.

"Peshewa search for her. Other braves help—those who not struck down with coughing sickness. But big snow come. Snow and wind. Her tracks be buried . . . and when they finally find her, it too late."

"Too late! Too late!"

Even in the midst of her own shock and sorrow, Rebecca was acutely aware of Kin-di-wa's agony. "Oh, no . . ." she moaned. "Oh, dear God, no . . ."

"And Little Turtle? Is Little Turtle still alive?" Kin-di-wa looked as if he meant to kill someone.

"He strong war chief, not little baby like Walks-Tall." Crow Woman made an effort to recover her dignity. "Little Turtle, great war chief of the Miamis, still lives."

Kin-di-wa turned abruptly and swept out of the lodge. Rebecca ran after him. "Kin-di-wa! Kin-di-wa, wait!"

But Kin-di-wa strode away as though he didn't hear her. Back along the fresh trail in the snow he went, shoulders rigid, back straight as a spear. Rebecca fell into step behind him, half-blinded by the tears streaming down her cheeks.

Kin-di-wa headed straight for their lodge, but he paused when he came to the entrance. Rebecca hurried up to him and touched his arm. Slowly, he turned to her. "Leave me, Cat-Eyes . . . go back to Crow Woman and Tecumwah. I would be alone."

"N—no, Kin-di-wa . . . Walks-Tall and Two Fires . . . they were my family too. Your pain is no greater than mine. We must share it together."

For a moment, she thought he was going to insist that she obey, but suddenly he groaned—a low tortured sound that seemed to come from his very soul. She took his hand and led him inside the darkened lodge. Then they collapsed into each other's arms and wept.

When the first storm of grief had passed and darkness had descended, Rebecca and Kin-di-wa sat before the lodge fire, staring into the flames. The lodge itself now seemed strangely large, empty, and silent, and Rebecca wondered how they would ever withstand this latest tragedy.

She wished someone would come and inquire about their journey, but no one came—out of respect for their sorrow, she guessed. The entire camp would probably wait until one or the other of them took the initiative to return to the land of the living, whenever that would be.

Rebecca sighed deeply. She felt as though she too had died and entered another world, a world of cold unhappiness and thundering guilt. She could not forget how often she had wished to have Kin-di-wa to herself. She could not forget her pettiness. When Kin-di-wa had been recuperating from his wounds and fever, not once had she allowed Two Fires to tend to him. She had even been envious that Two Fires had a son while she did not. And she had been overly critical of the kind of mother Two Fires had been.

She mourned the loss of Walks-Tall, but in some strange mysterious way, she mourned Two Fires's death even more. Walks-Tall, she had loved and appreciated. But Two Fires, she had scorned.

Rebecca wondered what Kin-di-wa was thinking as he sat so stiff and unmoving. Her husband's face showed no emotion now. Indeed, he might have been a statue. He simply sat and stared, as if he were alone in the lodge.

She moved slightly to make a noise, hoping he would notice. When he did not, she leaned over and rested her hand on his thigh. His muscles tensed, and he glanced toward her, but his eyes held such a look of misery that tears sprang once more to her own eyes. Only this time, she was mourning for her husband—not for Walks-Tall and Two Fires.

"I have failed my brother, Kat-a-mon-gli," Kin-di-wa said. "I have failed Black Loon, the brother who depended on me."

"Failed him? How? It wasn't your fault that Walks-Tall and Two Fires died."

"I have not found his murderer. I have not kept safe his woman and child. I have allowed his land to be taken, his village and crops to be burned, and I have brought no honor to his name or to his people."

Rebecca felt a surge of sympathy mixed with irritation. "None of what happened is your fault, Kin-di-wa. You mustn't think that way."

Kin-di-wa continued as if she hadn't spoken. "But the worst thing of all, is that I was not a good husband to Two Fires . . ." He paused, then glanced at her accusingly. "I never spoke words of love to her. I never invited her to share my buffalo robe. I never gave her secret looks, smiles, touches, such as I give to you. If I had, she would be alive today."

132

"Alive! Oh, Kin-di-wa, no! You cannot mean that; her death was a tragic accident!"

Kin-di-wa's eyes burned like two hot coals. "Do not play the fool, Cat-Eyes. Do you truly not know what happened to Two Fires?"

"She went out into the marsh in a snowstorm and got lost."

"Not lost." Kin-di-wa's gaze went back to the fire. "A Miami squaw does not lose her way in a snowstorm. Every moment, she knew where she was. She did not come back because she did not wish to."

"Are you saying . . ."

"That she killed herself? Yes . . . I am saying it. She killed herself because she had nothing to come back to—no child, and no loving husband for whom she might have wished to go on living."

"I don't believe it!" Rebecca jumped to her feet. "You're just saying that because you feel guilty. Well, I feel guilty too! I could have been kinder to Two Fires, and I'm sorry I wasn't. But am I to feel ashamed because I love you—because we shared secret looks, touches, and smiles? Don't do this to me, Kin-di-wa! Don't make me feel any more guilty than I do already!"

"It was I who should have been kinder to her . . ." Kin-di-wa picked up a small twig that had been lying near the fire. He snapped it in two. "She died because of me."

Anger rose hotly in Rebecca's chest. She had never resented Two Fires more than she did this minute. In death, the girl was succeeding where she had never succeeded in life: she was coming between them.

"Kin-di-wa, if Two Fires's death was not an unfortunate accident, if indeed she chose to die, then that is what she did—she chose to die! She could have chosen differently. She could have tried to win your affection. But the truth is—she always put Walks-Tall first, and when he died, she just gave up!"

Kin-di-wa did not look at her, and Rebecca had the awful feeling that he was slipping farther and farther away. A barrier was rising between them, and she had no idea how to stop it.

Quickly, she went to his side and knelt down. She took his hand between her own hands, thinking how cold and unfriendly it felt. She raised his hand to her lips and began to kiss his whitened knuckles. Tears slid down her cheeks, spilling onto his skin. She opened his hand and turned it over, kissing his palm—trying to reach him with her own grief, her own sorrow.

He pulled his hand away. "Do you think it will help if you make love to me? Do you think it will lessen our guilt—or merely make us forget?"

His tone was so cruel and sarcastic that Rebecca was stunned. He had never spoken to her this way, never pulled away from her before. A bitter taste came into her mouth. They had endured war, sickness, defeat, and hunger. Could they not endure this too? If he shut her out now, it would be an end to their love. Guilt and self-blame would grow like some poisonous weed between them, strangling their commitment, destroying their trust.

No! she thought. I won't let it happen. Everything else has been taken from us. Our love is all we have left.

She stood up and walked calmly to the other side of the fire, where he could not fail to see her. Then, very slowly, she began to undress. Off came her fringed leggings, then her sleeves, and finally, she began to undo the laces at the neckline of her doeskin.

He sat and watched her, his eyes narrowed to two slits, his body unmoving. She moved closer to the fire, so he could see the rosy glow of her skin. Unashamedly, she drew off her doeskin and stood proudly before him, her nakedness a gift that she hoped he would not refuse.

His glance dropped to her breasts, and Rebecca straightened her back and drew her braids languidly over her shoulders. She untied the thongs that bound them and shook out her hair, allowing it to fall in luxurious waves that reflected the gold-red light of the fire.

Still, Kin-di-wa did not move. He said nothing, and Rebecca realized that the battle had just begun. Her hand went to her throat. What if her husband did not respond? What if she was no longer able to arouse him?

She fastened her eyes on his, willing him to come to her. From throat to breasts to belly, she allowed her hand to move provocatively, carelessly, as if she hardly knew what she was doing. But she knew. She traced the path she wanted his hand to follow.

Her breasts, as she stroked them, gave evidence of her mounting desire. Her nipples became taut. A warm flush crept up her body from her loins. Kin-di-wa's glance strayed lower than her breasts. A muscle leapt in his jaw.

"Kin-di-wa," she moaned softly. "Come to me . . . come. Let us forget about grief and sorrow. Let us celebrate life."

Lightning flashed in his brilliant blue eyes. "What you do is wrong, Cat-Eyes . . . this is not a night for loving."

"This night . . . loving is the only thing that is right, my husband." She went around the fire to him, knelt down, and pulled his head to her turgid breasts. "Kin-di-wa, you must not turn away from me. Nothing must tear us apart—do you understand? Nothing. We do not honor the dead by cutting ourselves off from the living, or by giving pain to those who love us."

Indecision wavered in Kin-di-wa's eyes, then his arms went around her and a low growl emerged from his throat. He buried his face in her breasts. "Cat-Eyes . . . Cat-Eyes!"

It was all he could say. Over and over, he called her name, while Rebecca held and soothed him. Then Kin-di-wa swept her into his arms and laid her down on his buffalo robe. His hands tore at his buckskins, and when they were stripped away, he flung himself on top of her, this time no gentle lover, but a man being pursued by demons.

Hungrily, he devoured her flesh. His hands

searched and found. His kisses seared her soul. He opened her legs wide and thrust between them with the strength of a rutting stag. She arched her hips and rocked back and forth, drawing him into her, accepting his pain, his weakness, and his grief.

He is only a man, after all, she thought, made of flesh and blood, not bronze.

But as he rent her body with his spearlike thrusts, a tide of passion rose within her. She forgot where she was and why she was doing this. She forgot about Walks-Tall and Two Fires. She forgot everything but Kin-di-wa's violent ravaging of her senses. She sunk her nails into his back and urged him onward in mindless desire.

Wave after wave of rapture shook her body from head to foot. Kin-di-wa shuddered against her. She felt herself spiraling upwards—to a place where a cool sweet wind, fresh with the scent of green earth and springtime, washed over them. Dreamlike, they floated in a soft white mist, at peace with themselves and all around them.

"Kin-di-wa, look!" She urged him in her dream. On a far distant hill, glowing gold and green in the sunshine, a little boy and his mother were running and laughing . . . tumbling in the long wavy grasses. The little boy was plump and jolly, his black eyes bright with happiness. The woman was strange and beautiful, her long black hair streaming out behind her. She turned and waved, then swept the little boy into her arms and raced over the hill and out of sight with him.

The dream faded almost as quickly as it had begun, and Rebecca became aware of Kin-di-wa's body, sprawled out exhaustedly on top of her. She stroked and patted his hair. "Sleep now, my husband," she whispered. "Sleep and be healed."

But Kin-di-wa did not stir. She realized that he hadn't heard her; he was already fast asleep.

Six

Spring came to the Ohio Country in a slow progression of warming temperatures and awakening life. The Hunger Moon gave way to the Bird Returning Moon, and the sap flowed in the trees again, providing the sticky sweet syrup that gave flavor and goodness to so many Indian dishes. This year, it was welcomed with even more than usual thankfulness.

Flocks of honking waterfowl filled the skies, and buds pushed up from tree branches in total disregard of the freezing winds that still came roaring out of the northeast across the great lake. The Green Grass Moon tiptoed into the Ohio wilderness almost apologetically, Rebecca thought, but she could not disregard the stirring within her own mind and body as patches of muddy brown sprouted luxurious green mantles almost overnight.

"If it were not for spring," she said to Sweet Breeze one fresh April morning, "how would we poor humans ever survive?"

Sweet Breeze hugged her gathering basket to her slim bosom and breathed deeply of the rain-washed sunlit air. "We not survive," she said simply.

Rebecca pondered the deaths of all those who hadn't lived to see the springtime: Walks-Tall, Two Fires, two other small children, and three elderly inhabitants of the camp, all of whom, excepting Two Fires, had succumbed to the cough with the strange-sounding whoop at the end of it. Her own determination to go on living grew stronger.

"I can hardly wait to make a tonic from new roots and greens. Kin-di-wa and I both need something after this long hard winter." Rebecca hitched up her own gathering basket, wondering what to look for first—fresh beech leaves, wild endive, Frostwort, or Golden Thread.

"There be something to gather everyday now," Sweet Breeze said as she led the way into the forest. "We need roots and herbs for medicine, not only for food . . . Too bad Manitou no make root to take away sadness, make old men feel young again, and young men remember women who love them."

Rebecca glanced sideways at her friend. A suggestion of deep sadness marred Sweet Breeze's childlike beauty. Her large expressive eyes were luminous with unshed tears, and Rebecca knew she was thinking of the two people she loved most in the world—her father and her husband.

Little Turtle had survived the coughing sickness, but he rarely ventured out of his lodge, preferring instead to spend many long hours staring into the fire and brooding over the fate of his people. Rebecca didn't know what to say to ease Sweet Breeze's worry, but she did think it was time to once again remind her how helpful Apekonit had been.

"Apekonit would never have bought food for us if he didn't love you, Sweet Breeze. When Chenoten allows him to do so, he will come, for I know he hasn't forgotten you."

Sweet Breeze sighed. "It not only for myself I wish Apekonit to come—it also for my father. He need advice. Saginwash sending messages now to Miami, Delaware, Wyandot, Shawnee, and Pottawattomies."

"What kind of messages?" Rebecca's suspicions were immediately aroused. She recalled the stranger who'd come to camp several days ago, met with Little Turtle, and departed the same day in an almost secretive manner.

"Messages that say Saginwash no want treaty between Long Knives and Miamis. No want treaty between Long Knives and any tribe. Saginwash say 'don't go to Treaty Council in summer or fur trade be destroyed.'"

"What do they expect the tribes to do?" Rebecca exploded. "Go to war again? The fur trade is already destroyed. Besides, the Saginwash had their chance to help defeat the Long Knives, and all they did was stand by and watch the slaughter!"

Sweet Breeze bent down to pluck some green shoots and put them in her basket. "My father not want to be caught between two rutting bulls, fighting over territory. He sick of fighting—but he need to know if Long Knives will keep treaties made at Council."

Rebecca thought of the long string of broken promises from other treaty councils. "No one can guess what the Long Knives will do in the future, Sweet Breeze. Certainly not Apekonit and probably not even Chenoten."

"But Apekonit could tell my father what be in Chenoten's heart—how he think and what he feel."

Rebecca snatched up some green shoots herself, irritated by Sweet Breeze's naivete. "We already know what's in Anthony Wayne's heart," she snapped. "If it had been up to him alone, the entire tribe would have been wiped out from disease and hunger this past winter, and he would not have lifted a finger."

A long silence fell between them, broken only by inconsequential remarks about the herbs they were gathering. The sun moved across the sky, dappling the shadowed forest with splotches of light, and only when the scent of rain grew strong upon the freshening breeze, did they start back to camp.

By then, the sky was filling rapidly with churning slate-colored clouds, causing the tender green of new buds and leaves to stand out sharply against it. Rebecca balanced her heavily laden basket on one hip, hoping she would have time before the pending deluge to stop by Peshewa's lodge and give some greens to Crow Woman. The old woman had refused to come back to the lodge once shared by Walks-Tall and Two Fires. Too much sadness had occurred there, she said.

But now the sadness is over, Rebecca thought, and a sense of serene contentment, tinged with hope, stole over her. She regretted her bitter outburst to Sweet Breeze. It was spring, and only yesterday Kin-di-wa had reported seeing a fawn, whose mother he had carefully avoided disturbing. Even the deer were returning to their abandoned haunts, their instincts telling them they would no longer be stalked indiscriminately by an avalanche of hungry men.

They came into the clearing surrounding the camp, and Rebecca nearly skipped with pleasure, as she thought of Kin-di-wa's reaction when he saw her overflowing basket. She only wished Sweet Breeze could know the happiness of being near the one she loved.

Then Sweet Breeze's excited voice broke into her thoughts. "Look there, Cat-Eyes—someone comes!"

Rebecca looked up and saw a man on horseback galloping down the riverbank from the direction of Fort Miamis. A shaft of sunlight pierced through the clouds, and she set down her basket to shield her eyes so she could see him better.

He was a tall man, wearing fringed buckskins and hunting jacket—the sort of clothing worn by

Chenoten's soldiers when they weren't wearing their fancy blue uniforms, and as he reached a patch of sunlight in the budding trees, his hair shone red as fire.

Rebecca turned to her friend, but Sweet Breeze's basket of greens had already gone tumbling to the ground. Her mouth was open in astonishment, and before Rebecca could ask who the man was, her friend's face lit up like a star and she began running toward the approaching figure. "Apekonit! Apekonit!" she cried.

The rider saw her, dug his heels into his horse's flanks and turned him in Sweet Breeze's direction. Rebecca feared the horse would run down the girl, but at the last possible moment, the man reined in sharply, slid off the animal, and swept Sweet Breeze into his arms.

Sweet Breeze flung her arms around her husband's neck. "You come home, Apekonit! You come home to me!"

Apekonit held her to him, kissing and hugging her, then reluctantly disengaged his arms. Rebecca heard him say in a gentle voice, "Yes, I've come home . . . but not for long. All too soon, I must go back."

Sweet Breeze refused to let go of his shoulders. She stood on tiptoe, the top of her head barely reaching to his chin as she protested, "Oh, Apekonit, can I not say hello before I say goodbye?"

Apekonit looked sheepish. "I would have come sooner, Sweet Breeze, but General Wayne would not allow it. He only sent me now to bring an invitation to the Treaty Council. The Council will begin in mid-June."

He smiled down at his tiny wife. "At least it's all over, Sweet Breeze. Now, there'll be no more battles between our peoples, and once a peace agreement is signed, nothing will keep us apart. I swear it."

"But you no can stay—just for a little while?" Sweet Breeze's voice was trembling. "My father and I, we wait so long to lay eyes on you."

"For a little while," Apekonit promised, and Rebecca watched awkwardly as the two embraced again. She didn't know whether to stay or go, and while she was debating this, Sweet Breeze suddenly broke free of the embrace and turned to her. "Cat-Eyes—I almost forget! Come meet Apekonit!"

Rebecca hesitated. Surely, an introduction could wait; these two lovers needed to be alone. But Sweet Breeze took her husband's arm and drew him closer. Was it just her imagination, she wondered, or did Apekonit register a look of surprise, almost a certain hostility, when he looked at her?

"Cat-Eyes, this my husband, Apekonit—Captain William Wells, your people call him." Sweet Breeze's joy bubbled in every word. "Apekonit, this my friend, Cat-Eyes."

"Yes, I know of Cat-Eyes." The man with the double name and heritage studied her with a narrowing of his bright blue eyes and a tightening of his firm strong mouth. "You are Kindi-wa's woman, the one who came with him to

Fort Greenville."

"Yes, I am." Rebecca returned his probing gaze, noting that he was broad-shouldered, narrow-hipped, and quite handsome—though not nearly as striking as Kin-di-wa. "And I have heard much about you, both from Sweet Breeze and Kin-di-wa."

He nodded curtly, his arm tightening around Sweet Breeze's waist. "Your white name . . . is it Rebecca Simpkin, by chance?"

Rebecca was jolted by the familiar but erroneous last name. "Why—no. It's Rebecca McDuggan. Why did you call me Rebecca Simpkin?"

"Because if you are not Rebecca Simpkin, you look exactly the description of her: red hair, green eyes, a lovely skin color—and a shape few men would be quick to forget."

"Apekonit . . ." Sweet Breeze scolded. "You no should be noticing other women's shapes." She nestled into the curve of his arm, so dazzled by his unexpected presence she seemed blinded to the instant tension between him and her closest friend.

Rebecca felt herself coloring. "There is no Rebecca Simpkin, or if there is, it's some sort of strange coincidence."

"Coincidence?" Apekonit raised a doubtful eyebrow.

"Lots of people have red hair," Rebecca said pointedly. "You do yourself. Lots of people have green eyes. Why are you looking for this Rebecca Simpkin, if there is such a person?"

146

She dared not mention the reason she suspected.

Apekonit glanced down at Sweet Breeze, whose smile quickly faded when she saw the serious set of his mouth. Then he fixed his gaze on Rebecca. "Because a big bearded fellow named Will Simpkin is down at Fort Greenville looking for her. Says she's his wife—who was stolen away by Indians."

"That's a lie! I'm not his wife."

Sweet Breeze looked startled, but Apekonit's glance was keen and knowing, making Rebecca feel defensive. "But you have met the man."

"Yes, I've met him, and I'd rather be dead than married to him. I refused him more than once, and I can't think why he would bother to look for me, knowing how I feel about him."

"I think he does know how you feel," Apekonit grunted. "But he says your experience among the savages has addled your brain."

"Addled my brain!"

Apekonit nodded. "He says the savages stole you naked out of a rain barrel. Then they killed your father in a swamp when he tried to come after you. Is that true?"

Unhappy memories threatened to shatter Rebecca's self-possession, but she kept a tight control on her emotions. Will Simpkin couldn't hurt her now; Kin-di-wa wouldn't let him. "Well—yes. Some of it is true, as far as it goes. Will and Papa had gone to a salt lick and were attacked by Shawnee. Will ran off to save his own skin and left Papa to die of musket wounds. It was

147

Kin-di-wa who stole me out of the rain barrel and saved me from the Shawnee. But we became separated, and by some miracle I found Papa before he died and heard how Will abandoned him."

Rebecca paused breathlessly, seeing no need to tell Apekonit or Sweet Breeze how she and Kin-di-wa had become separated: Will had discovered Kin-di-wa making love to her in the Shawnee graveyard where they had taken refuge. He had practically killed Kin-di-wa, and then he had raped her.

"Apekonit . . . what this mean?" Sweet Breeze demanded. "Why you ask so many questions? Can this man hurt Cat-Eyes?"

Apekonit evaded the question with a dismissing gesture. "Do you also know a man named Jake Potts?" he pursued.

Rebecca's stomach lurched a second time. "He . . . I . . . yes, I did meet him. While Kin-di-wa was at Fort Greenville, the man stopped by our camp."

Apekonit frowned. "Well, now we know how Simpkin learned that you are among the Miamis. He and Potts ran into one another at the fort during the spring fur trade. They did some heavy drinking together—and a more troublesome pair of men, I'd be hard put to imagine."

Sweet Breeze tugged insistently at her husband's sleeve. "How so—troublesome, my husband? Cat-Eyes wife of Kin-di-wa now. If this man come to make trouble, Kin-di-wa show him what trouble mean."

"That's what I'm afraid of, Sweet Breeze." Apekonit's frown deepened. "Only the trouble could fall on Kin-di-wa and the Miamis, not the other way around."

Rebecca looked up at the low-lying rain clouds sweeping prophetically across the sky. She began to tremble. "You're right, Apekonit. Kin-di-wa must never meet with Will Simpkin. Not just because of me, but because Will is the man who killed his brother, Black Loon. Kin-di-wa came to my father's cabin seeking his brother's murderer. But Will's cabin was the next one downriver, and instead of finding Will, Kin-di-wa found me." She bit her lip. "He has never forgiven himself for failing to avenge his brother's murder."

"Damnation!" Apekonit swore. He glanced down at his worried wife. "You ask how this man, Will Simpkin, is troublesome. Now you know. The necklace he wears should have warned me. It's made of seven dried and shriveled fingers he had to have taken from a dead Shawnee. No live Shawnee would have traded away such trophies; Simpkin must be an Indian-killer from way back."

Rebecca shuddered, remembering the gruesome object. Will Simpkin never took it off—not even to rape her. "Do . . . do you think Will is headed here? Does he know where I am?"

"Jake Potts told him your name and your husband's. And he knows enough about Indian markings on clothing and weapons to identify you and Kin-di-wa as living among the Miami."

"Then I must find some way to get Kin-di-wa

away from here!" Panic swept over Rebecca as she realized anew the rippling effect her husband's killing of a white man might have: retaliation against all Indians, either through more bloodshed or through harsher treatment at the Treaty Council. "If we went away, wouldn't that help?"

Apekonit shook his head, looking more grim by the moment. "There is something else I have to tell you. The man called Will Simpkin won't risk coming here in search of you—because you are supposed to go there, to Fort Greenville, as soon as possible."

"Why?" Sweet Breeze stamped her foot angrily. "Why go to Fort Greenville? Who say she have to go?"

"General Wayne says so," Apekonit said quietly. "It's another reason why he sent me. He has issued orders: all white captives are to be returned to Fort Greenville so they may be escorted back to their families. And until this is done, there will be no Treaty Council."

Rebecca felt faint, but she managed to take a deep breath and straighten her shoulders stubbornly. "I have no family, Captain Wells. That order does not apply to me." *Forgive me*, she apologized silently to Aunt Margaret in far off Philadelphia.

William Wells gave her a sympathetic glance, but one that brooked no protests. "You have a white husband—or, at least, a man who claims to be your husband. And he has insisted that you be returned to him."

"He has no proof of our marriage!"

"Then you must go and explain that to General Wayne, though I can't promise you it will do much good. Will Simpkin has already told him that your cabin and all your belongings were burned when the Indians took you away. And he insists, backed up by Potts, that you are not in your right mind."

"Apekonit . . . can't you do something to help Cat-Eyes?" Sweet Breeze's expression was furious.

William Wells appeared as unhappy as his wife with his answer. "No, Sweet Breeze, I cannot. Cat-Eyes is not a Miami squaw—anymore than I'm a Miami brave. She's a white woman who was taken captive. And General Wayne's first step toward a peace settlement is that all captives must be returned, whether they want to be or not. The entire white nation demands it."

A shadow of pain and bitterness came into his eyes. "Too many white families have lost their loved ones to the Indians. Most of the captives, like me, have come to love their adopted families, but it makes no difference how we feel or what we think or what we tell our white relatives. They can't believe a white would want to stay among people they think of as savages. If we try to explain, they think we're crazy—that we've been fed some herbal potion. I can't lie to you: Cat-Eyes can argue all she pleases, but the way things stand now, it looks to me as if she'll probably be handed over to this fellow who claims that he's her husband."

Something snapped in Rebecca. "Will Simpkin

151

is not my husband! He's not, he's not, he's not!"

She turned and would have fled weeping into the forest, but Apekonit restrained her. His face was sad and gentle, as if he knew first hand what she was feeling. "I'm sorry to have to be the one to tell you these things, Cat-Eyes . . . but since there's no way out of this unpleasantness for either of us, let me give you some advice. You mustn't think of yourself this moment; you have to think of Kin-di-wa. His life is in grave danger. If he refuses to allow your return—or worse yet— seeks revenge on Will Simpkin, he'll die. General Wayne will not permit anyone to threaten the peace he has established. He'll permit no one to disobey him."

Rebecca broke away and ran, the freshness of springtime forgotten. Rain-drops drove into her eyes as the clouds chose that moment to open and release their pent-up fury. She ran blindly toward the trees and heard someone running after her. Apekonit's voice protested: "Let her go, Sweet Breeze, let her go. I think she needs to be alone now."

Hours later, in darkness, a thoroughly drenched Rebecca returned to her lodge. She was met by an enraged Kin-di-wa. "Where have you been? What is the matter with you—running off in a rain storm? I wanted to hold a feast for my blood brother, Apekonit, but now it is too late. Peshewa's mother has prepared one, and I had to make an excuse for why we could not attend . . ."

He paused, eyeing her shaking body with severe displeasure that soon melted into concern. "Take off those wet things. Or you'll be down with fever before morning . . . here, let me help you."

Rebecca stood numbly, allowing her husband to undo her laces and remove her dress. She was chilled to the bone and momentarily confused. Could it be that Apekonit and Sweet Breeze had told Kin-di-wa nothing?

Kin-di-wa wrapped a buffalo robe around her. "I made a stew. Come and eat. Then you must tell me where you have been."

"I . . . I went back to the woods to get my skinning knife." The lie came easily to her lips. "I used it to dig out a root and forgot to put it back on my waist thong."

"You were gone all this time retrieving a skinning knife?" Kin-di-wa looked incredulous.

Rebecca knelt down in front of the lodge fire. "I didn't know it was going to rain so hard—or that you wanted me to prepare a feast."

Kin-di-wa snorted and began ladling out a bowl of stew meat. "Can you not read storm clouds yet? The rain was so fierce it wiped out your trail."

"My skinning knife was farther away from camp than I thought. I'm sorry, Kin-di-wa." Rebecca fingered a piece of the steaming meat. "You—spoke to Apekonit? I met him when Sweet Breeze and I returned from our foraging, before I went back for my knife."

Kin-di-wa grinned, his ire apparently forgotten in his enthusiasm to impart good news. "He brought corn seed for us to plant. Not a great deal, but enough to get started again. And he brought an invitation to the Treaty Council. It is to be held during the Flower Blooming Moon but will probably last through the New Corn Moon, if it is like other Treaty Councils I have attended."

So he doesn't yet know, Rebecca thought. She was grateful to Apekonit and Sweet Breeze for not telling him. The more time she had to plan how to handle this problem, the better. "What do you know about Treaty Councils?"

"Talk, talk, and more talk . . . that is what treaty councils are all about," Kin-di-wa said. "The white man talks to cover up his greed, and the Indian talks to cover up his sorrow over losing his land."

"But—what happens to any white prisoners the Indians might have taken?"

"They are returned, of course." Kin-di-wa helped himself to a bowl of stew. "Fortunately, in this camp we have no prisoners, only a worthless white squaw who is making an old man of me before my time. Every time she is out of my sight, something bad happens to her."

Rebecca held her tears at bay and tried to smile at his teasing. Obviously, her husband was not as well informed about Treaty Councils as he thought. At least, he was poorly informed about this one. She wondered what he would do when he found out she was considered a prisoner, and that she had no choice whatsoever in the matter of being returned to white society.

"Is my stew not to your taste? Peshewa and I

spent half the day spearing that fish in the river."

Rebecca prodded her meat. "Is that what this is—fish? I thought there was something different about it. I wondered what strange meat you'd found now."

Kin-di-wa took the bowl from her hands. "A squaw who does not know fish stew when she sees and smells it must be thinking very serious thoughts. What is the matter, Cat-Eyes?"

"Kin-di-wa . . . is it really necessary for us to go to the Treaty Council?"

Kin-di-wa's blue eyes widened. "Of course! The entire tribe will be going. If we refuse to attend, it is the same as insulting Chenoten. He will believe we do not wish to make peace."

"Little Turtle can go . . . and Peshewa and all the rest. I was thinking maybe we could stay here—or go somewhere else instead."

Kin-di-wa put down their bowls, then moved closer to her. He slid his arms around her waist. "What is bothering you, Cat-Eyes? Can anything be more important than this Treaty Council? I cannot allow decisions which will determine our future and that of our children to be made by others."

Rebecca sighed. "I was hoping we might go away from here—far away. We could pack our belongings and go farther west, to the prairies or mountains you once told me about. We could go where no white men have ever been before."

Kin-di-wa's arms tightened. "You mean to the place of the golden eagles and the great herds of buffalo, the place the western tribes tell us is like

155

the Happy Hunting Grounds."

"Yes," Rebecca whispered. "Wouldn't you like to see it—to live there? To be free of white interference in our lives?"

"My little Cat-Eyes . . . I should like nothing better." Kin-di-wa lifted her face up to his, his blue eyes darkening. "But I have ties that bind me here. The Miamis are my people and I cannot leave them to an uncertain future . . . nor can I forget that my brother's murderer still lives."

"I thought you had forgotten your brother's murderer. I thought you had agreed to go to the Treaty Council to make a new beginning."

Kin-di-wa nuzzled her cheek. "You heard what you wanted to hear, little one, not what I said. I never promised to let the killer go free. I will not seek him out on a mission of vengeance, but if he ever crosses my path accidentally, he shall not live to see the next sunrise."

A shudder ran through Rebecca, causing Kin-di-wa to hold her more closely and look at her with concern. "You are still cold." He tested her brow. "And I think you are coming down with fever."

Rebecca brushed his hand away. "Please, Kin-di-wa—couldn't we just go away from here? I—I have bad feelings about this Treaty Council."

"There is nothing for you to fear." Kin-di-wa wrapped the buffalo robe more tightly around her. "You are my woman and I will protect you . . . and after the Council is over, we can go away if you wish. If Chenoten takes the whole of our land, the entire tribe may have to move

156

westward anyway."

Rebecca wondered if she might truly be coming down with fever. Her head was pounding, her throat felt tight, and the curved saplings that supported the lodge had begun to quiver and shake. "Kin-di-wa, I . . . I think I'm going to be sick."

She drew up her knees and put her head between them, while Kin-di-wa scrambled for an empty gourd. "Here . . ." He held the gourd under her chin, and her humiliation was so overwhelming she was able to conquer her churning stomach—for the moment.

"I don't know what's the matter with me . . ." she murmured.

"I know," Kin-di-wa muttered. "You have taken a chill." He got up to get more blankets and prepare a comfortable pallet.

"It was only a little rain . . . river water is colder, and I splash in that every day."

"You don't splash in it at night and for hours at a time." His preparations finished, Kin-di-wa came back to her and picked her up, cradling her in his arms as if she were a child.

"I can walk by myself," she protested, but the lodge was now spinning wickedly and her own speech sounded blurred and indistinct.

Kin-di-wa carried her to the pallet, laid her down, and piled skins and blankets over her. Then, as if that were not enough to warm her, he lay down at her side and flung an arm across her. "No more talk. You sleep now, and in the morning, I will go and find willow bark. Willow bark tea will cure your fever . . . but now, you need to rest."

Rebecca could not have agreed more. The problem of Kin-di-wa meeting Will Simpkin faded from her tired mind. It no longer seemed to matter that she must return to her own people. Her body had been taken over by some nasty alien presence, and as long as she was in its grip, she didn't have to think, to worry. Kin-di-wa would take care of everything.

Fever and chills kept Rebecca confined to the lodge for several days. Crow Woman, Sweet Breeze, and Tecumwah came by to look in on her and offer their services, but Kin-di-wa refused to allow anyone but himself to care for her. He bathed her in cool water when she was burning up, and warmed her with tea, blankets, and his own body when she shivered uncontrollably. He tended to every need—even the most embarrassing ones.

Rebecca was reminded of the time she had spent nursing him and found it almost pleasant to lie there basking in such loving attention. She knew what Kin-di-wa was feeling as he bent solicitously over her; she had felt the same concern for him—but she was in no hurry to get well again, to face problems it seemed easier to ignore.

On the fourth day of her illness, Sweet Breeze came into the lodge and shooed Kin-di-wa away from her side. "Go! Go find meat to make Cat-

Eyes strong again. I stay here and take care of her."

Kin-di-wa cast a longing glance at the sunshine outside the lodge. "Do you think it is safe to leave her?"

"It's safe," Sweet Breeze asserted. "Cat-Eyes need good red meat, not fussing husband."

Rebecca struggled to sit up. She resented anyone talking about her as if she weren't present. "It will be all right, my husband. Today, I am feeling much better."

"You are certain?" Kin-di-wa asked.

"I'm certain."

Kin-di-wa snatched his bow and a quiver full of arrows and quickly departed the lodge, looking, Rebecca thought, like a man being released from prison.

Wearily, she lay back down again. Sweet Breeze came to kneel beside her. "I sorry to send him away, Cat-Eyes. If you no wish him to go, I call him back—but I be hoping we might talk."

"Talk then," Rebecca sighed. She really was feeling better but didn't want to admit it to Sweet Breeze. The subject of her friend's conversation was one she still wanted to avoid.

"Apekonit leave to go back to Fort Greenville today," Sweet Breeze began. "But before he go, he want to know what you going to do about Kin-di-wa and the man called Will Simpkin."

"I don't know," Rebecca admitted. "I have thought about it until I am sick of thinking . . . and still I have no answer."

Sweet Breeze nodded sagely. "I suspect you

159

take fever because of worry. You strong woman . . . no take coughing sickness or other disease. No complain when starving. Now, one little rain storm, and—poof! You laid low like old tired squaw."

"Worrying can't bring on a fever," Rebecca snorted, but she wondered. Just talking about the problem made her head ache again. "What does Apekonit think I should do?"

"Apekonit think you should go away from here. You must convince Kin-di-wa to take you away—without telling him why. Because if he know why you want to go, he find reason to stay. He stay and kill murderer of his brother."

"Oh, Sweet Breeze, I've already tried! I thought we might go west. Kin-di-wa has always wanted to see the prairies and mountains." Rebecca tossed her head from side to side in weary remembrance of the conversation. "But he refused. He said he would never leave his people while things are so unsettled. After the Treaty Council, he'd be willing to go—not before."

"You should have gone three days ago, soon as Apekonit come. Then he could say to Chenoten, red-haired woman and Indian husband already gone. No could deliver orders for her return. She not living among Miamis now."

Rebecca choked back a sob. "Even if Will Simpkin were not involved, I doubt I could persuade Kin-di-wa to leave. He would want to go to Chenoten and argue; he wouldn't want to run away. He's never run from anything in his entire life."

Sweet Breeze smoothed back Rebecca's dis-arrayed hair. "Lie still and rest now, Cat-Eyes, or you become sick again just as you be getting better."

"But Sweet Breeze, what am I going to do?" Imploringly, Rebecca grabbed her friend's hand. "No matter which way I turn, I see nothing but obstacles."

"You think of something, Cat-Eyes . . . May-hap, you return to your people for a little while, then you come back to Miamis."

Rebecca was swept with horror. "Return to my people! I—I could never leave Kin-di-wa!"

Sweet Breeze looked down at Rebecca with enormous sorrowing eyes that reflected a great strength of character and determination. "You could not leave him—even to save his life?"

The full impact of her friend's suggestion was almost more than Rebecca could absorb at one time. She struggled to put the idea into words. "You mean if I . . . if I . . . return to my people willingly, I might save Kin-di-wa's life?"

She tried, for a moment, to think of what that would mean in terms of Will Simpkin, but her thoughts flew into a turmoil. If she fled Kin-di-wa and returned to Will, the problem would be solved—providing Kin-di-wa didn't come after her. But how could she stop him? He would have to believe she wanted to go back to her people, because if he ever saw Will or knew of his existence . . .

Sweet Breeze squeezed her hand encourag-ingly. "You think of something," she repeated. "It not for me to say what you must do, Cat-Eyes—but sometimes love must be tested by separation. It must walk through fire and never cry out. It must conquer every mountain in its path . . . and only then may you be worthy of it."

"Sweet Breeze . . ." Rebecca studied her small slim friend. "Love has been like that for you, hasn't it? It's been a test of courage."

Sweet Breeze nodded and smiled a beautiful shining smile that lit her face from within. "Yes, Cat-Eyes . . . but it be worth it. Apekonit go away from me again, but this time, I know he coming back. I see him at Treaty Council, and after that, we go home to Kekionga and build our lives again. Have many fat babies and be happy."

Kekionga. It was the main village of the Miamis which, before Anthony Wayne destroyed it, had lain in the juncture of three glistening rivers whose banks were planted on both sides with corn and vegetables for as far as the eye could see. How Rebecca wished she and Kin-di-wa could return to Kekionga too! Her courage wavered.

"Apekonit believe Miamis will not be robbed of all our lands . . ." Sweet Breeze continued happily. "Most, but not all. He think it possible for Miamis to learn enough white ways to live in peace. We learn to work land like whites, to read and write white language, to live in log houses . . ."

"Little Turtle will consent to this?" Rebecca had a moment's prophetic vision of a culture suddenly crushed and destroyed beneath the weight of a mightier but far less noble culture.

162

"Your father will not mind?"

"My father will do what must be done," Sweet Breeze said proudly. "And he will lead—not follow. He say maybe one day he even go visit white man's Great White Father, George Washington. He go visit big city of Philadelphia and learn all about white man's ways."

Rebecca closed her eyes, exhausted by surging emotions. Little Turtle was far braver than she was; she didn't want anything to change. She wanted to stay with Kin-di-wa and the Miamis and live contentedly together until the end of time. Why did life always force decisions and give rise to difficulties? Why, as soon as one found happiness, was that happiness so quickly threatened or snatched away?

"Sleep now, Cat-Eyes. I come back later and see if you need anything. Now, I must say goodbye to Apekonit."

"Go ahead, Sweet Breeze. Don't worry. I shall be all right . . . and tell your husband to 'go with Manitou.'"

The Green Grass Moon gave way to the Planting Moon, the beautiful month of May, and still, Rebecca came to no firm decision about what to do or what to tell Kin-di-wa. Every time, she thought about Will Simpkin, she felt physically ill. Her body manifested the symptoms from which her suffering mind could find no release. She became nauseated, could not eat, and experienced severe headaches and attacks of chills.

Kin-di-wa wondered if she was pregnant, and when she assured him she was not, he was disappointed. In marked contrast to her own desolation and fear of the future, Kin-di-wa embraced every positive attitude of hope and happiness the season offered. He hunted, fashioned arrows, dug a canoe out of an enormous log, and badgered her to plant the corn as soon as possible.

Rebecca suspected he had spoken to Apekonit about the possible outcome of the Treaty Council and now hoped that things might go better for the Indians than he'd expected. At least, he seemed determined not to brood about the Miami's past or future. The present is all that counts, he told her on more than one occasion; she must shake off her uncustomary weakness and appreciate the dewy mornings, the golden afternoons, and the sweet-scented evenings.

Most of all, she must appreciate the passion-filled nights, or the nights that could be filled with passion if she demonstrated more enthusiasm for them. She hated her own inability to respond more fully to his embraces, but something had frozen within her. The effort of keeping secrets from Kin-di-wa had destroyed her ability to be open and free and relaxed in their lovemaking.

On one occasion, she faked a response only to have him withdraw and look at her in puzzlement. "What is wrong, little Cat-Eyes?" he asked. "Do I no longer please you?"

Her heart twisted painfully. She wanted to

throw herself weeping into his arms and tell him how she couldn't bear for him to be knifed at the hands of Will Simpkin or shot before a firing squad of General Wayne's soldiers. But neither could she bear the thought of being parted from him. Instead of telling him anything, she put her face in her hands and complained about the terrible headaches that plagued her night after night.

"You must forget the past," he said gently, stroking her hair. "You must forget Two Fires and Walks-Tall, then these headaches will go away."

"I will try," she promised, but she hated herself for not telling him the truth about what was bothering her. And somehow things got no easier.

At times, she fled into the woods just to get away from his determined cheerfulness. Alone with the trees and the lush green vegetation, she was able to forget her nagging problems. Concentrating on the many species of herbs, wild flowers, trees and vines, she achieved a sense of peace and oneness with nature.

The creative hand of Manitou or the Great Spirit was manifested everywhere: from ferns, mushrooms, lichens, and grasses, to towering oak, hemlock, white pine, walnut, hickory, buckeye, and chestnut trees. The forest sprang forth with abundant varied life at every turning.

She took special pleasure in the delicate, multi-colored wild flowers. Violets, buttercups, and wood anemones carpeted the forest floor. The latter, the Indians called windflowers, because when the wind blew, they appeared to be floating. Kin-di-wa had opened her eyes to these tiny delights, and she could not walk among them without recalling the day he had told her their name.

"They are no more lovely than you are, Cat-Eyes . . ." he had said. And something soft and glowing had come into his eyes.

Now, one warm May afternoon, she walked among the windflowers and wondered how nature could be so oblivious to the agonies of humans. Sunlight filtered down through the green canopy of leaves, birds called in the trees, and squirrels leapt along the tree branches— mocking the sorrows with which she was burdened.

She sat beneath a flowering dogwood tree in full blossom. The dogwood was almost overshadowed by taller more majestic trees, but now, for this brief moment in spring, its beauty outshone all the others. Leaning back against the sun-warmed bark, she closed her eyes and was startled when, a few moments later, someone's hand caressed her cheek.

"Is this a windflower come to life?" Kin-di-wa asked softly.

"You startled me!" she murmured. "I didn't know you were following."

"Your mind was far away and very sad," Kin-di-wa said. Dressed only in beaded breechclout and moccasins, with two white feathers in his hair and a necklace of animal teeth circling his neck, her husband looked so handsome he took her breath away. His bronze chest muscles rippled fluidly, like a tawny cat's, as he sat down beside her, but his brow was furrowed with worry. "What can I do to make you happy, wife of my heart?"

The old endearment drew tears to her eyes. "You can kiss me, my husband," she invited.

He leaned over and pressed his lips warmly to hers, sending a thrill of desire rushing through her. In the patch of filtered sunlight beneath the dogwood blossoms, his eyes glowed a brilliant turquoise. "Your lips taste of honey . . ." he said huskily.

She took his face between her hands and kissed him again, seeking to tell him with the soft pressure of her mouth how much she loved him— how much she dreaded the thought of losing him.

He laid her back in the floating sea of windflowers and returned her kiss with a deep hunger that aroused her own long-suppressed passion. The sweetness of spring flowers, mixed with the pleasant sun-warmed scent of his body, filled her nostrils. "I love you, Kin-di-wa," she whispered. "You don't doubt that, do you?"

He traced the curve of her cheek with one finger. "Once, you said to me, 'we do not honor the dead by cutting ourselves off from the living, or by giving pain to those who love us.' Do you remember, Cat-Eyes?"

"Yes, I remember . . . it was on the night when we learned of Walks-Tall's and Two Fires's deaths." Rebecca wondered why he was bringing it up.

"I know you love me, Cat-Eyes, but why then have you taken a path on which I cannot follow? You are going one way and I am going another—yet you leave no trail for me to come after you, however much I try."

Rebecca hugged him to her breast, so he could not see her face. If I tell you what is in my heart, my husband, it will mean your death, she thought.

But Kin-di-wa drew back and leaned over her on one elbow. "Tell me what plagues you, Cat-Eyes. Your eyes are like green forest pools, hiding secrets."

Rebecca gazed into his probing blue ones, determined to try one more time to convince him to take her away. "Let's go to the western mountains, Kin-di-wa. Let's go today. There, I can be happy—we can both be happy! Everything will be right between us again. All sorrow will be left behind."

"This is what you truly wish?" he asked. "You want me to abandon my people?"

"I have abandoned my people for you . . ." Rebecca held her breath, watching the indecision, the battle of conflicting loyalties, raging in his eyes. It pained her to be the cause of so much struggle, but she would never ask him if it weren't necessary. Gently, she drew him down and moved her lips against his ear. "Please . . ." she whispered.

Kin-di-wa kissed her face, her lips, her eyes, her hair. "Demon-woman, she-cat . . . I can deny nothing you ask. I cannot live without your love, little Cat-Eyes, though I do not understand why you demand so much of me."

"You mean—we can go west? You're willing to go now?"

Kin-di-wa growled against her throat. "Yes, we will go now—this very day, if you insist."

"Oh, Kin-di-wa, you will not be sorry!" Joy raced through her. She wrapped her arms around her husband's neck and began to kiss him with such enthusiasm that he laughingly broke away from her.

"No, little one, I have waited too long for the spark of life in you to be rekindled. I will not waste it in hurried passion—the way animals mate during rutting season. I will take you slowly . . . so you know what you have been missing."

Then Kin-di-wa began to make love to her in a slow and gentle manner that soon set her senses reeling. First, he undid her braids and spread out her hair to make a cushioned resting place in the floating windflowers. Next, he helped her to disrobe. Then he took her in his arms and kissed and stroked her body from head to foot, paying special attention to the taut peaks of her breasts and the sensitive flesh of her inner thighs.

She tried to return his caresses, but he would not allow her to touch him. "This is the beginning of our new life together," he murmured. "If there is to be no one else but us in the world, if we are to go seeking our Happy Hunting Grounds on this

169

earth, then my woman must know to whom she belongs . . . she must surrender herself completely."

And Rebecca gave herself willingly to her husband, the master of her body and soul. She lay writhing in the windflowers as his mouth and hands carried her to eternal springtime. She fancied that she was the damp open earth, straining to receive his seed, and he was the Sun-God, drawing forth her sweetness. He planted his seed deep within her, in the rich fertile recesses of her most secret place, and she gave of body and spirit with sweet abandon—knowing that nothing on earth could equal the rapture she found in his arms.

Her hands clasped his naked hard buttocks and she rolled over, so that he was now lying in the fragrant windflowers. He had exploded once within her, but her desire would not be satisfied until he had done so again—this time, at her bidding. He had sought and possessed her, proven his domination. Now, she would demonstrate to him that she was mistress, with a passion equal to his.

With hands, mouth, and movements of her body, she awoke his sated manhood, until once again, his kisses grew hot and demanding. The wind stirred the branches of the dogwood tree, raining down white blossoms, and Rebecca threw back her head and cried out her ecstasy to the forest.

They lay together afterwards, entwined in each other's arms, as the breeze dried their sleek wet bodies. The scent of the fecund earth was everywhere about them, and as usual, Rebecca began to weep. Tears streamed down her cheeks. Whether she wept for happiness at Kin-di-wa's capitulation or because of the beauty of the act they had just completed, she couldn't say, but Kin-di-wa stroked her hair and chuckled.

"Never have I known a woman like you: you smile when you are miserable and weep when you are happy. What am I to do with you?"

She nestled closer to him. "Just love me, my husband—that is all I ask. This day has brought me great gladness and pleasure. I shall never forget it." She looked up into his bold blue eyes. "Whenever I see windflowers in the spring, I will think of you . . ."

"Windflowers have always reminded me of you," Kin-di-wa said. He plucked a handful of the tiny flowers and twined them in her hair, then kissed and caressed her a moment longer, until she drew away with a reluctant sigh.

"If we are going on a long journey, my husband, we have much to do. Little Turtle must be told."

A shadow of sadness invaded Kin-di-wa's expression, and Rebecca knew a moment of searing guilt. It would not be easy for him to walk away from all he cared about: his chief, his people, and his people's problems.

Quickly, she got to her feet and snatched up her doeskin. "Come, let's go tell him now . . ." Before you change your mind, she added silently.

They dressed and walked back through the

green cave of the forest. But before they reached the clearing near the camp, Rebecca paused and looked back the way they had come. She would always carry with her the vision of the forest as it appeared this very moment: lush, green, sun-dappled, and carpeted with windflowers.

She sniffed appreciatively of the mingled odors—wild flowers, leaf mold, distant pine, and the tang of the rich black earth.

"Are you coming?" Kin-di-wa asked.

"In a moment . . ." she turned to him smiling. "I want to remember everything, my husband. For this place we leave is my home too. But I know we will find someplace better."

Kin-di-wa took her hand. "Everything is better, now that my woman has learned to smile again."

Seven

Kin-di-wa would have strolled leisurely back to camp, had Rebecca not skipped on ahead, turning every few moments to call to him. "Come on, Kin-di-wa! We must pack. I don't want to wait another moment. Hurry, oh do hurry, won't you?"

She could not believe she had done it: convinced him to go away. He watched her, grinning and looking slightly stunned, as if unable to believe the change that had come over her. She was bubbling with happiness. Her feet seemed to dance away with her.

Oh, Kin-di-wa, she thought. If you only knew what this means to me! I will love you forever for this—even more than I love you already. This journey will be wonderful, our lives will be wonderful. I will make you so happy.

She ran back, grabbed his arm, and planted a

kiss on his cheek. They were coming into camp now, and he grunted a half-embarrassed warning. "Behave yourself. Miami squaws do not jump and laugh and shame their husbands by such wild displays of affection."

She fell dutifully into step behind him, but could not resist running a finger provocatively down his spine. His shoulders rippled, but he did not glance back at her, and she wondered if anyone else had ever seen the playful, teasing, gentle side of him. His pride, his arrogant pride would never allow such vulnerability to be revealed to others.

"Please walk faster, my husband," she giggled. "Or I shall leap upon your back and ride you into camp like a war pony."

She could tell from the set of his shoulders that he was probably scowling now, but he did walk faster in the direction of Little Turtle's lodge. Then, before they got to it, Rebecca saw Sweet Breeze crossing the clearing. The girl, with her gathering basket under her arm, was also headed for the lodge.

Impulsively, Rebecca darted around Kin-di-wa and raced in the direction of her friend. "Sweet Breeze, wait! I have wonderful news."

Sweet Breeze paused, eyes bright with questions, and Rebecca suddenly remembered her disheveled hair entwined with windflowers. Her face was probably flushed, too, and anyone looking at her would immediately guess what she and Kin-di-wa had been doing in the woods.

Well, what do I care if the whole world knows!

she thought ecstatically. I'm so happy I could burst!

"Oh, Sweet Breeze," she cried. "Kin-di-wa and I are going away. We're going to the western mountains—today. We're leaving this very day."

Sweet Breeze's face lit up. "Cat-Eyes, I so glad for you! Now, you no longer need worry about that awful man, Will Simpkin."

The mention of Will's name stopped Rebecca dead in her tracks. Sweet Breeze's brown eyes widened. She looked past Rebecca, and her hand flew up to her mouth. Embarrassment and dismay shone clearly on her face.

Rebecca wheeled around. Kin-di-wa was standing behind her. Rigid with shock, eyes blazing, he barked a single question. "What do you mean, she will no longer need to worry about Will Simpkin?"

"Nothing, Kin-di-wa, she means nothing!" Rebecca turned back to her friend for confirmation, but making matters worse, Sweet Breeze blushed a bright red crimson. Her eyes went to Rebecca, pleading for forgiveness.

"I so sorry, Cat-Eyes . . . I . . . I . . ." Sweet Breeze's shame got the better of her, and she turned and ran toward the lodge, leaving Rebecca alone to deal with Kin-di-wa's anger.

Rebecca's insides felt hollow. All life and feeling had suddenly drained out of her. She didn't know what to say. Kin-di-wa's eyes were a cold hard blue. "What did Sweet Breeze mean? What has my brother's murderer got to do with our going away?"

175

"N—nothing, Kin-di-wa." Rebecca tried to remain calm, to think of a reasonable explanation, but she could feel a guilty flush spreading up her cheeks. She became aware of the attention they were drawing.

Kin-di-wa became aware of it too. Several squaws who were sitting in front of a nearby lodge weaving mats from rushes, eyed them with interest. Among them was Tecumwah, Peshewa's mother, and Rebecca knew Kin-di-wa would not want so many witnesses to a public argument between them.

"Let us go home, my scheming wife," he said between clenched teeth. "Let us go home where you will immediately explain what this is all about."

Rebecca meekly followed Kin-di-wa back to their lodge, her mind fluttering anxiously like a trapped butterfly. Finally, she came to the only sensible conclusion: she must tell him everything and then beg him to go away as they had planned. If he really loved her, he would see reason. They could still depart this very day.

But Kin-di-wa was no sooner inside the lodge when he grasped her by the shoulders. "So my brother's killer is somewhere nearby. Why did you hide it from me? Why? And how did you find out?"

The look of bitterness and hurt in his eyes twisted her heart. "I don't want Will Simpkin to kill you, Kin-di-wa—and I don't want you to kill him. If you do, I'll lose you! Don't you understand?"

In a rush, she told him everything: how Will Simpkin was looking for her, claiming she was his wife, how General Wayne had ordered all whites to be returned to their families whether they wanted to be or not, how even Apekonit said she must go back. She left nothing out, not her fear for his safety, not her anxiety that she might be the cause of the Treaty Council's failure to establish peace, and not her guilt that she hadn't told him all of this sooner.

Then, she collapsed sobbing onto the mats. "I didn't mean to deceive you, Kin-di-wa. It's just that I was so afraid."

Kin-di-wa stood over her, fists clenched at his sides. Emotions of shock, anger, and amazement at his own stupidity raced across his face. When he spoke, his voice had a sharp cutting edge. "All this time, I thought you were grieving over Walks-Tall and Two Fires. All this time, you allowed me to believe that . . . You lived a falsehood every day. And today, amidst the windflowers, was the greatest falsehood of all."

Rebecca groveled at his feet, overwhelmed with shame. "I never lied to you, Kin-di-wa . . ."

"You never told me the truth!"

She glanced up at him in time to see his fist come up as if he meant to strike her, but it smashed down instead into his palm. Rebecca recoiled in pain. His fist might have been slamming into her heart. She lowered her head into her hands, wishing the earth would open and swallow her. "I'm sorry . . . so sorry. I only did it to save you from yourself."

Kin-di-wa dragged her up to face him, his expression contorted into an ugly mask of fury. "I am a man. I do not need saving from myself. I make a man's decisions . . . But you would turn me into an old woman!" His blue eyes narrowed. "Now, I see it. Now, I see how weak I have become. I have grown softer and more useless than Crow Woman."

"Loving a woman does not mean you are any less a man, Kin-di-wa!" She clung to him, trying to break through the stone wall of his bitterness and accusation. "Listen to me. We can still go away from here—go away and begin a new life. If we stay, I will have to go back to my people even if you kill Will Simpkin. Is that what you want? Do you want to lose me just for the sake of revenge?"

Kin-di-wa's fingers dug cruelly into the flesh of her arms. "Too often have I listened to you. Too often have I allowed my love for you to blind me. I should have killed that trapper who attacked you in the woods. I should have gone after my brother's murderer a long time ago. I am a Miami warrior. I must do what I must do!"

Rebecca could not believe he meant what he was saying. "Even—if it means the end of us?"

Kin-di-wa paused, but his eyes were implacable. "Can I do less than my brother would have done for me? Kat-a-mon-gli would never have allowed his love for a mere woman to weaken him, to keep him from his duty."

"A mere woman!" Rebecca stepped back, every muscle quivering. "Is that all I am to you? Is this how you really think and feel? Then you are a savage, Kin-di-wa. A stupid, bloodthirsty savage!"

Kin-di-wa stared at her a moment, the tension between them crackling like lightning. Then, he turned and strode out of the lodge.

"Kin-di-wa!" Rebecca cried. She ran to the lodge entrance. "Kin-di-wa! I didn't mean it!"

But Kin-di-wa never once looked back.

Rebecca had no more tears to shed by the time her husband did return. It was late the following afternoon. He'd been gone all night and most of the day, and Rebecca had wept herself dry and made what plans she could. Under the circumstances, plans were almost ridiculous, but nevertheless, she had made some, and as soon as Kin-di-wa came into the lodge, she told him.

"I have packed our things, Kin-di-wa." She gestured to two bundles. "I think we should leave immediately for Fort Greenville. You will be headed that way anyway, so I might as well go along. General Wayne will not be pleased if he has to send a detachment of soldiers to get me."

Kin-di-wa sat down cross-legged on the mats, his expression unreadable. "We will not leave to go to Fort Greenville until early in the Flower Blooming Moon. Then we shall go with Little Turtle and the rest of the tribe to the Treaty Council."

"So you will destroy the Council too," she said bitterly. "All in the name of vengeance."

"Woman, be still for once! I do not desire to

hear your opinion of my plans. I have discussed them with Little Turtle, and we have come to agreement on what should be done."

Relieved to hear he'd been talking to Little Turtle, Rebecca bit her tongue. If he chose not to tell her what he planned to do, she'd go crazy, but she sat very still, hoping he would relent.

Kin-di-wa did not look at her. He appeared to be studying the weave in the mats. "You and I will go to the Treaty Council where you will keep yourself well hidden among the women for as long as I tell you. My brother's murderer should be attending also, and I will find him and challenge him to fight. If I win, you will be returned to your people, but not to him. If he wins . . ."

Rebecca needed no explanation for what would happen if Will Simpkin won. Anger boiled up in her. "This is what you and Little Turtle decided? This is the best you could come up with?"

"If he wins, I will wait until he leaves with you and journeys far away from the Council—then I will go after him and take back what's mine."

Rebecca struggled to keep control of her temper. "Little Turtle agreed to that?"

"The last part he doesn't know about," Kin-di-wa grunted. "But I have sworn to Manitou that Will Simpkin shall never have you."

"And what if you win? You said I would go back to my own people anyway."

"Only for a time." Kin-di-wa turned dusky blue eyes on her. "Little Turtle says you must go back to insure the success of the Treaty Council, but after the Council is over, I shall come after you. Many times I have heard you speak of your aunt in Philadelphia. You could stay with her until I come."

Still trying unsuccessfully to quell her anger, Rebecca turned the plan over in her mind. It had so many possible flaws, things that could go wrong, but she could see that Kin-di-wa had given much thought to it. Too bad he hadn't allowed her to be a part of his planning. For that, she would never forgive him. "What makes you think General Wayne will permit you to challenge Will to a fight?"

Kin-di-wa's lip curled scornfully. "Is that not your people's way—to settle matters of honor with a sword or gun, at a certain time and place?"

"You mean dueling?" Rebecca of course knew of the practice, but didn't know Kin-di-wa or Little Turtle had heard of it. Duels were fought frequently in Philadelphia, but not here on the frontier. Disputes were more likely settled in the wilderness with fists and knives, not swords and pistols.

"Little Turtle says he will suggest the duel to General Wayne—as a way of settling our differences without threatening the Treaty Council."

"But what if he refuses?"

"Then, when my brother's murderer sleeps, I will slit his throat and steal away before anyone can catch me."

Suddenly, the sun-drenched lodge felt cold. Lanced with worry, Rebecca shivered. "Kin-di-wa, you haven't told Little Turtle that part of it either, have you?"

Kin-di-wa shook his head. "But the war chief of the Miamis will understand," he asserted. "He could do no less himself. I am trying to be reasonable, to understand the way the white man thinks, and to act according to his laws. But if the plan fails in any way, then there is only Miami law—and Will Simpkin shall not escape it, no matter what happens."

Rebecca sighed. She hated the plan and mistrusted her husband's logic. He was trying, she knew that, but he still refused to concede that there might be any other solution to the problem. She had been right all along: Kin-di-wa would never back down from a confrontation. He would not be satisfied until Will Simpkin was dead.

She watched him, sitting so rigidly, and felt a dull ache in her chest and throat. Tears threatened, but she would not permit them. Now, was the time to act, to make her own plans. She had no more time for tears.

The spring planting and preparations for the journey to the Treaty Council engaged everyone's attentions through the rest of May, but Rebecca still found time to meet Crow Woman alone one breezy afternoon around the first of June. She told the old woman she needed her advice on the gathering of medicinal herbs, then set off into the forest with her where no one else could hear their conversation.

Crow Woman tottered along self-importantly, obviously pleased to have been invited. Rebecca had always shown great interest in the old woman's knowledge, but after the deaths of Walks-Tall and Two Fires, she hadn't seen much of her friend, nor had she sought her out, and now, she felt guilty.

"How have you been, Crow Woman?"

The old woman flashed her toothless gums. "Better now since spring come. Joints not swell so much."

Rebecca noticed that Crow Woman's joints did indeed look troublesome. Her hands were gnarled and knotty, like the wood of old fruit trees. "Is there anything you can take to keep down the swelling?"

"Yes, yes . . . Bear's Foot, Boneset . . ." The old woman rattled off ten remedies before Rebecca could stop her. "Can always find something that works—except in winter."

"I guess there must be remedies for just about everything." Rebecca saw a way of approaching the topic she wanted to discuss and took it. "Come sit down on this log a moment so I can ask you some questions."

They sat down on a fallen log around which assorted ferns were waving like women's delicate fans. Rebecca smoothed the skirt of her doeskin. "Crow Woman, I have great need of your knowledge of plants and herbs."

"Is good you learn," Crow Woman grinned. "When I die, you teach others."

"Oh, you won't die for a long time yet . . . at

least, I hope you won't."

"What you want to know, Cat-Eyes? You want learn how to heal burns, cure bloody flux, stop pains of childbirth?" The old woman peered at her with beady black eyes.

"I—I want to know how to make a man lose his desire to—to make love to a woman." Rebecca flushed hot with embarrassment and plunged on with more bravado than she felt. "And I want to know how to make someone go to sleep when he may not wish to."

Crow Woman fingered a lacy fern, not quite able to conceal her shock. "You no want Kin-di-wa to mate with you any longer?"

"Oh, no, it's not Kin-di-wa I want to stop . . ." Rebecca paused in embarrassment. Every word she said just made it worse. "Crow Woman, I can't tell you why I need to know these things. You'll just have to trust me."

Crow Woman's grizzled white head bobbed up and down as she considered. "It not right to take away a man's mating power—to turn him into gelding . . . or to make him sleep unnaturally."

"I don't want to geld him, just remove his desire to mate for a time."

"Hunh! You not know much about men, Cat-Eyes. If man think he no have power, power goes away and may not come back again even when you no longer give him herb."

"But there is an herb that will do that—remove a man's power?" Rebecca persisted.

"Of course." Crow Woman hesitated a moment, then blurted, "Mad Dog Weed or Moccasin

Flower." She bent back the tip of a fern so it could not spring upright. "Either one make man-root go limp like this—like weak soft thing. And both together even better. Man no wish to make babies if you give him these in food or tea."

"Mad Dog Weed or Moccasin Flower. Where can I find these herbs and what do they look like?" Rebecca asked breathlessly.

Crow Woman sighed. "You certain you want to do this thing?"

Rebecca nodded.

"All right, then, I tell you . . ."

The old woman proceeded to describe the plants and the kind of habitats they favored, and Rebecca realized she knew them by their white name: Skull Cap, sometimes also called Hood-Wort, and Lady's Slipper. Both had been kept on hand by her own mother to soothe nervousness and excitability brought on by insect stings or fever. Mad Dog Weed was even thought to have some calming effect on persons who'd been bitten by rabid dogs or wild animals.

"They sound exactly like what I need," Rebecca said, "and I'm glad they aren't too hard to find."

"Not hard," Crow Woman agreed. "But take care, Cat-Eyes, not to be discovered. If a man learns he has been cheated of his mating, his rage be very great."

Rebecca suspected the old woman still thought she wanted to use the herbs on Kin-di-wa. Little did Crow Woman know; Kin-di-wa had not touched her since he learned about Will Simpkin. All his energies now went into an endless regime of physical exercise and practice with various weapons in preparation to face his enemy.

"Now, what do I use to put someone to sleep— a safe sleep that will cause no harm?"

Crow Woman sighed again. "There be many things you can use . . ."

Rebecca listened carefully, memorizing the names, descriptions, habitats, and suggested doses of several sleep-promoting agents. None of them worked instantaneously, and one had a particularly bitter taste, but at least, Rebecca now knew what to look for.

"*Winik,* Crow Woman." Rebecca thanked her friend as they started back to camp. "Please do not worry. I know what I'm doing."

"But your husband," Crow Woman cast her a doubtful look. "He know what you doing?"

"No," Rebecca admitted with some sorrow. "But believe me, it's for his own good—and for the good of all of us."

One week later, the Miamis left for Fort Greenville, and Rebecca found it a very different trip from the one she and Kin-di-wa had taken during the winter. This time, they went by canoe, and even though they had to portage around rapids and paddle against the current, the trip itself was easy and uneventful.

They stayed two days at Fort Defiance, now alive and bustling with soldiers, then proceeded up the Auglaize River in company with several dozen other canoes filled with Indians. The tribes were gathering from all over the Ohio and Indiana Country and even from beyond.

On the last night before reaching the outskirts of the Fort, they camped in a grove of tall beech trees, a welcome dry spot in land that was otherwise predominantly damp and swampy. Rebecca nervously perused the site for fresh herbs. She already had what she needed, carefully hidden away in a deerskin pouch, but Crow Woman had told her that freshest herbs worked best.

In addition to the plants recommended by Crow Woman, Rebecca also wanted something to calm a queasy stomach; she had been feeling slightly nauseated and unwell in recent weeks. She was certain that it was due to tension and nervousness. Even her last monthly flux had been affected by her state of mind. Her female bleeding had been thin and spotty, almost reluctant in nature, and she had suffered unusual headaches and cramps. Her next flux was due any time now, and further debility was the last thing she needed.

The sun was dipping behind the trees, casting long cool shadows, as Rebecca searched along the ground some distance from where a chattering group of squaws was preparing a communal meal. Suddenly, she was aware of being watched. She looked up to see the warm, friendly eyes of Little Turtle; he was sitting quietly on a stump nearby.

"So, little white woman . . ." The great chief spoke softly but his powerful voice still rumbled like distant thunder. "What do you seek?"

"Herbs . . ." Rebecca quavered. "Something to soothe my stomach."

"You have nervous stomach?" Little Turtle's eyebrows lifted. He ran a brown weather-beaten hand down one thigh, which was encased in an elaborately beaded, fringed legging. His leggings were ceremonial, Rebecca noticed, as was the breechclout he wore today, and the headdress, necklaces, silver earrings, feathers and armbands he would probably wear tomorrow on his arrival at Fort Greenville.

"Yes, I am a little nervous—thinking about tomorrow," Rebecca admitted. "You and my husband have made plans of which I do not approve."

Little Turtle gestured for her to come nearer. Rebecca did so, defiantly looking him in the eye. She noticed how thin and gaunt he was, though he seemed much recovered from the illness that had plagued him during the winter.

"You fear for your husband's safety . . . do you not?"

Rebecca nodded. "I am afraid Will Simpkin will kill him. Or General Wayne will kill him instead. Kin-di-wa has no intention of leaving the Fort without avenging the death of his brother."

"And establishing his ownership of you . . ." Little Turtle added. "But be not worried, little white woman. In the way approved of by your people—dueling—Kin-di-wa will kill the man who wears the Shawnee necklace. Then, as soon as Chenoten has done with flexing his muscles and making us bow down, Kin-di-wa can go

188

among your people and bring you back to us—
your chosen people."

"If he lives." Rebecca could not keep the
bitterness from her voice. She personally did not
believe General Wayne would even allow a duel to
be fought—between a half-breed Indian and a
white man.

"Put your trust in Manitou," Little Turtle
urged. "He will keep watch over Kin-di-wa." The
old man's eyes were warm and kindly, glowing
with quiet wisdom, but Rebecca felt too rebellious to take his words to heart.

"I do not believe Manitou thinks the way we
do. I doubt he would put revenge above reason."

"Not revenge—honor. Your husband must
uphold his honor. He cannot run away from a
man who took his brother's life and now
demands his woman. Does not your Good Book
say, 'An eye for an eye, a tooth for a tooth'?"

Rebecca was amazed at the extent of Little
Turtle's knowledge of her people. She wondered
if it had been Kin-di-wa, Apekonit, or some
passing missionary who had taught him one of the
Bible's more popular quotes. "It also says 'love
your enemy and do good unto him.'"

Little Turtle's eyes twinkled. "Someday, I must
learn to read such remarkable wisdom as one
finds in books. Especially in the Good Book.
Then, whenever I have need of advice, I can go
and find what I wish to hear."

Rebecca wondered if the great war chief was
mocking her. "I had rather look into my own
heart for advice—not into books. Not even the

Good Book," she said sharply.

The old man flashed a broad smile and nodded. "That be the way of all women, listening to their hearts . . . it be a woman's gift, her special blessing, but why then did Manitou make men so different do you suppose?"

Rebecca suddenly had no more patience for vague philosophies. She didn't understand what Little Turtle was getting at, and time was wasting away while they spoke. Still, he was the chief and worthy of respect, so she stood there silently, shifting from foot to foot, and hoping if she said nothing, the conversation would soon come to an end.

"Be not offended by a tired old chieftain, little white woman . . ." The smile faded from Little Turtle's face, revealing deep grooves of ancient sorrow. "Go about your herb gathering. I too have much to do and much to think about before the morrow."

Now that dismissal had come, Rebecca was ashamed of her disrespect and impatience. The image of the proud old chieftain sitting alone in the twilight suddenly tore at her heart. She wanted to fling her arms around him; she wanted to hug and kiss him, as a daughter might embrace her father. After all, she might never see him again. After tomorrow, she might no longer be welcome among the Miamis.

Yes, Little Turtle, she thought sadly, a woman must listen to her heart.

*　　*　　*

Rebecca slept little that night. She lay awake beside Kin-di-wa and stared up into the starlit sky, feeling totally alone and cut off from the man who lay beside her. Even his quiet breathing struck her as unfriendly. He had neither kissed nor embraced her since they had lain together in the windflowers. And he no longer looked at her directly.

Many times, she had felt his eyes upon her, watching, wordlessly watching, but when she glanced his way, he immediately looked somewhere else.

We have become like strangers, she thought, except strangers would never notice the little things I notice—how tense are the lines around his mouth, how furrowed is his brow, how lean, hard, and strong his body has become.

Her own muscles felt stiff and tense with worry, both for him and for herself. Where would she be tomorrow night? Would her plan work—or would it fail? She was tormented by the possibilities—the probabilities—of all that could go wrong. Over and over, she silently practiced the speech she intended to make to Anthony Wayne. If she could get in to see him.

General Wayne: My name is Rebecca Simpkin. I am the woman Will Simpkin has been looking for. You know the one of whom I speak—the tall man with the heavy curling beard and hair. The man who looks like a grizzly bear and wears the Shawnee necklace of severed human fingers . . . Well, what he says is true, General Wayne. He is my husband. Only I have an Indian husband too.

And my Indian husband swears he will kill my white husband. . . . Please, General Wayne, you must help me. I am willing to return to Will Simpkin, but you must lock Kin-di-wa in the guardhouse until we can safely get away. Until the Treaty Council is over. I will tell you where you can find him—he lies sleeping in our camp . . .

Rebecca tossed and turned on her buffalo robe. Then, she propped herself on one elbow and looked at her unmoving husband, marveling that he could sleep at a time like this. She longed to hold him in her arms for one last time, to mold her body to his. Oh, she would escape Will Simpkin and make her way back to him as soon as she could, as soon as it was safe! But what if her plan didn't work—and what if he didn't want her after she tricked him?

Kin-di-wa might feel betrayed. He might never understand. It made no difference. She would not go along with his foolish notions of honor. She loved him too much to stand by and do nothing while he risked his life for vengeance. If he killed Will Simpkin, he would die; of that, she had no doubt. And no matter what the cost, she must stop him if she could.

In the dark hour before dawn, as the first birds began to twitter, she fell into a half-sleep, but was still conscious enough to be aware of Kin-di-wa's arms stealing around her body. She nestled closer to him in drowsy appreciation of his warmth. "Cat-Eyes . . ." Kin-di-wa whispered, and she was instantly awake.

"Kin-di-wa?" she asked hesitantly.

Wordlessly, he turned her around to face him and then began to make love to her in an almost desperate fashion, as if he couldn't help himself. His mouth closed over hers, and his tongue probed deeply into her throat, communicating silently all he was unable or unwilling to say. She responded with equal fervor and desperation.

The language of desire seemed to be the only way they could share what was in their hearts, and as she traded steaming kisses and searching caresses, as her body became strongly aroused, she remembered random moments from their lovemaking in the past. Bittersweet. Their matings were always bittersweet—reflecting opposite emotions: joy and sorrow, happiness and anger, hope and fear.

Never had they mated in mindless response to nature's needs, the way animals always mated. Their whole relationship was fraught with pushing and pulling. Like air and water, they could never mix—yet never could they seem to resist the passion that flared between them.

She wrapped her arms and legs around him, knowing the rightness of what they were doing. A rising wave of excitement drove out every thought of past and future. Now, there was only the present: his hands and mouth upon her breasts, the feel of his lean-muscled body beneath her fingertips, the moistness between her thighs as her body prepared to engulf him in honeyed sweetness.

They joined together and began to move to some primitive ancient rhythm that stirred Rebecca to the depths of her soul. She was reminded of the pulse and sound of war drums: a slow steady beat that increased in volume and rapidity until the breath was wrenched from the lungs, the heart thudded in answering frenzy, and the body moved to its own deep dark demands.

Thus, did she move with Kin-di-wa, and release, when it finally came, was like an explosion of cannon-fire in her loins and in her brain. She was shattered and blown apart, intermingled with the man she loved—the man who would always be a part of her, no matter how far apart they were.

No words passed between them. Their bodies had said everything that needed saying.

And when the camp began to stir at dawn, Rebecca arose from their buffalo robe, gathered their things, and continued onward to Fort Greenville, to the destiny that awaited her.

Eight

Fort Greenville was located on high ground overlooking a stream running east, a valley to the north, and a large prairie on the southwest. The trees around it had been cleared away, and the fort itself was mighty and imposing. Certainly, it was much larger than any others Rebecca had seen in the wilderness. The main structure enclosed some fifty acres and had prominent bastions, projecting well beyond the walls of the stockade, at each of the four corners.

The inside of the fort, partially hidden from Rebecca's view as she stood with other tribal members at the south gate entrance, appeared to be a beehive of activity. Soldiers were drilling on the parade ground in front of rows of log cabins, a delegation of Indian chiefs was emerging from a large log structure that was possibly General Wayne's headquarters, and another detachment of soldiers was putting the finishing touches on a still larger structure that Rebecca assumed was the Council Lodge or meeting place.

Rebecca's attention was immediately drawn to the structure she believed to be General Wayne's headquarters, and then to an enticing display of open-air market stalls, where one could purchase or trade for furs, tobacco, foodstuffs, and clothing.

"Pull your blanket over your head," Kin-di-wa warned from behind her. "And stay back with the rest of the squaws."

Rebecca hastily adjusted the thin blanket she had brought for just that purpose but now found too hot to wear. It was, after all, warm and sunny—the twenty-third of June.

She faded back into the clutch of gawking squaws and children who were awaiting word from Little Turtle as to where to set up camp. Little Turtle, dressed in his finest ceremonial garb, had gone into General Wayne's headquarters more than an hour ago with several other chieftains of the Miami sub-tribes, the Weas and the Twightees, and hadn't yet emerged.

The patience of the Miamis exasperated her. Everyone stood so quietly, dressed in their finest most supple skins, with beaded designs and quillwork that no one was even noticing. Did anyone care or understand about their pride in their Miami heritage?

Having never completely mastered the painstaking art of quillwork, Rebecca wore only her everyday doeskin—and she was suddenly glad to be wearing nothing more decorative or confining. Her breasts were swollen and tender this morning, and her stomach more queasy than ever. She hadn't been able to eat and longed for a bowl of soothing herbal tea.

Finally, Little Turtle came out, holding a long white peace belt he did not have when he went in. Peshewa and Kin-di-wa hurried forward as he beckoned to them. They conversed in low tones as Rebecca anxiously watched. Then Peshewa strode back and motioned for everyone to follow. Rebecca glanced back at her husband. Wasn't he coming?

Several blue-coated soldiers, with polished boots, shiny brass buttons and gleaming white belts, came forward to conduct them to their campsite. Kin-di-wa and Little Turtle did not join them. Rebecca's stomach heaved alarmingly. Once they were encamped like the rest of the tribes, on the prairie or in the cleared space beyond the fort's big guns, would she be able to gain access to General Wayne's headquarters? And what if Kin-di-wa did not return to camp with her—but sought out Will Simpkin immediately?

She recalled how easily Kin-di-wa had swallowed a dose of one of Crow Woman's recommended sleep-inducing herbs, along with his breakfast. Another dose—the one she intended to give him at the campsite—should do it. Then, if he behaved in the normal manner of a Miami brave who became tired, he would merely lie down and sleep—unless he had important business to attend to first.

Rebecca sighed and turned around to follow the soldiers. If Kin-di-wa resisted his sluggishness, she hoped he would at least be too involved in Council preliminaries to think of pursuing personal matters.

First day requirements were rigid; each tribe was to be welcomed by General Wayne upon arriving, and then invited to establish a campsite. Afterward, they were expected to join in convivial feasting to recuperate from their journey. Then, a day or two later, they would begin the long process of speech-making—the serious business which would ultimately result in a treaty.

Surely, Little Turtle would not even mention the matter of a duel on their first day there! She had listened carefully to the news passed on by others, as they trekked into the vicinity of the fort, and had learned that the Council Fire had been lit on the sixteenth of June. As yet, no meetings of note had taken place. Instead, the tribes were still being welcomed—to the extent of each being allotted rations of meat, flour, and a modest supply of whiskey.

Meat, flour, and whiskey—what hypocrisy! Rebecca thought angrily. Why couldn't these items have been made available to the starving Indians last winter?

As she walked behind the escort of soldiers, Sweet Breeze suddenly tugged at the edge of her blanket. "Cat-Eyes, do you see him?"

Rebecca jumped. "Who?"

"Apekonit, of course . . ." Sweet Breeze craned her neck at a passing group of men. "Apekonit say he come to me as soon as we arrive."

"There are thousands of men in the area, Sweet Breeze. He probably doesn't know we're here yet." Rebecca cast a furtive glance at the masses of humanity encamped in and near the fort. Was Will Simpkin somewhere among them?

There were Indians in every manner of tribal dress, soldiers in both dress uniforms and casual hunting jackets, and traders and trappers in fringed buckskins and coon-skin caps. Naked children darted back and forth among the cook fires and lean-tos, and a group of young boys in war paint were racing each other to a distant oak tree. Horses, mules, oxen, and steers wandered freely, many of them hobbled, but still able to do damage if they lumbered into someone's shelter.

She was awed by the sheer numbers of people and animals. Despite the seriousness of the occasion, a festive air prevailed. Women were busily gossiping around their stew pots, from which savory odors exuded, and small circles of braves in ceremonial dress conferred beneath scattered shade-trees. The women, Rebecca knew, had come along to do the work while their men did most of the talking.

Outside the perimeter of the stockade, stood seven or eight additional log structures, but only braves wearing insignias of chieftaincy appeared to be leaving or entering the buildings. Rebecca wondered what was happening inside them as she, Sweet Breeze, and the rest of Little Turtle's delegation trudged across the large cleared area closest to the fort.

The soldiers led them down to a stream which forked out into two creeks. They crossed a wooden-planked bridge and found themselves in a pleasant breezy area where a small grove of trees had been left intact. Here, apparently, was their campsite. Sweet Breeze was pleased with the shady location, and immediately darted off to set up her father's lean-to, but Rebecca kept a worried look-out for Kin-di-wa, hoping he would come along shortly.

But it wasn't until she had unpacked their things and found several small stones to ring their cook fire, that Kin-di-wa came across the bridge with several soldiers bearing sacks of flour. Rebecca hurriedly poured a dark herbal tea from a water skin and offered it to her husband, trying as she did so, to keep her hands from shaking.

"You must be thirsty—mint tea flavored with honey is more refreshing than water."

Kin-di-wa took the gourd and drained it, giving her an inscrutable glance. "Put aside your nervousness, Cat-Eyes. It will be two or three days before everyone arrives, and most of the tribes will wait until then before they return their white prisoners. Little Turtle will also wait. He does not plan to bring up the matter of the duel until it is time to hand over the prisoners . . ."

Sensitive to the other source of her concern, he added, "I have heard that my brother's murderer is here, but I will not seek him out until the proper moment. And you must stay close to the other women and take care to keep yourself covered."

"Of course . . ." Rebecca said uncertainly. She didn't know how to act or what to say so as not to arouse his suspicion. "After—the duel, how long must I wait before you come after me?"

Kin-di-wa's glance softened. "Not long, little one. As soon as the Council is over, I will start east. The returned white prisoners will not be held here for the entire Council. Those whose families have already come for them will be released immediately, and those who have no families will be taken to Fort Washington first—then sent back east."

Her husband's hand came up to brush her cheek in a tender gesture, and she had to swallow against the sudden lump in her throat. Tears sprang to her eyes.

"Do not worry," Kin-di-wa said softly. "Will Simpkin is as good as dead. You will be back in my arms before the leaves change color in the fall."

Rebecca studied the smooth stubborn line of his jaw, emblazoning it on her mind. How confident he was! How sure of himself—as if nothing would dare to interrupt his plans. For a brief moment, she wanted to leave everything in his capable hands. Could her own plans have any more chance to succeed than his?

"How will you know where to find my Aunt's and Uncle's house in Philadelphia?"

Kin-di-wa almost laughed. "I will find it, Cat-Eyes. Nothing can keep me from you . . . but you may not even have time to go so far. It will take more than a moon for so many people to move safely through the woods or up the Ohio River, while I, going by myself, can move three times as fast. When you hear an owl hoot softly three times in succession, you will know that I am near and soon to steal you away."

"But—the owl is bad luck, is it not?" Rebecca remembered Kin-di-wa explaining this very thing to her a long time ago. They had heard the hunting owl one night before the battle of Fallen Timbers.

"Bad luck for everyone but you, Cat-Eyes. The Long Knives will lose face by losing one of their precious captives. Their anger will be great, so perhaps we will make it look as though you were carried off by a black bear. But really you will be carried off by one who loves you more than life itself."

As I love you! Rebecca thought. But the mere mention of a black bear reminded her of Will Simpkin. She tried to compare the two men: her husband and the man who claimed to be her husband. Wasn't Will taller, heavier, more barrel-chested, and certainly possessed of more ruthless strength and cunning? Oh, but Kin-di-wa was quicker, more skillful, noble, and far more courageous.

And perhaps that was the problem. Kin-di-wa would fight too bravely and courageously. Will would simply fight—as rudely and unfairly as necessary to win.

Suddenly, Kin-di-wa yawned, and this was enough to reawaken Rebecca's resolve. She had come too far to turn back now. "You look very tired, my husband. I have already prepared a resting place. Do you want to sleep awhile? Tonight, there will be visiting among the camps— stories, songs, maybe even dances. Why don't you rest now while I prepare a meal?"

"Have you more of that tea?" Kin-di-wa asked. "It quenches my thirst as nothing else can. What instruction has Crow Woman been giving you? I tasted some things in the tea I haven't tasted before."

"I cannot reveal an old woman's secrets, my husband." Rebecca struggled to remain out-wardly calm. "I will tell you only that Crow Woman has taught me how to use some herbs that are said to impart extra strength and vigor—if I have indeed used them properly . . . Go and lie down. I will bring you more of the tea."

Rebecca eyed her husband warily. So far he was reacting to the peculiar combination of herbs and sweetenings exactly as Crow Woman had said he would. There would be increased thirst so that he would want to drink more of the brew, he would feel refreshed when he drank it, and then he would find it increasingly difficult to keep his eyes open.

"I am not so old and tired I need to sleep in daylight," Kin-di-wa scoffed. "But I will sit down in the shade a moment while you pour out some more of Crow Woman's magic. If it is supposed to give me strength and vigor, I think I have great need of it."

Rebecca hastened to comply with Kin-di-wa's wishes, relieved that he suspected nothing. But by the time she brought him another gourd filled with tea, he was already fast asleep on a woven mat, with a rolled up buffalo robe under his head. She knelt down on the grass beside him. It was cool in the shade, and a sweet wind was blowing. The comforting sound of bees buzzing in nearby clover made what she was about to do, seem out of place and ridiculous.

She poured the tea out on the grass, then stroked his hair and spoke softly, so as not to awaken him. "Goodbye, my husband. Sleep now and take your rest . . . I shall find my way back to you as soon as possible."

Tears misted her vision. It was going to be so difficult to leave him! Until this moment, she hadn't realized how much a part of her he had become. Saying goodbye was like cutting off an arm or a leg—or cutting out her heart. "Please try to understand . . ." she begged. "Don't hate me for disobeying you . . ."

Gently, she bent down and kissed his cheek. His breathing was unusually deep and even—the slumber of a man drugged past his ability to fight it. If only the other herbs Crow Woman had recommended would work as well on Will Simpkin!

With one last look at her husband, Rebecca got to her feet and swiftly gathered together the few things she would need to take with her. Then, she crossed the makeshift bridge and headed toward the fort and Anthony Wayne.

"Sorry, l'il squaw-woman," the young soldier said, with a good-natured click of his polished boots. "The Gen'ral is just too plumbed busy to see you at the moment." He straightened the jacket of his blue uniform, made smart with its bright red facings, and grinned. "If'n you got a problem, why don't you jus' go get your chief an' maybe the Gen'ral will speak t' him. You savy? You understan' whut I'm sayin'?"

Rebecca removed the blanket from her face and hair. "I understand perfectly, Corporal, but will General Wayne understand why you are keeping a lady waiting out here in the hot sun?"

The corporal gawked when he saw her red hair and green eyes. The yellow plume of his black leather cap bobbed up and down. "Ma'am? Are you—are you a captive of the Injuns?"

"Of course," Rebecca snapped. "You don't think I'd be dressed like this if I were not." Go easy, she warned herself. The wife of a man like Will Simpkin might not be dressed much better.

"Well, now ma'am . . ." The corporal looked

unsure of himself. "I understan' that all captives are sposed t' be returned in some kind of ceremony a coupla days from now . . . but maybe I could speak t' my Lieutenant an' he could help you."

"Please do . . . my business with General Wayne won't wait a couple of days." Rebecca stood very straight, glaring at the corporal, and he departed rapidly into Anthony Wayne's headquarters, leaving her alone on the sun-drenched parade ground inside the fort.

From this vantage point she could see things she hadn't fully seen that morning: an impressive array of artillery to the east, the busy market stalls to the south, a large garden plot to the west, and the rest of the space filled in with soldiers' huts, officers' headquarters, bakeovens, powder magazines, a hospital, a guardhouse, an artificer's and sutler's shops—all enclosed by rows of sturdy log pickets.

Rebecca was impressed anew. If General Wayne meant to awe the Indians, he was certainly doing it. Even the uniforms of his men were bound to impress the pomp-loving tribesmen. A group of passing blue-coated soldiers eyed her curiously. They wore caps similar to the corporal's—made of leather with a roach of bear skin, cloth band, cockade, and feather. Only the color combinations varied. Some of the caps had roaches of black hair with white or red bands and plumes, while others had roaches of black hair with yellow or green bands and plumes.

She wondered if the varied colors differentiated the legions to which the soldiers belonged. Wayne was said to have four sublegions, each commanded by a different lieutenant, and she questioned whether she ought not to have approached a lieutenant first after all, rather than having gone right to the general himself.

The lieutenants were said to be occupying the four sturdy blockhouses. One of the two nearest blockhouses at the front corners of the fort was guarded by soldiers with white bands and plumes, and the other by soldiers with green bands and plumes. But before she could reason out the significance of this, a familiar voice distracted her.

"Well, now . . . so we meet agin', little squaw-woman."

Rebecca wheeled around to look into the pale hungry eyes of Jake Potts.

"Seems you an' me is fated t' keep bumpin' inta each other." Potts adjusted his coonskin cap, so the tail hung down behind, wiped one hand across his sweaty brow, and leaned against his long gun, the butt of which was sunk into the ground like a walking stick. His eyes roved over her possessively; he grinned as if he knew a secret.

"Go away!" Rebecca hissed. The shock of seeing him again was offset by nervousness; she didn't want the soldier to come back and find her talking to such scum. Her heart thudded loudly. If Potts was here, might not Will be with him?

Anxiously, she glanced around.

"Lookin' fer ole Will Simpkin?" The yellowed stumps of Potts's teeth caught the glint of the afternoon sun. "Well, don't you worry none. I'll find 'im fur ya. Him an' me come t' this little pow-wow jus' hopin' you'd turn up."

"I've come to see General Wayne," Rebecca said coldly. But her heart was now thudding so loudly she wondered if he could hear it. Will and Jake together. Somehow, she hadn't counted on facing the two of them. Of course, she should have guessed. Hadn't Apekonit told her of their friendship? Jake was the reason Will knew she was living among the Miamis.

"My, but you sure are purty," Jake said slyly, his hot-eyed gaze becoming ever more bold. "Looks t' me, like you even got a little more flesh on them sweet little bones o' yourn."

Rebecca was reminded of her swollen tender breasts, and a sudden speculation hit her: could she be pregnant? Never before had she experienced such disturbing body changes previous to the onset of her monthly flux. It had always proceeded routinely and been entirely predictable. But her last flux had been so scanty—not normal for her at all!

A flush crept up into her cheeks. Why should such a discovery come upon her now—at such an awkward moment? "Please leave me alone, Mr. Potts. I am waiting to see General Wayne, and if you continue to bother me, you may be sure I will complain to him!"

"My, but yur a hot-tempered little gal—an'

awful high an' mighty fur th' wife of a man no better'n me."

Rebecca was about to protest that a Jake Potts could not even begin to be compared to Kin-di-wa, when she remembered that now she was supposed to be married to Will Simpkin, a man indeed no better than Jake Potts.

The young corporal suddenly appeared at the door of General Wayne's headquarters. "Ma'am? The gen'ral says he'll see you but he wants t' know yur name first."

"My name? It's—it's . . ." Rebecca could hardly bear to say it in front of Jake Potts.

"Rebecca Simpkin . . ." Potts supplied gleefully. "She's married to a trapper by the name o' Will Simpkin—a friend o' mine."

Rebecca stared at him, a wave of nausea washing through her.

"That right, ma'am?" the corporal asked.

"Y—yes," Rebecca stammered, but it gave her such an awful feeling to admit to it, she nearly vomited on the spot.

"Miss or Missus?" The corporal waited patiently.

"Missus . . ." Rebecca whispered.

"Then follow me, Missus Simpkin, an' I'll take ya to the gen'ral."

A half hour later, Rebecca sat quietly on a puncheon chair, waiting for Will Simpkin to come and get her. She dug her nails into her palms, fighting back tears. Her speech to General Anthony Wayne, the Commander-in-Chief of the United States Army, had been the most difficult thing she had ever done. And all the while she had been speaking her carefully rehearsed lines, the famous man had sat quietly, calm and stately, taking in every word and nodding sympathetically.

She had wanted to hate him—had desired to claw at his immaculate blue and buff uniform with its showy gold epaulets, bright yellow braid, and shiny brass buttons. She had wanted to fling mud on the white ruffles at his neck and sleeves, and to trample his powdered white wig beneath her moccasins.

But the attentive blue-gray eyes that watched her did not match the picture of him she had drawn in her mind. This was no cold cruel monster who cared nothing for human misery. For all he was dressed so smartly, without a single wrinkle or hair out of place, Anthony Wayne looked tired—almost ill. He wore a weary unhappy expression, as if he wished he were anywhere but in the middle of a wilderness involved in a Treaty Council.

Yet his men spoke to him with respect, jumped to do his bidding, and did not look as though any one of them would dare to insult or malign him— even in private. She saw no trace whatsoever of his supposed "madness" and wondered how he had come to be called so. It could only have been done out of spite by someone who resented his firm discipline.

He had asked her if she had been well treated among the Indians, to which she responded yes. He had asked her if her Indian husband had treated her well also, and she could not bring herself to say no, as he obviously expected. Then, he had cocked his head and asked her the most difficult question of all, "Madam, you are returning to your white husband of your own free will then?"

She had nodded yes, unwilling to say more. He had already told her how pleased he was that she had come to him and given him the opportunity to avoid bloodshed. And she still felt that her instincts were correct: Anthony Wayne would never allow a duel, and he would insist she be returned to Will Simpkin.

Wayne had then sent a subaltern to find Will. At the same time, he had ordered a detachment of soldiers to escort Kin-di-wa to the guardhouse. Now, while she waited for whatever was to happen next, Rebecca could hear a loud voice outside on the parade ground. The voice sounded distressingly crude and familiar. "Where is she? Where's my woman? I demand she be brung out right now!"

A shudder ran down her spine. Could she really go through with this? She looked toward the inner room of the large log structure. It wasn't too late. Maybe she ought to run back to Anthony Wayne and tell him it was all a mistake, or more accurately, a lie. She fingered the beaded, fringed pouch—her collection of herbs. What if she had no chance to use them? What if she really was pregnant? What if Will Simpkin and Jake Potts together took her away and abused her unmercifully?

A soldier tapped on her shoulder. "Missus Simpkin, Gen'ral Wayne wants to see you one more time."

"Yes, oh yes!" Rebecca leapt to her feet and followed the man back into the inner room.

General Wayne stood up politely, waited for her to be seated, then sat back down behind the large crude desk, where several scrolls, an ink pot, a half-burned candle, and several other items took up most of the space. Through an open window, a sweet-scented breeze was blowing, ruffling the parchments in front of him.

"Mrs. Simpkin . . . my aid has located your husband, and Sergeant Billox is just now bringing up the Miami half-breed whose name, you say, is Kin-di-wa."

He nodded toward the window, which gave a partial view of the front entrance to the fort. Rebecca wsas riveted by the sight of Kin-di-wa, striding angrily past the main gate and flanked on both sides by soldiers.

She tore her attention away from the scene and looked at the doughty general who was studying her thoughtfully with his blue-gray eyes. "Mrs. Simpkin, I didn't realize when you first spoke of your Indian captor that I knew who he was . . . but I do know, don't I?"

Rebecca nodded. "We—he came here in the winter to beg food for the Miamis."

The immaculately uniformed general drummed his fingers restlessly on the tabletop. "I believe I knew him before then, did I not? Is he a friend of Captain William Wells?"

Captain Wells—Apekonit. "Yes, he is," Rebecca said. "He—they—Captain Wells and Kin-di-wa tried to arrange a peace agreement before the Battle of Fallen Timbers."

"Ah, yes, I recall now . . ." General Wayne shifted in his straight-backed chair. "But it failed, of course, and I assume this Kin-di-wa fought alongside the savages."

"He was badly wounded," Rebecca admitted, her emotions in a whirl. If only she had some sign, some suggestion of leniency from the general, she would refute everything she had told him and beg to be allowed to stay with Kin-di-wa!

General Wayne sighed. "Unfortunate. So many wounded, but it could not be helped. When one is faced with blatant defiance, one must slaughter the enemy—cut them down like flies."

He glanced up with a fierce expression that underscored his harsh words. "Well, Mrs. Simpkin, I won't keep you any longer from your husband. I simply wanted to tell you again how pleased I am that you came to me. If this fellow, Kin-di-wa, had laid a single hand on a white man, I would have had to deal harshly with him— friend of Captain Wells or no. I would have had to make an example of him, as I do of my own men

213

when my orders are disregarded."

"How—would you have made an example?"

"I would have shot or hung him, of course! It doesn't do to show weakness, Mrs. Simpkin, though I expect that sounds very harsh to a civilian—and a woman to boot."

In the little silence that followed, Rebecca clutched her doeskin pouch more tightly and threw back her shoulders. "No, it doesn't do to show weakness. I am ready to go now, General. It's been a long time since I've seen my husband."

"A pleasure to have met you, Mrs. Simpkin. Glad I could be of service."

General Wayne rose when she did, showing himself to be a gentleman in the manner her mother and her Aunt Margaret had often described to her. She forced a smile onto her stiffened lips.

"Thank you, General Wayne."

She came out onto the parade ground in the blazing sunlight, and the first person she saw was Will Simpkin, grinning hugely. His large body blocked her path, and she was assaulted by remembered impressions: bristling black hair brushing broad, well-muscled shoulders; a bushy black beard; curly black hair protruding from a fringed leather shirt that was open to the waist; and the sickening stench of an unwashed body which was damp with sweat even now.

Her glance fell to his necklace of dried,

shriveled fingers, strung on a rawhide thong and separated from one another by purplish-colored beads.

Quickly, she looked past him—only to be confronted by a pair of smoldering blue eyes. Kin-di-wa stood rigidly and silently off to one side between two rows of soldiers, three on his left, three on his right. She stiffened in surprise, having expected him to be in the guardhouse by now, not waiting in front of General Wayne's headquarters.

Will Simpkin stepped forward, little pig-eyes gleaming, and grasped her arm. "Good t' see ya agin', Becky, an' glad t' hear yur comin' along peaceable."

She flinched at his touch but could not take her eyes from Kin-di-wa. Why had they allowed him to witness her leave-taking? Why hadn't they jailed him immediately?

Kin-di-wa's eyes turned blue-black in color. The pain of betrayal churned in their depths, and she felt a jolt of pain herself. "Kin-di-wa . . ." she whispered.

"Come along, now, Becky . . . y' ain't gonna have no more t' do with that thievin' red-skin. I knew you'd choose me over him. T'ain't right, a white woman takin' up with a gol-durned animal." Will Simpkin tried to steer her past the soldiers, and someone took her arm on the other side—Jake Potts, still grinning his sly malicious grin.

Dear God! She had never dreamed it would be

as bad as this.

Her feet began to carry her forward, and Kin-di-wa's whole body tensed as she passed. Suddenly he sprang into the air, like a tawny maddened wild-cat. Rebecca felt herself jerked aside by Jake Potts and heard a heavy thud. Will Simpkin roared his outrage, then he and Kin-di-wa fell to the ground—hands going for one another's throats.

"Kin-di-wa! Kin-di-wa!" Rebecca screamed.

A flurry of blue-coated bodies descended on the grappling men. Will Simpkin shouted and humped his body in an effort to dislodge his attacker, but Kin-di-wa had him in a death grip. Rebecca could see his whitened knuckles as he strained to squeeze the life from Will. Then Will's hands got a tighter hold on Kin-di-wa's throat.

Rebecca screamed again and tried to squirm away from Jake Potts, but he held her tightly, his arms drawn across her breasts, his throaty laughter sounding loud in her ear.

For a moment, Rebecca couldn't see what was happening, then one of the soldiers raised his rifle butt and struck Kin-di-wa over the head with it.

"Stop it! You'll kill him!" she cried.

The rifle butt rose and fell again with an awful thunk! and Kin-di-wa collapsed on top of Will Simpkin.

"My God, oh my God!" Rebecca fought to run to her husband but could not escape Potts's iron-hard grip.

Immediately, an authoritative voice rang out. "Sergeant Billox! Take the prisoner immediately to the guardhouse, then present yourself in my headquarters!"

"Yes, sir!"

General Wayne's order brought instant response. Kin-di-wa was lifted bodily off Will Simpkin, and with a soldier on each side of him, grasping him under the arms, he was dragged off in the direction of a solid, windowless structure on the far side of the stockade. His head hung limply, and blood streamed down the back of his neck, staining his black hair and white feathers.

Desperate to help him, Rebecca pushed and shoved against Jake Potts. "Let me go to him!"

"Restrain that woman!" General Wayne thundered.

Two soldiers jumped instantly to help Jake Potts, and the general turned startled, angry eyes on her. "Your concern, Mrs. Simpkin, is admirable. But it's directed to the wrong man entirely!"

Rebecca was so stunned she could not reply. This wasn't what she had planned at all! Kin-di-wa was hurt: she must go to him at once! But as she looked around at the tense white faces, hardening against her, she realized she would not be allowed to assist her true husband. They believed she belonged to Will Simpkin; their sympathies were entirely with him.

Will got awkwardly to his feet and rubbed his throat. "Damn crazy bastard," he muttered.

"Mr. Simpkin . . . will you be so good as to take your wife and depart this fort immediately." It was an order, not a question, and the general's eyes flashed coldly. "I want no more incidents to threaten the good outcome of this Treaty Council. Now that you have what you came for, I expect you to be gone before nightfall. And I don't wish to see you again."

"My pleasure, Gen'ral . . ." Will picked up his coonskin cap and brushed it off. "I don't reckon I want t' stay aroun' here anyway—with so many thievin' rascals jus' lookin' t' take my scalp."

"Excellent," said Wayne. "We shall have no scalpings, you may count on it."

"General Wayne!" Rebecca finally found her voice. Her vision was blinded by tears, her chest was pounding, and she no longer cared what she said or did. "This is all a mistake—a terrible mistake!" She paused in uncertainty, put off by the tightening of the general's mouth and the growing coldness of his expression. "You will take care of him, won't you? You will see that he is all right?"

"Do you mean that Indian, madam?"

"Kin-di-wa . . . take care of Kin-di-wa." She had a glimmer of inspiration. "Let Captain Wells know that he is here!"

"Captain Wells will be told, madam." General Wayne bowed slightly in her direction, turned on his heel, and strode back into his headquarters.

"No more outa you, bitch . . ." Jake Potts's fingernails dug into her arm. "Y'all right, Will? . . . Th' bastard nearly killed you."

"Gotta mighty sore throat," Will grunted hoarsely. He jostled a soldier away from Rebecca's side. "Come on, let's git outa here."

218

By late afternoon, they were on a trail going south, and Rebecca was loaded down like a mule with the belongings of all three of them. Will walked in front of her, Jake Potts behind, and whenever she lagged a bit, Potts prodded her with the muzzle of his long gun.

"Git on up there, little squaw-woman . . ." he would order. Sometimes, he prodded her buttocks just for the fun of it, and Rebecca became infected with a growing horror. What had she done? What in God's name had she done?

The image of Kin-di-wa being dragged away haunted every step she took. He had lain so limp and helpless, the blood dripping down his neck and shoulders. What if they had killed him? How would she know?

Before they left, she had begged Will to find out if he was all right. She had pleaded with him to go and ask at the guardhouse. Will had angrily said no, but Jake Potts disappeared for a time, then caught up with them on the trail. He and Will conferred quietly for a few moments, but refused to tell her anything. What did it mean? Were they afraid that if they told her he was dead she would not go with them?

She wouldn't. There would be no purpose in it then. If Kin-di-wa was dead, she would kill herself, no matter if she was pregnant or not.

But as she trudged along, dispirited and afraid, she began to hope she might be carrying Kin-di-wa's child. She counted the days since her last monthly flux and discovered she was three days late already. Moreover, her last flux had been so abnormally scanty, she might already have been pregnant then—she must have been pregnant then! Before this morning, she and Kin-di-wa hadn't touched each other since the time they had lain together in the windflowers.

Could she truly be with child? Could new life be growing inside of her? She remembered how happy she had been that day when she learned they were going away together. She recalled every kiss, every touch, the way her body had responded so fully to his. Nothing would ever equal the rapture she had found in his arms—and now, he might be dead. And if he wasn't dead, he hated her. Oh, how he hated her!

She would never forget the look on his face, the pain in his eyes. He had felt betrayed. He had actually believed she preferred Will Simpkin, his brother's murderer, to him. She knew by his expression that he didn't realize what she was doing—that he saw only one thing: she was leaving with a man he hated, a man he had sworn to kill. She was leaving and she had tricked him, delivered him up to his enemies.

Would he ever accept her explanations when she returned? Would he believe her? Would he take her back? Perhaps, she should have confided in Sweet Breeze, Little Turtle, or Crow Woman. But no—this was something she had needed to do alone. And she must continue on alone.

Bitter resolve awoke in her breast. She would not allow Will Simpkin or Jake Potts to touch her. She would be crafty, cunning—slipping her secret herbs into everything they ate and drank.

Yes, she would protect Kin-di-wa's child at all costs. If he refused to take her back again, after what she had done, the child might be all she had left of him.

Dear God, she prayed. Please let me be pregnant. Don't disappoint me now. And help keep Jake Potts and Will Simpkin away from me!

Nine

An hour or more before sunset, they selected a campsite on the shores of a small stream.

"Git some firewood, and set up camp," Will nodded curtly in Rebecca's direction. "I heerd a turkey gobblin' back there aways, an' I'm gonna go after 'im . . . ya comin', Jake?"

Rubbing his knee, Jake sat down on a fallen log. "Can't walk another step. M' rheumatism is hurtin' somethin' awful. Must be a storm blowin' up."

Rebecca eyed him covertly, her suspicions immediately aroused. There were no signs of an impending storm; on the contrary—the light on the creekbank was pure liquid gold, and the sunset, could they have seen it through the trees, promised to be spectacular.

"Then set an' rest a spell—won't take me but twenny minutes t' git that big fat gobbler." Will tramped off in the direction from which they had come, and Rebecca busied herself with carrying out Will's orders. She did not look at Jake, but she could feel his eyes on her back. Her thoughts went to the skinning knife she had carefully strapped to her thigh.

"Come'ere, little squaw-woman," Jake Potts said.

Rebecca ignored him and bent to pick up a particularly heavy piece of firewood—as thick around as a man's wrist.

"Put that down an' come'ere!"

Rebecca straightened, holding the firewood tightly in one hand, where he would be sure to see it and understand the unspoken warning. "My husband has given me orders. I must obey them, Mr. Potts."

"Yur husband—hell! Will ain't yur husband, no more'n that god-damned Injun you left b'hind."

"That Indian?" Rebecca spoke before she thought. "Then he is alive. Kin-di-wa is alive."

Jake grinned slyly. "Wouldn't you like t' know, little squaw-woman? If he wuzn't, would you've come along so peaceable?"

"No," she admitted. "I would not have come at all if he were dead."

Jake laughed. "Jes' like I thought! I told Will that—told him there wuz somepin' funny 'bout you comin' along with no arguments! But he wouldn't b'lieve it! Th' gol-durned fool thinks you jus' up an' come t' yur senses—realized no respectable white woman would want to keep on beddin' down with a red-skin! . . . 'Course, you an' me know diff'rent on that score, don't we? Ya coulda' come away with me last winter!"

His eyes narrowed into two thin slits. "What I want t' know is—why did ya say yur Will's wife? Why did ya leave yur Injun? Was he plannin' on killin' Will, is that it? An' you didn't want no trouble? What did Will ever do t' him—b'sides claim you fer his wife?"

Rebecca maintained a haughty silence. As far as she knew, Will was unaware that one of the many Indians he'd killed had been Kin-di-wa's brother—and she would just as soon he never found out.

Jake Potts stood up and walked toward her. "Why, don't ya jus' put down that firewood an' be a little more friendly. I don't aim t' hurt ya none—I jus' want a little company."

Rebecca lifted her weapon and put as much menace into her voice as possible. "You'd better stay where you are, Mr. Potts. Will wouldn't appreciate you bothering me like this."

Jake grinned. "Ain't nothin' that says ya have t' tell 'im. B'sides, if ya think I aim t' stand by an' watch while he gits yur sweet little bones all t' hisself, ya kin think on that one again."

"If you take another step nearer, I'll . . ." She shook the piece of firewood threateningly.

"Ya'll whut?" He reached out and grabbed the stick before she could swing it. Holding onto it with both hands, she tried to take it back, and Potts gave a throaty chuckle. "I like a little mare with spirit . . . now, jus' gimme that stick b'fore

225

one o' us gits hurt."

Rebecca refused to surrender it, but just as Potts succeeded in yanking it away from her, they heard the sharp report of a musket, not too far distant.

Potts threw the stick on the ground. "Sounds like we're havin' turkey fer supper . . . too bad Will's got sech a good eye. At least, there's time fer a kiss or two."

Rebecca turned to run, but with lightning speed, Jake grabbed her. She caught a whiff of fetid breath as he tried to force his mouth on hers. She jerked her head backwards and then forwards—hitting him in the nose.

"Ouch!" He recoiled in pained surprise. His hand flew to his face. "Why, you little bitch! I'm through with bein' nice t' ya!"

"I'm through with being nice to you!" she spat. She curled her hands into claws—preparing to scratch out his eyes.

Potts seized her roughly, pinioning her arms to her sides. "Ya owe me, little bitch. Ya owe fer whut happened last winter—an' now, ya owe me fer nearly breakin' m' nose."

His mouth clamped down on hers, and though she struggled and squirmed and fought to be free, she could not escape his greedy lips. His tongue probed into her throat. He pressed her body against his, and just when she began to gag, sickened by his offensive onslaught, a triumphant cry echoed through the forest. "Git out th' stewpot, Becky! We're havin' us a feast!"

Potts immediately thrust her away and looked

in the direction of Will's voice. In that split second, Rebecca snatched up her piece of firewood, and by the time he turned back to her, she had moved out of his reach—but not out of striking range. He snorted disgustedly. "Later, bitch . . . we'll take up where we left off later—an' if you say anythin' t' Will about this, I'll tell 'im it wuz yur idea!"

Her idea! She'd rather be stricken with whooping cough than kiss a man like Jake Potts. But what if Will didn't believe her? As jealous and irrational as he had always been, he just might believe Jake's story and become impossible to handle.

Quickly, Rebecca picked up several more pieces of wood, which was plentiful along the creek, then rushed to begin building a fire. She mustn't give Will a reason to become mean and spiteful. One mean spiteful man was more than enough worry at the moment.

With another warning glance at her, Jake strolled nonchalantly back to his log, sat down, and pretended to be massaging his knee joints. A minute later, Will strode into view, holding his still smoking musket in one hand and a plump turkey in the other. "Whut'd I tell ya, huh? I knew this bastard wuz out there! Whaddya think, Becky? Ain't I as good a pervider as some no-good red-skin?"

Rebecca managed a polite response. "You were always a good hunter, Will . . . even Papa said so." This last she spoke quietly, but her stomach churned with nausea. How much more must she endure before this awful game was finished?

The mention of her father reminded her of how Will had run off and left Papa to die of gunshot wounds in a swamp. Yet she must behave civilly to him! The terrible scene came flooding back to her: Papa with one ear and half his face blasted away, mumbling deliriously. "Tell Becky . . . tell Becky not t' marry that damn scoundrel."

Papa had been trying to warn her how wrong he had been about Will—as if she needed a warning after all she herself had learned about him! Will had raped and degraded her. He'd killed innocent, trusting people. He'd lied about her being his wife, and now, he had the gall to compare himself favorably to Kin-di-wa!

Struggling to conceal her violent feelings, she hunted through Will's things until she found his iron caldron that had been dangling all afternoon from the pack on her back. Then she set about starting the fire with flint and tinder.

Will and Jake began cleaning and gutting the bird—a task she knew would normally have been left to her if the men hadn't been so anxious to eat. What else might they be anxiously awaiting?

The sun slipped lower in the west, and cool shadows gathered among the trees. Rebecca knelt down on the soft mossy ground beside the creek and submerged the caldron in the cold clear water. Angrily, she scanned the near vegetation— both out of habit and because she wanted to make certain of keeping a good supply of necessary herbs at hand.

She hadn't counted on having to slip herbs to

two men—but how else was she to protect herself? Likely, it would not even work. If they both suddenly lost their masculine powers, one or the other was bound to suspect something. Perhaps she'd been wrong not to blurt out the truth about Jake's interest in her. Maybe if she got Jake and Will jealous enough, they might kill each other and solve all her problems!

No, she must not count on the impossible. It would be better to somehow get rid of Jake so she could concentrate on deceiving Will—but how? And would there be enough time? If she didn't act quickly, it would be too late. Once the men had full bellies, their attention would be centered on her.

The weight of the container as she drew it out of the creek gave her an idea. She tipped out water until the caldron was half-full, then gingerly rose to her feet. Jake and Will were bent over the bird, paying no attention to her. Stealthily, she moved toward them.

"Whaddya think, Jake?" Will grunted. "Ya wanna head south t' Fort Washington an' then back east?"

"Hell, no! I don't think much o' towns an' villages . . . a man can't hardly breathe without someone lookin' down th' back o' his neck." Jake grabbed a fistful of turkey feathers and yanked them out with a vengeance.

"Yeah, I know how ya feel—but I wuz thinkin' o' Becky."

"Hah!" Jake snorted. "Now ya got yurself a woman, ya gonna go an' change yur whole life?"

Will scooped out a handful of bloody entrails from the cavity of the turkey. "Gonna make a honest woman outa' her. Gonna find me a preacher—in Gallipolis or Marietta."

Rebecca froze in the act of creeping around behind the men. She held the metal handle of the heavy caldron in both hands so it wouldn't creak. Had Will actually said he wanted to marry her?

"Yeah," Will continued. "Gonna git hitched. I don't want nobody questionin' my claim on her now that I finally got 'er—an' I don't want her t' go an' change her mind about me."

He *was* thinking of marriage! The very idea made her shiver. She was married to Kin-di-wa; there was no way she would ever marry Will.

"She changes her mind, jus' slap her around a few times," Jake said. "That's th' way I'd handle it."

Will chuckled into his beard. "If it comes t' that, I will. Had t' slap her around once b'fore an' show 'er who wuz boss. But I showed her—yes sirree—an' I'm lookin' forward t' tamin' th' little spit-fire all over again. . . . Becky!"

Will looked toward the neatly laid out fire, obviously expecting her to be there. "Where are ya? When ya gonna git that fire started? Gonna be too dark t' see iff'n ya don't git crackin'.'"

But Rebecca was now behind Jake Potts in the exact position she wanted. Holding the caldron in front of her by its handle, she began to spin quickly around, swinging the pot in a circle. The slight noise made both Jake and Will turn to look—and in that instant, she stepped closer. Clunk! Jake was struck full on the side of the head by the heavy pot.

"Becky!" Will leapt to his feet. "What in thunderation are ya doin'!"

Though he'd been knocked off balance, somehow Jake's body maintained its poise for a moment. He sat perfectly still on the log, a dazed look on his face, then slowly crumpled and fell.

"Ya killed 'im!" Will shouted. "Ya crazy woman, ya killed 'im!"

Rebecca was smitten with sudden weakness. She tried to put down the caldron, but her fingers seemed fastened to the handle. She could not unbend them. Will stooped over Jake's body and tried to pull him upright, but Jake was as limp as a rag doll. A bloody lump on the side of his head was already beginning to swell.

"Whut in hell come over ya, woman! Ya like t' killed my friend!" Will straightened up and glared.

A sour taste came into Rebecca's mouth. He was so big, so powerful—like an enraged bear. His eyes glinted red with fury, and she knew she had to reach him, to get through to his shocked brain, before he did something terrible to her.

"How dare you think of sharing me with him, Will Simpkin? Is this how you treat a woman who comes to you of your own free will?" The caldron clattered to the ground as Rebecca's fingers finally loosened, and she warmed to her indignant accusation. "I came to you—not to him. And I

231

won't stand by and allow myself to be attacked while you look the other way."

"Whut're you talkin' about?" Will growled, but his pig-eyes narrowed thoughtfully. "Did he—did he try somepin' while I wuz gone?"

"What do you think that scum would do? You obviously meant for him to try something, or why else would you have left me alone with him?"

Will nudged Jake's body with his foot. "Why, that no-good stinkin' polecat . . . an' I thought he wuz mah friend." Then he turned suspicious eyes on her. "But whut did you do t' git 'im excited? Wuz you twitchin' yur tail th' way wimmin do?"

"No. Of course not." Rebecca's cheeks burned. "I'm not that kind of woman."

"Hunh!" Will suddenly reached out and took her chin in his hand. He drew her closer. "All wimmin is that kind o' woman . . . torturin' a man with their looks an' their wanton ways. Lookit you—jus' looky. I ain't never seed a woman more wanton than you are . . . them big green eyes, that soft white skin . . . hair the color of fire . . . an' teats that'ud drive any man wild. Ol' Jake probably jus' couldn't help hisself."

"Do you intend to share me with Jake?" Rebecca stared into his eyes. "Because if you do, I won't stay here another minute. I'll go back to General Wayne and tell him. He won't permit such wickedness."

Will slid his arm around her waist, and she felt as if a bear had hold of her. The odor of sweat, leather, and musk—the scent of his sudden arousal—enveloped her like a fog. "Hell no, I ain't aimin' t' share ya with ole Jake. I'm jus' glad ya finally seed th' light. Yur my woman, Becky, an' I been lookin' fer ya ever since ya clouted me with that skull an' run away from me in that Shawnee graveyard."

The memory was hardly a warm one for Rebecca. She pulled away from him. "If you promise me you won't let Jake lay a hand on me, I'll try to be nicer to you, Will. Better still, why don't we leave him here and go on without him? If you're really going to marry me, I . . . I'd like to have some time alone with you."

Even in the semi-darkness, the gleam in Will's eyes was unmistakable. "Ya mean that, Becky? Y'ain't gonna go an' change yur mind? Ya finally learned yur lesson?"

Rebecca hated herself for lying to him. Even after all he'd done, he was still a human being—reaching out for warmth and contact. "I—I guess I have. I guess I'm ready to be with my own people. Kin-di-wa was—just a savage, you see."

"Kin-di-wa," Will snarled. "Whut didya ever see in 'im, Becky? Why, he wuzn't nothin' more'n a animal . . ."

"Wasn't?"

Will peered down at her, his eyes narrowing. "Wuzn't," he repeated firmly. "He's gone from yur life now, Becky! He's gone furever."

"D—do you mean he's dead?" Rebecca stopped breathing.

There was a silence before Will answered. She couldn't see his face for the darkness now, but when he spoke, his voice had a savage triumphant

233

quality. "Yeah, he's dead. Kin-di-wa's dead. That blow with a musket musta split his skull."

The world began to spin around Rebecca. It spun wildly out of control. Then it grew dark, darker than midnight, darker than the inside of the darkest cave. She dimly realized that something had happened. Will had told her something awful, but she couldn't remember what. She only remembered that somehow she couldn't breathe. All the air had suddenly been sucked from her lungs. She'd been struck a heavy blow and had fallen, and now she was in a deep well, a dark black hole, and she was alone, more alone than she had ever been in her entire life.

Someone began whispering, calling her name. "Becky . . . Becky, wake up!" the voice demanded.

But she didn't want to wake up. She didn't want to know what awful thing had happened. Here, in the blackness, nothing could hurt her. Nothing could cause her pain. "Consarn it!" The voice began swearing.

It wasn't Kin-di-wa's voice, the voice of her husband, her beloved. So she tried to ignore it. That alien voice had hurt her—said terrible things. Oh, where was Kin-di-wa? She wanted him so! Kin-di-wa would make everything better. Kin-di-wa would take her away to a place where flowers grew—floating pink-tinged flowers. It would be warm and sunny, a day made for love and laughter.

She allowed the blackness to carry her. She

floated on the surface of a smooth black river. It was so pleasant and peaceful. She could lie there and dream about Kin-di-wa. His eyes were so blue and changeable, expressing everything he thought and felt. His face was so noble and handsome, the lines and scars only making it more so. And his body—so straight and strong and well-muscled. How she loved his body! It was so lean and hard—so unlike her own. But how well they fit together!

She could see Kin-di-wa clearly, smiling and beckoning to her. The feathers he wore in his shiny black hair flashed whitely in the sunlight. His skin shone a pure shining bronze. He wanted her to come to him, to lie down with him in the windflowers.

Yes! Yes, she would go to him. But now, the darkness held her back. Kin-di-wa! She must go to Kin-di-wa. She tried to lift her feet, to move her muscles, but something—the darkness, the fog, something terrible—weighted her down and kept her from moving.

Kin-di-wa's image began to fade, to be swallowed up in blackness. She struggled and fought to get to him. He held out his hand to her, wordlessly beseeching. She reached out to him. Their fingertips touched; then he was suddenly blown away, having no more substance than a dried-up leaf.

The crackling of a fire awoke her. She opened her eyes cautiously, without moving, and attempted to discover her whereabouts. Her hand touched something soft—a buffalo robe. She was

235

lying on top of it, and another covering, her thin blanket, had been flung across her.

She turned her head and saw two figures sitting near the campfire. One of them, Jake Potts, was sitting on a log which had been dragged up close to the circle of orange light. She couldn't see his face; his head was lowered, supported by his hands, and a strip of something—maybe buckskin—had been tied around it.

Will sat off to one side but close to both her and the fire. He poked into the caldron suspended over the flames by means of a crudely built structure of sticks.

So she hadn't killed Jake Potts after all. Disappointment flickered. But—what had happened after she struck him with the heavy caldron?

She forced herself to remember. Kin-di-wa. Will had told her Kin-di-wa was dead.

Her heart twisted with such gripping pain, she could scarcely breathe. Could it really be true? Could she trust Will Simpkin to tell the truth? Will had no reason to lie to her; he believed she had come away willingly. Only Jake Potts had suspected her true motives, and he had refused to answer yes or no when she asked him if Kin-di-wa was dead.

Again, the memory flashed: how still Kin-di-wa had been while they dragged him off to the guardhouse! If he had not been dead, or close to it, he would have been fighting every step of the way.

But Kin-di-wa could not be dead. He couldn't be. She would not allow it. God could never be so unfair. He wouldn't take Kin-di-wa away from her when she needed him so much, when their love was so strong and beautiful, when all they wanted was to be together—with no one to interfere.

How could He permit this to happen?

And then, the answer came to her: God wasn't responsible for Kin-di-wa's death—she was. She had caused it to happen. She hadn't had enough faith, enough trust. She had doubted both God and her husband and instead had taken matters into her own hands. And now Kin-di-wa was dead. Dead. There could be no doubt about it.

Someone began to scream, a shrill cry of unbearable agony. Will and Jake jumped up and looked at her. She suddenly realized who was screaming, but the knowledge only made her scream louder.

Will dragged her to her feet. "Stop it, Becky, stop it! Kin-di-wa's gone—he's gone an' he ain't never comin' back! Ya might as well face it! Ya b'long t' me, girl—I'm gonna marry ya an' you'll forget all about that bastard!"

Rebecca screamed and screamed—until Will drew back his hand and cuffed her across the face. She crumpled onto the buffalo robe. The campfire, Will, and Jake whirled around her, and in the center of the spinning scene was the deep well of darkness, the black tunnel, the cave where she could hide. Gratefully, she allowed herself to be caught up and drawn into it—to be spun away into blackness. Only in oblivion could she find relief from pain.

Nausea awoke her this time. Her stomach was knotted with cramps, and her lips felt dry and swollen. She tried not to alert Will or Jake as she moved gingerly and opened her eyes. Birds were twittering, and the surrounding trees were clearly visible in the dim gray light.

She sat up. Will was asleep on half of her buffalo robe, his large body sprawled out on its side, his face and beard half-buried in last year's leaves. Jake Potts was a blanket-wrapped cocoon on the other side of the heaped ashes of last night's campfire.

She rose slowly to her feet, went to the stream, and lay down on her stomach beside it. The water was cool and refreshing. She scooped it into her hands and drank deeply, then bathed her face, neck, and arms.

Next, she combed her hair, using the comb Kin-di-wa had once carved for her, which she'd placed on a thong around her neck. She needed it desperately today—and all the days to follow. Not just so she could neatly arrange and braid her hair, but so she could remember Kin-di-wa in a happier time—so she could touch and use something he had once touched.

When she finished grooming herself, she sat for a few moments studying the shapes and colors of pebbles in the creekbed. How had the pebbles come to be there? Where was the creek itself going to and where had it come from? Did anybody know?

It was simply there, mysteriously, to meet her needs. But it wasn't water she needed now—it was Kin-di-wa. And Kin-di-wa was dead. She drew up her knees and rested her head on them and began to weep. Tears welled up from deep within and slid unchecked down her cheeks. She hugged her knees to muffle any sound and gave herself up to overwhelming grief.

The result of so much sorrow was only more nausea. Her stomach heaved and rolled, her head throbbed—and it was this reaction of her body that reminded her she might be pregnant. Four days late for a monthly flux which had always arrived promptly on the twenty-ninth day.

Could there be any doubt that she had conceived new life? She placed one hand on the soft mound of her stomach. It could not be her imagination. Her stomach did feel slightly fuller, almost swollen. And her breasts had undergone noticeable changes even before her last flux—the one that had been so unusual.

Yes, she was pregnant, carrying Kin-di-wa's child. The knowledge made her tremble. Kin-di-wa had been taken from her, but she had not been left with nothing. This child was the proof of their love. This child was the link between the past and the future. This child was Kin-di-wa and herself going onward—conquering pain, sorrow, and death. This child was all she had left.

"Becky? Becky—ya'll right this mornin'?" Will

lumbered up beside her, his matted hair and beard peppered with bits of leaves and broken twigs.

She wiped the tears from her cheeks. "Yes, I'm better . . ." Then, seeing the relief in his eyes, the change from worry to lustful interest as his glance swept over her body, she sought to focus his attention on other things. "How—how far are we going today, Will?"

"Soon as ya heat up th' rest o' that turkey, we're headin' on down t' Fort Washington . . . like I wuz tellin' Jake last night, we kin git hitched th' first place we meet up with a preacher . . . an' don't worry none 'bout ole Jake. I told him we're partin' comp'ny soon as we git t' th' fort."

It was as much concern as Will had ever shown to her, but Rebecca remained unmoved. She didn't want to marry Will. She didn't want him for a husband, and even if he'd accept Kin-di-wa's son or daughter, which she doubted, she didn't want him as father to her child.

"Will, I'm pregnant," she blurted. "I'm carrying Kin-di-wa's child."

Will recoiled as if she'd slapped him. "Whut? Whut did you say?"

"I am carrying Kin-di-wa's child."

Will hawked and spat contemptuously. "Well, I might've knowed it, th' way you wuz carryin' on . . . Yep, that explains it."

"Explains what?"

"Why you wuz wailin' 'bout that no-good Injun last night! I couldn't hardly understan' it. Ya come away with me by choice—wuzn't nobody forcin' ya. Yet there you wuz, actin' like you wuz outa yur head!" Will hunkered down close to her, his odor nearly gagging her. "Well, ya got t' git rid o' it, Becky, 'cuz it's an evil thing he done t' ya, an' th' child will be evil too."

"Evil! Get rid of it! What do you mean?"

"Don't ya know?" Will's eyebrows quirked. "He's put his mark on ya woman! He's planted his seed an' made ya his. He probably even had some old Medicine man cast a spell on ya . . . I knew it wuzn't natural, a white woman takin' up with a god-damned red-skin. He tricked ya, Becky! He fed ya potions an' herbs t' make ya crazy, so ya didn't know what you wuz doin' when ya gave yurself t' 'im . . . By God! Don't ya see it? Ya gotta git rid o' his evil spawn or y'all be marked fer th' rest o' yur days!"

Rebecca was too stunned to respond for a moment. How could Will believe—actually voice—such superstitious nonsense? Abruptly, she remembered Apekonit telling her the same thing: most whites could not accept that another white might come to find love and happiness among the Indians. And because they could neither understand nor accept it, they invented all kinds of ridiculous explanations as to why it sometimes happened.

"I don't know how to get rid of a baby, Will. And I don't want to get rid of this one . . . I—I have an aunt and uncle in Philadelphia who would probably be willing to take me in. Maybe, we should all part company when we get to Fort Washington. People go back and forth from there to Philadelphia all the time."

241

A strange excitement stirred in Rebecca, almost blotting out her grief. Going to her aunt in Philadelphia would be the perfect solution to the problem of her future. Eagerly, she voiced her rising hope. "Why, I could go on a flatboat up the Ohio River to Gallipolis, and then from there to Marietta, then on to Fort Pitt, and surely I can find someone going from there to Philadelphia . . . Why, I could be home long before the baby's due!"

She was startled when Will suddenly stood up, howling in outrage, and lifted her bodily to face him. "Yur plumb crazy iff'n ya think I'm willin' t' give ya up now, Becky! How many times do I gotta tell ya? Yur my woman an' nobody else's, an' y'all do exack'ly whut I tell ya! An' I'm telling ya—git rid o' that Injun's bastard!"

It was more than Rebecca could take. "No! I won't get rid of it. If you don't want my baby, you don't want me! So let me go, Will! Let me go to my Aunt Margaret, my mother's sister . . ."

Will crushed her to him. "Didja' or didja' not come away with me 'cuz ya wanted to—'cuz ya had some feelin' fer me? Yur own papa would've given ya t' me! That's why ya came, isn't it? 'Cuz ya had t' admit ya were wrong—givin' yurself t' a savage . . ."

Turning her head to avoid a faceful of Will's beard and protruding chest hair, Rebecca lost all sense of restraint. Something snapped inside her. "Oh, how can you be so stupid! I came to save Kin-di-wa's life! On one of your killing sprees, you killed his brother! So he was going to kill you,

242

and then General Wayne would have had to kill him—to shoot or hang him. So I said I was your wife to protect him, so General Wayne would lock him up . . . oh, what's the use? All I did was to get him killed anyway!"

Will's face grew livid. He shoved her away and sent her sprawling onto the creekbank. "You bitch! You whore! Ya think ya kin make a fool outa me? . . . well, little Injun cock-lover, let me tell you somepin'. Now, that ya got me, yur stuck with me—y'ain't never gonna git away!"

"B—but what about my baby? I refuse to give up my baby!"

Will hitched up his buckskins. "I don't keer about yur baby! I ain't playin' Papa to no red-skinned bastard!" A dangerous light came into his eyes. "Ol Jake an' me kin git rid o' that baby real quick—hell, ain't nothin' to it. A little rough handlin' is all it takes. Took me a pregnant squaw-woman once, nearly big around as a barrel. Oh, she begged an' she pleaded—told with her hands how she'd lose the baby if I took her rough, but I jus' went ahead an' did it anyways—good an' hard as I pleased. Sure enough, that ole baby popped out a few hours later . . . all blue an' funny lookin'—ugly as a vulture . . . It wuz lucky fer her it never did draw breath."

Shocked to the core, Rebecca struggled to sit up. How could anyone be so cruel? She crossed her arms protectively over her stomach. Will Simpkin and Jake Potts would never cause her to lose her baby. Never. She'd kill them first. Instead of Moccasin Flower and Mad Dog Weed, she'd put *Ki-ta-man-i* into their food. May apple, it was called by the whites, and the poisonous root worked quickly.

"Now, git up an' git us some grub . . ." Will snarled. "Y'ain't nothin' but my slave-woman now, miz Becky. Why'n hell should I bother t' marry ya—a woman half-crazy for a stinkin' savage? . . . Me an' Jake kin jus' take an' use ya til we've had our fill, an' then I'll sell ya t' some other trapper. Yeah, that's jus' whut I'll do—when I git sick o' ya, I'll sell ya!"

Fear made Rebecca move quickly to do his bidding—but before they departed camp on the trail going south, she satisfied herself that here, beside the little creek, no *Ki-ta-man-i* was growing.

They spent a shorter time traveling that day than they had spent the day before, and Rebecca easily guessed the reason why. All day long, Jake and Will told filthy stories, took long swigs from an earthenware jug they dug out of Jake's pack, and exploded into fits of coarse-sounding laughter. Jake complained that his head ached—that was how it started: the drinking which led to the swearing and telling stories.

Twice, Rebecca feared they were going to stop and rape her then and there, but Will always protested at the last minute, "No, let'er think about it first. Let 'er anticipate how it's gonna be—servin' two of us at the same time."

Will's mood grew meaner and more dangerous

as the day progressed. He was working himself up to a high pitch of jealousy and fury—a thoroughly vengeful state that matched the vengeance Jake Potts already felt toward her.

She did not know which man she feared the most: Will, whose glittering eyes betrayed both hurt and hatred, or Jake, whose equally hot-eyed gaze showed an even stronger streak of malice and cruelty—and a ruthless determination to make her pay for three things now: last winter, the bump on his nose, and of course, the lump on his forehead.

Desperately, she searched for *Kit-a-man-i* or some other toxic root, but the only herbs to be found were pleasant, beneficial ones. Could the herbs she had given them at breakfast do the trick? No, she thought with a sickening lurch of her stomach, there hadn't been enough time. The herbs Crow Woman had recommended did their best work when administered over a period of time—even several days, and then of course, the treatment had to be repeated regularly in order to maintain the desired effect.

Again, the realization struck her: had she been dealing with Will alone, she might easily have held him off. But dealing with two of them . . .

Every step she took weighed her down with anxiety and grief. By comparison, her bundles and packs seemed light. Yet she did not want to stop; she wished the trail could go on forever. And when Will suddenly barked, "Here, let's make camp here," Rebecca could not keep her heart from pounding, and her mouth from going dry.

The spot Will chose for their campsite was adjacent to the Great Miami River, whose shining waters provided an unmistakable path due south to Fort Washington and the Ohio River. Rebecca glanced longingly at the wide glistening stream. If only she could somehow escape, it would be a fairly simple matter to follow the river and arrive safely where she wanted to go. But time had just run out on her, unless . . .

She eased her packs and bundles to the ground, untied the caldron, and shoved it out of sight in a clump of underbrush.

"Awright, slave . . ." Will barked. He and Jake had already sat down and were now leaning back against a sturdy beechwood, the jug between them. "Make us a fire. Git us some grub—I got jerky an' flour in th' pack. An' bring me a chaw of tobacky."

"Jus' a minute, Will . . ." Jake's voice sounded slurred. "Make 'er undress first. If I gotta wait, at least I kin look . . . lookin' is half th' fun."

"Will!" Rebecca pretended she hadn't heard. "I can't seem to find the caldron. It must have come undone from my pack." She made a show of pawing through their things. "I—I thought I heard something fall a few minutes ago—back up the trail."

Will started to get up. "Ya stupid squaw! Ya think caldrons are easy t' come by? I had t' trade a heap o' furs t' git that one!"

"It can't be far, Will!" She made her voice sound contrite and fearful—which wasn't hard to do since her knees were shaking. "I'll just see if I can find it! It's got to be here somewhere."

Instead of bolting as she wanted to do, Rebecca merely inched toward the path they had been following along the river. She rattled brush and poked through clumps of greenery as convincingly as possible.

Jake's quarrelsome voice echoed after her. "T' hell with the caldron, Will. Make 'er undress. I'm gittin' tired o' waitin'."

"She kin find th' damn caldron first!" Will spat. "It cost me dear an' I ain't gonna lose it! . . . 'Sides, we got all night t' have our fun."

Rebecca heard a pop as the jug was unstoppered. Please dear God, she pleaded silently, let them be too drunk to realize what I'm doing.

"Oh, I think I see it back up the trail a little way . . ." She began to run—straight upriver to where the path jogged slightly to the left and was bordered by a thicket of brambles and wild raspberry canes she had noticed when they came from the other direction.

"Yes, I'm sure I see it now!" she called. "I'll have it in a minute . . ."

Certain they could no longer see her, she plunged headlong into the tangled growth beside the path. Head down, clawing away branches and vines, she kept going. The canes were thick with thorns that tore at her hair and clothing, easily penetrating to bare flesh, but the impulse to flee was so strong now that nothing could have stopped her.

Almost as if her suffering body was detached from her mind, she noticed that underneath the shiny green leaves, individual raspberries were ripening from green to a purplish color. Black Raspberries. Soon, the berries could be eaten— even now, several were ready.

On hands and knees, she broke free of the canes, and at almost the same time heard a muffled shout. "Becky! Where'n hell are ya?"

But the threat of that distant voice was hardly worth noting. They wouldn't find her so easily now, she thought triumphantly. Kin-di-wa had taught her a few tricks about losing herself in the woods.

She raised her head to scramble to her feet and found herself nose to cold wet nose with a creature that had a furry brown face and was now watching her with a pair of startled black eyes.

She gasped and drew back, unable to do anything but stare for a moment. The creature stared back. Its snout was shiny and black. Its tongue was a soft baby-pink. A white patch of hair on its chest stood out against the dark fur of the rest of its body. Unmoving at first, the animal seemed stunned by her sudden appearance in the raspberry patch it had been investigating. But then it rose up on its haunches, revealing its identity in all its awesome splendor.

It was a yearling black bear cub, large as a ten year old child, and before Rebecca could recover from the shock of discovering it, she saw a second yearling cub, shouldering its way nearer to its sibling.

Rebecca opened her mouth to scream and soundlessly closed it again. The cubs, although nearly full grown, must have a mother somewhere nearby. Mother black bears kept their babies with them for two full seasons. And Rebecca remembered something else Kin-di-wa had taught her: unless provoked, bears were normally gentle creatures, but she must never, under any circumstances, intrude on a mother bear and her cubs. A disturbed mother bear was the fiercest creature in the forest.

There was no other direction to go except backwards in the direction from which she had come. Any moment now, the mother might come lumbering into view, and Rebecca knew she was safer facing Will and Jake than a slashing set of claws. But going backwards into the lacerating canes was not as easy as she thought. The mass of growth behind her felt solid as a wall, and at her movement, both cubs uttered a warning "woof!"

A louder "woof!" came from behind them, and a large furry body, the largest black bear Rebecca had ever seen, reared up out of the greenery.

"Becky! Damn you!" Will's voice now sounded quite close. "Is this some trick yur tryin' t' pull?"

"We'll find ya, li'le squaw-woman!" Jake slurred. "Ya can't git away from us!"

"Here," Rebecca cried. "I'm over here! I—I tripped and fell!"

The sound of her voice startled both cubs and mother. All three reared upright, pawing the air with gleaming curved claws. Their heads waved back and forth, as if they smelled a noxious odor. Rebecca herself became aware of a heavy acrid smell, bear smell, mixed with her own sour odor, the odor of fear.

She gathered her body into a crouch, keeping her movements deliberately slow and unthreatening. The cubs watched her with a mixture of curiosity and half-grown bravado. The mother bear growled deep in her throat.

"Jake! Will!" Rebecca hissed. She moved cautiously to her left, seized a stick lying on the ground in front of her, and poked it experimentally at one of the cubs. The mother bear woofed her outrage—commanding her cubs to step aside and leave the intruder to her. But the cubs were too interested to heed their mother's warning. The one at whom she'd poked the stick took a swipe at the offending object.

Rebecca heard Jake and Will tromping and swearing on the other side of the canes as they looked for her. She moved further left, enticing the bears to follow by beating on the ground in front of them with the stick. "Come on, little brothers, that's it—this way," she crooned softly.

Somewhere to her left, the stand of cane ended. "Here!" she called again. "I'm right here!"

"If yur tryin' t' trick us, yur gonna be plumb sorry!" Will shouted. He was almost on top of her.

Rebecca stood up straight, raised the stick, then brought it down with a whistling sound smack on the tender nose of the nearest bear cub. At the exact same moment, Jake and Will broke through the canes at her back.

Depending on the sudden presence of the men to distract the bears, Rebecca darted left, then right. She zig-zagged away through the surrounding trees just as a thundering roar of maternal fury split the air.

"By God in heaven!" Will cried. "A she-bear an' her cubs!"

"Look out!" Jake screamed.

Rebecca did not stop to see what was happening. She raced from tree to tree, leaving the sounds of grunts, woofs, thuds, and unearthly cries of pain and horror far behind. The only sounds that mattered now were the pad-pad-pad of her scurrying feet and the thump-thump-thump of her pounding heart.

When she could run no farther, she grasped onto a tree and leaned against it to support her sagging body. The forest was now incredibly silent, with only the rustling tree branches, the far away chitter of a chipmunk, and her own ragged breathing to distract her.

Then over both these sounds, she heard another. Like a swell of music, a triumphant inner chorus rose to a crescendo in her grief-numbed brain: I did it! I made it! I saved Kin-di-wa's baby and I'm free at last. Oh, Aunt Margaret, I'm coming, I'm coming . . . Please be there! Please don't disappoint me . . . I'm coming home to Philadelphia!"

Part Two

Ten

"Becky, dear, wake up! Yeer missin' our entrance into Philadelphia!" The lilting Irish brogue of Molly McGuire brought Rebecca quickly to a state of full wakefulness. She sat up on the heaped bundles in the back of the dray wagon and cautiously stretched her stiff muscles, trying not to awaken the three youngest members of the McGuire family: six year old Patrick, five year old Joseph, and four year old Michael.

"What time of day is it, Molly?" Rebecca yawned and shivered in the crisp autumn air. She glanced skyward, but the sun was concealed behind thick gray clouds.

Molly raised one slender arm to shield her eyes as she too looked toward the sky. "What do you think, Tom?"

"'Bout noon, I'd say." Molly's strapping, black-haired, blue-eyed husband snapped his whip over the back of the sway-backed mare who was clop-clopping along the cobblestone street. Rebecca felt a moment's sympathy for the tired animal: day after weary day, across most of Pennsylvania, the little brown mare had been pulling the dray wagon—loaded down with Rebecca, the five McGuires, and all of their belongings.

"Noon already! I can't believe it." Rebecca was ashamed to have slept so long. They'd been on the road since before first light, but it seemed as if they'd been journeying only an hour or two. She smoothed down the wrinkled homespun dress that Molly had given her to replace her soiled doeskin. "How are you feeling, Molly?"

Her tiny friend looked especially thin and pale this morning. Indeed, Molly McGuire was hardly more than 'a rag, a bone, and a hank o' hair,' as she laughingly called herself, and her condition was hardly surprising in view of the fact that she'd borne five children in the last six years. The last two babies, dead of fever which had nearly taken Molly herself, were buried in the Ohio Country.

"Ah, 'tis feelin' better I am every moment now, t' see this fine city at last!" Molly brushed a hand through her lank brown hair and straightened up on the single crude plank where she sat beside her mammoth husband. "Yee've taken sech good keer o' me an' th' wee ones, Becky—I don't know 'ow we'd 'ave managed without ye'! Isn't that so, Tom?"

"Aye, tis so, lass," Tom agreed. "'Twas the will o' the Almighty that sent Becky-Girl to us at

Fort Washington."

"It was the will of the Almighty that sent you to me!" Rebecca protested. "I'll be sorry to leave you when we get to my Aunt's."

Molly turned sideways and patted her arm. "We'd be takin' ye' on with us gladly t' New York, Becky dear . . . but now ye' must think o' whut's best fer yeer own wee one comin' along in a short while."

"I know, Molly . . ." Rebecca caught and squeezed her friend's hand. "But I surely will miss you and Big Tom and the boys."

"As we'll miss you . . ." Molly smiled through brimming tears, then turned back to watch their entrance into the city.

Rebecca's hand dropped to her swelling belly. Over five months gone with child she was now, as nearly as she could calculate it—over five months since she'd lain with Kin-di-wa in the wind-flowers. Her heart constricted with familiar pain, but she dutifully pushed sorrow aside and concentrated instead on her present good fortune.

Yes, she had been very lucky to meet Molly and Tom McGuire one week to the day after escaping Will and Jake. Big Tom had been so distraught, with an ailing wife and three boisterous young-sters to transport home across an entire wilder-ness; he had eagerly accepted Rebecca's offer of help in exchange for food, protection, and passage as far east as Philadelphia.

If the McGuires hadn't needed her, Rebecca didn't know what she would have done. Getting to Fort Washington had been fairly easy; she had simply followed the Great Miami River. But the fort itself had been a dangerous place for a woman alone, without money or provisions. She shuddered to think of what might have happened to her had she not noticed the McGuires her first day there. Probably, she'd have found it necessary to join a family going west instead of east.

Anthony Wayne's stronghold overlooking the Ohio River had been swarming with adventure-seeking men, and the river itself had been log-jammed with flatboats full of eager settlers drifting westward. The Indians' defeat at Fallen Timbers had opened up the floodgates: there was no stopping the flow of settlers now. Only people like the McGuires, who had paid too high a price for free land, were desirous of returning east.

Rebecca wished Molly and Tom would be satisfied to stay in Philadelphia instead of going all the way back to New York. Their friendship and stalwart support was something upon which she had come to depend. Never once had the McGuires betrayed the slightest shock or censure when finally she broke down and told them her story. Rather, they had been sympathetic and kindhearted—as anxious to ease her grief and help her build a new life for herself as she had been to cook, launder, supervise the boys, and ease life for them on the long, difficult journey home to eastern Pennsylvania.

Three and a half months it had taken them: July, August, September, and half of October. Three and a half months—time enough for the child within her to make itself both felt and noticeable. Time enough to stop feeling guilty over what she had or hadn't done. Time enough to stop wondering what had become of Little Turtle, Sweet Breeze, and the Miami Indians. Time enough to ask God's forgiveness for enlisting the aid of three enraged bears so she could escape from Will and Jake.

Time enough for everything, except to stop loving the man who was lost to her, the man who'd been clubbed with a rifle butt because of her foolishness, the man whom she'd never be able to forget and whom she'd never again see in this life.

"Ye got a bellyache?" Young Patrick McGuire sat up beside her.

"What? Oh, no!" Rebecca realized she had been absent-mindedly rubbing her rounded stomach. "No, Patrick, me foine fellow, I'm feelin' fit as a fiddle . . . an' ye woke up jus' in time t' see the grand city of Philadelphia!"

Patrick giggled at her attempt to mimic his family's brogue. "Are we here then? This is Philadelphia?"

"You don't remember it?" Rebecca tickled his stomach. "Why, you were at least three when your family came through here going west!"

Two other tousled black heads—the three boys were the image of Big Tom—popped up in the creaking wagon. "Are we here? Are we here?" Joseph and Michael chirped excitedly.

"Becky-Girl says so," Patrick said in his father's voice of authority. "Be careful now, wi' yeer scramblin', or you'll tip over th' dray!"

The excitement in the back of the wagon made Rebecca more determined to forget her lingering sadness. Suddenly, her heart began to pound. She had both longed for and dreaded this moment: their arrival in Philadelphia, the largest city in the United States. She had spent her entire girlhood dreaming about coming to this city. But now, when the clop-clop of the old mare's hooves sounded so jarringly real and inevitable, all she could think of was how much she wished she were back in the Ohio wilderness—back in her lodge beside the river, with her husband's arms around her.

Sit up and look around! she scolded herself. This is no time for weeping over what is past and finished. You must get involved with the present!

Something fluttered in her lower abdomen: the baby stretching and moving. Michael scrambled into her lap, and all at once, it became easy to concentrate on the present. Wanting to see this place to which they'd finally come, Rebecca twisted and turned on the precarious load of blankets, bundles, and bedding. Her first impression of the city did not disappoint: never had she imagined it to be so grand and overwhelming!

The cobblestoned street down which they traveled was flanked by sidewalks made of flagstones, six-foot-square. Some of the side streets remained unpaved, but even these had boards or stepping stones laid across them. Houses and shops—red brick with white trim and roofs of tile or slate—rimmed both sides of the street. They were set back from the road the exact same distance, but appeared to be jostling wall to wall with one another for space.

Here and there, wooden houses painted in pleasing bright colors of red, yellow, and blue intruded. Several shops boasted awnings. Though none of the structures had front yards, most were blessed with porches bearing matched benches, facing each other.

Narrow walkways sometimes ran between the houses. Some had brick arches over them, and all were closed off by gates or doors. Rebecca speculated on where the walkways led—to gardens?

Then she noticed something curious: the street was higher in the middle than on the sides where open gutters emitted a terrible stench of which she realized she'd been aware for some time. The odor was indescribable—garbage, animal droppings, and all manner of human filth.

She wrinkled her nose in distaste, but no one else seemed to mind it. A woman, wearing a big white apron and a calico cap, swept her porch unconcernedly. A man carrying an armload of firewood from a nearby cart scurried down a cellar doorway. Several plainly dressed women, toting market baskets, stepped aside for an elegant lady in a flowing gown, shawl, and flowered hat. Both up and down the street, other people on foot, on horseback, and in buggies and dray wagons hurried by as though they never gave a moment's thought to the awful smell of the gutters.

Joseph pointed to a high post topped with an

iron gooseneck from which hung a square glass-sided lantern. "Yes, Joseph, that's a street lamp," Rebecca said. "It's lit with whale oil, and lamplighters light it every night that there isn't a moon."

She was pleased to be able to explain such a wonder to the little boy. Even though she herself had never seen street lamps, her mother had described them to her. "Philadelphia is better lighted than London," Mama had told her proudly.

"An' does each house 'ave its own water pump?" Patrick was quivering with excitement.

"I believe they do," Rebecca responded. "But most have them inside. Those you see up and down the street are public water pumps. They're mostly used in case of fire."

Patrick gawked at the tall wooden pumps with their long iron handles. Up and down the treeless street, the pumps were interspersed with white wooden posts for hitching animals. The posts also served to protect the walkway from the traffic in the street.

"The houses are so taaall," Joseph breathed in awe.

"They 'ave one floor sitting on top o' another floor, don't they, Becky-Girl?" Patrick said.

"Yes, they must . . . and maybe yet another on top of that one." Rebecca guessed. "Something like the loft a cabin has . . ."

She told the children to "hush now and be still," as Tom turned onto a larger busier street containing even more amazing wonders.

The mare skittered and shied at the noise and bustle: enclosed coaches, open carriages, dray wagons, carts, and light two-wheeled vehicles with room for no more than a single person were clattering to and fro. A man leading his horse-drawn cart shouted to Tom, "Git down an' walk yur nag, man! No drivin' allowed on High Street."

A richly dressed man on horseback galloped past, causing the mare to whinny nervously, and Tom reined her in and got down from his planking. "Guess I'd better walk 'er—even if others break th' rule. Where'd you say yeer Aunt an' Uncle lived ag'in, Becky-Girl?"

Poor Tom! Rebecca thought. The big man looked flushed and uncertain of himself. "Society Hill," she reminded him, then went on to give the street and house number. Could they possibly find the place by themselves?

"Go on up t' th' marketplace, Tom," Molly suggested. "Someone up there will likely know where 'tis."

"What a good idea, Molly!" Rebecca exclaimed. "I'm certain they don't live too far from there because my Uncle Hardin is a merchant!"

They were now headed in the direction of the Delaware River, and as they drew closer, the traffic increased. Rebecca was no less astounded than the boys to see two Indians bearing a strange-looking chair affixed to poles. The chair stopped in front of a shop over which hung a sign painted like the cover of a book. A beautifully-dressed lady stepped down and entered the store. The two Indians were left to stand waiting patiently for her to come out again.

Rebecca looked closely at the chair-bearers, but saw little resemblance to Miamis or any of the tribes she'd known in Ohio. These Indians, dressed in homespun trousers and fringed leather shirts, were evidently servants or slaves.

The number of black and brown-skinned people on the street also drew her attention. Having rarely seen any near Papa's farm, she hadn't realized there were so many Negro slaves in Philadelphia. Perhaps, the Quaker influence was lessening, for the Quakers, she knew, frowned upon slavery, the usual condition of Negroes.

Then Molly gave a little squeal. "Look, Becky, over there! 'Tis the top o' the Old State House!"

Rebecca looked to the left where Molly pointed, and there, not far distant, stood a row of large buildings. "Don't they call it Independence Hall now?" she wondered aloud.

"Oh, Tom!" Molly cried. "After we find Becky's kin, can we not drive past the very place where the Declaration was signed? I want to see Carpenters' Hall too and the County Courthouse. We'll likely niver be this way ag'in, an' th' boys must see an' remember these places whilst they 'ave th' chance!"

This mention of famous buildings and the Declaration of Independence gave Rebecca a moment of sadness—almost of guilt. Molly and Tom did not share her sympathy toward Indians and Negroes, for whom the noble sentiments in the Declaration would likely never apply. The

264

McGuires' enthusiasm for their growing young nation remained untainted, but even Rebecca felt a thrill of excitement when the lofty white spire of Christ Church suddenly loomed ahead of them down the road.

"Christ Church!" she pointed. "My mother once went to church there!"

As they drew closer, Rebecca went on to tell what she knew about this famous landmark with its neat white trim, red-brick facade, and gracious churchyard—the latter boasting long stone benches and a wrought-iron fence. President Washington himself worshipped here, as did Thomas Jefferson and other notables, including Betsy Ross who had sewed the first flag of the United States.

Benjamin Franklin, before his death five years earlier in 1790, had been a member of the church, and it was in Christ Church Burial Ground that he had finally been laid to rest beside his four-year-old son, his wife, Deborah, and others of his family.

Patrick, Joseph, and Michael were enthralled to hear that the pulpit of the church was said to be shaped like a "wineglass," but Molly looked disapproving, and after Rebecca finished telling all she knew of the place, Molly said, "Ye know, lads, Philadelphia is the only city where Catholics can worship freely ... We 'ave our own church here, St. Joseph's, where we ought to stop b'fore we leave."

Rebecca had quite forgotten the religious sensitivity of her friends. Regretting her tactlessness, she fell silent as Tom turned the corner and turned again—for the traffic was such that he could not get as close as he wanted to the market-building. It stood in the middle of the street near Christ Church.

Tom led the mare down a short dark street that ended almost at the river, then stopped and turned to Molly. "I'll jus' be steppin' inside o' this tavern here . . . an' askin' fer Becky-Gurl's people."

"Oh, Tom!" Molly protested. "I thought ye'd be askin' at th' market!"

"Now, Molly . . . 'tis a respectable lookin' establishment, an' it won't take but a minute." Tom tied the mare to a hitching post and went inside the tavern, leaving Molly and Rebecca to doubtfully study the sign that hung from a tall post in front of the two and a half story red-brick building.

The tavern was called "A Man Full of Trouble Inn," and the sign featured a man with a three-cornered hat and a woman, evidently the man's wife, leaning on his arm. The man had a monkey sitting on his shoulder and a parrot on his hand, while the wife held a bandbox with a cat on top of it.

After studying the sign for a moment, both Molly and Rebecca broke into giggles. "Aye, th' poor man is full up with troubles! That's fer certain . . ." Molly gasped, and Rebecca had to agree.

The sign said, "Est. 1759," and Patrick wanted to know what "est." meant. "It means when the tavern was built," Rebecca explained. "This building has stood here for thirty-six years."

Molly sighed. "How fine t' be able t' do sums like that in yeer 'ead, Becky. An' t' be able t' read as good as you do . . . I hope t' 'ave th' boys go t' school when we git settled in New York ag'in."

"They really should," Rebecca agreed. "I'm not sorry that Mama insisted I learn to read, write, and cipher when I was a child." Yes, she thought with a sudden sinking feeling: Mama's careful preparation for me to come to Philadelphia is finally going to be tested—but what fine gentleman will ever want to marry a woman who's pregnant with another man's child? A savage's child.

Wiping his mouth with the back of his hand, Tom came out of the tavern just then. "No trouble gittin' directions," he said. "Becky-Gurl's kin're well known. Th' tavern keeper told me right where t' go."

"T' hell, I'll wager, if ye coddle a taste fer the devil's own milk!" Molly huffed.

"Now, Molly . . . 'twas only a jigger o' ale. If I wuz really t' coddle m' taste, I'd 'ave stayed long enough for a mug o' flip." Tom took up the mare's reins and began leading the dray away from the tavern.

Rebecca smiled behind her hand. She herself had never drunk flip, but Papa had been fond of the rum-laced drink. It was made of beer to which a hearty dash of rum had been added, then it was sweetened with sugar, molasses, or dried pumpkin, and finally, a red-hot loggerhead was inserted

267

into it which made it froth and bubble—and taste slightly burnt or so Papa had said.

Why was she being assailed with so many memories? she wondered. Was it because her new life was about to begin, the life that she and Mama had planned so long ago?

Oh, she hadn't wanted to go west with Papa after Mama's death! She hadn't wanted to give up her dream of Philadelphia. But now, everything was so different. Everything had changed. What if she'd made a mistake? What if Aunt Margaret and Uncle Hardin didn't want her now?

As the dray lurched down the street, she summoned the last ounce of her wavering courage. Uncle Hardin was a prosperous merchant. If he didn't wish to claim her as his niece, the daughter of his wife's sister, then perhaps he would permit her to become a servant in his household. But no—Aunt Margaret had always seemed so kind and generous; surely, her husband would be the same!

Rebecca realized she knew nothing whatever about her uncle: Hardin Ezekial Stone. All of her correspondence and that of her mother had been with Aunt Margaret whom Rebecca only dimly remembered. Visits between them had been infrequent. Nothing had ever been said, but now that Rebecca thought about it, she wondered if Uncle Hardin and Papa had gotten along together.

Probably not. An illiterate Scottish immigrant and a prosperous Philadelphia merchant would have little in common. And Papa had never been very excited about the prospect of Rebecca going to live with her rich aunt and uncle. That had been Mama's idea.

The dray was now creaking down a quiet, lovely street where the buildings were larger, newer, and more ornate than any they'd seen previously. Polished brass door-knockers, insets of white marble, and delicate fan-shaped glass windows adorned the three-storied house-fronts. Tom stopped in front of an awesome home whose cornice was decorated with intricately carved swags and flowers.

"This 'eer 'as got t' be it, Becky-Gurl."

Molly smiled brightly. "Aye, 'tis a grand place, Becky." With a self-conscious gesture, she pulled her threadbare shawl around her shoulders. "Livin' 'eer, you an' yeer babe won't want fer a bloomin' thing!"

Rebecca was acutely aware of her own shabby appearance. Before she saw the house, she hadn't given a moment's thought as to how she looked, but now it occurred to her that she might actually be an embarrassment to her aunt. The cart itself looked out of place on this quiet, gracious street. "Will you wait here a moment, Molly—until I make certain it's the right place?"

"Aye . . ." Molly said stoutly. Her glance strayed to the gleaming brass house numbers.

"Oh, this is the right address," Rebecca explained. "But . . . but maybe they won't want me."

"Och! How could they not want ye? Yeer their own flesh an' blood!" Molly scoffed. She beckoned to Tom who was fussing with the mare's harness. "Go and knock on the door, Tom. Our Becky's lost her nerve."

"No!" Rebecca said. Her own vehemence startled her. But if someone were going to be made to feel small and bothersome, she'd rather it be her instead of good, kind Tom. Besides, first reactions were telling, and she wanted to judge them for herself. If Aunt Margaret looked the least distressed to see her, she'd hurry right back to the dray and go on to New York with her friends!

"I'm not such a baby I'm afraid to knock at my own aunt's door . . . here, boys, give me a hug and a kiss before I leave!" Rebecca quelled her uneasiness with the stiletto-sharp knowledge that the moment of parting had come.

"G—good-bye, Becky-Gurl," Patrick said manfully.

Making noises like whimpering puppies, Joseph and Michael threw their arms around her. Big Tom patted her arm awkwardly. He was never much for words—Molly did most of the couple's talking—but tears stood bright in his deep blue eyes. Rebecca was touched. She slipped down from the dray and came around the side to embrace the plucky, courageous woman who had come to be her good friend.

"It seems everytime I care about people, I'm forced to say goodbye," she whispered. Then she thought of Sweet Breeze and the others whom she'd left without a single word, and her sorrow became even sharper. "Goodbye, Molly . . . God bless you."

"'Tis God's blessing will be on you now, Becky. Lord knows, yeer surely in line fer a few o' His blessings." Molly thrust a bundle into her arms. "Here's a few things ye might be needin'—an extra dress an' a shawl, yeer old doeskin . . ."

"No . . ." Rebecca pushed the bundle away. "You keep them. You've done too much for me already."

A last quick hug and Rebecca broke away. The McGuires still had a long way to go, and she didn't want to hold them back. "Go on . . . go on now, Tom . . . there's no need to stay and wait. I truly am certain this is where my aunt and uncle live."

Tom looked relieved and nodded. "We'll jus' be goin' slow like down th' street, so if ye need to, ye kin call t' us."

Rebecca waited until the dray creaked into motion again and continued down the cobblestones with its load of wet-eyed waving passengers. Then she stepped up onto the porch and lifted the brass knocker.

A moment or two elapsed before the door opened, and a brown-skinned young woman in a bright calico dress and cap gave her a haughty bored look, as if she resented being disturbed. "Yes'm?"

Rebecca was so taken back she wondered if she might indeed have made a mistake. "I—I'm looking for Margaret Stone."

"An' who shall ah say is callin'?" The young woman drawled. She had large black eyes and bright white teeth. Her calico was immaculate, cleaner and of better material than the plain dress Rebecca was wearing.

"I'm Mrs. Stone's niece."

The woman—a girl, really—rolled her expressive dark eyes. "Then ah must be Presid'nt Washin'ton . . . Missus Stone don't have no niece that ah know of!"

"Prudy, dear, who is it?" A voice chirped from somewhere behind the girl. "Don't make them stand waiting on the porch!"

The girl stepped back. "It's jus' someone wants t' sell you somepin', Missus Margaret . . . Yo' better wipe yor feet b'fore yo' steps inside here!" she hissed at Rebecca. "There . . . on the foot-scraper."

Rebecca looked down and saw an iron device bolted onto the porch. If she hadn't been told what it was, she never would have known. Apologetically, she lifted her skirt. "I'm only wearing moccasins—not shoes."

The girl called Prudy opened wide the door. "Moccasins—hmmph! Missus Margaret's niece, indeed!"

Rebecca stepped into the house and found herself in a narrow hallway. Sparkling glass lamps, shining wood floors, and a graceful curving staircase competed for her attention. But then, from one of the doorways opening off the hall, came the sound of a soft tread, a rustling gown, and a high-pitched feminine voice.

"Well, who is it, Prudy, dear?" A small plump woman bustled into the hallway in a cloud of

perfumed air—roses, perhaps, or lavender—
Rebecca wasn't certain which. "Why, yes . . . yes,
who are you?"

Rebecca was unable to speak. It was her Aunt
Margaret: older, plumper, and with a different
hair style than she remembered, but still the same
delicate little woman with fluttery white hands,
lips and cheeks too pink to be natural, and hair
the same pale brown as that of Rebecca's mother.
Only this hair was tightly curled, almost frizzy,
and decorated with tiny pink and purple silk
flowers.

"Aunt Margaret . . . don't you remember me?"

Aunt Margaret's hand fluttered to her mouth.
Her blue eyes widened in their delicate webbing of
wrinkles. Her plump cheeks puffed out like round
ripe plums. "Oh, my . . ." she said. "Oh my, oh
my . . . can it . . . really be you, my little Rebecca?"

Rebecca didn't miss her aunt's shocked glance
at her clothes and her rounded stomach, but
neither did she miss the rising flush of joyous
color, the teary sparkle in the eyes, and the
turning up of the pink heart-shaped mouth. "Yes,
it's me . . . your niece, Rebecca."

"The only child of my dear dead sister! My only
kin in all the world!" Aunt Margaret opened her
plump white arms and Rebecca was enveloped in
moist kisses, sweet-scented hugs, and tender
wails. "Oh, my dear! Oh, my darling! . . . We
feared that you were dead! We thought never to
see you again! . . . Oh, how could your papa have
taken you so far away from us! Oh, he didn't

273

know, of course, how could he—when he never thought to ask? When he just up and left for the wilderness after your dear mama's death and there was no way we could reach him?"

Slightly dizzy, Rebecca pulled back. "Couldn't know what, Aunt Margaret? Whatever are you talking about?"

"Why, my dear . . ." Aunt Margaret dabbed at her eyes with a lacy handkerchief and beamed proudly. "He couldn't have known the wonderful truth, of course! Your Uncle Hardin has made you an heiress—willed everything he owns to you!"

"But—but . . . you mean, Uncle Hardin is dead?"

"Why no, dear!" Aunt Margaret's ample bosom rose and fell in its gauzy confinement—a pink and flowery print that looked somehow absurdly childish. "But after your poor mama died, we wanted to bring you here . . . to give you the life and marriage opportunities your mama meant for you to have. Your Uncle Hardin even changed his will! He was going to leave everything to Christ Church, but instead, he decided to leave it to you . . . so you could make a good marriage! After all, you're our only living kin!"

"Uncle Hardin changed his will?" Rebecca realized how dazed and dull-witted she sounded —as indeed, she felt.

"We tried to find you—sent a messenger all the way to Fort Pitt! But your papa—stubborn, ill-bred scoundrel, your uncle always called him— left no word anywhere along the way as to where he was going!"

Rebecca caught sight of the girl Prudy, standing off to one side with open mouth and wide shocked eyes. "I—I sent you a letter. Didn't you get it?"

"Oh, my, yes . . . we got it when it was too late. You'd gone to the Ohio Country, you said, and you were so sorry to have to cancel your plans to come and live with us. But you said you had to look after your papa . . . your poor grieving papa . . . why, where is he now, Rebecca? Didn't your papa come with you?"

Aunt Margaret peered behind Rebecca as though she somehow expected Papa to be standing right there behind her.

"I—I wrote you a second letter, Aunt Margaret, but I'm sorry—I never got a chance to post it. In it, I explained many things to you: Papa's death, for one . . ."

"Dead? Your papa's dead?" Aunt Margaret threw up her arms. "Prudy! Oh, my dear Prudy! Quickly, get me something—I'm fainting!"

Rebecca caught her aunt just in time while the girl, Prudy, rushed back toward the end of the hall, calling loudly. "Quick! Water! Spirits! Missus Margaret's havin' a faintin' spell!"

A flurry of footsteps sounded throughout the house. Rebecca helped her aunt into a large airy room and over to a slender wooden chair with a carved back and a seat covered in some rich, brocaded material. "Oh, my dear, no! Not the Hepplewhite! I shouldn't want to swoon or be sick on the Hepplewhite!"

Aunt Margaret groped her way to a sturdier chair, and sank down with a sigh of relief. "Oh, poor dear Angus McDuggan! Driven man, I always did say! Could never be happy to stay in a civilized place! First, he dragged your poor dear mama off to a farm—a farm, of all places—then he dragged his only daughter off to the wilderness! Oh, dear me, how did he die? Was it— savages?"

"Shawnee. They were Shawnee Indians," Rebecca said carefully.

"Shawnee!" Aunt Margaret clutched her bosom and leaned back in the chair, as Prudy and two other people rushed into the room. One was a tall sallow man with pinched features and a prominent Adam's apple. The other was an enormous black-skinned woman in the same type of calico dress and cap as Prudy's.

"Now, take a deep breath, Missus Margaret," the large black woman ordered. "Prudy, hand over them c'awn squeezin's. Henry-Luke, stan' by with th' water."

"Oh, my . . . oh, my . . ." Aunt Margaret gasped. She took a long swallow of the amber liquid in the fragile cut glass that Prudy held to her lips. "Oh, my!"

Aunt Margaret's eyes bulged and watered. Color rushed back into her pale papery skin. The tall sallow man—Henry-Luke—proffered the glass of water. Aunt Margaret took a sip then waved it away. "Go on, go on now, all of you! It was only a minor attack! . . . Can't you see I'm busy? This is my niece—my dear little Rebecca.

276

Escaped from the savages, no less!"

The three servants—or two slaves and one servant, Rebecca guessed—straightened up and stepped back. They looked frankly and disbelievingly at Rebecca. Prudy said, "Are yo' sure yo'ah all right now, Missus Margaret? Yo' done received a bad shock."

"Yes sir, a verah bad shock . . ." The big black woman confronted Rebecca with an accusing glance. "Missus Rebecca, yo' gotta be careful around Missus Margaret. She subject to faintin' spells an' such."

For a moment, Rebecca had the feeling that this woman and Prudy were the voices of authority in the Stone household, but then Aunt Margaret once more asserted herself. "That will be quite enough now, Bess. My niece could hardly be expected to know of my—condition. Thank heaven, it isn't serious. Spirits pull me out of it just fine. Now, go on along . . . all of you."

Henry-Luke left first, followed by Bess, the big black woman, and lastly, by Prudy, who seemed reluctant to leave.

"Are you really feeling better now, Aunt Margaret? I'm sorry to have startled you. Papa died a year ago last June, and well, I guess I've just adjusted to it by now."

Aunt Margaret motioned to the Hepplewhite chair. "Sit down, my dear, and tell me everything that's happened. I've worried about you so! I really did believe the savages had probably murdered you both!"

Not wanting to alarm her aunt further, Rebecca sat down and told only the barest details of what had happened over the past two years since she and Papa had first arrived in the Ohio wilderness. Midway through her story, Aunt Margaret had another fainting spell and had to be revived with "spirits," but then she remembered her manners and called for Bess and Prudy to serve tea.

Over a repast that consisted of tiny assorted sandwiches—minced ham, egg salad, and selected cheeses decorated with carrot curls—cranberry nut bread, butter mints, salted nuts, and tiny almond custards baked in china cups, Rebecca tried to think of a way to lessen the blow she most hated to give her aunt: that her child had been fathered by a "savage."

"And the baby, dear?" Aunt Margaret finally asked. "Who is the father of the baby?"

"It—it was a Miami warrior I married. A fine man whom I loved very much." And still love, she thought with wrenching sadness. "His name was Kin-di-wa—Golden Eagle, and he—he—I saw him struck down and killed at Fort Washington."

"I see . . . poor dear girl!" said Aunt Margaret, but this time, there were no hysterics or fainting spells.

Brushing back sudden tears, Rebecca saw a glimmer of something strong and hard in this woman who appeared to be so weak and foolish. Aunt Margaret sipped her tea thoughtfully. "A savage's child, you say . . ."

"I hope I haven't shocked you too much, Aunt Margaret, but—life is very different in the wilderness. It isn't what you would expect." Rebecca ran her finger down the handle of a fragile tea-cup—the most fragile cup she had ever seen. Indeed, even in Papa's house, they had drunk their tea, coffee, lemonade, or ale from pewter, never from delicate china such as this.

Aunt Margaret's expression suddenly brightened. "Perhaps, the child will look like you, dear! Couldn't you say you married—what was the name of that trapper you mentioned—Will Simpkin? Then no one would know your child is half-savage."

Rebecca started. "Quarter-savage, Aunt Margaret. Kin-di-wa was half-white and half-Indian."

"Ah, but savage is savage, dear—once it's in the blood. Why couldn't you just pretend the child was fathered by a white man? No one but you and I need know the truth!"

Rebecca sat up straighter on the Hepplewhite chair. Across the tiny tea table that had been placed between them, her aunt looked so hopeful as to be suddenly ten years younger. "I—I haven't told you everything, Aunt Margaret. That trapper, Will Simpkin, was a terrible man. He—he took advantage of me once, and he would have done so again if I hadn't managed to escape him. Not only that, he would have shared me with another trapper, a despicable man named Jake Potts."

"Shared you! Oh, bless my soul!"

Rebecca feared her aunt might suffer another attack, but the little woman's shock was so genuine, she didn't seem to think of fainting.

Rebecca pressed home her point. "I could never claim him as the father, Aunt Margaret. I think I'd become sick myself to call him so."

Suddenly, Aunt Margaret leaned across the table and placed her small soft hand on Rebecca's firmer, work-reddened one. "Oh, my dear, how you have suffered! It breaks my heart to think of it . . . well, we shan't fib about the child's father then, if that would distress you. But I can't think what people will say—I can't think what your Uncle Hardin will say!"

As though the mere mention of Uncle Hardin's name had conjured up the man himself, there was a noise of footsteps and voices in the hallway— masculine voices. "Margaret? Prudence! Oh, where is everyone when you want them! Can't a man and his guest be waited on when they walk through the door after a long hard day?"

"Good heavens! It's Mister Stone—and he's brought someone home with him! Roger Bakewood, I expect—a distant relative of *the* Bakewoods! Oh, I do wish we'd had enough time to think of what to say to him—your uncle, I mean, of course!" Aunt Margaret fluttered her hands and tried to rise from her chair, but the tea table impeded her efforts. "Prudy! The tea things—oh, do come and remove them! Whatever will Mister Stone think of this mess and disruption! He likes everything to be harmonious—clean and quiet when he comes home!"

"Here, let me get it," Rebecca said. She jumped to her feet and picked up the tea tray—laden with its delicate china and the remains of their meal.

"Oh, no dear, not you!" Aunt Margaret's face was panic-stricken. "The heiress to the entire Stone fortune mustn't clear dishes! Whatever will Mister Stone and Mister Bakewood think?"

"But it's no bother, I assure you . . ." Rebecca said. She had the tea tray firmly in both hands, but Aunt Margaret made a quick motion to rise from her chair. Her flailing hands struck the tray, and suddenly, china cups, saucers, and teapot went flying. Tinkles and crashes followed. Egg-shell thin porcelain struck the table, bounced off, and shattered on the gleaming hardwood floor.

Rebecca stared down in horror and was filled with even more horror when an outraged masculine voice shook the very walls of the house. "Good God in heaven, Mrs. Stone! Will you tell me what in thunderation is going on here this afternoon? . . . Who is this rudely dressed, clumsy wench—and what is she doing in my front parlor?"

Eleven

Rebecca turned and saw a short, beefy, florid-faced man holding a round hat and a silver-handled cane. His expression was furious—eyes bulging and mouth turned down at the corners. Even his jowels quivered with rage, and his bald spot had flushed a bright crimson. Rebecca fought the impulse to laugh as her embarrassment combined with amusement; despite his anger, the man looked quite ridiculous!

Beneath his chin, some sort of scarf had been tied in a large, neat bow. Masses of ruffles protruded from his chest. His jacket, the color of liver, had been cut away in front to reveal daffodil-yellow breeches—so tight he must have had difficulty in moving.

His stockings were white. Silver buckles adorned his shoes, and what remained of his thinning, gray hair had been tied into a queue that stuck straight out to one side, exactly like a pig's tail.

So this is Uncle Hardin, she thought. No doubt, on hearing that I am his niece, he will immediately wish to rescind his will!

A taller man, similarly dressed in cutaway coat, ruffles, and breeches of more subdued colors stood behind him, but Rebecca was too perilously close to either laughing or crying to pay much attention to him.

"Hardin, dear, and dear Mister Bakewood!" Aunt Margaret trilled. "Oh, do come in and meet someone special . . . We've had a little accident here, but Prudy can clean it up in a twinkling!"

Remembering the delicate china, Rebecca sank to her knees and began to gather up the pieces. "I'm so sorry, Aunt Margaret . . . your lovely china . . ."

Aunt Margaret grasped her arm with surprising strength and practically dragged her to her feet. "Leave it for Prudy, dear . . . Hardin, the most wonderful thing has happened! Our darling Rebecca has come to us at last!"

"Rebecca? You mean our niece, Rebecca McDuggan?" Uncle Hardin blinked in stunned disbelief. "B—but this can't be her! Why, she looks like a common bond-servant! And—has she gone and married already?" He looked pointedly at Rebecca's middle.

A flush devoured Rebecca's cheeks. She folded her arms self-consciously across the offending bulge of Kin-di-wa's child. "My husband is dead, Uncle Hardin, as is my father. Please forgive me for taking you by surprise, but I had no way of announcing my arrival beforehand . . . I'm sorry. I won't stay if it distresses you."

"Oh, my dear!" Aunt Margaret's hands fluttered about like butterflies. "Of course, you will stay! Mister Stone will be quite pleased once we've dressed you as befits a lady—an heiress, no less! Won't you, Mister Stone?" She took a step closer to her husband. "Oh, Hardin, you mustn't mind how Rebecca looks! She's had a terrible time of it—just terrible. But now, she's come to us at last, exactly the way we planned. And if she bears a son, why you can teach the lad your business. Won't that be *très magnifique?*"

"Stop using those damnable French expressions, Maggie!" Uncle Hardin exploded. "We may have broken away from the mother country, but the King's English is still good enough for me! . . . Besides, she's not a bolt of cloth to be sold, you know . . ." Suddenly shame-faced, Uncle Hardin's glance bored into Rebecca. His bulbous nose grew red. "I'm sorry to hear about your father, Niece. Damn fool he was, dragging his daughter off among blood-thirsty savages, but still I'm sorry to hear he's dead . . ."

"Thank you, Uncle," Rebecca said.

Into the little silence that followed, another male voice intruded. "Why, Hardin, old fellow . . . if your niece *were* a bolt of cloth, you'd have buyers aplenty to snap her up in a minute."

Both Uncle Hardin and Aunt Margaret turned to the man who had been standing quietly in the doorway, hat and cane under one arm. "Ah,

Roger, forgive us . . ." Uncle Hardin apologized. "You're witnessing a rather awkward scene, I'm afraid."

Roger Bakewood stepped into the room and, with his free hand, clapped Uncle Hardin on the shoulder. "On the contrary. I can't tell you how pleased I am to be the very first person to welcome your lovely niece to Philadelphia."

Before Rebecca realized what was happening, Roger Bakewood plucked up her hand and bowed low over it. When he straightened, he gazed deeply into her eyes. "Neither simple homespun nor impending motherhood can dim the beauty of this special lady."

Rebecca withdrew her hand and looked away from the pale gray eyes. Beneath heavy lids, Roger Bakewood's expression was—mocking? His full lips curved upwards in a half-smile that made her shiver. Yet she couldn't say he wasn't handsome; he stood as tall as Kin-di-wa, and the body beneath his fussy clothes was powerful and strong, though a trifle on the heavy side. He too wore his hair in a queue; it was chestnut-colored, almost wiry, with a curious life of its own.

"How sweet, Mister Bakewood!" Aunt Margaret exclaimed. "Our Rebecca is a pretty little thing, is she not? And when I am finished having Hardin's finest crepes and Indian silks made up into the new French fashions for her, she will doubtless draw the gentlemen like bees to honeysuckle. Don't you think so, Mister Bakewood?"

"Indeed." Roger's voice was husky and low. "But I shall be the first gentleman to request Hardin's permission to escort her about our fair city. You won't deny me, will you, old fellow? Your niece could hardly have a safer guide than I—a close friend of the family."

"And a Bakewood too—Philadelphia's most eligible bachelor!" crowed Aunt Margaret. A matchmaker's gleam came into her eye, and it did not escape Rebecca's notice—nor apparently Uncle Hardin's.

"Ah, quite, quite so, Roger! You would make the perfect escort for my niece." Uncle Hardin's expression became noticeably more pleasant as he surveyed first Roger then Rebecca in a thoughtful speculative manner.

Roger smiled and bowed, but Rebecca took a step backward. It was all going too fast, was suddenly too much. First, to be made an heiress. Then crepes, silks, escorts, and—possible marriage? She stepped further back and was dismayed to hear a crunch. Through her soft-soled moccasin, she could feel what she had done: further demolished a piece of china. "Aunt Margaret, I—I wonder if there's somewhere I might go and rest. You're all very kind, but I'm feeling a little dizzy at the moment. I think I'd like to lie down."

"How thoughtless of us, Rebecca dear! You do look pale—doesn't she, Hardin? . . . Prudy! Prudy! Oh, where is that girl? . . ." Aunt Margaret swished past Rebecca and started down the long hallway. "Prudy? Bess?"

Rebecca didn't know whether to stay or to follow.

Roger Bakewood took her arm. "Allow me to steady you, Mrs. . . . why, what shall I call you, my dear? What was your husband's name?"

Rebecca glanced up into his pale mocking eyes—then past him to where Uncle Hardin was toying with his hat and cane as if he didn't know what to do with them in the absence of his servants. It didn't seem like the proper moment to introduce another surprise. "You may simply call me Rebecca, Mister Bakewood. I have no wish to be reminded of sorrow every time my name is spoken."

"Then you must call me, Roger . . . for surely we'll become good friends." He bent over her hand again, this time lifting it to his full curved lips. His mouth, surprisingly warm and moist, pressed against her skin for an indecent space of time during which she struggled futilely to remove herself from his grip. When he straightened, he gave her another probing glance. She could only guess at its meaning—and shudder.

Aunt Margaret bustled back into the room, both Prudy and Bess in tow. "Ah, here we are, dear Rebecca. Bess, take the gentlemen's things, then clean up the broken china . . . Prudy, take my poor niece upstairs to the guestroom. It will be her room, now—unless, of course, she marries in the near future!"

"Yes'm," Prudy said.

*   *   *

The room to which Prudy led Rebecca was on the second floor and overlooked a small brick-enclosed garden behind the house. The room had a high ceiling, a blue-veined marble fireplace, and large four-poster canopied bed. A pewter chamber pot stood in one corner, and a pewter basin and water pitcher had also been provided.

As soon as Prudy left, Rebecca sat down on the bed and ran her hand over the soft, goose-tick quilt. She had never seen such luxury. Canopy, quilt, and curtains at the single window all matched the blue of the fireplace marble. Three of the walls were a pristine white; the fourth was covered with paper that was decorated with tiny blue flowers.

A table and two wooden chairs, not as fancy as those in the parlor but fancy enough, Rebecca thought, graced one wall. A door stood half-open along another wall, revealing a tiny empty room. Its purpose must be for storing clothes, she guessed, and wondered how many clothes one could possibly need to require an entire room for them.

The afternoon light was fading, and the room was almost dark. Rebecca lay down beneath the frilly blue canopy and pressed her fingers to her spinning head. So much had happened in so short a time! Could she really be lying on a bed in Aunt Margaret's house in the big city of Philadelphia?

She closed her eyes and thought about her Aunt and Uncle. Her sudden appearance had been a shock to them—but how shocking it had been to her to learn of her inheritance! She should have felt overjoyed, but instead, she felt uncomfortable, even afraid. Aunt Margaret had spoken of having new things made for her: fashionable gowns of crepe and Indian silk. And the gowns would require matching slippers and dainty shoes, soft lacy shawls and flowery bonnets. Perhaps, the finery would fill up that empty little room.

But am I ready for this? she asked herself. Ready for a life I know nothing about and challenges I haven't even thought of?

The image of Roger Bakewood came into her mind. She couldn't be mistaken: Aunt Margaret, Uncle Hardin, and Mister Bakewood himself had instantly thought of linking their futures—hers and his. Yet, he was a man she had only just met and one about whom she knew nothing!

Indeed, she knew nothing about her aunt and uncle either, except that Aunt Margaret cultivated a certain "feather-headedness" and claimed to be afflicted with fainting spells. But what could one make of Uncle Hardin? Was he as stern and forbidding as he seemed? What would he say when he learned the truth about her child?

Suddenly, she wished she had kept her soiled old doeskin. At least it had been familiar. It had spoken of home—the Ohio Country. How sad and strange! When she was there, she had thought of Pennsylvania as home, but now that she was here, she knew that her real home was Ohio. Was there no pleasing the human spirit?

Yes, she wished she had kept her old doeskin. It had been a link to a life she had loved, a time in which she had known great happiness. No matter that there had been hardships and sorrows! There had also been great joy. There had been laughter and kindness, generosity and cheerful sacrifice.

Most of all, there had been love, pouring over everything like pure golden sunlight. There had been passion too . . . rapture and ecstasy, colored like her moods, in every hue of the rainbow. Oh, how she missed that passion—the perfect blending of mind, spirit, and body! How she longed for the golden rapture of holding her husband in her arms, of feeling his body move against hers!

She sighed deeply as a great weariness stole over her. The softness of the goose-tick quilt was soothing. It was as if someone's arms enfolded her. Someone's hair brushed her face. She drifted . . . drifted. A familiar woodsy scent tickled her nostrils. Spring sunshine warmed her aching muscles. It was spring again, and this was Ohio—her true home, the place of her husband's people, the place of her husband.

"Let us make a child together," a masculine voice whispered into her ear. "Let us make a fine strong son or a gentle maiden, with her mother's green eyes and flame-red hair."

Rebecca turned toward the voice, her heart fluttering like a trapped bird. So long had it been since she'd heard that beloved voice! So long. She was sick with desire for the man who spoke to her. His voice was a caress on her skin. "Kin-di-wa— have you come back? Have you come to take me away with you?"

She saw his face: the strong stubborn jaw, the

sensitive mouth, the eyes as blue as heaven itself. Her fingers traced the white of his scars, the proud ridge of his nose, and came to rest on his lips. She drew him downward and pressed his naked chest to her breasts—but pain twisted in her bosom, sharp and new as the day she saw him struck down.

"Why do I still live when you are here no longer?" she asked sorrowfully.

"Ah, but I am here," he answered. "As long as you live, I live. I live within your memory, within your heart. You can summon me whenever you wish."

"But that's not enough, Kin-di-wa! Here—put your hand here." She drew his hand to her breast. "I want to feel your hands on my flesh. I want to taste your lips. I desire the sweet burning thrust of your manhood. I want to be your wife, Kin-di-wa!"

"Then come . . . let us make a child together."

"We have made a child already. If you were alive, you would know this."

"Ah, Cat-Eyes, Cat-Eyes . . . what foolishness is this you speak of? How can there be a child when it has been months since you've lain beside me and loved me? . . . You would not lay with someone else!"

She wrapped her arms and legs around him, remembering every curve and hollow of his body, every muscle—remembering how well they fit together, as if Manitou had known when he fashioned them that they would one day lie like this. "I would never willingly lay with another, my husband. Do you not remember that day in the windflowers? Our child was created then. I did not tell you because I did not know—until it was too late."

"For us, nothing can be too late, little one." His lips nuzzled her ear. "If our child already lives, then let us rejoice in his existence. Let him know and feel our love, even before he is born . . ."

"Yes, oh, yes, Kin-di-wa . . ."

Sensations that she had half-forgotten flowed over Rebecca in a rippling wave; her breasts blossomed beneath his kisses. Her loins grew warm and tingly. Her blood sang a sweet lusty song as it thundered through her veins. "Let me touch you, feel you, look at you," she panted. "Oh, Kin-di-wa! My husband, my only love . . ."

Kin-di-wa lifted himself above her. His eyes glowed a sparkling sun-lit blue. "You shall always have me, Cat-Eyes. No man shall ever take my place."

"No man . . . ever . . . I promise you, Kin-di-wa! Oh, take me, take me!"

In the exaltation of that moment, the sweet splendor of their joining, bells suddenly began to ring. Music flooded the room. The chimes started low and softly, then rose and swelled until each note was a crisp clear call—a call to banish sadness, to gladden the spirit and bring peace and gaiety.

But the sound ravaged Rebecca's heart. She bolted upright in the four poster bed, the image of Kin-di-wa abruptly banished. She had neither imagined nor dreamed the lovely fading music. It was six o'clock, the hour Mama had told her was always marked by the beautiful chime of bells from Christ Church.

How foolish she was! Disappointment flooded through her. For a single fleeting moment, she had thought the impossible had happened: Kin-di-wa had come for her. He had taken her away to a beautiful place where the wind always carried the distant sound of singing—and of bells, chiming out each golden hour.

"But it was only a dream . . . Oh, Kin-di-wa!" Rebecca bowed her head in her hands.

"Ma'am? Yo' awake now on account o' them bells?" White teeth and apron gleaming, Prudy stood in the darkened doorway. "Missus Margaret sent me up with a dress fo' yo' t' try on. I done let down th' hem an' I think it'll do jus' fine now—leastways, til yo' gits some new things."

"A dress? A dress for me?"

"Yes, ma'am. Yo' be wanted in th' dinin' room fer supper. Mister Bakewood is stayin' over an' Bess is puttin' out th' good china an' silver . . . here, let me git a candle lit, then I'll help yo' git dressed an' do up yoah hair."

When Prudy was finished, Rebecca scarcely knew herself. Her hair was caught up in a flowered comb and flowed in soft shining ringlets down her back. Her gown of gray Indian taffeta fit perfectly, though the style, Prudy informed her, was "jus' a littl' bit outa fashion."

A white gauze handkerchief, something called

a "fichu," was artfully tucked around her low bodice, and dainty slippers of soft gray kid adorned her feet. Prudy brought in a large looking-glass and propped it against the wall on the table. Reflected in it, by the light of two tall candles, Rebecca saw a stranger looking back at her—a stranger with a high, rosy color and eyes too green and large for her small sad face.

"Mah, but yo' sure are purty!" Prudy said admiringly.

Rebecca smoothed the shimmering material over her rounded stomach. "In this dress, I don't even look pregnant, do I? I look—like someone else."

"Oh, wait, 'til yo' tries on them new French fashions with their high waistlines. They'll be even mo' flatterin' than this 'ere ole thin'. Missus Margaret woah this three or foah years ago now, but she thought it might fit you 'cause it was allus a little too tight an' a little too long fur her."

"Is that why she doesn't wear it anymore—because it doesn't fit? It looks hardly worn at all."

"'Tain't th' fashion, I done tol' ya'. An' Missus Margaret is allus dressed in th' latest fashions. Here . . ." Prudy dropped a gray shawl with a blue silk fringe over Rebecca's shoulders. "This'll make it moah stylish."

The shawl fell to the floor on both sides. "It's very beautiful . . ." Rebecca murmured.

"Makes yo' look like a lady o' fashion now, Missus Rebecca."

"More like Margaret Hardin's niece?" Rebecca couldn't resist asking.

"Yes'm," Prudy grinned. "More like a heiress than a servin' wench."

They went down the curving staircase which was lit by the glow of shining glass lamps and candles protected from drafts by crystal shades. Rebecca was enchanted by the deep lustre of bronze and pewter, the soft sheen of silver. She walked as if in a dream. None of it seemed real: the rustle of taffeta, the delicate odor of mouth-watering foods, and the crackle of flames contained in marble fireplaces.

"Oh, my darling! You are simply *ravissante!* Isn't she, Mister Bakewood?" Resplendently dressed in a flowing yellow gown with a high waistline and a scandalously low-cut bodice, Aunt Margaret came toward her with out-stretched hands. "And when we finally dress you *à la mode Française,* you will be even more *ravissante!*"

"She is ravishing enough as she is," said Roger Bakewood. He lifted a goblet of crimson liquid in her direction.

Uncle Hardin grunted and lifted his own glass to his lips. He took a swallow and said petulantly, "Now, can we eat, dear wife? I confess to being half-starved."

"Of course . . . do come and sit down at table, Rebecca. We haven't much this evening—only *le boeuf* and *les pommes de terre,* but one night we shall have a true feast, one that would do proud the Empress Josephine herself!"

"I do wish you'd speak in English, Maggie!" Uncle Hardin groused. "Meat and potatoes is meat and potatoes, no matter what fancy name you call it!"

"Yes, Hardin dear, I'll try to remember . . ." Aunt Margaret showed Rebecca into the dining room where a very long table was covered with snowy white linen trimmed with lace. "Sit down here, my dear Rebecca. And Mister Bakewood, please sit across from her."

Rebecca was relieved to have the table, a bowl of ripe apples, and an array of glassware and blue-flowered china between her and Roger Bakewood. The man hadn't taken his heavy-lidded gaze from her since the moment she descended the staircase.

Aunt Margaret and Uncle Hardin took their places at opposite ends of the table, and Uncle Hardin moved aside a three-tiered candelabrum, the better to take stock of everyone. Aunt Margaret rang a tiny pewter bell, and Prudy swept in with the first course—not beef and potatoes, but cod's head with shrimp and oyster sauce.

Tomato pudding and artichokes seasoned with mace and cinnamon followed—then a hot sherried consomme. Prudy announced each dish before she served it, as if to do so might sharpen everyone's appetites. But by the time the beef and potatoes arrived, Rebecca could hardly eat another bite. She took a cautious sip of tart red wine and toyed with the pink, juicy meat on her plate.

Roger Bakewood leaned forward and broke the silence. "You do not care for Philadelphia

297

beef? It is said to be the finest in the world."

"Oh, it's very fine, I'm sure—but I'm not accustomed to eating so much at one sitting," Rebecca explained. "Besides, I over-ate at tea."

"Nonsense, my dear," Aunt Margaret scoffed. She chewed and swallowed a large bite of beef, then motioned with her knife. "You barely ate a thing! Why, how will you nourish your child if you don't partake of everything that is offered?"

"I'm certain my child will not go hungry this night!" Rebecca's hand dropped to her swollen abdomen, then slid away in embarrassment. She was amazed at such open discussion of her condition—something she had not expected before a stranger like Roger Bakewood, or her uncle either.

"And when shall the child be born?" Roger Bakewood asked.

"In February, I think—early to mid-February," Rebecca answered honestly.

"So soon then. Such a little time to get settled into your new life here. Tell me, my dear Rebecca, do you think you can adjust?"

Rebecca put down her fork. "Adjust? How do you mean?"

Roger drummed his fingertips impatiently on the tabletop. "Why, adjust to being an heiress, of course. And to living in civilization. I trust that your life in the Ohio Country was quite different from what can be found in Philadelphia."

Rebecca cast a sidelong glance at her uncle, but he was eagerly spearing a third helping of artichokes, and Aunt Margaret was spooning out more potatoes. "Yes, it was quite different, but since I was a little girl, I have dreamed of coming to live with Aunt Margaret. My mother went to great pains to teach me the social graces."

"Why, anyone can see that you are not lacking in social graces, dear girl! What I meant was—do you realize what it means to be an heiress?"

Rebecca studied the hooded gray eyes of the man across from her and wondered what he was thinking. "I suppose it means that my future is secure—that I and my child shall not suffer from want."

Roger Bakewood leaned back and wiped his hands carelessly on Aunt Margaret's lacy tablecloth. "It means that and more, Rebecca. It means that every money-hungry young blade in Philadelphia will be pursuing you. Have you given any thought to that possibility?"

"Given any thought to what, Mister Bakewood?" Aunt Margaret interrupted. She and Uncle Hardin were seated too far away for easy conversation. Roger repeated his statement more loudly—drawing Uncle Hardin's irate agreement.

"Damn right you are, Roger! Why, all the penniless schemers and nameless no-accounts in this town will be looking to sweep you off your feet, Niece! They won't care a hoot for your welfare—and even less for your child's! They'll only care for your inheritance: my four ships, my warehouse, my smaller investments, and of course, my summer house in the country!"

Rebecca was stunned. She had no idea Uncle Hardin was so rich. Mama had only mentioned a shop and two ships. Timidity and awe overwhelmed her. "But Uncle Hardin. I have no wish to marry again . . . so your—things shall be quite safe. Really, I have hardly recovered from the loss ōf my first husband. I've nothing to offer a second."

"Nothing to offer!" exclaimed Aunt Margaret. "Why, you have youth, beauty, a coming child, and now, you even have money. Tell her, Hardin! Tell her why you made her your heir! Because you, Rebecca, are our only living blood relative, yes, but also to gain us our rightful place in Philadelphia society!"

"Margaret." Uncle Hardin cleared his throat. "This is hardly the time and place for such a frank discussion."

"Now, Hardin, what better time is there—when a man who is ideally connected is sitting right at our table? . . . You see, dear Rebecca," Aunt Margaret began. "Your Uncle Hardin is a very successful merchant and businessman. But he has always lacked—certain refinements. Why, he came from a long line of lowly shoe-makers, and his mother's family were nothing more than . . ."

"That will be enough, Mrs. Stone!" Uncle Hardin's fist came down hard on the table. The goblets and silver jumped. "Our niece and Mister Bakewood can hardly be interested in the origins of my family! Besides, this is the land of opportunity and equality. We have no classes or titles here. America isn't England or France. We've done away with all that nonsense . . . Why, of what concern can it be to me if the Washingtons, the Biddles, the Cadwaladers, or the Thomas Jeffersons refuse to invite me to their endless round of parties and dinners? Why, look here—I've a Bakewood sitting at my table! That's good enough for me!"

"You're very kind, old man . . . but I'm a Bakewood without Bakewood money." Roger Bakewood said. "I have a name and no money. You have money and no name—but your dear wife has a point. You need only some further relationship—a well made marriage, for instance —to break into that inner circle. And of course, while it may be unfair to settle all your hopes on your lovely niece, she could be the key, you know. And she could make herself a fine future in the bargain."

"You see, Hardin? Dear Roger understands precisely! And I thought you did too—or have you forgotten why you agreed to make Rebecca your heir?" Aunt Margaret dimpled and gave her head a little shake. The yellow silk flowers danced on the nest of her frizzy brown hair. "Why, what's wrong, Rebecca dear?"

Rebecca felt unwell. The heavy meal, combined with dismay over what she'd just heard, was upsetting her stomach. "N—nothing, Aunt Margaret. I'll be fine in a moment." She took a hurried sip of water.

"Oh, my dear!" Aunt Margaret was immediately contrite. "Please do not think us lacking in feelings for you! It isn't that we are cruel or cunning—wishing to direct your future to our own ends. But your dear mama and I had always planned for you to come to Philadelphia and marry well. And you wanted to come! After your poor mama died, we thought if we made you an heiress your chances of making a good marriage would increase! And so would our chances of being more fully accepted among the first families of Philadelphia. Why, your Uncle Hardin was even planning to turn over the management of his smaller investments to whomever became your husband!"

"Really, Hardin, old boy . . . that is most generous of you." Roger Bakewood gulped a mouthful of wine, then lowered the goblet from his thick red lips. "Had I known that, I would have proposed to your niece at once this afternoon. Of course, the man who finally weds her will be getting a real beauty as well as a bargain."

Rebecca bowed her head and listened in disbelieving silence. They were talking about her as if she were a piece of goods, something to be bartered and sold to the highest bidder. No wonder Aunt Margaret hadn't wanted anyone to know about Kin-di-wa! It would be difficult enough to arrange a marriage for a pregnant niece—let alone a niece who'd been married to a savage!

Uncle Hardin pushed back from the table. "Let's go into my study and have a brandy, Roger . . . I never did like carrying on a conversation in front of women."

"But we haven't yet had the syllabub and apple tarts," Aunt Margaret cried. "You wouldn't want to miss the syllabub—Bess made it so well this evening."

"Damn the syllabub, Maggie! A man needs brandy, not curdled cream doused with sweetenings and cider!" Uncle Hardin stood up.

"She made it with wine, not cider, Hardin. Just the way you like it . . . but all right, if you insist." Aunt Margaret also stood up. "Rebecca and I will take our sherry and dessert in the front parlor, while you men retire to the study. Come, Rebecca."

Rebecca followed her aunt out of the dining room. She had no desire for sherry and syllabub. The baby kicked and moved, and suddenly, the clumsiness of her pregnancy dismayed her. Never had she felt so awkward and out of place! But at least, in the front parlor, she'd be free of Roger Bakewood's speculative scheming gaze.

Aunt Margaret sat down on the Hepplewhite, and Rebecca drew back another chair from the flickering fire in the black marble fireplace. More than a dozen candles bathed the room in a soft golden glow, but the room itself was stuffy and overly warm. She removed the gauze handkerchief from her bodice, revealing her creamy white cleavage.

"Oh, my dear, if you had done that in front of Roger Bakewood, he would have proposed to you on the spot. Your breasts are quite exquisite!" Aunt Margaret glanced down at her own plump bosom. "Mine, I'm afraid, have lost their shape. They hang down like pendulums now, except when my waist is tightly cinched." She indicated her waist, which appeared to begin right below her bosom, then began fussing with the lace at her neckline. "Did you know that the Empress Josephine sometimes allows her breasts to be fully exposed? 'Tis said to be all the French rage! But of course, here in America, only some have gone as far as that—those of us with bosoms like yours. Perhaps, you ought to try it!"

Rebecca purposefully tucked her handkerchief back into her bodice. "I have no desire to attract attention, Aunt Margaret, nor do I understand your great interest in everything French."

"Why, whom else are we to copy? Not the English, certainly! I detested English fashions all those years we were forced to wear them."

"Why not design your own fashions then? American Fashions. Made out of sturdy American cloth."

Prudy came in bearing a tray with two small glasses of sherry. Aunt Margaret took one, but Rebecca was feeling too rebellious and irritated to be any more polite than necessary. She shook her head no and Prudy departed.

Aunt Margaret sipped and made a face. "How dull sherry is! I'd much prefer a brandy—but of course, that wouldn't be considered proper for a lady. Ah, well . . ." She took another sip. "Interesting that you should mention adopting a distinctly American mode of dressing. I hear that President Washington feels the same way. He has even instructed Martha to wear nothing but homespun, linen, or cotton—fabrics produced right here in America."

Rebecca idly rubbed her shimmering taffeta.

"Doeskin. The President forgot doeskin, the softest, most comfortable, and most American material of them all."

"Doeskin?" Aunt Margaret downed her sherry in one quick gulp. She fanned herself with a plump white hand. "Isn't that something only savages wear?"

"I wore it, and it was lovely! As lovely as this gown I'm wearing now—and far more practical."

"Oh, my dear! Please don't say such things in front of your Uncle Hardin or Mister Bakewood—or anyone else, for that matter. Your past is best forgotten, you know. For the sake of your child, as well as your own sake."

Rebecca sighed. "Then please don't rush me into marriage, Aunt Margaret. I'm not ready to marry again. Perhaps, I never shall be."

Aunt Margaret fanned herself harder. "Never? But never is such a long time, dear. Doesn't your child deserve a father?"

A father, Rebecca thought. No man could be the father to her child that Kin-di-wa would have been. "My child will have a loving mother, and he will have you and Uncle Hardin and—he will have this inheritance you are all so concerned about."

"Oh, of course he will have all that, dear niece! But a man like Roger Bakewood—he could give your son or daughter so much more! A name. Prestige. Acceptance into society. Money counts for very little when one is snubbed wherever one goes."

"Do they really snub you?" Rebecca thought

of Indians and Negroes, and yes, even people of odd faiths, like the McGuires, for whom acceptance would always be a struggle. What could Aunt Margaret and Uncle Hardin possibly have in common with them?

"They take no notice of me," Aunt Margaret said mournfully. "They don't invite me to tea or to their dinner parties. They don't even speak to me or smile at me in church! And I'm as fashionably dressed as any of them! Lord knows, if we had had children, what slights they would have had to suffer—and what opportunities might have been denied them!"

Now Rebecca felt sorry for her aunt. The plump little woman in her flowery stylish gown now seemed suddenly pathetic. In her agitation, her breasts sagged noticeably, and a web of wrinkles marred her carefully made-up complexion. How could anyone be cruel to this little creature who tried so hard to be gay and charming? How could anyone dislike her?

Rebecca arose from her chair and crossed to her aunt's side. She bent down and hugged and kissed her. "Oh, Aunt Margaret. I can't promise you I'll marry Roger Bakewood tomorrow, but I will promise you I'll think about it—if indeed he asks me. I guess I'm being selfish, not thinking of what's best for you and for my child. I guess I'm still grieving for what I've lost, instead of appreciating what I've found."

Aunt Margaret enveloped her in a sherry and rose smelling embrace. Tears glistened in her bright blue eyes. "Oh, my dear Rebecca! You did love your savage, didn't you? Think of it, a love such as that—where a beautiful young woman would give up everything for the man she loves!"

"Yes, Aunt. I did love him—but at the time, I was giving up very little."

Aunt Margaret patted her hand. "Well then, perhaps it was meant by God to have happened like this. Your savage was taken away from you, but a golden future lies ahead."

"Yes, a golden future," Rebecca repeated, but she wondered, as Prudy brought in the syllabub, why she felt so cold and dead inside. For the moment, even her child was still and quiet. Does it matter what I feel anymore? Does it really matter what happens to me?

And the answer came winging clearly into her head: *All that matters now is what happens to my baby. My child is the only future Kin-di-wa that I will ever have. My child is all that counts . . . and for my child, I will do anything—even marry the devil himself.*

Twelve

Roger Bakewood lost no time in pursuing his advantage over other possible suitors. The very next morning, as Rebecca was trying to persuade Bess to allow her to help prepare the noon meal, Aunt Margaret summoned her from the kitchen. Roger Bakewood awaited her in the parlor. Wearing a light colored broadcloth coat with pearl buttons, and breeches of the same fabric as the coat, Roger looked handsome, stalwart, and authoritative.

"Dear Rebecca!" Aunt Margaret took Rebecca's hand and drew her forward. "Mister Bakewood has come to take you for a ride about the city in his post chaise!"

"My cousin's post chaise, dear Mrs. Stone. He has kindly lent it to me for the occasion." Roger made a slight mocking bow. "I could only have provided a buggy—but a buggy is hardly worthy of the beauty of your niece."

Aunt Margaret smiled and patted his arm. "Oh, but you will have your own post chaise one of these days soon, Mister Bakewood. I feel certain you will!"

"A buggy would have been fine," Rebecca murmured. "I rode into the city on a dray wagon."

"A dray wagon! Mercy me," Aunt Margaret exclaimed. "It's a wonder you didn't arrive here black and blue from such discomfort. Oh, you will so appreciate the smooth ride of a post chaise!"

"But, Aunt Margaret, perhaps the ride should wait until another day—didn't you say we were going to Uncle Hardin's shop to select fabrics for my new wardrobe this morning?"

"Why, yes, I did!" Aunt Margaret recalled. "Well, we can always do that this afternoon or tomorrow. I shouldn't want you to miss this wonderful opportunity—to see Philadelphia, I mean, of course."

But Rebecca knew exactly what her aunt meant: this was an opportunity for her and Roger Bakewood to become better acquainted—possibly even engaged, if Aunt Margaret had her way. Rebecca sighed and graciously gave in. "I suppose I would much enjoy seeing Philadelphia —if you think I am dressed well enough."

Roger Bakewood bowed low. "You will outshine every lady we pass in the street," he assured her.

"You must take one of my capes, dear child," Aunt Margaret insisted. "It's rather nippy this morning. And a cape will cover up that old blue day dress I lent you. Of course, the fabric of the dress is very good, but the style is hopelessly out of fashion."

Prudy materialized out of nowhere with a cape of fine deep-blue camlet and a small bonnet of chequered straw, causing Rebecca to wonder if everyone but herself had known that Roger intended to call on her that morning. "Missus Margaret," Prudy interrupted. "Yo' wants ah should go along with 'em—to pertec' Missus Rebecca's rep'tation?"

"Oh, I'm sure that won't be necessary, Prudy! Mister Bakewood is most trustworthy, and my niece is no longer of an age to require a chaperone. Besides, chaperones have gone out of style too, have they not?"

Prudy shook her head and rolled her eyes disapprovingly as she helped Rebecca into the cape. Rebecca wished the girl would go along, but perhaps Aunt Margaret had other tasks for her to accomplish. She tied the bonnet under her chin and wondered how she looked; she certainly felt like a wealthy lady, wearing so many fine things.

"There now, I guess I'm ready."

"Do enjoy yourselves!" Aunt Margaret bubbled. "You've got a perfect day for sightseeing—brisk but sunny."

Roger took Rebecca's arm and led her out to the carriage. It was an enclosed, three seater affair, drawn by a well-groomed horse whose coat was the exact same color as Roger's. The driver jumped down from his seat atop the vehicle and opened the door for them. Roger helped her step inside and sit down on the plush black leather, then he got in and sat beside her.

A moment later, they were proceeding briskly down the street. Roger smiled and patted her knee. "I thought today we would merely ride past the major points of interest in our fair city. Some other time, we can explore each one individually."

To discourage his bold familiarity, Rebecca made her voice sound icy. "That sounds very nice, Mister Bakewood. But how can you spare the time? Surely, you have better things to do than escort a pregnant woman around Philadelphia."

Roger reached for her hand and enclosed it between his two large ones—which were surprisingly soft and white. "I thought we had agreed you were to call me Roger—as I am to call you by your first name."

Rebecca bristled. The man was really too sure of himself, too over-confident, but then Aunt Margaret and Uncle Hardin had given him reason to behave that way. "All right, Roger . . ." she said coolly. "Tell me. How do you spend your time?"

Roger chuckled a shade too heartily and squeezed her hand. "The way any gentleman does—the way your uncle does, in fact. I look after my investments, such few as I am fortunate enough to have. This requires that I pass a great deal of time at William Bradford's London Coffee House, which we shall soon pass at the corner of High Street and Second. There, I read the newspapers, trade and barter, gossip with other gentlemen and merchants, and attempt to discover what is happening in the marketplace. I am also on the board for the new university, and in that position, I . . ."

As Roger Bakewood talked, Rebecca studied his face. It wasn't plump exactly, but his cheeks, chin, and neck were thick and gave the impression of both power and indolence. His eyes, the most prominent feature of which were heavy lids, were cold and guarded—the color of gray slate. His lips were too full for a man's and rather dissipated, as if he lacked good character. She would not like to be kissed by those lips.

"So that is what I do with my time, dear Rebecca," Roger finished, and she realized she hadn't heard the last part of what he'd just said.

"Um—then how is it you're a Bakewood with no money, as you said last night? Have your investments not been good ones?"

"My, but you are direct," said Roger Bakewood. "I admire that in a woman."

But judging from the quiver of his full lips, Rebecca suspected that he did not admire it at all. He looked out the window and said, "Ah, there is Christ Church."

Rebecca seized the moment to withdraw her hand from his. "So it is! My mother used to worship there. I knew it the moment I first saw it—yesterday, on my way into the city."

"Well then. Christ Church. So you've already seen it."

"Not inside, of course," Rebecca admitted.

"But let's use this time to get better acquainted, Roger. Isn't that why you asked me to come for this ride?"

Roger looked surprised and displeased. "You know," he said. "You aren't quite the country bumpkin you pretend to be, are you?"

For the first time since she'd met him, Rebecca smiled. "Is that what you were hoping I'd be—an innocent country lass who could easily be swept off her feet? Come now, Roger . . ." She attempted to sound faintly amused and sophisticated. "I saw how interested you became when you learned not only of my inheritance, but also of the investments Uncle Hardin is willing to turn over to whomever I might marry."

The full lips compressed into an angry line. The nostrils flared. Then suddenly, Roger Bakewood smiled. "All right, Rebecca . . . I shall tell you my sad little story. I shall also admit that I am interested in your inheritance *and* in your uncle's investments. I can see there's no point in trying to deceive you. Indeed, if we are totally honest with each other, we might strike a bargain much sooner than I had dared anticipate—a bargain that would benefit us both."

"A bargain?" Rebecca had been enjoying her ability to puncture this man's self-conceit, but now she felt less sure of herself. "What do you mean—a bargain?"

"My story first, dear lady." Roger recaptured her hand and told his story, interrupted now and then by the need to point out some Philadelphia landmark they were either passing or approaching: the Second Street Marketplace, the Free Quaker Meeting House, St. Peter's Protestant Episcopal Church, and the country area called the "Northern Liberties," where Peggy Shippen used to go riding before she met and married the traitor, Benedict Arnold.

Rebecca was completely fascinated, both by Roger's story and by his intimate, gossipy knowledge of the city and its inhabitants. She even forgot he was holding her hand. Gradually, her sympathies stirred. Roger Bakewood, a descendant of an aristocratic English family, had suffered greatly because of his father, an ardent Tory.

During the Revolutionary War, his father had thrown the weight of his share of the family fortune toward the British, while his brothers and his own father, Roger's grandfather, openly supported the colonists. Of course, after the war was over, the rest of the family surged to power, and Roger's father paid heavily for his misplaced loyalties. Before his death, five years previously, he had lived as a social outcast and had even planned to return to England—as soon as he could raise the money.

"It was quite pitiful," Roger concluded. "My father died an embittered man, and shortly thereafter, my long-suffering mother followed him to the grave. I was left alone, with no money and no prospects—with little, in fact, but my father's debts: large sums of money which will take years for me to pay back."

"But surely, your uncles must realize that you

are not to blame for your father's errors! Why couldn't they step in and help you!"

"Ah, sweet Rebecca," Roger raised her hand to his lips. "How incredibly naive you are! This may be the city of Brotherly Love, as some do call it, but it is actually quite a closed society. There are the rich, the intellectuals, the politicians—the new aristocracy—on one side, and there is everyone else on the other. Of course, no one actually admits it, but old loyalties and family ties die hard."

"But—but I thought from what Aunt Margaret said, that you are accepted into Philadelphia society."

"Well . . ." Roger glanced out the window.

They were riding through the Northern Liberties now, and Rebecca caught sight of a row of trees: red, yellow, and gold against a bright blue sky.

"Well, what?" she questioned.

"Well, I am accepted by my cousins, and even my uncles are softening toward me. They respect what I have accomplished thus far on my own, and have even hinted that they might come to my aid at last. But first, I must make some improvements—reform my social life, as they delicately put it."

"Reform your social life? What does that mean?"

"They want me to settle down," Roger said. "To become a family man. To stop chasing skirts, if I may be so bold to state it plainly."

Rebecca wrenched her hand from his. "Do—

316

do Aunt Margaret and Uncle Hardin know of your—loose ways?"

Roger's thick lips turned upwards. "Of course not, dear lady. I am very careful to be discreet in my vices. Truly, I harm no one—it is only that I have never yet met a lady with whom I wish to share my life and my fortune, such as it is—until this moment."

Rebecca recoiled into the far corner of the carriage. "At—at least, you are honest, Mister Bakewood!"

Roger moved over on the seat and boldly pressed his thigh against hers. "I shall always be honest with you, lovely lady. You see, I have nothing to lose—and everything to gain. If we were to marry, I would gain the wife and family my proper relatives wish for me to have, and which by having, might open their pocketbooks and provide a whole new range of business opportunities for me. I would also gain some valuable investments to add to my little empire . . ."

"Y-yes, I can see that," Rebecca stammered. "But what would I gain?"

Roger's hand again came down on her knee. "Why, a husband, of course. And the undying gratitude of your aunt and uncle for all I would then be able to do for them. They would be included in all the gatherings of my prestigious family—which would quickly result in other invitations to the gatherings of all the prestigious families in Philadelphia."

But what of love? Rebecca wanted to ask, but

she was distracted by the pressure of his hand on her knee. Before she could remove the offending member, his other hand came down on top of hers, and he smiled a slow, insolent, provocative smile. "Of course . . . there is one other thing I forgot to mention, dear lady. You would also gain a father for your bastard child."

"What? What did you say?" Rebecca gasped. This time, she succeeded in wrenching both hands and knee away from him. "My child is *not* a bastard! How dare you say such a terrible thing?" Roger's look of cynical amusement and triumph made her even angrier. "If you truly think my child is a bastard, you may take me home at once, Mister Bakewood—and I shall tell my aunt everything you just told me!"

Roger Bakewood leaned toward her. "Now, now, my dear—do calm yourself. Do you know how exquisite your beauty truly is? Why, your coloring is magnificent—especially now, when you are upset and angry. Your eyes, I vow, are fiery emeralds. When we marry, I shall somehow contrive to purchase emerald earrings and a necklace for you to wear to all the elegant dinner parties and balls we shall be attending."

"Mister Bakewood! *My child is not a bastard!* There's no need for me to marry just to spare him shame!"

Unruffled by her outburst, Roger sat back in the gently swaying carriage. A shaft of sunlight coming through the window lit his chestnut hair, but cast his face in dark shadow, making him look almost evil. "Then, why, pray tell, do you refuse to speak his father's name? Why did your aunt say you'd had such a terrible time of it? Last evening was the perfect opportunity to discuss your background, your experiences, and how and why you suddenly turned up on the doorstep of your only relatives. Yet not a single word was mentioned. Why, pray tell, is that?"

Rebecca felt trapped. If she still refused to speak, Roger could only conclude the obvious: that her child was indeed a bastard. He might even mention this possibility to her uncle or to others—causing no end of damage. But could she trust him with her secret? With all this talk of marriage, now was the time to find out!

With as much dignity as she could muster, she faced him levelly. "No, Mister Bakewood— Roger, my child is not a bastard. But he is something of which you may not approve. His father—my husband—was half white and half Miami Indian."

A single tear slid down her left cheek, then another down her right. Angrily, Rebecca wiped them away. "So my child will be a 'breed,' a 'savage,' people will call him. They will probably snicker and laugh at him behind their hands! They will discuss his shortcoming in their proper voices! . . . Really, I don't know why I didn't go back to my husband's people after his death, instead of coming east. There, among the Miamis, my child would be accepted and loved, not mocked and scorned."

Roger removed a lace-trimmed handkerchief from his breast pocket and ceremoniously handed it to her. "Among the savages, your child would live as a savage. He would never know anything but savage ways—and would probably die like a savage too, the way your husband no doubt died. No, my dear, you made the right choice in returning to civilization. And you are very wise not to speak of your child's father."

Rebecca dabbed at her eyes and blew her nose. "It wasn't my idea, but Aunt Margaret's. She would like to keep it secret forever, but I was only waiting for the right moment to say something. Aunt Margaret is afraid of what Uncle Hardin—and you too—will think."

Roger stroked his chin. "Well, of course, I can't say for certain, but I doubt that your uncle will be pleased. Gossip can hurt a man's business, you know—especially a man who's struggling so hard to be accepted."

Rebecca lowered the handkerchief. "But you—what do you think?" she asked, and it seemed to her at that moment, that something very weighty was hanging on his answer.

Roger studied her a moment, his hooded eyes inscrutable. Then he took both her hands in his and drew her closer to him in the carriage. "I think you are a very courageous and beautiful woman who needs the immediate protection and care of a strong man—one who will look after you and your child and behave as if the child were his own." His grip on her hands tightened. "I am the man you need, Rebecca. No scandal could long distress you—or your aunt and uncle—if you became my wife. I shall not allow a single word to be spoken against any of you."

The alien odor of scented soap, bay rum, and Roger's masculine presence tingled in Rebecca's nostrils. Confused and frightened by his nearness, by his overwhelming self-confidence, she tried futilely to pull away. "But I—I can always keep the truth a secret—forever!"

"Were you able to keep it secret from me?" Roger's arm slid around her waist. "Eventually, your uncle must be told. He may be quite shocked and irate, but in that regard I can help. I feel certain he will not disinherit you if the truth comes from me rather than from you—especially when I tell him that we are soon to be married."

Roger's lips were now level with hers—those thick disgusting lips! Half-mesmerized, Rebecca forced herself to look away from them. "Roger, you are going too fast! I only came to Philadelphia yester—"

He made a sudden movement, and she was caught in a crushing embrace. His lips invaded her mouth in a brutal, passionate onslaught. She gasped and struggled. His hand searched beneath her cape and found her breast. Relentlessly, it kneaded and squeezed until, with a shudder of revulsion, she managed to shove him away. "Roger! Stop it! Stop it this instant!" Her stomach heaved with nausea. Shaking, she turned toward the window. "Dear God! I've only just met you—I thought you were a gentleman—I—I . . ."

A hot flush crept up her cheeks. Whatever was wrong with her? Everytime she turned around, some man started pawing her. Will, Jake, and now Roger actually acted as if they'd been invited to rape her!

Roger's ragged breathing filled the carriage for a moment, then stilled. "Rebecca . . ." he said reasonably. "Rebecca dear, please forgive me."

"Forgive you?" The image of Kin-di-wa came into her head, and guilt sliced through her like a skinning knife. Somehow, even now when he was dead, she was still betraying him—at least, she felt as if she were betraying him.

"Yes, forgive me. I was quite overcome by your beauty. You are a stunning woman, you know. I have never met anyone more desirable."

"Roger, I am not desirable. I am pregnant."

His hand brushed the ribbons on the side of her bonnet. "My dear, you are a pagan goddess . . . you must not blame me for being unable to keep my hands off you."

"But if you do not . . . I promise you, I shall never marry you!"

"Ah, well, then," Roger sighed. "Perhaps, it is just as well I must go away for several weeks. A mill I am building in Lancaster requires my attention."

Rebecca glanced back at him. "Is there really a mill—or have you changed your mind about marrying me, after all? Did you ever intend to marry me? Or did you only intend to tumble me in the back of your cousin's post chaise at the very first opportunity?"

Roger exploded in a mirthless shout of laughter. "There is really a mill, my dear! And I haven't changed my mind about marrying you. But you do need time to have your wardrobe made, and to think on all we've discussed today. After I return to Philadelphia, I want you to be ready."

"Ready? Ready for what?"

"To be escorted to dinner parties and teas, of course! To meet my prestigious family. And most importantly, to become Mrs. Roger Bakewood. If the baby is due in February, we should certainly marry in January—or even sooner, if it can be arranged."

Rebecca's temples began to throb. Her muscles ached with tension, and she realized she was trembling. "Please don't speak of marriage anymore today, Roger. Perhaps, it is good that you are going away; I do need time to think."

Roger bent down and nuzzled her cheek. "You shall have three weeks, my darling."

"Please don't call me darling."

"Ah, but darling—you must get used to it . . . And now, shall we take a ride past Independence Hall—maybe even stop and see the Liberty Bell?"

Roger was gone, not three weeks, but six. Aunt Margaret's household was in an uproar getting ready for Thanksgiving, when Rebecca received a message that Roger would call on her that very afternoon—the eve of the much celebrated holiday. Surprisingly, the message came from Henry-Luke, Aunt Margaret's gardener, stable-hand, and general all-round handyman.

Henry-Luke came up to Rebecca in the wind-swept courtyard, where she had gone to escape the heat and confinement of the house—as well as Aunt Margaret's fainting spells, which were beginning to get on her nerves. A tall scarecrow of a man, he bowed and cleared his throat. His Adam's apple bobbed. "Missus Rebecca. Mister Bakewood wants I should tell ya' that he'll be callin' on ya' this afternoon."

Rebecca smoothed down the folds of her new green cape. "How do you know he is back in the city, Henry-Luke? I've had no word from him since he left—and neither have Uncle Hardin or Aunt Margaret."

Henry-Luke shifted his feet, and it occurred to Rebecca that she really didn't like this man, didn't trust him. There was something sly about his eyes. She'd never seen him smile. Unlike Prudy and Bess, who were noisy and somewhat bossy but whom she was coming to like very much, Henry-Luke moved about the house and courtyard like some thin, hungry cat—watching, always watching as if he intended to steal something. Or as if he had something to hide.

"Seed him a few minutes ago on th' street when I wuz comin' back from tendin' the carriage horses. Mister Stone's stable is three blocks away

324

from 'ere, y' know."

"Yes, I know it is . . ." Rebecca said. By now, there was little about Uncle Hardin's properties she didn't know. In between endless hours at the dressmaker's, she had made it her business to try and learn something about the life in which she now found herself. "I'm just surprised Mister Bakewood would stop and speak to you instead of sending a messenger directly to me or Aunt Margaret."

"Well, the truth is . . ." Henry-Luke shifted his feet. "Mister Bakewood and me is old friends. He wuz th' one whut done got me this job—he recommended me t' Mister Stone."

"Oh, I see. How kind of him." Rebecca toyed with her new fur muff which hung from a strap on her wrist. For some reason, she didn't quite like the fact that Roger and Henry-Luke were so friendly. A servant should not have divided loyalties, she thought, then wondered why she suspected that Henry-Luke was disloyal to his employer. Certainly, she'd never heard Aunt Margaret or Uncle Hardin complain about him.

"You want I should take any message back t' Mister Bakewood?" Henry-Luke asked eagerly— too eagerly, Rebecca thought.

"No, that won't be necessary. I'm sure you have plenty to do to get ready for Thanksgiving. Bess and Prudy have been working since sunup."

"Suit yourself, ma'am. I wuz jus' tryin' t' be helpful." Henry-Luke crossed the courtyard and let himself out at the back gate. Rebecca wondered where he was going. As tall and thin as he was, he gave the impression of skulking—of appearing and disappearing out of nowhere.

Despite her warm cape, Rebecca shivered. Her long-sleeved stylish dress was only light muslin, and the day was raw, gray, and windy. Dry leaves skittled along the flagstones. She decided to go back inside and see how she might help with Thanksgiving preparations. It seemed so ridiculous that she had nothing to do today when there was obviously so much to be done. If only Aunt Margaret, Prudy, and Bess didn't have such ingrained ideas about the proper occupations for a "lady"—especially a pregnant one.

No working in the kitchen, no cleaning or laundering—and no toting firewood. Rebecca reflected that if she wasn't so busy with her new clothes and surroundings, she would be quite bored. She had even begun to look forward to Roger Bakewood's return with its promised round of parties and balls—if indeed he still intended to pursue his courtship of her. It was a prospect that was daily becoming more attractive as boredom loomed ever closer.

Taking her time and breathing deeply, Rebecca walked slowly toward the house. Along the Miami of the Lake, the trees would all be naked now, she remembered, but the women would still be gathering the last nuts and roots of the season. They would be banking the fallen leaves against their lodges to shut out cold and snow. They would be gathering as much firewood as possible.

How different life was there! Among the Miamis, her life had meaning and purpose; her tasks were necessary. Here, all her time was spent on frivolities: shopping for just the right bonnet or gloves, experimenting with new hairstyles, and endlessly fussing over insignificant details of her adornment. She had no purpose whatsoever. No one really needed her, no one depended upon her, she had no true responsibilities. But of course, the baby would change all that.

Beneath her cape, she patted the firm round curve of her abdomen. The baby kicked in response, and she was suddenly impatient with being pregnant. She wanted the baby now—wanted to hold it, to love it, to rock it to sleep. Her arms ached to embrace her child. Would it look like her—or like Kin-di-wa?

She stopped walking and closed her eyes, and Kin-di-wa's image leapt into her mind. For a moment, he was actually there before her in the courtyard. Flashing his knowing smile, he stood so straight and proud. She wanted to rush into his arms and once again feel his familiar warm embrace, smell his clean woodsy scent, and press herself along the lean hard length of him. She grew dizzy and opened her eyes.

I must stop doing this! she berated herself. I must stop imagining that he is still alive.

But she wondered if she would ever succeed. Over and over during the past weeks, she had experimented with forgetting Kin-di-wa. She had tried to go a whole day without once thinking of

327

him with longing. Now, she tried again to put him out of her mind—to think instead about Roger.

Kin-di-wa was in the past; Roger was the future. And Roger was an attractive man, or so Aunt Margaret kept telling her. More importantly, he would accept her child as if it were his own. Roger would keep both her and the child safe and free from want. Her baby would never go hungry, as Walks-Tall had done. And Roger would introduce her to a whole new way of life—a life of gaiety and laughter. No more would she ever have to worry about hunger, disease, or starvation.

A sudden strange sound from behind made her turn around. Henry-Luke's voice came loud and angry. "G'wan! Git outa 'ere, ya' stupid stray!"

The sound came again, a low whine of fear and suffering. Then Rebecca saw a small shadow of a dog dart through the back gate and skitter behind some evergreen bushes. Brandishing a three-tined pitchfork, Henry-Luke came through the gate after it. "Where'd he go, Miz Rebecca? Where is th' little bastard? I'll git 'im this time fer sure."

Involuntarily, Rebecca's glance went to the evergreens, and Henry-Luke began to prod among them. "Come on out! Come on! Ya' cain't git away from me! Yur time has come, dawg!"

Rebecca was spurred into action. She crossed the courtyard hurriedly and reached Henry-Luke just as the dog tried to make a run for it. Henry-Luke lunged with the pitch fork, but Rebecca grabbed his arm just in time. "Don't, Henry-

Luke! Let the poor thing go!"

The dog dashed to another concealing clump of shrubbery, and Rebecca noticed that it was running on three legs. The fourth leg—the left front paw—appeared to be injured, and the animal itself was so thin as to be almost a skeleton.

"Missus Stone don't want no stray in her garden," said Henry-Luke. "I chased 'im away from 'ere b'fore, an' this time I'm gonna finish off th' little bastard!"

Henry-Luke's eyes gleamed with menace—an expression that Rebecca recognized instantly as the killer instinct. He easily shrugged her hand from his arm and went after the dog again. "Henry-Luke!" she shouted. "Leave this courtyard immediately, or I shall complain to Mister Stone!"

Henry-Luke looked back at her—disbelief etched on his sallow features. "Complain to Mister Stone of what, ma'am? I'm jus' doin' mah duty."

"Leave the poor creature alone! Can't you see that it's hurt and probably starving?"

"It don't belong in 'ere. I'd be doin' it a favor t' kill it."

"You'd be doing me a favor if you'd leave the animal alone. I demand that you leave it alone, and I will take full responsibility for whatever happens."

Henry-Luke glared at her a moment, then tossed his pitchfork on the walkway, where it fell with a clang and a clatter. "Y'all be lucky he don't bite ya' an' give ya' some horrible disease. Mister and Missus Stone won't like ya' fussin' with it—an' neither will Mister Bakewood."

"That's my affair, Henry-Luke—not yours. Now, please go back to whatever you were doing. I will see to the dog."

But Henry-Luke stood defiantly, glancing from her to the place where the dog was hidden. Rebecca brushed past him and, with some effort because of her pregnancy, got down on her knees on the flagstones and called softly. "Here, boy . . . here, boy! It's all right now, you can come out."

"Gawd almighty!" Henry-Luke swore, but Rebecca paid no heed to him.

She snapped her fingers and patted the stones. "Come on now, boy—no one's going to hurt you."

The shrubbery shook and a small white muzzle appeared, then quickly withdrew again. "Henry-Luke, will you please leave us alone now? He won't come out while you're still here."

"Son of a bitch," Henry-Luke growled. "I don't like takin' orders from no woman who come 'ere dressed like a servin' wench."

"Henry-Luke!" Rebecca did not take her eyes from the shrubbery. "You will take orders from Mister Stone's niece, or I will make certain that you are dismissed!"

"Yes, ma'am." Henry-Luke's footsteps echoed angrily down the flagstones toward the back gate. The gate creaked once, then was silent, and

330

Rebecca was left alone with the dog.

"Come on, boy . . . he's gone. He can't hurt you now. Come out, and I'll look at your leg and find something for you to eat. Poor starving little dog . . . I know what it is to be hungry."

The shrubbery shook again, and this time, the little white muzzle was followed by the rest of the dog—a pure white dog, or a dog that would be white as soon as the dirt, grime, and blood was washed away from it. Whimpering softly, the dog came to her, and Rebecca saw that it was covered with nicks and cuts, as if it had been in a fight. Its lame forepaw trembled. Indeed, its whole body was trembling.

"Poor thing," Rebecca crooned. "Your ribs are poking right through your hide." She reached out to pick up the dog, but it shrank in terror. Rebecca ignored her cramping leg and back muscles and stroked it gently for several minutes. Warm brown eyes glanced gratefully up at her. A warm dry nose nudged her hand. "Poor creature, I believe you've got a fever."

At last, the dog allowed Rebecca to pick it up and carry it into the house, where Bess quickly overcame her shock and heated some broth to feed it, all the while shaking her head, "Oh, Lawd . . . as if I ain't gots enuff t' do th' day b'fore Thanksgivin'. Now, I gots t' nursemaid a half-daid dawg!"

"No," Rebecca said firmly. "I will nursemaid the dog."

And that was how Roger Bakewood found her

later that afternoon—playing nursemaid to a small white dog that she had decided to christen "Snowflake."

"My dear," Roger protested. "Aren't you afraid of disease? Of contaminating your child?"

Rebecca sat in the front parlor with the sleeping dog—bathed, bandaged, and brushed down with straw—in her arms. She was rubbing the tiny spot between its two perky ears, and every time she stopped, the dog awoke and licked her hand pleadingly. "Snowflake is not diseased," she explained with some impatience. "He's merely been mistreated."

"He is a sweet little thing," said Aunt Margaret. "Tiniest, skinniest little dog I ever did see!"

"If you ask me . . ." Roger turned his back to the two women and looked out the front window. "It's a disgrace that you would take such chances! Of course, you weren't here in Philadelphia in 1793 during the terrible outbreak of Yellow Fever, but I shouldn't be surprised to one day learn that the disaster was caused by the number of strays we had running about our fair city!"

Aunt Margaret clapped her hands to her bosom. "Oh, do you really think the fever was caused by stray dogs? Dr. Rush—*Benjamin* Rush, Rebecca dear—said it was caused by coffee that had spoiled down on the wharves."

"Perhaps, it was caused by all the filth and garbage in the gutters," Rebecca suggested. "I wonder sometimes how you Philadelphians can stand it." She wrinkled her nose against the odor of refuse that had wafted in when Roger was admitted to the house. Even the cold weather seemed to have little effect on obliterating the noxious smell.

"But it's much cleaner now than it used to be! Isn't it, Mister Bakewood?" Aunt Margaret asked.

Roger turned back from the window, a scowl upon his face. "If your niece thinks our city is so dirty, dear Mrs. Stone, she can always return to her precious savages."

"Oh, dear me!" Aunt Margaret gasped. "How—how did you know Rebecca had lived among the savages?"

"Because she told me so, didn't you, Rebecca?"

Rebecca refused to show surprise at Roger's lack of manners. He was angry with her, she guessed, but wasn't certain why. Was it because she hadn't leapt to her feet and embraced him when he entered? But he had, after all, kept her waiting for his return for six weeks instead of three—and hadn't even bothered to apologize. "I told you that my husband was half-Miami by blood, Roger. I didn't tell you where I had been living—but yes, I was living among the Miamis."

Aunt Margaret looked much distressed, and suddenly, Rebecca was angry with Roger for upsetting her. Gently, she held up the sleeping dog. "Aunt Margaret, would you take Snowflake out to his box in the kitchen? Mr. Bakewood and I need a few moments alone with each other."

"*Me,* dear?" Aunt Margaret eyed the dog

warily. "He won't bite, will he?"

"Of course not—but he does like to have his head scratched. And be gentle with his sore leg."

"Oh, my! Maybe I should call Prudy! I've never done anything like this before!" Aunt Margaret came to Rebecca and gingerly took the dog in her plump white arms. "Why, he hardly weighs as much as a human baby! I had an opportunity to hold one last summer, and oh, it was the sweetest thing! A little girl named Susannah . . . of course, I expect I shall have to get used to holding babies now, so I might as well begin with a little dog! Am I doing it right, Rebecca dear?"

Rebecca couldn't help grinning. "You're doing it perfectly, Aunt Margaret."

Aunt Margaret glanced back and forth between Rebecca and Roger as if uncertain whether to leave them alone together in view of recent developments. "I won't allow anyone to bother the two of you—unless of course, Mister Stone comes home. He's due home shortly, you know . . ."

"Don't worry," Rebecca said. "We'll be finished with our conversation long before Uncle Hardin arrives."

When Aunt Margaret had departed the room and gone down the hallway with Snowflake, Rebecca arose from her chair. "Why did you say that, Roger? Why did you let her know you knew about my baby's father?"

Roger remained standing in front of the window, his large body blocking the light. "You haven't told her then, I take it. Or your Uncle

Hardin either."

"Told them what?"

"Told them that I'm willing to marry you immediately—regardless of who your child's father was."

"I've been trying to decide whether I'm willing to marry you!" Rebecca snapped. She was newly amazed at Roger's haughty self-confidence. "You don't write to me, you send no messages, you come three weeks later than you said you would, and still, you seem to expect a warm welcome."

Hands behind his back, Roger rocked back and forth on his heels. He was impeccably dressed as usual—his ruffled shirt a snowy white, his coat bright blue, and his breeches a matching darker blue. "I was hoping for something other than total preoccupation with a mangy little dog."

"And I was hoping for an apology—or at least, an explanation." Rebecca turned her back on Roger and crossed to the elegant black marble fireplace. She ran her finger down a shiny silver candelabrum which stood on the mantelpiece. In the silver, she could see her flushed angry face. "Do you have an explanation?"

Roger's footsteps sounded behind her, and then his hands came down on her shoulders. "Lovely Rebecca . . . of course, I do. And I have an apology too." He turned her around to face him. "Forgive me for being gone so long—but the work on the mill must be completed before the first snow. Indeed, I must go back right after Thanksgiving."

"But, you said we would be attending parties

and balls. And I would be invited to meet your family."

"It's your welfare I'm thinking about, my darling. The mill will begin earning a tidy profit just as soon as it goes into operation. Why, the farmers must store their grain until it's finished—unless they want to haul it miles away over bad rutted roads . . . You see, my dearest Rebecca, when we marry, I want you to have the best of everything . . ."

"And will it soon be finished?" Rebecca hated to sound shrewish, but she wondered how they would ever have time to get to know each other better, if Roger was gone so much. If indeed, they did marry, she'd be marrying a stranger.

"Ah, well . . ." Roger's pale eyes darkened. "That is difficult to say—for you see, I've run out of money."

"Why—how could that happen? And how can you possibly hope to finish the mill then?"

Roger's fingers pressed into her shoulders. "It's nothing terribly serious, my dear—only that one of my other investments has suffered a reversal. Time will set it right, of course, but I am temporarily short of capital. Yet, the mill must be finished before winter sets in. I can't afford to wait until spring!"

Rebecca shrugged away from Roger's touch. "So what will you do—ask Uncle Hardin for help?"

Roger pursed his full lips then smiled. "Do you think he will give it to me? I wouldn't want him to think I was marrying you for your inheritance—though I should be able to secure a bank loan against it, once our banns are announced."

Rebecca felt a shudder of dislike. Roger was much too direct and calculating. Yet, she could hardly blame him for wanting the mill to be successful since it would mean so much to their future life together. "Roger . . . I need to get to know you better before I can consent to marry you. Don't you feel the same way? Don't you want to spend more time with me?"

Roger quickly drew her into his arms. "My dear, I want nothing more! I know you must feel disappointed that my time is so limited just now— but I shall see you this evening and tomorrow, and by Christmas, I should be free to spend all my time with you! Why, the holiday season will be the perfect opportunity to introduce you to all my friends and family. The parties and balls are magnificent then!"

Rebecca put both hands on Roger's chest and leaned back from him. The round bulge of her mid-section further deterred any intimacy. "It really isn't so much the parties and balls, Roger, though I admit I was looking forward to them. It's—well, how will I know you truly want to marry me for myself and not just for my uncle's money?"

Roger's eyes glanced down at her bosom, modestly concealed behind a gauzy fichu. "All the money in the world, my dear, could never convince me to take an ugly woman into my bed." He bent his head and kissed her neck, and when he straightened, his eyes were smoldering. "Of course, we cannot pretend to love each other yet—but should that prevent us from marrying? I think not. Don't forget, this is 1795, a very modern era. Passion and convenience may take the place of love, until such time as tenderness and affection have a chance to grow and be nourished."

Rebecca wondered whether Roger was capable of tenderness and affection. "I—I never believed I could marry for anything but love."

Roger's finger traced her neck. "Security, comfort, social position—these are excellent reasons for marriage, my sweet. And if your pregnancy now robs you of passion, think of what you will feel after the child is born. I'll wager your body will once again crave a man's knowing touch."

As he said this, Roger's hand slid down to her bosom. "I promise you, I know far better than any savage how to please a woman."

"Roger, please . . . what if someone should come in and find us?" Rebecca pushed his hand away, but Roger suddenly tugged on the fichu concealing the deep cleavage of her bodice.

"Just one look, my pretty little bird—one touch, and I shall leave you alone!"

The fichu floated to the floor, and as Rebecca watched it in stunned disbelief, Roger pulled her to him and began to kiss and fondle her.

A harsh voice from the doorway made both of them jump. "And is this how you repay my friendship—by compromising my niece?"

"Uncle Hardin!" Rebecca gasped.

"Why, Hardin, old boy . . ." Roger said. "Your niece was only demonstrating the favors she once bestowed on a savage. Of course, the man was her husband—but never fear, I plan to marry her now myself."

Thirteen

For several agonizing moments, Uncle Hardin merely stood and gaped. Then he exploded. "God in heaven! What do you mean, Rebecca's husband was a savage? Mrs. Stone said he was a trapper, and that I shouldn't speak of him until the girl had more time to recover from the sorrow of his untimely death!"

Oh, dear! Rebecca thought. She had wondered why Uncle Hardin never asked questions about her child's father, and now, she knew. "Uncle Hardin . . ." she began and stopped. Without the fichu, she felt naked. Roger had managed to pull her bodice so far down that her breasts were almost totally exposed; even now, he was still casting lustful glances toward them.

Uncle Hardin's expression was both shocked and accusing. "Well, Niece . . . were you indeed married to a savage?"

"Yes, but . . . well, that is . . ." Hastily, Rebecca turned away and adjusted her gown, then snatched up her fichu. Before she could further elaborate on her answer, Roger stepped forward.

"It's even worse than you imagine, Hardin, old boy. She was married to a half-breed. The man wasn't even a thoroughbred."

Rebecca whirled around. "He was every inch a thoroughbred! He was the perfect example of all the best qualities of his people!"

"Really now . . ." Roger said. "And were you married in a church, as befits every proper white woman—or at least those of good breeding and refinement?"

"In a church? There are no churches in the wilderness, Mister Bakewood!"

"Not even married in a church!" Uncle Hardin's face quickly drained of color. He staggered to a chair and sat down without bothering to remove his coat or to put down his hat and cane. "Why then . . ." he groaned softly. "My entire fortune is destined to fall into the hands of a bastard."

Wishing Roger would disintegrate on the spot, Rebecca crossed the room to her uncle's chair. "I don't know what you mean by 'bastard,' Uncle Hardin. Kin-di-wa and I married according to Indian custom—by agreeing to live together and love each other every day of our lives. He was unable to give me all the proper gifts that ordinarily accompany an Indian marriage, because everything the Miamis had was destroyed by Anthony Wayne. But our commitment was no

342

less firm or proper because of the lack of presents. I assure you, my child is not a bastard."

"My dear . . ." Roger had the effrontery to approach her and slide his arm around her waist. "What your uncle means and what you yourself must realize, is that here in Philadelphia no such agreement between a white woman and a heathen savage would ever be recognized as a marriage. You were—how shall I put it delicately—living in sin?"

Rebecca jerked away from him. "That's putting it neither delicately nor truthfully! You, Mr. Bakewood, are an ignorant, ill-mannered lout who has said enough for one afternoon!"

Roger stiffened. "I've said only what needed to be said. As I have already told you—I care not one whit who fathered your child or whether or not you were properly wedded. I am willing to marry you anyway, to shelter both you and your questionable offspring. Once you are under my protection, no one will dare speak a word against you. Everything I own shall be yours and the child's, and I will defend you both to the death!"

Taken back by Roger's unexpected gallantry, Rebecca stifled her sharp retort. If only Roger wouldn't rush her so! If only the man wouldn't touch or try to kiss her! Every time he pawed her, she only became more set against him. She hated the feel of his hands and mouth. Oh, if only she didn't feel so confused and vulnerable—so worried and afraid for her baby's future! She needed time to think, to decide what was best for everyone.

Uncle Hardin cleared his throat and sat straighter on his chair. "Well, sir! When I came in and saw you making unseemly advances toward my niece, I thought I should have to challenge you to a duel! But now that I know your intentions are honorable, I'm inclined to thank you, rather than challenge you. If you were to marry my niece, you'd be doing us all a mighty fine favor."

"I would be doing myself a favor to marry your lovely niece . . ."

"Please stop it!" Rebecca cried. "I've already told you; it's too soon . . . I can't begin to think of marrying anyone—least of all a man I hardly know!"

Uncle Hardin stood up. His cane clattered loudly to the floor. "Why, Niece, marriage is the only way out for you now! The only way to protect your good name, and my name too, I might add. A quick marriage to Roger here—a man I know and trust even if you do not—would put an end to speculation before it started. Marriage will insure the child's legitimacy!"

"Marriage? Did someone mention marriage?" Aunt Margaret bustled into the room. "Why, Hardin dear! I didn't hear you come in!"

Roger bowed and a slight smile quirked his lips. "Dear Mrs. Stone. You did indeed hear properly. We been discussing the advantages to all of us if your niece and I were to marry."

"Oh, my dear Rebecca! I would be so happy if you married Mister Bakewood!" Aunt Margaret enfolded Rebecca in a violet-scented hug. "I can't think of anything that would please me more!"

"Why then, it's settled!" Uncle Hardin boomed. "And to make the event even grander, I shall add a tidy sum of money to the investments I was already planning to give Rebecca on the blessed occasion of her wedding."

Roger beamed and smiled. "Hardin, old man, you are much too generous."

"Wait! Wait a minute, please! I haven't said I was willing to marry Roger!" Rebecca looked from one to another in desperation: did none of them want to understand? "I—I loved my husband very much! He—he was everything to me! He was my lover, yes, but he was also my dearest friend. He was my heart, my soul, my very being . . ."

Aunt Margaret patted her arm. "Yes, yes, dear . . . we understand. Why, in time you'll feel the same way about Roger! Don't you see? Your husband is dead now, my poor dear Rebecca, and you must do what is best for yourself and for your child. You must forget him, or at least try to put your grief behind you. Really, my dear, it's for the best . . ."

Forget Kin-di-wa. Rebecca shook her head violently. She would never forget her husband. And she could never be happy with Roger. But as she looked around at the three decided faces, she felt a wave of weakness wash over her. Her knees began to tremble. There was no way to fight it— no way to deny it any longer. Kin-di-wa was gone, and she would likely never know happiness again. What was the use of fighting? Perhaps she really

345

was incapable of deciding what was best to do under the circumstances.

"Please excuse me . . ." she murmured, and without waiting for permission, started toward the stairs.

"Rebecca!" Roger cried in a commanding tone.

Rebecca did not stop, but she heard Aunt Margaret's lilting voice calming and soothing her ardent suitor. "Dear Roger . . . give her time. She seems to be a sensible girl, and I'm certain she'll come around."

Uncle Hardin snorted. "If she does not come around, I'll cut her off without a half-penny! I'll not see all I've worked for go to ruin. Roger's the perfect match for her, and if she refuses to marry him, why, no one else will have her! Pregnant with a savage's child!"

"Hush, now, Hardin . . . she'll hear you!"

"T'would be a good thing if she did!"

Roger Bakewood did not stay for supper that evening but was invited for Thanksgiving dinner, along with two couples who were friends of the Stones. "Of course, they're not anybody, you understand," Aunt Margaret whispered in an aside to Rebecca. "But we must make do with what we've got until the doors of more important people open to us."

Rebecca sighed with pity and irritation. Her aunt was so preoccupied with social position that she judged everyone in terms of status, rather than in terms of loyalty, goodness, or simple friendship. But Rebecca realized that it was neither the time nor place for a lecture on the value of friendship for its own sake. She dutifully dressed in a gown of sheer peach silk that Aunt Margaret insisted she wear and then dutifully sat at the table next to Roger. He paid her extravagant compliments and exerted a most proprietary manner through all eight courses of a sumptuous meal that included roast goose with gravy and chestnut stuffing, pigeon pie, and broiled chicken with mushroom sauce.

After dinner, the gentlemen retired to the study for brandy, and Aunt Margaret led the ladies into the parlor for sherry and dessert. When everyone had been seated, one of the women, a Mrs. Fotheringham, adjusted the puce-colored skirt of her gown, patted her tight gray curls, and smiled at Rebecca—revealing large, horselike, yellow teeth.

"Oh, my dear! What terrible things you must have seen in the wilderness!" She leaned forward and lowered her voice. "They say the savages are particularly curious about white women. Their own women rarely wash and smell to high heaven, you know, so when they come across a white woman, they can't resist stealing her away and ravishing her! ... Tell me, did you see any savages up close? I hear they run around naked, their male ornaments hanging down right in plain view—God save their heathen souls!"

"Why, Nettie!" Aunt Margaret cut in. "Of course, Rebecca saw savages—but only from a distance, didn't you dear?"

Rebecca had a sudden desire to shock Mrs. Fotheringham right out of her puce-colored slippers. Not wanting to embarrass her aunt, she fought determinedly to quell it. "The Indians I knew neither smelled to high heaven nor went about totally naked," she said quietly.

"Ah, then you did mix in with the savages!" Mrs. Fotheringham shot a triumphant glance at the second female guest, a sour-faced woman named Mrs. Trumbull.

"Oh, no! She never mixed in with them!" Aunt Margaret insisted. "Her papa would never have allowed that."

"Actually," Rebecca said. "After Papa died, I lived among the Indians for a time—and a finer, more noble race of people I have yet to meet."

"Noble! Oh, dear me!" gasped Mrs. Fotheringham. "But wasn't it savages who killed your papa and your husband?"

"I lived among the Miamis. It was Shawnee who killed my father, and soldiers of the United States army who killed my husband."

Aunt Margaret sprang to her feet. "Sherry? Would anyone like more sherry? Or coffee? Tea? Perhaps another tart?"

Mrs. Fotheringham licked her lips avidly. She ignored Aunt Margaret's question and focused her attention on Rebecca. "But why would soldiers kill your husband, dear—unless he was a criminal or a traitor, or something even worse."

"My husband was not a criminal or a traitor, Mrs. Fotheringham. He was . . ." Rebecca was interrupted by a choking sound. Aunt Margaret's face had gone white as milk, and one hand clutched her lavender-swathed bosom as if she dared not breathe—or as if a fainting spell was imminent. She made an effort to recover her composure and looked pleadingly at Rebecca.

"He was a *coureur de bois*—a woods runner," Rebecca finished hurriedly. "And his death was a tragic accident. So tragic, I find it too painful to talk about."

"My yes, of course! How thoughtless of me!" Mrs. Fotheringham frowned and leaned back in her chair. "A *coureur de bois,* you say—such a romantic occupation!" She held out her goblet to Aunt Margaret. "I believe I will have a touch more sherry, dear Maggie, and do have another glass yourself. You look quite pale, my dear, and the sherry is *très bon,* as always."

"It came from France, dear Nettie! Oh, how could we ever survive without our little *trésors,* our luxuries, from France!"

Aunt Margaret's relief was so visible that Rebecca winced. She wished that her aunt had more courage, more backbone and determination —but then a wave of protective maternalism engulfed her. For herself, she cared not at all what people thought or said, but when it came to her child . . . Oh, how could she bear it if anyone spoke a word of censure or ridicule against her innocent child?

Rebecca was glad when the men rejoined them, and the evening drew to a close. The Trumbulls departed first and then the Fotheringhams, leaving only Roger who requested a few moments alone with her while Henry-Luke was bringing round his buggy.

Aunt Margaret and Uncle Hardin retreated to the upstairs, and with an uneasy feeling, Rebecca sat down on the edge of the exquisite Duncan Phyfe chair her aunt had recently bought in New York.

Flicking an invisible piece of lint from the snowy white lace on his shirt front, Roger turned his back to the fire and studied her for a moment before speaking. "My dear Rebecca, you are a vision in that peach silk."

"A thick-waisted vision, no doubt." Rebecca tried to sound prim and distant.

"Nothing can dim your beauty, my dear, except perhaps unhappiness."

"If my beauty depends on my happiness, Roger, then I must be ugly indeed!"

Roger's lip curled upwards in a faint half-smile. "If you think you are unhappy now, how do you think you will feel when all Philadelphia knows about your sordid past?"

Rebecca stood up. Why did Roger always go for the jugular? It was this very trait that made her so uneasy about him. Kin-di-wa had always been direct and disarming, but he had never been deliberately cruel. "I'm very tired, Roger . . . if you insist on discussing my past again, I'll say good-night."

Roger came toward her with outstretched arms, but she quickly side-stepped his embrace. Anger swelled in her chest. "Don't touch me, Roger, I warn you. I refuse to be touched

350

anymore against my will."

He stopped a foot short of her and bowed his head. "Ah Rebecca . . . why do you try so hard to resist me? Your beauty is a silken cord that binds me to you . . . and have I not yet made it plain that I would be bound to you forever?"

"Why don't you save your pretty speeches for someone more innocent and gullible than I am, Roger? It's my uncle's wealth that attracts you. And the only thing about you that attracts me is the promise of safety and security—a good future for my baby."

Roger advanced another step, and Rebecca caught the scent of whiskey and the sour odor of perspiration mixed with expensive male cologne. "My dear stubborn girl," Roger said. "I had hoped for something more than mere business between us . . . I had hoped for some growing emotional attachment—or at the very least, some flare of passion."

"There will hardly be time for all that before the wedding. Indeed, if there is to be a wedding, I must insist that we be practical."

"Practical?"

Expressions of hope, surprise, and suspicion warred on Roger's face, and these hints of uncertainty gave courage to Rebecca. She took a deep breath. "Yes, practical. I—I feel that I could agree to marry you if you would agree to—forgo your rights as my husband."

"Forgo my rights?" Roger's eyebrows shot up in astonishment. His full lower lip thrust out petulantly, making him look like an angry frog.

"Madam! Do you mean I am never to bed you—is that what you mean?"

Watching him flush to a dark angry crimson, Rebecca knew she could never endure love-making with this man, could never agree to share his bed—no matter if Uncle Hardin threw her out into the winter snow. She would never agree to wed Roger unless he gave her his promise, as a gentleman, that he would not claim his marital rights.

"That is exactly what I mean. You must never make love to me. Never."

"But—how can you demand such a thing!"

"Because your advances are . . . distasteful. I've tried to let you know this. I've tried to explain how I feel. But you always refuse to listen. You keep pushing yourself at me, Roger—and I've decided I've had enough."

"But, my dear! Surely after the wedding . . . and after you've lost this abominable bulge : . . your womanly desires will return! I've suggested this to you before! You have only to trust me in this matter . . ."

Rebecca's hands flew to her extended womb. "This bulge is not abominable to me, Roger. It's the only reason I'm consenting to marry you at all. For my child, I'll do anything—except lie down with a man I don't love. I—I thought I could do even that, but . . . I find I can't."

"Can't or won't?" Roger's powerful hands caught her shoulders and she had the feeling he was about to shake her—or to force himself upon her then and there.

"Can't and won't," Rebecca insisted. "But I will be a good wife to you, Roger, I promise. I'll care for your house and entertain your guests. I'll speak kindly of you and never complain or criticize. No one will ever know that we're husband and wife in name only. It will be our secret. And, of course, as my husband, you will control and manage whatever is mine, whatever comes to me from Uncle Hardin and Aunt Margaret."

Roger's hands dropped away from her. He frowned and grunted. "Why, this is monstrous! It's unheard of! It's . . . it's . . ."

Rebecca allowed him to spit and sputter but did not soften her expression or determined stance. Now that she knew what she wanted, she did not intend to back down. In a few moments, Roger's outrage dwindled as he realized she could not be bullied. "All right then, I agree . . ." he conceded wearily. "After all, there's always the chance that after we're married you'll change your mind."

"You mustn't count on that, Roger . . . I want your word as a gentleman. You will make no attempt to touch me as a husband touches his wife, either before or after our marriage."

Roger gave her a small tight smile. "If that's really the way you want it, my dear, then yes . . . you have my word on it as a gentleman. And now, hadn't we better inform your aunt and uncle? It takes time to plan a wedding—even a wedding of mere convenience."

The wedding date was set for the third week of January. Rebecca wanted a small affair—a quiet

353

ceremony at Christ Church—with only Roger, one or two of his cousins, and her aunt and uncle present. Roger wanted something more lavish with a large reception afterward so he could invite his influential friends and family to witness his "settling down."

Mindful of her ever advancing state of pregnancy, Rebecca explained how awkward she would feel meeting so many strangers at one time. But Roger was adamant in his wishes. He found eager support from Aunt Margaret and Uncle Hardin: "But my dear Rebecca!" Aunt Margaret exclaimed. "This is our opportunity to make our entrance into 'genteel' society—and we do so want to make a good impression! Why, people will be offended if they aren't invited to the wedding."

Hoping to get the engagement and pending marriage off to a friendly start, Rebecca politely gave in. But Roger, angered by her initial arguments and still brooding over their secret bargain, left for Lancaster immediately after Thanksgiving and did not come back to Philadelphia until two days before Christmas.

On his return, he pressed Rebecca to attend a round of holiday parties and dances with him. "No, Roger," Rebecca gently insisted this time. "I think what we really need is some quiet time for ourselves before the wedding—so we can get to know one another better."

Roger scowled through all of an otherwise sunny Christmas Day, then informed her, that as the mill in Lancaster was not yet completed, he must try to make it operable while the weather still remained fair. Rebecca toyed with a be-ribboned ivory cameo she had just received from him as a Christmas present and smiled through her disappointment, "Please do what you think best, Roger."

"Dear Rebecca!" Aunt Margaret commiserated on the 27th of December, the day after Roger's departure. "How disappointed you must be that Roger could not at least have stayed over until New Year's!"

Aunt Margaret stroked the snoozing Snow-flake who was curled up in a contented, white heap in her lap. The little dog nosed the plump caressing hand, and Rebecca had to smile. Since that day when she'd sent Aunt Margaret into the kitchen with Snowflake, the two had become inseparable. Rebecca might have been jealous had she not had the anticipation of her baby to fill the empty void around her heart.

She bent her attention to the tiny stitches she was taking in the flounces of her baby's christening gown. "Yes, I am disappointed, Aunt Margaret. But Roger is only thinking of our future. The mill will prove quite profitable if he ever gets it open."

"But perhaps you should have agreed to attend a few parties. That would have kept him in town, I believe!"

"I suppose so," Rebecca agreed. "But why do parties interest him so much? I can't possibly dance the newest dances in this condition, even if I knew them—which I don't. Besides, I thought

355

you were the one who likes parties—not Roger and certainly not me."

"Oh, yes, indeed I do! But Roger does too, my dear, and of course he wants to show you off. He wants you—and us too, the dear boy—to have our first taste of Philadelphia society as soon as possible!"

Rebecca put down her stitching. "Oh, Aunt Margaret, I'm sorry. I never thought about all of us attending those parties—I mean, if I had realized, of course, I would have agreed to go!"

"That's all right, dear," Aunt Margaret said generously. "There will be plenty of time for parties after you get married—and we will have the opportunity to meet Roger's friends and family at the wedding. Besides, you're feeling quite awkward and uncomfortable these days, aren't you, dear?"

Putting one hand to her aching back, Rebecca sat up straighter and smiled. "Does it show so much? I feel as if I'm as big as a buffalo."

"A buffalo! Imagine that! Why, I've heard the creatures are indeed huge. And I do love to hear you speak of all the exotic things you've seen in the wilderness . . . but do remember dear, be careful what you say in front of others. They aren't so broad-minded as I am—or as your Uncle Hardin and dear Roger."

Broad-minded was hardly a word Rebecca would use to describe Uncle Hardin or Roger or even her aunt, but she kept silent. She owed them all so much. She had walked into their lives with nothing more than the coarse homespun on her back, and they had provided her with expensive gowns, lovely surroundings, more money than she'd ever dreamed of, and—most important of all—a secure future for her baby.

A sound of someone clearing his throat came from the hallway, and Aunt Margaret looked up in annoyance. "Henry-Luke! Why ever are you standing there listening in on our conversation? Is there something you need?"

Henry-Luke's nose was red, as if he'd just come in from outside, and he rubbed his hands together before pulling a letter from his sleeve. "B'fore he left yesterday, Mister Bakewood give me this t' give t' Missus Rebecca. I wuz just a-bringin' it t' her is all."

"Well, why didn't you say so?" Forgetting the sleeping dog in her lap, Aunt Margaret began to rise and Snowflake spilled to the floor. Henry-Luke's glance went to the animal: his eyes narrowed. Snowflake began yipping and trying to tunnel out of view under Aunt Margaret's skirt.

"Goodness gracious! Whatever ails my poor baby?" Aunt Margaret hurriedly side-stepped, nearly upsetting her chair as she tried not to step on the dog.

Rebecca held out her hand. "Give me the letter, Henry-Luke, then you had better go."

Henry-Luke came into the room and handed Rebecca the wax-sealed parchment. His close proximity made Snowflake yelp in abject terror and make a flying leap into Rebecca's lap. "Please go, Henry-Luke!" Rebecca said sharply.

The man smirked and moved closer to Rebecca's chair. "You want I should take th' critter out an' git rid o' it?"

Before Rebecca could answer, Aunt Margaret recovered both her footing and her dignity. "You most certainly will not take Snowflake out to be gotten rid of!" She stalked over to Rebecca who was trying to keep the frantic dog from ruining the delicate lace of the christening gown on which she'd been working. "Here now, Snowie Baby, come to Mama . . . why, whatever has upset you so?"

Aunt Margaret gathered the animal to her plump bosom and glared at Henry-Luke. "Go on along now, Henry-Luke! You scared the poor thing half to death."

Henry-Luke shot a venomous look at Rebecca, accusing her with his eyes. His expression said that she was at fault—both for bringing the dog into the house in the first place and for fueling his mistress's anger. "I'm a goin', Missus Stone. Like I said—I wuz only bringin' in a letter that Mister Bakewood wanted me t' give t' Missus Rebecca."

After Henry-Luke's departure, Rebecca broke the wax seal and opened the letter. Why would Roger be sending her a message today? She'd seen him only yesterday before his abrupt departure. Quickly, she scanned the letter's contents.

"Well, what does it say, dear? Is the dear boy missing you so much already?" Aunt Margaret sat down again with the dog and readjusted the pink ribbon around its neck. The ribbon matched her dress.

Rebecca handed the letter to her aunt. "It says

358

that we are invited to attend a ball. One of Roger's cousins wants to hold a ball to announce our forthcoming marriage."

"A ball!" Aunt Margaret's eager hands snatched the letter, and Snowflake had to once again scramble to keep his position on her lap. "Oh, how splendid!"

Rebecca gathered up her sewing. She didn't think it was splendid. She had a vision of herself standing in a group of beautifully dressed, wealthy women. They were all thin and lovely, while she was heavy and awkward—a subject of ridicule and speculation. Everyone would be asking questions about her first husband and about her experiences in the wilderness. And they would be wondering how on earth a pregnant widow had ever managed to snag Roger Bakewood, the notorious womanizer and bachelor.

"Why, this is *très merveilleux!*" Aunt Margaret exclaimed. "The ball will be held at the end of the second week of January—only a week before the wedding! And Roger insists we must all attend!"

Rebecca winced at the sound of her aunt's French. By now, she knew that Aunt Margaret only used it when she was pathetically trying to fit herself into the image of the cultured lady she had always dreamed of being. "Of course, we shall attend, Aunt Margaret. I wouldn't dream of denying you that pleasure."

"Oh, but we must have new gowns! New slippers and new capes!"

Rebecca thought of the wedding finery already on order and sighed at this new expense. "Not for me, Aunt Margaret. All my gowns, slippers, and capes are new as it is."

"But not elegant enough, my dear! Don't you realize what this affair will mean to all of us? This ball will be the talk of the entire town! . . . Oh, your future my dear—yours and Roger's—will be quite assured after this!"

And probably yours too, Rebecca thought unkindly, and she felt a twinge of guilt. Who was she to criticize her aunt's yearnings for social prominence when she herself was marrying not for love but for money and security?

New Year's Eve came and went with another awkward dinner party with the Fotheringhams and the Trumbulls. After that, everything centered on The Ball, as Rebecca began to think of it. Even the preparations for the wedding ground to a standstill as the household scrambled to make ready for the closer event.

Despite Rebecca's protests, Aunt Margaret ordered a magnificent gown to be made for her in a sheer green silk that exactly matched the color of her eyes. Sea-green, Aunt Margaret called it. The gown had short cap sleeves, a high concealing waist, and a scandalously low-cut bodice.

Over the gown went something called a pelisse which was made of green velvet and had a quilted border. A matching silk chemise, matching slippers of softest kid, and fingerless gloves called "mitts" completed the outfit. In Rebecca's opinion, such finery was much too elegant and expensive. But Aunt Margaret assured her that she would be stunning and attired in the very latest fashion.

At least, Rebecca thought dourly, the gown's high waist would allow plenty of room for her enormous mid-section, and the lovely velvet pelisse would provide warmth from the bitter cold winds that swept across Philadelphia through the early days of January.

The evening of the ball arrived, and Rebecca allowed Prudy to dress her and arrange her hair in a becoming mass of shining red ringlets and long flowing waves that were intertwined with silk flowers and greenery. The baby, catching Rebecca's mounting excitement, thumped and squirmed so hard in his mother's womb that even Prudy noticed it.

"Law'! That chile knows his mama is goin' somewheres." Prudy slipped an emerald-green mitt over Rebecca's outstretched hand, then helped her to wiggle the long funnel of satin up her arm. "Wonder if'n he knows his mama is gonna be the prettiest lady there."

"He?" Rebecca gave a last determined tug at the mitt with her free hand. "Do you think it will be a boy?"

"Sure better be . . ." Prudy snorted. "It oughta be a boy whut looks jus' like his pappy."

"His p—pappy?" A lump rose in Rebecca's throat, impeding her question—but she didn't trust herself to repeat it.

Prudy's brown eyes grew soft. "Yo' deserves it, honey. I seen th' way yo' big green eyes gits that faraway sad look in 'em, like you wuz thinkin' o' someplace else an' someone yo' loved an' lost. A little fat baby boy whut looks jus' like yo' husban' would make yo' smile an' laugh ag'in. He would take away yoah pain."

"Oh, Prudy!" The urge to weep and confide in someone overwhelmed Rebecca. There was so much pent up hurt, guilt, and grief that she could never share with Aunt Margaret. And she had so much fear and unease about the future—about her marriage arrangement with Roger. How could she possibly be planning to marry a man she didn't even like—a boorish man who was impatiently awaiting her downstairs at this very moment? "Oh, Prudy . . ." she repeated.

"Now, honey . . . don't yo' go an' cry an' make yoah eyes swell up. Yo' is doin' th' right thin' marryin' up with Mister Bakewood. All wimmin is slaves, yo' know, not jus' me an' Bess. We all gots t' dance t' th' tune o' someone—a pappy or a husban'. Better t' choose a man with prospec's o' gittin' rich than not t' marry at all. 'Specially in yoah position."

Struggling to hold back her tears, Rebecca wriggled her fingers through the other mitt. "Yes . . . yes, I suppose you're right."

"Sure, ah'm right, honey. Now, you jus' go on t' that ball an' hold yoah head up high, an' don't let those folks intimidate yo'. Iff'n they gives yo' any o' them sly glances and talks b'hind yoah back, why yo' jus' remember yo' gots a sweet little chile growin' inside o' yo'—a chile whose gonna be th' spittin' image o' his pappy . . . an' that's th' onliest thin' that counts—that sweet little chile . . ."

Rebecca blinked and straightened her shoulders. "You're right, Prudy. That's exactly what I've been telling myself all along."

Roger's cousin lived in a large, brick, three-storied house on South 3rd Street. Its shutters gleamed whitely in the darkness and candle-glow spilled gaily from its many-paned windows as the elegant carriage Roger had borrowed for the occasion drew up in front.

Sudden panic seized Rebecca as Roger helped her down onto the cobblestoned sidewalk. The walks and roadways were slick with a thin film of ice that immediately chilled her toes through her thin slippers and made her momentarily afraid of falling and injuring the baby.

"Roger, your hand, please . . ." she requested, as Roger turned to assist Aunt Margaret.

"It's only a little ice, my dear . . ." Roger ignored her plea and continued to help Aunt Margaret. "There, now, my dear Mrs. Stone, are you quite all right?"

"Oh yes, dear Roger, thank you!" Aunt Margaret hurried forward, took Rebecca's arm, and began to steer her toward the steps and the wrought-iron railings in front of the house. "Oh my, it is quite chilly tonight, isn't it? Let's hurry and get inside."

More certain now of her footing, Rebecca still trod gingerly. "Shouldn't we wait for the men?"

Roger and Uncle Hardin came tardily to their rescue. "Damned if it isn't a little slippery," Uncle Hardin grunted.

Roger grasped Rebecca's free arm and strode confidently toward the door with its delicate fan-shaped inset of sparkling glass. The door swung open as if by magic, and a man with ebony skin and gleaming white teeth ushered them inside. The mellow sounds of chamber music and the murmur of many voices came from somewhere behind him.

The man-servant took their capes and great-coats, and a maid emerged from nowhere to lead them up a wide carved staircase. A tall, elegant, blond woman came down the stairs toward them. Jewels flashed at her throat and in her hair. She held out her hands to Roger. "Roger, dear cousin-in-law! The black sheep of the family . . . so you've finally decided to turn respectable!"

"Augusta . . ." Roger bowed deeply. "Allow me to present to you my future wife and in-laws."

The woman was older than Rebecca, and her face was layered with powder. Still, she bore herself with an easy grace and was slender as a reed in a high-waisted blue gown with an elaborate embroidered train. She smiled thinly and nodded. "Yes, Mr. and Mrs. Stone . . . and this must be their poor little niece, Rebecca."

The woman's glance swept over Rebecca with haughty amusement, and Rebecca felt her cheeks flush crimson. Aunt Margaret stepped forward eagerly. "What a stunning home you have, Mrs. Bakewood! Why, this beautifully carved newel post here—wherever did you find such splendid mahogany?"

"It came from Santo Domingo, I believe . . ." Augusta Bakewood's hand trailed carelessly across the newel post and came to rest on a small piece of ivory that protruded slightly from the gleaming wood. "Here is the ivory amity button which marks the place where the deed for our home has been sealed for safe-keeping. Your newel post also has such a button?"

"Why, n-no . . ." Aunt Margaret stammered, and it was obvious to Rebecca that her aunt had never heard of the custom of sealing one's mortgage into one's newel post.

Mrs. Bakewood smiled and her voice dripped condescension. "Well, I suppose that's a practice only among the oldest and wealthiest Philadelphia families."

"Oh, we shall have to take it up, won't we Hardin? I do declare—one could hardly find a safer place than a newel post for such a valuable paper!"

"Yes, yes, indeed!" Uncle Hardin agreed. He coughed and looked acutely uncomfortable.

Mrs. Bakewood plucked at Roger's wine-colored velvet sleeve. "Your future in-laws are simply charming, Roger. Samuel will be most pleased to meet them."

"And where is Cousin Samuel?" Roger inquired in a subdued tone.

"In the ballroom upstairs, of course. If all of you will follow me, I'll take you up and introduce you to our guests. They haven't all arrived yet, but

I can promise you the evening will be anything but dull. Indeed, we have quite an unexpected surprise for you . . ."

"A surprise! *Enchantée!*" Aunt Margaret bubbled.

"What was that you said, dear?" Mrs. Bakewood asked.

Aunt Margaret repeated the French phrase. "Oh, you mean how enchanting!" Augusta Bakewood said. "But my dear Mrs. Stone—I didn't know you spoke French fluently. I shall have to introduce you to one of our French guests. The two of you should get on very well together."

Rebecca saw a ripple of fear cross her aunt's face and, for a moment, she wanted to strangle Augusta Bakewood. Poor Aunt Margaret! She had come to this magnificent house with as much eager anticipation as a child on her first visit to a sweet shop. But soon she would discover how hard and tasteless the pretty sweets could be. As for herself, the evening's adventure was going no worse than Rebecca had expected. Acceptance into Philadelphia society could hardly be won in a single evening. Indeed, perhaps, it could never be won.

"Come along now, dear fiancée." Roger seemed not to notice Rebecca's breathlessness as they mounted the wide carved staircase. "You will be quite amazed at Samuel and Augusta's ballroom."

Rebecca was not only amazed, she was struck with awe. The ballroom occupied the greater part of the second floor and was made to seem even larger by enormous gilt-framed mirrors that reflected hundreds of candles and a magnificent crystal chandelier.

"Waterford!" Aunt Margaret gasped.

"Of course, dear Mrs. Stone . . . a mere bauble we've had for several years now," said Mrs. Bakewood. "Now, wherever is Samuel, do you suppose?"

The ballroom was filled with lavishly gowned women and formally attired gentlemen. It smelled of heady perfumes, savory foods, and had an underlying odor of burning wax.

As Rebecca and Roger entered, faces turned in their direction. Conversation ebbed, and even the musicians fell silent and did not begin to play again as they finished a popular piece.

A large heavy-set man who bore a marked resemblance to Roger started across the floor toward them. "Ah, Roger! So our guests of honor have arrived."

Roger drew Rebecca forward. "Cousin Samuel . . . my future wife, Rebecca. As I've already told you, she's a recent widow and the niece of two very fine people, Hardin and Margaret Stone."

Painfully conscious of everyone's stares and the awkward silence, Rebecca was almost afraid to look Samuel Bakewood in the eye. Her glance leapt past him to a tall man who stood behind him and off to one side. Instead of velvet coat, ruffled shirt, skin-tight breeches, and buckled shoes, the man wore fringed buckskins and embroidered moccasins. Two white feathers protruded bravely from the back of his neck. Long black hair was pulled back from his face and secured by an embroidered headband.

He was starkly handsome, with aristocratic features, and as she stood there, mute with shock, his burning blue eyes sought hers.

Samuel Bakewood came toward her, momentarily blocking her view of the tall man in buckskins. Bakewood half-turned, smiled, and gestured in the direction of his Indian guest. Rebecca dared not trust her eyes, yet neither could she look away as the Indian's expression darkened to a well-remembered scowl.

A buzzing sound assaulted her ears. Voices rose and fell around her. Deep within her body, a trembling began. It spread rapidly to her limbs, and when she tried to speak, nothing came out but a gasp. It can't be, she thought frantically. I'm imagining this—I must be.

But the tall blue-eyed man was walking toward her. He stopped in front of her and looked down into her eyes, his broad-shouldered body only inches away from her groping finger-tips. She had the sensation of being alone with him—as if all time had suddenly stopped. The present faded into a babble of voices: Roger's, Samuel's, and several others.

Someone said, "Rebecca and Roger are soon to be married—next week, in fact."

Someone else, perhaps it was Augusta, added, "We wanted everyone to meet Roger's bride and his future in-laws. We're so pleased dear Roger is finally getting married and settling down to raise a family. Of course, the wee ones will be coming along more rapidly than normally anticipated . . ."

A titter of nervous laughter followed.

I'm going mad, Rebecca thought. I must be dreaming. This is impossible.

The man's blue-eyed glance swept her face, dropped down to her heaving bosom and then fell to the bulge of her child. Our child, she thought breathlessly.

His glance came back to her face. She swayed and wondered if she was falling—falling into the depths of those brilliant, piercing, blue eyes. Then a husky beloved voice broke through the wall of disbelief and unreality.

"So, little Cat-Eyes . . ." the voice said softly. "So . . . we meet again."

Fourteen

Augusta Bakewood grasped Rebecca's arm. "My dear, you've grown so pale. Is anything the matter? . . . I take it you already know one of our other guests. Perhaps we should not have attempted to surprise you, but when we heard that an emissary of the defeated Little Turtle— one of his fiercest warriors, no less—was here in Philadelphia to meet with President Washington, why, we thought it would be amusing to invite him this evening . . . are you not amused, dear?"

Rebecca couldn't answer. Her body felt hot and cold at the same time, and the ballroom was spinning around her. *Kin-di-wa*. Kin-di-wa was alive and standing in front of her. Kin-di-wa was here in Philadelphia.

Then Kin-di-wa spoke to her again, this time in the smooth guttural tones of the Miami language. "Do not allow this ugly, ill-mannered woman to disturb you. She is vicious and small-minded, as is her husband, as are all whites, and I am sorry I came here tonight."

Rebecca was momentarily stunned by his condemnation, but she was still too overwhelmed to wonder or worry about it. Hardly conscious that she did so, she responded in the Miami tongue. "Kin-di-wa! How is it possible you are really here? How is it possible you still live?" She made a movement to throw herself into his arms, but his dark expression stayed her.

"Do not tell me you have been grieving for me, Cat-Eyes . . . Is not this what you have always wanted?" His eyes blackened to pools of hatred, as he took in the whole of the ballroom with a short wave of his hand. "Is not this the reason you betrayed me? I ask you only one question: if you wished so much to return to your people—why did you choose to run away with my brother's murderer? I would have brought you here myself had I known you were so unhappy. There was no need to turn to my enemy."

"No, Kin-di-wa, no! I went away with Will only to protect you—not because I wanted to come home! I was afraid you would be killed! I never meant . . ."

"You never meant *what,* Cat-Eyes? You never meant for me to be bludgeoned senseless? You never meant for me to rot away in a blockhouse for two full moons? You never meant for me to be denied revenge for my brother's death or to wish for my own death because of your treachery?"

Kin-di-wa's words, spoken in a low, despair-ridden tone, had the effect of wounding Rebecca to her very soul. Her senses clamored for her to throw her arms around him and to assure herself that he was truly present—bone, flesh, and muscle. But the dark slant of his eyebrows, the harsh lines around his mouth, and the hatred in his eyes, made her immobile. She wondered if she were dreaming, and only the sound of the language—the musical flow of Miami words— convinced her she was not.

"I thought you were dead," she whispered. "Or I would have come to you. I only intended to stay with Will until the Treaty Council was over. After that, I meant to leave him and come back to you . . . It was the only way I could see to protect you, to save you from yourself."

"And who was there to protect you? Or did you not want to be protected?" Kin-di-wa's scorn-filled glance fell to her bulging waistline. "It appears I did not torture myself needlessly. You went willingly with my brother's murderer and willingly you lay with him. And did you soon tire of his lovemaking too? Or did he tire of yours? . . . Where is he, Cat-Eyes? I do not see him . . . But mayhap it is just as well he isn't here—for if he were, I should have to kill him. And Little Turtle would once again be displeased with me for failing to keep my temper—and for ruining an important mission."

Rebecca was so dismayed that she didn't know what to say. She was dimly aware of the shocked silence of those surrounding them, but nothing mattered but that Kin-di-wa should understand the reasons behind her past actions. Timidly, she reached out to him. "Kin-di-wa, I'm sorry! I never meant to hurt you! You must let me explain!"

But Kin-di-wa's gaze was icy cold and unwavering. "No, little Cat-Eyes . . . what I have seen is explanation enough." He turned abruptly to Roger's cousin and made a small informal bow that struck her as almost ludicrous. "You must excuse me, sir," he said in perfect English. "I regret I must leave immediately."

"What? What's that you say?" Roger's cousin sprang to life. He, Roger, Amanda, Aunt Margaret, and Uncle Hardin had been listening open-mouthed to the mysterious exchange, and now all of them stirred as Samuel Bakewood sputtered his protest. "Why, you cannot go yet, Golden Eagle! You've only just arrived, and everyone is waiting to meet you. Why, President Washington insisted I show you a good time. After all, when you go back home to your chief you'll want to be able to tell him how we civilized folks entertain!"

A muscle in Kin-di-wa's jaw twitched threateningly, but his voice remained calm and polite. "I will tell the great Chief Little Turtle that he must come to see civilization for himself. It is beyond the understanding of a lowly savage of no rank."

"Oh, I would hardly call you lowly." Amanda Bakewood stepped forward and slipped her arm through his. "I would say you are quite the most fascinating man here, and I *must* introduce you to my lady friends before you go rushing off."

Kin-di-wa stiffened as if torn between his desire to get away and his sense of duty and obligation.

Rebecca thought Little Turtle must have given him strict orders: go among the whites and learn everything you can of them. Go and learn—and in the process forget about the white woman who betrayed you.

"Come, come . . ." Amanda spoke as if she were addressing a child. "One turn around the ballroom, and you can go rushing back to your little room at the Man Full Of Trouble Inn. That is where the President insisted you stay, is it not?"

Rebecca's ears pricked: was that where Kin-di-wa was staying—and where she might find him alone? Somehow, she could not imagine him sleeping in a real bed inside the confines of wood and brick.

"It is where I try to sleep," Kin-di-wa answered. "But sleep does not come easily when I cannot see the stars."

Grinning broadly, Amanda led him away. "My goodness! Do you mean you are actually accustomed to sleeping outside under the sky?"

Rebecca couldn't hear Kin-di-wa's answer for Roger was suddenly hissing into her ear. "Stop staring at him like that! Everyone is watching!"

Reluctantly, she tore her glance away from the retreating buck-skinned figure and realized that indeed, everyone's attention seemed to be focused in their direction.

Samuel Bakewood smiled. "Forgive us for not warning you, my dear . . . but how were we to guess that you might actually know the fellow— and know his language?"

"Yes, I do know him . . ." Rebecca said quietly.

She was still in a state of shock. "Actually, I'm married to him. He's the father of my child."

There was a gasp behind her, then a rustle of silk and a thump. Rebecca turned and saw that Aunt Margaret had finally and honestly fainted dead away.

"Oh, my dear! How could you do this to us?" Aunt Margaret wrung her plump white hands and twisted her rings from front to back and back to front again. Her eyes were swollen from weeping, and she was making little hiccuping sounds in her throat. The Hepplewhite chair creaked with her agitated movements—as if in protest.

"A disgrace! You've disgraced us before all of Philadelphia!" Uncle Hardin paced up and down the parlor, then turned to waggle a finger at her. "You've ruined everything! Not just for us—but for yourself and Roger!"

Rebecca sat perfectly still and allowed the accusations to flow over her like rain-water. Part of her was contrite: she disliked causing anyone pain. Part of her was indignant: after all, she'd only told the truth. Still another part was joyful: Kin-di-wa was alive! And yet another part teetered between hope and despair: could she find Kin-di-wa and win his forgiveness?

Roger turned from the fireplace. His thick lips were pursed in concentration: he had been silent since the moment they walked into the house— following a hurried departure from his cousin's. "I don't believe anyone really heard Rebecca say that he was her husband. And we can thank you, dear Mrs. Stone, for having the good sense to create a diversion—and an excuse for getting out of there."

"A diversion?" Aunt Margaret blinked. "Oh, but it was so embarrassing to faint in front of everyone! And I was so looking forward to this evening! . . . Did you see that marvelous banquet we never got a chance to sample? Curds and creams, jellies, sweetmeats, at least twenty kinds of tarts, trifles, floating islands, whipped sylla-bub, Parmesan cheese, three kinds of punch . . ."

"Damn the food, Maggie!" Uncle Hardin exploded. "Don't you realize what happened tonight?"

Aunt Margaret sniffed and dabbed at her eyes with a lace handkerchief. "Of course, I realize! Why do you think I fainted in the first place? And why do you think I'm crying now?"

"But I really doubt that anyone heard a word she said," Roger repeated. "Except for Cousin Samuel . . . and he gave me his word before we left that he would not repeat it—not even to Amanda. Especially not to Amanda."

The impact of what he was saying finally struck Rebecca. "But what I said is true, Roger. Kin-di-wa—Golden Eagle—is my husband, and this baby I'm carrying is his child."

"No!" Roger exploded. "That savage is not your husband. He *was* your lover. You never married him in any ceremony remotely com-parable to a religious or civil contract."

"But . . ." Rebecca began and stopped. There

was no point in revealing yet that she intended to go back to Kin-di-wa. If he would take her. She doubted that any of them would understand what she had been trying to tell them all along: she loved Kin-di-wa, and she was married to him—heart, soul, and body. She didn't need a piece of paper or a ceremony to tell her what was in her heart.

Roger smiled in an unsuccessful attempt to be jovial. "Hardin, old boy . . . It's my conclusion that your niece and I can still be married as planned. We'll just pretend that nothing ever happened tonight and go ahead with the wedding. If there is any talk, it will soon die down . . . we need only hold up our heads and proceed as naturally as possible."

"Oh, Roger! . . . Do you really think we can go ahead with the wedding?" Aunt Margaret's face grew radiant.

Uncle Hardin looked doubtful. "Well . . . I don't know. Someone *might* have heard."

"Might have, yes . . . ." Roger conceded. "But if the marriage goes forward, they will simply realize they were mistaken. If we hesitate or postpone it, on the other hand, gossip will most certainly arise."

Rebecca knew she must speak. It was unfair to allow their hopes to be raised—only to dash them down again. She cleared her throat and dug her fingernails into her palms. "Roger, Aunt Margaret, Uncle Hardin . . . I must say something. I—I don't think I can marry you after all, Roger. I'm truly sorry, but I don't love you—as you

378

already know . . . This marriage was only for the sake of convenience, so my baby would have a protected future and so you would—also have a better future."

Uncle Hardin stopped pacing and stared at her. His jowls shook. "And if you don't marry Roger, what kind of future do you think you'll have then?"

Rebecca hesitated. "I—I don't know. But seeing Kin-di-wa again tonight made me realize that I can never marry someone I don't love. I would be miserably unhappy. And I would probably make Roger miserably unhappy too."

"But my dear . . ." Aunt Margaret verged on tears again. "What on earth will you do? Of course, I couldn't understand a word you and your Indian were saying to one another, but I had the distinct impression that he wasn't as happy to see you as you obviously were to see him."

"He wasn't happy," Rebecca admitted. "He was angry over something I did. You see, I never quite told you the whole story, Aunt Margaret . . ."

"What does it matter what the whole story is?" Roger interrupted rudely. "There's only one issue here: do you intend to go traipsing after your so-called husband when he goes back west to his people?"

"Well . . . I don't know that either," Rebecca spoke truthfully. She remembered how she had followed Kin-di-wa to Fort Greenville despite his refusal to take her with him. "I—I need very much to meet with him—to speak to him alone."

"Oh, no you don't, young lady!" Uncle Hardin bellowed. "Don't think you're going to invite a savage into my house!"

Aunt Margaret leaned forward and fanned her face anxiously. "But Hardin . . . Amanda and Roger Bakewood invited him to their house."

"As a curiosity, madam! Only as a curiosity! They did not invite him as a friend—and certainly not as a prospect for a future member of the family!"

Roger sat down on the new Duncan Phyfe. "Quite right, Hardin old man. They invited him only to amuse their friends—at my or our expense, of course. I told them—in confidence you may be certain—that Rebecca had lived among the Miami savages for a time. So naturally when they heard that this fellow was a Miami also, they gambled on the possibility that perhaps the two had met. Oh, Cousin Samuel denied it, of course, but—"

"But I thought this invitation meant you were reconciled with your family!" Aunt Margaret wailed. "I thought it meant we were going to be accepted among them! Isn't that why they gave the ball—so they could meet us and we could meet them and everyone would know that everything in your past had been forgiven?"

"In my past, madam?" Roger lifted one eyebrow. "And what have you heard about my past?"

"Oh, dear, I guess I shouldn't have said that . . ." Aunt Margaret put her hand to her mouth. "But, well, you see . . . I had heard some things . . . about your morals . . ."

"We're wasting time here!" Uncle Hardin thundered. "Niece, you must tell us once and for all! Are you going to marry Roger? Because if you aren't—for whatever reason—I'm changing my will in the morning! I won't see all I've worked for go to ruin. The fact is, Roger's a Bakewood, and Bakewoods stand by their own. Black sheep of the family or no, they'll accept him back in the fold as soon as he's safely married—and they'll accept us too because we're willing to stake Roger's future."

Rebecca was sickened. It was shockingly clear to her that her aunt and uncle would stop at nothing to move upward in society. They not only knew about Roger's loose background and his crass motivation for marrying her, they applauded it. And their love for her was conditional: if she played along with their scheme, her financial future was assured. If she did not, they would send her packing.

Oh, how had she willingly allowed herself to become a part of this? How had she consented to trade her future happiness for something so cheap as money? Was this the heritage she wanted to give her child? Did she really want her son or daughter to consider a full belly and fine clothes to be more important than love or happiness?

Kin-di-wa's image flashed in her mind. Willingly, she had endured cold, hunger, grief, and war for him, and willingly, she would endure it all over again just for the chance to be near him. Few goals in life were worth so much—but love was surely one of them. If she had to sacrifice everything, her inheritance, her security and that of her child's, so be it. She wouldn't let Kin-di-wa leave without her. She'd beg for his forgiveness. Indeed, she'd follow him all the way back to the Miami of the Lake in the dead of winter, if necessary!

"Well, Niece?" Uncle Hardin was waiting for her answer. Roger gave her a confident stare, and Aunt Margaret smiled tremulously through tear-filled eyes.

"No, Uncle Hardin," she said. "I will not marry Roger. Go ahead and change your will. I'll marry no man but Kin-di-wa—if we aren't already married."

Rebecca sat on the edge of her bed in the darkness and waited for the household to settle down. A short distance down the hall, she could still hear Aunt Margaret weeping and Uncle Hardin speaking gruffly. Gradually, the noise subsided, but Rebecca sat waiting patiently— knowing that sleep would be long in coming to anyone in this house tonight.

Her decision had been greeted by pleas to reconsider from Aunt Margaret, a rash of swearing by Uncle Hardin, and a fearsome silence by Roger. Finally, Roger had stood up and pointed a shaking finger at her. "You're going to be sorry," he had rasped. "I'll not become a figure of ridicule—turned down by a pregnant woman whose child is a savage's bastard. Mark my words, if you refuse to marry me, you'll live to regret it."

And with that, he'd snatched up his greatcoat and left.

Poor Roger, Rebecca thought now. His disappointment was obviously bitter, but no doubt he'd soon get over it. He'd never been in love with her, and perhaps, Uncle Hardin would be willing to lend him the money he so desperately needed—the money he wouldn't be receiving as a wedding gift.

Rebecca had far more sympathy for Aunt Margaret. Her aunt had begged both her and Uncle Hardin to reconsider. "But, Hardin," she had pleaded. "Even if Rebecca has disappointed us, she's still our niece. We can't just throw her out into the cold."

"Do you take me for a monster, madam?" Uncle Hardin had grumbled. "Of course, we'll feed and shelter her—but not a penny will she receive unless she relents and marries Roger. This is our one chance, Maggie, to become somebodies instead of nobodies, and I'm not about to throw it away without a fight."

But Aunt Margaret and Uncle Hardin will have to remain nobodies, Rebecca thought sadly. There was nothing she could—or would—do to help them, no matter how low they stooped in an effort to persuade her. Not that she expected them to stoop very low—her aunt and uncle weren't wicked; they were simply foolish and shallow. Oh, why couldn't they find in each other the happiness they were seeking elsewhere?

Rebecca held her breath and listened but could

hear no one moving or speaking. Silence had swallowed up the house. She slid off the bed and gathered up her velvet pelisse and her sturdy warm cape to go over it. A shaft of moonlight coming through her window illuminated the path to her door. The room was cold, but Rebecca felt warm and wet with perspiration. If she could remember the way to the Man Full Of Trouble Inn, she would soon be seeing Kin-di-wa!

Down the stairs she crept, hardly daring to breathe lest someone hear her. Aunt Margaret would say she was mad to think of going out alone so late to a public inn. Uncle Hardin would plant himself in front of the door and forbid her to leave. But nothing on earth could keep her from going. She had to see Kin-di-wa tonight—she must. What if he departed before she saw him? What if she never had the chance to tell him how much she loved him? What if he left never even knowing that the baby was his and that neither Will nor Jake had succeeded in laying a hand on her?

On top of all that, she had to see him because she couldn't bear to be apart from him any longer. He was alive. He was still hers. And she belonged beside him.

She reached the front door and was stealthily opening it, when something sounded behind her. Expecting the worst, she whirled around and saw only Snowflake leaping down the steps toward her. The patter of his paws sounded like raindrops on the polished hardwood floor.

"No, Snowie, you stay here . . . go on back up

to Aunt Margaret."

The little dog whined and wagged his tail. His whole body shook with his message: he was desperate to go outside. Otherwise he would never have left the little pink and lace pillow Aunt Margaret had installed beside her bed for him.

"No . . . I can't take you now. You'll have to stay here." Rebecca shrugged into her pelisse and tugged her cape over the top of it. The air from the open doorway was frigid. "Go on now, Snowie . . . go back to bed."

Rebecca backed through the doorway, blocking the path to freedom with her unwieldy body. She eased the door shut on Snowflake's nose and heard him whine and scratch. Then came his high-pitched yelp. Quickly, she opened the door again before he could alert anyone else to his problem.

"Oh, Snowie! . . . all right then, but hurry up!" Rebecca stepped aside and allowed the little dog to dart past her skirt. His white tail waved gaily as he disappeared down the icy front steps.

"Missus Rebecca? Is that yo' lettin' in all that cold air?"

Rebecca froze. Clad in a ghostly white nightgown of coarse-spun linen, Prudy came toward her down the darkened hallway.

"I—I'm just waiting for Snowflake to come back in," she faltered. "He insisted on going out."

"Jus' a minit, an' I'll lights a candle," Prudy said.

"Oh no, don't bother!" Rebecca pleaded. "I'll only be a moment."

But the ghostly figure retreated back the way it

had come, and a light flickered, grew bright, and moved toward Rebecca. Her heart fluttered and thumped. What explanation could she offer for still being dressed in her ballgown—having never changed for bed?

Prudy held up the candle, and the light spilled across Rebecca. "Lordy, Missus! Why is yo' got yoah cape on—an' yoah pretty new clothes? Surely, yo' wuzn't goin' out alone at this time o' night?"

"I—I was just letting Snowflake out, as I said. And I haven't yet felt like undressing." Rebecca's cheeks flamed at the lie, but she stared into Prudy's shocked brown eyes with an air of defiance—daring her to argue.

"An' ah wuz jus' woke up by a vision o' angels—come t' sing me a fanciful tune!" Prudy scoffed. "But ah guess ah deserves t' be told a falsehood fur askin' sech stupid questions. You're runnin' off t' meet up with yoah Injun, isn't that what yo' is doin'?"

Rebecca was swept with shame. "Yes . . ." she admitted. "Forgive me for fibbing. Does everyone in the house know what happened tonight?"

"Yas'm, honey, they shoah does. An' ah don't blame yo' fo' wantin' t' git outa here and go t' him. But . . . here now, close that door. Ah'm catching mah death o' cold."

Rebecca reluctantly eased the door shut behind her until she heard a whine and remembered Snowflake. She reopened it a crack, and the little dog slipped through and danced around her ankles—pleased with himself and her. It wasn't often he had company in the middle of the night.

"Come on back t' the kitchen," Prudy urged. "An' ah'll fix a nip o' tea."

Rebecca followed Prudy's white-clad figure down the hallway to the shadowed recesses of the kitchen. She didn't want tea. She wanted to leave the house immediately, as soon as she'd persuaded the girl to pretend that she hadn't seen or heard a thing.

Prudy set the candle in its pewter holder down on the work table where Bess did all her chopping, kneading, and mixing. "I shoah could use a cuppa tea mahself . . . is it all right wif yo' if I have one too?"

"What?" It took a moment before Rebecca remembered that Prudy was a slave and not allowed to help herself to food or drink without permission. "Oh, yes, do have some . . . but don't make any for me. I really can't stay, Prudy. I must go to my husband. He'll likely be up and gone before dawn, so if I don't go now, I may miss him."

Prudy paused in the act of stirring up embers in the kitchen fireplace. "Is yo' really an' truly married t' him, Missus Rebecca—or does yo' jes' wish yo' wuz?"

"Of course, I'm married to him!" Rebecca was indignant. "We're married in every way that counts. I don't care what anyone else thinks of our arrangement. Before God and my husband's people—most of all before ourselves—we're married."

"Then why don't he jus' come here an' claim yo'?"

"That's something I haven't time to explain right now, Prudy. He has his reasons, as I have mine for wanting to go to him. All I ask is that you don't alarm Aunt Margaret or Uncle Hardin." Rebecca pulled her cape more snuggly around her shoulders to let Prudy know she didn't intend to change her mind about going out.

Imperturbed, Prudy reached for the tea strainer. It hung from a hook on the wall. "An' whut shall I tell Missus Margaret in th' mornin'? Shall I tell her yo' is gone fur good?"

Rebecca shrugged her dislike of this line of questioning. Thus far, she hadn't allowed herself to think past the necessity for seeing Kin-di-wa tonight. She didn't want to think past it. Until she knew whether her husband would forgive her, nothing else mattered. Deciding not to marry Roger was as far as she could go in deciding her future—the rest was up to Kin-di-wa.

"Why tell her anything? Pretend you know nothing. That should be easy enough, since I haven't said what I plan to do."

Prudy's glance dropped to the strainer that glinted silver in the flickering light. "Ah jus' don't wants nothin' bad t' happen t' yo', Missus Rebecca. Ah don't wants yo' t' git hurt. Yo' oughtn't t'be roamin' th' streets alone at night— runnin' off t' a man yo' thought wuz dead an' who nevah let yo' know diff'rent."

Rebecca was deeply moved by Prudy's concern. Sometime, when she had more time, she would explain everything to her. She would finally rid herself of the terrible burden of guilt and sorrow she'd been carrying for so long—much as she carried her unborn child. "It will be all right, Prudy. I promise. Kin-di-wa is staying at the Man Full Of Trouble Inn. I know where it is. I won't get lost."

Prudy's eyes became two round black stones. "But yo' cain't go there alone, Missus Rebecca! Why, that ain't fittin'!"

"I'm going, Prudy. There isn't anyone else I could ask to go with me."

"Yo' ain't asked me! I could go wif yo'. Two wimmin out alone at night has sure gotta be safer than one. Ah' could even go rouse Henry-Luke an make 'im come along an' look after us both!"

Rebecca started. "No! Not Henry-Luke." The last person she would want to accompany her would be the tall, sly handyman who was so friendly with Roger Bakewood.

"Then it's settled that at least ah'm comin'!" Prudy laid the tea strainer down on the table. "Y'all wait right here til ah gits dressed."

Rebecca waited with mixed emotions. Prudy could get into a great deal of trouble for taking part in this scheme. If Uncle Hardin found out about it, he might even whip her. Bess and Prudy were always treated well, but given severe provocation, there could be exceptions. Rebecca had about decided to insist that Prudy stay home, when a man walked into the kitchen—a man she had never before seen.

"Wh—who are you?" she stammered.

The black face under the workman's round felt hat broke into a white-toothed grin. "It's me—

389

Prudy! Doan ah look like a lady's man-servant in these ole clothes o' Henry-Luke's?"

Grinning despite her surprise, Rebecca studied her friend. Prudy wore a pair of breeches made of mattress ticking and a patched and faded home-spun jacket. Several layers of clothing peeked out from underneath, but the identity of these was perhaps best not discovered.

"You—look perfectly fine to me!"

Prudy took a long curved butcher knife from the knife block and stuck it somewhere inside her coat. "Wished ah had me a pistol. Then ah could pertec' us from anythin' that came after us."

Rebecca shook her head disapprovingly. "I've seen you wield that knife on a piece of meat. I doubt we need anything else, especially a pistol that you wouldn't know how to fire anyway. Hurry now, we'd better go . . ."

Snowflake pattered after them down the hallway, but when they got to the door, Rebecca bent down and said in her sternest voice, "Go on back to bed, Snowflake. You can't come with us. And don't you tell Aunt Margaret where we've gone either!"

The little white dog licked her fingers, then, as if he understood everything she'd told him, turned and pattered toward the steps. Rebecca closed the heavy front door behind them and filled her lungs with the icy cold night air.

They arrived at the Man Full Of Trouble Inn without incident. Other than occasionally slipping and sliding on patches of ice and having to avoid a night watchman on his rounds, they had no difficulty making the journey. A full moon showed them the way; not even the cold deterred them. The exhilaration of doing something so dangerous and foolhardy kept them unaware of how frosty it actually was. But once in front of the inn, beneath the sign depicting the man for whom the inn was named, Prudy began having qualms.

"Yo' cain't jes' march in there an' ask fer yoah husban', Missus Rebecca. Why, if they's anybody still awake, they's gonna be a-drinkin' an' a-carryin' on."

"Now, Prudy, this is supposed to be a respectable establishment," Rebecca argued. "Besides, the presence of a trusted man-servant should be enough to discourage any problems."

"But Missus Rebecca, how yo' gonna explain goin' up t' a man's bed chambah at this hour o' th' night? Won't it look mighty peculiar an' compromisin'?"

"I suppose it will, but I didn't come this far to back out now." Rebecca was about to go marching straight for the door when it suddenly swung open, emitting the sound of male laughter and a shaft of golden light.

Quickly, she stepped back into the sheltering shadows, dragging Prudy with her, as two men exited the Inn. The taller and brawnier of the two stumbled and almost fell, then lurched forward, leaning heavily on his buddy's arm. A portion of their conversation carried clearly to Rebecca's ears. "Whut ya say, Jake, ole fren'? Let's go fine us a couple willin' wimmin to finish off our celebratin'. I mean, I ain't had me a piece o' sweetmeat fer longer'n I care t' think about."

"Ain't no woman gonna look at th' two of us, Will," the other man hissed savagely. "Me, whut only gots one eye left, and you whut is all clawed up. I ain't settin' myself up t' be laughed at by no saucy bitch. B'sides, I'm savin' up all I got fer the one that done this to us."

The two men paused a moment in front of the sign, and in the cold light of the moon, Rebecca saw them clearly—two familiar-looking backwoodsmen with coonskin caps and full growths of beard. They turned in her direction, and fear exploded in her chest. She had to bite her tongue to hold back a scream. Despite a patch over the right eye of the shorter one and several deep ugly scars on the face of the taller one, she would have recognized them anywhere: Will Simpkin and Jake Potts.

Oblivious to her and Prudy's presence alongside the inn, Will scratched his well-padded chest, swaying where he stood. "Wuzn't that a piece o' luck though! Findin' out where she lives our second day in town!" He staggered closer to the sign pole and leaned against it. "Little bitch . . . little red-haired whore. All these months it took us—but we're finally gonna git our revenge."

Jake Potts pinched his hawklike nose between his fingers and blew out a stream of mucus onto the cobblestones. He wiped his nose with the back of his sleeve. "Allus did say, you wanna know somepin' jes' go an' ask at every tavern in town—somebody gonna know. Ain't no secrets in taverns."

Will looked up at the sign. "Too bad we ain't stayin' in this one—the Man Full O' Trouble Inn. Y' see, Jake . . ." he grunted mirthlessly. "I'm plumb full o' troubles myself. I mean, until a hour ago, I wuzn't even certain she wuz still alive! Becky could've ben killed or dragged off by some maraudin' Injuns or even 'ave gone someplace else b'sides back to her aunt an' uncle . . ."

"Yeah . . ." Jake snorted. "She could'ave ben clawed half t' death by bears like we wuz. No tellin' whut might'ave happened t' her. Guess it wuz plumb lucky we finally caught up with 'er."

Will drunkenly hugged the signpost. "Whut do ya think we should do now, Jake? I mean, b'sides stealin' her away. I want she should pay, dammit! She's gotta pay fer all she done t' us!" He leaned back and took a swing at the post as if it were a person, and though his fist did not connect, Rebecca cringed and shook.

"We'll think on it t'morrow . . ." Jake laid a hand on Will's shoulder. "We'll think on it . . . maybe her aunt and uncle would pay plenty t' git whut's left o' her back again after we git done with 'er. We'll scout th' place first thing t'morrow an' see whut's t' be done."

Will unwound himself from the signpost. "Gawd A'mighty! I cain't wait t' see 'er face when we grabs 'er! I bet she thought we wuz done fer when she sicked them bears on us!"

"We almost wuz done fer," Jake said darkly. "That she-bear almos' blinded me—an' that's somepin' a man don't fergit."

Rebecca was overwhelmingly grateful for the concealing blackness where she and Prudy hid. If Will were to see her face now, he'd discover all he could possibly wish to see there: sickening shock and gut-clenching horror. Her chest was so constricted with fear, she had no sensation of breathing.

Zigzagging drunkenly, the two men moved off down the street. As they passed beneath a whale-oil lamp and out of ear-shot, Prudy moved soundlessly toward Rebecca. "Yo' see why yo' cain't go in there, Missus Rebecca? T'ain't safe wif scum like that about!"

Rebecca started. Did Prudy realize that the men had been talking about her? But her friend's next words dispelled that notion. "Huh! Wonder where th' night watchman is now, when we need 'im? Who ever th' poor girl is that those men're lookin' foah, ah hope she keeps her doors locked tight an' nevah goes out on th' streets alone! . . . Now, come on, Missus Rebecca . . . let's jus' go on back 'ome where we b'longs!"

But now that Will and Jake were gone, Rebecca's courage came flooding back in stronger measure. Kin-di-wa was sleeping in the very inn where Jake and Will had learned the whereabouts of her aunt and uncle and of herself. Now, it was even more important that she get to him—and get away with him. Now, there was no time to waste.

394

In a town where it had taken Jake and Will only two days to find out where she lived, how long would it take before they found Kin-di-wa—or he found them? They might even run into each other on the streets.

"You can go home, if you want to, Prudy—I'm going inside the inn." Rebecca started walking.

"Missus Rebecca—wait! Why don't ah go inside th' inn an' say ah gots a message fer yoah husban'? An' then ah'll bring 'im outside t yo'!"

"Prudy . . ." Rebecca summoned up her patience. "That's a fine idea but we can't stand out here talking on the street. I'd much prefer to say what I have to say to him someplace where it's warmer and more private."

"Ah know! Yo' kin wait fer 'im inside th' stable! Nobody'll bother yo' there!"

"The stable?" The idea appealed to Rebecca immediately. Kin-di-wa could slip out to join her without causing any disruption inside the inn.

"The stable's likely 'round back or down this way, ah expect." Prudy gestured vaguely behind them.

"I'm sure I can find the stable, Prudy . . . all right. Go ahead. I'll wait for him there. Tell him . . . tell him Cat-Eyes wishes to speak with him. And be careful . . . don't let anyone guess you're a woman."

Prudy drew herself up straight and said with dignity, "Ah knows jes' how t' handle this, Missus Rebecca . . . don't yo' worry none about it!"

Rebecca kept to the shadows and went looking

for the stable. She found it farther down the street overlooking the Delaware River. A single whale oil lamp illuminated the entrance, but once inside, Rebecca found the darkness forbidding. The smell of hay and straw and the pungent odor of horses tickled her nostrils. She heard a few low nickers and a clatter of hooves. Then her eyes adjusted to the darkness, and she could see that the stable was half full.

Its occupants turned their heads curiously in her direction. Timidly, she moved down the row of animals, searching for a bale of straw or something on which she could sit. At the very end of the stable, she found five or six bales stored up close to the wall. The floor itself was littered with straw and Rebecca sat down on a bale and gratefully burrowed her feet into the scattered debris. Only her feet reminded her that this was January—possibly the coldest month of the year.

She waited with nerve endings all a-tingle. Seeing Will and Jake had come in the nature of a physical blow, but she could not take time to worry about them now. What should she say to Kin-di-wa? She quivered with nervousness. Her insides might have been made of whipped syllabub or calves' foot jelly.

She rubbed her hands together beneath her warm cape. Then she studied the plume of frosty air in front of her face. Her breath and that of the horses made the stable seem almost warm. Looking up, she saw that a stray moonbeam had worked its way through the broken shingles and slats of the roof; a silvery pool of moonlight lay on the floor in front of her.

Suddenly, she became aware that she was no longer alone. Someone was walking toward her through the tunneled darkness. She strained her eyes to see clearly and held her breath. Her bosom heaved with churning emotions. "Kin-di-wa," she whispered. "Is that you?"

Fifteen

The tall figure came to a standstill in the pool of moonlight, and in the silver glow, she recognized him. "My husband," she breathed. She wanted to stand up but didn't trust her legs to hold her.

"You should not have come here, Cat-Eyes," he said.

Was there a slight tremor in his voice? Reaching up, she grasped his hands. "I came because I belong to you—as you belong to me. Where else should I be but here? I love you, Kin-di-wa . . ."

Her voice broke. Clinging to his hands, she pulled herself upright, and now, it was easy to see him. The line of his hair, the ridge of his nose, the crest of his cheekbones were brushed with silver. Only his eyes remained dark and shadowed. Dispassionately, he pulled his hands away. "You betrayed me, Cat-Eyes—there's no longer room in my life for you."

The way he said "you" sliced through Rebecca's heart. Though she stood close enough to embrace him, she sensed that he would only push her away. His pain was too great to be soothed by her touch. Only the truth could ease him. "Kin-di-wa, the child is yours—not Will's or Jake's. I realized I was pregnant the day I went away with them."

For a moment, he didn't speak. "Then you did not become pregnant on that day—or rather, that night—when you abandoned me to my enemies."

"No, Kin-di-wa . . . I was already into my second month by then. The child will be born next moon, in four or five weeks at most. Perhaps, it will even be born earlier."

Kin-di-wa's eyes searched her face. She tilted her face to the moonlight to show him she had nothing to hide, then took his hand and guided it to the firm fullness of her unborn child. The baby chose that moment to thrust a foot against his father's hesitant fingers. "You see, he knows it's you . . ." she whispered. "He knows it by the joyful beating of his mother's heart."

Fleetingly, a look of wonder invaded Kin-di-wa's face, but then his mouth tightened and turned downward again. "And does he know that his mother is unworthy of him? That she betrayed his father by lying with other men?"

Rebecca kept Kin-di-wa's hand closed over the bulge of their child. The child might reach him even if she failed. Knowing her husband as she did, she knew he could never deny his child. "I never lay with Will or Jake. I never intended to lie with them. Crow Woman instructed me in the use of herbs to take away a man's desire. But before the herbs were even needed, I found a way to escape."

This was not precise truth, of course, but the details could all come later. For the moment, Rebecca simply wanted to cut through his disbelief—to make him know that she had never been unfaithful to him. Never since the day she'd met him had she desired another man.

"That is most difficult to believe, Cat-Eyes. Neither man is stupid in the ways of the forest. Though I have taught you well, I doubt you could have hidden your trail so carefully that they could not find you when they came after you."

"They didn't come after me . . . I—I provoked a she-bear with yearling cubs and led her straight to them."

Kin-di-wa's glance probed her soul. "The bears killed them?"

"I—I didn't stay to find out," she evaded. "I ran away and hid. Then, because I believed that you were dead, I followed the Great Miami River down to Fort Washington. I joined a settler family coming back east, and they brought me here to Philadelphia where I found my aunt and uncle."

"But who told you I was dead?" Kin-di-wa's hands gripped her forearms. "Why did you not return to Fort Greenville to discover for yourself whether I lived or died?"

"Will told me . . . after Jake went back to check. I was frantic and begged them to find out.

They didn't tell me right away, and I thought it was because they knew I would never go with them once I knew of your death . . . It didn't take them as long as it took you to discover that I was only trying to protect you," she added bitterly.

A silence followed her outburst, then came a long low sigh. "Ah, Cat-Eyes . . ." Kin-di-wa's arms slid around her waist. He pressed her to him, and his chin brushed her hair and came to rest there. "I could not believe you had done that to me—turned me over to my enemies and denied me revenge on my brother's murderer."

Her heart fluttered with hopefulness at his changing mood. "I only did it out of love, Kin-di-wa. Perhaps, I was wrong and foolish . . . perhaps, I should have had more trust in you . . ."

"No," he nuzzled her hair. "I was the one who was foolish . . . I put my desire for revenge before everything, even my duty to my people. I—not you—brought all this suffering upon us. It is I who am shamed, for my love was not as strong as yours. It was not . . ."

"Hush, my husband . . . I will not allow anyone to speak against the father of my baby." Rebecca leaned back to look into her husband's face. Happiness and relief surged through her. He was no longer angry, and she was filled to bursting. Eagerly, her hands moved up his velvety-soft buckskin shirt and entwined themselves in his hair. "Kin-di-wa, oh my beloved, my dreams have been haunted with the memory of you. I have wept so many tears, I have longed so much to be near you . . ."

"Little one, ah little one . . ." His warm breath caressed her face. Slowly, like the figure in her dreams, he bent his head. His lips touched hers. They moved in a circle around her mouth, then closed over her mouth.

She was lost in his deep probing kiss and felt the impact of the intimacy all the way down to her chilled toes. A warmth spread through her—as if she'd downed several goblets of Aunt Margaret's French sherry in quick succession. Her limbs began to shake.

His voice rumbled huskily. "You are cold?"

Unable to speak, she shook her head no. Cold was the furthest thing from her mind. Her body was aflame with desire and the sensation strangely embarrassed her. How was it possible that she—a woman almost nine months pregnant—could go weak-kneed with a single kiss?

His arms enfolded her and lifted her off her feet in one swift movement. Cradled against his broad chest, she could hear his thudding heart. He looked around the stable once then moved closer to the stacked bales of hay. With one swift kick, he collapsed the nearest one.

Breathlessly, she waited to be laid down in the sweet-smelling mass, but then he paused. "This is no good. You will take cold, and the child in your womb will be harmed."

She thought he was having second thoughts about the wisdom of their making love in her condition. "It won't hurt the child . . ." she hastened to assure him. "I'm strong and healthy, and the child is too."

But her words had no effect on him. He spun around and strode toward the door.

"Wh—where are we going?" she quavered.

"I think it is time to enjoy the white man's comforts," he responded in a mysterious passion-laden tone.

Nervousness and excitement warred in Rebecca's consciousness, but not for anything or anyone would she have stopped him—no matter where he took her. She wound her arms around his neck and reveled in the feel of his living strength as he carried her effortlessly out of the stable, down the street, and around the corner to the entrance of the Inn.

He kicked open the door and carried her inside. Candles in pewter holders lit the interior, and a small fire glowed in a tile-enclosed fireplace. Rebecca had a quick impression of cleanliness and warmth as Kin-di-wa purposefully threaded his way through empty chairs and tables, passed the cagelike structure of the bar, and headed for a staircase.

"Mister Golden Eagle, sir!" A bald-headed man jumped up from a table in a corner of the inn. He left another man, with whom he'd been sharing a pitcher of ale, and came running after them. Eyes as round as china saucers peered worriedly through thin wire spectacles as he looked from Kin-di-wa to Rebecca and back again to Kin-di-wa. "Pardon me, sir, forgive me, but where are you going with—this lady?"

Kin-di-wa looked down at the short, bald innkeeper and gave him the barest whisper of a smile. "This lady is my woman, and I'm going upstairs to my bed with her."

"Upstairs!" The innkeeper's voice squeaked.

Rebecca stifled a laugh. "It's true . . . I am his wife, and we're going upstairs to bed." She smiled her prettiest smile. "Really, it's quite all right . . . If it's for the sake of my virtue that you worry, why—as you can see—I am already pregnant."

The little innkeeper stared at them speechlessly, and Kin-di-wa brushed past him and mounted the stairs. He carried Rebecca down a narrow hallway, turned into a spacious bedchamber, and closed the door firmly behind them.

Rebecca was breathless with giggles as he set her down on her own two feet. After months of being "proper and refined," and even longer months of being gloomy, laughter now poured forth from her. Her fingers struggled helplessly to remove her cape. "Oh, Kin-di-wa! The poor innkeeper looked so shocked! I doubt he believed a word we said—unless, of course, Prudy explained about us."

She stopped giggling and drew a deep breath. Where was Prudy? In the excitement of seeing her husband, Rebecca had forgotten all about her friend. "Kin-di-wa? . . . Where's the messenger I sent to you?"

Suddenly practical in his concern for her, Kin-di-wa had already left her side and was laying another log on the fire in the tiny bedroom fireplace. The fire's rosy glow provided the only light in the room and revealed the only furnishings: a sturdy four-poster bed, a single cherry-wood chair, a washstand with basin and pitcher, and a pewter chamber pot.

Kin-di-wa stood up straight and began to undo the lacings of his buckskin shirt. "Do you mean he who has skin the color of a raven's wing? Pah! What a weak excuse for a man! I sent him back to your aunt and uncle. He didn't want to go, but I told him I would take his scalp if he argued."

"Did—did she, I mean he go back there, do you think?"

"You do not see him, do you?" Kin-di-wa slowly removed his shirt and the warming expression in his eyes made her put aside her fears for Prudy's safety. At least, the girl had a knife to protect herself—and her disguise had fooled even Kin-di-wa. It was best she had gone home quickly; now, she could not be punished for having taken part in this escapade.

Rebecca drank in the sight of her husband, standing so tall and handsome before the fire. His bared broad chest was as sculpted with muscles as she remembered; his shoulder-length hair was as black and glossy. An embroidered rawhide band held back his hair from his aristocratic face. She wondered what had become of his two white feathers, then guessed that they had already been removed in anticipation of sleeping. But to sleep, was not why they had come to this warm, sheltered room.

Involuntarily, her glance strayed to the bed. Disdaining quilts or blankets, Kin-di-wa had spread his buffalo robe across the mattress of the large canopied four-poster. Other skins were heaped to form a pillow. He followed the direction of her gaze, and his brilliant blue eyes sparkled hungrily. "Sometimes, in the middle of the night, I get up and move my bed to the floor. White beds are too soft, and I must remember that I am Miami."

"But you are white too . . ." she reminded him softly. "It isn't so wrong to enjoy the comforts of the white man . . . have you not enjoyed your visit to Philadelphia? You must tell me about it . . . and about Sweet Breeze and Little Turtle too. I— I never heard everything that happened at the Treaty Council either."

She berated herself for babbling mindlessly— but was swept with a sudden shyness, as though this man were a stranger.

"Later, Cat-Eyes. We will speak of such things later."

His tone was a warm invitation. They moved toward one another—pulled by a force that was stronger than either of them. Blue fires leapt in his eyes; she could feel the heat of his passion even before he touched her. His hand trailed down the folds of her velvet pelisse. "What manner of covering is this? I have never known anything that felt like this."

"Velvet . . . It's called velvet." Swiftly, she undid the fastenings and slipped out of the concealing garment. Cape and pelisse slithered half-way to the floor before practicality gripped her. She caught the garments and laid them across the nearby chair, then wondered what he thought of her revealing gown. When she raised her eyes to his, she knew. He looked both intrigued and disapproving.

"Why do your aunt and uncle allow you to go about dressed like this?" His fingers ran lightly over the plunging neckline, causing her to shiver with anticipation.

"Here, in Philadelphia, this dress is considered to be the height of fashion."

"So I noticed earlier this night . . ."

His fingers dipped into the valley between her breasts, and she thought she would swoon at the sensation. Then he rubbed the filmy material of her gown between his thumb and forefinger. "The color of your dress is the same color as your eyes. What does one call this sort of covering?"

"Silk . . ." she breathed.

"Hardly a covering at all," he murmured.

"Another garment is worn beneath it—at least by modest ladies. It's made from the same material as this one."

"Are you wearing such a garment?"

"Yes . . ."

"Then I would see that one too . . ."

Rebecca began to undo the trailing ribbons beneath her bosom, but her fingers were all atremble. He reached out and undid the ribbons for her. "Thank you," she whispered.

He helped her remove the fragile flowing gown. It too went across the chair. Now she wore nothing but her silken shift.

"I am sorry that doeskin doesn't come in the color of new spring leaves—the color of your eyes." His fingertips caressed her bare arms. "It is a color you should always wear." Next, his hands moved up to dislodge the carefeul order of her hair. The little mass of curls came tumbling down, and he luxuriated in the flowing red tresses. "But I think I like it better when the flowers in your hair are real . . ."

"One cannot have everything, my husband . . . especially in winter." She removed the disarranged silk flowers that had held her curls in place and set them on the mantelpiece.

His fingers wound themselves in her hair as if he couldn't get enough of feeling it. Then, with one lazy finger, he traced her lips and trailed down her chin to her neck. He stopped when he reached the cameo affixed to a ribbon at her throat. "And what is this?" he asked.

She stiffened. The cameo was Roger's Christmas present to her; she'd forgotten she'd worn it to please him this evening. Reaching up, she clawed the bauble away from her suddenly burning skin. But Kin-di-wa grasped her hand before she could toss it into the fireplace. He took the cameo from her and turned it over in his palm to look at it. "Who gave this to you, Cat-Eyes?"

"R—Roger Bakewood," she answered truthfully, but not wanting to say more.

His eyes compelled her to continue, and she realized that if she did not, if she refused to be honest with him on this matter, everything they had gained tonight would surely be lost again. "The reason for the ball this evening was to announce our forthcoming marriage. We were to have been married at the end of next week."

His eyes darkened, but somehow he managed to control his emotions and did not turn away from her. "He was one of the men who came with you to the gathering?"

She nodded. "The other was my uncle. You must not have heard the introductions . . ."

Anxiously, she studied his face. In the glow from the fire, his cheekbones were a dusky rose, and each nuance of expression was unerringly revealed. His expression now was jealous, as she might have expected—but also oddly patient. "From the moment I saw you come into that room, Cat-Eyes, I heard nothing that was said to me . . . I would hear you tell me about this man . . ."

She was jolted by Kin-di-wa's willingness to listen and discuss the matter calmly. Had they both learned some difficult lessons from what had happened between them? Rebecca took his hand and walked over with him toward the bed. On the very edge of the bed, she sat down and drew him down beside her. It seemed easier to tell him this way, without having to face him or look up at him.

"I don't love Roger Bakewood," she began. "If the truth be told, I loathe him. But I had no money and no way to provide for our baby . . ."

In a short time, the telling was done, and despite the cultural gaps between them, and Kin-di-wa's difficulty in fathoming the strange ways of the whites, Rebecca felt she had said all she knew how to say.

"So you saw marriage as your duty . . . as a

matter of honor—even though you didn't love this man and didn't intend to share his bed." Kin-di-wa summed up her explanation without passing any judgment.

"Yes!" She turned to him with suddenly brimming eyes. "That's exactly the way it was! It was—it was like you having to marry Two Fires!"

"Little Cat-Eyes . . ." He brushed a tear from her cheek. "I wonder you did not remember how badly that affair turned out."

For a moment, the tragedy of Two Fires's death was fresh and alive again between them. Then Rebecca grasped her husband's hands. "But I did remember, Kin-di-wa. When I saw you, I knew I couldn't go through with it . . . and tonight I told Roger I could never marry him. No matter if you were willing to take me back again or not."

"Willing?" A slow suggestive smile enlivened Kin-di-wa's stern features. "I will demonstrate to you my willingness. Since you cannot seem to close your mouth and end your explanations, I will close it for you."

Kin-di-wa leaned forward and kissed her, and in the blinking of an eye, her long suppressed inner fires were rekindled. Kin-di-wa had not rejected her. His forgiveness washed over her like soothing balm. She drew him downward, his lips still devouring her mouth, and they lay back on the soft warm buffalo robe.

His kisses became warmer, more insistent. They covered her face, her hair, her throat. His hands moved gently across her body. Gently, they explored her swollen breasts. Pregnancy had enlarged them, and desire now made them even larger. He filled his hands with them, lightly stroking her nipples beneath the sliding silk.

He put his ear to her distended abdomen and communed silently with their child. She fancied he told the baby to sleep now and be still, so he could gently pleasure its mother. The absence of kicks and flutters told her the child obeyed.

Her body was filled with a rapturous languor as he stroked her from head to foot. She knew he must feel some urgency for when she tried to touch him, he pushed her hand away. But other than that single motion, all his movements were cherishing. He massaged the muscles of her legs and thighs, then turned her on her side and massaged her back and neck muscles.

She hadn't realized how stiff she was with tension until his hands brought relaxation. She closed her eyes and languidly floated off on a warm green sea and was gently rocked in a silvery mist. His hands and mouth were her entire world. He touched, stroked, kneaded, and kissed. His tongue was feather-soft and beguiling.

She could not have said when he removed her shift or helped her change position, or when the heat in her loins began to spread throughout her entire body. Yet the heat was gentle and controlled—like the heat of a low-banked lodge fire. And she had no doubt that soon she would be consumed in it.

Opening her eyes, she saw him poised above her. His extended arms kept the weight of his body from crushing their child. Never had his eyes been so brimful of love and passion. Never had they glowed with such blue intensity. He caressed and cherished her with his glance and in the breathless moment following, slid into her body and filled her with—himself.

Tantalizingly, he moved within her. Her hips rose to meet each slow and measured thrust with a gentle thrust of her own. Their child was a passenger on this journey to dizzying heights—forgotten and yet not forgotten. Release came in undulating waves, like the shuddering of a dogwood tree in spring as it rains down wave after wave of blossoms.

Rebecca would not have been surprised had she discovered dogwood blossoms in their bed. The memory of that other time—when their child had been conceived—lingered on the fringes of her consciousness like the scent of blooming flowers.

Kin-di-wa removed his body from hers and lay down on the bed beside her. He enfolded her in his arms. Her heart was still thumping rapidly, and her skin was sheened with wetness. She murmured her repletion, and he whispered against her ear. "Did I hurt you, little Cat-Eyes?"

"You could never hurt me . . . our bodies were made for loving."

"But the child . . . did I hurt the child?"

"The child slept—as all good children sleep when their parents wish to be alone with each other."

He nipped gently at her ear. "I only hope the babe sleeps as well after it is born."

"It will. Or I shall lace it into its cradleboard

and hang it from a nearby tree!"

Softly, they laughed together, and Rebecca thought she had never been so happy, so completely satisfied and filled with bliss. The child stirred to life within her, and she was reminded of the tenacity of living things. She was swept with awe that her body should have become a vessel for new life. It was a sacred mystery: because she and Kin-di-wa loved, a child had been conceived. The life force surged onward, sweeping them before it, as it moved in ancient rhythms only God Himself could understand.

Kin-di-wa's hand rested on the child, and when the babe stretched and moved, it seemed to her that her husband stopped breathing—the better to be aware of what his hand was feeling. "The child is strong," he said finally. "And I do not think it will long be content in the confines of its mother's body. After it is born, we shall return home again—perhaps, we should even wait until spring."

A chill fell over Rebecca as she thought of Jake and Will, and for a moment, in a spirit of total honesty, she wanted to tell him what she had seen and heard outside the inn tonight. But fear came rushing in too quickly. There were two of them against one of Kin-di-wa—and she was not about to lose her husband a second time. "I don't want to wait, Kin-di-wa. I want to leave for home tomorrow—as soon as I see Aunt Margaret and Uncle Hardin to tell them goodbye. If we leave right away, perhaps we could be half-way home by the time of the birth . . ."

"No, little Cat-Eyes," Kin-di-wa's voice was firm. "So far it has been a mild winter, but we cannot expect the mildness to continue. You are too far along to embark on such a dangerous journey. Will not your aunt and uncle also insist that you stay here?"

"My aunt and uncle will be very disappointed that I am not marrying Roger . . . I doubt I will be welcome anymore. And I doubt even more that you will be welcome . . ."

Kin-di-wa kissed her shoulder. "Then we can stay here, little Cat-Eyes. President Washington invited me to stay as long as I wish. He made arrangements with the innkeeper to see to all my needs. He says he hopes that if he treats me well, I can persuade Little Turtle to come to Philadelphia . . . There should be no difficulty persuading our chief. He has always had a burning interest to know more of the white man's ways, and now that we have made peace, I think he will accept the invitation of the great white Father."

"Why didn't he just come with you?" Rebecca was curious despite her worry over how to get Kin-di-wa to change his mind about staying in Philadelphia.

"He did not want to appear too eager. And he did not want to be here in Philadelphia to witness the triumphant return of Chenoten."

"General Wayne is coming here?" She sat up in astonishment—though why the general should not come to Philadelphia was beyond her power to answer. Until the building of the new capital on the shores of the Potomac River was completed, Philadelphia was still the center of culture and government.

"Chenoten left shortly after I did—only I did not have to transport legions of weary soldiers through the forest and across the mountains as he did. I expect he will arrive in a few weeks." Kin-di-wa reached out and ruffled her hair. "The Treaty Council was completed early in the Moon of New Corn, little one. We lost all but a portion of land running along the Miami of the Lake, and of the land we kept, we had to give up places for the building of forts so that white soldiers will always be among us. But at least, now there will be a time of peace—and we can only hope that it will be a long time before the greed of the whites grows strong again."

Rebecca sighed. She had read in a Philadelphia newspaper a brief article concerning the treaty terms. The article had pointed out that the Indians were lucky to be receiving twenty thousand dollars worth of goods, and an additional nine thousand and five hundred dollars annually, for lands that did not rightfully belong to them in the first place. The article had so angered her, that she had refused to read any more newspapers. Divided among so many tribes and sub-tribes, the goods and money would not go very far.

"How did Little Turtle respond to the treaty terms?" she asked, but what she really wondered was whether the Miami chieftain's proud spirit had yet been broken. She could not forget how hopelessly defeated he had looked during his illness last winter.

Kin-di-wa played with a lock of her hair, turning it this way and that, to see how it reflected the golden light from the fire. "His speeches were eloquent—or so I heard from the soldiers guarding the blockhouse. He gained permission for us to return to Kekionga and was even given his own piece of land there. He also succeeded in having Apekonit named as interpreter to our people . . ."

"But that's wonderful! Apekonit will make a fine interpreter! And Sweet Breeze will be so pleased to have her husband living among the Miamis again."

Kin-di-wa nodded. "Yes, it is wonderful, for I am certain we will need an interpreter we can trust." He paused. "Apekonit has also asked me if I will assist him—and I have been giving the matter much thought."

"Oh, Kin-di-wa, you must!" Rebecca seized her husband's hands. "You have so much to offer the tribes! Your mastery of English, your knowledge of history and how my people think and why they do what they do . . ."

Kin-di-wa shook his head and smiled ruefully. "You are as bad as Little Turtle. He said these same things when he sent me on this mission: use what you have been given, my son. It is a new day now, and we have great need of your gifts—those gifts that make you more than a simple warrior."

Rebecca smoothed back her husband's hair and kissed his forehead reassuringly. "I think Little Turtle speaks with wisdom—as he has always done. The day to be a warrior is gone; now, it is the day to be a diplomat."

"A diplomat?" Kin-di-wa's eyebrows shot up questioningly.

"One who solves problems with words instead of muskets," Rebecca explained.

"I don't know, Cat-Eyes . . ." Kin-di-wa shook his head again. "I still find it difficult to be comfortable when my feet are trying to walk in two worlds. Sometimes, I think it may be possible for whites and Indians to live in peace, but too often, the hatred rises up in me, as strong as it ever was . . . and then I want to reach for my weapons again and drive your people from my lands. I do not know if I have the great strength of character and purpose possessed by Little Turtle . . ."

Kin-di-wa shot her a burning blue glance. "When he made his mark on the treaty papers, after all the others had done so, he said, 'I am the last to sign this treaty, and I shall be the last to break it.' From that moment, Little Turtle turned his thoughts to how we might live peacefully and even learn from the whites—but I—I could still be persuaded to take up the war club again."

"Oh, my husband . . ." Rebecca drew him into her arms. "You are no less a man than Little Turtle just because you have doubts! These are weighty problems you grapple with—and most men deal with petty things that would only make them ashamed if they thought about it."

Rebecca remembered Uncle Hardin's efforts to be accepted into Philadelphia society. She hugged her husband tightly. "I would not wish you to be other than you are. Doubts and all, I love you, Kin-di-wa . . . I am proud to be your wife."

Kin-di-wa nuzzled her breasts. "When I know my woman loves me, all my doubts go away . . ."

Rebecca lay back on the bed, and no more words were spoken except those that could be spoken with their eyes, their mouths, and their bodies. A long time later, when the fire had died down in the hearth, and early morning light was creeping in at the shuttered window, Rebecca remembered that she still hadn't asked her husband about Sweet Breeze or Crow Woman or the rest of the Miamis.

She roused Kin-di-wa from a deep restful sleep and began to bombard him with questions. They tussled like children on the buffalo robe as he scolded her and answered her questions at the same time: everyone at the Miami encampment was well and would be happy to see her again. They had food enough to last the winter. Yes, he was certain Sweet Breeze would forgive her for leaving so quickly without saying goodbye . . . and yes, most important of all, Apekonit had already rejoined his wife and Sweet Breeze was expecting a child.

This last information made Rebecca's heart leap with happiness for her friend. She wondered when Sweet Breeze's baby was due: their children could be playmates for each other.

A sudden loud rap at the door spoiled her joyous thoughts as a rumble of thunder spoils a summer outing. Kin-di-wa rolled off the bed with the quick alertness born of sleeping in the wilderness, and Rebecca grabbed her pelisse from the chair-back and quickly covered her nakedness.

"Mister Golden Eagle, sir? There's someone downstairs waiting to see your—um, wife."

Kin-di-wa gave her a questioning look to which she responded, "It—it's probably just my friend— my man-servant. Actually, Prudy's not a man, after all, but a woman dressed up in a man's clothing." Noting her husband's puzzled expression, Rebecca hurried to explain. "We thought it would be safer if she looked like a man instead of a woman . . . Anyway, she's probably just worried about me and came to make certain I'm all right. I'll dress quickly and go down to see her."

Kin-di-wa spoke to the innkeeper on the other side of the door. "My woman—my wife—will come down in a few moments. Tell the visitor to wait."

Rebecca scrambled into her shift and gown, threw on her pelisse, and hastily tied back her disheveled hair with a ribbon. She'd not thought to bring a comb or anything else with which to freshen herself. Perhaps, Prudy could return home and get her some things. She would not want to face her painful meeting with Aunt Margaret and Uncle Hardin when she was looking so disreputable.

By the time Rebecca was ready, Kin-di-wa too was dressed and he held the door open for her. She went ahead of him down the hallway, then down the steps, and into the main room of the inn. She hoped Prudy would not be angry at having been abandoned by her or threatened by Kin-di-wa.

But it wasn't Prudy who stood before her. Looking slyly arrogant and accusing, it was Henry-Luke. A sense of evil foreboding made her shiver: why would Henry-Luke come here to the inn—where was Prudy?

BLANK PAGE

Sixteen

Henry-Luke said nothing for a moment—but his glance swept over her like icy fingers discovering all her secrets. Conscious of her dishevelment, Rebecca squared her shoulders and shot him a haughty stare. "Where's Prudy, Henry-Luke?"

"Back at yur aunt's an' uncle's—prayin' they don't sell 'er t' some big cotton plantation down South." Henry-Luke's eyes glinted, as if he hoped that was exactly what would happen. "Damn fool gurl shoulda knowed better—stealin' my laundry an' dressin' up in it t' take part in sech a damn fool scheme."

Rebecca's heart sank; Prudy had been discovered after all. And Henry-Luke was enjoying every minute of the poor girl's trouble. "It's not your business to judge her, Henry-Luke. She only did what I commanded her . . . and I intend to explain everything to my aunt and uncle this very morning."

Henry-Luke's lip curled. "That's why I came, Missus Rebecca. Yur aunt's outside in Mister Bakewood's carriage cryin' her eyes out—th' poor woman."

"And my uncle—where is he?"

"He's already down to th' London Coffee House on business. He was madder'n a hornet when he found out about you and Prudy, but he said he'd deal with th' whole thing later. It's just lucky we caught her is all . . . tryin' t' sneak back inta th' house in th' middle of th' night."

"We?"

"Bess an' me . . . Bess thought it was a thief come t' steal th' silver an' pewter."

Rebecca frowned. Her dislike of Henry-Luke was rapidly turning to pure hatred. On her own, Bess would not have made a fuss or alerted the entire household to the escapade. "And I suppose it was your idea to borrow Mister Bakewood's carriage to come and get me this morning, wasn't it?"

Henry-Luke grinned. "Yes, ma'am. But only 'cause poor Missus Stone was in sech a terrible state. She said she plumb couldn't wait 'til Mister Stone got through with business."

"Well . . . you may go out and tell your mistress that I shall be out to the carriage in a moment. I—I have business upstairs, and . . ."

"What is it, Cat-Eyes? Is something wrong?"

At the sound of Kin-di-wa's voice, Rebecca whirled around. She hadn't heard him come into the room. "Oh, Kin-di-wa! My aunt is most

424

upset—she's come in a carriage to get me . . ."

Kin-di-wa's warm grip on her arm made Rebecca fall silent. His glance warned her that there was no need to share their problems with the innkeeper, a tavern maid, and two other men—seamen by their dress—who were just coming into the empty dining room. She allowed her husband to escort her back in the direction of the steps and out of obvious earshot of the others.

"Do you wish to go and make things smooth with her?" Kin-di-wa eyed her with concern. "I shall stay here and wait for your return . . . or I could go with you, if you wish. President Washington is going to see me again today, but I can send a message that I am delayed."

Rebecca sighed. She didn't want to let Kin-di-wa out of her sight now that she'd found him again and they were reunited. But it seemed that their responsibilities to others must somehow be dealt with first; then they could truly savor and enjoy their reunion. She smiled into his bright blue eyes. "Why don't you let me go and speak to my aunt while you go and speak to the president. I will come back here later today. Then—I will know better about our future."

Kin-di-wa nodded. "That is best. Bring your clothes here when you come—something warmer and more sturdy than silk. Though you may keep one garment of silk, if you like." His expression spoke more than his words about what use she might make of one silk garment. "We shall talk about our future tonight."

She resisted the impulse to kiss him in public,

but allowed her fingers to brush his fringed sleeve. He would understand the underlying meaning of the casual gesture. She turned and walked toward Henry-Luke. "I am ready to see my aunt now. Please lead the way, Henry-Luke."

The curtains were drawn in the carriage. Rebecca noticed this immediately as she came out of the inn into a dim gray morning that threatened snow. Poor Aunt Margaret probably hadn't wanted anyone to witness her disgrace—having to fetch home a pregnant niece who had spent the night with her savage husband.

Henry-Luke opened the carriage door for her, and in her anxiety to watch her footing, Rebecca did not take any special note of the hand that reached out to help her step up into the vehicle. But the hand proved to have amazing strength, for no sooner had Rebecca grasped it, when she was hauled into the carriage with unexpected speed, grazing her shin bone in the process.

"My goodness! Aunt Marga . . ." The words died in Rebecca's mouth.

There was no one in the carriage but Roger Bakewood who quickly pulled the door shut behind her. Then someone—probably Henry-Luke—leapt into the driver's seat and the carriage jolted forward almost before Rebecca could catch her breath. She was thrown back against the seat opposite from Roger's. "Roger!" she exclaimed. "Where's Aunt Margaret?"

It was not surprising that Roger should have

chosen to come along on this little jaunt, but it *was* surprising that Aunt Margaret was not present as expected. Rebecca looked around the plush dark interior, half expecting Aunt Margaret to materialize out of nowhere.

"Ah, Rebecca . . ." Roger's nose was unusually ruddy in an otherwise ghostly pale face. Dark circles ringed his eyes. Rebecca caught a strong whiff of brandy and noticed that Roger too was still wearing his elegant velvet dress clothes from the previous evening. "Ah, Rebecca," he sighed again. "Would that I could have been the one to put the bloom in the lovely peaches of your cheeks. Wrinkled and mussed as you are, my dear, you are a breathtaking sight this morning."

Rebecca leaned forward in the rumbling carriage. "Roger, where is my aunt? Henry-Luke said she was concerned about me. Was she too distraught to come herself? Is that why you came alone?"

Roger coughed and cleared his throat. "Ah, yes . . . your dear Aunt Margaret. Why, I believe she's still at home, lying abed in her chambers. Do not concern yourself with her, my dear. I doubt she'll rise today before noon—especially after the strain of last night."

An ugly suspicion rose in Rebecca's mind. "Does she know where I am, Roger? Henry-Luke said . . ."

Roger snorted drunkenly. "My good friend and spy, Henry-Luke . . . What an accomplished liar he is! You must never pay much attention to anything said by Henry-Luke. One of the things for which I pay him is to spin any tale I tell him to."

"You pay him!" Rebecca's unspoken hazy fears became startling realities. "Henry-Luke is in your employ? But, of course, he would be, wouldn't he? He said he used to work for you—and the truth must be that he never quit!"

Her mind jumped with the possibilities of why Roger Bakewood had recommended Henry-Luke to her aunt and uncle for employment in the first place. The reason had to be Uncle Hardin's money, of course! Roger had simply found it convenient to know everything that was happening in the Stone household so he could somehow use it to his advantage.

Another conclusion came sailing home to her. Unthinkingly, she blurted it aloud. "Henry-Luke discovered Prudy stealing back into the house, didn't he? But instead of telling my aunt and uncle, it was you he told, wasn't it?"

Roger nodded, grinning as he never did when sober. "Yes, my dear, he came to me directly. Scared the little chit, Prudy, half to death, he did, and she willingly told him everything. No doubt, she hoped to spare you the shame of having the entire household roused to get up and go after you."

"Then no one—except Prudy—as yet knows where I am."

"Precisely." Roger reached out suddenly to pat her hand. "Nor shall they know what's happened to you even when Prudy breaks down and tells them. If they come hurrying to the Man Full Of Trouble Inn, all they'll be able to find out is that you've already gone off with someone who claimed to be your aunt."

Rebecca snatched her hand away. "I don't understand, Roger. What do you hope to gain by this—this kidnapping in broad daylight?"

"A wife, my dear, a wife . . ." Roger's blood-shot eyes gleamed redly. He looked a little mad.

He's too drunk to know what he's doing, Rebecca reasoned, but perhaps, he could still be reached by reason. "Roger . . . please try to be sensible. I am already someone's wife; I stayed with him in the inn last night. The innkeeper knows about us, and soon, everyone else will too."

"That matters little, my pretty sweeting . . . once, your savage husband is safely out of the way, no one will be too surprised if we go ahead with our marriage."

"Out of the way! What do you mean by 'out of the way'?" There was a sudden jounce as a carriage wheel struck something in the road, but it was nothing compared to the jounce Rebecca felt in her heart. Had Roger gone completely crazy? Would he stop at nothing to achieve this marriage?

"Oh, don't look so stunned, my dear—I am not a murderer. But it will take little, it appears, to secure the services of two evil-looking men whom Henry-Luke found prowling about your aunt's and uncle's early this morning . . . Really, Rebecca. You arouse the most amazing passions in men. They couldn't say enough bad things about you when Henry-Luke cornered them with his pitchfork. Of course, when they discovered that Henry-Luke shared their sentiments about your character, they had even more interesting things to say. Indeed, as soon as I drop you off with a friend of mine, I intend to have a chat with them myself. Will Simpkin and Jake Potts, I believe their names are . . ." Roger watched her with a bleary-eyed stare—no doubt hoping to see the effect his words had wrought upon her.

But Rebecca was past caring what Roger saw or thought: her whole being centered on her concern and fear for Kin-di-wa. Why hadn't she told him about Will and Jake being in the city? Forewarned and forearmed, he might still have a chance against the two men. But expecting nothing, he could hardly be more vulnerable to any plan that Roger, Henry-Luke, Jake, and Will might hatch.

And wherever Roger was taking her, it was obviously to a place from which she could not easily escape to warn her husband.

The carriage drew to a standstill, and Roger grasped her arm. "You should have worn your cape, my dear. I wonder you are not cold with only your pelisse and your gown."

In truth, Rebecca did feel cold, but it was a coldness of heart not body. Henry-Luke opened the carriage door, and for one wild desperate moment, Rebecca toyed with the idea of making a run for it. But where could she go and how could she move fast enough to get away from Henry-Luke? His sly eyes were filled with malicious triumph as he handed her down onto the sidewalk before a large, shabby-looking, row house in a part of town she didn't recognize.

"Come, my dear . . ." said Roger. "My friend, Lisette, is awaiting you."

Between her two captors, Rebecca mounted the steps to the house. Roger opened the door without knocking, and Rebecca stepped into a hallway whose predominant color was red. Crimson flowers bloomed on the garish wallpaper. A crimson-gold carpet runner graced the floor. Someone called, "Rogere, *mon cher* . . . is that you?"

A woman in a scarlet gown came toward them. Rebecca stared. The woman's gown was cut to the latest French fashion once described by Aunt Margaret. Her neckline ended beneath her bosom, and the rouged tips of the woman's fully exposed breasts projected boldly outward like the prow on a sailing ship.

"So Rogere . . ." The woman pouted through scarlet lips. "Thees is the preetty little pregnant bird you wish to marry as soon as she is free. Well, breeng her along upstairs and I—your dear friend Lisette—will see that she does not fly the nest while you tend to beezness."

Rebecca turned pleadingly to Roger. "Please do not leave me here, Roger. This—isn't a proper place for a lady."

431

"Ho! So your bride turns up her preety little nose at my house—does she not?" Shaking her glossy black curls and rolling her painted eyes, Lisette seemed to enjoy Rebecca's discomfort. Her heavy French accent became even more exaggerated. "Why, I assure you, *ma petite jeune fille,* thees house ees very proper. Rogere and many other important gentlemen spend much time here—sampling my favors and those of our other ladeez. Come, now . . . or I shall 'ave to send for Beeg Lucifer who has a temper you cannot even imageen. He would love to break your preety little neck if you do not obey me."

"Roger . . ." Rebecca begged.

But Roger's attention was fastened on the bobbing bared breasts of the scarlet-gowned woman. "Lisette, my dear, I knew you would not let me down . . . after the chit is locked away upstairs, perhaps you could spare me a few brief moments alone with you . . . and send Natalie down for Henry-Luke."

"Of course, dear Rogere . . ." Lisette fluttered her abnormally long black eyelashes. One scarlet-tipped fingernail tapped the heart-shaped black silk patch by her mouth—as if she were inviting Roger to kiss it. "Has our pregnant leetle bird refused to give you the loveeng attentions you so enjoy? Well, do not fear . . . Lisette will see to all your needs."

Henry-Luke smirked. Clearly besotted, Roger grinned and swayed. Realizing she had no choice, Rebecca followed Lisette up a curving red-carpeted staircase. The woman led her into a dark shuttered room where red brocaded drapes, wall hangings, and bed coverings subtly proclaimed indecent purposes.

Lisette gestured to the four-poster which was canopied with red silk. "Lie down and rest, *chérie*. Een your delicate condition, one can never have too much rest. I weel take care of Rogere . . . unless of course, you prefer I send heem up to you."

Rebecca quickly sat down on the edge of the bed. "No . . . no. I think I had better rest."

Lisette swept through the open door and closed it behind her. Rebecca heard a key turn in the lock and was left alone with nothing but the lingering odor of the woman's musky perfume.

It seemed an eternity before anyone came to the room again. Rebecca alternately paced the floor and perched on the bed, resisting the impulse to lie down and close her eyes. Her nerves thwanged with exhaustion, but she could not sleep. Visions of Kin-di-wa lying wounded and dying in an alley somewhere haunted her thoughts. She was sick with worry and shame.

Once again, she had betrayed her husband's trust and placed him in great danger. If only she had told him about Will and Jake! Of course, the two men might refuse to do Roger's dirty work unless he agreed to turn her over to them. That at least, she was certain Roger would never do. But could Will and Jake be persuaded to murder Kin-di-wa for money?

No, she guessed. In all likelihood, Will and Jake would be happy to do the evil deed for nothing—for the mere joy of ridding themselves of the man she loved. Once Kin-di-wa was dead, Roger might even promise to give her to them after all, but without any intention of ever keeping the promise. She would no longer be surprised at anything Roger did.

Aching with despair, Rebecca walked to the shuttered windows and examined them, but a sheer two story drop to the cobblestones below made escape impossible. She tried unsuccessfully to pick the door lock with a solid gold hairpin that she found lying atop the heavy walnut dresser. Then she searched the dresser itself—hoping to find some sort of weapon. There was nothing but scented lingerie: multi-colored silk chemises so fine and sheer that they would conceal absolutely nothing beneath them.

Wearily, Rebecca sat down on the bed and fingered the red silk coverlet. Her other hand rested on the mound of her child beneath her pelisse. Was it only last night that her body had thrilled once again to her husband's touch? Was it only last night that she and Kin-di-wa had reaffirmed their precious love and renewed their commitment to each other?

Tears ran down her cheeks. It did not seem possible that after so much pain and suffering, she would have to endure losing Kin-di-wa again. There had to be some way out of this predicament, but not a single idea came to her. Dread and sorrow had turned her into a wooden statue, with wooden thoughts and responses. She could do nothing but sit and wait—wait for someone to unlock the door and tell her that it was over: Kin-di-wa was dead and she belonged to Roger—or to Will and Jake, or to whomever would at long last have her when there was nothing much left to have.

When the key turned in the lock again and the door swung open, Rebecca started. But it was only Lisette bringing her a tray of food. The smell of beef and gravy overpowered the odor of the woman's perfume as she set the tray on a small round table before one of the shuttered, heavily draped windows.

"Half of the afternoon ees already gone, *chérie*. You must come and eat or the leetle one will not be strong. Seet here, and I will eat weeth you." Lisette drew up two chairs and removed the pewter lids from two plates of meat and vegetables.

Despite her anxiety, Rebecca sniffed appreciatively. She was starved—but how could she eat not knowing what was happening to Kin-di-wa? Warily, she approached the table and sat down. Lisette poured wine from a crystal decanter into two gleaming goblets. She placed one before Rebecca and took a thirsty swallow from her own. Then she sat down and began to eat with delicate gusto.

Rebecca watched and wondered if a plea for

help or sympathy from this woman would work. She ate a few bites of food herself, only dimly noting the tenderness of the beef and the buttery flavor of the onions, turnips, and potatoes.

Lisette poured more wine for herself and gave Rebecca a guarded look that revealed nothing of her feelings. "Rogere is not a bad man, *chérie*. Why do you find heem so repulseeve?"

"I love my husband," Rebecca answered. "Roger only wants to marry me for my money— my uncle's money," she amended.

"Ah, so . . . That ees the reezon my poor dear Rogere has decided to abandon me and my ladeez—moneey, the source of all evil een men— and also the source of all good."

Rebecca doubted that money could be a source of good in anybody. Nevertheless, hope began to worm its way into her consciousness. Could this painted French doxy have some feeling for Roger? If so, she might be willing to allow Rebecca to escape.

"My—husband was supposed to see President Washington some time today. Then I was to meet him back at the Man Full Of Trouble Inn this afternoon. Whatever Roger is planning . . . if I could get to my husband in time . . . I know I could persuade him to leave Philadelphia immediately . . . the two of us together . . ." Rebecca trailed off uncertainly. Kin-di-wa could already be dead while she was sitting there dreaming up plans. Jake and Will might already have waylaid him coming to or from the inn.

Lisette finished her second glass of wine in a single gulp. "Eet ees impossible," she snapped. "Rogere and I are old friends and one does not betray one's friends . . ." Her glance was dagger-like in its intensity. "Whatever you may theenk of me and my house . . . the one theeng I am ees loyal."

"Yes, I can see that," Rebecca murmured. She regretted that she had earlier implied any criticism. Had she been more discerning of possibilities for escape, she might have made a friend instead of an enemy out of this woman.

Lisette arose from the table and picked up the meal tray. "Do not even theenk of escape, my preety leetle bird . . . Beeg Lucifer is taking the buckboard down to the waterfront to peek up some supplies, but I and my ladeez shall be here for the rest of the day, and of course, thees evening. For however long Rogere wishes you to stay, you weel stay . . . ees that understood?"

Rebecca nodded dumbly. Then Lisette smiled, and for a moment, beneath all the paint, powder, and black silk patches, she was almost pretty, as she must have been when young and innocent. "Still, it ees a peety . . . If it were not for you, Rogere might one day marry me. I am more suitable for heem than an eennocent like you— and what ees more, I love heem, the same way you love your husband . . . eef there ees such a theeng as love, that ees. Personally, I have come to doubt eet."

This last comment killed any hope Rebecca

437

might have held onto. When a woman no longer believed in love, there was no hope to be had in her. And the same was true of a man also. As Rebecca had painfully discovered, the loss of love from one's life could twist and distort one's whole set of values. It could lead one down paths one never intended to follow.

Lisette paused on her way to the door and nodded in the direction of a small cold fireplace Rebecca had barely noticed. "Oh, *chérie,* how thoughtless of me! You have no fire and no wood to make one—and eet ees beginning to snow outside . . . I weel geeve you a cape to wear until Lucifer can breeng up some wood."

Lisette departed the room, taking the tray with her. Rebecca remained seated in the chair, studying the little smoke-blackened fireplace. Its hearth was littered with gray ashes, but she felt neither hot nor cold—only empty. Was her entire life to be as bereft of warmth and happiness as the fireplace was bereft of flame? Had she grown wise too late?

A moment later, Lisette returned with a dark-colored woolen cape that had a small fur-lined hood. She flung it around Rebecca's shoulders. "I am sorry, *ma petite.* Thees will 'ave to do until Beeg Lucifer comes back from the docks. The buckboard ees even now at the door awaiting heem . . . He has no time to be breenging up wood."

"Really, you should not have bothered," Rebecca said with little spirit. "I'm not cold."

438

"Of course, you are cold! Eet ees snowing outside, I tell you!" With a whirl of her musk-scented gown, Lisette went out of the room again. Her voice trilled loudly in a strange false way as she passed down the hallway. "Poor Lucifer! Having to go so far eento town een such bad weather!"

Rebecca turned to look after her—and noticed that the door to the room had been carelessly, perhaps purposefully, left wide open.

No one stopped Rebecca as she hurried out into the hallway, down the steps, and out the front door as quickly as her feet could take her. The empty buckboard stood close by on the street. Partially concealed behind a curtain of whirling snowflakes, a sway-backed horse waited patiently for commands. Rebecca debated whether to try and drive the vehicle herself or whether to run and hide down some alleyway. Had Lisette meant for her to escape? Had she intended for her to use the buckboard left so conveniently in front of the house?

She peered over the side of the wagon and saw several barrels and an old tarpaulin rolled into a large shapeless mass. The sight of the tarpaulin made her decision easier. She grasped onto the side and put her foot into one of the large wooden spokes of the big back wheel. The spokes enabled her to climb up and over the side—although in an awkward breathless manner. Once inside the

wagon, she struggled frantically to unroll the tarp
and wrap it around herself, as she huddled behind
the barrels.

She barely had time to cover her head as an
enormous black man came around the side of the
building and headed toward the wagon. The
man's deep bass voice made her flesh crawl with
fear as he climbed aboard and clucked to the
horse. "Git on up there, Brownie, old nag . . . The
mistress will have her brandy and sherry no
matter if it snows or not."

The wagon lurched forward over the cobblestones, and Rebecca spent a cramped, cold,
uncomfortable three quarters of an hour before
the wagon came to a stop again. It creaked and
shuddered as the man dismounted. Rebecca
listened for his departing footsteps before she
dared pull back the tarpaulin and dust the snow
from the cape of her hood which had been
peeking out unbeknownst to her.

The wagon stood on a rise overlooking the
frozen Delaware River on her left. To her right,
stood a long low building which could only be the
warehouse inside which the big black man had
presumably disappeared. Fearful he might return
and find her lingering there, she scrambled
hurriedly out of the buckboard.

The warehouse could not be too far from the
Man Full Of Trouble Inn, she guessed. Hazarding
another guess as to the proper direction, she
started down the street along the river in search of
it. The swiftly falling snow concealed her foot-

prints almost as soon as she made them; it also wet through her fragile slippers. Her feet were chilled to the bone by the time she recognized first the stable, then the corner of the inn.

Gratefully, she stumbled through the door and into the welcoming warmth of the dining room. Several patrons—two men and a stylishly dressed woman—looked up from steaming mugs of hot buttered rum whose fragrance taunted Rebecca's appreciative nose. With frankly curious stares, the three silent patrons regarded her snowy figure, and Rebecca held up her head and swept over to the innkeeper. He peered at her from inside his little caged-bar with its neat pewter mugs and plates standing upright on shelves along the wall behind him.

"Sir . . ." she said quietly. "Is my husband here, do you know?"

The innkeeper tilted his wire rim glasses, the better to take disapproving note of her damp disheveled appearance. "I don't believe so, madam. He left this morning right after you did, and I don't believe he has yet come back."

Rebecca's stomach fluttered. "I'll just go up and check the room then."

"Wait, madam . . ." the innkeeper objected, but Rebecca was already hurrying toward the stairs. Kin-di-wa could easily have slipped inside the inn and gone up to the room without the innkeeper noticing. At least, she wanted to believe that, in view of what might have happened to detain him. Surely President Washington would not have kept him so late in the afternoon, especially in such bad weather.

Rebecca flung open the door to the bedchamber. Someone stirred on the bed. Another figure rose from the chair beside the fire. The muzzles of two muskets glinted as they pointed straight at her heart.

"Waal, now . . ." drawled the familiar voice of Jake Potts. "Ain't this a sweet surprise. We thought we wuz gonna catch th' rooster but we caught th' hen instead."

Rebecca blinked and swallowed against the rise of terror in her throat. "Wh—what are you doing here?" she croaked.

"Git in 'ere, an' close th' door," Will growled from his position on the bed. "No need fer that innkeeper t' hear. We had enuff of a problem convincin' 'im we wuz frien's o' yurs an yur Injun."

Rebecca was too shocked to move. Jake Potts crossed the room and closed the door behind her. His smile became an evil leer as he looked her over with his one good eye. Will moved to a sitting position on the bed and laid his musket across his knee as he too scrutinized her in the poor light. "Becky, Becky . . ." He shook his head. "You shouldn't oughter have treated us as nasty as you did. An' I see you done went ahead and d'cided t' have that baby after all."

Rebecca's hands flew protectively to the bulge beneath Lisette's cape and her own pelisse. "If you think for one minute, Will . . ." A loud rapping at the door interrupted her.

"Madame Golden Eagle?" The little inn-keeper's voice was laced with indignation. "You rushed off before I had a chance to tell you about your visitors. Is—is everything all right in there?"

"N—No!" Rebecca cried, but before she could elaborate, Jake swung his musket around to prod her stomach.

"You tell him everythin's just fine!" Jake hissed. "Go on, tell him!" The muzzle of the musket prodded deeper.

Rebecca fought to control her panicked breathing. "E—everything is just fine, sir!"

There was a moment's silence behind the closed door. "Madame Golden Eagle . . ." The inn-keeper still sounded indignant. "I realize that your husband is a guest of President Washington who kindly recommended him to stay at this inn. The President knows we have an excellent reputation . . . and—it's because of our reputation that I feel compelled to point out to you that it really isn't proper for a lady to entertain gentlemen callers alone in her room . . . I mean without the presence of her husband . . . so I must respectfully request that you . . ."

"Tell 'im yur husban' should be 'ere any minute," Jake snarled softly.

". . . that you entertain your visitors in the pub and dining room until your husband returns," the innkeeper finished.

"Why, yes, that's an excellent idea!" Rebecca hastened to agree. She stared defiantly at Jake, suddenly realizing that this was a public inn. Her best protection—and Kin-di-wa's too—would be to have plenty of witnesses around to forestall the carrying out of Jake's and Will's plans. Surely, they wouldn't harm her or Kin-di-wa in front of others!

"Please do not worry, sir," she called out in a stronger voice. "We shall be down directly."

Jake's single eye burned with rage, and Will snorted and rolled off the bed. "Shit and damnation!" he muttered.

The innkeeper's voice intruded through the door again. "Oh, and one more thing, Madame Golden Eagle . . . a man and woman—your aunt and uncle—came to the inn looking for you at about midday . . . I told them you'd gone out and were expected back later this afternoon. They said they too would be coming back . . . You will be here to receive them, won't you? They seemed quite distraught."

"Yes—oh, yes, of course!" Rebecca had an almost overpowering desire to laugh at the expressions on the faces of the two men in front of her, but the laughter died in her throat as Jake stepped toward her menacingly.

"Very good then, Madame Golden Eagle . . ." the innkeeper said. "I shall await you all downstairs."

"Little bitch!" Jake's hand snaked out and grabbed her upper arm. His fingers dug into her flesh through her cape. "We're gittin' outa here right now! An' you better think o' some excuse t' tell that nosy upstart innkeeper!"

Will came toward them. His bristling hair and beard quivered with anger, and the marks of bear claws stood out redly on his face. "Little she-cat! Little whore! . . . Where we gonna take 'er, Jake? That Bakewood fellow said we wuz t' finish off th' Injun b'fore we got our money. 'Course, it wuz Becky we really wanted, an' now that we got 'er, I say t' hell with th' money . . . t' hell with th' Injun too."

"We'll find someplace . . ." Jake's tone was coldly determined and full of venom. "A town this big has got t' have places where they don't ask too many questions—long as ya ain't too stingy with yur money. An' we kin still make a heap o' money. I ain't fergittin' her aunt and uncle. You think they won't pay plenty t' git 'er back again—after we're through with 'er, that is?"

"Leave my aunt and uncle out of this!" Rebecca cut in furiously. "Besides, they won't want to pay! They've already disowned me for refusing to marry Roger!"

"Oh, that don't sound too likely . . ." Jake steered her toward the door with Will bringing up the rear. "Didn't that little innkeeper say they come 'ere lookin' fer ya? Maybe, they already done reconsidered."

Propelled into the hallway against her will, Rebecca bit back stinging tears. What a fine mess she'd made of things this time—not only for herself and Kin-di-wa again, but also for her aunt and uncle. Her only consolation was that perhaps

Will and Jake would be unable to surprise Kin-di-wa so easily now that the innkeeper knew about them. Kin-di-wa would recognize the description of the two men—wouldn't he? Or would Jake's eye patch and Will's scars—their most noticeable features now—throw him into confusion? How would he ever find her in the middle of a snowstorm in Philadelphia?

Down the steps she walked with wooden, still half-frozen feet. Jake kept her elbow firmly in one hand and his musket in the other. Will lumbered down the stairs behind her, and she became reacquainted with his distinctive obnoxious odor. He stunk of filthy buckskin, unwashed body, beard, and hair, and, she imagined, decayed fingers. She'd already caught a glimpse of his Shawnee necklace protruding from beneath the double or triple layers of clothing he wore as protection from winter weather. Jake Potts also smelled—but not quite as badly as Will.

As they came into the pub and dining area, Rebecca noticed that the little innkeeper was back in his bar-cage, but the patrons had already departed. She wished they had remained. Jake gave her a little shove toward the cage, his meaning clearly imprinted on his face. She searched her mind for a reason why she should be going out with Will and Jake. Then she wondered what would happen if she made a stand then and there—if she simply refused to go with them.

The innkeeper looked at her expectantly. His disapproval of her appearance, her behavior, and her relationships with men shone in his eyes. "Yes,

Madame Golden Eagle?"

The noise of the outside door being opened distracted Rebecca. She half-turned, along with Will and Jake, to see who was entering the inn. At the same moment, the innkeeper said, "Well, I see your aunt and uncle are returning . . . and here's your husband coming in too!"

Seventeen

For a single breathless moment, Rebecca simply stood and stared as Aunt Margaret and Uncle Hardin came into the inn, followed by Kin-di-wa. All three wore a layer of fresh white snow—Kin-di-wa's layer being thicker than the others. They stamped the snow from their feet, stopped, and stared. Surprise stole over their faces. Then Rebecca saw Kin-di-wa's hand move slowly toward his hunting knife. Sheathed in leather, the lethal blade hung from his waist thong and was the only weapon he had with him.

"Don't any o' ya move!" Jake Potts commanded. He aimed his musket at Aunt Margaret who stood dead center of the three snow-clad figures.

"Or we'll blow yur haids off . . ." Will asserted. He trained his musket on Kin-di-wa, as if the others were hardly important. "We got our shootin' pieces all primed an' ready."

Uncle Hardin gaped and sputtered. Nervously, he took off his hat, brushed the snow from it, then clamped it back on his head. "Why, this is absolutely outrageous! I demand to know the meaning of this!"

Swathed in a bright red cape with a fur-lined hood, Aunt Margaret extended her fur muff toward Rebecca. "Oh, my dear! Who are these men?"

Out of the corner of her eye, Rebecca saw the little innkeeper cowering in his cage. Only Kin-di-wa, it seemed, had the presence of mind to remain still—though Rebecca felt certain that he had already sized up the situation, knew exactly who the men were, and had hatched a plan to deal with them. Thinking to help by creating a diversion, Rebecca pulled away from Jake and Will and rushed to her aunt's side.

"Roger sent them to kill Kin-di-wa!" she cried. "So he could marry me and get Uncle Hardin's money after all."

"Roger? Roger hired these men?" Aunt Margaret gasped. "I don't believe it!"

"Impossible!" Uncle Hardin snorted.

"Shut up, all o' ya!" Jake motioned to Rebecca, Aunt Margaret, and Uncle Hardin. "Move away from that Injun feller there . . ."

"Oh, dear . . ." Aunt Margaret turned and peered out from under her hood at Kin-di-wa. "Is—is that your Indian who came in with us? Why, it is your Indian, isn't it?"

"It sure as hell is," growled Will. Looking as

riled and dangerous as the black bear who'd left its mark on his cheek, Will squinted his eyes at Kin-di-wa. "An' it seems t' me we kin take keer o' him right now. Quit hidin' behind them white folks, an' git on outside, you slimy red bastard!"

Kin-di-wa pushed his way between Aunt Margaret and Uncle Hardin, but Rebecca would not allow her husband to be exposed to the line of fire from the two men's muskets. She blocked his passage with her body and glared at Jake and Will.

Kin-di-wa forcibly steered her to one side. "If you do not harm these others—especially my woman—you may do what you like with me. Although I suggest that you not do it here, in front of witnesses."

"No, Kin-di-wa!" Rebecca cried, but to her surprise, Uncle Hardin clamped remarkably strong hands down on her shoulders.

"You must stay out of this, Niece," he said. "This is a matter to be settled by gentlemen—not by a pregnant woman."

A protest leapt to Rebecca's tongue, but a piercing glance from Kin-di-wa silenced her. "Your uncle is right, little one . . . you must trust this matter to me. These men will not shoot me down like a dog in the street—not where everyone can see them. I think they would rather try one at a time to take me, just to prove that they can do it."

"Yes, sir!" Uncle Hardin startled Rebecca with his staunch agreement. "Fight like gentlemen, one at a time—that's the only way!"

A crooked grin revealed Will's broken rotted teeth. "Gen'lemen, hunh . . . why not?" His eyes fastened on Kin-di-wa. "Filthy red-skin—I kin take ya an' crack yur ribs b'fore ya even know whut hit ya."

Blue fire crackled in Kin-di-wa's eyes. "At least, that would be a better death than a bullet in the back—the way you killed my brother."

Will looked surprised, then pleased. "Hah! I almos' fergot that one o' them worthless savages I kilt over th' years wuz yur brother. Whut a shame you wuzn't with 'im so I coulda got ya' both at th' same time."

"There is also the matter of all the harm you have done—and tried to do—to my woman," Kin-di-wa said quietly.

Rebecca thought Kin-di-wa's restraint was almost eerie. She knew how her husband felt about Will Simpkin, yet it seemed to her that of all the men in the room, Kin-di-wa radiated the most calm assurance. His lithe body, clad in clean embroidered buckskins from which the snow had melted quickly, seemed poised to explode at any moment, yet his anger was coolly held in check.

Will grinned. "Then let's fight—both fer yur brother an' fer yur woman."

"Don't be a fool!" Jake said to Will. "We kin take him an' Becky with us, an' git rid o' both of 'em whenever we want. Don't fergit th' money . . ."

"I ain't fergittin' nothin'!" Will suddenly roared. "But I want this Injun t' suffer now .·. . I wanna hear 'im beg fer mercy. An' I wanna see

452

little Miz High an' Mighty Becky cry 'er eyes out fer 'im."

Will shot Rebecca a look that bespoke months of frustration and an unfulfilled desire for revenge. Rebecca shivered. Will wanted her to suffer even more than Kin-di-wa. He wanted to take from her the one thing she held most dear: her husband.

"Yeah," Will said in a tone of pure hatred. "I want Miz Becky t' watch me kill her Injun with mah bare hands."

"Gentlemen!" Uncle Hardin broke in pleadingly. "Might I not suggest a duel! That's the way we gentlemen settle things in Philadelphia! Oh, of course, there's been talk of bans against the practice—but gentlemen still find it a fair and just way to settle arguments and matters of honor. Why, I'd even be pleased to serve as second to my niece's ah—er—husband. And you sir . . ." he pointed to Jake, ". . . can serve as second to er— this other fellow."

"Hardin!" exclaimed Aunt Margaret.

Even Rebecca was shocked. But she also found something very endearing and plucky in the way her gruff unsentimental uncle was attempting to arrange things to help Kin-di-wa. Heretofore, Uncle Hardin had demonstrated nothing but prejudice toward Indians in general and Kin-di-wa in particular.

"No duels . . ." Will spat. "I wanna fight 'im with my bare hands. An' I wanna fight 'im here and now."

Jake's ferretlike little eyes slid from Will to

Kin-di-wa and back again to Will. He seemed to be trying to decide whether to chance Will's fury by protesting further. His hands tightened around his musket. "All right . . ." he said at last. "You fight 'im—an' if there's anythin' left over when you're through, then I'll git my turn at 'im."

"But that's not fair!" Rebecca cried.

"Outside, gentlemen, outside!" The innkeeper rushed out of his cage. "Please don't tear up my establishment!"

Kin-di-wa moved toward the door, never taking his eyes from Will. "Come, yellow dog . . . let us see if you fight as well as you shoot men in the back."

Will handed his musket to Jake. He shoved up his buckskin sleeves and flexed his enormous muscles. "Who you callin' a yellow dog? This dog is gonna tear ya t' pieces."

Kin-di-wa backed out of the inn, followed by a grinning Will. Outside, it was snowing furiously and growing dark; no lamps had yet been lit on the street. Rebecca broke away from Uncle Hardin, but Jake blocked her way with the barrel of his musket.

"After me, little she-cat. An' don't try anythin' funny. I'll be watchin' ya every minute."

Uncle Hardin and Aunt Margaret followed Rebecca out onto the sidewalk. Their carriage stood in front of the inn, and the three took shelter from the rising wind and blowing snow by standing near it. Jake strode away from them a little further down the street. He hitched his own musket over his shoulder, securing the weapon in place by means of a leather strap. Then he aimed Will's musket at Kin-di-wa.

Warily, the two men circled each other in the middle of the street. Will was bigger than Kin-di-wa, Rebecca noted dismally. His body was thicker and heavier. But the two men were about the same height, and Kin-di-wa moved with a quick easy grace. Will lumbered in a slow awkward manner, no doubt confident that once Kin-di-wa came to him, he could easily enfold him in a crushing embrace.

The little bald innkeeper hurried to stand beside Rebecca. He had stopped to put on his coat, but he had forgotten his hat, and snow quickly began to cover his hairless pate. The snow was now coming down so fast and thick that it was difficult to discern the quicker movements of the two combatants.

They lunged and feinted at one another, but whenever Will seemed about to grab his opponent, Kin-di-wa leapt backward, as graceful as a dancer.

"C'mon, ya son of a bitch!" Will shouted above the wind. His hand went to his belt, and Rebecca guessed what he was doing even before she saw the glint of the blade he had withdrawn.

"Kin-di-wa! He's got his hunting knife!" she screamed.

"Oh, dear! Oh, dear!" cried Aunt Margaret. "It isn't fair for only *one* to have a knife!"

Uncle Hardin put his arm around his wife's shoulders. "There, there, dear! I'm sure Rebecca's Indian knows what he's doing."

But Rebecca wondered. She had watched Kin-di-wa fight Indian-style on more than one occasion, but thus far her husband had made none of the quick unexpected movements of hand or foot that could send his opponent sprawling. Nor did he reach for his own hunting knife. She couldn't guess at his strategy—unless he meant to tire Will before he downed him.

Kin-di-wa seemed to be goading Will to come after him, much as Rebecca had goaded the big black bear into making an attack on Will and Jake. He leapt and turned in the whirling snow, keeping just out of Will's reach—and out of slashing distance of his knife.

Rebecca's heart thumped against her rib cage. She felt she could scarcely breathe. It was growing harder to see by the minute. The scene took on the aspect of a nightmare. The two figures, coated now with white as they moved through the curtain of falling snow, made an eerie sight. Kin-di-wa moved silently, but Will could be heard grunting and cursing under his breath.

Then Will gave a disgusted cry and lunged at Kin-di-wa. Kin-di-wa leapt to one side, and Will lost his footing on the snow-slick cobblestones and sprawled face downward with a thud. Immediately, Kin-di-wa was on his back. He crooked one arm around Will's neck and jerked backwards and upward. Will pounded the cobblestones with his fists as he fought Kin-di-wa's efforts to break his neck.

Half-mesmerized as she strained to see through the heavy snowfall, Rebecca almost missed the movement from the shadows beyond Kin-di-wa and Will. Uncle Hardin and Aunt Margaret gasped, and Rebecca pulled herself together and shouted. "Behind you, Kin-di-wa! It's Jake!"

Jake came forward swinging Will's musket in a lethal arc. Kin-di-wa let go of Will and ducked. The heavy barrel of the musket sliced through the snow-splattered air where Kin-di-wa's head had been only the moment before. Kin-di-wa lost his balance, toppled sideways, and fell heavily onto the cobblestones.

Had he struck his head? Rebecca couldn't see. But then Kin-di-wa struggled to his feet, swayed dazedly for a moment, and staggered away. Once again he assumed his wary half-crouched position, but she was afraid that the fall had cost him his clearheadedness.

Beside Rebecca, the innkeeper squeaked, "God in heaven! It's snowing so hard and getting so dark I can hardly see a thing!"

Neither could Rebecca. The wind had suddenly shifted and was driving the snow into their eyes. She tugged her hood forward over her face and could just make out Will getting slowly to his feet and rubbing the back of his neck with one hand. He blundered several steps in the wrong direction before turning back toward Jake and Kin-di-wa.

A long, skinny, dark object flew through the air between Jake and Will. It had to be Will's musket. Jake's sudden holler confirmed Rebecca's guess: "Let's kill 'im, ya stupid bastard! B'fore he kills one o' us!"

Will caught the musket. He laughed and

lumbered several paces to Kin-di-wa's left. Jake moved several paces to the right. Slowly, they circled their prey—leaving no easy escape for Kin-di-wa in any direction.

Will lifted his musket and took aim; Jake had already taken aim with his musket. To Rebecca, it seemed as if the two men were aiming at each other. They could never be so stupid, she thought, but in the snowy blackness it was hard to tell. Everything had become distorted and dreamlike. She could only be certain of one thing: Kin-di-wa, standing dead center between them, would be caught in their cross fire.

She ran toward her husband. "Kin-di-wa! Kin-di-wa!"

Trying desperately to reach him, she stretched out her arms and hurled herself against the wind and snow. Her feet left the ground, and she thudded against something solid—Kin-di-wa's body, she hoped. Her own body twisted, and she felt herself falling, dragging him down on top of her. The icy cobblestones rushed up to meet her. Too late, she thought of her child.

She slammed against the stones just as musket-fire thundered above her. Smoke and flame seared a burning bright arc through the darkness. She grappled with a warm familiar weight; it had to be Kin-di-wa she'd knocked down. He groaned and pulled back from her. The bright after-glare of the gunfire revealed a spidery stream of red glistening on his forehead.

Darkness descended again, and his ragged breathing sounded loud in her right ear. "Cat-

Eyes! Are you all right?"

She tried to speak but could not catch her own breath. She wanted to say she was fine and to ask how he was. Most of all, she wanted to find out what had happened to Jake and Will. If they hadn't shot each other, wouldn't they be loading their guns for a second try?

"K—Kin-di-wa!" She could say nothing else. A tearing sensation ripped through her lower abdomen. A knifelike pain drove into her tailbone, stabbing her with wrenching intensity. The pain blotted out all her other concerns; it was worse than any she had ever felt. "K—Kin-di-wa," she managed to gasp. "I—I think the baby's coming!"

The pain consumed her. It came in waves. The waves started low in her back, then spread around the curve of her extended belly and peaked with several sharp tugs at the very core and center of her being—somewhere deep within her lower abdomen. She was dimly aware of activity around her: Kin-di-wa removing himself from her body, figures rushing toward her, voices talking all at once.

Uncle Hardin was shouting jubilantly, "They're dead, by thunder—they're dead!"

The little innkeeper was practically jumping up and down. "Never saw nothing like it! They just pointed their guns and shot! Never even saw each other. Guess they were a mite too anxious to put a ball in you, Mister Golden Eagle!"

"Oh, Rebecca! My poor dear niece!" Aunt Margaret was sobbing. "Is she all right? Did they kill her too?"

Kin-di-wa's steady voice cut through the confusion. "Get a torch or a lantern. My woman has been hurt . . ."

The cold driving snow—or was it sleet now?—stung Rebecca's face. Kin-di-wa bent over her; she felt his arms gently maneuvering themselves around her. He lifted her just as another pain grabbed and tore at her insides. She stiffened and moaned. Helping hands—Uncle Hardin's?—supported her on the other side.

"But where are you taking her?" Aunt Margaret hovered somewhere nearby. "If she's hurt, we must get her home directly!"

"It's the child . . . the child is coming." Kin-di-wa was a rock to which Rebecca clung through her awful pain.

"Oh, my goodness! Then bring her along to the carriage! Our house isn't far—she can't have the baby in a common inn where there's no one to care for her!"

"I will care for her . . ." Kin-di-wa said.

The wave of pain receded. It ebbed along the edges of Rebecca's consciousness, gathering momentum for another assault. But in the temporary lull, she dared to try her voice. "It—it will be better at my aunt's, Kin-di-wa. All—all the baby things are there, in a chest by my bed."

"I'm afraid there isn't time, little Cat-Eyes."

A light bobbed in the darkness. The little innkeeper came running toward them, holding up a lantern. In its wavering gold light, Rebecca saw her husband's face. Blood was still trickling from an ugly swollen cut on his forehead. She wondered who would care for *him*.

"I think we have time . . . Please let's go to my aunt's." She bit her lower lip against the beginnings of another wave of pain. Never having had a baby before, she didn't know if there was time or not—but suddenly she wanted the warmth and luxury of her own bed, her own room at Aunt Margaret's. Prudy and Bess would be there. Help would be available for both her and Kin-di-wa.

"This time, you must have faith in me," Kin-di-wa snapped. "I know what is best." His tone implied that she erred once again in not placing her trust in his judgment. Perhaps, back there in the street, he had been planning to drop to the ground at the crucial moment when Will and Jake had fired. Perhaps, she had risked her life—and the life of their child—for nothing.

Kin-di-wa carried her toward the inn, while Uncle Hardin scurried ahead to open doors and clear a path through tables and chairs. Aunt Margaret followed behind, wailing and fluttering. "Oh, what shall we do without Bess and Prudy? I've never delivered a baby! Why, I might get sick and faint!"

Rebecca had a sudden giddy impulse to giggle, to laugh until her sides split with humor instead of pain. Aunt Margaret had never sounded so helpless and foolish. The whole world was ridiculous and foolish. Who would ever think that two grown men—experienced backwoodsmen—would miss their target and shoot each other? Who would ever believe that Jake and Will were finally dead? The wave of pain crested and made her gasp. She forgot what had seemed so funny.

"Push . . ." Kin-di-wa commanded. "The baby is coming . . . you must push."

Firelight flickered on the ceiling of the same bed chamber where only last night Rebecca had lain with her husband. Beneath her clutching hands, she could feel the soft texture of Kin-di-wa's buffalo robe.

"I—I can't!" She was afraid of any more pain. The pain was tearing her body to pieces.

Kin-di-wa held her knees apart. Her rumpled, soiled ball gown—the lovely gown that matched her eyes—was tangled and twisted and pushed up somewhere around her breasts. Rebecca wanted her husband's sympathy, but his attention was fastened on that place she could no longer see in her anguish, the place from which her child was soon to emerge.

"Cat-Eyes—you must push! The child is almost here!" Kin-di-wa looked up. His eyes darkened. His nostrils flared. "You mustn't give up yet, Cat-Eyes. It is almost over. One more push—that is all I ask of you!"

She hated to disappoint him, but she wasn't brave. She wasn't strong. *He* was brave and strong. She was weak and scared—worse than

Aunt Margaret who at least had taken charge of heating water to bathe the baby when it came. Everyone, even Uncle Hardin and the innkeeper, was doing something. They were all taking part. Only she held back. She didn't want to push, couldn't stand the pain. But with one last look at her demanding husband, she pushed.

The pain rent and tore her body. Something gave way. Something slid out. The pain eased a little. Something lay throbbing between her legs, and Kin-di-wa's hands made a scooping motion. She saw a dark wet head, a tiny waving fist. She heard a hiccup and a cry.

Kin-di-wa's blazing triumphant eyes met hers. "We have a daughter, Cat-Eyes—a perfect, beautiful daughter."

Rebecca held her newborn baby to her naked breast. The delicate rosebud mouth opened and closed, opened and closed, but failed to grasp that for which it searched.

"Brush her cheek with your nipple," Kin-di-wa urged.

Rebecca did as her husband suggested, and the baby suddenly latched onto the nipple. Tiny fists clenched tightly. The baby sucked, sputtered, and swallowed; lost the nipple, found it, then sucked again in total bliss and concentration.

"So small and yet so determined, like her mother." Admiration filled Kin-di-wa's voice.

Through a veil of tears, Rebecca studied her

husband's face. "No, she gets her courage to try new and difficult things from her father."

Kin-di-wa's burning blue eyes mirrored his sudden scorn. "Pah! A man chooses what he will live and die for; a woman has no choice. Too often her choices are made for her. But she is no less courageous in facing life and death than he is—indeed, as all men know, she is more courageous . . ."

Remembering her fear and pain, Rebecca stroked the silky soft skin of her daughter and was filled with shame that she hadn't been braver. "I could not have borne this child, if you had not given me strength."

"Ah, Cat-Eyes . . . If it were left to men to suffer as you have suffered, there would never be any children."

Rebecca pondered this a moment and decided that Kin-di-wa was right. She had labored long and hard to bring this tiny scrap of humanity into the world—but the poignant joy and wonder she felt flooding through her now, made it all worthwhile. She would do it again in a minute. Well, maybe not in a minute . . . but she would be willing to do it again someday soon.

"What shall we call this daughter of ours?" Kin-di-wa asked. "I think she will be a great beauty."

Rebecca studied the sucking mouth, the slightly squashed nose and the squinted eyes, with amusement. The baby's skin was still flushed from birth, and it was too soon to tell the color of her eyes. But her hair was definitely going to be black. Long, silky, and black as midnight. "I should have thought of a name before . . ." she sighed. "Now, I am too tired."

"As soon as she finishes suckling, you must sleep, Cat-Eyes. A name will come to us . . . There is no hurry."

No, there was no longer any hurry to do anything. Rebecca did not know if she could keep her eyes open long enough to wait until the baby finished suckling. Every bone and muscle in her body ached. Exhausted, she laid her head back on the pillows that Aunt Margaret had heaped behind her. The room was warm, quiet, and restful—lit only by a single candle and the fire in the fireplace. The bed was clean and neat, and so, at last, was she.

I really must thank Aunt Margaret for working so hard to make things comfortable, she thought. Her aunt had shied away from helping with intimate details of the birth—overseeing the delivery, cutting the cord, and removing the afterbirth. But she had made herself indispensable in other ways. It was she who had bathed and cleaned the baby, as gently and surely as if she'd been performing such delicate chores every day of her life.

Rebecca smiled as she drifted into sleep. The little dog, Snowflake, had served a purpose she'd never imagined when she brought it into Aunt Margaret's house. Snowflake had helped her aunt to grow up and to gain confidence in herself. The little animal had taught Aunt Margaret how to care for others and to make herself useful.

Or perhaps, Rebecca thought ruefully, I am the one who has grown up. At least, I've learned not to judge others so harshly.

When Rebecca awoke again, morning sunlight was streaming through the window. Aunt Margaret stood before her holding a whimpering blanket-wrapped bundle. "I'm sorry, dear, but nothing I do seems to soothe your little girl. I think she's hungry."

"Oh!" Rebecca sat up. Her breasts had an aching fullness, and with a sense of relief, she reached for her daughter.

"I've brought up your breakfast too—on a tray. After you've fed the baby, you must eat every bite if you want to get your strength back."

"Thank you, Aunt Margaret. Thank you for everything." Rebecca opened the neckline of a voluminous white linen nightshirt Aunt Margaret had borrowed from the innkeeper. She put the complaining baby to her breast.

Aunt Margaret sat down on the edge of the bed. "She's so tiny . . . and so beautiful! Thank God she is healthy too!"

Her aunt echoed Rebecca's own sentiments. Despite being several weeks ahead of schedule, the baby seemed remarkably strong as she sucked vigorously at the swollen breast. "Where is Kindi-wa—and Uncle Hardin?" Rebecca asked.

Aunt Margaret lifted an ill-fitting white apron and smoothed the folds of her bright red gown. Its color was close in shade to Lisette's, and Rebecca couldn't help wondering what Aunt Margaret would think if she knew that a "fallen woman" shared her tastes in clothes—at least, her taste in colors. "They've gone to speak with the authorities about Roger Bakewood and Henry-Luke. Prudy told us what she knew of Henry-Luke's involvement in this matter."

"Oh, yes, Roger and Henry-Luke . . ." Rebecca had quite forgotten them, but now she felt a surge of guilt. She ought never to have agreed to marry Roger—a man she didn't even like, much less love. Her stomach fluttered nervously. "Kin-di-wa . . . he seemed content to let the authorities deal with Roger?"

"Why, yes, dear—he did." Aunt Margaret suddenly looked worried. "You don't think he'd do something rash and foolish—take matters in his own hands, do you?"

Rebecca had a moment's impulse to leap out of bed and go after her husband, to take matters in *her* own hands again. But she forced herself to remain calm and consider the matter reasonably. "I'm sure Kin-di-wa will do what's right, Aunt Margaret. He won't do anything foolish."

And hearing herself say it, Rebecca knew it was true. Kin-di-wa sometimes did crazy things for the sake of honor, but he never did them without first giving careful consideration to the consequences of his actions. Well, almost never. And anyway, she had the feeling that now he would be more careful and temperate. She and Kin-di-wa both had learned some difficult lessons.

Aunt Margaret sniffed, and Rebecca saw tears welling in her eyes. Her aunt's face crumpled, as if a cheerful, painted mask had suddenly been stripped away. "Oh, Rebecca . . . I'm so sorry about Roger. It's all my fault! If I hadn't been so anxious to rise in society, none of this would have happened. I've been a fool—and I helped to turn your uncle into a fool too!"

Rebecca put out her free hand to pat her aunt's arm. "You couldn't have known what sort of man Roger is . . . Indeed, I'm not so certain he's all that bad. He—he's just misguided, perhaps even unbalanced. He thought your money could put everything to rights in his life."

"Well, your uncle and I are no better! We thought our money could buy status and happiness." Aunt Margaret looked so shamefaced and so miserable that Rebecca longed to comfort her.

"Are you really so unhappy, Aunt Margaret? Does it mean so much to you to hob-nob in the houses of the rich?"

Aunt Margaret wiped her tears away with one plump hand. "I thought it did—but I was wrong. Why, I never felt so out of place in my life as when we went to that ball given by Roger's cousins. Augusta Bakewood is so condescending, looking down her nose at us! . . . Who does she think she is anyway? This is America, for heaven's sake—not England or France. We've never had an aristocracy, and thank God and the constitution, we never will!"

Rebecca hid her smile by nuzzling the fuzzy dark hair of her daughter. "But Aunt Margaret, do you think that Indians—and Negroes too—were created equal to you?"

Aunt Margaret looked stunned. She turned startled eyes on Rebecca. "Oh, my goodness! I never gave a moment's thought to it. But—but . . . Why, I've got to speak to Hardin about this! Why, Bess and Prudy . . ."

"Are slaves, aren't they?" Rebecca finished softly.

There was a moment's silence, then Aunt Margaret jumped to her feet and clapped her hands together. Her face was shining. "Oh, Rebecca . . . I realize I've been blind, but all of a sudden, I have so many wonderful ideas! First, I'm going to free Bess and Prudy and start paying them wages for their work, and then . . . Why, only the other day, I was reading about a movement in Congress to ban the slave trade. Many states have already done it, you know—and I don't know why your uncle and I couldn't lend our support to the effort . . ."

She stopped talking and beamed at Rebecca. "Oh, my dear! Do you know what your Uncle Hardin said to me last night?"

Rebecca could hardly wait to hear. "What?"

"He said, 'You know, Maggie . . . it seems to me we've been very wrong in the way we've handled this matter of Rebecca's Indian. The fellow is really a decent sort of chap—a gentleman through and through. It seems to me we've been wrong about a number of things, my dear.'"

"Uncle Hardin said that?"

"Yes, he did!" Proudly, Aunt Margaret straightened her shoulders. "He's a fine man, is your uncle! Never afraid to admit when he's wrong—something I'm only just learning. Indeed, I wouldn't be surprised if he reinstated you in his will."

"Oh, Aunt Margaret . . . I don't care about Uncle Hardin's money—unless he'd be willing to let me use it in some way to help the Indians . . ."

"To help the Indians! Why, I don't know, dear, but it sounds like a wonderful idea! You may be certain I'll suggest it to him!" Aunt Margaret gave her a conspiratorial grin, and Rebecca's heart swelled with happiness.

Then she thought of leaving her aunt and uncle to go back to the Ohio Country with Kin-di-wa and knew a pang of sadness. But at least now, so many problems had been resolved. So many doors had suddenly been opened. A cold clean wind was blowing through all of their lives. "Oh, Aunt Margaret . . ." she said again. "I'm so happy!"

Later that night, Rebecca and Kin-di-wa shared a late evening supper alone together. Aunt Margaret and Uncle Hardin had gone home, after securing promises from both of them that, in another few days, they and the baby would all move to Uncle Hardin's house and stay there until spring—the time Kin-di-wa believed to be best for traveling.

Rebecca sipped from a glass of sparkling red wine—compliments of the innkeeper—and regarded her husband with great affection. The baby was sleeping on the bed beside her, and Kin-di-wa was hungrily demolishing a plate of potted goose, which the innkeeper had assured them was his cook's best dish.

Disdaining chairs, Kin-di-wa sat cross-legged on the floor in front of the fire, and his preoccupation with his dinner gave her the chance to study him. The cut he'd suffered the night before had turned a bluish yellow, and there were tired lines around his mouth and eyes, but these were his only flaws. His skin shone bronze in the firelight, his hair gleamed a shiny black, and his eyes, at long last free of worry and sorrow, were as blue as a summer sky.

He caught her staring at him and pushed away his plate. Then he rose in a single graceful movement and came over to sit beside her on the bed. "What are you thinking, Cat-Eyes? Your eyes are sparkling like green stones—the kind I saw a woman wearing at that party the other night."

"Emeralds," Rebecca supplied. "Those stones you saw were probably emeralds." She pushed aside the memory of flashing jewels and shimmering silks, things for which she had never felt much hunger. Had the ball at Augusta Back-wood's been only the night before last? It seemed so long ago now, and so much had changed since then. "And I was thinking how happy I am that we're together again," she added, acknowledging her deepest hungers.

Kin-di-wa brushed back a tendril of hair from her face. "And I am thinking how beautiful you are."

He bent and kissed her, and in the warm afterglow of the kiss, Rebecca sipped again from her wineglass and gave vent to her curiosity. "What happened today when you went with Uncle Hardin?"

Kin-di-wa's eyes narrowed. "We took steps to see that the man who hired Will and Jake will be punished."

"You mean you took legal steps."

"Legal? What is the meaning of 'legal'?"

"I mean that Roger and Henry-Luke will be punished according to the laws of white people, not according to *your* laws."

Kin-di-wa sighed. "Yes, my little Cat-Eyes. They will be punished according to your ways, not mine . . . By this afternoon, they had already been caught and taken wherever it is your people take their wrong-doers."

"Oh . . ." Rebecca hadn't known that Roger and Henry-Luke had been apprehended. The knowledge gave her a sense of relief, but also one of sadness. She hoped that Roger would somehow repent and become a better man as a result of this experience. Perhaps he might even one day find happiness with the woman who loved him and would no doubt stand by him: the prostitute, Lisette. But for Henry-Luke, she could entertain little hope. The man had seemed cunning and evil the very first time she'd met him.

"Did you think I was going to kill them and take their scalps?" Kin-di-wa raised one eyebrow questioningly.

"No . . ." she said in a small voice. "But—I worried just the same."

Kin-di-wa took the glass of wine from her and set it on the floor. Then he took her hands in his and looked into her eyes. "My killing days are over, Cat-Eyes. So also are my days of vengeance. I swear to you—I shall never again bear malice against another, be he white or Indian."

Rebecca blinked back tears. It seemed all she ever did anymore was weep—but oh, what joy was in these tears! "Nothing you could say would make me happier, Kin-di-wa. I have longed to hear you say those words. I want nothing more for us than peace—and to go home and work for peace between our peoples. You will accept Apekonit's offer? You'll become an interpreter?"

Kin-di-wa nodded. "My skills are humble, but I know they are needed . . . And I had rather labor on the side of peace than on the side of war." He glanced down at their sleeping daughter. "Or what future shall we give our daughter, our little Wind Flower?"

"Wind Flower?" Rebecca was startled, but the name struck her as exactly right. Indeed, it could not have been better. She smiled and squeezed her husband's hands.

The child who had been conceived on a bed of windflowers stirred beside them. She stretched and opened her eyes. They were blue at this moment, but a subtle shading in them made Rebecca wonder if they might not turn green eventually. The baby tried to focus in her parents' direction. It seemed to Rebecca that she was concentrating with all her tiny might—and then, quite unexpectedly, she smiled.

"It is only the—ah—workings of her body," Kin-di-wa said with uncustomary delicacy.

But no one would ever be able to convince Rebecca that Wind Flower hadn't actually smiled. What baby wouldn't smile—knowing how much she was loved?

Rebecca could not keep back a smile of her own. I too am loved, she thought, and for a moment, the secret of all joy and happiness in life was stunningly revealed to her: open yourself to love. Open yourself to trust. It is only in risking everything that you have the opportunity of gaining everything.

"Tell me why you are smiling . . ." Kin-di-wa asked.

"I am smiling . . ." Rebecca said. "Because . . . because . . ." Her profound discovery escaped being put into words.

"Because you love me as I love you . . ." Kin-di-wa prompted. He kissed her fingers lingeringly. "Now that is something to smile about." And the look that stole into his eyes was proof that he understood her far better than she understood herself.

Aglow with happiness, Rebecca leaned back and closed her eyes. She thought of their future—

stretched out before them like a shimmering golden path. The long dark night of their separation had ended. Now the dawn had come, more splendid and breathtaking than any they had known before. "Yes, my husband, I love you," she whispered. "And nothing will ever part us again."

Epilogue

Dear Aunt Margaret,

Kin-di-wa and I arrived safely, here at the Miami's main village near the headwaters of the Miami of the Lake, several weeks ago. Little Wind Flower survived the long journey well. She could not be in better health or spirits.

Of course, nowhere on earth is spring more beautiful than in the Ohio and Indiana Country: the wind is sweeter than honey. Wildflowers carpet the forest floor, and new life abounds at every turn. I am filled with joy to be home again!

My dearest friend, Sweet Breeze, gave birth to a

baby girl at almost the same time I did. The baby is named after me—Rebecca. It is really quite amazing: I gave my child an Indian name and Sweet Breeze gave hers a white name!

Surely our daughters are the sign of a bright new future. Kin-di-wa and Sweet Breeze's husband, Apekonit, or William Wells as the whites call him, are working day and night to improve the lot of the defeated Miamis and to safeguard the peace established by the Greenville Treaty.

Fort Wayne—the fort built here by Anthony Wayne before he returned to Philadelphia—has become a bustling trade center. The trade goods and farm tools that you and Uncle Hardin sent back with us have stirred a great deal of interest. Little Turtle, the Miami chieftain, has become an outspoken supporter for improving Miami methods of agriculture. Indeed, he plans to travel to Philadelphia next year so that he can learn more about the white man's way of doing things.

Perhaps Kin-di-wa, Wind Flower, and I can accompany him for a visit. We do not want our daughter to grow up never having known her white heritage. She is a child of both worlds: white and Indian. Kin-di-wa and I want her to be proud of who she is and to cherish the differences between our cultures. And, of course, we want her to know all of you—our family.

Give my love to Uncle Hardin and to Bess, Prudy, and little Snowflake. Write soon. I miss you—but never have I felt more content or more hopeful. Affectionate regards.

Your niece,

Rebecca